Between Shadow and Oblivion

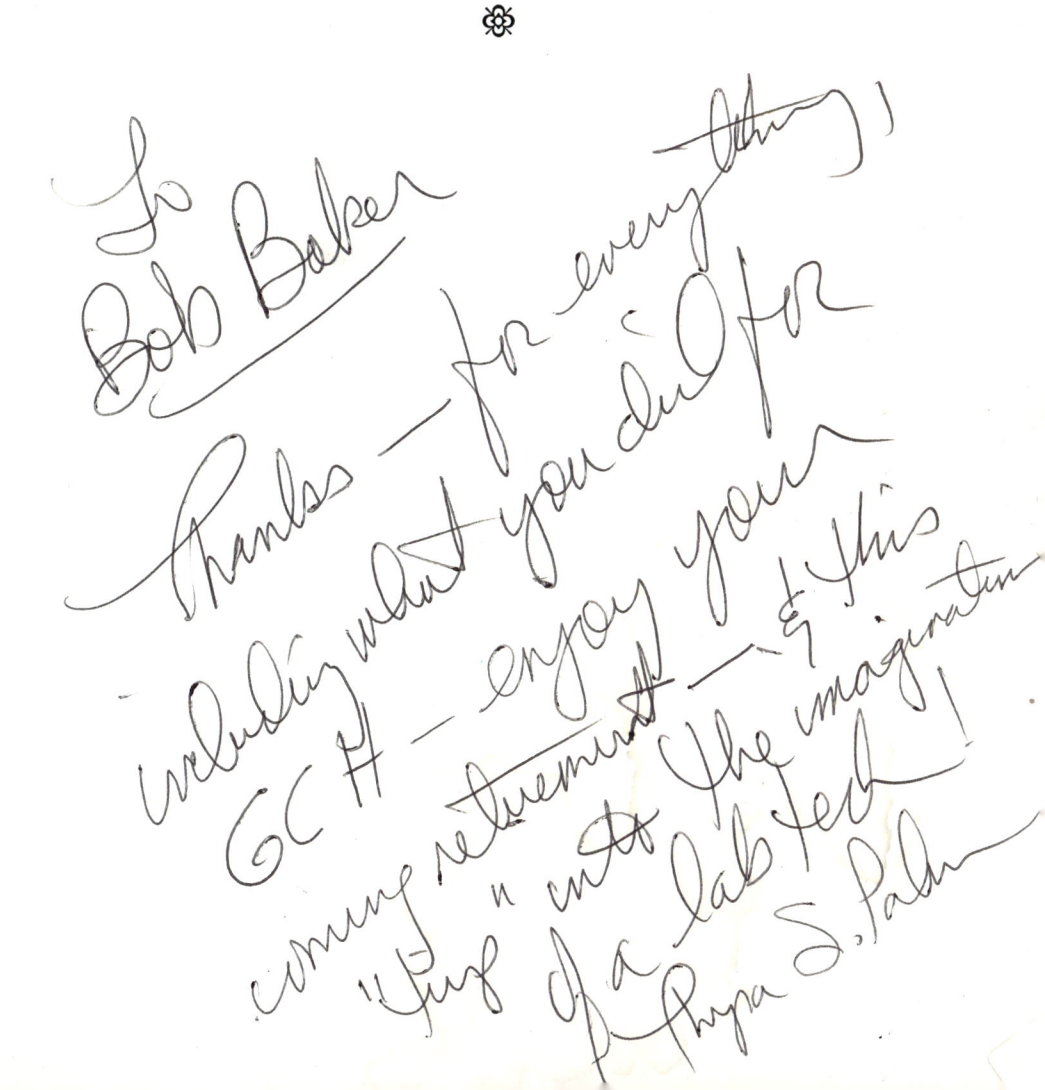

Between Shadow and Oblivion

Compiled by T.S. Palmer

Writers Club Press
San Jose New York Lincoln Shanghai

Between Shadow and Oblivion

All Rights Reserved © 2001 by Thyra S. Palmer

No part of this book may be reproduced or transmitted in any form or by any means, graphic, electronic, or mechanical, including photocopying, recording, taping, or by any information storage retrieval system, without the permission in writing from the publisher.

Writers Club Press
an imprint of iUniverse.com, Inc.

For information address:
iUniverse.com, Inc.
5220 S 16th, Ste. 200
Lincoln, NE 68512
www.iuniverse.com

ISBN: 0-595-19822-8

Printed in the United States of America

Dedicated to my crazy, wonderful co-workers who read, reread, and critiqued every chapter as it was written…to my family who supported, encouraged, and inspired me every step of the way…to BJ and Linda…to Gloria, in Heaven, it's finally a done deal. I miss you…my thoughts to yours.

I am the Alpha, and the Omega…the Light will ever overcome the Dark.

I

❀

….The silver-black jet sped on its way, flying just ahead, and above, the gathering storm clouds. It was doing its best to out race not only the trailing bad weather, but the slow approach of night as well. The sleek craft flew through the skies, seemingly impervious to the reaching fingers of Nature's irrepressible forces.

Inside, stretched out upon one of the plush couches, a young woman was blissfully unaware of the nearing storm outside the plane. She slept quietly, one arm flung above her head. Her slender form was curvaceous, her long legs drawn up slightly, and her features were hauntingly beautiful, even in repose. Her hair, dark and curling, tumbled over the pillow's surface, glinting as it picked up highlights from the lightning flashes now visible through the window. Her name was Elizabeth (Beth) Phelps, a successful business woman, on her way home after an absence of a few weeks…an important company merger deal securely tucked away in her laptop. She thrived on the fast-moving, and intense world of corporate dealings, but all she wanted now was the familiarity of home, and the solidarity of family and friends.

Seated close by, in the semi-darkness, a man and another woman watched her slumber in contemplative silence. At a nod from the woman, the man stood, and crossed over to where Beth was sleeping. He stood over her, gazing down from his imposing height. He was a powerfully built individual, with an arrogance evident even in the softening shadows of the inner cabin. He glanced back at the other woman, trying to gauge her mood, and wishes, without any words. Seeing his look, she rose, and joined him. She was nearly as tall as he was, and the darkness failed also to mask the beauty that was hers, or the aura of power that radiated from her. She frowned slightly, probing the sincerity of Beth's sleep, seeking any hints that the slumbering woman was aware of their nearness. Satisfied the woman was indeed sound asleep, she looked back to the man beside her, nodded, and returned to her seat.

He looked down at Beth for another few seconds, then slowly knelt down beside the sleeping female. Gently, he lifted her left hand, and brought it to his lips. Turning the hand over, he softly brushed his lips over the palm, inhaling the subtle scent from her skin. A flash from outside the window caused him to look up, his eyes alert. The eerie brilliance of the lightning accented the sculptured masculine features…his dark eyes seemed lit by inner flames. He brought his attention back to the sleeping woman, and a slight smile played about his full lips, softening somewhat the arrogance and sternness there.

The flickering light from the storm was now illuminating the interior of the jetliner with a surreal brilliance. His finely shaped head was being contrasted like the bust of some ancient pagan king…or, one of the gods of antiquity. His strange eyes seemed to glow…the intensity increasing in strength. He bent over her, seeking her lips, slightly parted in her sleep. He deepened the kiss, taking in her soft breaths, and staking his unspoken claim upon her mouth. She murmured indistinctly, but did not waken.

He released her mouth, and bent closer to her right ear. "Sleep well, my Elizabeth…sleep deep, and dream well! Yours will be dreams filled with all manner of strange, wondrous things…things now within your heart that even you are not aware exist there. These hidden desires will now make themselves, and you will be able to see, and experience all that will truly fulfill you as a woman." He murmured, stroking the dark curls. "Sleep…dream…see the destiny that can be yours alone. You will no longer be able to deny what you truly desire…they will always be there, no matter how vigorously you may deny this when awake! Hear me, Elizabeth…you can have it all! You have only to see…believe…and choose!"

Beth stirred again, a little more restless this time, as if trying, even asleep, to draw back from the power of his presence. Then, her sleep deepened again, and her mind slipped off into the nether world of our unconscious dreams.....

…In a landscape of compelling, entrancing beauties, Beth found herself walking along a small, well defined footpath. She took a deep breath, feeling her senses becoming intoxicated by the multitude of scents. All around her were flowers and plants, shapes and colors almost overwhelming to the mind. She rubbed her palms over the cloth over her thighs, feeling a tingling beginning in each palm. She looked off to the right, seeing a vast lake, and the surrounding meadowlands. The trees were beyond majestic in their height, and girth…strings of precious gems dangling from their far-flung branches. She could see large, moving herds of deer, horses, and fine cattle. The horns of the cattle were of purest gold…the crowning antlers of the male deer glistened with the sheen of solid silver…the strength and beauty of the horses was enhanced by the great snowy wings the possessed.

She looked to the left, seeing a line of imposing mountains marching off in the near distance. The large forest that led to the mountains seemed thick, cool, and oddly quiet. She felt a pull, beckoning her to enter the forested areas. She shook her head, and looked all around, feeling a strange eagerness…a sense of great anticipation that was growing within her. She felt as if on the very edge of discovering that which would give her the happiness she'd never dreamt possible. Beth opened her arms wide, as if trying to embrace everything about her…to bring it all even closer so that she might sample each and every pleasure offered.

She took another deep breath, then let it out slowly. She didn't know which way to go…what to do first. At her feet, literally, in unimaginable abundance, were treasures beyond known comprehension. She tilted her head, becoming aware of a low murmuring that tickled at her ears…voices that whispered that all she saw here could be hers to possess. All she had to do, they breathed, was listen, look…and make the correct choices when offered to her. She glanced up at the sky, hearing the chorus of voices telling her to simply follow the path, into the forest…follow it, and find the greatest wonders. It was there, they promised, she would find the one thing that would grant her all her hidden heart's desires.

Beth began to ran, hesitating no further, skimming over the path as though she possessed the mythical winged sandals of Hermes himself. She wasn't sure exactly sure, but she *knew* that the end of this path would be everything she would ever desire in all her lifetimes! As she ran, she felt her usual icy control, and the strict guidelines she'd lived by, being stripped away. In their place was growing a mounting, surging excitement that she'd never experienced before. She was in the grip of a strange fever…she was powerless to resist. Whatever lie ahead, she *had* to continue on…to find what the voices had murmured so enticingly about to her. She went deeper into the cool shadows of the great forest…feeling its darkness surround her, embrace her like a long lost lover. She went around a sharp bend in the path, then stopped suddenly, gazing at the barrier before her.

Cloaked in the deeper shadows of the giant trees, rising like a sculptured mountain, was a great palace. Constructed of huge, gray granite blocks, it seemed both out of place in the silent woods…yet, so very much a part of the unusual makeup of this strange, beautiful place. Beth stood there, feeling a gentle breeze caressing her heated cheeks…cooling, soothing the fevered skin, but not completely killing the deepest embers. She could hear the continuous whisper of the leaves, stirred by that same breeze, and found herself sighing. She could feel an inner heat growing...a sense of arousal she'd known only in the throes of a passionate embrace. Her eyes widened slightly, her nostrils flared as though catching the scent of an approaching lover.

Slowly, Beth walked forward, her feet feeling heavy, as if weighed down by lead...her legs acting as though they were carved from rigid wood. It was like something, or someone, was trying to prevent her reaching her goal. She pressed forward, feeling her heart rate increasing...again, it woke a memory within her of a sexual encounter. She had to reach the doors. She was convinced that it was there, somewhere within the interior of that imposing structure, that all her questions would finally be resolved. The breeze quickened, becoming a substantial wind...swirling around her tall figure, tugging at her clothing with invisible talons. The scents that permeated the air grew stronger...perfumes of Nature, unmatched by Man.

Beth reached out, her fingertips now brushing against the doors themselves...she'd finally reached her objective! The doors loomed over her, fantastic works of solid bronze adorned with what looked like embossed Celtic loops and ornate knots. The cool metal seemed to actually begin to warm at her brief touch, and the massive doors opened slowly, without a sound. She stood there for a second, or two...then stepped forward. Instantly, she felt the unmistakable sensation of her upper right arm being grabbed from behind.

Beth jerked her arm away, looking to see who had come up behind her...there was no one there. She lifted her left hand to her forehead, wincing as a sudden intense pain shot across her head, from ear to ear. She began to feel this urge to back away...to run back to the open meadows. She mustn't go in there!...danger was within that looming palace...and it wasn't merely a danger to her physical self...her immortal soul was also threatened! She grasped her head with both hands now, panic rising as the pain grew. What was going on here?...where was all the beauty and pleasures, the treasures?

Suddenly, her mind was calm…the pain and panic completely gone. The wind had dropped once again to the flesh-soothing sensation of before…the aromas serene, yet enticing. Beth lifted her head, and looked at the open doors. She passed through the gleaming doors, and entered a vast courtyard. She looked around, turning as she looked, wondering why it was so quiet…so empty. There wasn't any sign of people, animals…of any living beings. Yet…she could catch the faint strands of music…of conversation…and, it was coming from the large windows high above her head.

She decided to go in the main doors, at the top of the sweeping steps that led out of the courtyard. She'd find someone who'd tell her what was going on around here…where her desires really were hidden. As she walked across the courtyard, towards the stairs, she began to notice that her footsteps were echoing throughout the courtyard's confines. The sound was growing in volume the closer she got to the bottom step. It was rapidly turning into a crescendo of sounds, like the roaring of great guns in a war. The sounds were also taking on a physical reality…of pain! The echoing, screaming noises were attacking all her senses…like white-hot pokers thrust into her flesh, into her very spirit! Beth clapped her hands over her ears, trying to block the sounds, and the pain.

Finally, it was just too much. "Stop it!…please! I can't stand anymore! Whatever you want of me, I'll do!…just please stop!" she cried out, spinning around, clutching the sides of her head.

Within a heartbeat, all was silent. The shadows seemed to grow, deepening in their intensity, swimming over the stones towards her. They engulfed her, becoming even darker…wrapping her in a strangely comforting cocoon. All her fears, and pains seeped away from her, and she drew in a deep, cleansing breath. Then, she felt herself lifted up by unseen arms, and cradled like a beloved infant, against warm velvet softness. I t was like being cuddled next to a thick down pillow…yet, she could feel the underlying hardness as well.

She slowly lifted her head, unsure of what she'd see. What she did see, though not clearly, were two glittering eyes...like twin marbles of polished jet, bathed in dark flames, and holding a universe of hidden emotions in their bottomless depths. Beth found herself feeling both exulted...and terrified! She suddenly knew, deep in her soul, that she'd found what she'd been being guided to...her ultimate destiny. It was only now, though, that she began to heed that inner voice that was asking...at what price?.......

...The tall young woman stiffened, turning from her study of the planes outside the terminal window, seeking whatever it was that had given her the sudden jolt of pure fear. All she saw, however, was the normal activity of the large metropolitan air terminal, and her friends. There were several other people sitting around as well, all engaged in sitting, talking, reading...and in the case of a few, sleeping in their seats. She swung her gaze back to the window she'd been facing, her expressive azure eyes wide with concern, impatience, and a little confusion.

One of her companions, Kristine Howell, had seen the sudden turning, and noted the expression overlaying the sculptured facial features. The attractive redhead frowned, wondering what was up. She stood up, crossed the floor, and came up behind the other woman. "What's up, Sandy? You've been as skittish as one of your colts all day...and now you look like you've seen the devil himself! What is it?" she asked her friend softly, putting a calming hand on the other's forearm.

Sandra Phelps-Usher shook her head, hands clasped tightly together in front of her body. "I know I've been jumpy today, Kris...you don't need to remind me of that little fact! I can't tell you why, though...at least, nothing concrete." The tall brunette looked back out the window, her brain barely registering the coming and going of the various airliners. " I can only tell you that I'm worried...really worried! I just had the weirdest sensation...of fear, and loss! And I haven't the first idea of why

I would even begin to feel anything like this!" She glanced back at Kristine, the ice blue eyes troubled and scared.

"What are you scared about? What is there here…now…that could possibly be so frightening?" Kristine lifted her hand, palm up, trying to get her friend to see how silly she was being.

Sandra shrugged, rubbing her forehead with the fingers of her left hand. "To be honest…it's this trip Beth's been on for the past three weeks! For some reason I don't understand, it has me…afraid! More deeply afraid then I ever remember being, Kris…I just wish that plane would hurry up!" She drew a deep breath, trying to relax her tense body. "I know, when I finally see my sister, I'll finally relax!"

Another of her companions, a buxom blonde, shook her head in mild exasperation at her cousin's attitude. "For crying out loud, Sandy…give it a break, will you?" Lynda Parker gave her a stern look. "Look, every time Beth goes away on one of these lengthy business trips, it's always the same!…you get all worried, and worked up. Listen now…you have talked with her several times a week, haven't you? Everything was fine with her, wasn't it?" She watched as Sandra slowly nodded. "So, okay then…chill out!"

Lynda's younger sister was also one of Sandra's waiting companions. Leslie Robinson frowned at her sister, then spoke to Sandra. "Much as I hate agreeing with my sister on anything, Sandy…in this case I make an exception. I'm sure everything is fine with Beth…the plane's just a little delayed because of bad weather. When Beth's plane lands, and the two of you are together again, you'll be fine! Just try, and relax a bit…okay?"

Sandra wanted to protest, but had to smile, a trifle lopsided, at herself. She knew she did have a tendency to overreact where any family, or friends were concerned. It had been like that all her life, but more so since the unexpected death of her business magnate father, Richard, just a little over a year ago. This unhappy event was followed only a month later by the tragic auto-accident death of her ex-husband, Ted. Sandra had become somewhat fatalistic in her attitude towards a great many things in her life. This was very evident where her twin sister, Beth, was involved.

Sandra turned back towards the great glass panes of Denver's Metro Airport, looking up at the darkening skies. They'd already been told a few flights would be delayed because of the storm approaching from the East. She knew standing there, trying to locate one plane amongst all the coming and going traffic was impractical...but she couldn't stop herself. That one plane held the most important person in her life right now...her twin sister.

Beth had been overseas, in London, tying up all the loose ends to a very lucrative business deal with a prominent British firm. Sandra knew exactly what her sister would say if she could see all the tension and fear Sandra was exhibiting right now. She smiled ruefully, almost hearing the cool, clear voice telling her to stop being so emotional...stop letting her logic, and common sense, be over-ridden by unfounded fears, or emotional superstitious anxiety attacks. Sandra sighed, admitting once again to herself her marveling that they were indeed twins. She believed whole-heartedly with in the special "bond" said to exist between identical siblings. She'd even experienced a few such links herself as they were growing up. Beth, with her usual concise logic, always dismissed such ideas. The reason, she said, they responded so quickly to one another's feelings or needs, was because they'd grown up together...they knew one another completely.

Elizabeth, or Beth, was the older of the two, by almost an hour. To see one of the sisters was to see a mirror image of the other. Tall, slim, well-built...they showed their heritage from their late Italian mother in the dark curling hair, and beautiful olive-hue complexions. The high cheekbones, and entrancing blue eyes came from their father's side. From both parents, they'd each inherited quick, analytical minds...very useful, for both of them, in their business dealings. A deeply passionate nature was also an inherited quality from both parents. Beth learned how to channel all this emotion into a cool, calm demeanor that allowed her to always keep the controlling hand where the family's business ventures were involved. Sandra's nature was the polar opposite.

Identical as they were in appearance, friends and family really had very little trouble telling the two apart. Despite their physical similarities, the sisters' personalities were as different as the proverbial night and day. Beth's cool, calm attitudes were balanced by Sandra's fiery, often impulsive nature. When they had been growing up, it had always been Beth who'd been the leader, the decision-maker…Sandra devotedly following wherever her twin led. Sandra was, in truth, every bit as capable as Beth, but she acknowledged, early on, her own limitations, and Beth's superior skills in negotiation and legal intricacies. Sandra had never felt any kind of resentment, inferiority, or envy where her sister's talents were concerned…in fact, she was immensely proud of all her sister was capable of bringing into reality where the family businesses were the primary interests.

To most who were meeting the sisters for the first time, it was always Sandra who came across first as the warmest because of her open nature, and giving ways. Beth was often tagged an "ice princess", especially by many of her rivals and disgruntled opponents in the corporate world. In reality, Beth had as warm a soul as her twin…but simply chose not to allow the world to know it. The world at large saw a talented, beautiful woman…aloof, cool, professional, and extremely capable to head the vast business conglomerate she did.

It had been just this calm exterior, and sharp business acumen, that had led to her father selecting, and grooming her as his heir to the corporate throne he'd inherited from his father. Sandra was second-in-command, and had accepted this decision with her usual whatever was in the best interests of all attitude. Richard Phelps had instinctively known that it would take a very cagey, somewhat diabolical opponent to put anything over Beth…the family would not suffer with her as its head.

Beth had graduated, first in her class, from the prestigious Harvard law school…and had entered the world of corporate law as easily as she had stepped onto the dance floor at her debutante ball when she'd been seventeen. She'd confounded, and impressed...and irritated...all rivals with her immediate grasp, and resolution, of every problem, or challenge placed before her. She learned all that was needed about the reins of power from her equally-gifted father. Now, at age thirty-two, she was the undisputed head of a multi-billion dollar empire that went around the world in its interests, and properties.

Sandra had harbored no ill will with her father's choice...she knew her personal skills lay in other directions then those for Beth. There had never been as respected, or charming a Vice-President, or P.R. head for the firm then what Sandra had turned out to be. She, and her personally-selected staff, saw that no part of the human equation in every aspect of running the business was ever overlooked, or neglected. Her main interests, however, was in the smooth running of the huge stables of Blackmoon. The bloodlines developed over the years had become among the country's champions, and were sought out by overseas parties as well. Sandra felt her greatest satisfaction when viewing the results of the efforts of careful breeding. Seeing one of their horses, or one of the offspring of one of their animals, take top honors in racing, dressage, or any of the world equestrian events...she experienced a warmth, and sense of accomplishment she really didn't get that often in the corporate world.

Together, these two unique women had proven to the business world, family, friends, and themselves, that their father's trust in them had not been misplaced. They kept their close relationship as sisters, and together had been able to handle anything the world had thrown at them...even the sad deaths they'd experienced. But...only the Fates know when that one challenge...that will tax any and all strengths and convictions...will one day appear. It is then, and only then, that we learn the true depth of our character, and the solidity of our faith.

Sandra sighed again, glancing at her wristwatch. She looked out the window...she didn't like the looks of the heavier cloud cover rolling in over the airport...she was beginning to hear the faint rumbling of thunder in the near distance. She took in a deep breath, hugging her arms about her upper torso...everything was fine, she murmured to herself. Why couldn't she shake this feeling...of what? Nervousness...anxiety...or something deeper? She shook her head, trying to get rid of this ever-increasing sense of oppression...and danger.

Leslie had been watching her cousin closely. She turned to her own sister, a frown of concern on her pretty face. "You know, Lyn...I don't think I've seen Sandy this uptight! Why do you suppose she's so worked up this time?"

Lynda looked up at the silent Sandra, then shrugged impatiently. "It's just this storm...She's always been worked up during storms...like they get inside her, and stir something up. Beth always had to practically sit on during a bad thunderstorm when they were kids." Lynda brushed an errant lock of hair back behind one ear. "Sandy's never been real fond of the darkness. Don't worry, Les...she'll be fine...just as soon as Beth gets in!"

Kristine spoke up, lowering her voice so Sandra wouldn't hear. "I think her attitude's a little different this time, Lynda...she may really sense something actually wrong!" She winced a little at the expression on Lynda's face...she knew the blonde was extremely skeptical about certain things. "No, really...this time she really may a reason to worry...I'm beginning to feel that way myself! And I honestly don't have a concrete reason to feel this way! Maybe...maybe there *is* something to worry about!"

Lynda threw her hands up, shaking her head. "Please...don't start! Look, Kris...I know how you, Garalynn...and Sandy all feel about that psychic crap, but I just can't swallow *any* of it!" She stood up, hands on hips, an expression of determination of her attractive features. "All we have here is a plane delayed by a storm!...end of explanation! Don't make it into anything else!"

Leslie could see the beginnings of an argument starting…she stood up, stepping in between the other two women. "Cool it, you two!…not here, not now! This is not the time for one of your famous fights about what is, or what isn't! Cool it!" She hissed, hoping to stave off a scene.

Lynda was about to retort back when the paging system for the airport blared into life. "Sandra Phelps-Usher…please pick up the nearest white courtesy phone. Mrs. Phelps-Usher…please call the main desk!"

A startled look on her lovely face, Sandra turned , walking towards the line of courtesy phones that lined one wall of the terminal they were in. Her friends watched as she picked one of them up, and began speaking into it.

"Wonder what that's all about?" Leslie declared, cocking her head to one side.

Lynda shrugged her slim shoulders. "Hard telling…though, I'm sure Sandy's giving a little to whoever's on that phone! She *hates* being paged in public!"

"You suppose it has anything to do with Beth?" Kristine wondered aloud.

"I say we all wait!…and not create problems where there aren't!" Lynda retorted back, feeling more then a little irritated.

"Hush up!…here she comes!" Leslie stated, seeing her cousin hang up the phone, and start back towards them.

Sandra waved at them as she neared. "Gather up your stuff…we're out of here!"

"Whoa…what's up now?" Lynda was a little surprised….Sandra seemed relieved, but still unusually tense.

"It seems that Beth is coming in by private jet…but not to *this* airport!" Sandra started walking towards the terminal's main entrance. The others could seen the set to her broad shoulders…the tension there…all was not well, and they knew the signs of incoming emotional storms.

"Private jet?...but I didn't think Beth took the corporate jet when she left. Did she request it to come get her?" Kristine was a little puzzled, as she hurried to keep up with her friend.

"Was that Beth on the phone just now?" Leslie asked, slipping her light coat on as they walked.

"No...it was her executive assistant...Rachel. She's been trying to track me down for a couple of hours. I didn't bring my cell phone along today, and she finally got the idea to check here. Beth called here, from the jet, and told her about the change in plans so she could let me know." Sandra kept up a brisk walking pace...an indication of her inner emotional meter. "The jet's going to land at Blackmoon's private airfield...I'm to have the car there to pick them all up, and back to the mansion."

"Them?...who's all on that jet?" Leslie asked as they walked through the main doors, and out into the darkening outside. She shivered a little as the late August wind took a uncharacteristic cold turn.

"Don't ask me...Beth never mentioned bringing any guests the last time I talked with her!" Sandra looked for the limousine, waving so the driver would see them. "And it's not the corporation jet...that's still in the hanger. This is so unlike Beth...all the changes, and mystery, I mean!"

They all watched as the big car slowly pulled to a stop in front of them. The young driver, Stephen, jumped out, and opened the doors for them. The four women got in, and he closed the doors, then got back into his seat behind the wheel. He started the car, and eased the long vehicle down the long terminal drive, then out into the stream of traffic on the main highway.

Lynda looked across the space inside the luxury car, and frowned. "Sandy...did Rachel say why Beth changed her plans? I mean...it's so unlike Beth to alter her travel itinerary in any way once she's got it set up!"

"If you want to know the answers to that, Lynda...I suggest you come out to Blackmoon with me...and ask her yourself!" Sandra declared, settling herself more comfortably in the deep seat.

"You know...I think I just might do that!...I'm nosy! Besides...my ever-loving husband's probably still there, playing with your horses, Sandy!" Lynda was referring to her veterinarian spouse, Keith Parker...chief vet for the Blackmoon stables.

"You just want to see your husband, Lynda...but I smell a mystery! And that's something I can't resist!" Kristine declared, crossing her arms across her chcest. "I think I'll come along, too!"

"Well...I guess I'll come along just not to be left out! Besides...I haven't sampled one of Dolores' super meals in a long time. Can I use the car phone, Sandy? I want to call my babysitter, and tell her I'm going to be late."

Sandy smiled, nodding, and then buzzed Stephen, telling him that everyone was going back to the mansion. Then, she laid her head back, suddenly tired. Why had her sister changed all the travel plans so suddenly? Acting on impulse was something her twin *never* did...why now? Another twinge of uncertainty, and fear, swept through her stomach again...what was causing this? Maybe, once she and Beth were back together, she'd feel herself again...or not?.......

.....Garalynn Gagnon walked around the spacious library. She wasn't too certain when the other members of the family would be back, so she'd retired to the room she loved best in all of the breathing-taking rooms of the Blackmoon mansion. The butler, Rolland, had promised to let her know when the others showed up.

The leggy blonde took in a deep breath, letting it out with a sigh of satisfaction...she loved it here. She'd been coming out to Blackmoon since she'd first met the sisters, at age ten. This place had always given her a strong sense of belonging, and home, whenever she was here. The only child of Richard Phelps best friend, he'd brought her here to live, for real, when her parents were killed just after she'd turned fifteen. Richard had legally adopted Garalynn into his family, promising her she'd never be alone. The sprawling mansion, and surrounding acres had become as much her home as it was Beth's, and Sandra's. She was now thirty-three, a successful lawyer, and maintained a permanent residence in central Denver, though she still had quarters always ready for her in the mansion. As close as she was, to her adopted sisters and Blackmoon, she still wanted her independent lifestyle, and the chance to prove her personal capabilities. Richard Phelps had fully understood this...it was a trait he'd encouraged in all his family, to be all they could. He had graciously allowed her the space she felt she needed...but, as with the other two girls, he kept a close, protective watch over her well-being, and happiness.

Garalynn looked about the room, realizing again just how much this one room meant to her. To her, this room held the true essence that was Blackmoon's spirit...encased within fine leather, the history of the family, and all its endeavors, was nestled amongst countless volumes of history, folklore, religions, archaeology, and so forth. The total background of all the generations of the Phelps family's hopes, dreams, and physical accomplishments all enclosed within this one room. Garalynn remembered that she had once tried to count all the books in the library, when she was thirteen...she'd given up long before coming close to the end. Books, scrolls, tomes, and relics were not easily numbered at a glance. They were guarded by one of the finest security systems in the country...befitting one of the most valuable private collections in the world. It was a room that inspired deep thinking, quiet reflections...curiosity about cultures and worlds long gone by...or simply one of the best places to relax, and escape the outside pressures.

The library was an unusually constructed room, in the shape of a huge octagon, with the door being the eighth side. Three walls were ceiling to floor bookshelves, holding the bulk of the volumes to be found in here...in all sizes, worth, types, and descriptions. Since Blackmoon Manor had first been built, each succeeding generation of the Phelps family had not only added to the manor house itself, but also to the contents of this special library. The bookshelves were constructed of Lebanese cedar, remarkable for their unique color, and distinctive fragrance...adding to the unusual aura the room radiated.

Predominate in the type of books found here were those dealing with almost every aspect of history, lore, and ancient legends. A great many were devoted to many ancient, and vanished civilizations, or cultures. Several dealt with the local Native American histories and legends, many that dealt with the area today known as Blackmoon, and the surrounding lands. Garalynn always felt that stepping into this room was like touching a small piece of History itself.

The other four full walls were paneled in the rich cedar, with a few simple though elegant paintings, and a couple of the usual hunt trophies. The rest of the wall space was covered with specially constructed shelves, and displays cases. Safely protected behind bullet-proof glass panes were some of the remarkable artifacts, from all over the world, that the family had collected since Blackmoon's conception. While the bulk of the valuable relics the various generations of Phelps had found, or helped find, had made their way to museums all over the world...many of the more unusual ones had found their way into this incredible collection. Many of the Phelps ancestors, up to and including the present, had boasted avid historians in their numbers. Many had been seekers, also, of all the unknowns of their respective eras, and worlds. There had been more then a few who'd backed archaeological expeditions to distant points of the globe most people had never heard of before. Some had actually been members of such expeditions, and all had brought new members back to expand the Blackmoon collection.

So acute was this family's interests...some called it an obsession...with all things historical, spiritual, psychic mysteries, that one entire level of the manor house had been painstakingly built to resemble an actual tomb. This tomb had been discovered over seventy-five years ago, by a Phelps backed, and manned, expedition to an obscure corner of what, in antiquity, had been referred to as the Valley of the Queens. Here, following a vague reference in a scroll found in a court official's tomb, they'd located the artfully concealed resting place of a prince of the fourth dynasty (approximately 2560 b.c.) in behind the tomb of a minor second wife of a ruling Pharoah. The name of the prince wasn't one of the most notable, or did his tomb rank as one of the most artful, or fabulous...as was the finding of Tutankamon's. But...there had been something...or so the media of the day had hinted at in their coverage of this event. In a highly unusual gesture, the ruling government had allowed the Phelps expedition to take the entire contents of this tomb, and transport them halfway around the world, to the confines of the Phelps family holdings. What had caught the attention of the archaeological world, and the press, was the fact that it had been the government themselves who'd suggested such a thing. Much was made of this unprecedented happening, and it had been hinted more then once that the powerful, and wealthy American family had "bought" such a favor of the foreign government. Nothing was ever made public, however, and the event gradually left the minds of the general public, though there were still those in the world of museums and archaeology who pondered it...some had even requested seeing this unique room, called simply enough the Tomb. But, few outside the family itself ever did see it...it was under the most stringent of guard at all times. The entire room had been designed to resemble the location the tomb had been found in, and was reputed to be among the finest representations ever seen.

Garalynn had been in the Tomb several times, but she'd found it to be a very unsettling event each visit...she'd never stayed long. It didn't mean as much to her, as it did Sandra, the present generation's history buff. Sandra considered the Tomb Blackmoon's true soul. Garalynn knew, however, that this library was the real heart...sprawling, warm, grand with age like a dowager empress...enigmatic with unspoken riddles, and mysteries. This was Blackmoon...and all it represented...and promised.

She turned her attention to the painting over the small fireplace. It had been commissioned by Richard Phelps a year before his death, and showed the manor house as it was today. Each time she looked at it, it reminded her of the story he'd told her, Sandra, and Beth about how their home had come to be, and where it had gotten its unique, mysterious name. She could almost hear the deep voice as he unfolded the fascinating, haunting story.......

...The first Phelps to settle here, and start the building of Blackmoon had been an Englishman named Joshua Logan Phelps. His family was originally from some forgotten town near southern Wales, and had come over to the young America in the late 1790's. Young Joshua had left his family home in Delaware, and headed west in 1803, seeking his fortune. At nineteen years of age, he was considered a level-headed, practical man, who feared little in his world. His parents didn't understand why he wanted to leave the comforts of home, and the benefits of a prospering business in shipping...but they granted him the right to seek his goals in his own way. He wasn't afraid to strike out, on his own...to make his dreams a reality.

He headed inland, sometimes traveling with others seeking to carve a new life...other times alone in the solitude of the wilderness. He followed tales of where wealth could be found, for those willing to work...being drawn to find that special place that was to be his alone. He trekked for many months, living through his share of illnesses, pains, hunger, perils...and the times of supreme joy when he viewed the unspoiled beauties about him. He fought down those times, when tired and discouraged,

He'd begin to wonder if he'd ever find what he was looking for so doggedly. From trappers, other pioneers, and friendly indians he met along the way, he learned the skills vital to survive this beautiful, rugged, sometimes savage land.

More then once, he'd been tempted to stay in one spot, or the other…or with one particular group. Then, that unfathomable urge would arise again, driving him to continue his journey. He'd find a place, and feel like it was finally the one…only to have that mysterious inner force propel him on further. A power beyond his comprehension was pulling him towards a place not yet discovered.

At long last, he entered into that area that would become modern Denver, Colorado, and its surrounding suburban environs. Here, at long last, he found himself at the end of physical endurance…and past the boundaries of emotional strengths. He could go no further. He now had serious doubts that his dream place would ever exist…that he would ever see it. He began to have thoughts of returning to Delaware, and the family that waited for him.

At this time, through a couple of trappers he'd been keeping company with, he was introduced to the local tribe of Cheyenne. The trappers had helped him learn some rudimentary words to help him communicate with the tribe's elders. The Cheyenne welcomed the travel-weary, heart-sore man into their midst. He decided to accept their offer to stay with them for awhile…at least, until he could finally decide what to do.

During his stay with tribe, sharing their semi-nomadic life, he struck up what would be a life-long relationship with the shaman, or medicine man, of the group…a wise old man called Two Feathers. The two became fast friends, and Joshua stayed in the old shaman's guest lodge. It was from Two Feathers that Joshua learned of the rich history of the Cheyenne, as well as their deeply reverent religious beliefs devoted to the living world around them. It would turn out to be this wise man who would unknowingly be that catalyst that would show Joshua his true goal.

Joshua, and Two Feathers, were sitting outside the shaman's lodge early one August evening. They were relaxing after eating, smoking and talking. The old man had gazed up into the star-filled sky, and in a low voice, asked Joshua if anyone had ever told him of the story of the Dark Eagle's Nest. Joshua recognized that name…he'd heard a few of the braves mention it when they talked about one of the mountains in the foothills of the tribes summer camping grounds.

Joshua told Two Feathers he'd never heard the tale, and asked if the shaman could relate it to him. The old man took a deep draw on his long pipe then slowly let it out, letting the tobacco waft its sacred smoke about his head. He held the pipe up towards the heavens…an offering to the Spirit. Then, he held the pipe out to Joshua. The white man took it, and drew in on the pipe…this was one of the rituals he enjoyed. He released the smoke from his lungs, and watched the tendrils drift upwards, caught in the soft breeze.

Two Feathers began the tale…the coming, and going, of a great warrior, filled with the greatness of the Spirit himself. He had come to their forefathers generations ago, over twenty by their counting. This warrior had been called the Dark Eagle…a name given him by the elders of the tribe. The warrior had lived with the tribe for a time, teaching them many things. He showed them how to better read the stars…for more the just directions. Also, to understand all the aspects of sun and moon…how they could be used to find good camping, good hunting…and when was the best time to move, to hunt, to plant, and to prepare to defend their homes and families. He also taught them how to recognize friend from enemy, and how to keep their lives safe, protected, and fulfilled.

He also told them stories…of the future, and what it held for them, and their descendents. He told them that they would soon see new races of mankind…with skin colors of black, white, and even yellow…but mostly it would be the white skins who would impact the most on their world here. There would be many greedy men who would covet the riches they had here…but there would be many great men who would prove to be their great friends. There was so much he told the, Two

Feathers told Joshua…all passed on from one generation to the next by the shamans, they storytellers of the tribe.

Two Feathers paused, taking a sip from the filled waterskin beside him, then took up the narration once again. When it came time for Dark Eagle to leave the tribe, he told them he would come once again, though it may be many generations into the future. He warned them also of a great evil…an evil that would one day threaten all that decent people held dearest in life. He taught the shaman what to look for…the omens and signs that would point to this great evil's approach. One sign that would serve as a warning would be when the moon turned black. Now, Two Feathers explained…this thing had happened before, and the shamans before him had all known it to be a bad sign…but for what reason had remained mysterious. Now…thanks to the Dark Eagle…they knew it was a warning that the evil was close.

Joshua was intrigued…he sensed a deeper meaning behind this story. He pressed his wise friend for more details. Two Feathers settled his back a little more comfortably against the saddle he was using as a back prop, and smiled…the children of the tribe all acted this way the first time they heard the tale. He told how the Dark Eagle had told them what to do when the black moon appeared…in fact, he'd even taught them how to predict when such a time would occur.

When the signs pointed to a possible black moon appearance, two braves would be selected by the chief and the elders. These two warriors would, on the night of the dark moon, ride out of the village, and up into the foothills…to the highest peak there, the one now called the Dark Eagle's Nest. There, they would be confronted by a guardian…and he would set them on the next leg on their journey. It was a journey to find that which would protect their homes and families from the approaching evil, the shaman said…but one from which they might not be able to return.

If they were successful, however…the black moon would pass, and the great evil would never appear. The two warriors were messengers, to the Spirit, for the protection and safety of the tribe…the price for the greater good. Two Feathers went on to say that Dark Eagle had cautioned them not to panic if a black moon did show…it was merely a warning, a sign to be on their guard. It was not the great evil itself…merely a warning, and a reminder, that it was always out there…waiting. The forces of the Spirit…the light of sun and moon…would always be their weapons against the forces of darkness.

When Two Feathers stopped talking, there was silence between the two men for a brief time. Joshua was running all he'd heard over in his mind…he'd never heard such a tale before this. He wasn't sure why…but this intrigued him almost to an insanity. He had to learn more. He pressed Two Feathers, feeling himself driven inside again. The old shaman was puzzled by the intensity of his friend's need, but shrugged, and started to tell about the time he himself had first heard the tale…and had first seen the actual event.

He had been a boy of seven summers, when the shaman, who'd been his father, had prepared the tribe for the appearance of the black moon. He remembered the night it had really happened…even though he'd heard his father, and the chief, telling all the people that everything would be all right, he'd still been terrified when he'd looked into the sky, and seen that amazing sight. He'd felt as though the world was actually going to end!…it couldn't go on without light from *both* sun and moon, could it? He'd wondered if the moon would ever shine again. He told Joshua he'd watched as the two braves had ridden from the village, and into the almost overpowering darkness. He'd been filled with a sense of terror he'd never felt since then.

Now, he stated, he'd lived through three black moons in his lifetime, and he'd learned that however dark it seemed to get…eventually the light did return, and the darkness retreated like a whipped cur. He'd come to believe that the time of the black moon was actually a test for his people…of their faiths, and their beliefs in the Spirit they turned to for all things.

Joshua had asked about the two braves...had they returned?...did anyone really know what truly happened when they went to that mountain? The old indian had sighed, and shook his head, slow and sad. Those two men had never been seen by the tribe again...in fact, in all his memory, there had only been one time a brave sent to the Dark Eagle's Nest had ever been seen again...and that had been before he'd been born. He recalled his father speaking of a hunting party finding one of the two selected braves a few says after the black moon had passed...near the foothills.

The man had been near death...from exposure, and loss of blood. His body bore terrible wounds, and strange markings. The wounds had been of such a severity that Two Feathers' father had been shocked the man was alive at all. The man had died shortly after the hunting party had brought him back to the village...after babbling incessantly of a great cavern, an undying light, and a glowing god. The tribe had finally decided that his mind had been driven mad due to his injuries...and whatever had happened up on that dark, and unknown mountain peak.

After Two Feathers had stopped speaking, there was silence...the two men were each wrapped in thoughts they could not yet put into speech. Joshua finally spoke, in a low, halting voice...asking something that he'd been wondering about. How, he had asked, had the shamans known how to both recognize the signs of a black moon's coming...and how to select the two braves to go to the mountain. Two Feathers had replied that the strange warrior had left the shamans something to use...something that would always guide, and help them to know such things. Joshua asked if he would be allowed to know, or see such a thing.

Two Feathers sat quietly foe a few moments, pulling on his pipe, and thinking deeply. Finally, he nodded, sighing. He pulled himself to his feet, motioning for Joshua to wait here, then the old man went into his lodge. After a few minutes, he came out, carrying a large, tube-shaped piece of cured white wolf's hide. It was stiff, shiny with age and use, with a few bare patches where the fur had been rubbed off, or had fallen off due to age. The shaman had sat down next to his saddle once again, and laid the hide tube across his legs. His gnarled, but still strong fingers had gently untied the laces, slowly and reverently opening the flap of hide.

Once the flap was fully open, the old man had paused, closing his eyes, and muttering a short prayer under his breath. Joshua couldn't hear everything, but he caught enough to know it was to the Spirit…for guidance and protection. Then, Two Feathers had reached one hand in, and slowly pulled out another piece of cured hide…buffalo this time. He put the outer hide aside, and smoothed the new one over his lap, and down past his knees. His hands went over every inch of this buffalo hide, chanting another brief prayer…to keep his eyes clear, and his thoughts focused. Joshua couldn't understand any of this one…it was in a dialect he didn't recognize at all.

Two Feathers opened his eyes, his prayers over, and motioned for Joshua to come closer. The white man did so, gazing intently at the open buffalo skin…there were many symbols, and marks all over the hide, in colors he'd never seen on any other hide, or clothing in the village. There were unusual groupings of marks, some resembling unique pictures with strangely familiar implications. He reached out to touch the hide, but the shaman shook his head…only the medicine man was allowed to handle the sacred hide, he'd stated quietly.

Joshua understood, and just stared at the intriguing cloth…this was it, his mind told him…this was what he'd been after. His destiny was just a few inches away. He sat back, thinking…then asking Two Feathers if he could tell when there might be another black moon. The medicine man gazed at the hide, his fingers moving over selected groups of marks, or symbols. Then, he looked up into the night sky, seeking and finding various stars. He compared the stars, after locating them, to the hide, then reached his fingers into one of the pouches he always had at his belt. He took a pinch of the dried plant spores, and tossed them into the nearby fire. They flared up, with a bright flash, and he stared into the flames…seeing things evident to his eyes only.

After a few seconds, he turned his gaze to Joshua. The white man had been taken aback by the intensity of that gaze, wondering what his friend had seen. Two Feathers nodded slowly, and began to speak. He told Joshua that the Spirit had come to him just then, and had told him to tell Joshua anything he wanted to know…that Joshua held a special role in the future events of the tribe, and their future descendants. He began to translate the various markings, and symbols, pointing out each as he talked. The marks…picture words…were part history, part prayers…part instructions. The instruction part told the tribal elders what to do when the tribe was threatened, and what to look for when selecting the two braves. It took over an hour for the old shaman to explain just the rudiments to Joshua, but he found himself holding back on some of the finer points…he just couldn't break the training of a lifetime, which stated that no non-tribal person could learn the secrets of the sacred hide. Two Feathers wondered what it was about this white man that so impressed the Spirit…would he ever learn all the moods the Spirit could manifest?

It was while they were finishing up that Two Feathers realized there was a definite pattern to the night sky…he looked hard at one group of stars, then back to the skin. He rolled the hide up quickly, and excused himself to Joshua…he stated that he had to go into his lodge for some rest. Then, with one last hard glance at the sky, he left the puzzled white man sitting by the low fire.

Joshua leaned back against the log he'd been using as a backrest, thinking over all that he'd learned in the past couple of hours. Could this really be the key, his quick mind asked…is this where my destiny really lies? He turned his head in the direction of the foothills, and the mountains beyond. He couldn't see it, but he knew the general spot the Dark Eagle's Nest…his startling blue eyes narrowed slightly, thinking about the story he'd heard tonight. He was an intelligent man…he knew most folk legends were largely tall tales…but there was always a basis of truth. If he carried out the plan that was beginning to form in his mind, he could be in a very perilous arena. He stood up, dusting his leggings off...it was time for bed. Perhaps tomorrow...

In his lodge, finally alone, Two Feathers stoked up his small fire, then placed the hide carefully on his bedroll, smoothing it out. He settled down in front of the fire, crossing his legs, and reaching for his large medicine bag. This bag held the dried roots, herbs, etc. that he used in the rituals that were his ways of insuring the welfare of his people, and village. He reached behind him, pulling out the buffalo horn shaman's headdress...it had been passed from father to son, in his family, for nearly ten generations, and was considered a source of great power. Two Feathers used it only in the most serious medicine rites. He had to learn the truth...to see the reality that the Spirit had been trying to make him see tonight. Once he learned that, then he would know the right way to deal with his new friend...and this mysterious role Joshua was to have.....

.....As the days slipped by, and the seasons once again began their eternal changing, Joshua used the time to perfect his skills in tracking, hunting...and when necessary, fighting. He wasn't sure just what had really happened the night he'd learned of the Dark Eagle story, but ever since then, Two Feathers had declared his intention to make Joshua familiar with all aspects of Cheyenne spiritual beliefs, and comfortable with all forms of ceremonies used by the tribe. He'd become quite a trapper, amassing quite a number of valuable pelts. He utilized his trapper friends to gradually convert his hides and pelts into a very comfortable fortune. Not needing to spend any of the gold he received from the trading posts near the tribe's hunting grounds...he found it no problem to build it up for the plans he'd made. He'd become a valuable and respected member of the tribe, and had cemented this position when he'd been allowed to marry the granddaughter of his good friend, Two Feathers. Her name was Silver Deer, and she was more beautiful then any woman Joshua had ever seen. He'd sent word back to Delaware, with some Army engineers passing through, about his marriage, and let his family also know a little of what he'd planned to build out here. He knew they'd probably be shocked at what had happened, but he loved Silver Deer deeply, and intended to keep anything from interfering with his happiness...or his plans.

When the first signs of spring began to be noticed, Two Feathers announced to the tribal elders that it would soon be time for a black moon, and they must begin the selection of the warriors who would ride to the sacred mountain. There was great competition among most of the braves, and their families...it was a point of great honor to be chosen. There was also a significant undercurrent of anxiety...and fear. That this was for the good of the entire tribe, and a point of honor, all acknowledged. No family, however, wanted to lose a member...most found their minds, and spirits, unsettled and confused as they made their daily prayers to their Spirit.

Joshua had requested to be considered as one of the two riders...Silver Deer had tried repeatedly to dissuade her husband from this path, but failed. Two Feathers, and the chief, Iron Wolf, had patiently explained that, though now a member of the tribe, Joshua had not been born so, and therefore was ineligible. Joshua had nodded, understanding their words...but it didn't alter his decision, or determination one bit. He was being driven by an inner force that would not be silenced.

Then, early one spring evening, he'd been dozing in the lodge he shared with Silver Deer, dreaming about the buffalo hunt the next morning. Suddenly, he was jerked from his light sleep by screams, and wails coming from all parts of the tribal area. Joshua bolted from his lodge, scooping up his musket and powder horn as he did so. He stopped just outside, seeing everyone standing around their fires, gesturing upwards, and staring into the darkening night sky.

He looked up, and stared in disbelief...a thin crescent of blackness was beginning to creep across the face of the full moon. Joshua gripped his musket tighter…it was beginning. He didn't hesitate…seeing the chief and Two Feathers talking with the two chosen braves. He grabbed the reins of his horse, tethered beside the lodge. Silver Deer saw his movements, and realizing what he was going to do, tried to stop her husband. He pushed her away, then swung up on top of his horse. Digging his heels in, he urged the startled animal into a gallop, and disappeared from the firelight. Iron Wolf tried to stop the reckless man, but ended up jumping out of the way to avoid being trampled. Two Feathers signaled to the two braves, who quickly mounted, and rode off into the consuming darkness of the lunar eclipse. Two Feathers put a gentle arm about the shoulders of Silver Deer. He tried to comfort the trembling young woman…but he seriously wondered if they'd ever again see the strange white man who'd become such a part of their lives.

Five days passed, and there was no sign of either the two braves…or Joshua. It seemed, Two Feathers sighed, that the tribe must begin to plan a funeral rite for the missing husband of his granddaughter. The ceremonies for the spirits of the two braves would be performed at sunrise the next day…perhaps he should persuade Silver Deer that Joshua should also be included. He had told his granddaughter that they would probably never see her husband again, but the beautiful young wife had steadfastly refused to give up on Joshua. In her heart, she told her grandfather, she would know if he'd met an ending somewhere in the sacred foothills…she knew he was still very much among the living, and she would wait for however long it took until he returned to her.

Then, on the sixth day, two things happened that caused Two Feathers to wonder if his world was turning topsy-turvy. First, just after sunrise, one of the two braves rode slowly back into the camp…his horse exhausted, and lathered. The young warrior slid off the back of his animal, and collapsed at the feet of the astounded chief, and the equally amazed shaman. He was covered in dirt, and blood…and was trying, with the last of his strength, to pull a small pouch from his loincloth. Two Feathers had knelt next to the man, pulling out his medicine bag, intending to tend to the numerous injuries. The warrior pushed the shaman away, shaking his head slowly. He handed the small pouch to his chief, then slowly laid back on the grass, closed his eyes, murmured a few words only the two men standing over him could hear…then died.

Iron Wolf couldn't believe this…his brave had chosen to die rather then let his injuries be taken care of. He stared at the pouch he now held…made of the hide of some animal he wasn't familiar with at all, with black and white stripes. Two Feathers reached out, taking the pouch from the chief's hand, and tugged at the strings closing the top of the small leather item. Once opened, he tilted the bag over, and dumped the contents out into his hand. All there was inside was one large golden coin…bearing on one side a large bird with upswept wings, surrounded by flames. On the other side was the engraving of a single tree, with wide swept branches. Neither man had ever seen such a coin, not even from the trappers, or pioneers they came into contact with. Iron Wolf motioned to a trio of warriors, and they bore the body away…taking it to the man's family for burial preparation. When they were once again alone, he looked at the shaman, and quietly asked if Two Feathers had heard what the dead man's last words. The old man nodded, wondering what the significance of those soft words held…all the warrior had murmured had been "He is coming back!" Neither man knew what to say…this had been an event totally unexpected…they were to feel the same way later that same day.

Just before sunset, the entire tribe stood outside their homes, staring at the apparition riding slowly down the center pathway of the village, headed for the large lodge of the shaman. Two Feathers, Iron Wolf, and Silver Deer gazed t the approaching rider…the two men wondering if their eyes had suddenly taken to hallucinations, the young woman feeling a joyous relief blooming inside her heart.

Joshua Phelps slowly rode his horse towards the trio, stopping only when he was directly before them. For a few moments, he gazed down at them, sitting tall and proud above them, his bearing sure and resolute. Then, moving slow and graceful, he swung down from the back of his horse, and stood in front of them. Two Feathers, finally regaining use of his voice, hoarsely asked where he'd been...where he'd gone that dark night. Joshua didn't answer...he seemed to be taking counsel within himself. Then, he solemnly shook his head, and opened his arms to his young wife. Silver Deer threw herself into those arms, and lost herself in her husband's impassioned embrace.

As the young people embraced, Two Feathers looked hard at his grandson-in-law, wondering. It was only now that Joshua's appearance really registered with the old medicine man...there were a few changes. Joshua's long brown hair, usually worn tied back in a long queue, was now nearly all shorn off. There was now only a single, long braid...coming off the right side of his bared skull. Dangling from the end of this braid was a gleaming silver disc, bearing an unusual design...similar to the bird engraved on the gold coin the dead brave had brought back with him. Joshua's everyday deer-hide vest had been replaced by an intricately beaded long sleeved shirt, of white buffalo hide, with long fringes on the sleeves...the fringes made of black wolf hide.

Physically, Joshua appeared quite well, although a bit tired looking. It was his eyes, however, that truly revealed the extent of whatever he'd gone through over the past six days. They were still the deep, startling blue...but, now, they held the gaze of one who'd looked on things for which there were no words. They now seemed to see completely through anyone he was talking with...probing deep into the individual's soul, and bringing out into the light any secrets concealed there.

What he'd seen, or done, on that mountain, he never said. He did, however, put everything down in a private journal, which he then concealed in a place known only to himself. When asked about it, he told Two Feathers and Silver Deer that when the proper time came, the journal would be taken out, and given to the person who could make the best use of its contents. Until that time, he stated, not even members of his own family would be permitted to read it. The contents were of a nature that could cause great distress...and even greater fear! Though they all finally had to settle for that vague, unsettling explanation, the tribe realized that something special had indeed happened to their strange friend.

From that day on, until the time of his death, Joshua carried a unique aura about with him...one of power, prosperity...and destiny. His personal fortunes definitely improved, and continued so during the rest of his lifetime. He had already accumulated a sizable personal fortune...to which he now added a large amount of gold...source never revealed. As the years passed, and the trickle of westward bound pioneers increased, Joshua took his wife, and infant son, and left the tribe's summer campsite. With the help of his trapper friends, Joshua established a trading post, along the trail-way that wound through the foothills near the Dark Eagle's nest.

As the young nation developed, and expanded, the trading post also grew, and spread out into a thriving compound, made up of several families and others who'd decided to join the fast-growing town. The trading post had quickly become a mainstay for the Army, who'd set up a fort, to guard the trails west...and also for pioneers, prospectors, trappers, etc., who were all heading west, to build new lives, or find their fortunes.

Joshua had also traveled back to his family's home, on the east coast, and, with his brother Ethan, revamped the family's shipping firm...making it one of the best all along the east coast. Once this was done, and running well under Ethan's capable hands, Joshua headed back to his business, home, and family in the Colorado territories. He seemed to have been gifted with an uncanny ability for acquiring more and more wealth, power, influence, and a growing group of devoted friends, employees, and followers. As the family grew, Joshua made sure that all members of his brood became involved in the entire circle of the many businesses and interests of the family. And yet, underlying all this, there was always the still unrevealed mystery of the Dark Eagle's Nest...unknown, and tantalizing to those in any way familiar with the family's history. Joshua was asked often about it, and merely smiled slightly at each inquiry...his personal involvement with that dark, looming mountain would stay his private knowledge, to his death. In fact, on his death bed, he steadfastly refused to say anything that would illuminate, or remove the lingering mystery.

Joshua Phelps died in the late months of 1857, at the age of seventy-three. Two of his family of five children were at his side...his two oldest sons, Seth and John. Per their father's last requests, the two men split the running of the business between them, with the other son and two daughters all receiving healthy shares of the profits...also per the conditions and wishes set forth in their father's will. John remained in the area of the original trading post, now called Denver. Seth traveled back East to oversee, and run the family interests there. The brothers maintained a close relationship, even over the distance separating them. This helped the family to keep the various businesses strong, making their respective holdings even more lucrative, respected, and successful. When Seth passed away, leaving no heirs, John turned the businesses over to various family members...the most successful, the shipping firm, he bequeathed into the hands of his older sister's oldest daughter. This caused a great stir among the community, and some of the older family members...placing such power and responsibility into the keeping of a female. John's will was strong, and as the acknowledged head of the family, his word was resolute and final...the legacy remained as designated.

The family's influence in politics as well as business now, stretched from one shoreline to the other...and was beginning to make its presence felt overseas. Their major fortunes, and loyalties, still remained strongest in the nestling hills of the Denver skyline, and the surrounding areas. As each succeeding generation came along, they made the family's position in the growing city's community more secure, more well-known in the workings of home city, state, and country. By the present era, and generation, the Phelps name was well-entrenched in the corporate world, and well-respected and secure in the world outside the sphere of business. The once humble cabin that Joshua Phelps had first built for his family was now replaced by a baronial-styled manor house, surrounded by a vast scope of lands, buildings, and smaller homes. The main grounds of the estate took in about twenty-five acres, meticulously tended by a small army of gardeners, and landscape experts. The rear of the manor house loomed over an exceptionally beautiful maze of gardens, and statuary. The pride of the grounds crew, however, were the formal gardens, about a quarter of a mile from the main house. These gardens were five acres within themselves, and had become quite a tourist draw. The family had graciously opened these living marvels of landscaping, and horticulture, to public viewing about thirty years ago, and they'd quickly become quite a favorite for those enamoured of the beauty of nature's gifts.

The estate had been given the name of Blackmoon Estates shortly after the death of Joshua's son, John. It had been improved, and expanded with each generation, and was now considered one of the finest homes in the entire state. There were the usual tennis courts, pools, and a huge stable complex. There was a full-time manager, and crew, responsible for the smooth running of all aspects of Blackmoon…for the senior members, there were comfortable residences built in, and around the central thirty acres of the estate. There was a full-time staff of twenty-five who lived within the confines of the manor house…in the spacious, and comfortable servant's wing, added onto the main house nearly fifty years ago. The rest of the working staff of Blackmoon lived in the nearby Denver environs…this group totaled fifty members in all.

So…in this way, Blackmoon Estates came into being…an impressive holding, and a lasting tribute to one man's courage, and determination to succeed. It was beauty personified, dignity and family integrity become tangible, and power incorporate to all who saw it. Within the scope of its influence, it never failed to awe, inspire…and above all, to intrigue. For, with all else it entailed, this sprawling home carried the very essence of mysteries unsolved…the tangible scent of hidden dangers, and the undeniable lure of something beyond human comprehensions……..

……The butler broke into Garalynn's reverie, holding a small silver tray out towards her. "I took the liberty of bringing you some of the bordeaux that you're so fond of, Miss Garalynn," Roland said, smiling gently at her. He'd been head butler here since all the girls had been small. Since the death of the father, he'd taken it upon himself to make sure they were all comfortable, and well looked after…they'd become like his own daughters, and there was very little he wouldn't do for any of the three women.

Nodding her thanks, Garalynn took the offered glass, and walked to one of the over-stuffed chairs scattered throughout the room. Sinking into it gracefully, she swung her long legs up onto the matching ottoman, and settled back with a deep sigh. She sipped her wine, and rested her head back against the chair's headrest. It had been a long, hard day at Phelps Inc…She was helping Beth's staff to keep things going efficiently while the CEO was over in London, besides her own duties as Vice-President in the legal department of the home company of the Phelps Conglomerate. Garalynn had worked for her adopted father's company since she'd passed the bar, in corporate law. Richard Phelps had convinced her to join her adopted sisters in the firm, and she'd agreed. She had originally planned to accompany Beth on this latest business deal, in London…but at the last, Beth had asked her to remain behind…she wanted a level hand on the controls while she was gone.

Garalynn took another sip of the fragrant wine, savoring the full-bodied taste on her palate, enjoying the warmth it brought to her tired body. She sat her glass down on the end table, and settled her head back again with a sigh. The quiet solitude of the room, combined with the relaxing qualities of the wine, was beginning to work their influences over her weary senses. She could feel herself growing drowsy. Her head snuggled deeper into the pillow headrest of the chair, and her eyes closed. Her mind allowed itself to drift, feeling the gentle fingers of sleep caress it, and her surroundings faded away....

..."Garalynn?...wake up! Come on now...wake up!" The cool, clear voice, layered with tones of amusement and warmth, came at her consciousness like a splash of cold water.

Garalynn say up abruptly, feeling her heart racing with the suddenness of her movements...looking up at the tall slender woman bending over her. "Beth?" She rose from the chair, and embraced her sister. As they separated, Garalynn noticed that there was another woman, and a man, also in the library with Beth.

Garalynn hugged Beth once again. "I guess I fell asleep...it is so good to have you home again! I though Roland was going to let me know when you arrived?"

"It's not his fault...he didn't see our car drive up...we came in the private drive, up behind the mansion itself. He didn't know we were here until he saw us in the hallway just a few moments ago. Some friends of mine offered me a ride home, in their private plane. I took them up on the offer...I really wasn't up to crowded terminals, and jet liners, so their offer was a god-send. By the way, here they are now!" Beth turned towards the silent couple, motioning for them to join them. "Garalynn...I'd like you to meet Lord Sean Dresden, from London...and his sister, Tamara. Tamara...Sean...this is my sister, Garalynn Gagnon. She's one of the firm's vice-presidents...as well a one of my dearest friends!" Beth smiled at her sister once again, squeezing her hand.

"Forgive me if I offend...but I thought you said your sister was your identical twin, Elizabeth!" The tone was cool, and Garalynn detected unsettling undercurrents in the silken voice as Tamara Dresden gazed at her.

Before Beth could reply, Garalynn smiled slightly. "Beth's sister, Sandra, *is* her identical twin, Tamara…I am her sister by adoption!" She stated quietly, holding her hand out. "I'm pleased to meet you both…and let me be among the first to welcome you to the States, Denver, and Blackmoon. Have you been here before?…to Denver, I mean?"

Sean stepped forward, taking her hand in his, and lifting it to his lips…his dark eyes never leaving hers. "It's rare that we have such a…*beautiful* welcoming committee, dear Garalynn. I assure you that had I known Denver had so many lovely females…I would have visited this city a long time ago!" His voice was a pleasant baritone, caressing her ears with an almost physical touch.

Garalynn nodded, her voice suddenly unable to articulate. This was one of, if not the, most physically handsome men she'd ever met. Tall…about six feet, five inches…urbane, dressed in the finest example of European style, he was an impressive man altogether. But…she felt as though his very presence was threatening to overwhelm her senses…his touch was causing irrational sensations to swirl inside her entire body, and her thoughts were jumbled. She'd been drawn to him almost immediately when he'd touched her hand…with all the blind, illogical obsession of a moth to a flame! She gently pulled her hand away, drawing a deep breath…closing her eyes for a brief second to reground herself. She looked back at him, once again anchored in her mind. She still felt an attraction towards him…as she would any good-looking man…but that momentary obsessive feeling was now gone.

Garalynn gazed into his eyes, seeing the compelling quality deep in those dark depths…their gaze complimented his powerful physique. Overall, she had to admit…it was definitely a most unforgettable first impression! And yet…she had this sudden sensation of something dangerous, and unsettling.

"My apologies, Garalynn...I trust my remarks in no way offended?" Tamara said smoothly...Garalynn could have almost sworn the other woman purred! "I wasn't aware that Elizabeth had more then the one sister. To be sure, Elizabeth has mentioned you a great many times...but always as her legal department head, or as her chief assistant, never as a sibling!" She gazed intently at Garalynn, as though subjecting the lady lawyer to some sort of special scrutiny. "Your name...most unusual, most rare...Scandinavian, isn't it?"

"As a matter of fact...it's Norwegian...my mother was born in Oslo." Garalynn returned the intense gaze...making her own probing of the other.

If her brother made a striking first impression, Tamara Dresden was definitely right up there as an equal. She was as fair as he was dark, and almost equaled her brother in height. Her golden-tanned skin seemed to almost glow, like the soft glimmerings of rich velvet. Long, platinum-blonde hair hung in straight lines down the sleek back, to the slim hips. She was beautiful, the ethereal beauty of an angel...her features an artist's dream become flesh. But, with all this physical perfection...it was the eyes that first caught, and held the viewer's attention. They were as golden and clear, like the finest crystalline amber. They seemed to gaze out on the world, and all it held, with a singular serenity. Garalynn, however, felt something quite different than that...though she agreed they were uniquely beautiful eyes, it was true. But...when she has first looked into their depths, she'd found herself suddenly very afraid! It had seemed, in the first moment they'd locked gazes, that she had seen the sum total of man's consummate terrors in those crystalline orbs. Then...the impression was gone, a veil dropped, and all that remained was the intriguing eyes themselves. For reasons as yet unknown, Garalynn found herself instinctively on her guard...and a fear rising within her she'd felt only upon waking from a particularly wicked nightmare...there was also a distinct feeling of familiarity.

She tilted her head to one side, looking closely at the other woman. "This will probably sound very cliché...but, have we met somewhere before?" Garalynn felt she was right in this. "I can't shake this feeling that we've known each other, very well...from some other time!"

Tamara shrugged her slim, strong shoulders...but Garalynn saw the millisecond of tension come and go in those glittering eyes. "I don't believe so, Garalynn...I have a very good memory for faces, and I doubt very much if I would have forgotten one as lovely as yours!" This last spoken with an unmistakable thread of sexual warmth...Garalynn felt a slight shudder of warning slip through her body...she'd had her share of approaches from gay women, but she'd always graciously allowed them to known her preferences lay elsewhere, and had in fact, become good friends with some of them. They were respectful of her wishes, and had been grateful she'd afforded them the same courtesy. She drew a deep breath...this was not going to her liking. She knew this was not a woman to cross, in any way!

Tamara saw the hesitation on Garalynn's face, and knew she'd caused a little indecision within the other woman...she smiled to herself...when others were off-balance, she was always the one in control. "Perhaps...I have one of those faces, as they say!" She replied coolly.

Garalynn shook her head, knowing it wasn't to be explained away that easily, then she turned back to her sister, and the man standing next to her. "By the way, Beth...where's Sandy? I thought she, and the others, were meeting you at the airport today!"

Beth smiled, thinking of her twin. "She's hopefully on her way here, from the airport, even as we speak, Garalynn...at least, if my secretary was able to track her down after I talked with her. We flew into the company's private airfield, and the car brought us here. I had called, and asked my secretary, and told her to let Sandra know the change of plans." She shook her head slightly, a wave of amusement going through her as she envisioned her twin's predictable response. "I'm sure I'm going to hear all about it when she does get home! Oh, good…I'd asked Roland to get us some refreshments, and here they are now!" She turned as the male servant entered the room, carrying a large serving tray which he sat on the large coffee table in the center of the room.

"Here's the drinks, and light snacks you requested, Miss Beth…shall I have the maids get guests rooms prepared?" He smiled, glad to see one of his girls back home.

"Yes…have them get two in the hall around the corner from my room ready…Lord Dresden, and his sister, will be here for an indefinite stay." Beth was grateful for Roland's always reliable, and considerate, anticipations.

He nodded, and left the room. Beth gestured for Garalynn, and her guests, to take a seat around the table, then sat down on the couch with Garalynn. She was anxious to hear about how things went in her absence. Garalynn poured some coffee, and answered a few of the questions Beth sent her way. Tamara relaxed in the easy chair across from the two sisters, sipping at the tea she'd poured for herself. She felt Sean's presence behind her chair, and glanced up at him. She saw how intent his gaze was as he watched the interaction between the sisters…his dark eyes warm with an inner heat.

Seeing that the other women were momentarily distracted with their personal discussion, she murmured softly aside to him. "Your interest is becoming too apparent, dear brother…take care it does not become an obsession! Elizabeth's good will is critical to our plans going smoothly…do not cause any problems that would interfere with tasks at hand!"

"How is it going to cause problems by simply enjoying the sight of a beautiful woman, my sister?…or, in this case, *two* such beauties! Why not enjoy *all* that might be offered?" was his low reply.

Her eyes narrowed ever so slightly…a subtle warning in her silken voice as she looked up again. "I agree with the statement of their beauty, Sean…but don't presume too much! I don't think Elizabeth is as open to certain things as you would hope, Sean...and I will not have you antagonize her at this stage! Don't spread your vaunted charm too thin, brother...remember the primary goal here. I will not tolerate anything going wrong due to your oversized ego!" She took a deep breath, and quickly answered a remark directed her way by Beth.

After a few moments, when Beth's attention was back to Garalynn, Tamara looked back at her brother. "Sean...there is something here...something I hadn't anticipated...and it revolves around this Gagnon woman! I cannot fully fathom it as yet...but I shall! In the meantime...do not give me any other problems to fix! Remember the reasons we've been sent here...and indulging your personal pleasures was not included in those plans! There is a task we have to complete before we're allowed to return home...and get back to our normal way of life!"

"You seemed inclined towards personal pleasures a few minutes ago, dear Tamara...you are hardly in a position to criticize my likes!" He'd bent closer to her head, keeping a watchful eye on their two companions. "I am very aware of why we are here, *and* your precious timetable, and how important it is we adhere to it totally! Stop treating me like a spoiled, willful *child*! I am as anxious as you to get this all over with, and get the hell out of here!" His handsome face contorted with dark feelings for a brief second, then returned to his customary expression of cynical humor. "But...I still see no logical reason not to enjoy what might very well be offered! You should do so more often...it might help you be less...intense!" He hissed as her slender fingers dug into the muscles of his jacket covered forearm.

"Take care, brother...you tred on very uneasy ground! And that is all I will say on that...for now! You speak of not being treated like a child!" She looked up at him, the golden eyes flashing, though the silky voice was soft, and cool. "Make sure your actions are not those of a child, Sean...and you won't be responded to as one! Now...lower your voice before we're overheard!" With that, she dismissed her brother in her mind, and focused her attention back on the sisters.

Garalynn had picked up on the brief exchange between Tamara and Sean, though she hadn't been able to make out any of the conversation itself. She'd seen the brief expression of anger on Sean's face, quickly replaced by one of abject obedience. She'd been aware of Sean's staring at both Beth, and her…and while she was flattered an attractive male was showing an interest in her…it had also, in some unusual way, frightened her. She didn't want any sort of attentions from this man!…but, she had no logical reason why. She shook her head, trying to shake this feeling!…she didn't like this at all! Why should she feel like this?

Beth rose from her seat, crossed the room, and lightly placed a hand on Sean's arm. "I'm sure the staff will have your rooms ready. Come…let me show the two of you where you'll be staying. You can freshen up, and then we can sit down to a real meal!"

He smiled down at her, pushing his momentary anger with his sister away…his dark eyes burning a suggestive path down her slender throat. "Of course, my dear Elizabeth! I must admit, I do find myself quite ravenous…for many things!" His eyes then swept over Garalynn, a clear meaning of the glance in them. He grinned as she turned her head away. He slipped a strong arm about Beth's trim waist.

Garalynn watched as the couple started towards the library's doorway. She found herself very troubled…her thoughts jumbled and unclear, something very unusual for her indeed. She found herself very apprehensive where her sister was concerned…especially where it involved the obvious attraction between Beth and Sean. Maybe she should have a good old heart-to-heart with Beth. She started towards the door, thinking to catch up with the couple that had just left, and ask Beth to see her later. Her mind was occupied with this, so she didn't hear Tamara come up behind her.

"My brother, and Elizabeth, make quite an attractive couple...don't you think? I think something quite spectacular could come of their being together...don't you agree, Garalynn?" A strange, subtle smile seemed to come and go about the lovely mouth as Tamara spoke up.

Garalynn turned her head, instantly on her guard once again. "My sister would make any man look good, with her on his arm, Tamara...as would her twin! I'm proud of how beautiful both my sisters are...and I will do anything I must to keep them both safe, and happy!...anything!" The tall lawyer said quietly, yet firmly...sending a clear message to the other woman. "Tell me...you all seem very familiar with one another...have you two known Beth long?"

"Oh, yes...nearly six years now! We first met her when she accompanied her father on a business trip to London in April of 1995...the first meeting for both Aranax and Phelps. My brother, as you could probably tell, is quite smitten with her. We were both quite happy to learn she would be the negotiating agent on this latest deal between our two firms." The tone of the voice was quiet, but Garalynn's sharp senses picked up on hidden undercurrents of silent mirth...as though Tamara was enjoying some huge, private joke.

"So...Aranax is your family's company?" Garalynn asked, starting after Beth and Sean again.

Tamara walked along beside the other woman, her eyes sliding up and down the lithe figure. "Yes...it's been in the family for over eighty years...one of many that we've accumulated over the past few decades." The tall blonde seemed bored with the conversation now...she was more interested in getting to learn more about her companion at the moment. Tamara was possessed of acute sensory powers...far above those of most humans...these sensitive powers were telling her there was indeed something special about this woman, but what?

Garalynn stared ahead, watching the fast disappearing forms of her sister, and Sean. "Tamara...this may sound pushy, but...just how long are you, and your brother, planning on being here, in Denver?" She glanced at the other. "I ask this because I'm sure Beth will want me to arrange some activities…I usually handle that sort of thing for her."

Tamara gazed at her, long and deep…she'd picked up on the unconscious defiance, and challenge in Garalynn's quiet words. Then, she tossed her head back, laughing…the sound like the tinkling of breaking glass. "To be quite honest, Garalynn…I'm not really sure. We do have a schedule I'd set up, and I do prefer to adhere to it…but, then, one never knows about schedules…do they?" She glanced once more after Beth and Sean, than back to Garalynn. "I appreciate your offer of…activities, but we'll have to play it one day at a time. I must say, though…I am beginning to feel that this trip will prove both entertaining, *and* profitable!…in more ways then one!" With a last smile, and nod, she hurried down the corridor after her brother, and Beth.

Garalynn stood where she'd been left, now thoroughly convinced there was something far from the norm going on here. This brother and sister from England…why did they seem dangerous? And why did it seem she'd known them before, especially where Tamara was concerned? Maybe, she thought…this was just because she was tired…that there wasn't anything, other than a bad first impression? No…she shook her head, this was real. Whatever it was, if this duo meant harm, in any way, to either of her adopted sisters…they'd answer to her in a big way!…..

II

❈

……Using the special pliers, the groomsman gently pulled the offending stone out of the big stallion's left front hoof. Holding the horse's bridle, running a soothing hand over the withers to settle the big animal, Sandra bent forward slightly, examining the hoof after the stone was removed. The soft center of the hoof's underside looked reddened. She straightened up, frowning, and stroked the proudly arched neck. The shiny coat felt like rough silk under her fingers. The big horse nipped at her hip pocket, nickering softly.

She chuckled, reaching into that pocket, and pulling out a couple of carrot chunks she always had when around her horses. "You think you're so smart, don't you?" She smiled as the soft lips tickled her palm, taking up the sweet pieces. She glanced over at the groom. "I don't like the way the center of the hoof looked, Tony…that stone was in there long enough to cause some inflammation. Have Dr. Parker look at it when he gets here, please?"

Tony Alonzo, her chief groom, nodded, taking the lead straps from her. "Sure thing, Sandra. I'll take him over to the infirmary, and have him ready for the doc. Come on, Treste!" He led the sorrel stallion away.

Sandra washed the grit off her hands in the watering trough. Straightening up, she shook the water from her hands, and looked around the huge compound. She was always at her happiest whenever she was around the beautiful, intelligent animals in Blackmoon's stable complex. She'd found, more times then she could count, that being with her animals, especially when she was troubled about something, helped focus her mind, and allow her to sort the best way out to handle the problem. She felt a quiet surge of pride, looking around the busy complex. She hadn't done half bad with what her father had bequeathed her…she whispered a silent "thank you" to him, in her mind.

The stables themselves consisted of a huge five-sided courtyard…the arched entrance, the offices, infirmary, and the stables, divided into those that held the prized brood mares, those for the yearlings and new acquisitions, and those for the thoroughbred studs. Each of the sections of the stable complex had their own exercise yards, with runways that led to grassy meadows for each section…separate from those of the other sections. The major wealth of the stables lay with the studs, each one a multimillion dollar franchise. The ledgers showed five such stallions currently at stud within the Blackmoon complex…the top one being an Arabian named Zarif Royale, Sandra's personal pride, and joy. He was the finest of the horses she herself had had a hand in breeding, and raising. He stood at nearly eighteen hands high, and not a single dark hair marred the snowy white perfection of his stunning coat. He could stand so still, and proud, at times, he seemed carved from purest marble. The purity of his color, as well as his size, made him a standout in his breed. The powerful chest, long strong legs, and graceful arched neck all proclaimed his desert heritage. Dark, watchful eyes looked out over this world where he was an undisputed king.

Zarif had always held a special place in her heart, ever since the night he'd been born. She'd been there, with the vet, to help his dam, Anaka, bring him into the world. In that minute, woman and horse had bonded…Sandra knew, in that moment, that she'd never let Zarif leave Blackmoon, or her. No matter what happened, or what anyone might offer for the big horse, she'd never get rid of him.

As she stood there, thinking of her special horse, her attention was distracted by a car coming in the archway. It stopped in front of the infirmary, and a tall, slender man, with graying hair, got out. He reached into the car, and brought out a large, black bag, and turned in her direction. Seeing Sandra standing there, the man waved, and walked over to where she stood.

Reaching her side, he bent down, and kissed her cheek. "Good morning, you pretty thing…you're looking as good as your horses!" He grinned at her.

She poked him in the ribs, grinning back at him. "Thank you, doctor…at least, I think thanks are in order!" She shook her head at him, then looked up as a thought came to her. "Oh, Keith…I almost forgot. I had Tony take Treste over to the infirmary…we removed a stone from his left front hoof, and it looked a little inflamed to me. Could you check it out for me? Oh…and guess what else? It appears one of your little 'ladies' is going to present us with a new foal way ahead of time!" She grinned again at the expression on his lean face.

Dr. Keith Parker, chief veterinarian for Blackmoon, and Sandra's cousin-in-law, simply shook his head, letting go with a deep exasperated sigh. He slapped a palm to his forehead in mock horror. "Don't tell me…let me guess…Windsprite! That mare never sticks to anyone's schedule!"

Sandra laughed, enjoying his company as always. Then, catching sight of Beth, Tamara, and Sean entering the courtyard, she stopped, chewing slightly on her lower lip, and taking a deep breath. Keith glanced down, puzzled by the sudden silence. He followed her gaze, and whistled softly under his breath. Sandra was not surprised to see a healthy male appreciation mirrored in his eyes as he watched the approaching trio. That fact seemed to make her sadder.

"That's quite a little beauty…though, not so little, huh? Guess she's one of the guests Lynda told me about, right?" He glanced down again at her…in time to see the flitting expression of pain, and anger slip across Sandra's lovely features.

Her eyes betraying her inner turmoil, Sandra nodded. "Yes…her name's Tamara Dresden…the man's her brother, Sean. Their family owns the British firm we just closed a major deal with. Apparently…they're both old friends of Beth's!" She glanced at Tamara again. "You really think she's that beautiful?"

He slipped a supportive arm about her shoulders. "Say, what goes on here? It's not like you to be jealous! Come on now…tell a pal…what's going on here?"

"That's just it…I'm not sure what *is* wrong…if anything! Look…I am the first to admit I can't warm up to them…especially Tamara! And, I know that fact bothers Beth a great deal! " She turned away, putting her down a little. "That's not true…she has told me it hurts her! She wants us to get along so desperately…but, Keith, I just can't! I can't give you a concrete reason, but I don't trust either of them!" She lifted her head, staring into space. "Keith…you know there's nothing I wouldn't do for either of my sisters…especially Beth! But, I can't do this…maybe if she wasn't so…so obsessive about him! And, I just don't like it!…at all!"

Keith was more than a little surprised at this declaration…totally unlike the warm, and usually open-minded woman he'd come to know. He took a deep breath, and chose his words carefully. "Sandy…do you think you might just be a…little jealous? Before you jump down my throat," he held a hand up to stop her near outburst. "You and Beth have always enjoyed a close relationship, and even your late marriage did nothing to change that. Look…I don't know these people, but maybe there's something that makes you feel, deep inside, that this relationship *could* change all that! And, since she's his sister, your feelings have included Tamara as well!"

Sandra glared at him. "Look, Sigmund Freud…don't be psychoanalyzing me, okay? You're an animal doctor…*not* a human one!" She stepped back, rubbing her palms along the sides of her jeans.

"Besides...I already tried that argument on myself! It's *not* that, I'm sure...I'm just not sure what it is! Now...hush!...here they are!"

"Keith!...how wonderful to see you again! It's been far too long! How are you doing?...I chatted with Lynda a few days ago, but didn't ask about you!" Beth gave him a warm hug, then stepped back, slipping an arm through Sean's. "Keith...I'd like you to meet two very special friends. This is Tamara, and Sean Dresden...Tamara, Sean...this is Keith Parker, our vet, and cousin!"

Keith nodded to Tamara, and shook Sean's hand. Then, he looked back to Beth, and smiled. "You're right, Beth...it has been a while. But, then...you don't usually show up, down here in the stables, on a week day morning! By the way...your little mare's ready for some easy riding now. That tendon pull seems to have healed up very nicely!"

"Wonderful...I've missed my rides on the weekends. I suppose I could use another horse, but Diamond has always been my favorite. I want to take Sean, and Tamara, on a ride around the property very soon!" She smiled warmly up at the big man standing next to her. He grinned down at her, his dark eyes caressing her as always. Keith just nodded...what goes on here? Beth acts like she's drugged!...were the thoughts going through his mind.

Sandra was about to say something when she saw one of the trainers, Doug Traylor, bringing Zarife out into the courtyard. She knew she hadn't given any orders for the big horse to be brought out, so she walked over to see if anything was wrong with her horse. Zarife saw her coming, and whinnied a greeting, tossing his proud head up and down.

Rubbing the animal's nose, Sandra looked at Doug. "Doug...what's Zarife doing out here? He's supposed to be down at the exercise pasture today...is anything wrong with him?" She asked, smiling a little when the stallion put his head over one of her shoulders, and pulled her up against his chest...his answer for a hug.

Doug was a little uncomfortable, glancing over at the others before speaking. "He was out in the pasture, ma'am...but your sister there asked me to bring him up this morning."

Sandra turned to Beth, a look of surprise on her face. "Beth?...why would you want Zarife brought up? You know you can't ride him...and why didn't you say something to me about it?"

"Tamara and Sean saw him out in the pasture the other day, and expressed an interest...so I asked Doug to bring him up this morning. As for not telling you about this...it didn't seem all that important to tell you first...after all, what's the harm?" came the unusually cool answer. "It's nothing to get all excited over, Sandra!"

Sandra couldn't believe what she was hearing...yes, it wasn't such a big issue, but the way her twin was acting was what was bothering Sandra the most. Beth acted as if no one else's feelings mattered at all. Sandra drew a deep, shaky breath. "Beth...you know that I want to be notified about anything concerning any of the horses!...especially where Zarife is concerned! And, you also know...he is *not* for sale, under any conditions, or to anyone, no matter who!" She absently stroked the big horse, trying to regain her inner focus.

Beth's slender brows drew together in an angry arch, and her blue eyes narrowed in displeasure. "You had best watch the tone of your voice, Sandra!...*I* am the head of the family, let us not forget!...and if I choose to show one of *our* animals, then I shall do so!...is that understood?" She stepped closer to her sister, jaw set and eyes like flint. "I think you need to rethink your priorities through, my dear sister...this is just an animal, *not* a person! Start acting more with logic and cold, hard facts...you might find more to your life than animals, or failed relationships!" Ignoring the shocked expression on Sandra's face, Beth turned to Doug. "Take Zarife back to his pasture, Doug...than have the grooms get three horses ready for us! I want to show Tamara and Sean the west woodland before dinner. We'll wait in the office until they're ready." She looked back at her sister, expression blank and uncaring. She nodded once at Keith, then slipped her arm through Sean's. The couple turned, and walked away, leaving two very shocked people...and one very amused one.

Zarife had pulled back, snorting and tossing his head when Beth and Sean walked by him. Sandra settled him down by stroking his neck again. She was staring after her twin, trying to understand what had just taken place...and why.

Tamara looked at the big horse for a few moments, then smiled at Sandra, the golden eyes cool and amused. "Sandra...I wouldn't be too upset with your sister...she's still a little unsettled from the plane trip, after all. And, she does tend to get a little irrational...and defensive when she's around my brother!" Tamara reached a hand towards Zarife, but paused when the stallion's ears went back. "A truly beautiful spirited animal...I quite understand your feelings towards hum, Sandra. I have one, or two, *pets* back home that I would be loathed to part with under any circumstances!" She looked back to Sandra, and smiled again. "Let this matter lie...think nothing of it, and everything will be fine! Elizabeth will probably have forgotten all about it in the morning! Well...I must be going! A pleasure to meet you, Dr. Parker! Adieu...for now!" With a wave of one slender hand over a slim shoulder, Tamara left them.

Sandra and Keith stood in silence for a few seconds, then she turned towards him. "Did I just hear what I think I heard?...was she trying to tell me how to act with my own *twin* sister? And telling me as though she were speaking to a child?"

The doctor shook his head. "I can't answer you, Sandy...I don't get any of it at all myself! Beth sure wasn't the Beth I've known for years." He looked at Sandra, and took her by one arm. "Look, Sandy...you've got to keep yourself calm here...you look like you're about to explode a blood vessel! I have to agree with you...something really isn't normal here...but, until you can first prove it, then find out what and why, you can't say or do anything!"

"And just why do you say that?" She asked, her voice low and cautioning. "Letting people walk all over my feelings has never been one of my strong suits, Keith…and Beth, above all others, knows that!"

"Is it worth straining your relationship with Beth further?…maybe losing it all together, Sandy?" He put his hands on both shoulders, and looked into the angry, and hurt, blue ice eyes. "It's obvious, even to me, that Beth *is* more than a little involved with this guy Sean…and not just on an emotional level! Whatever is going on with the two of them definitely has your sister acting totally not herself! Cool, calm, and collected…*that's* the Beth I know, not the snobbish, uncaring woman we just interacted with, Sandy. And, unfortunately, you're going to be the one bearing the brunt of her irrational emotions…at least, until you and she sit down, and talk it all through! And you will, you know…you two have always been able to talk your troubles, and disputes, over, and settle them! Just hang in there!"

She shook his hands off her shoulders, moving away. She stopped by the water trough, watching Doug lead Zarife back towards the stallion's private paddock. "You haven't been around here the last ten days, Keith…you don't know how she's been, especially when the Dresdens have been around! She had made a point of practically alienating most of the servants!…telling them they haven't been doing enough to make Tamara and Sean feel welcome…that they'd all better start doing their jobs better, or they could be replaced! Keith…some of those people have been with us since we were born!"

"That doesn't sound like our Beth, that's for sure!" He came up behind her, staring after Beth and Sean…or, at least, in the direction the couple had disappeared.

"That's only a small part of it…she's accused Garalynn of flirting with Sean…trying to take him away! Our sister has been staying at her condo in the city…trying to steer clear of both Beth, and the Dresdens! Beth hasn't even been going into the office during the week…even for a token show! She's had everything important faxed here, to her personal office…then has me, or her secretary here, handle it so she's free to be…to be with him!" Sandra crossed her arms over her chest, her jaw working in stressed agitation. "She's been like a yo-yo!…fine one moment, the next like…" her voice died away, and she looked at Keith, her eyes wide, pain-filled and worried. "Sometimes…sometimes, I almost wonder if they haven't drugged her in some way, Keith!"

He shook his head. "That's one concept I refuse to accept where Beth, or you, is concerned, Sandy…at least, until someone shows me hard proof! Maybe, it's what Tamara said…a combination of jet-lag, and her obvious feelings for this Sean! I will say one thing…for the record, I don't like him! Maybe it's unfair…since I just met the guy, but there's something too perfect, too arrogant about him!" He looked towards the office, and the show arena. "Something about him gives me the creeps!"

Sandra sighed, rubbing one hand over her forehead. She was suddenly very tired, and wanted to leave. "Well…whatever, I guess it's going to up to me to set things straight once again. I think I'm going to have to have a one-on-one with my sister…or else, one hell of a good row!" She turned as Doug Traylor came back from the paddock, and approached them again.

He told her the big stud was back in his pasture, and asked if there was anything she needed him to do now. She shook her head, thanked him, then left the two men alone by the watering trough. Doug looked after her, wishing he could help. "Miss Sandra's pretty worried about her sister…isn't she, Dr. Parker?" He asked quietly.

Keith knew the question came from a genuine concern, not a wish for idle gossip between Blackmoon employees. Doug had been working for the family for several years, and was close with all of them…especially Garalynn. "Yeh, I'm afraid she is just that, Doug! But, knowing her as well as I do, and how much her sister means to her…I know she'll find an answer to things. That's part of Sandy's special charm…she always finds the way where anyone she cares about is involved!" He clapped the other man on the shoulder. "Well…got to get to work!

Horses wait for no vet!...see you, Doug!" Keith headed for the infirmary, and the start of his day's work.

The trainer stood there, still looking in the direction Sandra had left in...thinking over all that he'd seen, and heard in the past few days. He knew Beth's actions of late had been out of the normal, and Sandra was worried about that fact. There was something about the two guests at Blackmoon that had him uneasy...especially the drop-dead gorgeous Tamara. Unknown to anyone else, Doug often walked the gardens at night, troubled much by a chronic insomnia. It was during one of these nocturnal strolls that he'd come across Tamara...though unseen by her. The fact that she was walking around, in itself, was not a fact of alarm. He knew that as well as anyone. But, what was unusual, and a little alarming...Doug had watched her, on more than one occasion, performing some strange, ritualistic type dance...always in the center of the formal gardens, always in the moonlight...and always totally nude! The silver moonlight had bathed her lithe body, making the golden skin shimmer...but he swore he saw dark patches on her body, of some dark, shiny liquid. Her hands always looked stained with the same dark fluid...but he could never find any trace of it anywhere in the garden. And, he'd examined the central areas closely after she'd gone back into the manor house. He'd wondered if it was just some sort of special make-up she used for the erotic dancing he'd witnessed. He hadn't said anything, to anyone, about this almost nightly spectacle...one, because she had been nude, and he knew how it would sound. But, the main reason he'd kept silent...the movements she'd make as she danced called to him, in a way as ancient and mysterious as time itself. He'd resisted moving to join her, each time he'd watched the strange and unsettling dance...but he couldn't help thinking that there *had* been a time, perhaps centuries ago...that he *hadn't* resisted, that he had joined, and his very soul had suffered for it! He decided to continue watching the enigmatic woman during her midnight revels...he owed it to the family that had come to be as his own.

"I'm not sure there's really anything to watch out for…it is only a gut feeling, after all, " he murmured to himself. "But…if those two *do* mean some kind of harm, or something bad for the family, then they'd best watch out! There's a lot of people, here at Blackmoon, that have a special place in their hearts for the ladies we call 'boss'. And, *none* of us will take someone trying to hurt any of them kindly at all!" He frowned, thinking. "No…not kindly at all!"……

…..Beth trembled, senses reeling, held captive in the tight circle of Sean's powerful arms. His lips leisurely tantalized the side of her slender throat. His left hand had pulled the neckline of the beige silk blouse she was wearing…down, and to one side, leaving the top of her right shoulder bare. His mouth slid down to this new territory, his warm breath searing the flesh there, causing her to shudder delicately, his tongue flicking lightly over the goosebumps appearing. His right arm wrapped securely about her waist, he held her tight against his body, bending her ever so slightly backwards.

He murmured against her skin, the movement of his lips bringing forth more shudders, and a slight increase in her breathing. "Has your anger disappeared?…or do you insist in maintaining this irritation with your sister? Instead of allowing yourself to be immersed in the pleasures I have vowed to surround you with, my dear." His tongue flicked along her collarbone, trailing the pulse point until he came to where the shoulder met the base of the throat. There, his mouth gently latched onto the pounding pulse, letting her just barely feel the drag of his teeth along that throbbing.

Beth opened her eyes, his words snapping her out of a near trance. She pulled her hands back from his broad shoulders, and pushed against his chest. "Sean…let me go! I can't do this!…not here!…not now! Someone could walk in!" She looked towards the door of the empty stall they were standing within.

His deep voice rumbled against her ear, temptingly slow and seductive. "And would that be such a disaster?...for someone to see us in the act of love? You are far too reserved, my dear Elizabeth...spontaneity is an essential basis for true passion to grow, and manifest itself!" He drew her back against him, his lips gently engulfing her earlobe, driving her senses into a whirlwind again. "Love will not long be denied, my sweet girl...even by someone with a will as great as yours' professes to be!"

She felt her head spin, then she gasped, pushing him away. His arms allowed her to leave their circle this time, as he watched her closely. She stepped back, shaking her head. "You...you don't understand, Sean...I can't allow myself to lose control! Too much, and too many people's welfare depend on that control always being there. Besides, no one here would understand at all if they came in on me...on us...it would be inappropriate, Sean! I know how stupid this sounds, but my dignity, and how other s perceive me...I 'm sorry, Sean." She smoothed her hair back into place, adjusting her blouse as well. "I just can't understand the way I acted towards Sandra today! It was as if I didn't care a thing about her wishes, or feelings...or anything! It was like I was deliberately trying to provoke an argument with her! She was right...this is her world out here! She has the final say...not me! I have to talk to her...soothe everything back to the way it is usually."

Her blouse fixed, she bent and picked up her windbreaker from the straw covered floor. As she straightened out, Sean stepped closer, the knuckles of his hand brushing gently over her left cheek.

"There will soon come a time, my Elizabeth, when you will care *only* for what I think, what I feel...and how those feelings can make you feel, and react! It will be the things that *I* can show you...teach you...give you that will come to be the only ones of value in your mind, and heart!" He smiled, his dark eyes holding her blue orbs, reaching deep into the cerulean depths. "Forget this little incident...it means nothing! It will blow over, like the insignificant dust it is! Talking further about it will only drag things out, cause more bruised feelings, and blow everything out of proportion. Trust me…I know what I'm talking about here!" He spoke to her without the usual arrogance behind his words…rather, his words were firm and measured, as if from a depth of certainty only he possessed.

Beth was about to reply when Tamara's light laugh broke in on their preoccupation with each other. "Ah, so this is where the two of you disappeared!…how interesting!" She looked around the spacious stall, smirking. "So…are we still going riding today? I got bored waiting in that office…what interests have you two been involved with in here?" Beth stiffened, picking up on the subtle undercurrents of sarcasm and ridicule.

"Of course, we're still going riding! I was just showing Sean around while the horses were getting rigged. You wait here…I'll go see what the delay is all about!" Beth hurried out of the stall, suddenly feeling trapped and suffocated.

Tamara watched her leave, then slowly turned back to where her brother still stood…a brother who was suddenly very apprehensive, and cautious. He looked away briefly, unable to see the slight smile on his sister's face. Tamara smiled even more, seeing this discomfort. She walked about the stall, running her fingers over the various pieces of tack hanging about the interior. She glanced at her silent brother from time to time. Finally, she stopped in front of him, a smug expression on her lovely face. "Was my entrance ill-timed, dear brother? Elizabeth appeared unsettled…and you look as though you wished you were anywhere, but here, with me! Is there something amiss?" Her voice was light, consoling…and as deadly as a hidden poison.

He shook his head, feeling his throat go dry, knowing his danger. "She's still upset over the argument with his sister, that's all…she'll be fine!" He answered. "She's a little shyer than most of the women I've been involved with, that's all!"

"Oh?…shy? So…I am to take it that her 'nervousness' was in no way due to you then…is that what you're saying?" Tamara raised one shapely eyebrow. "Has your great charm lost some of its strength,

Sean?...you weren't trying to exert any of it over Elizabeth? Why, Sean...are you nervous as well? Surely...you haven't done anything to feel that way...have you?"

Sean looked away again, clenching and unclenching his fists. "Alright, Tamara...you can stop this now! I know why you're acting this way...you think I went against your wishes...that I moved too soon for your precious plan!" He steeled himself, staring into the golden eyes. He feared little in this life...but his sister was something he did. "I an just as capable as you about taking advantage of an opportunity, Tamara. I can make the decision to move ahead...I an capable of being in charge of a situation!"

She tossed her head back, her laughter ringing out, clear and mocking. "Oh...really? Well, then, Sean...go ahead...tell me what to do next?" She gazed at him, the smirk lingering about her lips belied by the anger in her eyes.

His lips were white now, the frustration and anger coursing through his body making him unwise. "You have no right to talk to me in this fashion, Tamara! This precious plan of yours can't work without me, and you know it! You had better start treating me as my position, and rank, warrants!"

Her eyes went blank, and her laughter ceased. The slight smile remained on her lips, but it was merely a sham. "Sean...this should be obvious, but I will say it for your benefit...once, and only once! I will treat you in the manner I feel you have earned to this point. You will take whatever I decide to give you, in whatever manner I choose to give it in...and you will not argue the point further! You will follow my orders...any orders...to the fullest letter, or you will pay the consequences! Is that all clear?" The voice was light, cool, and seemingly innocuous...Sean knew otherwise, but his anger had been pushed too far.

He reached out, grabbing her arm, and jerking it up harshly, pulling his sister up close to him. "I said you will not speak to me like that any more!...do you hear me? I am just as in charge as you, and your ways are not the only ones to be followed here, Tamara! You told me to make Elizabeth care for me…care deeply. I have succeeded quite admirably, dear sister, and I saw no reason not to push the situation a little! What is the harm, Tamara? It can only help to make her even more pliable to our wishes…and that will help the plan become reality even better!"

"So…that's the way it is? And, of course, the fact that *your* personal pleasures will also be well served has nothing to do with anything…does it? As long as the goal is reached, then what does it matter if a step, or two are omitted? What does it matter that any unplanned step, that could destroy all we're here to accomplish, is inserted into our schedule? So it ends up taking us longer to find what we're here to find. As long as you are satisfied…what does it matter that it will take that much longer for us to go home, or that the longer we're forced to stay here, the greater the danger to *us* becomes?" Tamara was almost purring…a warning sign he should have been wise enough to pick up on, and heed. "You're right, Sean…you were supposed to make Elizabeth care for you, and you *have* succeeded very well, indeed! But, remember…how, and when, this situation was to be pushed further was discussed, and decreed, by the *family*…before we came here! The decisions as to how things were to proceed were left to *my* discretion! Keep that in mind at all times, and everything will go smoothly. And…you will be able to realize all you hope…when I say it is time! Now…let my arm go!"

He didn't listen, didn't take the chance she'd given him to retreat gracefully…his dignity, and everything else, intact. "You are always so sure of yourself!…aren't you, dear Tamara? Sooner, or later…that smugness will be your undoing!" He released her arm, his eyes flashing with dark anger…yet bleak with the knowledge that he was helpless against his sister's cool, dispassionate power. He took a deep breath, letting it out, ragged and harsh. "You know I can't do anything against you, Tamara…at least, not at this time! Why must you take such pleasure in demeaning me at every turn? You need me, for full success…and I need you to realize all I desire! We should not be competing with one another, Tamara. To realize success fully, we need cooperation between us at all times!"

"That's quite true, Sean. Do as you are told, follow the plan laid out for us, and all will become fact! Don't make me have to remind you of this again!"

He glared at her, trying to come up with a suitable response. Then, he relaxed, a sudden thought coming to him. "Tamara...you're still trying to get back at me, aren't you? Even after all these many years, you haven't forgotten...or forgiven! You are still determined to make me feel all the pain, frustration, and loss you declared I caused you all those...gods, Tamara! My hand...you've cut my hand!"

He clutched his right hand, grimacing in real pain...shocked that she'd been able to hurt him. He carefully began peeling back the riding glove he'd put on earlier. Now bearing several rips, with thick blood beginning to ooze out through the tears, it looked as though a savage animal had shredded it with its claws. He glared at his sister, dropping the ruined glove to the floor, and wrapping his hand tightly with his handkerchief.

Silent, Tamara stared at him, her eyes devoid now of any expression. She'd moved with an inhuman speed, and Sean had had no chance to move away. She knew his hand was in no way seriously injured. She'd meant it only as a lesson. With leisured grace, she pulled her own glove back on, and brushed her long hair back behind her ears.

Finished with wrapping his hand, he looked sullenly at her. "Damn you, Tamara...this was not necessary!" He held his bandaged hand up with a jerk. "I wouldn't have done anything to you...you're my sister! Must you always have the last word in everything?"

"Since mine is usually the best one...yes. That was just a sample, Sean...never forget that! You may be stronger than most everyone else...but *I* can hurt you! You'll be fine, and you know that! That little cut will be healed by tomorrow...just keep it covered, and out of sight, until that time. Don't defy me again, Sean…or the next time may be worse then even you could bear! Don't forget who is in charge…I'll not say this again!"

He wanted to scream his anger, and frustration at her…see that cool self assurance melt away, dissolve into tears. But…he knew he couldn't…it wasn't the time for him to declare his "independence" from either his sister's domination, or his family's influence even from a distance. So, hanging his head in resignation, he acknowledged her superior status, and his place in the scheme of things. Though every inch of his body desired nothing more than to strike back, Sean knew his task at hand now was to get back into his sister's good graces…and that meant subjecting himself to profound humiliation at the hands of his sister…he had to apologize. His time would come, he told himself…then, we would see who is best.

"Forgive me for my anger, Tamara…and if I stepped out of line where Elizabeth is concerned, then I apologize for that also. What are your orders now?" He bowed his head, swallowing his pride…at least, outwardly.

Tamara gazed at him, gauging the depth and sincerity of his words…she sighed, realizing he was simply trying to placate her, his desires still foremost in his thoughts and feelings. "For now…we'll overlook this for now, Sean. There is far too much at stake to indulge in insignificance, and not enough time. I truly hope you do mean what you say, brother…for your sake! As for Elizabeth…continue to court her as you have been doing, Sean, and do not let your hormones get too agitated…you'll have what you desire most soon! But…when *I* say so, do you understand?" She half-turned away, then looked back at him, eyes half-closed in seemingly lazy contemplation. "And, Sean…a few moments ago, you were about to refer to an incident in our past, to which I say…don't! Never bring anything about that event…ever again! To do so may make you the recipient of unending, excruciating pain…and you know I can make that a fact! Simply do as you're told, and everything will be fine!" She made as if to leave, but he stopped her...gently, and with total deference this time.

"Tamara...I have to ask this, forgive me. Aren't *you* ever uneasy being here?...even just a bit? I mean...there is so much here that is unsettling to the senses, sister! Can't you feel it? Not to mention, having to curtail our usual routines, and putting up with the...well, you know what I mean! Haven't you felt the need to...it's nearly driving me wild! How can you always be so calm?" His handsome face looked stressed, and a little pale under that dark tan.

She put her hand over the fingers on her forearm, squeezing them a little as if trying to reassure. It was strange, and unusual to hear the gentleness in her voice after what had just transpired. "You let those thoughts dwell too much in your mind, Sean...you always have! There is a great deal more to life than those desires you allow to rule your every step! I'll try and make this as simple as possible...simply follow your orders, complete the tasks assigned you with your usual flair, and we'll soon be on our way back home!" She reached out, stroking his cheek with a tenderness seldom exhibited by her towards him. "I know the need you speak about, Sean...I feel it as well, believe it, or not. I have simply learned how to focus better then you. Don't let it worry you...I'll see to everything when the time arises! Haven't I always taken care of you?...I don't intend to change all that now, dear brother! Do as I said...make Elizabeth become so dependent on you, on your presence, that she must have it always! Just do it as I will relay it so...alright?" She sighed, removing her hand, and drawing herself to her full impressive height. "You, above all others, know what will happen if this is pushed too hard, too fast...and fails as a result! Or...have you forgotten some of the others? We cannot fail this time, Sean...the penalty is too great! You know that as well as I! Ours is not the *forgiving* sort of family...remember that!"

"When I think of all we stand to gain...or lose...Tamara, it actually unsettles me almost past endurance! And when I feel that tension...the need becomes even greater! I wish we were home now! Despite all Elizabeth's allure, and all our family can gain…I wish only that we were home…among our own, and away from the auras of *this* place!" Sean shook his head, trying to regain his calm, and usual arrogance. His face was ashen, and sweaty.

"You can control it, Sean…we all have to when the necessity arises. However difficult it is, we have all had to, from time to time. Don't worry about it any further…I'll see to the necessary arrangements. Remember, Sean…control is the most vital link in all we've done, and in all we've yet to do! Should the need become overwhelming, then I'll make sure it's handled…discreetly, and efficiently. Now…return to the manor house…I'll make your excuses to Elizabeth, and tell her we'll ride another day. Now…go, and keep that hand out of sight!"

Sean quickly left…being around Tamara just then was proving unsettling, and somewhat frightening. He'd decided against his desire to challenge his sister…for this moment, at least. He hadn't given up on the idea of that challenge…oh, no! He fully intended to regain his rightful place, and see his dear sister receive all that was coming to her, at his hands. The time would present itself, and he'd take full option on all it gave to him! His sister…indeed, his entire family…would one day bow to *him*!

Tamara walked out into the bright October morning, taking a deep breath of the fresh mountain air. The welcome Indian summer had made the breezes balmy, and the air made her feel ever vital, and alive! In the few days they'd been at Blackmoon, she'd come to appreciate all that it meant to the Phelps sisters. The underlying beauties, and strengths impressed her…strength was something she understood very well. But…she didn't allow her appreciation to distract her mind from the pursuit of the goal their family had sent there to accomplish…beyond the business dealings.

She glanced around, satisfied that there didn't appear to be anyone who could have overheard the conversation between her, and Sean. She looked towards the center of the courtyard, and saw Sandra coming back out into the square. The distrust, and dislike from this one of the Phelps sisters had been all to obvious. It was proving to be a small irritant, but hardly an impossible one, she was sure. She'd overcome greater obstacles than Elizabeth's obstinate twin sister…this was not going to beat her now!

She hummed a little tune to herself. "Her only worth is how we can utilize Elizabeth's feelings for her sister to our best interests. Should she become more of a problem…she can always be eliminated altogether!" She said softly to herself. A small noise broke in on her concentration.

She quickly turned her head, and saw the trainer she'd seen earlier that morning, with Zarife. Doug Traylor, trying hard to slip around the corner without being heard, or seen, paled when he realized he'd been seen. He grabbed hold of the bag he was carrying, and ran out of sight, around the corner of the stable. His actions, expression, and body language…it all told Tamara that he most probably had indeed over-heard what had transpired between her and her brother. She also realized now that she'd seen him before this time, and earlier that morning. Her head lifted, and her eyes narrowed as her memory supplied her the information she required. She had been sure, once or twice, that someone might have been spying on her midnight walks…but not really positive. Now…now, there was no longer any doubt…it had been this man!

Tamara stood there, quiet and pensive…but only for a moment. She lifted one hand, running her fingers through her thick mane, feeling the breeze rippling the long tresses, like strands of liquid silver. She stared into space, a brittle smile playing about her lips. His eaves-dropping didn't bother her over-much…it was simply an unplanned annoyance, that would need to be dealt with, sooner or later. Personally, she always preferred sooner. She took a deep breath, and sighed…she did so hate loose ends!….

….Lt. David Collison looked about the spacious apartment, shaking his head, tired and out of sorts. He'd been more than ready to all it a day when this call had come over his car radio…he'd cursed softly, and turned his car back in the opposite direction, reluctantly answering the call's request for all units to report. He looked around again, trying to visualize what this place looked like when in order. It must be quite a place to see…when clean, in order, and intact. Right now, however, there wasn't one single piece of furniture that wasn't in ruins. No wonder the neighbor who'd called it in said it had sounded like a full-fledged battle zone. He'd already spoken with the two troopers who'd first responded to the call, and his partner, who'd beat him there, was speaking with the landlord, and the neighbor who'd summoned the police.

David shook his head again, and reached into his coat pocket, dragging out his battered, ever-present notebook. He'd frequently said he didn't think this job could shock him any more…he had a bad feeling this case was about to prove him wrong. He opened his notebook, and frowned, looking around. This crime scene seemed different from others…despite the wreckage, there really wasn't definitive physical "trace" to go with here. The lab boys were already there, and starting their meticulous task of gathering even the most minute bits of "trace"…the necessary atoms of evidence that was needed to both identify the perpetrator, and the events leading to the actual crime itself. The lab crew had lifted a few prints so far, those of the victim, and a few others as yet unidentified.

Another bit of unsettling evidence…for the amount of damage done to this room, it had to have taken twenty minutes at least to achieve this level. Yet…the neighbor who'd called the police said it had been only a minute, or two, that she'd heard both the crashing, and the curdling screams. She, and her husband, had both gone to the door, when the noise had abruptly ceased, but neither of them saw anyone leave…they'd been afraid the killer, or killers, were still in the apartment itself. David knew there was a back entrance to this floor of the building, and had a couple of his men checking it out for any evidence. He also had some men checking on the street, and the surrounding buildings, for any possible witnesses. So far…nothing.

David looked towards the overturned sofa…and the sheet draped lump lying on the floor beside it. One of the troopers had used what he could find to cover the body, after they had entered the apartment to find the destruction. The officers had said they found it there, and being good men, had made sure nothing was touched, or moved in any way. David had looked at the body when he'd first arrived, and had gotten quite a surprise. The man lying under that sheet had been literally torn to pieces…not one single inch of his body didn't bear some terrible laceration, or ripping cut. In fact, David had thought they'd resembled a victim he'd looked at last summer…the result of a wild mountain lion attack. The thing that had surprised him the most was the lack of something…there was little, or no blood!

The lab boys had told him, that except for a very few small spots, they'd found no traces of blood anywhere, even when using luminol, which would allow even minute, invisible traces of old blood to be seen in the dark, with fluorescent light. The coroner, still going about his portion of the investigation, had told David that, in his preliminary findings, it looked as though this victim had had *all* bodily fluids drained…but there was no trace of any fluid, anywhere in this room, or the entire apartment…thus far, at least.

To David, there was only one obvious reason…the victim hadn't been killed in this room. The body had been brought here, and the room destroyed, to make it look like this was the site of the murder…to throw the police investigation off. The big question was…why? What was there about this particular victim that someone went to great lengths to be sure no one would find out the truth behind the killing?

He walked back over to the sheet-covered body, squatted down beside it, and pulled back one corner. He stared at the ruin that had been the guy's face, seeing the wide, staring eyes. Whatever those eyes had last seen had clearly shocked, baffled, and terrified the man. That look of fear was all too familiar to David…it had shown up too often in his line of work. But…there was something else in those dead eyes' expression, he thought. There was something beyond the sense of bafflement…beyond the fear, beyond the terror. David was convinced that this man totally disbelieved what he'd seen, and that disbelief had been so huge that the man's mind couldn't accept it! David shook his head, dropping the sheet back in place, and standing with a soft groan. This was not going to be a good one, his brain told him.

He saw his partner, Sgt. Patrick Reynolds, using his penknife on a spot next to one of the pictures hanging on the wall by the fireplace. He walked to join Patrick, looking over one burly shoulder. "What you got there, Pat?" He asked, trying to see what the older man was after.

"Bullet-hole…just trying to see if we got lucky, and got a good bullet! Hold on…" Patrick slowly lifted the tip of his knife up, using it like a hook to gently pull the trapped piece of ammunition out. With a triumphant groan, he let the small bit of metal come out, and fall into his open palm. He gently dropped the bullet into an evidence bag, and grinned at David. "Looks good…little or no damage to it. Ballistics should get a good shoot here!"

"Well…it'll be one of the few good things we have been able to come up with here!" David declared, sticking his notebook back in his coat pocket. "Pat…what do you think really happened here? I mean…there's an awful lot of things that don't add up here!…you know what I mean?" He looked at his partner…he trusted this man beyond all others he'd worked with, and knew his instincts were truer than most.

"I think someone's trying to throw us in a wrong direction…for whatever reason, we don't know yet, but I think that's what's going on here. It's obvious this guy wasn't killed here…unless they did so with drop cloths over everything to catch even the tiniest drop of blood. But, even that wouldn't answer about all the other bodily fluids, would it,

Dave?" Patrick sighed, running one burly hand back through his thinning hair. "Dave, I'm not really sure what happened here! We've taken a total of five 9mm slugs out of this room…from the wall, one of the chair backs, and from the fireplace mantel. There was obviously a fire fight here…probably when all the furniture was wrecked, too. So…if there *was* a fight here, and shooting…chances are the killing was done here, if you think that way. Except, again…no blood! Unless, as I said…someone's just trying to make it *look* that way…and it was done somewhere else!"

"So…was it here, or not?…looks like we've a riddle to solve, as well as a murder, right, Pat?" David looked over at the body. "You ever seen someone killed like that before, Pat?…like someone just lost it, went crazy, and just started hacking!"

"The only time I've seen anyone close to being cut up like that was over in Vietnam…after some Cong had gotten through with them! But…even that was more methodical, more understandable. This is just…I don't know. There's something about this killing that gives me the creeps!" The older policeman shrugged his shoulders…he didn't feel comfortable here…there was a presence, an aura that make his flesh crawl.

"Yeh…I think I know what you mean…I can't shake the thought it was some kind of animal, and yet an animal doesn't use a gun! And, so far, there's been no sign of any kind of animal being in the apartment!" David shook himself…this was getting too afar of what they were supposed to be doing here. "You know…it still bothers me…the lack of blood, or any *real* trace of physical clues! I can't help but think…well, let's just focus on what we *do* have." He looked at Patrick. "Any ID on this guy as yet?"

"Yes…he had a wallet in his pants pocket., with about one hundred fifty in it…which kind of rules out robbery, huh? There were four credit cards, too. The guy's name is…was Douglas Traylor. Dave…there was a Blackmoon employee card in his wallet." Patrick smiled crookedly at the grimace David's face went through. "I had one of the uniforms call out there…seems the guy was one of the head trainers at the stables there. Been there about thirteen years. The estate manager said someone from the family would be coming over to identify the body."

"Great…just fucking great! Blackmoon…why me? You know what that means, don't you, Pat? All the big brass will be sticking their noses in on this one…screwing any leads we get, and trying to tell us how to carry on the investigation! Now, I really wish I hadn't gotten this call!" David said disgustedly…he hated politics in any form, and especially when the upper level bureaucrats interfered with the normal routine of the department.

Patrick knew his partner of five years was upset when he used that certain curse word…David seldom used it otherwise. "Well…look at it this way, pal…maybe you'll be able to actually go out to Blackmoon! Hear it's quite the place inside…never been myself, though we've seen it from the outside lots of times!"

David sneered…he had very little use for the "idle" rich, even those as philanthropic as the Phelps family. He glared at his partner's grinning face. "Go ahead…smile! You won't be long when the pressure from up top starts beating down, to get this case solved ASAP!…and get the murderer under wraps! And from what we *haven't* been able to find out about this case, it's going to be a heel of a one to crack!" He turned towards one of the uniformed policemen who'd just come up to them. "And what the hell do you want?"

"Sorry, Lt.…the guys down at the front door called up to say there's someone from Blackmoon down there…about this guy!" The officer heartily wished he was somewhere else.

"Tell them to let whoever it is come up to the hallway here…but I don't want them in here, you hear? I hold you responsible…understand?" David gestured towards the hallway. He looked back at Patrick.

The big sergeant shrugged, then, looking back at the body, his demeanor changed to one of nervousness. "Dave...we've been partners a while now, right?"

"Sure...over five years now. In fact, you're the one who put me up for these lieutenant bars!" He stepped closer, sensing something was wrong. "What is it, Pat?"

The older man waved his hand, trying to make little of what he was feeling. "I think, maybe, that I'm just a little spooked by this one...too many things that don't go together...you know? Dave...have you ever known me to be jittery, or flaky about a case before?"

David grinned, gripping the other man's shoulder. "You're just flaky about everything, Pat!" Seeing that his attempt at humor wasn't working, he dropped the joking, and gazed at his partner, and friend. "You're one of the steadiest, most incisive cops I've ever worked with, Pat...I learned to trust your gut feelings over a lot of so-called evidence! Now...where is this leading to, buddy?"

Patrick jerked his thumb over one shoulder, in the direction of the body. "It's just that...well. No one deserves to die like that!...and it scares the crap out of me!"

For a moment, or two, David felt his thoughts being taken into a dark area that he seldom allowed his mind to go into...then, he shook his head, angry for letting himself to think such things. "Forget it, Pat...this is just a very nasty scene, and we're going to find out that all we're dealing with here is some kind of wacko!" He gripped Patrick's hand, and grinned. "Come on...you'll feel better once we wrap things up here, and head for home!"

Patrick smiled slightly. "Yeh...you're probably right...about everything!" He looked around the room one last time, then saw the gurney at the door. "Looks like the ambulance guys have arrived...okay for them to come in now?"

"See if the coroner needs the body for anything else here first...I think he's done, but make sure. And, Pat...while you're at it, pass the word around that everyone's to keep their traps shut on this one! Anything anyone outside of the department needs to know will be in the official press release! This one's going to be hard enough without flapping gums...not to mention it's going to be sensitive because of the possible involvement of Blackmoon, and the Phelps family!" He nodded to his partner. "That reminds me...got to go out to the hall...someone from Blackmoon is on their way up!"

David headed for the door...besides going to meet the person from Blackmoon, he found he suddenly needed some fresh air. As he stepped outside of the doorway, he couldn't resist one last look back inside...he saw the ambulance attendants lifting the sheet covered body up onto the gurney, and suppressed a shudder. He shook his head...he was letting Patrick's nervousness get to him. He turned back towards the hall, and ran smack into the tall, slender woman who'd just come up behind him. He grabbed her buy the shoulders, preventing her from tumbling back over the large potted plant against the wall. "Sorry...didn't see you there! Afraid you can't go in there, ma'am...it's an official police crime scene. You have business around here?" He looked at her closely...there was something familiar about her.

Sandra Phelps-Usher drew a shaky breath, settling herself from the near fall. Then glancing towards the open doorway. She paled a little, seeing the covered body on the gurney, coming through the doorway as she watched. She shook her head, bringing her attention back to the tall man holding her by the shoulders. "My name's Sandra Phelps...and I was asked to come here to...to identify an employee of ours!" She looked at the gurney. "Is...is that Doug?"

"If your employee's name was Douglas Traylor, and this is where he lived...then it's my sad job to inform you Mr. Traylor meet his death approximately three hours ago...by person, or persons, unknown." He couldn't take his eyes off her...she was so beautiful. "Do you feel up to identifying the body?...I warn you, it's not a pretty sight!"

She took a deep breath, then slowly nodded. He stopped the gurney, and gently lifted the sheet. Sandra's eyes widened when she saw the ruined face, but there was enough for her to recognize that it was her trainer, and friend. "Yes…that's him!…that's Doug!" She looked away, staring up into David's dark blue eyes. "What happened here? Who would do that to Doug?…he was one of the gentlest men I knew!"

"We're not sure of any of that right now, Ms. Phelps…we'll know more once we have all the evidence gathered together…and finished with all the interviews. Come on…let's get away from here…find somewhere quieter to talk!" He took her by the elbow, and gently steered her back down the hallway, away from the proximity of the crime scene. He knew there was a small lobby down the hall, and figured it would be better to question her there.

Once there, he got her settled in one of the chairs, then sat down across from her, and took out his notebook. "I know this is not the best of times, ma'am…but I do need to ask you a few questions," he asked, gazing at her…she was really nice to look at her, his brain kept saying to him.

She shook her head, feeling herself regaining control. "It's fine…whatever I can do to help catch the monster who did this, I want to do!" She looked away a moment as a thought came. "Oh, God…Garalynn!"

"Ma'am?…who is this Garalynn you mentioned?" David made a quick notation of the name.

"My sister…she was…involved with Doug! I don't know how I'm going to tell her he's dead, let alone *how* he died! This is going to just about destroy her!" Sandra closed her eyes, hearing her sister's anguished cry already, in her mind.

"I'm sorry about that…ma'am, do you know anyone who was out to get Mr. Traylor? Did he owe money?…did he gamble, or do drugs?" He stopped talking as her lovely face darkened with sudden anger.

"Drugs?...Doug hated drugs! His kid brother died from an overdose a couple of years ago, and he's been an avid anti-drug supporter ever since! Believe me...my sister would have nothing whatsoever to do with a man who did drugs, or gambled! The last time I talked with Doug, he was very up about the fact his loan at the bank had been approved. In fact, he was scheduled to sign the final papers tomorrow!" Sandra's anger died as she thought about Doug, and Garalynn.

"A loan?...did he say what this loan was for? That might give us a motive to go on!" Patrick remarked, joining them in time to hear the last statement.

"It was for his own horse breeding ranch...he'd purchased some land a couple of years ago, just on the northern outskirts of Pueblo. I helped co-sign the papers to approve it for him!" She answered, feeling a sadness she thought she'd never feel again soon...the same one she'd felt with the deaths of her father, and ex-husband.

"You were going to help one of your trainers open his own breeding ranch?...not afraid of the competition? After all, he knew a lot about *your* business, didn't he?" Patrick asked, feeling that was stretching good working relationships a little too much.

Sandra stared at him, her brows drawing together. "Doug was a good employee...a good friend, and probably would have ended up being a member of the family! He and Garalynn were very much in love! I would have done anything to help him succeed in the business he loved...just to make my sister happy!" She wasn't sure she liked this burly looking policeman...she especially didn't care for what he seemed to be implying.

David could tell this wasn't going well...he knew Patrick could be a little blunt for people's tastes at times. "I'm sure that area is one we don't have to pursue, Ms. Phelps...but we do have to ask those kind of questions, you know. When exactly did you see him last?" He shot a look at Patrick that told the older man to keep quiet.

"Last night...at the stables. He's been helping me with one of our new studs, and then he was supposed to have today off! Most of the time, Doug stayed at the stables...he was only here, at the apartment, on the weekends. He had always been somewhat of a loner, until he and Garalynn started seeing one another." Sandra stood up. "Look...I really have to get to my sister's...I don't want her to hear about this from the television, or radio! I don't think I can tell you anything else right now...but I'll be happy to answer any questions you might have at another time, if that's okay?"

"Of course...I want to thank you for coming over for the ID...I know it wasn't easy at all!" David stood, and gestured towards the elevators. "Come on...I'll walk you out to your car!" With one last look to Patrick, who was grinning suddenly, David took a grip on Sandra's elbow once again, and led her towards the nearby elevators.

They didn't speak on the ride down to the main floor, or as they walked out to where Sandra's sleek black Mercedes was parked. He held the door opened for her, then closed it quietly. He smiled at her, nodding, and she smiled back. She started the car, looked up at him again, shifted gears, and then drove off. She glanced in the mirror, and smiled to herself, seeing him still standing there, watching after her car.

"You have the look of a teenager who suddenly discovered what girls were really all about!" Patrick came up behind him, grinning broadly.

"Shut up, will you, Pat? Let's get back to the precinct. I want to see everything as it comes in, about this case. I want things to move fat with this one, Pat...it's important!"

He shook his head again...something important was happening here...but he wasn't sure what. He turned, and headed back into the building.

Patrick grinned broader, shaking his head, and following his partner...he hadn't seen a reaction to a woman like that, from his usually stoic co-worker, since David's divorce four years ago. Maybe things were looking up...Patrick started to chuckle, then remembered what awaited them in that building. Suddenly…nothing seemed very funny at all…

…..Beth stood by the windows of the balcony off her bedroom, arms crossed, hugged close to her body. Staring out at the cool fall night sky, she felt the breeze caressing her face, moving the floor length curtains, stirring the dark curls above her ears…cooling slightly the fever she'd felt for the past few days. The sky seemed so full of stars, so peaceful and quiet she could almost hear every beat of her own heart. She leaned her head against the side of the balcony doors, sighing…she wished she could just go to sleep. She'd been restless, unsettled, the past couple of days…ever since that stupid argument with Sandra. She didn't understand why she'd actually tried to provoke her twin into that altercation. She also couldn't believe how close she'd come to succumbing to Sean's desires…in that stall! Beth was no novice to sex, or passion…but any relationship she'd been involved with had always been under her control, and by her choices and terms. With Sean, however…the passion was constantly threatening to take over…to rip her precious control from her grasp, and throw her well-ordered world into a chaos that had always been abhorrent to her. To Beth, who valued her cool logic, and calm control, above all else…this was a situation that was disturbing and terrifying.

She closed her eyes, trying to push thoughts of Sean, of that day in the stall, away from her mind…but it was proving a harder task then she thought it would. Just the idea of him here, in her room, putting his arms around her, pulling her up…she shook her head, trying to dampen the fire that tried to consume her since that day in the stall. Her relationship with Sean had been an affectionate one, especially since she'd realized she was falling in love with the big man. But…they had not progressed beyond kissing, and occasional petting…not that she hadn't thought about it, but she had been content to let it go as it was, liking the romantic overtones that seemed to be there. Now, though…everything seemed to be rushing towards a definite change, and she wasn't sure she either understood…or really wanted.

"What is the matter with me?" She clasped her hands to the sides of her head, trying to squeeze the thoughts away. "I never have trouble sleeping…this is ridiculous!…what is wrong with my head?"

Gradually, her self control did once again assert itself, and she drew a long, deep breath, opening her eyes. "I wish I knew what was going on with me of late. First…that idiotic fight with Sandy…and the way I jumped all over Garalynn! I wonder if I could be coming down with some sort…no, that's a stupid idea as well." She gazed up at the stars, wishing they held answers for her.

"Maybe all I really need is some time alone…I usually take time off after a long business trip, but not this time." She mused out loud. "But…how would I explain it to Sean, or Tamara? They're my guests…Sean especially is sure to be offended! They might even leave before I returned." She turned from the balcony doors, leaning on the back of a chair, feeling the fever starting up again. "I can't…I can't let him go! But…I can't go on like this either! Dear God…what is wrong with me?"

She straightened up, hugging her arms tight about her body. She turned back to the balcony, leaning again against the door frame. For a few moment, she simply stood there, feeling the breeze, watching the edges of the curtains move with the wind like living fingers…enduring the sensations as the silk of her negligee seemed to stroke her body. The wind seemed to be whispering to her, hushed and soft. That realization made her stop, a memory surfacing…a dream tugging at her mind, and heart. She turned her head, finding that the whispering beginning to creep over her entire body…like unseen fingers stroking her flesh, awakening it to an anticipation…an arousal she'd never dreamed possible.

Her eyes drifted towards the bedroom door, her heartbeat quickening, a longing growing deep inside her. She looked away from the door, telling her mind to take back control of her rebelling body. The feelings coursing through her, however, were proving stronger than reason, and her gaze went back to the door. Something was calling...beckoning...to her, promising a fulfillment, an ecstasy she'd never achieved before this. She walked slowly to the door, grasped the knob, and turned it. The door opened, and she found herself in the hallway. Beth turned to her right, walking quickly now, and headed down the deserted corridor. When she cam to another, branching off to the left, she turned that way, hurrying along, until she came to the door at the end of the hall. She found herself a little breathless, as the excitement she remembered in her dream manifested itself in the real world.

She stood before the door, her hand lifting to knock...then, she paused, realizing what she was about to do, and wondering where all her good sense had gone. She took a step back, away from the door...arguing with herself, clasping her hands together as her agitation...and arousal...grew. Then, just as she had half-decided to return to her room, the door opened, and Sean stood there, gazing down at her. He was clad only in pajama pants, his bared chest showing the hard, well-defined lines of the muscles there. His dark eyes held her motionless, their glittering intensity blocking all else from her sight...and from her mind.

Beth was suddenly aware that she was standing in front of this man's bedroom, wearing only the sheerest of negligees. She was mortified to think what he must be thinking of her at this moment. She gazed at his handsome face for a moment more, then turned, intending to retreat back to the safety of her own bedroom. Before she could accomplish this, Sean's hand reached down, and captured hers, bringing it slowly up to his lips. His eyes never leaving hers, he backed slowly, pulling her into the bedroom, then gently closing the door.

He'd been thinking about Beth...very intensely, in fact. He'd been thinking about his growing longing for her...how desperately he needed her, needed her lovely body for all that it could give him. Tamara's words, however, had also been pounding through his mind, warning him of the consequence of further disobedience, or defiance. Then, as if in answer to his desires...here was Beth, standing at his very door! She'd come to him, of her own volition...surely, a sign that his wishes were to be fulfilled, wasn't it? Did he dare to defy his sister's words?...yet, wasn't such a sign begging to be acted on? Dare he allow such a sign from the gods to be wasted? He led Beth to the large sofa in his room, and gently pressed her into sitting down. He sat down beside her, his eyes caressing her figure.

Beth felt like a giddy schoolgirl, on her first serious date...frightened and yet, very intrigued. "I...I'm not really sure why I'm here...at this time of night," she glanced down at her attire. "Or...or dressed like this! You probably think...I should go, Sean...it's late!" She stood up, her hands clasped in front of her body.

He stopped her, gently pulling her back onto the sofa. He touched her cheek, smiling gently, but the depth of emotion within the dark eyes was anything but gentle. He wasn't going to let this opportunity pass. "You're here because it's been predestined that we come together...share the joy of one another. You came to me, tonight, because your souls felt mine calling to it, and knew where it was meant to be!" He drew closer to her, his hand leaving hers, and sliding seductively up her arm. "If you hadn't come to me, Elizabeth...I would have found a way to come to you! You are here now...let that be the only thought you have. Relax...I promise...you'll feel nothing, but absolute pleasure!"

The dark, shining eyes fascinated her once again. The warmth from his body seemed to spread throughout her own, flaming her own inner flame even higher. She lifted one hand, running her open palm over the broad chest. Feeling the smooth skin, the hard muscles...her sense coming fully alive at the touch of the velvet-like texture of the golden-hued skin. She brought up her other hand, gripping both of his shoulders, feeling the corded muscle there ripple as he moved slightly. She lifted her hands, cupping his face, lifting her own towards his, whispering his name.

His dark head bent down over hers. As their lips touched softly, Beth felt a surge of panic, and tried to pull back. His arms tightened bout her, and he deepened the kiss, his tongue forcing its way into her mouth. The embrace drew any further resistance from her, and her arms slipped up, and around the sturdy neck. He pushed her back onto the sofa, laying her full length on the cushions, his hands caressing the sweet hips through the silk of her negligee. Sean's hands were hot through the fabric, and Beth wanted that heat...wanted to feel it searing her skin. Before she could act, though, Sean seized a strap in each hand, and with a sudden tensing of the powerful shoulders, he tore the gown into two pieces.

Sean pulled the ruined garment away from Beth's body, and threw it on the floor, his hands reaching once again for her. He stood as his hands slipped about her slim waist, and he brought her up with him. With an easy motion, he picked Beth up in his arms, and carried her towards his bed. He lay her gently on the bed, slipped his pants off, and stood beside the bed, towering over her recumbent form. She gazed up at him, seeing the power and strength in the tall body...his desire evident, erect, and awesome. He allowed her to look at his naked body for a few moments, then lay down beside her on the bed...pulling her tight against him. She turned towards him, her arms slipping around to his back, her fingertips digging into the firm flesh. She murmured words she wasn't enough aware of saying, seeking his heat...needing his touch. He kissed her, gently stroking his hands all over her trembling body, causing whimpers of desire and need to slip from her imprisoned lips.

He brought his mouth next to her ear, his breath stirring the silky hair. "This is the only time I will seek your body with gentleness, my love. Soon...you will know how to truly please me...to give me everything I will ask of you! You seek me tonight, with all the fires hidden within you...fires you yourself aren't aware you're capable of reaching, Elizabeth! I will show you those fires...you will feel their flames...and the bonds that bind you to this so-called civilized world will be forever severed! From tonight on…you will desire nothing that does not come from me! You will feed the power within me…the power that has always been rightfully mine…and the world will be ours!" He kissed her lips again, demanding her total surrender.

Beth's arms wound about him, trying to bring him even closer…all her doubts, fears, hesitations suddenly gone. She was in the grips of a passion she hadn't believed possible to feel…and she didn't want it to end! Her fingers worked their way deep into his thick hair, holding his head tight to hers. The kiss was intense, almost savage. He gathered handfuls of her dark hair, his mouth slipping along her jaw-line, nipping at her chin, then down along the line of her throat, locking onto the pulse point. His hands began to explore her body in earnest.

She felt her body coming alive as it never had before under those skilled hands, and demanding mouth, lips. Every touch, every stroke was a demand…a call to the slumbering spirit within her…a passionate, savage, almost feral spirit she didn't know lived inside her soul. She moaned, deep in her throat, wanting that dark spirit to return to the hidden darkness it was spawned within. But…its strength was too great…her need was too intense, and her soul was being consumed by the mindless desire that darkness conjured. Her will was abandoned to a wanton lust Beth had never experienced before this…the lovely executive wanted nothing, but the pleasures Sean was holding out to her body. Her body arched up into his, urging him on…seeking that ultimate peak.

Sean smiled darkly to himself…she was responding as he knew she would…she really had no choice. He kissed her lips once again…this is what he'd needed, Tamara and her plan be damned! He'd been granted a golden opportunity, and he intended to make the fullest use of it! He started sliding down the gorgeous body under his, his lips leaving a moist trail, over breasts, abdomen, and stopping just above the mound of dark curls. His hands kneaded the long thighs, feeling the muscles shudder as his lips kissed their way all around Beth's heated center. Then, his hands slid under her firm cheeks, and lifted gently, bringing those curls closer to his avarice mouth. His tongue slid into the glistening moisture, separating the passion swollen folds, and locating the throbbing bundle of nerves that was Beth's core. He drew it completely into his mouth, and then thrust a finger into her warmth. Beth's voice failed her completely as a wave of heat began to build within her loins. Her senses felt as though they'd reached an overload of feelings…she wasn't sure she could endure much more, and remain sane.

Sean felt her climbing, seeking that top peak, and he grinned. He pulled back suddenly, hearing her gasp of frustration. Her chest expanded, a scream of sexual need about to explode…then Sean's mouth covered hers again, and the scream died, turning into a moan deep within her chest. He bent over Beth's quivering breasts, tongue teasing the hardened nipples even more erect. Then, in a swift move, he engulfed one with an avid mouth. As he took a deep pull, suckling like a newborn, he felt Beth's hands hold his head tighter against the captured point. Her eyes were closed, her mouth open, and her mind completely awash in her own desires.

He lifted his head, and Beth's body felt the loss of contact…she whimpered deep in her throat. "Sean…please…I need you!" Her voice was husky, the tones both seductive and needful. Her hands cupped the sides of his face.

"Ssh…soon, my love…when you're really ready!" He smirked, his eyes full of all the desire he was feeling…and the secret satisfaction. He bent over her again, kissing along the rounded base of her left breast, grinning to himself as he felt her heart rate go even faster…she was so close.

Beth felt as though she were sinking into a bottomless abyss, eyes closed, body writhing with longing…desperately needing a release from this overload of sexual energy, and physical pleasures. Sean's hands slid up and down along her sides, over the rounded hips, and down the sleek outer thighs. They caressed along the inner thighs, coming close but never touching that aching need the woman beneath him wanted filled.

He lifted his head, letting his hands continue their soothing…their arousing of every inch of Beth's flesh. The smile was now gone from his face…his expression was dark, probing…almost menacing. Beth's eyes were closed, her body floating in the sea of pleasure he'd brought her into. She didn't see the look on his face, or the subtle changes beginning to take place. If she had even been able to open her eyes…seen Sean at that moment…it would have snapped her from the sexual trance in which she reveled. But, Sean had no intentions of allowing that to happen. He kept his hands moving, working the pressure points he knew would keep her at a level of arousal so intense she was practically begging him for release. He kept bringing her up, but always, just at the right moment, stopping, keeping her from that final peak. Her body was in such need, every muscle was shuddering…she reached out for him, aching so much she possessed a strength she didn't know was possible for her. He responded, grinning wolfishly…he had the chance for his personal success quite literally in the palms of his hands.

Sean tilted his head back, breathing deeply…control, he had to maintain control…he was too close. Tamara's words flashed through his head…how important it was that the time be right, for everything. But…the feel of Beth's pliant body…the intoxication of her scent…his own demanding needs. He yearned for full expression so much! His sister couldn't hold out against this…this need anymore than he…not at a time like this, he just knew that! His hand shot out, switching the bedside lamp off. Beth opened her eyes at the loud click, and looked up at him, panting slightly. Even in the darkness, she could still see his eyes…their dark fires calling once again to her awakening passions.

His mouth claimed hers again, demanding total surrender. The power he'd always relished at moments like this…it was building deep within his loins. Soon, he'd take complete possession of the lovely body under his. His mouth moved from her lips, across the collar bone, and fastening on the pulse point at the base of her neck. His breath felt as though it was searing her skin with its heat. Sean moved her body, shifting his own, positioning himself. Feeling the rapidity of her heart's beating, the deepness of the breaths she was taking...his fingers and lips could feel the rising heat of her blood. He knew it was now time!

He slid one knee between her legs, then slid in, using his hips to widen the spread of her long legs. Her legs lifted up, wrapping around the powerful hips...drawing the strong body tighter against hers. With a powerful thrust of those hips, he entered her eager body, feeling the heated, moist welcome. He wasted little time...there was little to be spared now. He began moving faster, plunging into her with all the smooth, even power of a well-oiled piston. His hands were holding onto her hips, pulling her closer with each stroke, deepening the penetration. Beth's body was responding, unconditionally...holding nothing back. He was going deeper...faster...harder...touching her in places she'd never been touched before now. She could hear her rapid, harsh breaths, her lungs desperately seeking air. Her heart was going faster and faster...the blood coursing faster, and hotter, throughout her body. That blood was stoking those inner fires, bringing the heat ever higher...the essence within each drop of blood building in strength, and purity. Beth clasped his back, raking the golden skin with her nails, wrenching a groan out from between his clenched teeth...a groan that grew into a low, rumbling growl.

With an animalistic roar, Sean stiffened...one last, hard thrust of his hips, and he released his pent-up heat deep into her body. He moved slower now, easier, breathing deep. His mouth moved lower, and his lips circled the nipple of her left breast. He sucked hard, pushing deep into her once again, and feeling her finally being allowed to reach her own pinnacle at long last. As white-hot flashes surged through her body, Beth felt her mind go void for a few seconds...her body's awareness of things also suspended. As she arched tight against his body, he bit deeply into the full breast, feeling the warm, salty tang as her blood gushed into his mouth.

Beth felt herself sinking deep into a strange lethargy…drifting into an eerie limbo as he took a few deep pulls on her breast with his hot mouth. She was awash in a strange undulation, nothing real to her, but the connection with his flesh. In what seemed like an eternity, but was actually only a few seconds…she finally came back to herself. Once again, she was aware of things, and sounds about her. She snuggled down into the bedcovers, feeling the warmth of his body nestling close over her. She murmured indistinctly, rubbing one hand over his shoulder, then slipped off into a gray sleep.

Propped up on his elbow, just above her slumbering form, Sean watched her, his teeth bared in a self-satisfied, arrogant grin…lips and teeth stained with a dark crimson tint. Still breathing deeply, he watched over her coma-like sleep. His smile widened, one of triumph, rather than tenderness, or sated passion. His expression was akin to that of an addict who'd finally received his "fix". He shifted positions, and now lay next to her, leaning his head against the headboard. His tongue slid over his lips, and teeth…cleaning all traces of the stain away. He thought about what had taken place…Tamara was not going to be happy. He had gone against her wishes…her planned schedule…but, surely, she'd understand that this had been an omen! Dropped into his lap, a gift from the gods, so to speak…even Tamara had to see that. He'd taken what the Fates had seen fit to give him, and he'd made good use of it! He'd show her…his sister wasn't the only one who could make the best use of an opportunity! He pulled Beth closer, inhaling her scent…now a mixture of perfume, sweat, and the faint copper tang of fresh blood. He bent over her, his tongue gently laving the swollen nipple, cleansing all traces of blood from the fragrant flesh…deftly and delicately, so as not to awaken her. The licking motions were, also, causing the healing process to speed up.

When he was through, he smiled, knowing there would be little or no sign of any kind of injury to the tender skin. He lay back down beside her, snuggling close, his mouth against one ear. "You are truly mine now, Elizabeth…in more ways then you can ever imagine. None can tear us apart…ever! You've given me the greatest gift tonight…the essence of your true being! And, this is only the beginning…you can never leave me. Together, we will create the ultimate power…and my family will have no choice but to grant me the ultimate rank. The prize will be mine again…and I'll never let it be taken from me again!" He caressed the dark curly hair, staring off into space. "My sister will never know she's losing…until she loses! There may be risk here, my Elizabeth…but the stakes are worth it! Don't worry…I'll always be by your side…especially if things work out the way I wish!"

He nodded, settling his head on the pillow next to Beth's. It would be risky, the idea that had come to him tonight…but the possible rewards outweighed any, and all risks…even his sister's formidable displeasure…..

…..Tamara stood on her balcony, arms outspread, eyes closed…reveling in the sensations caused by the night breezes over her skin. She was completely nude…her preference during the night hours. She didn't need as much sleep during the night as most, preferring to spend the dark hours either walking in the gardens here, or on her balcony, communing with the stars. She felt strangely restless tonight…unsure as to the cause, she'd come out onto the balcony, and opened her body to the embrace of the night.

The night hours were the only time she allowed any of her impressive emotional guards to relax…the only time she allowed the past to intrude on the present. She gave herself up to the powers of the darkness, becoming one with all the sights, sounds, and smells. She opened her eyes, gazing up into the sky. It had been such a star-filled night as this that the only man she'd truly ever loved had made love to her for the very first time.

She could still hear that deep, calm voice...murmuring words, and vows, of eternal love...promising her all the joys, and beauties that such a love as theirs would bring forth. They'd been so deliriously happy then...so complete...the world, and all it held, spread out before them. No one before, or since, would ever share such a unique, spiritual magic. And, then...the great revelation came...for both of them. A revelation that touched each of them, but in far different ways! They had tried, several times, to talk it out...fix it all back to the way it had been before, to the joys they'd shared in the days before this. There had been changes...confrontations...arguments...and, ultimately, a fearsome betrayal! Now...as she had before him...she was again alone.

For a second, she allowed the loneliness, and the pain, to be evident on her beautiful face, knowing no one would see. Her voice was soft as she gazed at the far away stars. "If only you'd allowed yourself to see things from my view, my poor lost love! Why was it so hard to acknowledge that my way was perhaps better than the one you chose? Mine offered us everything...all that was possible could have been ours, for all time! Yours...yours was the way of service...menial chores, trials, and sacrifice...and what was at the end of this path of pain?...nothing! A feeling of peace, you said...the sense of belonging, of family." She shook her head, clasping her hands together, and resting them on the balcony railing.

"Did your peace bring you all that you thought, my love? We might still be together, savoring the bliss of our love, if you had only opened your eyes! But, no...your mind and soul would not be swayed...and now, we are ever at odds! You must remain in the prison your way brought you...and I must go on alone, without your love! How could you have allow this?...did you really love me, that you could let me go? Now...when I allow myself expression, it's meaningless affairs with insignificants. How I still miss you, my love...how foolish you are!"

In the midst of this reverie, something brushed her mind...like the barely discernable whisper of the wind's fingers. At once, her faculties were all completely alert, her guards back in place. She gripped the balcony railing, peering out into the darkness, seeking the danger. She narrowed her golden eyes, channeling all her concentrations outwards...trying to locate whatever had triggered her senses. She opened all the unique faculties, allowing everything to wash over them.

After a few moments, she felt that soft brush again, and narrowed in on its location. Her eyes widened when she realized where this sensation was originating from right now. She took a deep breath...realizing what this meant, feeling her anger surging within her. The sense of peace, of quiet, she'd been experiencing flew away into the night sky...she felt her anger threatening to escape its bindings. She stared back into her bedroom, fixing her gaze on the distant door. She'd warned him...now, she'd show him the price such blatant disobedience could bring.

She walked back into her room, reaching for the light robe hanging on the bedpost at the foot of the huge four poster bed. She was seething inside...she just couldn't believe he'd be so arrogant...with her. She slipped the robe on, walking towards the door, determined to settle this once, and for all. Than, as her hand touched the doorknob, her anger dissipated...her customary calm once again asserting itself. She stepped away from the door, and leisurely approached her bed. She removed the robe, hanging it back over the one bedpost, then slipped under the covers. Relishing the feel of the cool linen over her skin, Tamara stretched a little, then switched off the bedside light. The darkness wrapped itself about her, almost caressing the long, lithe form...and she smiled softly into that darkness. Charging out to confront him would have bee a colossal waste of her time...and powers. It wouldn't have changed the fact that the deed had already been consummated. And, to attempt to face someone with his considerable powers, without her own being at their best...could be suicide, even for her. She'd been placed in charge, so long ago, because she'd seldom allowed permitted herself to be shaken, out-maneuvered, or taken off-guard…especially by her own brother! That was why the head of their family, and the true power behind Aranax had chosen her as leader for this most important task. Sean would simply have to learn, once again, how very foolish…and dangerous, it was to go against their family's wishes.

"Fool!…blind, selfish, unheeding fool! Will your ever truly learn? All you have ever thought of, your entire lifetime, has been solely your own desires, and wants! How do I make you see the importance of following orders?" She mused out loud, trying still again to figure her sibling out. "You lost everything you had, once before, because you refused to put family before self! Wasn't that punishment enough?…do you think yourself so powerful as to challenge that very source of all we are?…all we have? I am going to have to use extreme measures to make you see, Sean…but, it will not be easy here! Oh, Sean…why must you always act like you're the only one that matters?"

She closed her eyes, willing the sleep to come over her body…letting the combined elements of the night, and the dark, soothe her spirit. She'd take this premature event, and incorporate it into her already mapped out plan, and make the most of it. As for her wayward brother…may the gods who steered the course of one's lifetime be there to try and save him this time!…..

…..Stretching his powerful arms high over his head, Sean expelled a lusty sigh of satisfaction. He'd risen early, and come out onto the broad veranda at the rear of the manor house. It was a beautiful Indian summer morning, and the maid had brought his breakfast out there, setting the well-ladened tray on one of the tables there. He was enjoying the mild weather, and the beauties of this autumn day.

He felt fantastic…in fact, better then any day since they'd arrived in Denver, and here to Blackmoon. He still felt as though he weren't at his very best yet, but it was a vast improvement over the past few days. He'd really been getting more and more tense as the time they'd been away from their home, and their usual daily routine, became greater. He reached for a warm muffin, biting into with great relish. It felt so good to be making decisions based on *his* thoughts, and wishes. He had always chafed at the thought of being a submissive...last night had been just the beginning to his reassertion. Yes...his time was definitely coming again! Thoughts of last night brought a wide grin to his lips, and his eyes sparkled lustily. Beth had proven to be all he'd imagined, and even more than he'd hoped. True...she'd been a little hesitant, at first...but, as the night had progress, after their first time, she turned out to be quite an adept pupil...and soon matched his passions with her own. She had turned out to be his equal in all things sensual, and sexual...and just the thought of her made his blood burn, and his breathing deepen. He wondered if she'd awakened yet. He'd carried her back to her own bed in the early hours of dawn...she'd been asleep in his arms, murmuring softly at the movements.

Sean took another bite of the fresh blueberry muffin, savoring both the taste, and the different textures against his palate. He'd always been a connoisseur of foods and drinks...relishing in the varieties he'd found throughout the world, especially those that actually brought a surge to his ever-present libido. Food, in itself, could be both sensual and sexual...and he enjoyed the comparisons. He'd found the food served here, at Blackmoon, to be among the finest he'd ever had, outside of his own home.

He breathed in the cool, fresh air. Why is it, he wondered, that the air was fresh in Fall as at no other time of the year? It held a crispness... a newness that filled his lungs with power and enjoyment. He sat down at the table, pouring himself a large cup of the aromatic coffee. He sipped at the dark liquid, his eyes moving over the various sections of the gardens. He delighted in the many colors of the trees, still glowing in their autumnal dress. It wasn't his home...but Blackmoon was indeed a most beautiful place to be.

His thoughts turned to his sister…he'd be facing her soon…and felt a momentary twinge of uneasiness. He shrugged it away…there was no way she could know it yet! He would not allow her to interfere with the plan he'd put into motion last night. He knew she'd most likely be furious…or at least, as furious as Tamara ever allowed anyone to see her be. But…he was certain he could explain it in such a way that she had to agree with the logic behind his actions. Beth's coming to him last night had been a sign that this was meant to be…meant to happen when it did! As logical as she always was, Tamara would see that, and the rightness behind his actions, and reasoning. He'd simply taken what had been freely offered…she'd have done the same…wouldn't she?

He took another drink of the coffee. As his eyes lifted a bit, he saw the distant, brooding mountain…focal point in the spread of mountains and hills that made up a great portion of the estate's rear acreage. The sight of that cloud-shrouded peak brought back some of the uneasiness he'd confessed to Tamara a few days before. He knew the story of that particular mountain, the legend that surrounded it. Beth had told him the story more then once. He brushed a hand over his eyes, trying to settle himself again. He wanted to think only of the pleasant things he had been…like those of last night. The mountain brought up thoughts he wished gone…for good. He put his cup down, and reached across the table, towards the plate of crisp bacon.

Tamara seemed to suddenly burst out of the bright sunshine, overshadowing even the great peak behind her. "Having a good breakfast, dear brother? May I join you?"

Sean paled. Though her tone was light, he'd easily picked up on the dark undercurrents…she was very angry! "Tamara…sister! How marvelous you look this morning! Please…do join me! The food is as good as this great morning!…fresh, and succulent. Not like that we have at home, but it more then suffices." For some strange reason, the confidence he'd been experiencing faded away…the sense of power as well seemed gone. "You're up earlier then usual…for you. Is everything all right?"

She continued to stand by the table, looking down at him. He could now clearly see a stark, and dreadful anger swirling in those golden depths. He went even paler, realizing how great her anger must be to allow him to actually see it manifest. "All right, you ask? Suppose you tell me, dear brother!...tell me how right everything is after last night! Did you sleep well, Sean? Was it a restful sleep? Were you perhaps troubled by dreams?...the kind of dreams a disobedient brother might suffer?" She sat down across from him, graceful and deadly. "I think, perhaps...you have things to tell me, Sean?...about last night?"

Sean swallowed hard...he was in a fearful trap. "Tell you?...about last night, Tamara? I don't think so, dear sister...I mean, what is there to tell?" He gulped the last of his coffee down, and placed the cup on the table, reaching for the thermal carafe of coffee before him. "I slept like the proverbial baby!"

Her arm shot out, knocking his hand away from the carafe. "Enough!...your lying disgusts me! Tell me the reasons you saw fit to disregard my wishes last night, Sean...make me see the need, and the logic for changing the timetable!" She sat back, composed and calm. "Go on, Sean...tell me!"

Sean felt his throat constrict...she knew everything! He rubbed his palms nervously over his pant leg. He should have known. How could he have been so foolish, so dangerously foolish to believe she'd never realize what he'd done. He'd been so confident...so smug...last night, thinking himself the victor. How?...how had she found out so soon?...what had given him away? He rose from his seat, slowly, watching her carefully. He knew, better than most, how deadly swift her seldom viewed rage could explode. "Tamara...I can explain...it was Beth who came to me! I didn't seek her out last night, Tamara...I swear!"

Tamara followed every movement he made, her golden eyes never leaving his dark ones. She appeared relaxed, undisturbed...but he knew that was only a mask for the outer world. He spread his hands, palms up in supplication. "I know what you said...that the schedule had to be followed at all costs! I fully intended to do just that! But...when such an opportunity is placed within your hands...Tamara, how damaging could it truly be that this happened *before* you said? It can only help us!...make her even more willing to help us accomplish our task here! Can't you see that?...don't you agree?" He stared at her unblinking eyes, trying to find something to break that icy gaze. "Tamara...what difference does it make?...*really* make?"

He never saw it coming...her hand slashing up through the air, connecting with side of his jaw. His head snapped to one side with the force of an explosion. She gazed at him, expression blank...but deadly. "If you *ever* thought, with your head...the one between your shoulders, not between your legs...you'd known the answer without having to ask me!" She continued to stare at him, daring him to retaliate. "Sean...you know why we're here...what we're after. You know that one of the most important things is *not* to draw any unwanted attention to ourselves...that we have to be cautious in every action we take, or do! Maybe last night's events, in reality, aren't all that important...but the place they hold...held...in the plan we were to follow is what matters!"

He shook his head. "I don't understand, Tamara...what difference could it possibly make as to *when*? It's not as if what happened influenced anything...other than Beth's feeling towards me, that is!" He looked at his sister, a frown on his handsome, dark face. "Why is it so vital?"

She sighed, motioning for him to reseat himself...she'd try once more. "I will tell you, once again, what we have all been told...there is *always* a reason for anything we are told to do, and how we're to do it! A thousand times that has been *pounded* into your mind...and still you act like an adolescent on a hormone high!" She sat back in the chair, arms crossed over her chest, gazing out over the garden area. "Let me try and explain it so that even you has to understand all of it! Things are going well in this business deal, and the alliance we're trying to establish with this family, Sean…your courtship is a key link in firmly securing our goals. Now, I want you to think…last night, you allowed yourself *full* expression, didn't you?"

He lowered his head, not wanting to meet her eyes…how did she always find out the truth? "Yes…it's been *so* long, Tamara…I couldn't help myself! It helped me, Tamara…helped me to regain the balance I've felt myself losing ever since we came here! I apologize."

"Apologies are so easy for you, Sean…it's just another way to manipulate others for your own means. Listen to what I'm trying to say to you…full expression is dangerous for us, except for specific conditions…correct? What would have happened if Elizabeth had seen?…really seen? That attention we seek to avoid would have burst forth, and then what would you have had to do? To prevent us from being found out…our goal never realized…you would have had to done something to her, wouldn't you? And that, dear brother, would have caused even more unwelcomed attention! Sooner, or later…we would have been exposed, and what then? Now…do you begin to understand?"

"The plan we are to follow…the time it indicated would have helped eliminate any such …problems? How is that possible? If it's going to happen, what difference as to the time?" Sean was finding it hard to see how a plan made out so far in advance could select a time that the danger of exposure, or attention, would be less than another time. "I still don't think it makes that much difference, Tamara. Be honest…would *you* have turned down something so fair, so delicious, I it had been offered so freely to you?"

Tamara looked away, disgusted with his one-track way of thinking. "Sean…you are my brother, and that fact is the only one that saves you right now! Listen, and listen well…the reason I am upset about last night is because of the time factor! If you don't understand what I mean by that, then I do not choose to discuss it further! Simply follow my orders from now on…do you understand *that*?"

The big man shrugged his wide shoulders. "Yes…I understand. But…Tamara, I want *you* to understand…what happened last night ensures our success here! Beth will do anything I ask of her now…she'll help us, in anything we need. She didn't see anything she shouldn't…I can assure you of that, Tamara. All she was focused on was the sex…a fact most women having sex with me have in common!" He smirked a bit. "My success rate with the ladies is…"

He was cut short, pulling his head back a bit as she stood up. "Please…I haven't had my breakfast yet, dear brother! Hearing your self plaudits always has the affect of making my stomach roll! One other thing, Sean…did the thought of a possible morph cross your mind? After all…that is always a risk with full expression, as well as self exposure. Were…are you prepared to face that event, should it happen?"

Sean snorted, shaking his head. "A morph?…after only one time? Tamara, we all know that it takes more then just one time!" He stood up also, rolling his shoulders a little to ease the tension. "I think you're overreacting…there's nothing to be so fearful about where that matters!"

"That is a word you should know has little meaning for me, Sean! As I said before, I don't intend to talk about this again, so I will say one last thing, and that is all I want to hear about it! If you took the necessary precautions, brother…then we have nothing to worry about, however ill-timed your actions may turn out to be! Let's hope certain signs do not reveal themselves…it could be most unfortunate to try and explain!…but of course, you thought about that, didn't you? Or, did you perhaps have another itinerary in mind?" She smiled, hard and cool, as his face reddened. "Yes…I am fully aware of what you'd planned, Sean…a surprise for the family, which will never be realized!"

She sat down again, and poured herself a cup of coffee. She gestured for him to reseat himself as well. "Well?…no glib explanation?…no self-serving reasons, dear brother?"

He stared at her, so golden and vibrant in the sunlight…so unassailable, and so damned correct! He drew a deep, shuddering breath as her words finally began to sink into his brain. He had risked everything last night...and would it have been worth it if Beth *had* seen? Why was it always him who seemed to make the miscalculations? Why was Tamara always so right? He sat down, heavy and awkward.

"You're right...as usual, Tamara! But...what's done is done, so carrying on about the right, or wrong, of my actions is mute at best!"

"How so like you to put everything in its proper perspective...seeing only what *you* consider important!" She simply sighed, shaking her head. "Still...I suppose there is no choice, but to go forward...keep alert, though! The plan will proceed...with no further deviations, I trust?"

"Exactly...you can count on that, Tamara!" He was more than happy that his sister seemed inclined to letting this pass. "Everything will be just fine...she will be completely mine, from now on, Tamara! You'll see...everything is going to be fine!"

"I hope so, Sean...for both our sakes! If something *does* happen, however...*I* will see to it, do you understand? I want no interference...from anyone!" She stared at him, her intent all to clear in those hypnotic eyes.

He felt his anger stirring. "Don't talk to me like I was a child, Tamara! I'm a grown man, capable of making the right decision, and acting upon it! If I've made a mistake, than *I'll* take care of it!" His face flushed with a sudden surge of anger, and irritation.

"You know...there have been many times I've had the thought that it would be much better if you weren't my brother! Maybe...we just might have to have a family meeting when we return home...*if* you persist in this type of behavior, Sean!" She gazed up at the mountain, calm and serene despite her words.

His deep voice dropped to a whisper, filled with a tone of deadly resentment, and menace. "You're pushing too hard, Tamara...don't! Remember to whom you are speaking! Push me too far, and learn what happened to others who made that fatal error!"

Tamara laughed, light and carefree. "And...need I remind you who *is* in charge here, Sean? Think very carefully, and long...recall what happened to those who tried opposing *me*! Now...which of us has the most to fear?...or, to lose, dear brother? Face it, Sean...you have never been able to best me!...in anything!"

He glared at her, wishing he could throttle that slender neck...watch that unsettling gaze fade from those golden orbs! How satisfying it would be to have her, helpless, in his hands!...to hear her actually gasping for mercy...from him! His fists balled at his sides, and the cords stood out in his neck as his rage built so high he was sure his blood vessels were going to rupture! But...grinding his teeth in impotent fury, he closed his eyes, and turned his head away. As great as his anger, resentment, and hatred was for his sister, he knew he dared not move against her. His fear of her, and the power he knew she possessed...she would destroy anyone who stood in the path of a task set her by the family...even a sibling! He didn't dare give her a legitimate reason to call forth that power...that terrible rage that was hers! He bowed his head, and nodded...mutely cursing the tall woman before him.

Tamara smile slightly...she was under no illusions where her brother's acquiescence was involved. She knew she held his loyalty simply because, right now, he had no other options open to him. For now, though, that was enough...as long as he obeyed her from now on, she would be content. She sipped her coffee, then looked back at him. She was surprised to find herself feeling a twinge of pity for him, seeing the tight, pale expression on his face. She stood up, walked around the table to where he now stood, his fists now pushed deep in his pants pockets.

She placed a gentle hand on his shoulder. "Why do you continually challenge me, Sean? We're family...we must work together! Please...work with me, and we'll get this over, and we can return home! Don't you want that as much as I?"

He had to nod, startled at the tone of her voice. "Yes...very much! But, Tamara...I want Elizabeth as well! I will do whatever you wish, from this moment on…but I want to know that she will remain mine! It cam only make her more an ally, sister…the fact that it sees to a need of mine should make no difference, so long as the plan goes as laid out! Alright?"

She sighed again…still the grating undertones in his voice, and still the self-indulgence. No matter how old he would grow to be…it would always be in terms of *him*, no one else mattering. "Sean…you will never learn, never change. You were in charge once, remember?…you allowed that colossal ego, those unquenchable lusts, to get in the way of the task Father set you. You lost everything!…and very nearly took the entire Paris family down with you! The only reason you didn't *lose* your life was be cause Mother spoke up for you in the family council! You're are lucky everyone holds her in such high regard!" She lowered her head a bit, bringing her right hand up, and slowly making it into a rock hard fist. She placed this fist against her chest. "*I* am the one now, Sean…and I will not allow you to take this from me! You will do nothing that could even remotely ruin the plan, or cost the family further pain, or loss of success!" She stared him down, making him lower his eyes. "As for dear Elizabeth…what's done is done. We will make the best of it. You may do with her as you wish, Sean…at least, where the sex is concerned! She would have to many questions if you suddenly held her at arm's length, after last night. But…it will be limited to sex, and nothing else!…no further full expression, unless *I* deem it so! Understood?"

He understood…he'd been given the last pardon he would ever receive. Any misstep on his part, from now on, would be meet with the full fury of his sister's unforgiving rage. He brightened, though, at the thought of having his way with Beth whenever he desired her. Not being able to indulge himself all the way wouldn't be easy…but he could do it.

He watched his sister as she drank some more of the coffee, inhaling the fragrant aroma with obvious pleasure. Watching her, seeing that ever-present cool composure, Sean had to admit, reluctantly, that he did admire how she always stayed so calm, so in control…at least, the greater majority of the time. Hers was a multi-faceted personality, a complexity not easily discerned by those around her. He looked up as she switched on the radio sitting at the far side of the table.

A few words, just being finished by the newscaster as the radio came to life, caused him to glance at the manor house, then leaned over the table. "Tamara...did you catch the late news on the television last night?" He asked quietly, cautiously.

She looked at him, gauging what he was really asking. "Not really...the set in my room was on, for a while...but I didn't pay much attention. You know very little about the media interests me, Sean...what are you getting at?"

"They were talking about that murder a day, or two ago...the one that involved that trainer that worked in the stables here." He answered, watching her closely. "He was the one who brought that white stallion up that day, for us to see...remember?"

"The one who was named Douglas?...yes, I remember. Poor man...were there any details on the newscast?" She glanced at him, face calm and unexpressive.

"He was killed in his apartment, in downtown Denver. Apparently, there was quite a lot of damage done to the place. I'm sure if the police do have some solid leads, they won't allow them to be leaked to the media!" Sean was quite certain he could venture a guess as to what had really happened.

"Isn't it terrible?...people can't even be safe in their own homes! I'm sure Sandra especially is going to miss him...he apparently was a great help with her horses!" She smiled slightly, looking over her shoulder at her brother. "I wish the authorities all the best in bringing the killer, or killers, to justice!"

He was very sure now. "Yes...I have a feeling they'll need all the luck they can find, to solve this murder! I wonder...why was he killed? And, from what little the media did reveal, it was not an easy death! Makes you wonder, doesn't it?...what do you suppose he did to warrant such a hard ending?" His voice was quiet, not seeking any sort of response...just stating a fact, or query.

"Why bother ourselves over some unknown man's death? What was there to even mark his having been here?...nothing remarkable at all! You wonder over things of little significance, brother. Forget him...history already has!" She gazed back at the mountain, her thoughts far away. "Our task is close at hand, Sean...I can almost taste the succulent victory now!"

"Tamara, I can't help, but worry...about our task, that is." He stepped a little closer to her, his face serious. "Do you really think we'll realize success this time? We have failed so many times already!"

"We failed because it was not the time for our success...there is a scheme to all things, Sean...you know that. Right now, we hold all the cards, so to speak. All the real power is in our hands now, Sean...or, soon will be! Think about it, Sean...no one, here, is even really aware of what it is we seek! And, what few who could suspect us...they aren't even sure what the objects we're after even look like!" She smiled at him, her poise and confidence reaching out to him. "I see no logical reason to think we won't find victory this time, Sean! This time we shall find them...find them all!...and we shall reap all that was promised us! There won't be anyone who can stop us, or even compete with us, once that has been accomplished! We need only be patient, and let things come to us as they are meant to do so!"

He looked over his shoulder, towards the manor, to be sure they were still quite alone. Then, he leaned closer, lowering his voice. "How can you be so sure?...what if there are others who know what we know? And, you know what I'm talking about, Tamara! For all we know, they've..." He was cut off as she whirled towards him, her eyes narrowed and gleaming.

"Do you take me for a complete idiot, Sean? Don't you think I would have had certain things checked out before we came here? If there were even a chance that that had happened, we never would have come!" She drew a deep breath, calming herself. "I can assure you…if there were any reason to suspect *they* were involved, in an active way…I would have known it instantly!" She pointed a finger at him. "Just do as I have told you, Sean…keep our little Elizabeth happy, and out of the way, until we truly need her! I do, however, stress again that things be kept under tight control…do I make myself crystal clear, Sean?"

He stiffened a little at the last few words, but kept his mouth shut. "Yes…it is very clear, Tamara! You needn't explain again…all will be as you have stated!"

She nodded, satisfied for now. "If that's true, than it's been a good morning, my dear brother! Now, you had better get around…remember, we're supposed to go with Elizabeth to see one of her family's research sites this morning."

"How do you do it, Tamara?…be so calm, as though nothing is wrong, that there is no danger? You *know* the danger, here, is all too real!" He declared, stubbornly refusing to keep his fears silent.

She shook her head, sighing…he would never learn. "Danger is what keeps the blood coursing through our veins, Sean…that, and the knowledge that ultimate power is only a hand's span from our grasp!" She leaned forward, suddenly quiet and deadly serious as she gazed into his face. "Sean, you think *I* am the one who threatens you…who seeks only to demean you! You are so far from the truth…though, make no mistake, if you foul up again, I will not hesitate to retaliate! Sean…if we do not find what we were sent to find, then we're *both* through! No power in this known universe can save us if what we're here to get falls into the hands of others! And, I don't think I need explain whose hands I refer to, do I? Now…go, get yourself ready." With a final warning look, she turned from him, and walked back into the manor house.

He watched her leave, disappearing into the confines of the house, then he sighed, deeply and sadly. He glanced once more up at the mountains, and felt once more, that unexplainable brush of fear. He tried to shake it off…to clear it from his mind forever…but failed. Deep within his soul, he had to admit he didn't possess the iron will, and fathomless courage that his sister had always. That was one of the reasons their family had entrusted the leadership of this mission to Tamara. He accepted that, albeit grudgingly, but vowed silently that he would regain all that had been stripped from him, and that would be soon! Though…to be truthful, as long as his sister was alive, he really wasn't sure how that would finally happen!

He sighed again, his good mood of earlier completely vanished. Then, in an ironic twist, it surfaced again, and he started to grin. Tamara had given her blessing…he could satisfy himself, with Elizabeth, whenever, and as often, as he desired! She had cautioned him, however…but he really though she was being just a little too cautious…especially her comments about a morph! He would restrain himself, as she wished, although…a thought came making him grin even wider. She didn't know everything…he might still have a hidden ace up his sleeve!

He squared his wide shoulders, and started walking into the house. He'd do all he had to in order for their family to reap the benefits. After all…success for the family meant more for him! And, once the outcome was a success…when everyone was lulled into a more complaisant mood and position…then, he'd make his move! He would become the ultimate victor, in the ultimate game!……

…..With a soft, quick breath, Beth came fully awake, and sat up in her bed, one hand to one temple as dizziness washed over her senses. She closed her eyes, now clutching the sides of her head with both hands, making herself breathe deep and slow.

After a few moments, the giddiness left her, and she raised her head, opening her eyes. She looked around, a little surprised to see she was once again in her own room, her own bed. The last thing she could recall was being in…her face reddened as the thoughts of last night flooded her mind. Sean…he must have carried her back here, after their last time together last night…but why? Was he embarrassed to have anyone know they'd slept together? Or...was he simply trying to make things easier for her? Her eyes widened a bit as she realized that it would have been *she* who would have been embarrassed for anyone to find out what had happened last night, not him. She sat up straighter, realizing that normally that would have been the truth! She usually hated even the risk of anything that would make her look anything less than in total control. In fact, Beth had to admit to herself, it was usually she who initiated any romantic encounters, and she who controlled the dynamics of the situations. Not last night...she'd had no control whatsoever over the events of the previous night.

She glanced at the bedside table, seeking the clock...ten o'clock. "Ten?...god, I must have overslept! Why didn't Maria wake me?...I told her I had that meeting this morning, at the research plant! Tamara, and Sean...they must be waiting!" She rubbed her hands over her face, trying to shake the last vestiges of the lethargy still lingering over her entire body.

She pulled her hands away, looking at them strangely, suddenly aware that her sense of touch was more acute than ever. The texture of the skin of her face had come through her fingertips in a new wave of awareness...as though she could feel each individual cell, feel every drop of blood as they moved through capillaries, veins, and arteries.

She shook her head, chasing those feelings away. "Lord...I feel so damn tired this morning! And, my head...it feels like it's going to explode!" She rubbed her temples, grimacing a little at the throbbing centered there.

Taking another deep breath, she arched her back, trying to stretch the tightness out of her muscles. She threw off the bedcovers, and swing her long legs over the bedside, readying herself to rise. She had to sit still, however, for a few moments, as another wave of dizziness swept over her. When it seemed as though everything was fine again, she stood up...gasping as she grabbed at the corner post of the four poster bed because the entire world suddenly seemed bent on spinning out of control. A minute, or two, and the vertigo utterly vanished. All that remained was a slight nausea, a suddenly raging thirst, and the beginnings of a ravenous hunger deep in her body.

She straightened up, and headed into the adjoining bathroom. She picked up a glass off the vanity, and filled it from the sink faucet. She thirstily drank the cool water down rapidly, and than another. She felt a little better, her mind not so fuzzy. Right now, her body craved a good, hot shower. She walked over to the big, double stall shower enclosure. Opening one of the clear glass panel doors, she reached in, and turned the water on. With a soft "whoosh", the water gushed from the ornate spouts set all around the stall walls.

She adjusted the water temperature until it was just as she liked it. Dropping her negligee to the floor, she stepped into the stall, pulling the door shut as she did so. As the air temperature warmed within the shower, clouds of steam began forming, swirling about her lithe body. She tilted her head back, closing her eyes…letting the water surge all over her tired, aching form. As the heat started its way through her body, she felt herself feeling better all the time…her mind becoming clearer all the time. She reached for her body sponge, and one of the bottles of shower gels lining the long shelf on one wall. In a few moments, she was enjoying the heady kiwi scent, spreading the foaming suds all over her body…the fragrance wafting all through the shower stall.

Beth sighed with pleasure, the ill feelings leaving. Then, as the sponge moved over her breasts, she winced. Frowning, she pulled the sponge away, and stepped under one of the streams of water, rinsing all the soap off her body. Once done, she lifted her hand to her left breast, running her fingertips lightly over the firm flesh. Just under the bottom of the areola, she felt a small, hard lump…tender to the touch, and definitely something that was not there the day before! She wasn't able to see it clearly, because of the location, so she turned the water off, then stepped out of the shower stall.

She stood before the floor-length mirror, close, nervous. She cupped the left breast in her hand, lifting the soft globe up slightly so she could see the underside in the mirror. She didn't really see anything clearly, but there did appear to be something like a large mosquito bite, or maybe a spider bite. She rubbed the fingertips of her other hand over the slight reddened area, feeling the sting as they ran over the spot. What was going on here?...when had she gotten a bite there?

She walked back out into her bedroom, trying to calm her mind as it was creating worst case scenarios...this was crazy! She sat down in the old over-stuffed chair she always had in her bedroom...the one their mother had always sat in, cuddling them close as she told stories, or when calming their fears. She drew her knees up, hugging them tight with her arms. She had to calm herself...she wasn't going to solve *anything* if she allowed herself to panic.

Gradually, the feelings of alarm, and fear left her. She began turning her thoughts inwards, calling on her slumbering memories. The events of last night flooded over her, and she ducked her head, cheeks flaming as she realized where the bite mark probably came from, and who'd inflicted the tender mark. It had been so glorious...so passionate...so liberating! She didn't know making love could be that...that intoxicating, that addicting! That she could, and did, respond so wantonly was yet another revelation for her mind to absorb, and digest. He had called forth a fire from her inner being she never fathomed possible for one of her reserved and calm nature. She found her breath quickening...her body aching for the sight of that magnificent body again, the searing, addicting caress of those skillful hands. She hid her face in her hands, trying to settle her world into its usual calmness.

Beth took her hands away from her face, sitting up. She had to get herself up, and back into her customary calmness. She'd overcome harder obstacles than her suddenly wayward emotions...she'd regain her focus, and then everything would be fine, back to normal.

She got up from the chair, picking the discarded towel up from the floor, and focused her mind on the tasks for the day...though the memory of her suggestion to Tamara and Sean about visiting the research plant made her pause. Sean...her mind drifted towards last night's memories...she shook her head, this had to stop! She was a grown woman, not some love-struck teenager. Suddenly...she felt certain she was no longer alone in her room. She whirled about, eyes searching every foot of the bedroom, seeking whatever had triggered her senses. Nothing, and no one...yet, something *had* alerted her, but what? She stood there a moment, towel dangling from her fingertips, thinking hard, trying to remember what had first caught her attention. Then, it came to her...a scent, wafting delicately under her nostrils...a perfume...no, a man's heady cologne! She walked to her bed, and knelt beside it. She sniffed the bedcovers...yes, it came from them! Her brain supplied the answer...it was Sean's. He must have rubbed against the covers when he brought her back here last night. Beth lifted her head at that thought...how had her olfactory sense become so acute? How could she have picked up so faint a trace of scent after hours? It was as if her sense of smell had been magnified a hundred-fold! In fact...she was picking up on several scents as she stood there, some she knew she'd never usually pick up on. What was going on here?

As she rose again to her feet, she realized *all* her senses seemed unusually acute this morning...in ways they'd never been before! She swore she could hear the kitchen staff talking, and moving around, two floors below her!...her imagination must be working overtime here! She raised one arm, drawing in a deep breath as her nose moved over the forearm.

She didn't remember her skin having so sweet a fragrance before now...a sweetness that went far beyond that from the bath oils she'd used. The oils were scented with chamomile, and lavender, with just a hint of fresh mint. This aroma was akin to a rose petal. And yet, more then just a rose...it was like when the petals began to drop from the rose. One last strong burst of fragrance released into the air, before they died…the scent of life, and death!

Her head jerked up…she'd clearly heard someone else's voice speaking those exact words…but whose voice? She was still alone in her room. "Alright…enough is enough! I obviously didn't get enough sleep last night!" Beth shook herself, getting a grip on her emotions. "I'm going to get dressed, have a good breakfast, and get things back on track! Things will be fine…I'll be fine, and everything will once again make sense. And as for Sean…I'll handle that when I have to!"

She tossed the towel on the bed, and headed for her dressing room to get ready for her day, confident once again that she had everything under her usual control……..

……..Kristine walked around the classroom, looking over her student's shoulders, gauging their work. The fifteen art students were all engrossed in a charcoal study of the nude male model poised on the dais at the front of the spacious room. She paused every now and then, giving a pointer here and there…praising an especially good job…answering a question about technique, or composition. Occasionally, she had to reassure a student still a little embarrassed about gazing at the well-built, undraped young man standing before all of them.

She glanced up as a bell rang. "That's all for this session…make sure you all take your supplies with you. Give your sketches to Andrea, and she'll put them in the locker until next session." She smiled at her students. "And, don't forget…I'll be gone all next week, so don't be too hard on your replacement instructor!" The class all laughed…they were all too enamoured of their lovely art professor to take any offense at the light remark.

Kristine watched as they all gathered up their things, and then headed for the door, chatting with one another. She answered a few questions from a couple of lingerers, and dismissed the model. She gave a few instructions to her assistant, and then sat down behind her desk. It was Friday, and she had a few things to finish up, paper-wise, before she started her vacation.

Sometimes...not often, but sometimes, she regretted going into the world of full-time teaching. Her love of art, and her consummate skill as an artist, made her an excellent instructor, as well as a very popular one. The University of Denver had been her choice when a student herself. She counted herself very fortunate when, a few years after her own graduation, the dean of the university had offered her the chair of the art department. It was like coming home all over again. By the time they'd offered her the position, she'd already had several successful shows as an artist, and a few of her paintings hung in select private collections all over the country. Kristine was sure this fact had been very instrumental in their approach to her.

She looked up as the door opened...and was surprised to see Sandra, and Garalynn walk into the classroom. She stood up, a smile on her lips. "Well, hi there, you two! What are you doing out this way?...especially this time of day?"

Sandra stopped by the desk, picking up one of the sketches. "Hmmm...nice scenery, Kris! From memory?...or, visual aids?"

"You know I believe in dealing only with the real thing, Sandy!...eat your heart out!" Kristine grinned, well used to her friends' teasing about her use of live models in her classes. "Now...what's up? You two don't usually take time out, in the middle of a workday, just to go visiting! What's up?" Kristine sensed a tension emanating from both her friends, though both women were doing their best to appear just the opposite.

"Just thought you might be up for an impromptu dinner party this afternoon...about five? Unless, of course, you already have plans?" Both Sandra and Garalynn were very aware of the lovely art teacher's current involvement with a prominent judge...an honest, hard-working, thoroughly charming man that all her friends highly approved of, and liked quite well.

"No...no plans tonight. John's got a law enforcement seminar he's giving at the civic center tonight. A get-together really sounds like fun! We haven't had too many of those since...well, in quite q while!" Kristine changed her words hastily, realizing what she'd been going to say might offend.

Sandra looked away, chewing a bit at her full lower lip. "You don't have to be so cautious...everyone here knows what you were really going to say! We haven't been doing anything we all used to, since our guests from England showed up! *Nothing* at Blackmoon has been the same since they came into Beth's...and my, life!"

Garalynn took hold of Sandra's arm, squeezing reassuringly. "That's what I've been trying to say ever since they arrived...I don't trust them!" She looked over at Kristine. "That's one of the reasons I suggested this dinner, Kristine. I think everyone needs to get a few things off their chests, about the Dresdens...and without Beth around!"

"Garalynn...I told you that unless we have some kind of hard proof that they *are* up to something, Beth is not going to listen!" Sandra declared, a trifle heatedly.

"Say...what is this? You two never argue...what brought this on?" Kristine glanced at Garalynn. She knew the lady lawyer was the one who'd open up first about any problems.

"The Dresdens are most likely the root of all problems at Blackmoon right now...especially any of those between family members!" Garalynn smiled at Sandra, showing no offense taken at the heated words. "They seemed determined to monopolize Beth...and she seems equally determined to allow them! I have hardly seen Beth at the office in the last four weeks! If I have needed to get in touch with her about business matters, I either leave a message with her secretary, or contact her at the Blackmoon office! And, when that has happened, either Tamara, or Sean...or both, has been present!"

Kristine was greatly surprised at Garalynn's words. "Even during business meetings? What justification did Beth give for that? I mean…she's always dealt with business matters with an 'only those who need to know' type of attitude!"

"Her reasons were that since they're here, and interested in all aspects of the company's running, they should be present at anything that deals with the company!" was the quiet reply from Garalynn. "I'll tell you one thing…being around them, especially the sister, is getting to be almost creepy!"

"Look…let's talk about this later, over dinner! Let's get rolling…the others will probably beat us there!" Sandra waved, heading for the door.

"Hey, wait, I have…what others? What's the big rush?" Kristine looked at Garalynn, hands on hips.

Garalynn merely picked up Kristine's briefcase, and handed it to her. "The others are Lynda, and Leslie…we're all meeting at my condo. They're bringing part of the food, and we'll get the rest on our way there!" Garalynn gestured towards the door. "As for there being a rush…everything will be explained there, after we eat!"

"Alright…but this had better be a damn good dinner!" Kristine declared, thoroughly mystified, and a little exasperated……

….."And that's why I suggested we all get together here…in a quiet place where we can't be interrupted, or over-heard!" Garalynn looked around the table. She'd just finished explaining why they'd wanted to meet.

Lynda sat back, putting her crumpled napkin on the table. "I'm not really sure if I understand all of what you're trying to tell us, Garalynn…or you, Sandy. Do you really think either of the Dresdens are trying to manipulate Beth? Don't get me wrong…*I* don't like, or trust, either of them!" Lynda looked over at her silent cousin. "But…do you have any real evidence that something bad is going on here? You know…like, drugs, or blackmail…or something?"

"Do you really think someone who's doing what Sandy said would be so stupid as to leave any kind of proof around to be found? You're the one who's the mystery story fanatic here, Lyn…use your head!" Leslie glared at her sister, than turned back to Sandy, and Garalynn. "There's just one thing I don't get…how could Beth, of all people, allow herself to be used, in any way! Sandy…you know how strong-willed your sister can be, in any situation! What would they hope to gain? The business merger was already an accomplished fact…what more did they need?"

"Now, who's not using their head? You gain control over Beth…you gain control of one of the largest industrial conglomerates in the world!" Lynda stated, a grim smile on her face. "I think, using that logic, plus Beth's behavior of late…well, Sandy and Garalynn may well have a legitimate claim to make! We may all have something very real to worry over!"

Garalynn rose from the table, walking over to where her grand piano stood, and slipped onto the bench behind the instrument. Her nimble fingers began to lightly skim over the black and white keys, drawing a soft, pleasant melody from the piano. In moments of deepest stress, the music she could coax from the keys helped ground her emotions, allowing her to cope with almost any, and all problems facing her.

She looked back at the table, continuing to play the piano. "I am convinced, and very afraid, that the Dresdens are going to be far more trouble than we could ever imagine! There's an evil about them…an evil for which there are no words!" She drew a deep breath, her fingers unconsciously bringing out a darker, more intense melody, reflecting her inner feelings. "I believe, through ways we would never believe, or could, only guess at…they have gained control of Beth's mind, and free will! I also believe their goals may be far worse than just taking control of the company…far worse, for her, and quite possibly others!"

Sandra looked down at her hands, clasped in her lap. "Tamara, and Sean have been here over four weeks now…and the only time my sister has not been with one, or both of them, has been when she's asleep! Although, if I'm going to be perfectly honest with myself, and you…I am pretty sure most of her nights of late are now being spent with Sean!" She glanced up at the collective gasp from her listeners.

"She's sleeping with him?...our Beth? Are you sure about that? I just can't believe that!" Lynda couldn't believe how calm Sandra was, talking about this.

"Beth's reserved, Lynda...not dead! She's a normal, healthy woman, and Sean's a handsome, incredibly charming man! Like him, or not...Sean has a very pronounced sex appeal. Most women would think her crazy if she *didn't* accept the chance to sleep with him!...including me!" Leslie shrugged her shoulders, shaking her head.

Kristine spoke up. "The thought that Beth could be under anyone's influence never entered my head!...until today! But...I have to admit that the idea of that kind of thing going on *does* supply some possible answers to questions I've had of late!"

"Questions?...what questions?" Lynda asked, giving her sister a final scowl.

"The last time I was out to Blackmoon...about a week ago...Beth went out of her way to point out that my continued presence there was not appreciated! She'd found Sean helping me adjust a stirrup, on my saddle, and stated that he was just a little too interested...and that it was *my* fault! At first, I only thought it was just her jealousy...cripes, we all know how she feels about him! Then, as she went on and on, I realized she was serious! She really believed I was trying to get him! I didn't say anything to her, at the time...just went for my ride. I left as soon as I got back...didn't see her at all before I left." Kristine tilted her head to one side, thinking back. "As I think back, now, I realize she was odd, in several ways, that day! She was constantly complaining that everyone in the house was being way too noisy!...too slow, and she was forever thirsty! I remember asking her if she felt all right, and she snapped my head off, saying she was fine! She said it was none of my business how she felt, how she ran the company, or her personal affairs...and that if I knew what was good for me, I stay the hell away from Sean! The strange thing was, other then that one question about how she was feeling...I never mentioned a thing about the business, or her personal stuff! Beth knew me better than that!...or, I thought she did!"

Sandra banged her open palm down on the table top, startling all of them. "Why didn't you tell me about this before today, Kris? Dad always told you all that Blackmoon was your home as well as ours! Beth knows that...at least, she used to!" She stood up quickly, and started pacing back and forth across the big room. "This is just another thing, in a growing list, that illustrate just how much my sister is changing! To be honest, I'd begun to fear that Beth is on drugs!"

"Beth?...on drugs? Sandy...I think you're over-reacting a little about this!" Leslie stated, frowning at the absurdity of that idea.

"I don't agree, Leslie...there's a very good chance that that is exactly what might be going on here! In fact, even Keith's wondered that same thing a couple of times. He says her actions have been way left of her normal actions!" Lynda said, lifting a cautionary finger. "He told me that he's seen times when she's very euphoric...than, the next time, she's tense, jittery, suspicious...the way an addict gets when they aren't getting their drug! Maybe, if Garalynn and Sandy are right, that's how they're controlling Beth...with drugs!"

"I don't agree that drugs are involved here, Lynda...though, I do agree her odd behavior did start when they arrived here! I don't think, either, that Beth's suffering any type of break-down. I do, however, believe they are creating a dependence within her, and that the dependence is based on this obsession she has with Sean!" Garalynn said, stopping her playing on the piano keys. "I think this dependence is being influenced by something insidious, and deadly! The sooner she is permanently removed from their sphere of influence, the better for all of us!"

Lynda shook her head, waving off the intensity behind Garalyn's words. "The only part of what you said that I agree with is getting them away from Beth!...getting them the hell out of Denver! I'm not sure about this evil you spoke about, but I do think they're a bad influence, especially that Tamara!" She looked around the table at them all, nodding. "That is one very strange lady, whom I want nothing whatsoever to do with!...she's creepy! So...how do we get rid of them?"

"Lynda...you and I really aren't involved in this. We can't really do, or say anything where Beth's concerned! At least...not until we know what *is* going on here! I think that's where we all need to concentrate any efforts we put forth...finding out what has changed Beth's actions. Once we discover what, and who is causing all this, we can figure out any actions needed...right?" Leslie was admitting to herself that she was a little frightened of any head-on confrontation with Tamara...that woman unsettled her very much!

"Let's put everything on the table, so to speak, and see just what we're dealing with...at least, what we know to be happening! First...there's the arrival of the Dresdens, from England. A physical fact no one here can deny, or overlook...right?" Kristine looked around, seeing everyone nodding. "Okay...three weeks after their arrival, we all have noticed uncharacteristic mood swings, neglect of work duties in someone who has always been a workaholic, and this growing attraction..." she paused, seeing everyone's expressions. "Alright...this obsession with Sean! Beth says she's not ill, but her physical appearance says otherwise. Anything else?"

"After everything that's been stated, or hinted at here today, I think you may be understating things a bit!" Lynda glanced at her companions. "So...what now? What do we do?...is there anything we can do?"

Sandra bowed her head for a few seconds, then looked up. "I'm not sure what we can do...until we can make Beth see the dangers, all we can do is stick close, and be there for whatever does happen. Beth being who she is, is not about to listen without firm, unshakable proof! I've talked to Dr. Hodges, the family physician, and he wants her to come in to see him...but, so far, she's had an excuse for every time he's asked her to come into the office. She says she's not ill, so why waste both their time? She tells me I'm being a hypochondriac!" Sandra lifted her glass of wine, and took a sip. "She's talking about finding them some property around Denver...so they can build a home to stay in when they come from England! I know what she really wants...for Sean to decide to stay here permanently! You know...all I have ever wanted for my sister..." She glanced at Garalynn. "For *both* of my sisters...is for them to be happy! I can see that Sean *does* make Beth happy...but, is it a good happy? Am I wrong about the way I feel?...do I just butt out, and let things develop as they will? But...what if I'm right? If I do nothing, what will happen to Beth?" She could feel the frustration welling up within her. With a sharp cry, she flung her glass against the wall. The red wine slid down the textured wallpaper, the red stain ominous against the pale ivory of the paper.

"Displays of temper aren't going to help, Sandy. We have to do what Leslie said...find out the real cause of Beth's actions, and do something about it! If there is some sinister force at work here, we have to discover what it is, and eliminate it!...no matter how angry it makes our sister with us!" Garalynn shook her head, understanding Sandra's inner turmoil, but knowing they had to keep themselves calm, and in control.

"And the Dresdens?...after all, they *are* the problem!" Lynda was positive she was right, and the solution as a simple one...get rid of Tamara and Sean.

"They'll stay as long as things are going their way...especially where my sister is involved!" Sandra said in a flat tone, wiping up her mess with a towel Garalynn had handed her.

"There has to be a way to point out to her what's going on, Sandy! God...even the manor house staff doesn't care for the Dresdens! They're afraid of them...even Dorie, and she doesn't fear anyone, or anything!" Leslie declared, speaking of the head cook at Blackmoon.

"I know...but as long as Beth wants them there, everyone's keeping quiet, out of love and respect for her! I know she's the only one who hopes they stay for good!" Sandra sighed, wishing for a way out of this.

"Beth's does want them to stay, yes...I believe it's not totally due to he infatuation with Sean, Sandra. I believe it's also because she can't help herself! She *needs* them here, especially Sean!" Garalynn's tone was grave...her eyes determined and sad.

Sandra's face was beginning to show all the pent-up stress. "Just what is that supposed to mean?...what are you getting at, Garalynn? You've been saying things like that for the past few days now! Spit it out, will you? No fancy lawyer talk...just plain English! What are you trying to say?"

Garalynn took a deep breath, sitting back down on the piano bench. "I wish I could just lay it all out in front of all of you...but, I can't! It's not clear in my own mind yet. Call it a gut reaction, or instinct...intuition...but I know I'm right! Without a doubt...they are dangerous!...not just to Beth, but to all of us! The longer they stay, the greater the danger...the more deadly the outcome! They are a more serious danger than any of us realize!"

"Well, I don't know about danger, but they're not being totally honest with us...of that I am sure! Tamara'a just a bit *too* perfect...too poised, and way too sure of herself! Every time I've been around her, she's managed to scare the crap out of me...without saying a word! Those eyes of hers...I swear they look right into your soul!" Leslie shivered, thinking about the tawny beauty.

Lynda nodded, for once agreeing with her sister. "And Sean...he can really rattle you...except when he's not around that sister of his! Than, he's almost fun to be around...charming, sexy, and...what am I doing!" Lynda shook her head. "When he's with Tamara, though...then he's more dangerous than charming! I've felt that come from him, even through his touch! To be honest, though, it's sometimes difficult to resist him!"

"If we're all honest...I think we've all felt that...that pull from him! And, I know if we gave in to that pull, he wouldn't hesitate to take advantage of any of us, despite of how he's supposed to fell about Beth!"

Sandra looked at Garalynn. "And how do we tell Beth that?...that the man she loves wouldn't even think twice about sleeping with any of her friends...or either of her sisters!"

"You're all missing the blatant truth!...he's a dangerous man! Not as dangerous as his sister, perhaps...but dangerous nonetheless! Tamara is...she's a danger none of us could imagine!" Garalynn felt a kind of desperation inside when she thought about her adopted sister, and the two strangers.

Sandra raised her hands, shrugging her slim shoulders. "Well, until Beth sees it the way we all do, there's no way she's going to believe her precious Sean is anything but perfect! I wish I could just wave my hand, and everything would be back to the way it was before they came! I wish I knew what was the right thing to do, say something or keep my mouth shut!" Sandra sighed, her shoulders slumping a little. "My sister's happier than I remember her ever being. All our lives, especially after Mama died, Beth has always taken care of me. She's never really had the kind of happiness a woman looks for, or dreams about...until now! Do I stop that happiness, for reasons I'm not sure about...am I being unreasonable, or jealous? If I'm right, and I do something about it, then I will be the destruction of the happiest time my twin sister has ever had! Yet...if I keep silent, she could be in the greatest danger she's ever been in before! What do I do?"

"Look...none of us can come up with concrete reasons as to why we distrust Tamara, and Sean...but we all know there *is* a reason! We all want Beth to be happy...but we also want her safe!" Leslie came up beside her cousin, placing a gentle hand on her shoulder.

Sandra covered Leslie's hand with her own, and gave a squeeze. "I'll tell you all this...I'm not sure just how much more of this uncertainty I can handle! Normally, in any other situation, I'd simply go to Beth, and we'd discuss it...like we always have done in the past! But now...well, the few times I have tried to talk about things, her reactions have been anything but encouraging! If I pursue this further, I risk wrecking the most important relationship in my life! If I don't, I could lose my sister! I wish I knew what to do!"

Garalynn came over to Sandra, gripping her other shoulder. "Your indecision should tell you something…have you ever had that where Beth is concerned? You have always been blessed with an instinct that has guided you throughout your life, Sandra…and that instinct has seldom been wrong! Let it guide you now…you know it's wrong for Beth to be with Sean! You know, in your deepest soul, that he will be her ruin!…if not death! And don't ever forget about Tamara…she's a greater danger than Sean!"

Lynda had had about enough. "Would you stop saying that? You've been hinting at something for ages now…just spit it out! Say what you think…you're driving me buggy!"

For q few moments, Garalynn just stood there, gazing at Lynda. She appeared to be taking some sort of inner council with herself. Finally, she squared her shoulders, and looked around at all of them, She could see the expectation on their faces. "You're right…I've been talking, without saying anything! You've heard me say that I felt I'd met Tamara, and Sean, before, right? What I *haven't* said was that every time I've felt that sensation, there's also been the strong feeling that wherever it was that we *did* meet, it was a time of danger…and death! I know, as sure as we are all standing here now, that they represent the intentions of evil…in all the possible definitions of the word!"

For a few seconds, the group was all quiet, taking in what their friend had just told them. The words seemed to touch something within each of them…a something that stirred ancient fears, and thoughts best left buried, or forgotten. Leslie tried to speak, and found she had a lump in her throat. Kristine sat there, eyes wide and fearful, heart beating faster and faster. Lynda stared at Garalynn, a frown of uncertainty on her face. Sandra stood there, trying to piece everything together in her mind.

Lynda finally broke the unsettling silence. "If it was your intention to scare the hell out of everyone, Garalynn...congratulations, you've succeeded! What's the purpose for any of what you've said?"

Garalynn whirled to face her. "Get it through your head, Lynda...I'm not trying to get at anything, or scare anyone! I just want to keep my sisters safe, especially Beth right at this time! I can't give any of you any more reasons than the fears in my heart! But, as sure as I am alive, and speaking...the Dresdens *are* a genuine threat!" She turned towards Sandra. "Sandy, you know I don't usually speak before I'm sure...but this time I can't wait! I know that I'm right, and that one day I'll have the proof to convince you all! I can only hope you'll believe me now!"

The others all looked at one another. They could see how earnest, and determined their friend was at this moment. They all knew her to be steady, levelheaded, not prone to wild speculations and fears...was she right? Was the danger real?

Sandra sighed, suddenly very tired. "I think this has been talked out as far as we can right now...let it go for now! All we can really do is watch, and try to find any clue to what's really happening! Let's just keep Beth in our prayers, and hope the powers that be are watching over her!" She looked at her companions, and they all nodded. "Let's drop this, and do something...anything, to get our minds off this! Any ideas?"

"Well...there's a special show at the planetarium this evening, and I can get us all in for free! We all used to like going there as a group, and we haven't been in a long while...how about it?" Kristine spoke up.

Lynda looked around the group. "I don't see any arguments...so, lets get going! I definitely need something different right now! Lead the way, Kris!"

Everyone pitched in, and the room and table were soon cleaned up. That done, they gathered up their belongings, and headed out the door. Just the idea of doing something together had brightened their spirits. They were anxious to put the dark thoughts behind them. As she was about to close the front door to her home, Garalynn experienced a sudden chill. She paused, then shook it off, deliberately emptying her mind of any fears, Whatever it was…she didn't want to face it right now!………..

****

III

❃

….Beth leaned forward, hugging close over the neck of the horse she was riding. She loved the feel of the wind slipping past her ears, with a low even "whooshing" sound…loved the feel as it wound it way through her dark hair. She felt the movement, and strength, of the animal under her, as they raced through the autumn forest, the thick leave cover being kicked up by the flying hooves.

She glanced back, over one shoulder. She could see that Sean was steadily gaining on her, the spirited gelding he was riding stretching its long legs to the limit with every stride. The vivid hues of fall's colors sparkled in the sunshine, leaves softly drifting down from the trees overhead, or spurting up into the air, kicked up by the racing horses.

The air was crisp, and clean like no other time of the year. Finally, as her horse reached the bank of the river that wound its way throughout the estate acreage, Beth drew her mount to a stop. The horse tossed its head, blowing, and Beth laughed, happy and a little breathless from her ride. She waited for Sean to fully catch up with her.

As he reined in next to her, he smiled at her , his admiration clear in the dark eyes that raked over her form. "You surprise me, Elizabeth…I didn't realize you were so accomplished a horsewoman! I am impressed!"

She smiled, blushing a little, looking away, suddenly shy. "I don't usually ride so recklessly…but the day is so perfect for riding, I couldn't hold back! It must be the air…autumn here is always so invigorating! It makes one feel so vital…so alive!"

Sean swung down from his horse, with an easy grace that most big men didn't possess. He tied his horse's reins to a nearby bush, then walked over to her, and held up his arms. Grasping her slender waist, he swung her down from the saddle, and pulled her up against his tall form. He gave her a slight hug, a little kiss, then reached for the reins of her horse. Gathering up those of his mount, he smiled again at Beth, and began to walk towards the river. She walked beside him, feeling so small next to him, despite her own height of five foot ten, but basking in the waves of pure sensual energy that always seemed to radiate from him.

When they reached the riverbank, Sean guided the two animals forward so they could drink their fill from the clear, rushing waters. He slipped a strong arm about Beth's shoulders, pulling her closer against him. He felt unusually happy, and peaceful today…and very tender towards the woman with him. He leaned over, kissing the top of her head, enjoying the scent of her hair. She sighed, snuggling closer, slipping an arm about his trim waist.

Sean took a deep breath, drawing the cool air into his lungs, savoring the crispness, the cleanness. He was glad he accepted Beth's suggestion for an afternoon ride, and it fit in well with Tamara's plans. She needed Beth out of the way for a couple of hours, and made it clear to Sean that they didn't need to hurry back. Sean had felt unusually tense, and restless the past few days. This was longer than he'd ever gone, from his usual routine, and he had been feeling stressed and confined. He felt a little better after the ride, and gave Beth a broad grin, letting her know he was glad she made the suggestion. She smiled back, feeling happy and more content herself. Her own inner turmoil of the past few days seemed to have finally resolved itself.

Beth drew in deep, happy breaths. She'd always enjoyed riding, but never as much as today. She watched as Sean knelt down on the river bank, and scooped up some water in his cupped hands. He brought the water up to his mouth, liking the sharp cold on his lips, the coolness that slid down his dry throat. She lowered her head a bit, watching his profile from under her lashes. She couldn't find a single line she didn't love. She looked away suddenly, overwhelmed by the surge of feeling that went through her...the sense of arousal. She seemed to have absolutely no control over her emotions lately, and today seemed no different...the slightest thing seem to set her off. All Sean had to do of late was merely brush against her...her heart started racing, her breathing became rapid, and her knees felt like they couldn't hold her up much longer. She'd see him enter a room, and it frequently took all her dwindling willpower to keep from running to him, begging for his touch, and his love.

Her body's demands took total dominion, especially since that first night they'd made love. The inferno he'd placed within her flamed brighter, higher, hotter...more intense each day. He fed that flame every night...she was becoming more and more enslaved, reveling in the state, her struggle against it weakening all the time. She knew something was happening within her...could feel the strange changes...but, she didn't care anymore! All that mattered was Sean. When he was anywhere around, this insanity ruled everything within her. When there was a rare time he wasn't around, she was better able to think clearly, handle her affairs with her usual control. For a brief time, she was correct, and everything seemed fine. Then...something would trigger that bewitching flame within her body...and her logic, common sense, and control would be consumed in its heat!

Sensing a subtle change in the air, Sean looked up at Beth. His wide grin faded, to be replaced by an intense look of arousal. He stood up, recognizing the fires in her eyes, feeling that familiar surging, that eagerness...that hunger he'd been holding under tight control, keeping it from full expression as Tamara ordered. True...he and Beth had been together every night, but he'd kept his passions bridled, not allowing himself to let go the way he truly desired. He wanted her so much…in the way he enjoyed the best, but he was trying to accede to his sister's wishes. But…it was so hard…and his need was so strong!

In the end, it was his need that took complete control…surging within him stronger than it ever had before. It pushed his sister's words, and his fear of her anger, into the furthest reaches of his mind. He surrendered to its demands without further hesitation, and stepped closer to Beth. Taking her in his arms, he pulled her tight against his hard body, inhaling the provocative scent of her. Seeing his intent clear in her eyes, Beth gave a small gasp, and involuntarily took a step backward.

His arms slid around her waist, pulling her back against him. His head bent over hers, claiming the full lips. There was little gentleness in the kiss. It was one of urgency, and fully aroused passion. Her arms slipped about his neck, and she returned the embrace with a fire to match his own.

Bending her slightly backwards, his lips seared their way down her throat, ending at the apex of the pulsating artery. Her fingers dug into the heavy muscles of his broad shoulders, locking his body to hers. He lifted his head slightly, looking down into her face. The dark fires crackled in the depths of his eyes, and he could feel his desire growing stronger…deeper. His gaze shifted to the neck of her blouse, and he raised one hand to it.

Swift as thought, that hand gripped the neckline, and jerked down, and out. The buttons popped in all directions, and the fine linen tore. He stripped it from her, and tossed it to the forest floor. She could feel the cool air against her heated skin. She looked up at him, smiling ever so slightly, lips parted, and arched herself tighter against his powerful body. Every touch, every movement…she encouraged the desire within him to continue to grow, even as her own began surging.

Sean kissed the side of her neck, lingering again over the pounding pulse point there. His mouth moved down, as he bent her backwards again…one hand slipping down to her bra-covered breasts. His powerful hand cupped one full breast, kneading it firmly, his thumb working over the tightening nipple. Beth could feel the heat of his mouth, even through the cloth of her bra...a searing heat that fanned her own desires higher, and hotter. She gripped his head with both hands, her nails sinking into the skin of his scalp, gripping the thick hair firmly. She heard his grunt...then a low, deep growl...he was so close.

Sean quickly removed the interfering clothing, and immediately took the erect nipple deep into his mouth, intent on arousing her even more...to bring the pure essence once more into her surging blood. As he took a deep pull on her breast, Beth felt herself slipping into that intoxicating, mind-drugging limbo he always brought forth. It no longer frightened her, though, because she knew it would soon bring that total, consuming passion he alone had ever given her. She arched her back, pushing more of her breast into his avid mouth, feeling his talented tongue working on the nipple, causing even more heat to go directly to her very center. She murmured in his ear, encouraging his efforts, telling him of her love, and desire. She was more than ready to join with him again...her body was calling to his, seeking the connection that took them to that crest of pleasure, and ultimate fulfillment. She lifted his head, wanting to kiss his lips again...but stopped when she saw his face.

His teeth were bared, clenched so tight she could almost hear the teeth grinding with the pressure. His lips were drawn back, in an animalistic snarl of pain...and in an expression of near fear. His facial muscles contorted...Beth thought she was losing her mind...for a second, it was like seeing a beast straight from the bowels of Hell itself! In another second, though, the terrifying vision was gone...she shook her head, believing she only imagined that sight. Sean was in so much pain, his muscles so contorted...she knew she'd only imagined it.

She heard him groan loudly, his arms loosening their grip on her waist. She fell back, right into a pile of leaves, and twigs. She struggled to sit up, gazing wildly up at him, as he stood there, clutching at his head, outlined in the setting sun's rays. His breathing was loud, irregular, and harsh with barely suppressed screams. She could hear him whimper as he tried to regain control. His features, though twisted in pain, no longer resembled any kind of beast, and she was sure now she'd only dreamed what she thought she'd seen.

As she stared, bewildered and concerned, he stiffened, throwing his head back, and dropping to his knees beside where she was sitting. He bent forward until his forehead was cushioned on some leaves, another deep groan issuing from him. He still had his hands tight on either side of his head, grinding his teeth, and thrashing his head from side to side.

Beth propped herself up with her open palms, staring at Sean in confusion, and growing apprehension. He continued to throw his head from side to side, speaking throatily in a language she'd never heard before. Suddenly, he rose to his knees, throwing his head back, and howling with the intensity of the pain that was racking his entire body now. He reminded Beth of a trapped animal! She continued to stare, not knowing what to think, or to do.

Sean slumped back to the ground, moaning. Beth crawled over to him, wrapping his arms about his prostrate form, and lifting his head into her chest, cushioning it on her bared breasts. She rocked him gently, crooning softly, trying to reach him through his agony. His arms slipped around her, seeking solace from the pain in her gentle touch, and warmth. Beth just didn't understand…what could do something like this to a man as strong as Sean?

She drew him closer, rocking him like an infant. She whispered softly: "Sean, I've got you!…it's okay. I'm here, and I'll take care of you! I have to get you back to the manor house, then we'll be able to take care of…of whatever this is! Hang on, my dearest…we'll get through this!"

Lost in the world of his pain, understanding only the tone of her voice, and the warmth of her body, Sean merely groaned in reply. Every cell in his body was being attacked, and he wasn't conscious of anything else. Beth hugged him once more, then gently lowered him completely to the ground. She had things to do!

Beth reached down, grabbing her bra, and torn blouse. Quickly putting them back on, she pulled the blouse together as best she could, then went to where the horses were standing. She led them over to where Sean was curled up, and dropped the reins there, bending down to slip her arms about him again. She managed to get him to his feet, swaying and incoherent. She had just retrieved the reins when both horses began snorting, tossing their heads, pawing the ground. She calmed them down, speaking soothingly to the now nervous animals, then started the task of getting the stricken man onto his horse again.

It took a few minutes, and tries, but finally, he was in the saddle, slumped over the horse's neck, still muttering deliriously. Beth was still having trouble with the horses, stepping about restlessly, and both animals were covered with a nervous lather. Beth was an accomplished rider, but it took all her skills to quiet the two horses so she could mount, and get going. She led the horse Sean was on, talking to both to keep them as calm as possible...she discovered it was the sound of her voice that kept Sean calm as well as the horses.

She dug her heels in, and started the long trip back to the manor house. Sean was still bent low over the neck of the horse he was riding, still groaning. Occasionally, he growled, like an animal in pain...at which sound the horse under him laid back its ears, and bared its teeth. A few quiet words, and a firm hand on the reins kept the big horse under control. She wanted to ride fast, and hard, to get the man she loved to medical care, but she knew that it had to be slow, and careful. Both horses were still very skittish, taking extra time for control on her part...and Sean simply wasn't up to a rapid ride through the forest. Beth drew a deep breath in, calmed herself, and headed for the stables, and home......

.....Tamara stepped into her brother's bedroom, her lovely face showing no trace of fear, or concern. She crossed the room quickly, making no sound at all. Standing beside the bed, she gazed down at Sean's sweat-beaded face, her eyes quiet and unreadable. She seemed calm, but there was a tangible aura of tension about the tall, lithe body. She glanced over to the other side of the bed, where Beth sat in a chair, her right hand holding Sean's left...her face worried, and tear-streaked. Beth had looked up when Tamara entered, watching the other woman draw closer to the bed. When the tall blonde still didn't say a word, Beth stood up, putting Sean's hand down at his side, and coming around to the other side of the bed.

"I've contacted Dr. Hodges, our family physician...he'll be here shortly. I wanted to take Sean directly to the hospital, but he wouldn't allow me. He insisted that he only needed to rest...that you would know what to do!" She looked into the calm face, wondering what the other woman was thinking. "I'm very worried, Tamara...I've never seen an attack, or seizure, like that before! He was in so much pain I honestly thought he was going to die! Has anything like this happened before?"

Keeping her eyes on her brother's face, Tamara's tone of voice was light, casual...as though nothing were wrong. "He's had a few similar...seizures, though perhaps not as intense as you say this one was. It's an inherited condition, Elizabeth...from our father's side of the family. The attacks have usually been brief, and he's recovered from them in a mater of a few days...rest, and quiet is what he needs to have now!" She turned, facing Beth. "I don't think your physician need bother himself in coming here, Elizabeth...though I do thank you for the thought! I have the necessary...medicine for him! I simply have to get it refilled...we seldom carry much with us. You don't need to worry any further. As I said...all he really requires now is rest, and quiet!"

"What he needs is to be checked out by a doctor, Tamara! I can't believe that what I witnessed, out there in the woods, was just a simple convulsion! And, if Sean does have some sort of medical condition, why hasn't he mentioned it before now? Why wouldn't he let me know about something like this? We love one another!" Beth couldn't believe Tamara was treating this so casually.

"His pride, Elizabeth...such a foolish thing, but so vital to a man! I'm sure he'll explain it all to you soon...after he's gotten his strength back. I really must insist that you cancel your doctor's visit...if he could speak, I know that Sean would second this request most strongly!" Tamara smiled slightly, patting Beth's arm.

Beth couldn't believe this. "Tamara...I have had some medical training, and I am telling you that what happened to him, out in the woods, was something quite serious! I insist my physician see him! As your hostess, I take my responsibility towards the two of you very seriously! I also happen to be in love with him...I insist Dr. Hodges see, and examine him! Now...if you'll excuse me...I had ordered some tea...I'm going to see what's holding it up!" Beth turned, and walked out of the bedroom.

Tamara waited until the door was closed, then swiftly bent over her brother's still form. "Sean...open your eyes! It's Tamara...look at me! We don't have much time!"

Slowly, Sean opened his eyes, focusing on the face of his sister. He groaned softly, grinding his teeth together. She watched him in silence, feeling his efforts to fight back the waves of pain, and now nausea. She put her hands on the top of his head, concentrating, probing into his mind with her special gift...searching for the cause of this pain. She drew back, with a gasp...her eyes darting about the room as if seeking the cause in the room. They were completely alone...how had this happened? She knew now, beyond a doubt, what had happened to Sean was no accident...it was a deliberate attack from their ancient enemy! But how?...how could it have happened, here, without her sensing it first? The area had been deemed clear...no signs of their bitter foes. And how had they gotten to Sean? For such an attack, proximity of touch was required...yet, Elizabeth stated they had been alone!

Sean looked up at her, breathing shallowly. "Tamara...I cannot stand this anymore! The pain...it is beyond anything I've been through before! It's tearing my insides apart with claws of fire!"

She replaced her hand over his forehead, her alert mind linking with his, and giving him some of her strength, and calm. "You *are* ill, Sean...but you're allowing the fear you feel to help this tear at your insides! Take of my strength...calm your fears, and rid your mind of all of them! There is too much to do, and at stake, for you to allow this 'sickness' to win over your will!" She shook his upper arm. "Get control of yourself...it will help ease the pain!"

Sean drew his hand over his face, taking a deep, though shaky, breath. "How can I be calm, Tamara?...this is an attack! You know that...I saw your face when you touched my mind...you know it *was* an attack! How is that possible?" He laid his head back, trying to follow her instructions to calm himself. "You know I am never 'sick'! How could this happen, Tamara?...you said it was 'clear' here!"

Tamara gripped his chin, forcing him to meet her gaze. The golden eyes were flashing. "Stop this!...it will not help! You leave yourself open to attacks, Sean, when you allow yourself to panic! I admit...this most probably *is* an attack...and I cannot tell you how it happened! This area was cleared years ago...you know that...and there has been no sign to show any further 'contamination'! Even now...I sense nothing! And, you know I would if it were true! What I do not know...is how any of them could have gotten close enough to actually touch you, to cause this! Did you see anyone else, besides Elizabeth, anywhere around where this happened?"

He shook his head, feeling the pain easing as Tamara's powers began to push it from his mind, and body. "There was no one...I would have sensed them. There was no one, Tamara! We must leave here at once...before it happens again!"

She slapped his cheek, jarring him out of his near panic. "Be still!...you invite another attack by allowing such fear to cloud your mind!" She straightened up, thinking hard and swift. "There is another possibility...one I should have foreseen before we left home." She sat on the edge of the bed, bending close to him. "You know we've had to forgo our regular...routine since we've been in this country, and city. Under usual conditions, an abstinence never causes problems! We've always had the means to keep everything calm, and efficient...until this time!"

"So...what is it? What is causing this?" Sean was trying to keep calm.

"Something has managed to 'infect' you...causing an imbalance within your body!" She bent closer, looking directly into his eyes. "Sean...your little 'transgression' with Beth the other night...it may have been the indirect cause of this!"

"How?...she's not one of them! Are you trying to say what I'm suffering is some kind of allergic reaction?" He snorted, thinking his sister had lost her mind. "That was only one time, Tamara...and nothing happened! That was three weeks ago!"

"I haven't worked it all out in my mind yet, Sean...but I feel sure your attack, and that night, are connected!" She stood, looking around the room. "There are currents about this place...currents of power, and strengths I'm not familiar with, dear brother. And what bothers me most...these currents weren't here when we first arrived! To be honest...I didn't pick up on them until I was touching your mind a few minutes ago!"

He stared at her. "You didn't pick up on...Tamara, what are you saying?"

"I told you...I haven't worked everything out yet! But...I will tell you what I think!" She looked at him, her eyes hard. "When you decided to disobey me, and take Beth fully...you opened the door to these currents, to the forces I now realize exist in this place! I'm not entirely sure how they work...but I will learn!"

He shook his head, not believing. "I don't believe this!...how could they get to me with only one time! That's not possible!...I'm not without powers myself, you know, Tamara! I would have sensed them!"

She clenched her fists, keeping her emotions, especially her temper, under tight and sure control. "You still don't understand, do you? It's why you were told *not* to get intimately involved until told to do so!...why full expression is something to be realized only under the right conditions! Because, my dear brother...when you allow yourself full expression...you drop your guard! It can't be helped!...it's the nature of the deed! That is why I said you probably were 'infected' that night! Whatever you were 'marked' with, it incubated within your body, and finally 'attacked' you!...when you were about to disobey me once again!"

He paled...she knew what he had intended to do, out there in the forest. "Tamara...I...I am sorry! I've been feeling so uncomfortable the past few days! I thought it might make me feel better!...I wasn't really trying to go against your orders!"

She shook her head. "I should be furious with you, Sean...but, you have suffered enough, and in a way...your illness has alerted us to the fact we *do* have enemies close by, and that will have to be dealt with! At least now...we won't be entirely taken by surprise! Now...get yourself under control...before Elizabeth comes back! It's going to take your words to convince her to cancel this physician's coming over! Right now, especially, we can't afford any further complications that such a visit *could* raise!"

He looked away, swallowing hard, trying to steady his breathing. "What do we do now, Tamara? I can't go through this again!" He looked back at her. "How can we stay here now?...with an enemy we can't see, *or* sense! We're too much at risk here now!"

She shook her head...he really was disgusting, with all this fear. "Be silent, Sean...it won't happen to you again...that I promise! I have been alerted, and have adjusted my sensory mechanisms accordingly...the next time 'they' try, if at all...I will be more than ready to repel their efforts! As for you..." She put a gentle hand, which further surprised Sean, on his shoulder. "All your system needs now is a little building up…your abstinence has weakened you more then anticipated. Once you're back to full strength, you'll be able to ward off any further 'attacks'. Just, please, do as I instruct you, Sean! Any further disobedience now could prove fatal!"

"I will *not* disobey you, Tamara…not in this! You're far more experienced in these matters than I! But…do you really think it could be…fatal?" Sean went pale…he fought the fear off, remembering what his sister had said about letting fear rule him.

She glanced up…her mind had been occupied with arrangements. "Yes…most definitely!" She started to turn away, then looked back at him as he sat on the edge of the bed. "If the 'attacks' don't kill you, Sean…I will! Keep that though ever in your mind…it should dissuade any further 'ideas' you may come up with! Now…do as I said, with Elizabeth! I have to see to the necessary arrangements…for your 'treatment'!"

Sean stared at her…he couldn't believe what she was purposing…even though a large part of him was elated at her words. "Here?…now? Is that wise, Tamara? This, we know now, is unfriendly territory for us! You're the one who always goes on about keeping a low profile…keeping risks down! Do you realize if we do what you're suggesting…Tamara, I can't believe *you* are willing to take this large of a risk!"

She frowned, wondering why she tried…once he got something in his mind, he became fixated on it. "Of course I realize any, and all, risks, Sean! Do you think I'd suggest something like this without having it all planned out, in my mind, before acting on it? This is merely a minor inconvenience…a small adjustment to the schedule already laid out! Everything will work out fine…keep calm!" She took her chin between the thumb and forefinger of her right hand, thinking. "Let me see…I think about forty-eight hours should do it! Yes…that's more than enough time to get everything arranged for your 'treatment' You can hold on until then, Sean…you just keep your little paramour from screwing things up, with her physician!" She turned, and headed for the door.

"It will be fine, Tamara...Elizabeth will do anything I say! Don't worry...I know what a physician, or a hospital, would mean for us!" He stretched his arms up over his head, really feeling stronger. "You infused me with some of your energy, didn't you? I can handle her now, with ease!...don't worry!" He laid back, getting ready for Beth's return.

She gave him one last glance, her hand on the doorknob. "Be very certain that you do, Sean! It's more important than you could possibly realize. Rest now...I'll return shortly!" Then, she opened the door, and went out into the hallway.

Beth was out in the hallway, talking with one of the maids, who was holding a large tea tray. She turned as she heard the door open, then close. She motioned for the maid to take the tray into the room, then looked at Tamara. "How's Sean? I was just coming with the tea."

"He's much better...you'll see when you go in. Oh, and he's asked me to ask you to please cancel the physician...he doesn't need it! Once he takes the family medicine, he'll be fine! I'm going, right now, to make the necessary arrangements to get that medicine. Your concern, Elizabeth, is both understandable, and appreciated...but very unnecessary!" Tamara was all smiles, and glowing charm.

Beth stared...beginning to get more than a little irritated at this continual blocking of her efforts to help the man she loved. "I don't happen to think it *is* unnecessary, Tamara! I intend seeing this through! I am sorry to go against your, and Sean's, wishes, but I feel I have no choice! I only want what's best for him!"

"If that is true, than you'll agree to *his* wishes, Elizabeth...cancel the physician's visit!" Tamara lifted her head, bringing the full strength of her eyes on Beth's. She reached up, swift as thought, lightly touching the other woman's temple with the tips of her fingers. "You'll see...in a couple of days, he'll be fine! If not...then we'll talk about a physician seeing him...alright?"

Beth started to speak, but suddenly found it difficult to think clearly...the sharpness of a migraine beginning to make its presence known. She put a shaky hand to her temple. "I...I guess we could do that...even though I really don't like waiting! But...if you, and Sean, feel this strongly about it, we'll try it your way first! Excuse me...I want to see how Sean's doing!" She nodded to Tamara, then went into the bedroom.

Tamara watched as the tall brunette went into the bedroom. After the door closed, the blonde stood there for a few moments, thinking. "I have to admit...there is more to you than I first thought, Elizabeth! There is a steel shaft in the center of your spirit...no wonder my brother is so taken with you. I'm sure he counted on you being a weapon against me...but, as usual, *my* will prevails!" She smiled to herself, idly twirling a blonde lock with the fingers of her left hand. "Yes...you will do as we wish, Elizabeth...as *I* wish it to be! Though...to be honest, it isn't as if you really had a choice in the matter!...your destiny was decided long ago!

With that cryptic remark, Tamara turned from the door, and walked down the hall towards the room she was staying in. She had some very important calls to make...to get things underway for Sean. As she hurried along the corridor, she thrust aside any lingering resentments, or anger, for her brother. There was no room, in her mind, for anything but the tasks at hand!.....

.....Five days after these events, Patrick shoved his head into David's office at their precinct. "Hey, Boss...you free to handle a call from a couple of upset parents?"

David glanced up, scowling, hands resting on one of several piles of papers on his desktop. "Parents?...why?...someone murder their kid?"

Patrick came into the office, and stood in front of the desk. "Well...we're not sure *any* kind of homicide's been committed...yet! Seems their daughter, her boyfriend, and one other boy, went backpacking a few days ago, and no one's heard anything from them since they left! The parents want us to look for them...says he's sure something's happened to them!"

"That's Missing Persons...why'd they call Homicide? Give the call to Andrews, in Missing Persons...I don't have the time to go looking for wayward teenagers! This Traylor case is giving me ulcers!" David sat back in his swivel chair, groaning...he was really beat!

Patrick walked over to the coffee pot his partner always kept perking in his office, and poured a cup. He took a big swig, grimacing a bit. He glared at David, holding the cup out towards his partner. "Call this coffee?...or furniture glue? No wonder you look like Hell! It tastes at least a week old! You age wine, you know!...not coffee!"

"Shows what you know...it's only three days old! Besides...I happen to like coffee with a full body! Now, quit changing the subject...why did we get that call about those kids, and not Missing Persons?" David stretched his arms over his head, trying to get the kinks out of his back.

"Missing Persons is short-handed...and the father's a personal friend of the police commissioner, who convinced the chief that since Homicide has more personnel than Missing Persons...well, we got picked!" Patrick took another drink, shaking his head again at the taste.

"Great!...as if our work load isn't heavy, or crazy, enough! How am I suppose to free up men to go baby-sit some bigwig's kids when we're barely able to check out the details of the legitimate cases we have on the tables!" David rubbed his temples...he hated politics, and the games that went with them. He was wishing he'd really gone through with taking his vacation now...but, he'd let the chief talk him into postponing it for a few months. Bad decision.

The big detective sergeant pulled up a chair, and sat down, leaning his elbows on David's desktop. "I know what you're getting at, Dave...and I have to agree with you...most of the time! But, I'm a father myself, and...well, I can't help, but put myself in this guy's place! If it were my daughter who was missing, I know I'd be pulling any string, calling in every favor...anything that would help me find her! This city's been jumpy ever since details of the Traylor case hit the media...people are seeing all sorts of things, in their minds...and every little odd thing is getting looked at as if it's another crime! But, I shouldn't have to point that out to you, Dave...you already know that, inside!"

David scratched behind one ear. "Yeh...I *do* know that, Pat! If I had any kids, I guess I'd probably be feeling the same way! Speaking of the Traylor case...I'd still like to find who leaked the news to the papers...*before* we were ready to make a public statement! I'd especially like to know how the Chronicle got copies of those pictures they printed! I don't get it...I've never seen so much media hype given to a homicide! At least...not since that movie star was arrested for his wife's murder, out in Los Angles!" He ran his fingers over his eyes, rubbing them...they were tired, and a little bloodshot from lack of sleep. "There's a lot of weird things going on lately...wonder if it's a full moon?" He tried to joke...but his mind kept going to the Traylor murder. "Have Nate and Jack check this missing kid story...they can see if there's anything really needing Homicide's investigating. If they don't think so, then it goes to Missing Persons...I'll talk with the chief about it!"

Patrick nodded, agreeing. "Well...heard Internal Affairs is looking into the press leak problem...sure would hate to be the poor bastard who did it once they get their hands on him...or them! You know...what you said about the Traylor case, and it making the city antsy! It's a good thing they don't know there's been a second murder, with the same M.O. They'd be in a feeding frenzy then!" Patrick took another drink. "You know...this actually gets better the more you drink it! You know...I thought the Traylor case was bad, but what was done to that night watchman a couple of nights ago was worse! And...it makes even less sense then the Traylor one! Why would anyone break into the University museum, trash the place, then do what was done to that old man? Do we know yet if anything was actually taken?"

"Well, as far as the curators have been able to determine, nothing of any real value is missing...just a few amulets, and talismans. But, you're right…it sure as hell wasn't worth what happened to that man!" David leaned back, thinking absently about that second murder…like the first, there was evidence of a struggle, but again, little or no blood, and that look of horror on the victim's face…what had the two men seen that had terrified them so prior to their deaths?

"Yeh…well…if the press finds out about this second killing…what do you supposed triggered this?" Patrick shook off a slight shudder…he'd had a bad feeling ever since the Traylor case started…a feeling of his own frailty, his eminent death. He'd never had a feeling, from a case, like this before. He wished he could get rid of it as easily as he probably would this coffee!

David stood up, suddenly restless. He walked around the desk, and went to get a cup of coffee for himself. He stood there a moment, cup in one hand, coffee pot in the other…gazing into empty space, thinking. "Pat…do you ever ask yourself…why here, in Denver? If this kind of thing had happened in L.A., or New York, it would still be news, but people wouldn't be surprised it happened there! Here…it's taken the entire state by surprise! I can't help, but wonder…why here?"

"This sort of thing is going to be a shocker anywhere, Dave…guess we're just the 'lucky' cops who got stuck with it this time!" Patrick tried to lighten the mood.

The tall policeman paced his office, taking large gulps of his coffee, his thoughts busy and deep. "Pat…why do I feel so intense about this case? Why this feeling that this is one we *have* to solve?…if we *never* solve another case, in our lives as cops, *this* one we have to finish!"

Patrick nodded, cradling his cup between his large hands, gazing down into the dark brown liquid. "I know…I know. I've had the same kind of feelings, ever since we first walked into that apartment! I just want to see it over, and done with!" He glanced up, grinning a little lop-sided. "There's something about this one, Dave…like I said, it scares something, deep inside me, and I don't know why!"

David gazed at his partner for a few seconds, then shook himself, and returned to his chair behind the desk. He sat down, rifling through some of the paperwork piled on top of the desk. He held up a large manila envelope. "See this? In here are *all* the bits, and pieces, of evidence, and data on the Traylor case…everything! Tons of information…and not one clear-cut clue to pint us in a definite direction! For the love of God…I can tell you just about anything you'd want to about the victim, even what he'd eaten just prior to his death…except *why* he was killed, and *who* killed him! Nor, do we know any common denominator tying him to the second victim…but, I promise you…there *will* be something that ties them together!"

Patrick looked at David, his expression one of agreement…and sympathy. "And, just to spice things up…lets not forget all the 'helpful' pressure from upstairs!"

"Pressure?…the chief's on my back like he's one of my backbones! And, the commissioner's chewing on the chief's butt like it's prime porterhouse!" David looked up, a memory stirring. "What about these missing kids, Pat? Even if they are some bigwigs, it's unusual for us to be called…what about it?"

"I'll have Nate and Jack get right on it…Ben took all the necessary information down already. The father said he'd gone to pick them up, at the agreed meeting place, and they just never showed! He said he waited for a few hours, then checked at all the homes to see if they'd showed up there…nothing!" Patrick stood up, and headed for the door. "I'll make sure Ben gives Nate and Jack all the info."

"Yeh…make sure I get a copy of that, too, Pat." He rolled his eyes at the smirk on his partner's face. "I just want to be filled in on anything this department's working on, okay? Did the father say whether, or not, anyone had contacted the rangers? If those kids went backpacking in the hills, then maybe the rangers know where. Have Ben call them…if nothing else, they can help in the search!" David looked out the large window in his office. "Something tells me it's important we find these kids, Pat. It scares me, but I think there's a chance they're connected with these murders...and if that turns out to be true..." David didn't finish that thought...he couldn't. The implications were too much to consider.

Patrick wasn't sure why...but his gut reaction was to agree with his partner's grim prediction. "You want anything Nate and Jack find...or the rangers...called into you?"

"And only me!...I want the chances for any further 'leaks' kept as low as possible! The fewer people having all the facts, the better!" He sighed, his fingers fidgeting with the edges of some of the papers on his desk. "Pat...you remember saying, at the Traylor apartment, that this case gave you a real funny feeling, in your gut?"

"Yeh...but I admit, I was a bit spooked by the scene, Dave...though, I *did* mean it!...still do feel that way! Why?"

David sighed again, his head slumping down deeper, between his shoulders. "I have to tell you something...when I first walked into that apartment, I got the damnedest sensation!...like, this was all meant to be! The moment I saw all that mess in Traylor's place, things started going off inside my head!" He shrugged, staring at the wall. "I feel like the answers...the *real* answers...are right here, in front of my nose! Something inside me keeps saying that I should know the reasons, the causes of *all* this!...but, I don't know *what* it is I'm supposed to know!" The big man slammed his hand down on the desktop, his frustration coming to the surface.

Patrick stood at the doorway, a faraway look on his rugged face. "You know...I find myself wondering more and more, since we started this case...do we *really* want to know the reasons? I believe that there *are* things we're not supposed to know! There's a strangeness about this case...a fear! I don't want to know the answers!...yet, I know we have to solve it!...even if it means our own deaths...we have to solve it!" After his last words, Patrick stood for a few moments, staring out the window, then, with a last look at David, he walked out of the office, closing the door behind him.

Behind him, staring at the closed door, and the wall, David felt that strange feeling brush his mind again. What was it he was supposed to know? Maybe, Patrick was right…did he really *want* to know?…….

……Beth sat down at the table, smiling across it at her sister, who was just finishing up her breakfast. One of the servants placed a well-filled plate down in front of Beth, while the other maid poured another cup of coffee for Sandra. Sandra noticed that her twin seemed unusually relaxed this morning, less worried and tense. Sandra also thought her sister looked a little thin, her eyes clouded.

When the second maid was through pouring a cup of coffee for her, Beth held up a hand. "Thank you, Mary…will you tell the garage to have the car ready in about half an hour?…thanks!"

"You're looking calmer than I've seen in the past few days…Sean's better, I take it?" Sandra asked, breaking off a piece of another warm croissant, eating it with relish…a feeling of warmth that her sister seemed more her old self.

Beth's eyes brightened. "Yes…it's like some sort of miracle, Sandy! It's as if he'd never been sick at all! I don't really know what the medicine, and treatment, was that Tamara got for him, but it certainly worked! In the past six days, he's gone from a man who looked one step away from death to his usual, robust self! The weakness, and the pain…all gone! I can't tell you how relieved I feel!"

Sandra smiled, somewhat sadly…her sister's feelings were so clear, so obvious from her expression, and words. There was a glow that Sandra had never seen before…the glow of a woman in love, and utterly fulfilled. "Well, obviously it wasn't as bad as you thought…and I'm glad for that fact…for you, Beth! You said Tamara spoke of a family illness?…did she give you any more specifics? That must have been it, since she was able to fix him up so quickly! I think, hon, you tend to over-worry a bit where he's concerned, don't you think?"

Beth's wide smile faded, and she glanced away, biting at her lower lip. She looked back at Sandra, reaching across the table and taking one of Sandra's hands. "I really wish you liked him better, Sandy. I know you're worried about my getting hurt, but that's not going to happen with Sean! He loves me, Sandy...and I love him! We share the kind of love that comes only once in someone's life! It would mean so much to me if the two of you could at least be friends!"

Sandra heard the pleading behind Beth's words...the yearning. It bothered her that she couldn't grant her twin's request. "I suppose I can at least try, Beth...but, I'll tell you straight off...only for you! I don't promise anything...but, I will give it the best try I possibly can!...okay?" She gazed at Beth, her heart aching as she saw the depth of feelings her sister had for this man. "You really *are* in love with him...aren't you?" She wished she didn't trust Sean, and his sister so much.

The expression that came over Beth's beautiful face told Sandra, more than her sister's words, how deep her feelings for Sean went. "I feel as if he were the air I breathe, Sandy...and the blood that keeps my heart beating! When he's not with me, it's like a part of my body is missing! I don't think I would want to go on living if he was ever taken from me...from my life!"

Sandra's heart skipped a beat at those words. Biting back a response, Sandra stood up quickly, walked around to where Beth was sitting, and hugged her tightly. Beth was pleased by the gesture, but sensed something else was behind the intensity of the embrace. When Sandra released her, Beth gazed up at her, an unspoken query in the cerulean eyes that matched her own.

Seeing that look, Sandra smiled softly, shaking her head, touching Beth softly on the cheek. "I have to get going...meeting Garalynn, in town, to go over the Stimpson writ, and plan our strategy before court this afternoon. You take it easy today, hear?...I don't want you over-doing it!" She straightened up, her eyes still on Beth's face. "Are you sure *you're* okay? You look tired, pale…and thin, Beth!…are you eating okay?"

"Of course!…I've just been so worried about Sean…haven't been sleeping real well!" She squeezed Sandra's hand. "I'll be fine, now that he's better…stop worrying about me! Go to your meeting…we'll talk later!" Beth smiled, love for her twin shining from the crystal blue eyes.

Sandra wasn't sure she believed Beth, but she did have to get going. "I'd like that…see you later!" With a wave over her shoulder, Sandra left the dining room.

Beth got up, going to the archway, watching her sister walk down the hallway, towards the main foyer. Sandra's long, energetic stride was something Beth had always loved watching…graceful, and athletic, saying much about Sandra's inner spirit, and personality. Beth sighed, turning back towards the table. She hoped Sandra meant what she'd said…about trying to get along better with Sean. She really didn't understand the reason behind her twin's mistrust of the Dresedens…she only knew she wanted them all to get along. It was important to her that the people she loved got along.

Beth did admit, to herself, that part of the problem was her own irrational actions of late…but she couldn't seem to control her emotions. Her outbursts of jealousy…her mood swings…her paranoia…she didn't understand them, but she knew they were all to real! She didn't know why she'd been snappish, every so often, at her twin…and over the most ridiculous things! She'd even accused her sister, Garalynn, of trying to seduce Sean away from her! She loved both her sisters…Sandra most of all. Sandra was as much a part of Beth's heart, and soul, as anything could be…except, that now her heart was filled with Sean.

So…why did she sometimes act as if Sandra meant little, or nothing at all? Beth shook her head, determined to correct her own actions in the future. She wanted everything to go smoothly, from this point in time on……..

......Garalynn sat at the table, sipping her iced tea, waiting for Sandra to arrive at the casual, but warm bistro known as Jean Claude's. They had used the restaurant many times as a meeting place, and Garalynn had always liked the fact that the atmosphere here never failed to relax her, and ease her mind. Sipping her tea again, she skimmed over the newspaper she'd brought with her. It was filled with the usual hype...sports...want ads...and miscellaneous trivia.

On page three, however, she found an article...an editorial...written about the apparent lack of progress on the part of the police department in solving the Traylor murder. It went on to hint, quite broadly, that this might not have been the only murder committed, recently, in such a lurid fashion. Garalynn closed her eyes, swallowing hard...trying to get past the picture she'd carried with her for the past few weeks...Douglas Traylor's casket, and that roguish face she'd grown to love so pale, and cold, in death's final embrace. She couldn't get that ugly image from her mind...at least, her heart murmured, she hadn't been the one who'd identified the body, at the murder scene, or later, at the hospital morgue. Sandra had chosen to take that unpleasant task from her. In fact...her family and friends had banded together to convince her *not* to see her lover's body, until it was safely at the funeral home. Though she'd felt as though she'd let Doug down, she'd not seen him until he was ready for his funeral. She'd stood by his coffin, Sandra and Kristine standing beside her, her fingers slipping softly over the cool flesh of his cheek, and forehead. She'd felt so detached...so calm...she couldn't believe she was so calm. She'd felt Sandra's hand at the small of her back...lending silent support, and understanding. Sandra had been through this, with her dead ex-husband's death in that auto accident...Garalynn knew that her sister understood, on a level no one else could...all the nuances of emotion, or lack of, that Garalynn was going through.

The beautiful lawyer shook her head, pushing the hard lump in her throat down once again, closing her eyes, getting her heart and breathing a little more under control…she knew it would take a while, but she would get through this! She just missed him so much…and the odd thing…she missed the sound of his voice, and the scent of his skin, the most! She opened her eyes, feeling a little calmer. She quickly turned the page, before she could read anything more about the case.

When she got to page five, she saw another item that caught her attention…a story concerning missing teenagers, one of whom had a father on the city council. She slowly read the short article, then closed the paper, her hand resting on the folded newspaper, staring into space. She was experiencing another of those odd sensations she'd had, on and off, over the last few days. They were very strong, very clear…even waking her up on occasion. Akin to strong electrical pulses moving along her arms, hands, legs, and face…they came without warning, without apparent cause. She'd seen her doctor, fearing some sort of neurological disorder…he'd told her all the tests he'd ordered came by showing no problems. He'd given her a tranquilizer, stating that these sensations could be a result of stress. She'd taken the medication as directed…and still the sensations came. It was almost like…like someone was trying to speak to her…to gain her attention…to tell her something.

She shook herself, getting angry…feeling the frustration growing. "Stop this!…get a grip, for God's sake! This is just what Dr. Ortega said…a result of all the stress, overwork…and Doug! You're allowing your mind to make things up!…get a hold of yourself!" She muttered to herself, tossing the offending paper onto one of the extra chairs at the table.

She jumped suddenly as someone touched her on the shoulder. Looking up, she saw Sandra standing there, a concerned look on her face. The lovely Phelps sat down next to her adopted sister. "Hi…everything alright? You looked like you were a million miles away…and you're pale as a ghost! And, what were you muttering about just now?"

Garalynn shook her head, trying to re-orient herself. "No…just thinking out loud, about something in the paper."

Sandra gazed compassionately at her sister…her closest friend. "You saw that article about Doug's case…didn't you?…the one that says the police aren't really trying to find the killer." She reached over, clasping Garalynn's hand. "Hon…you know they're doing all they can! Have faith!…they'll find the person who took him from you, and make them pay!"

Garalynn felt the tears prickling behind her eyes…she looked away. "I *do* have faith, Sandy…I just miss him so much! We'd just admitted our feelings for one another…had just made love for the first time…and now…I try not to be angry, or want revenge, but it's not easy." She looked back, eyes bright, and managed a shaky smile. "I try…all I can feel right now, though, is a sense of injustice! All I can hear, in my mind, is…it's not fair!"

"Yes…it's *not* fair!…but, then, sometimes life seldom is…fair! Garalynn…nothing I , or anyone else, can say is going to take that pain from you…at least, not right now! The only thing I can say is that you have to believe is that what happened is for a reason…however bizarre that reason may turn out to be. There's a reason for everything in this world…there has to be! Take your memories, Garalynn…for now, let them be the anchor that keeps you steady…they *do* help see you through!" Sandra smiled slightly…sadly…thinking back to how she'd felt when her husband had died. Her ex-husband, she reminded herself…though, at the time of his accident, he'd been on his way to her. They had decided to see if they could try again, with each other, and their life together. She shook her head…Garalynn needed her full attention right now.

"You're right…I'm just tired…too much work, and stress…I'll be fine! You know…what I was really thinking about when you walked up was this article." Garalynn picked the paper back up, and opened it to the item she had been reading.

Sandra took the paper, and quickly read the item. "Those poor parents!…they must be frantic!" She glanced at her sister, seeing the concern. "It's probably just teenagers being teenagers...an adventure, you know...a lark. They get interested in something, and lose all concept of time! I'm sure, between the police and the rangers, they'll be found...*and* be all right!" She reached a hand out, and grasped Garalynn's. "I think you feel too much...for too many people! It's one of the best traits you possess...but sometimes, I think your intensity is going to burn you out one day! You need to learn how to temper it...just a little bit!"

The lady lawyer sighed, closing her eyes for a moment. "I admit...sometimes, I have a problem with my emotions taking over!...and, lately, that seems to be happening quite a lot!" She opened her eyes, and smiled a crooked smile. "Maybe...I'm more tired than I think!" She put her free hand over the one of Sandra's that covered her other hand, leaning forward. "Sandy...I'm going to tell you something...and it's probably going to make you think I've gone off the deep end! But...I *have* to tell someone!"

Sandra gripped her sister's hands, trying to calm her...and herself. "Take it easy, will you? Now...go ahead...tell me what's got you edgy!"

Garalynn took a deep breath, shuddering a little. "I...I seem to be ...be hearing things lately! It's like someone's been trying to talk to me, but I can't quite make out the words! And, yet...each time it's happened, I've looked all around...and the only one who's been in the room is me! I'm always alone!" She clenched her fists in frustration.

Sandra grasped Garalynn wrists, bringing the clenched hands back down on the table top. "Settle down!...you're starting to make *me* jumpy! Look...like you yourself said, you're stressed out! Plus...you've suffered a personal loss! And...this thing with Beth, and the Dresdens sure hasn't helped any!" Sandra drew in a deep breath, feeling a twinge of fear that Garalynn's mind really might be suffering. "I think you need a break...like maybe, away from here for a few days? You want some time off? I know we can make adjustments to the work load so you can have a vacation...just say the word, and I'll see to it! Helps to know one of the 'bosses' personally, you know!" Sandra tried to lighten her sister, and best friend's mood.

Garalynn laughed, smiling. "I'll think about it…I promise, Sandy. You're right…the idea of getting away is very appealing. Maybe, my mind's just too tired, also…there's not a time I can say it's at rest. There's too much I…" her voice died away as her overworked mind seemed to be picking up on a low hum. She looked around, her eyes widening.

Sandra saw the expression, and knew something was happening. She tightened her hold on the other woman's wrists, using her thumbs to rub soothing circles on the soft skin of Garalynn's forearms…sending a message of support, and reassurance. "Hey…it's okay!…I'm here!"

Garalynn stared wildly into the deep blue eyes that reached out so lovingly to her from across the table. She took a shuddering breath in, settling her inner frenzy. "I know…you've always been there for me! Thank you."

Sandra smiled back…but her eyes clearly showed her worry. She knew she'd been concentrating too much on this thing with Beth. She hadn't been there when her other sister had been in need, also. She told herself that that had to change…Garalynn meant as much to Sandra as Beth!

As the waiter came to the table, and began taking Sandra's order, Garalynn kept the thoughts steady, and to herself. Saying what had suddenly occurred to her, without any proof right now, would only hurt, and anger. For the time being, she would keep her own counsel…keep an eye on how things unfolded…be there when the things she now realized would happen…happened. She knew that the feelings she had now were *not* just the end products of a tired, stressed mind. The sense of danger was more then a sense…the dangers were real!…….

…..Kristine pulled her horse to a stop, then swung gracefully down from the saddle. "Hold up a minute, Garalynn!…I've got a stirrup that's bad!"

Garalynn turned her horse back, reining to a stop where Kristine was tugging on the adjustment straps, getting her right stirrup to the proper level. Garalynn had called Kristine after she left the meeting with Sandra...she wanted a little break before heading back into the stress and hectic schedule of the office. They'd met at Blackmoon, and gotten two horses to go for a fast ride. Garalynn had felt it would help refocus her energies...re-center herself. "I told you, back at the stables, that it looked wrong! You should have let Tom look at it, like he suggested!"

Kristine glared up at her, continuing to tug on the strap. It finally loosened, and she hooked it at the correct level for her legs. She straightened up, dropping the stirrup back into place, and dusting her gloves off. "There!...finally!" She looked up at the sky, noting the lengthening shadows...it was getting late. "I think we'd better head back...you still have to get to the office for that five p.m. board meeting!"

Garalynn nodded, but pulled her reins to the reins. "I know...but, let's have one last run, okay? I know a couple of short-cuts that will get us back to the stables in plenty of time! Come on!" She pointed to a not too distant hill. "I'll race you to that hill...the one that overlooks the cabin! Last one there has to unsaddle the horses when we get back!" With that statement, Garalynn dug her heels in, and her horse shot off.

"Unsaddle the...hey, that's not fair! You cheater!" Kristine jumped into the saddle, and spurred her horse to quickly follow.

Laughing, exhilarated by the chase, the two galloped their mounts through the quiet, color-bedecked woods. They both felt tensions, and irritations melting away in the excitement of the ride. The pounding hooves, and the fresh, cool air was like an intoxicant to their spirits.

Spurring up the small rise to the top of the hill, Garalynn pulled back on the reins, bringing her horse to a stop on the very crest. She laughed, a little breathless, looking over her shoulder as Kristine rode up behind her. Looking at one another, they both laughed, and Kristine shook her head, acknowledging her friend the winner. She pointed an accusing finger at Garalynn. "You cheated...next time, it will be different!" She was about to say something further when her attention was taken by something in the open glen just below them. "Say…what's going on down there? I didn't think anyone was up at the cabin this late in the year! Garalynn…look!…what's up?"

Shading her eyes, the other woman raised up in the saddle a bit, and peered down into the area Kristine was pointing at. "No one is supposed to be up here…except the caretakers. The cabin compound was closed three weeks ago. I wonder who all those men are…hey, one of those cars is a police cruiser! Come on…we'd better ride down, and see what's going on. I wasn't informed that the authorities, or the rangers, were coming onto Blackmoon property…and all permission has to go through my office!"

As the two women rode into the clearing, they were met by several uniformed policemen, and three forest service rangers. All the men had tensed up at first, at the unexpected entrance, but everyone relaxed a little when they saw the two women. Both Garalynn and Kristine could sense that something big was going on here.

Patrick walked up to the two horse, and flashed his badge at the women. "Mind climbing down from those horses, ladies? This area is part of a police crime scene, and only authorized persons allowed. I'd like to ask you both a few questions, if you don't mind!" He smiled at them, trying to set them at ease.

Complying with his request, the two women swung to the ground. Looping the reins over one arm, Garalynn brushed some of her hair back behind one ear, and looked at Patrick…her expression grave. "There's a few question *I'd* like to ask, too, officer…like who gave you permission to come onto private property, unless you have a warrant? I'm the lawyer for the Phelps family, and whether a warrant, or permission…all things like that are to go through me! And, to my knowledge, no one's called to ask that!" She looked around the open glade, noting all the equipment, and the activity. She looked back to Patrick. "Again…what is going on here?"

Pocketing his shield, Patrick grinned…he liked this tall beauty. He pulled an official-looking paper out of his inside coat pocket, and handed it to her. "Here's our warrant, ma'am…and we also had permission from the Phelps family…we talked with Sandra Phelps about forty-five minutes ago. After we told her what we had found, she was very happy to cooperate with us, and the rangers."

As Garalynn and Patrick moved off, continuing their discussion, Kristine stayed with the horses, looking around the clearing. She knew that just over the next rise was the cabin compound, with the large main cabin, two guest cabins, garage, storage barn, and the caretakers small home. The entire cabin area included fifteen acres, of which this clearing was part. She wondered what had happened that would bring both rangers, and police here. She watched as a couple of men unloaded some strange-looking mechanical equipment from a van. To the other side of the clearing, she saw a man walk out from behind a large clump of bushes, and stop to talk with a man pouring a thick, whitish material into a depression in the ground. 'Taking impressions,' she told herself. What was going on here? She had an uneasy feeling about all this.

Her observations were cut short as Garalynn rejoined her, taking the reins of her horse from Kristine's hands. "Come on…we've got to get back to the mansion right away, and see Sandy!" She turned back to Patrick. "Thank you for filling me in on things, Sgt. Reynolds…I'll pass it all on to my clients as soon as I get with them! We'll be in touch…come on, Kris…let's go!"

The two women quickly mounted their horses, and rode off. As they were leaving the clearing, Kristine called out to Garalynn, who was riding slightly ahead of her. "Are you going to tell me what's going on back there?…or do I have to guess? What are the police, and the rangers, doing here? What were…*are* they looking for, Garalynn?"

Garalynn glanced back at her companion. "All I can say right now is that what's going on back there has to do with those missing teenagers! Until I can talk with Sandy, and Beth, I can't say anymore!…even to you, Kris! Right now…the most important thing is to get back to Blackmoon as soon as possible. The police will get back with us there!"

"How can it be connected to those kisd? The newspapers, and the TV media, said they were back-packing in the eastern foothills…Blackmoon, and it surrounding acres, are in the *western* hills! I don't see how it could have anything to do them! What exactly did that policeman say to you?" Kristine could see how tense her friend was at that moment.

Garalynn didn't answer…she just kept riding. Kristine didn't understand her friend's silence, but she was intuitive enough not to push, or pry. In truth, the reason Garalynn wasn't responding had nothing to do with a desire for silence…she honestly didn't…couldn't hear Kristine.

When Kristine had started speaking, it was like someone had suddenly switched off all sound. Garalynn could see Kristine's lips moving, could see trees and such being passed…but, she heard nothing! At least…not in the conventional way of hearing. She was. however, "hearing" something in her mind. This time, it was clear…not just a hum, and jumble of sounds. This time, it was a deep. Clear voice, speaking slowly, and in a language she'd never heard before…yet, instinctively knew.

"Be most cautious, my sister! Guard thyself, and those thou loves! Keep close, and ever vigilant…the dangers lie close, and are most real! Keep thy vigil sharp…or thou will face greater sorrows…even death!"…….

…..David Collison got out of his car, and stood there, watching the dwindling forms of two women riding out of the clearing he'd just driven into. He looked at Patrick, and frowned, motioning to his partner. When the other policeman joined him, David pointed in the direction Garalynn and, Kristine had ridden. "Pat…who was that? What were they doing here?"

Patrick looked after the now disappeared forms. "One of them was the lawyer for the Phelps…she's also the adopted daughter of Richard Phelps. The other one is a close family friend. They were out riding, and found us here. They came to check us out, and I showed them the warrant, and gave them a quick explanation as to why we were here, Dave. They're on their way back to the mansion...I told them we'd contact them there, later."

Nodding, David looked around, absently reaching into his coat pocket. "Well...lets get this over. That the ranger who called us?" He pointed to a forest ranger leaning against the white van.

"No...the one that called us is over there, sitting in my car. He's not feeling the greatest right now!" Patrick waved his arm, and the man sitting in the open rear door of the sedan, head in hands, slowly stood, and started walking towards them.

"His name's Jerry Hansen. He's actually the one who found them, and then called us!" Patrick called to the man. "Hey, Jerry...the lieutenant's got a few questions for you!"

The stocky man, wearing the drab green of the Forest Service came over to where they stood, and stopped. David was a little shocked at his expression...pale, sick, and angry. He nodded at Patrick, fumbled in his shirt pocket before jerking out a folded paper, and handing it to David. "This is a copy of the report I'll be filing with my superiors...figured I'd save time if I made copies at the start! Name's Jerry Hansen, lieutenant," he held his hand out to David.

The tall policeman took the offered hand, and shook it firmly. "Dave...call me Dave. Patrick says you were the one who found them?"

Jerry nodded, taking off his mountie-styled hat, and wiping the sweat from his brow with the fingers of his right hand. "Actually, it was one of the caretakers up here who called our ranger cabin...said he'd seen some kids fooling around up here, and that he wanted us to check it out! My partner, and I were the ones who responded...we have an agreement with the Phelps to check things on their property before the cops are called in. I'll tell you something, Dave...I sure wish to hell it had been someone else who'd gone into that...that cave! Dave...what's in that cave is enough to make anyone think they'd walked into some horror flick! You know...those God-awful cut-and-slash thrillers the kids are all nuts about these days?"

David could see how affected the ranger was...his frown deepened. He looked around, glad to see that the flood lights were not yet in place. It would be dark soon, and he didn't really relish the idea of thrashing about in this area without good light. He brought himself back to the present. "You said you got a call from a caretaker?...up here, in the woods? Who was it that called?"

Jerry pointed towards the nearby hills. "Just over that hill is where the Phelps family has their cabin complex...quite a large one, I might add. It's closed up for the season right now, but there's always a caretaker around. This one that called us happens to be a friend of mine. He had been kind of isolated up here the past few days, getting things ready for winter...he hadn't heard anything about those missing kids. When he got back into town, to pick up some more supplies, he read about them, and that's when he called our office. He said that the pictures of the kids he'd seen in one paper looked like the ones he'd chased away from the cabin complex area a couple of days earlier. He said they'd left, grumbling, but very much alive, and healthy!" Jerry pulled a rumpled pack of cigarettes from his jacket, and pulled one out.

"So...that's why you came up here?...but why here. If that cabin's over the hill?" David asked, pulling his lighter out, and handing it to the other man. "Wouldn't the logical place to look first be over there?"

"Well...I happened to remember that last year, right about this time, we'd gotten a tip about a college frat party up here! See...it's kind of a tradition for at least one of the fraternity houses to try, and stage a party up on Blackmoon property...been going on for about twenty years. Most of the time...it's set to happen inside a large cavern up here, and most of the time, it's pretty harmless. I guess that's why the Phelps family has never really complained about it!" Jerry drew in, then slowly exhaled, the cigarette smoke spiraling up into the cool air. "Anyway...when Ted told me about those kids prowling around the cabin area, well, I figured maybe we'd better check things out. I thought we'd probably find that our missing teens got involved with a good old fashioned beer brawl!"

"You knew the cavern was in this area then?" David was trying to get things settled in his mind. "Ever had any trouble here before?"

"No…just a few parties, like I said. The cave's really a cool place for partying…open, lots of room, even got a hot springs. Actually…it's a fantastic spot for camping. The Phelps family has built in some redwood benches, tables, and such for use when they're up at their cabin. It's been the 'in' place for forbidden trysts…but, I gotta tell you…I wish I'd followed my gut instincts, and called you guys first! I wish to God I'd never stepped into that cave!…and I know I won't again!"

David and Patrick looked at one another at those last words. David looked back at Jerry. "I think that's all we need form you for now, Jerry…you'll have to come to the station, and sign the formal statement, but you can do that tomorrow. Thanks for all your help, and cooperation!" He turned as one of the uniformed officers came up to their group. "Yes?…what is it, Peters?"

"The coroner asked me to tell you to come right in when you got her, Lt. Collison…he's been in there for nearly three hours now!" The young officer jerked his right thumb over one shoulder, in the direction of a large clump of bushes.

"Right…come on, Pat!" A last nod to Jerry, and the two policemen started walking towards the bushes. "You talked with the coroner yet, Pat?"

"Yeh…he thinks they've been there a couple of days…although he said determining the correct date is going to be real difficult! He' hoping, once he gets them back to the pathology lab, he'll be able to pinpoint time of death more accurately!" The sergeant shook his head, reaching out, and pulling back on a large bush…disclosing the entrance to a large cave. "You know, Dave…Jim said something that really threw me at first…that they looked like…well, like they'd been mummified!

We found back-packs in there that helped identify them…but they looked like they'd been in that cave for a hellava long time!"

David had been about to enter the dark tunnel, but stopped at his partner's last words. "Pat…have you been in there?…I mean, you've seen them, right?"

Jaw set, anger and disgust clear even in the stance of his stocky body, Patrick nodded slowly. "Yeh…though, like Jerry said…I wish I hadn't! You, and I, have seen some pretty ugly things, Dave…as cops, you can't help it! I didn't think anything could get under my skin anymore…I was dead wrong! What's in here makes the word monstrous seem tame! You can't describe what's in here, Dave…the words just don't exist! Hell…I didn't even care that everyone saw me lose my lunch after I was in there!…because everyone else did, too! It does something to you…what's in here! I think you'll understand when *you* see it!"

Not knowing exactly how to respond, David just nodded, accepted the flashlight Patrick held out to him, and began walking into the cave. Both men flipped their hand lights on, and walked on. After a few moments of walking, David was getting a little surprised at just how deep the cave went into the hill. He suppressed a deep shudder, feeling the walls closing in on him as they went along.

Finally, the cave's depth ended in a large, airy chamber. Here, they found they didn't need their lights, as the generator-powered lights built in by the Phelps family had already been switched on. There were a lot of eerie shadows, and David had a fleeting impression of subtle movement amongst those shadows. He shook hid head, dispelling the gathering cloud of doom, and fear that was threatening to drop around him.

Patrick nudged David, pointing over to where one man was bending over something behind a group of rocks. They walked over to where he stood, nodding at him as he turned towards them, straightening up. As they joined the man, who was the medical examiner, David glanced over the man's shoulder. He stopped sharply, eyes widening...feeling his stomach lurched wildly. He looked away, swallowing hard.

When he felt steadier, and that his internal organs weren't going to try and exit his body, he touched the coroner on one shoulder. "For Christ's sake, Jim...what the hell are you working on? I mean...what *is* that thing?"

The medical examiner, Jim Petty, glanced over his shoulder, then brought his eyes back, a deep sigh issuing. He removed one of the latex gloves he was wearing, and ran the fingers of that hand through his thinning red hair. "Quite a sight for these parts, huh? I can't remember ever being called in on a case like this, Dave! As for *what* it is...near as I can determine, out here, is that it is...*was* a young, white male, approximately eighteen to twenty years of age, and in fairly good physical development. There was a backpack found near the body...the ID in it makes him one of our missing teenagers. The other male, black and approximately the same age, is out in the ambulance already...pretty much the same condition as this one here!" Jim looked back at the shriveled, leathery-looking body. "I don't think I've ever seen something like this...at least, *not* in what was, a few days ago, a healthy, well-built young man! Dave...every drop of fluid has been drained from their bodies!...and I mean *every* kind of fluid! Blood, spinal, urine, cellular, and lymphatic...all gone! It's crazy!...and I don't have a clue yet as to *how*! If I had seen these bodies, without any knowledge of the missing kids...I'd have told you we were looking at two mummies!...that they'd been here for hundreds of years, instead of only a couple of days! This is absolutely beyond my experience!...nothing comes close!"

"You said the bodies had been drained...was that what killed them? Or, were...were they *alive* when that happened? And...why *does* the body look so...so old?" Patrick felt his own stomach crawling a little, looking at the body he'd seen an hour before.

"The fluid depletion is what makes the body look so shriveled, and old, Pat...as for the cause of death...until I do the complete autopsy, that's still hanging! As weird as this may sound, I'd have to say he…both of them, were literally consumed by something!…source unknown! It's like dried fruit, Pat…suck out the moisture, and you get a prune! Or, in this case…something resembling a centuries-old mummy!" He removed his other glove, motioning for one of his two assistants to take over. "The total lack of fluid is unheard of, Dave…unless you're talking about a professional embalming! I don't know of anything that has the ability to extract every drop of fluid produced, or stored by the human body! And, to boot…something that does that very, very fast! I have a lot of speculations…and very little concrete facts! The only things I can definitely state right now is this…both males were tortured before they were killed!"

"Tortured?" David looked at the body again. "How can you tell something like that? It's hard enough to recognize that it's *human* let along tell what happened to it! Hell, I can barely make out where the eyes are supposed to be!"

"That's because of the fluid depletion…plus, the fact that his eyes are gone, Dave! They've been removed somehow…but as yet, I cannot find any sign that they were torn, or cut out! As for what I said about torture…both male bodies bear definite, precise lacerations along the complete length of all their extremities, as well as the length of the torso itself!" Jim replied, placing a few plastic bags inside his black leather bag.

"What do you mean…precise laceration?" David said, stepping out of the way as two attendants brought a stretcher in, and started loading the body into a black body bag.

"Someone, with all the precision of a trained surgeon, or pathologist, made incisions along each arm, and leg. These incisions cross-sected nerve pathways in such a way as to cause extreme pain…at the same time, minimizing blood loss! The incisions on the torso, however, were in such a way as to maximize blood loss…pain was minimum to moderate. Yet, none of these incisions would be the ultimate cause of the total fluid removal! This is going to be a very interesting autopsy!" Jim shrugged his shoulders, easing the tension in the muscles...he sighed, feeling drained right at the moment.

David could feel his frustrations rising, along with his confusion. "Dammit, Jim...none of this makes any sense! Where's the girl?...wasn't there a missing girl...or, did you not find her with the two boys?"

Jim nodded, low and deliberate. He glanced at Patrick, whose face went grimmer, and darker then it had been already. Jim gestured across the cave chamber, to the far wall, sheathed in shadows, behind one of the log tables set up in the cave. "We *did* locate her body...over amongst that clumping of rocks. But...well, before I say anything, maybe you'd better take a look yourself!"

Puzzled by both the coroner's words, and his tone of voice, David walked over to the formation of rocks that Jim had indicated. As he neared the grouping, he noticed the largest of the rocks resembled a table, or an altar...and there was something stretched out on top of it! He stopped beside the rock, fighting his churning stomach. He gulped hard, tasting bitter acid. "Sweet God above! Jim...what kind of animal does this to another living being?...let alone a young girl?" He shifted his gaze to the other men who were now beside him.

"The worst kind of animal, Dave...the two-legged, *human* variety! You understand why I said you had to see for yourself? I couldn't explain it enough for you, or anyone to really understand!" Jim stared down at the still form draped atop the rock table. "And, I hope I never have to try on any other case...not like this!"

In silence, the three men gazed at the heart-pulling, gut-wrenching sight laid out in front of them. Stretched out full-length, arms outspread...poised like a diver preparing to spring off a board into the water below, a young woman lay on the cold rock. Nude, she looked as though she was merely asleep, features serene and still. It was a horrible irony, to the men looking at her, that there was not one sign of fear, or suffering she must have experienced. David had the flitting thought...she looked like she'd been about to embrace a lover bending over her.

The young woman's body was not shriveled, or twisted like the young men's...her flesh still held the faint blush of her life, even now. He body, bared to the world, showed all the clean sculptured lines of her blossoming womanhood. None of the men, though, really noticed her nubile beauty...they could only stare, each feeling a different degree of horror, at the atrocity that some twisted mind had visited on this lovely young woman.

Her legs and arms were bare of the injuries Jim had described found on those of the young men...though, David could see faint traces of some brightly colored substance, in some sort of design, along her extremities. It was her torso that held his full gaze, though he wished he could look away! From navel to throat, she'd been neatly, but completely, cut open...like someone gutted an animal!

The gaping wound screamed its silent rage at the men...shrieking at them, asking the centuries old question...why? Feeling his gorge suddenly rise, David jerked away, bending over, and retching violently. The other men stood by quietly, understanding...they'd both reacted in similar fashion, even Jim. When he felt a little better, David straightened up, turning back to the pitiful sight. He bent over the body, seeking answers. He found a mark on her forehead, in that colored substance he'd noticed on her arms and legs. He lightly touched the mark...it smudged slightly, so he pulled his fingertip away, not wanting to ruin a possible clue.

Jim nodded. "I saw that mark, too. Got a couple of good, clear pictures. It looks like a deliberate design...like the kind we found on those Satanic cult victims a couple of years ago...remember? I'm going to show it to some experts...see if that's what we've got here. Anyway...whatever it turns out to be, I've a feeling it's significant! And, somehow, I think it's also tied in to the other cases I've been working on recently!"

"You think it's got some sort of religious significance?" Patrick wondered, remembering back to that Satanic cult...that hadn't been as gruesome as this case so far, but it had been a very bizarre case to work!

David wiped his forehead with his handkerchief, stuffing it back into his hip pocket when done. "If they haven't already, have the lab boys go over each rock in this place, especially this one! Jim...make sure copies of those marks get shown to the History department at the college...and the monsignor over at St. James...he's one of the best historians around, especially where obscure designs, and tribal clan markings are concerned. Maybe, he can also give us some insight to go on...anyway, it's worth the effort at this point!" He glanced again at the dead female. She'd been so young, so lovely...what a waste! He found himself angered that someone had so brutally ended her young promise, and he swore he'd bring the person, or persons, to justice.

Patrick nodded, and left to go see that things were progressing the way he knew David would want them. Jim cleared his throat, bringing his attention back to the older man. "Dave...how are you going to tell this to the chief?...he nearly lost it with those cultists, as I recall...couldn't believe anything like that could happen in Denver. He's going to freak for sure when he finds out about this!"

"Especially since one of those two boys is...*was* the son of a city councilman! I can hear it all now!" David spread his hands to his sides, showing his frustration, and anger. "What can I say?...I have to tell him the truth! He'll think I've flipped...until he reads your report, then he'll go ballistic! In fact...the entire city will freak when they hear about this! There was enough media splash about Traylor's murder...after this gets out, *and* the story about that night security guard at the museum...I really think I'd like to be anywhere but Denver when all this hits the fan! But...all I can do is tell the facts, then ride with the tidal wave that happens!"

"I'll do as thorough, and as fast, a job as possible, David...that should help! By the way...thought you should know...we haven't been able to locate the heart yet!" Jim stated gravely.

"Heart?...what heart?" David stared at the coroner, a little confused.

"Hers...you didn't notice it was missing? Very neat job, too...incredible smooth, precise surgical cuts...someone knew what they were doing here! Anyway...we haven't located it anywhere in the cave, as yet...but they're still going over every place they can see, and think someone would try to hide something like that!" With that, Jim picked up his sample bag, and headed out of the cave.

"Jim...hold up! I'll walk out with you. Have to see about getting in touch with the parents, and having them come in for an identification...formal one, I mean!" David suddenly didn't want to be in the cave. He gestured to one of the other officers. "Wills, I want you to let Patrick know I'm going to see about contacting the parents, okay? Tell him I'll see him back at the station afterwards."

"Whatever you say, Lt....you going to have them come up here?" The other policeman looked around the cavern, trying not to let the uneasiness he felt be apparent.

"I'd don't think so...no reason they have to see how we found their kids! It's going to be bad enough when they have to view the bodies back at the morgue! Catch you all later!" A half-hearted wave, and David left with Jim.

Wills shook his head, hands on hips, and looked at his partner. "I'd sure hate being the one who has to tell mothers and fathers their kids have been gutted!...*and* mummified! He's got one hell of a job ahead of him!"

The other policeman agreed. "Glad it's him, and not me! What a mess!"

The other five men in the room, listening intently to the conversation, all nodded, not envying David his gruesome task. All of them were wondering, deep inside, just what it was that they'd come up against in this case. There was an air of uneasiness among all the men at the station of late...too many strange, and terrible things had been happening, and none of them thought it was going to be easy to solve...or stop!.....

****

IV

❀

......Beth stood just inside the entrance to the room call The Tomb, in the basement level of the mansion itself. At their requests, she'd brought Tamara, and Sean, downstairs to view the special room...and all the ancient treasures it housed. In fact, this was where she'd been when Garalynn and Kristine had shown up at Blackmoon, before they'd gone for their ride. The house staff had told Garalynn that they weren't exactly sure where Beth was...they'd seen her with the Dresdens, and assumed the trio had gone out.

Beth had retrieved the special, electronic "key", from her mansion office, and headed for the special elevator that went to the basement. She really didn't want to go into the Tomb...the room had always made her very uneasy, but she couldn't refuse Sean's tender request, backed up by Tamara's sweet plea.

Once she had the key, they'd all taken the private elevator, and headed for the basement level, Beth telling them a little about the elaborate security measures that the family had installed because of the Tomb being inside Blackmoon itself...and almost all of them controlled by the one specialized key she held. First, Beth turned the motion sensors covering the hallway leading to the Tomb, then she led them down the corridor, until they stood in front of the ornate entrance to the Tomb. Here, she pushed the second button on the key, and deactivated the lasers that guarded the main doors, and switched off the alarms also connected to the doors.

Once this was all accomplished, Beth flipped the small switch at the base of the electronic control. This was the trigger that opened the twin bronze doors. These doors were supposedly copies of the ones found in the actual tomb, discovered so many years ago in Egypt. Made from bronze plates, decorated with pure silver, they looked as thought they each weighed a ton. Yet, each door was so perfectly balanced that, once unlocked, a single fingertip could open, or close the massive portals.

As she was opening the doors, Beth gave Tamara and Sean a brief background about the room they were all about to enter. "My great-grandfather was the one who started construction on this room. He'd been one of the original members of an expedition sent, and had one of the other members, a museum curator and artist, work with the architects in building it. They used sketches from the original site as blueprints, and whenever possible, the original building materials from the site were transported to this country for the construction here. It's been enhanced over the years, and is considered one of the finest re-constructions of an ancient burial site in the world!" Beth

swung the doors wide, and gestured for them to go on in.

"You're about to see something that is, in even the tiniest details, the exact twin of what they found at the original site. Our father told us it took them nearly three full years to build this room. It was filled, for the most part, with the actual relics found in the tomb over in Egypt...an amazing feat in itself since most relics usually stayed in the country in which they were found! Actually, the Tomb is more than just one room...it takes up most of the entire basement level of Blackmoon itself!"

Tamara walked into the room, and stood there, gazing at the still-dark room. "I've read quite a bit about this room, Elizabeth. I must admit I was quite surprised to learn about the actual relics being here, and not in some museum in Egypt!" She looked back at Beth, who was just about to turn the lights on. "How *did* your family manage such a remarkable feat?"

"I really can't tell you that, Tamara…I don't know all the reasons. I do know, though, that everything was legal, and above board! The permits, and contracts, are all locked away in the safe in my office here in the mansion. In fact…it was the governments of Thebes, and Cairo, who were the ones to suggest the relics be brought, and stored, here in the Tomb. As to the real reasons…well, I'd have to say my great-grandfather took those to the grave with him! Now, enough talk…behold, the past of ancient Egypt, and the Pharoahs, come to life!"

She flipped the switch, and the hidden lights came on, illuminating the entire room. Tamara and Sean found themselves standing in the center of a room…a room that had dwelt in a world that had ceased to exist over two thousand years ago. Before the coming of Christ, and the coming of age of most of the world's "civilized" cultures…this room's inspiration had been constructed to hold the body of a king. There was an aura within this room…of lost majesty, strange and hushed religious rites, and the stories of a people long admired for their architectural accomplishments. I t was almost as if one could step outside this room, and actually view those accomplishments…whose bearing and construction still amazed, and awed a world today.

There seemed to be muted echoes in this room…distant, far-away echoes of the funeral party as it approached the tomb. One could almost hear the wails of the mourners in the procession…the low beatings of the great drums, and the almost supernatural keening of the rams' horns. There was the hint of the rich incense borne by the leopard-skin covered high priests in ornate censers…the ethereal scent of the myrrh, and precious oils used to anoint the royal corpse. The tangible feeling of power permeated the atmosphere of this room…a reverence and adoration…of superstitions, and religious devotion…and through all this, an underlying current of awe, and fear.

The walls had been constructed of strong steel columns, covered in hardwood sheets. These were, in turn, covered by slabs of sandstone, to approximate the stone walls of the real tomb. Everywhere, carved into the sandstone, then painted in vivid hues, were the hieroglyphics...the ancient picture-language that gave the modern world a glimpse into the day-to-day life of the ancient kings, and the people they ruled. The construction was of such a superior quality that to look around, one would truly believe they stood within the center of a structure comprised totally of giant blocks of stone!

There were many articles of furniture scattered throughout the room...chairs, foot stools, and small tables. Made of the finest teakwood, and cedar, they bore many detailed symbols, both of the dead ruler's power, and the deference he bore for the many gods of that ancient time. Also seen tossed, and piled about the room were many chests, of various sizes and shapes. All were magnificently carved, and detailed...many in precious gems, and electrum...am amalgam of gold and silver. One small chest, about the size of a breadbox, was made of solid gold, and bore a king's ransom in jewels on its gleaming, polished surface.

Also throughout the room, in various spots against the walls, statues stood, silent and impressive. They were carved from sandstone, granite, marble, and alabaster...ranging in size from one foot high to the tallest four, each of which stood nearly ten feet tall. These colossi stood, one in each of the four corners of the room, as silent, stern-faced guardians...daring anyone who would disturb the king's rest to enter the forbidden room.

Off to the left side of the room was a small altar, with a five-foot statue on a small, raised dais behind it. This statue was a man's well-muscled body, with the head of a hawk...bearing the blue and white double crown upon its beaked head. It was carved from polished black onyx, with eyes of fire rubies. The altar itself was of white marble, with delicate veins of gray-black marble running through it. On the floor before the altar were four foot high vessels, resembling goddesses, of dark gray alabaster. Each of these vessels bore the royal cartouche, or insignia, of the buried king. In between each of the vessels was a small, sealed pot of myrrh, and henna.

Directly across the room from this altar was another small, raised dais...of blood-red sandstone, it was comprised of three narrow steps...leading to the small, solid gold chest. Upon the lid of this chest reared the uraeus...the rearing cobra, and vulture that symbolized royalty. Only the Pharoahs, their family, and the gods were entitled to wear this most sacred symbol on their foreheads, or place it on their belongings.

The other two walls held a variety of chests, a small hunting chariot, furniture, personal items, and even a royal bed, along with a dismantled "sky boat"...for the dead king to use in his travels across the sky with the god, Ra. Everywhere anyone could look in this room, it was filled with all the things the ancients deemed necessary for the everyday living of their buried king. The pomp of the royal court could almost be felt here...the rank, and the power of the person entombed here all too real. All in all, it was a sight that could, and did, take one's breath away. It inspired awe, respect...and for a select few, a yearning for that long-lost life.

Opposite the doors, the final wall was the focal point of the entire room. Here, isolated from all the rest, stood a high dais, stark and starling...carved from a solid block of black obsidian. In the muted lighting, it loomed out of the faint shadows like a crouching lion, flanked on either side by a seven- foot statue...both representations of the king in the full flower of his youth. In the direct center of the platform was a great, fantastically carved marble sarcophagus. White, with thick lacings of black throughout its surface, it was an awesome sight that drew the eye. The base of the sarcophagus held more hieroglyphics, featuring the cartouche of the ruler held within its cold embrace. At the four corners of the sarcophagus stood the royal canopic jars...each the figure of a winged goddess, and each holding a mummified major organ of the entombed monarch.

Stepping up upon the top level of the obsidian dais, one could stand beside the stone coffin, and look down on the lid…which was carved to show the real features of the king inside. It had been first carved, then covered in a thin coat of plaster, and the royal artists than went to work, bringing the carven features to life. The ornate headdress was bright with light yellow hues, black striping…and inlays of lapis, amethyst, gold, silver, and turquoise. The crook and the flail crossed the chest of the dead king's likeness, royal hands gripping them tight, and strong…symbols of a ruler's power of life and death over his subjects. The crook, and flail were covered in gold plate, and bore a few rough-cut rubies and sapphires. How awesome must this personage have been when he was in the full bloom of life, and wrapped in the rich mantle of his royal power. And even today, here…the sense of power was all too real. It was a power, not just of this mortal plane…but one that went beyond time and space, into a vanished world of the ancient gods themselves! Standing there, beside that sarcophagus, one could almost grasp what it must have been like…to be hailed as a king, and worshipped as a living god!

Sean finally broke the silence, letting the breath he'd been holding out, his eyes wide and enthralled. "Magnificent!…it is beyond mere words! No one can adequately describe this, Elizabeth!…it must be seen to be realized, and believed!"

Tamara ran her fingertips lightly over the lid of one of the chests. To her, the cool metal fastened on the still fragrant cedar seemed to caress her fingers with a strange, warm current. Her eyes narrowed, and she smiled slightly, understanding. When she spoke, her voice was hushed, strangely saddened…filled with echoes of the past. "It *is* overwhelming. I quite understand, and agree, with all the precautions your family has set up, Elizabeth. There's a fortune beyond reckoning within these walls…a sense of power, and life more than anyone could comprehend!

It definitely cannot fall into hands that would be unworthy to even touch it!"

Beth nodded, agreeing, but she shivered slightly as she looked around the room...she'd never been at ease here. "Yes, you're right...but, I don't think that will ever happen, Tamara...it's been tried, but never accomplished!" She shook herself a little, then looked at her companions. "I'm sorry...I've never been comfortable in this room, ever! It tends to make me very uneasy! I feel like the priests who'd laid the dead king to rest are still within the room, waiting for the moment when they sealed the tomb for all eternity!...gives me the willies! If you really want any information about anything in here, Sandra is the one you need to talk with, Sean! She's quite expressive about the things in this room...says she feels as if every relic in here is trying to tell its part in the king's life, and power. She's quite the historian in our family...especially where ancient Egyptian myths, and history are involved!"

Tamara sighed deeply, causing Sean to give her a sharp glance. He could see the almost dreamlike mood she was enwrapped in...what could be wrong, he wondered.

"Think of it, Elizabeth, " she said, her golden eyes darting about the room. "A time when power was absolute, and held within the hands of one man! It fills me with so much happiness to see it all...and yet, also with much sadness!" She gestured towards the obsidian dais, walking to its foot, and gazing up at the great sarcophagus. "The title of King carried with it all any man could desire, or dream about!...and the privilege of 'divine right' was a fact, not merely empty words! When this ruler spoke, his words were law...and death was the penalty for breaking that law! There was a simplicity to those times...not the political maneuverings, and interpersonal games governments seem drowning in today! There was an order to things...a protocol that stated the way things were meant to be, and anyone who went against that order...that rightness...was punished!" She sighed, her eyes never leaving that stone coffin. "The way of maat…divine justice, and a proper order to all aspects of life. How I miss such a way of life!"

Sean stiffened…had Tamara lost her mind, talking in such a fashion? Beth frowned, now sure how to take the way Tamara was behaving…her words were so emotional, so unsettling! She tilted her head to one side, staring. "I suppose you could say it was a simpler life back then…though I've honestly never heard anyone else state it quite that way! Personally…I think it was a crueler, must more oppressive way of life, especially of you happened to be a servant, or a slave back then! Unless you were a member of a royal family, or one in power somehow…all you were was so much fodder, to be crushed underneath the king's heel! All you existed for was to serve whatever ridiculous, unreasonable…or perverted desire the king wished! Things might not exactly be paradise today…but I think we're learning…at least, we're trying to conquer war, injustice, world hunger, and the ravages of disease! We've eliminated a lot of diseases that wiped out entire populations back then! I think we're slowly getting to where we're meant to be!"

Tamara whirled to face Beth, eyes flashing, and nostrils flaring. "You honestly think the human race is *better* today? How can someone of your breeding, and position…not mention intellect!…even *think* of subscribing to such a lame concept of how life is meant to be lived?" Beth had never seen such an open display of strong emotion from Tamara. She stared, very shocked. Sean was bluntly astonished at his sister's behavior…he couldn't remember seeing her this animated.

Tamara walked to the center of the room, whirling around to face them, arms open as if to embrace the entire room. "Open your mind, Elizabeth…cease to be a sheep, as you obviously have your entire life! This is an opportunity for you to learn the true meaning of life!…to take your rightful place in the natural, and true, scheme of things as the universe had decreed them to be! The truth…it is so strong in this room, it's almost stifling!" She looked at the altar, her eyes gazing into a past she seemed to actually be able to see! Her voice came to them as though it traveled through the centuries of time to the present. "There is an inhumanity that exists today...that has existed for centuries! It surpasses any evil that lived in the past...any abomination that crawls about today! It has dwelt in the minds, and hearts of men, throughout all time! It has grown stronger over those milleniums...and threatens to forever destroy the rightness...the order that should be! But now...as no other time before this, as we are now finally in the true, new millenium...there is finally a chance to utterly destroy it!...to rid mankind of its influence for all eternity!"

"Tamara...what on earth are you talking about? I don't understand anything that you're saying! What is wrong with you?" Beth was completely mystified...and beginning to wish she'd never agreed to bring them down here. She was starting to get some very uneasy sensations about her friend, and she didn't like how they made her feel.

"I'm saying that most people are blind!...and fools to boot! Make no mistake...the evil I spoke of is real, Elizabeth! Its agents are clever beyond mere intelligence...coating their filth in layers of sweetness, trickery, and subtle lies! It has been spoon-fed, throughout the centuries, to the world's peoples. It has been accepted by a large percentage as the only way!...the only viable, tangible truth!" Tamara stared straight ahead, not really seeing the other two persons in the room. "But...it's *not* only truth...the way! Mankind has to see that, and accept the fact that there *is* a better way!...a way to put everything back in order! And, while there is still time to save mankind from their ultimate destruction! There is another choice...it is so easy! And nothing will be asked from them, save their belief, loyalty...and obedience!"

Beth's uneasiness was increasing in volumes. "What on earth are you talking about? Tamara...I really think it's time we leave here! I'm not sure what's going on, or what's set you off...but I don't think I want to hear any more!" Beth started towards the doors, but stopped when she got to where Tamara stood.

"You make it sound as though the human race is out to destroy itself! If you're talking about people who haven't received Christianity as their faith, then you obviously aren't able to accept the fact that different cultures have their own religious beliefs! I'm a Christian, but that doesn't mean I'm going to beat up on my neighbor because they happen to be a Jew…or Moslem…or Buddhist…or whatever they were raised to believe in as a deity! I have always believed that it didn't matter what name was given…it's all one in the same…a power that created everything! I don't need a name to believe! I honestly believe that whatever, or whoever, is the true God…they don't care what we call them!…as long as we believe, as long as we keep faith with those beliefs!"

"You are so wrong, Elizabeth! I was not necessarily referring to the Christian belief, and practices as they are known. You say I said mankind is on a path to destruction…and for the most part, I'm right! The human race has been bent on that path of destruction since *before* the last great cataclysm that changed the world more than three-hundred centuries before the birth of Christ! It is as radical a change as when Christ first introduced His teachings to the world…and as profound! And, do you know what makes it so overwhelmingly sad, my dear Elizabeth? That path that your race is bent on?…it could so easily have been avoided!…a fact that many enlightened souls have already discovered, to their everlasting joy, and the eternal salvation of their souls!"

"Three-hundred centuries?…what happened three-hundred centuries ago? What cataclysm are you talking about?…the flood the Bible mentions?" Beth was getting more confused, and more agitated with every passing moment. "Tamara…you may be enamoured of the past, but I prefer end this conversation! I like the world I live in, here and now…and I wish to let the past *stay* in the past! And, don't forget…it's *your* race as well as mine!" Beth stared at her, shaking her head in disbelief.

"As you say, Elizabeth…but the past has always held much that is dear for me, and always will! There were cultures, and civilizations then that your scientists are working feverishly to learn about, and understand!...and why is that? I'll tell you why...they're all just starting to realize that the past is the key to the future! Those ancient cultures were as fine as any we have today, and in many ways, steps ahead of what we have now, despite all our technologies, and sciences! Architecture, science, meteorology, geology, finance, medicine...bold and many steps have been made today in these areas, true. But...the ancients made just as bold, Elizabeth!...and scientists today are attempting to ascertain *how* they did this! All life is a circle, Elizabeth...what we think as new may turn out to be a repetition from a far-flung past! It is a never-ending facet to life, and will be so eternally!"

Sean stepped forward quickly, slipping an arm about Beth's shoulders, throwing a bewildered look at his sister. "That's one of Tamara's pet theories, Elizabeth...the family's quite used to her getting on her 'soapbox' whenever the past, or history, is brought up! She whole-heartedly subscribes to the statements, by a well-known British archaeologist, that things that happen today are nothing more than a repeat, or reflection of things long ago!" He hugged her slim shoulders, trying to use her attraction to him as a distraction from this conversation. "She really gets caught up in them when she starts talking about them...don't you, sister?"

"Yes...I do tend to get rather vocal!...but can you say I'm wrong? Look at all the evidence! The ancients had the abilities to predict times of famine, or plenty...times of war...the births of heroes, leaders, and even holy teachers! Even here, in what they called the 'new world', the Aztecs, Incas, and Mayas rivaled the architectural perfection found in Egypt. Where did these skills come from? Those ancient cultures were the backbones of what the world is today amazing...laying the foundations for the marvels we have today, and serving as inspiration for countless more to come! I mourn the endless secrets lost, and all due to the greed, and carelessness of Man!" Tamara sighed, shaking her head, the long white blonde tresses rippling like molten silver.

Beth stepped away from Sean, breaking his embrace, surprising the big man. She scowled at the woman before her. "Well...pet theory, or whatever, I've had enough of this kind of conversation! I think it's time to go...and now!" She took a step towards the door. "You're both entitled to your opinions...as I am mine! But...when it starts to be a source of arrogant debate...then I say, it's time to step back, regroup, and let things go! I don't know why you're so passionate about this, Tamara...in fact, I really don't want to know! I'm beginning to think you're not who I thought you were!"

Tamara gazed at Beth, Gauging the depth of this startling opposition. Raising one shapely eyebrow, she clasped her hands together behind her back, and nodded slightly...her control once more back in place. "I suppose you're right, Elizabeth...we should go! Talking about the past is wonderful...but sometimes, too painful! After all...we can't change anything in the past...can we?" She smiled disarmingly at the suspicious, and uneasy woman...then glanced at her tense brother. "I do apologize to you, Elizabeth...for anything I said that could have offended you, or made you in any way ill at ease! I do get somewhat emotional when talking about ancient history...it appeals to me in a way I can't explain. It calls to me, like a beacon...reaching to something in the deepest corners of my inner soul! I think it's one of the very few times I can lose control of my emotions! Forgive me?"

Sean nodded, silently backing his sister...though, his internal turmoil was making it difficult to keep his mouth shut. He couldn't believe the way his sister had been acting today. What on earth was going on here? Was this part of her "master" plan?...or had she really lost all perspective? Had caring for him, during his recent "illness", taken more out of her then either of them realized? He was more than a little scared...if Tamara lost it, what hope was there for the "plan" to succeed?

As for Beth...she was just plain confused!...and she didn't like that feeling one little bit! She was thoroughly convinced now that she never should have been the one to bring Tamara down here. Clearly...the

Tomb had unleashed some pent-up feelings within Tamara that were extremely unsettling. And, there was something else she was sure of now. "I'll tell you what, Tamara…the one thing I'm sure of is that you've not exactly been honest with me! I feel as though you've deliberately misled me, and my family…for what reason, I'm sot sure! Maybe this is a somewhat irrational, emotional reaction on my part…but that's the way I feel! I want the truth… *why* did you really come here? Did it have to do with what's here, in the Tomb?"

Instantly on the defensive, Tamara stiffened, looking hard and deep into Beth's staring eyes…crystal blue points of glittering defiance. Realizing fully what it was that was going through Beth's mind, Tamara smiled slightly. She stepped closer to the other woman, grasping her gently by the upper arm, looking directly into her tense, and guarded face. "Elizabeth…I asked you to forgive me if I'd upset, or offended you in any way! It's a failing of mine…this preoccupation with the past, and its peoples! Believe me…I've *not* spoken anything with the intention of deceiving…there is nothing hidden from you, by either me, or Sean! All that is important to you…you know! I believe you Americans have a saying…what you see is what you get!…that, I promise, is the truth, Elizabeth!" She brought the overwhelming power of her hypnotic eyes on Beth, using her considerable willpower to bend Beth back into a more *compliant* attitude.

Sean, still not fully understanding, but trying to back Tamara, placed a gentle hand on Beth's shoulder, smiling lazily at her…his dark eyes smoky, and intense. "I don't think you need to be alarmed in any way, dearest! It's just Tamara's way, when she talks about the past. Believe me…we are keeping nothing from you…and our only interest in seeing this room was to see all the wonders we'd heard were kept here! And, I have to say…everything we'd heard, or read…didn't come close! It's a fantastic place, Elizabeth!…absolutely mesmerizing!"

Before Beth could attempt an answer, Tamara spoke up. "This has turned out to be an unfortunate misunderstanding! I think we need to find something to get our minds off this! I've an idea...something to brighten things up!" She glanced first at Sean, then smiled at Beth. "Sean...it's such a beautiful afternoon...why don't we put off our trip into the city, and you take our lovely Elizabeth for a long stroll through the wonderful formal gardens? The freshness of the air, and the beautiful colors...all should brush the unpleasant feelings away! What do you think?"

"Dinner will be served soon, Tamara...and I'm not really in the mood for a walk in the gardens! It will be too cool, and getting dark! I think I should put the time before we eat to better use! If you don't want to go to the city, then I can clear up some paperwork in my office here!" Beth started to leave.

Sean reached out, taking her in his arms. Despite her inner tensions, and her unease with Tamara, Beth felt that all-too familiar heat begin within her body. This time, however, she pushed him away, determined not to succumb control of her emotions to him again. "I said...I wasn't interested right now, and I meant it!" She snapped, tossing her head back, staring at him, angry and determined. She looked back to Tamara, eyes wide, jaw set. "I said it was time to leave, Tamara...I won't say it again!"

Tamara held one hand up, cautioning Sean to keep silent. She walked slowly towards the agitated woman, stopping directly before her. She reached out, gently brushing the fingertips of her right hand over Beth's left cheek. "You've a right to be upset, Elizabeth...I've spoken out of turn, and disregarded the hospitality of the house that has welcomed us, and the hostess who is our friend! Forgive me...be angry, or upset with me, if you must...but, please, don't take it out on Sean! He loves you very much, you know!"

Sean, taking the subtle cue from his sister, stepped forward, his arms slipping around Beth's slender waist, from behind, encircling her tenderly. He bent his head, and kissed the spot just below her ear, his lips lingering over the pulse point there. The kiss drew a startled gasp from

Beth, distracting her as it was intended. He turned her, gently, within the circle of his arms, until his mouth could claim hers. The drugging kiss broke down the remainder of Beth's resistance, and her arms wound about his neck, drawing him in even closer. When they finally broke apart, he held her, sensing her legs wouldn't stay erect much longer. He stood there, holding her, a slight smile playing about his sensual lips. She gazed up at him, once more completely under his erotic spell.

"Now…since our 'misunderstanding' is resolved, why don't we all go back upstairs? Then…you, and Sean, can go on that walk!…alright?" Tamara smiled, gesturing towards the doors.

Both Beth and Sean nodded, and the trio headed for the twin doors. Beth turned off the lights, reset all the security measures as they walked down the corridor, and headed for the elevator. In a few minutes, they were back in Beth's office, and the lovely executive was putting the key back into its place in her wall safe. Then, she excused herself so she could go get her jacket. When she'd gone, Tamara walked over to where the safe was concealed, and looked at her brother, over one shapely shoulder. She stood there .like that, for a few seconds, then crossed the room, and sank gracefully into one of the chairs.

"Well?…what was all that? Just what was going on down there? You're the one who goes on, and on, about discretion, low profiles…caution! You came perilously close to losing it down in that room!…and almost gave Elizabeth the reason she needed to get rid of us altogether! What is going through your mind?" Sean ground his teeth, trying to keep his temper under tight control.

She gazed up at him, her face smooth with unconcern, eyes calm and expressionless. "For now, I don't choose to give you an explanation, Sean…when I think the time is right, for you to know, then I'll do so! I had my reasons…that's all you need to know at present, Sean!" Tamara stared into space, thinking. "Sean…I know I restricted your behavior, where Elizabeth was concerned…but, tonight, I think you *need* to push her a little! The situation requires *full* expression once again!...to make sure, once and for all, that she doesn't defy me again!" She had to smile at the surprised expression on the dark, handsome face. "Don't look so shocked, dear brother! You've followed my orders, since that first time...you've had sex with her every night, but nothing more! Now, as a little reward as well as a necessity...I think you can go all the way! Normally, you know I wouldn't dream of suggesting such a thing!...full expression can be dangerous for us, even under ideal conditions! This is necessary...total cooperation is essential, now more than ever! Time is beginning to be a factor against us...thanks to you! It's seems most fitting that you be the one to put things back into the realm of *our* control! Ah...I see my suggestion pleases you! How transparent you can be at times, my brother!"

He scowled, then gave her a grudging smile. "I have never enjoyed hiding my feelings, or desires, Tamara...even though I know how the family views such unbridled emotions, in public. I, personally, have always thought such inhibitions a needless burden...hiding one's true passions is wrong! To experience the true pinnacle once again *will* be quite satisfying, I assure you!" He knelt before her, his face concerned again, and placed a hand over hers. "Tamara...*you* have abstained for such a long time, sister! I do not desire *you* becoming ill, like I did! I'm not sure I'd be able to care for you with the same efficiency as you did for me! Tamara...are...are you sure *your* strength is all right?...are *you* secure?"

She leaned forward, touched by the sincerity of his concern...free of any ulterior desires or agenda. Her slender fingers smoothed the thick black hair off his brow, and touched his cheek ever so lightly. "Put your fears, and worries aside, Sean...I'm really quite fine! My needs don't require anything, at this moment. When I took care of some loose ends a while ago, I also took care of some ...personal requirements! As for indulging in *your* favorite pastimes...there hasn't been anyone that piqued my interests of late! Though...that may change. Since we've been here, I…well, no matter. You should know *my* personal stamina is the greatest in the family! Don't worry about me anymore, Sean…simply see to your lover tonight, in the way I told you…and enjoy the repast!"

He grinned, sudden and roguish. "Of that you have nothing to worry about, dear sister! I will enjoy her lovely body very much! She's actually become quite possibly the best lover I've ever had! Her inner passions have come out…remember when you told me about that? How bringing the dark fires out of someone, who wasn't even aware they possessed them, was the ultimate sexual satisfaction? How long before *you* take a lover in that…forgive me, Tamara! I meant no harm!" He paled, drawing away from her, out of her reach. He drew a quick, shaky breath…her expression wasn't a forgiving one.

The explosion he expected, and feared, never realized. She stood up from the chair, slowly, her face blank…but the golden eyes were deadly. She continued to stare at him, one finger lightly touching his hair, as he stayed on one knee. "You know, in your heart, that that was an improper thing to say, or question, Sean…that's the *only* reason I let it pass!…but, never again!" her voice was a silken whisper of sound, settling deep within him, chilling as if ice had been suddenly formed there. "Do not seek to know too much about my desires, Sean!…such seeking would bring little satisfaction…only a terrible void where none would hear your screams!"

Ashen, his mouth cotton dry, Sean Stood up, nodding as he did so. The absolute fear he was feeling was akin to a tsunami washing over him. He didn't feel anything but that fear…not even the usual resentment towards her ordering him around like some mindless, insignificant servant. At this moment, all he wanted was to get away…far away from this person…but the simple act of standing took all the strength, and energy he was able to generate out of the terror surrounding them. He just stood there, staring. At that moment, Beth walked back into the office, jacket over one arm. She was about to speak to Sean when the distinctive beep of her cell phone began to be heard.

She smiled, shrugging, and pulled the small phone from her jacket pocket. She spoke softly into the mouthpiece, nodding unconsciously. Then, conversation over, she flipped the phone closed, and looked at the two of them. "I'm sorry, Sean...I'm afraid that walk is going to have to wait after all!...that was my sister on the phone! She's on her way home...and the police are on their way here, also! They contacted her earlier, about some urgent matter, and now they want to speak with both of us! Sandra wants me to be here when they arrive." She took Sean's hand, rubbing the back of it with her thumb. "I'm sorry...we'll take our walk later, after they leave! Now, if you both will excuse me, I need to get around for the police!" Beth squeezed his hand once, nodded to Tamara, then quickly left the room.

Sean stared after her, not knowing what to say, or how to feel. Tamara stood there, thinking, eyes narrowed. After a few moments of silence, Sean looked back at his sister, and took a deep breath. "Tamara?...Tamara, look at me! The *police* are going to be here, in this house! Why are they coming here?...why now? What are we going to do?" He felt as though the walls were closing in on them.

"Keep silent, Sean! This is hardly the time for you to behave like a panicked child, afraid of its shadow! There could be any number of reasons the police were coming out here!...and none of them connected to us! Stop supposing their visit here involves us in any way! And, if it does...we'll handle it, Sean! Stay calm!" Tamara didn't look at him as she spoke, one manicured fingertip tapping against her chin absently.

"What about Elizabeth?...she's walked out on me! How am I supposed to follow your orders if she won't cooperate? Are you listening to me?...Tamara!"

"I heard you, Sean!...I'm sure all the house staff heard you! I wouldn't be surprised if half the city of Denver didn't also hear you! The police won't be here all night, Sean...keep your voice down, and your wits about you!" She glared at him in disgust. "How can such a strong man be so cowardly? The opportunity, with Elizabeth, will present itself once again...this is merely a delay! Now, go to your room...get ready for the authorities' visit...I have other things to see to right now!" She gave him one last glance, her eyes clearly showing her disappointment with him, then left the room. Sean stood where she'd left him...in the center of the room, hands hanging at his sides. He wondered what things it was she had to see to.......

......Sandra turned, eyes wide with disbelief, and horror. She stared at the three police officers standing in the room with them, in the family's main den. David was one of the policemen, and she found his presence strangely reassuring. He smiled slightly at her, encouraging her. "I can't believe this!...are you sure it's them? What were they doing on Blackmoon property? I thought they were in the eastern foothills?"

Garalynn sat back in her chair, closing her eyes, and wishing this was only some awful, bizarre dream. Beth, sitting behind where Sandra was standing, bent her head forward, closing her eyes in sorrow. Kristine wished she was anywhere, but here at this moment...she couldn't believe what David had just told them.

"Unfortunately...that's something we don't know as yet! We'll be checking with some of their friends...see if they can give us any information. We do know that some of the group they go...*went* around with did say there'd been some sort of dare, and it involved Blackmoon property. One of the fathers told us about the dare...we're looking into it. Look...I know how upsetting this all is...happening on your property, and *how* it happened...and, we're not here to accuse anyone of anything, but we *do* need to ask a few questions! Sometimes, even without knowing it, people around a crime scene may know something, however small!" David was directing his words towards Beth, but his eyes seldom left Sandra, who was now standing by the fireplace.

"We're probably going to be having men out at that cave for quite some time…it's a designated crime scene until the person, or persons, responsible are brought to justice! Part of the on-going investigation will involve talking with the employees working on Blackmoon property," Patrick stated, then saw the troubled expression slip over the sisters' faces. "It doesn't necessarily mean anyone here is a suspect, ma'am…it's just SOP…standard operating procedure. Like the Lt. Said…someone may know something relevant, without knowing they do! You never really know when, or where, the one clue needed to solve the case will pop up!"

"There won't be any problems talking to any of the people working here, Sgt. Reynolds…I'll let everyone know to be as cooperative as possible. We have a good group of people working for us, and most of them are very desirous of finding the truth behind Doug's murder…they'll especially want to help where these kids are concerned, I assure you! Do you wish to start questioning people tonight?" Beth looked at Garalynn, and nodded to her. "Garalynn…can you put a list together for the police?…you know, of all the people working here? Do you think you'll need any of the off-sire employees' names, Lt. Collison?" Beth turned back to the tall officer.

"It probably wouldn't hurt, ma'am…just in case we turn up any leads after we talk to the ones here, and at your cabin compound! Any help you can give us will be greatly appreciated!" David nodded, smiling at Beth…his dark blue eyes on Sandra's face, however…he just couldn't stop looking at her.

Sandra walked over to the desk, and opened one of the side drawers. She flipped through some of the folders there, then pulled one out. She straightened up, and handed it to David. "You'll find all the addresses of non-company employees in here…the ones who don't already live here, on the estate."

"Non-company?" The third officer, Det. Sgt. Bill Sisto, asked, puzzled.

"The staff who work in various areas on estate property are designated non-company…any others, working at any of the plants, or the corporate offices, are listed on the rolls as pro-company!" Garalynn explained. "It was the family's way to keep records clear, and separate…pros are treated well, but nons are considered almost family!"

"Exactly how many employees are we talking about?…total, I mean!" Patrick asked, accepting the folder from David.

"Here, on the estate?…or, overall total?" Beth asked.

"I think all we need, for now, is the number who'd be working on estate grounds…I wouldn't think any of the others would have reason to be here. At least…well, *would* they?" David looked at Sandra, who smiled back at him. He grinned, wide and hopeful…suddenly, he felt very good inside.

Sandra smiled again…she liked the way his eyes crinkled at the corners when he smiled. "No…not unless they'd been summoned here, for one reason, or another. As for the number actually on the estate…well, I believe, at last count, it was about fifty-six. I think that's about right, don't you, Beth?" Sandra looked at her sister, eyes narrowed a little as she tried to think.

Beth agreed, standing up. "I think that's the right number…but, you'll find all the information you need in that folder, Lt. Collison." Beth's attention was beginning to drift…she could not keep thoughts of Sean, and being with him, from creeping into her suddenly hazy mind. She touched fingers to her suddenly throbbing temple. "If you'll excuse me, Lt. Collison…I have some guests waiting for me, and I am suddenly not feeling too well!" Sandra's head jerked around…she couldn't believe her twin was going to leave now, and for what?…Sean! What was Beth thinking?

David nodded, misunderstanding…he thought her sudden ill feeling was due to the news they'd just received. "That's fine, ma'am…we'll check back if we need anything further. We'll also keep your family posted on the way the investigation is progressing. I mean…we're going to be around for a while!" David replied, slipping his notebook back into his pocket.

"I'll walk you out, Lt. Collison...unless you want to start talking with the staff tonight? The house staff is as good a place as any to start, I would think!" Sandra glanced at him, her lovely dark head tilted slightly to one side.

"I think you're right...come on, Pat. Bill...take this folder, and divide the names between the men of the team. I want everyone busy on this right away, okay?"

"Whatever you say, boss...I'll have the men get right on it!" Bill took the folder, and headed out of the room.

David looked after his fellow officer, feeling strangely alone. Then, he looked back to the woman waiting patiently beside him...he suddenly knew...in his heart, he knew. He didn't say anything, just nodded to her, and the two of them left the room.

"Well...I think I'm going to go change out of these riding clothes! See you all in a bit!" Kristine left, heading for the room that was always kept ready for her in the mansion.

"Garalynn...I'll be out for a little while. If you need me, I'll be somewhere around the garden area!" Beth hurried from the room before the other woman could even think about voicing any objections.

Alone in the room now, Garalynn sighed, shaking her head. Like Sandra, she wished Beth wouldn't get deeper in this relationship with Sean. "You're headed for serious trouble, my dear sister! I wish you'd listen, to both Sandy, and me!...like you use to, in the past!" She murmured out-loud, picking up her briefcase, and leaning it on the edge of the desk top.

"Is everything all right, Garalynn?...or, do you often carry on conversations with an empty room?" The clear voice startled the tall blonde woman.

Garalynn whirled, staring at the woman framed in the doorway of the den, surprised she hadn't heard her. "I didn't hear you come in,

Tamara! When did you arrive here?" She drew herself up straighter, on her guard. "If you're looking for Beth...I believe she's gone looking for you, and your brother!...something about the gardens, I believe!"

"Yes...I saw her in the hallway. She, and Sean, have gone for a walk...in the gardens! She told me all about the police's visit, and what they had found. Dreadful about those teenagers, isn't it? To think something like that could happen in this day, and age!...it's almost beyond believing, isn't it?" Tamara walked into the room, stopping behind one of the tall, wing-backed chairs. She placed her hands together, resting them on the edge of the chair back. "I was coming after something Elizabeth had left in here for me...but, seeing you here...there's something I've been meaning to ask you!"

Garalynn's chin lifted a little, a hint of defiance, and alertness showing. "If there's something I can help you with, I'm 'happy' to do so, Tamara. What exactly do you want to know?"

Tamara smiled...this woman really thought she could control the situation between them, how amusing! She pushed some hair back from her face, and gazed intently at Garalynn. "I'd very much like to know what it is about you that makes me absolutely sure we *have* met before!...as you yourself said when we first meant! I know I shrugged it off at that time...but, I was wrong to do so! Now...the thing that interests me is *where*, and *when*! In what lifetime could our paths have crossed? And, what could have happened then that has you so *hostile* towards me now? I sense a new sort of awareness about you now, Garalynn...one you most certainly didn't have when we first met. I think there are many things we need to discuss!...what do you think?"

Garalynn's mind felt a subtle probe of energy...and, amazingly, her mind struck back, thrusting the uninvited "visitor" from its depths. She stared at the woman she now knew was a dangerous enemy...though, why and how she knew this, she wasn't entirely certain. "What makes you feel I'm *now* so hostile towards you, Tamara? Is there...what reasons would I have to be suspicious, or anything like that? After all...we've hardly spent *any* time with one another! You, and your brother, have been far more interested in Beth than any of the rest of us!...isn't that true?"

Tamara came around the chair, approaching the spot where Garalynn stood. She tilted her proud head back a little, appraising the lady lawyer's body language, as well as trying once again to ascertain the thoughts she now held. Garalynn held herself steady under the scrutiny, sensing some darker power trying to overcome her resistance...knowing she had to stay steadfast. She hid the slight shudder that rippled through her lithe form when she felt the brush of something...dangerously sensual. Her eyes never left the golden eyes across from her...though, she was now seeing things in those glittering depths she'd hoped she'd only imagined before. Something reached out to her from those fathomless orbs...something almost tender, promising. She felt, like the softest of fingertips, a caress across the high planes of her cheekbones, and down the slender column of her neck. Her heartbeat increased, and she heard her breathing become slightly harsh, and rapid. Than, her brain screaming for her swirling sensibilities to right themselves, Garalynn shook her head, and stared defiantly into Tamara's eyes. Though the two women hadn't spoken a word in the past few moments, Garalynn's mind made it very clear she wasn't falling victim to whatever power the other woman was attempting to exert over her.

Tamara's eyes widened, and she frowned...she wasn't used to being put off by anyone, let alone a...what was this? "We both know there is something between us, Garalynn...a something that's been there since the beginning, I now realize! I see it in your eyes...we *have* met before!" She shook her head, the long white-blonde hair rippling slightly. "I'll tell you a little secret, Garalynn...I have the ability to 'look' into other's minds, and view their innermost thoughts, wishes, feelings...desires! There has been almost no one I couldn't do this with...until I came here! And, now...I find there are *two* people who possess the unbelievable ability to keep me out! You…and your sister…Sandra!" She gazed up at the magnificent eland trophy head over the desk. "I can't explain it…yet! But, secrets have never stayed hidden forever from me! There is something *unique* about the two of you…and it's not something of the blood, as the two of you are sisters by adoption, not birth! No…this is something you share…from a time before now! It's something…not quite mortal! I'm intrigued, to say the least…and determined to unclose the secret! Unless, of course…you chose to reveal it to me, all on your own? Why don't you tell me, Garalynn?" She reached out, softly, briefly, touching Garalynn's cheek.

Garalynn jerked her head away…she couldn't allow herself to fall into the seduction of this beautiful, and deadly woman. She looked at Tamara. "I think your imagination is working over-time!…there's nothing to tell! Anything you may be sensing, coming from me, is nothing more than the heartfelt desire to see you, and your brother, gone from *all* our lives! And, the sooner, the better! Oh, and this ability you say you have…to read minds?…don't try it with me ever again! I can't stop what you try with others', Tamara…but, here and now, I'm serving notice to leave me, and mine, alone!" She turned to leave, then looked back, jaw set. "You know, though, Tamara…you are correct about one thing! I do have an incredible hostility towards you! I'm not really sure as to the underlying reasons…but I do know I don't trust you, or that brother of yours! Call it a 'gut' reaction…but I *do* know neither of you is whom you appear to be! I will find out what's going on here, and stop you *before* you can harm either of my sisters, I promise! Stay away from me…and my family!"

"That's going to prove a little difficult, my dear…seeing as how Beth and Sean are now very much in love with one another! You can't speak for *her* wishes…now, can you?" Tamara had an arch lilt to her voice…her eyes bright with a crystalline flame. "I think this is a decision you should consider very carefully, Garalynn…you don't want to make an enemy of *me*! I can offer you so very, very much! And, the alternative...it is so very dark!"

"Beth's mind isn't too clear these days...but that will all be taken care of once the two of you are out of her life...all our lives!" Garalynn clenched her fists, feeling the nails dig into the palms of her hands. "Hurt either of my sisters, Tamara...in *any* way, and I swear...the repayment will surprise even you!" Her expression, and tone of voice, held a quality, unknown to her, that caused Tamara to pause, smile gone.

Garalynn gathered up her things. "Just remember what I said, Tamara...stay away from me, and my family! There's no way you're going to take anything more from us, and I mean...anything! Despite what you may feel...or want! Just remember that!" And, than, she was gone.

Tamara stared after her, eyes narrowed...how dare she defy her! She closed her eyes, opening her mind to everything around her. She slowed her breathing, making it very slow, and deep. Her incredible senses reached out...through the room, the manor house, and the immediate surrounding areas. After a few seconds, she opened her eyes, and smiled slightly...everything was clear. The strange sensation, however, persisted...she was being watched! After a few more moments, she shrugged it off...putting it down to the feelings she had during the conversation with Garalynn...the woman had a spirit! She sighed...this wasn't going to be quite as easy as she first thought...but total failure never entered her mind! When she desired something...she always got it! Whatever the secret was that Garalynn, and Sandra, were keeping from her...she'd uncover! As for the other...she smiled to herself. She'd *never* failed there!...it was simply a matter of patience, and she had an eternity of that! She walked from the room, humming a little tune to herself.

The room was now totally silent. Then, barely audible at first, a low hum began to stir...coming from all corners of the large den. A white-hot glow began to be visible...growing ever brighter, as the hum grew ever louder. When it reached an ear-splitting whine, it suddenly vanished with a loud "ping". The light returned to normal levels, and all was as it had been. A low sound...much like a deep sigh of sadness...echoed, then died. The room was once again wrapped in the normal silence of an empty room.......

......Sean drew Beth's hair through his fingers, watching how the early moonlight made each chestnut strand glisten as though wet. He glanced down at her, leaning into the hollow formed at the juncture of his chest and shoulder, her eyes half closed. He had been a little surprised when she'd walked into his room, and stated she wanted to go on that walk...the evening shadows had started creeping over the gardens. He'd felt that fire building in her, and was startled by the intensity...something had stirred her inner fires, and they were seeking the answering flames of his body. They'd walked a little through the ornate gardens, caressing and kissing as all lovers from time eternal had done. When they'd reached a secluded area, they'd stopped, and sat down on one of the large marble benches there. He'd taken her into his arms, seeking the softness of her lips. She'd answered with an intense embrace of her own, pressing herself against the hard muscles of his upper body. Then, they'd just snuggled close, his arm about her shoulders...no words, just silent sharing.

Beth opened her eyes fully, looking up at his profile in the moonlight. She shivered, with gathering emotion, as she realized how the gathering darkness made that profile even more alluring...more mysterious. She wanted...suddenly, she was afraid...of the darkness, and him! She sat up, breaking the strangely gentle embrace.

"It's gotten really dark...I think we'd better go back inside, Sean. I need to check with Sandra, and Garalynn, about this police thing!" She looked away, not wanting to see the startled confusion she could feel radiating from the aroused body beside hers.

Sean pulled her back, up against him...he wasn't going to let her go inside before they settled something between them. She'd aroused his passions…they needed expressing, not banking! He felt her shiver, and knew it wasn't from the cool night air wafting about them. "Hush, my love…we have more pressing things to address right now…and right here! No need to feel cold…I'll warm you up very soon, and that's a promise!" He bent over her, and kissed her…hard, and driving.

Beth pushed him back, that odd fear growing…with an odder sense of embarrassment as well. "No!…not here! Sean, let go of me!…I want to go inside!"

He just grinned, broad and ruthless…holding her prisoner against the powerful muscles of his chest. He looked down, into her face, his white teeth flashing in the moonlight. "There's nothing you can do to forestall the inevitable, Elizabeth…despite these feeble, and insincere attempts to deny what your passion dictates! My poor love…still trying to follow what your emotions tell you is the *proper* way!" He kissed her again, bruising her soft lips with the intensity of his caress. He drew back, nipping at her lower lip a little. "Admit it, Elizabeth…you want this as much as I! The idea of making love out in the open appeals to the adventurer within you! The forbidden is always the sweetest fruit!"

She pushed harder against that immovable chest, not wanting to hear his words…to have to admit the truth behind them. She could feel the upsurge of her passions, feel the falsity of her feeble protests. Yes…he was right…she *did* want this, and the thought they could be discovered only added a height of emotion to the level she was feeling. She stopped pushing her hands against his chest…feeling the fingers of those hands spreading, seeking to touch every inch of his body. Her lips parted slightly, a whisper of sound escaping between them…his name. He gently cupped her chin, raising her chin so he could fully see those beautiful eyes. His head tilted down over hers, and their lips met. The kiss was an affirmation…an acknowledgement…a surrender. The slight chill to the night air was quickly being replaced by a searing, drugging warmth.

Sean smiled to himself, feeling the last vestige of resistance disappear from the soft, firm flesh under his hands. His desire had become so strong that his hands trembled slightly as he undid the buttons of her jacket, then her blouse. She gasped a little, feeling the cool air tickling her now bare skin. She felt the goose bumps popping out, drawing a shaky breath as his hands cupped her trembling breasts, the nipples hardening. His hands were quickly replaced by his lips, drawing the nipple of one breast deep into his mouth, while his hand teased the tightening nipple of the other. His mouth was eager, not willing to wait any further to taste her skin. She arched her back, holding his head to her.

Pushing her back onto the bench, Sean felt his own heat growing, and it brought a growl forth, from deep in his throat. Moving over her body, he quickly stripped the slacks, then panties, from her body. Covering the trembling body with his own, his hands, and lips continued their stroking, caressing, and arousing. He could feel her body's rising towards the peak…and each time, he'd slow his caresses, bringing her back from that which she sought so ardently.

Finally, Beth arched the entire length of her heated body up against his. "Sean…please? I feel like I'm going to lose my mind!" Her hands gripped his head, pulling him to her…kissing him with a savage intensity she'd never shown him before.

He drew back slightly, face dark with passion, and contorted with the ferocity of all he was barely keeping a rein upon. Moving quickly, he pulled her hands up over her head, holding them there with the strength of one hand. He watched her eyes widen in surprise, and bent over her mouth as she was about to speak. His mouth captured hers, his tongue slipping smoothly into her mouth, teasing yet forceful. She responded, her mouth as avid as his.

His lips slid down, resting on the pulse in her throat. He smothered a small moan, savoring the heat from the throbbing artery. He could tell how fast her heart was beating, each pulse vibrating against his lips. He smiled grimly…it was almost time. He stroked his free hand down the contours of her body, drawing another gasp from her…then he slipped it in between her thighs. Her hips bucked, then began moving in rhythm with his stroking fingers.

The sounds of her moans gained in frequency, and the increasing movements of her body told him it was just about the right time. Sean moved over her, slipping his hardness into her body, tantalizing one nipple with the heat of his mouth again. A few fast, hard strokes, and he felt her reach her peak...this time, he stroked her over the edge, into the precipice of mindless pleasure. As her body stiffened, and her eyes closed, he bit down on the captured nipple. His mouth curved into a dark grin as he tasted the warm saltiness of her blood. His entire system tingled, like an electric current hummed through it. His mouth could taste the pure essence in the blood...and he savored it, like a connoisseur of fine wines.

He took a few deep pulls on the breast, feeling his loins tighten, then surge with an explosive suddenness as he achieved his own peak. He lifted his head from the breast he'd been attending, panting slightly, and looked at Beth. Head back, mouth slightly open, and eyes closed...Beth appeared unconscious. He placed one hand over her heaving chest...feeling the slowly decreasing heartbeat. He pulled his tongue all around the surface of his lips, finding faint traces of the blood he'd drawn from his unknowing lover. His body quivered at the taste, feeling each drop of blood burst into a life all its own as he swallowed them. He bent his head over the limp body he held, and drew the still swollen nipple into his mouth once again. His tongue laved the tender spot gently, lovingly...easing any soreness from it even as it cleansed the blood traces from the supple flesh. She murmured softly, snuggling closer. When he was finished, he looked at her...she was fast asleep.

Sean looked into the starry night sky, his breathing returning to its normal rhythm...eyes still a little glazed, and body pleasantly satiated. He felt wonderful!...a sense of well-being, power, and satisfaction like he hadn't been able to experience in some time. He felt like hurling his triumph into the face of the Heavens themselves!...daring anyone to oppose him! But, wisely...he simply smiled, and looked back at the sleeping woman in his arms. The moonlight gilded her tanned skin, and she appeared like a marble statue. Sean felt a strange warmth come over him...a tenderness long lost to him. He touched the damp, dark curls tumbling over her forehead, brushing them gently back into place.

Tamara should be pleased how things went tonight. From now on, he knew Elizabeth would do whatever she was told. Securing someone's cooperation, or loyalty, had always been an easy task for him...his rare failures were usually due to the physical demise of his then lovers. But...as he gazed at her face, feeling something very alien to him, Sean was sure Beth wouldn't be one of his failures. This feeling, however...he had to shake it off. He wasn't sure what it was, but it interfered with his thoughts...and he wanted it gone!.......

****

V

❀

.......Sandra walked into the library, stopping as the man waiting there turned towards her. It was late the next morning, and the butler had just informed her about the officer's visit.

She smiled, recognizing the policeman. "Hello again, Lt.Collison…we seem to be seeing each other quite often here these days, don't we? I am glad to see you, though I could wish it were for other reasons! Any breaks on the case yet?"

David grinned…some of the tiredness he seemed to always be feeling melted away just being around this woman. He cleared his throat, bringing his attention back to the moment. "I wish I could say we'd broken the case…that we'd made some arrests…but, no such luck! We had to tell the families last night…and that was a pretty bad scene! Is your sister going to be joining us this morning? What I mean is…I'll wait to say what I came to say until she gets here, if she is coming."

Sandra shook her head, motioning him to take a seat. She sat down on the loveseat, and looked across the coffee table at him. "No…my sister won't be joining us today. She's not feeling very well this morning. I'll be sure to tell her whatever you say, don't worry. You know…I don't mind repeating how upset my entire family, and the staff, is about all this! I still can't believe it's happened!"

David leaned forward, resting his elbows on his knees. "We have learned one thing…a couple of their friends told us that one of the reasons they were at that cave had to do with a bet! I'm sure you're aware that the cave's been used by groups of kids, for parties and initiations…we think something like that may have been the basis for *why* they were there! But…as to *what* happened to them after they got there…that's still up for speculation! I wish I could tell you more, and better information…but so far, we're just not sure of anything! Anyway…I just wanted you to know!"

She gazed at him. "Thank you…for the thought, at least! Look…can I ask you a question, Lt. Collison?" She smiled reassuringly as he nodded. "Why is it I get the strong impression you're more than a little ill at ease here? Why?…is it me? What can I do to help make you more relaxed?"

He sat back, a little surprised at her insight. He looked away, grinning a little sheepishly. "It's…I guess it's this house!" He returned his gaze to her face. "I've been in a few luxurious places, but nothing like this one! It's the most beautiful *home* I've ever seen! Your family must be proud of it!…God, that sounds so dense!" He shook his head, not believing how he was stumbling around. He wanted to always be on his best around this lovely woman…but he wound up feeling like a teenager, with his first love.

Sandra continued looking at him, the crystal blue eyes warm, thoughtful…and curious. "I can't help, but think that there's more to it than that! But…no matter, I'll just make sure you're comfortable whenever you *are* here!" She stood up, and walked to the desk.

He also stood up, and was about to follow here when the relic shelves caught his attention. He'd looked at it several times while waiting for Sandra, and something about it had been nagging at his mind. Now…when he looked at the shelves now, it clicked in place inside his brain. He stepped closer to one of the display cases, and peered into it intently. It contained several small alabaster vials…one especially held his gaze.

Sandra came up beside him, puzzled as to why he was staring so intently into the display case. "Something interesting to you, Lt.?"

He pointed at the vial. "What is that? It's so small…but I think it's somehow very important!" He glanced at her.

She quickly punched in the security code, than opened the glass doors. She carefully lifted the little bottle out, and held it out to him. He took it from her, slowly, afraid to actually be handling a piece of history. He turned it, in his hands, checking out the inscribed symbols closely. Sandra watched his examination, wondering why he was so intent on that particular vial.

"That's an oil vessel…used to store one of the sacred oils the priests used during one of the consecration rites in the temples. This particular vial is made from alabaster, and was thought to be from the temple to Sekhmet, in Luxor." She looked into his grave face…she could see the importance this vial held in his eyes. "What is it about this bottle that has such interest for you, Lt. Collison? What is it?"

David handed the vial back to her, and watched as she carefully replaced it in the case, and re-secured the alarm system. He nodded his head slowly, as if something had been made clear at last…yet, he felt more confused then ever as well. "I'm not sure…there may be some significance, or not!" He lifted his eyes to hers. "That large marking on the vial?…the one that looks some sort of weird bird?" He directed his finger at the symbol he was referring her gaze towards. "Well…it looks almost exactly like a symbol we found painted on the forehead of that young girl in the cave!"

She didn't say anything, just kept looking at him. He stepped away, throwing his hands up in frustration. "Sorry…please forget what I said…I never should have said that out-loud! Guess I'm more tired than I think!" He saw her confusion. "What I just told you…it falls under evidence marked 'need to know only'!" He stared into space, back in the cave again.

Sandra's eyes were a dark dusky blue, fastened on the tired, sad face of the man standing beside her. She could feel a warm current running between the two of them…a feeling she hadn't felt in a very long time. She reached out one hand, placing it on his left upper arm, squeezing it once. "Don't worry…I'm good at keeping secrets!" Sandra tilted her head to one side, frowning a little as a memory surfaced. "Did you say that the girl had this mark on her forehead?"

"I'm pretty positive that the two marks are exactly the same…yes! Does that mean something to you?" He was wondering what was causing that serious look on that perfect face.

She shook her head, not wanting to answer just yet. She walked over to one of the bookcases, and ran her fingers over some of the volumes, searching for a specific title. "I am not one hundred percent certain…but I do remember a reference somewhere about special symbols, or marks. They were dealing with selected persons, or items…and the part they played in certain religious matters." She began going up and down the shelves, pulling out certain volumes, and then shoving them back. "Now, where did…oh, wait a minute!…what I'm looking for is in one of the scrolls kept in the Tomb! Come with me, Lt.…it will only take a few minutes to check this out!"

He nodded, willing to go anywhere with this beautiful, charming woman. He was also willing to take any, and all help he could get concerning this case. They headed for Beth's manor office to get the key. Once they had that, they headed for the basement level, and the Tomb. Once at the ornate bronze doors, Sandra unlocked them, and deactivated the security systems. She opened the doors, and switched on the lights as she, and David walked into the room. They both stopped dead in their tracks, staring at the carnage all around them.

"Ah…this might be a stupid question…but, is it *supposed* to look like this?" David said softly.

The lid of the sarcophagus was off, laying on the floor, next to the dais. Sandra hurried across the room, up the stairs, and bent over the opened marble coffin, anxiously examining the mummy held within it. It seemed fine, but the wrappings had been disturbed, as if someone were searching among them. She saw a few of the jewels, and amulets always hidden amongst the funeral wrappings…as protection…of royalty, scattered about the interior of the coffin. That puzzled her, as each one was considered quite valuable…monetarily, and historically. Why hadn't the intruder taken them?…if they weren't the target, what was?

She turned, looking quickly about the room. Sandra felt almost as if she herself had been violated. She winced, seeing broken pottery, statues gouged, and other relics with holes and cracks all over them. And again…she was struck by the mysterious sight of an unbelievable fortune in precious gems, and metals, scattered all about the room…still in the room, not stolen away! Real thieves would never have left the fortune she saw thrown around the room…historical robbers would never have damaged the ancient, and priceless antiquities also still present in the room. Why break in then?…and how had *anyone* gotten by the elaborate security measures? What was going on here?

David came up behind her, gently taking her by the wrist. "Try not to touch anything else, Sandra…I'll call this in, and get my guys out here right away! Is there a phone near that I can use?" He looked at her. "You okay? Can I get you anything?"

She shook her head, feeling numb. "I'll be fine…I think! I can't believe anyone could be so vicious!…or stupid! These things are a part of our history! How could someone trash such treasures? Stealing I could understand, even if I wouldn't ever forgive! I mean…isn't that what most thieves would do?…steal, then fence, or get paid by whoever hired them? Why this?" She walked down the steps, and bent over, picking up one of the four small goddess statues that had originally guarded the corners of the sarcophagus. "Why this?" She murmured softly, her fingers gently caressing the relic.

David came up beside her, one hand reaching out to gently touch the back of her head, fingers stroking the silken tresses. "Sandra...listen to me...we'll get whoever did this, I promise you! Now...where's that phone?" He spoke quietly, knowing how much shock, and pain, she was in right now. "Listen...can you tell what might have been taken?"

She gestured towards the doors. "There's a phone in the hidden control panel...that's behind that war shield hanging on the wall! Huh...wonder why they left that hanging?" She shook her head, shoulders slumping...it hurt her heart to see the once beautiful room's demise. "I'm not sure anything was really taken...I'll have to check the contents of the room with the manifest my father had drawn up. And, with this mess...that's not going to be an easy task! The manifest is in the small door on the back of the altar...I'll get it!" Sandra headed for the small altar, and David headed for the concealed phone.

Sandra knelt behind the altar stone, and pushed the concealed button. The hidden drawer opened, revealing a rolled scroll. She removed this, and stood up, opening the scroll on the top of the altar. She began slowly going over the long list written on then scroll, looking up as she read each item, and locating it amid the wreckage.

David joined her. "There will be a unit out here in about thirty minutes. How's it going?" He looked down at the opened scroll. "That's the manifest?...why is it done up as a scroll?"

She smiled, glancing up. "My dad's idea...make it look like it belonged here! I think it's going to take a while to reconcile this list with the contents of the room, Lt. Collison...I'm afraid I'll have to be in the room while your men are going over it!"

He shrugged. "No problem...and the name's David! Can I ask you something?...what exactly were you bringing me here to see?"

"There's a few scrolls kept here...some dealing with the actual steps necessary during some of their religious rites, as well as a copy of the Scroll of Ani! What I was after is on one of them...the Ani scroll, I think!" Sandra replied, closing the manifest scroll, and straightening up with a soft sigh.

"Scroll of Ani?...speak English, please!" David chuckled, half kidding.

"Well...it's actually referred to as the Papyrus of Ani...and is also known as the Book of the Dead. It was first discovered, in 1888, by a British archaeologist, Dr. E.A. Wallis Budge...and they've been working on its translation ever since. The book of the Dead, of which the Ani scroll is just one, is made up of about two hundred books, or 'chapters'...all of which being a collection of spells, hymns, charms, invocations, and prayers that dealt with all forms of spiritual, and philosophical writings, and beliefs." Sandra gazed into space, thinking back to her old Antiquities professor, and his passion for this particular subject. "Most of the influential Egyptians made sure a copy of the Book of the Dead...or the 'chapters' they felt most important, were entombed with them at their death. The royals had the most impressive, and extensive copies placed inside of their tombs."

"Sounds like it was pretty important to them," David said softly, a little awed by the respect in her voice as she spoke about the ancient papyri. "Is there...I mean, was there a copy in the tomb all this is from?"

She nodded, gesturing towards the sarcophagus. "Yes...it's underneath the mummy itself...in a special pouch. You know...the Ani papyrus, the original, was nearly eighty feet in length! The passages on it were considered a necessary guide to the afterlife for the newly deceased. It's considered by many experts as one of the finest interwoven representations of poetry, allusion, symbolism, art, and language in all the world...even though it was first written nearly thirty-five hundred years ago! The origins of the Book of the Dead are thought to be traced back to what are known as the Pyramid texts, used solely for the use of the king, and his family...then they were called the Coffin texts, and could be used by anyone able to afford a proper sarcophagus. They started to be called the Book of the Dead about 1550 B.C.E. You know, David...the passages within the Ani scroll were really more than mere guidelines on how to enter the afterlife…they actually held how one's life should be lived. Very similar to what the Islamic Koran, and the Christian Bible held out as the correct, and accepted ways to enter their respective Paradise, and Heaven."

"And this scroll is what you were going to show me?" David put a gentle hand on her shoulder, bringing them both back to the matter at hand.

"Not that scroll specifically…though, now that I think about it…it probably could answer a few of your questions about religious symbolism. The scroll I was after, though, is…or, rather, *was* in one of the chests near this altar stone. I'll have to go through everything, as scattered as they are, in order to find the right one!…sorry!" She shrugged her slim shoulders, her cerulean orbs lifting to his darker blues.

His hand squeezed the shoulder it rested on, the thumb slowly massaging the firm flesh beneath the silk blouse. "Don't be…if we're meant to find it, then we will! Look…I better get upstairs, so that I can guide the unit down here. I'll be back shortly…you keep looking that manifest over…we'll talk about anything you find *is* missing later, okay?"

At her nod, he smiled, and headed for the doors. Sandra watched him leave…continuing to watch even long after he'd disappeared from sight. She wondered about this quiet, warm stream of emotions he evoked within her. Then, her smile widening, she shook her head, and went back to her examination of the manifest……

……Sandra sat at the small table in the sun-room, wearily rubbing her eyes. She looked up as David entered the room, and sat down at the table, across from her.

He grinned in tired appreciation as she poured a large cup of fresh coffee, and pushed it towards him. "Thanks…I can sure use this!" He took a healthy swallow, and sighed in gratitude. "My men are almost done in the Tomb, and your security guards are standing by to close everything up when there are done! Oh…and that museum guy really worried me a few times! I thought he was going to have a heart attack three, or four times as he examined the damage to all those relics! That insurance fellow didn't look too good either!...he kept muttering, and using his calculator!" He took another drink of coffee, and gestured towards the manifest scroll, and large notebook open, on the table, in front of Sandra. "Find out anything?"

She cut a piece of the pie sitting on the table, slipped it onto a plate, put a fork on the plate, and pushed it all to David. "Yes...although what I've ascertained so far is missing doesn't really make too much sense! One thing that *is* missing is a section of the Sun Stone."

He took a big forkful of the fresh apple pie, and grinned...it was really good! "I think this is about the best pie I've tasted in quite a while! Can't remember the last time I had home-made cooking!" He looked up at her. "Did you say a piece of stone? Did it have jewels, or gold on it?"

"No...nothing like that. It did have a number of carvings...prayers, and stuff like that. It was supposed to have come from a truncated pyramid called the Ben. The Sun Stone was very sacred to the ancient Egyptians, David...they believed it marked the very spot that the Creation began...where the Sun was born! I'm not positive about this, but I think the experts say it was from about forty-four hundred B.C.E. It's worth, in a historical, or religious sense, is priceless!"

"Someone went to all that trouble to steal a hunk of rock? Look, Sandra...even if it is worth a lot...historically!...it doesn't make sense to go through all this to steal just that! Would they ask for ransom, you think?" David was a little incredulous.

She giggled at the expression on his face. "I think most experts in the field of Egyptology would have a stroke hearing you call it a hunk of rock! Asking for ransom is a very definite possibility...there have been many art thefts that were just for the sake of seeing how much the owners were willing to pay to get them back!" She glanced back at her notebook. "The chest that held the Sun Stone fragment is also missing. It was about the size of a standard television set, and did have a few jewels on the lid. There were also four scrolls in the chest...containing prayers from the Book of Thoth, considered very powerful among the hierarchy of the priesthood!"

"So...so far, we have a missing hunk of...the Sun Stone!" He frowned a little at her sudden grin. "A rock fragment, a chest, and some scrolls...not much of a haul for any professional thief! And yet...no amateur could break through that security! Anything else?"

"Yes...the final object kept in that particular chest...a small pouch, made from woven hemp fibers. According to the manifest, it held three amulets...the amulet of the Heart, the amulet of Life, and the amulet of the Eye." She read from the notes she'd made in her notebook.

"And what was so special about those things? Were they made from gold, or had jewels?" He saw her expression turn a little cynical. "Okay...so I'm overly concerned with monetary matters! It's just that it's been my experience that money...in *any* form...is frequently the motive behind a lot of crimes! So...what was so special about these three amulets?"

"Well, amulets, and such were always buried with the dead...sometimes right in the mummy wrappings themselves! They were carried, on their persons, by the living...in all classes! Amulets, and talismans were for all sorts of reasons...luck, protection, healing, spiritual. For the dead, they were almost always for a safe journey to the afterlife...to allow their soul, or *ka*, to speak, and interact with the gods, and other departed...to help them enjoy a long life in their heaven. These three were considered among the most important, or beneficial...and therefore, sought out as most valuable, or necessary!"

"Would they have been important to someone who, say...wanted to perform some kind of religious rite?" David had a sudden flash of that mark he'd seen...and a memory of another, older case with similar markings, though not the murders.

Sandra glanced at him, a little surprised by his perception. "Actually...to someone who still believed, or followed, the old ways, such things would be invaluable! And, though many people today would find it unbelievable...there are many who still *do* adhere to those ancient beliefs, and practice their rites!"

"Complete with...*blood* sacrifices?" He looked away, seeing that mutilated body, back in the cave. "That's sick!"

Sandra understood his reaction...it was one most decent people would experience, and show. "David, there's something you have to understand...religion, in all its aspects, governed each day of their lives! Political, military, domestic...personal!...everything was first, and foremost, under the gods' rule! They believed that their time, here on earth, was merely a preparation for their *real* life...the one they would have when they went to the afterlife! That's why the Pharoahs, especially, devoted so much time to their tombs, and the contents held within them! Everyone was like that...even the so-called poor quarter held their dreams of a better life...*after* they died! If they followed the teachings of their gods, and the necessary steps listed in the Book of the Dead on how to prepare one's life for the final judgement...they would earn that good life after death!" She rose from her chair, and walked over to the window. "Offering sacrifices was something that was not only expected...it was a necessity! And, an offering of blood was considered one of the greatest! After all...what was being offered...sacrificed...was life itself, and that the ancients held in highest esteem!" She looked back at him. "However abhorrent it may seem today...giving the gift of blood, especially that of a human...was the highest token of devotion possible! Most of the time, just like what is in our own Bible's Old Testament, such sacrifices were oxen, horses, sheep, birds, or fowl...very few of the ancient gods *required* human sacrifice, though there were a few throughout history's annals. Few of them, however, were the gods of ancient Egypt! When a blood sacrifice *was* a human being...the circumstances were very unique, or special!"

"But...why? Why kill anything, let alone a human being? I've read where some cultures actually sacrificed their own *children*, for God's sake! What did they think they'd get out of something that...that grotesque!" David was trying hard to understand...to keep his anger, and disgust, under tight control.

Sandra returned to the table. She understood what he was trying to say...and definitely, what he was feeling. She'd been exactly the same, when she first learned what ancient cultures had done in the name of their respective deities...even Christianity had its dark periods, when zealous devotees of the Christian beliefs wiped out entire villages, or persecuted members of other religious dogmas. But, as she had learned more and more of the history of the world she lived in, she'd come to understand, if not accept, the reasonings behind a number of those ancient spiritualisms. Her father had taught her, as had her professors, that life...all life...was indeed a circle. Part of understanding that circle, to help know where we might be headed in our own lives today, was to understand where we had been, historically speaking. A knowledge of the past helped to form a hope, or belief in the future...aiding our own souls to be more rounded...more complete in all things.

"The priests...not just of the ancient Nile religions, but of most *all* historical religions were convinced, from time beyond knowledge, that there was special powers contained within each drop of blood, especially *human* blood!" She poured herself another cup, and warmed his up. "They felt that this power was almost the ultimate power mankind has sought for centuries! There's even been writings found that some groups suspected that the key to immortality was in the blood!...whether human, or not, they didn't specify! Anyway...by offering what they held in such reverence, and no small amount of fear, was to insure their getting the attentions of the deity they were supplicating. It would be the surest way to be sure they'd receive all they hoped for, and all they asked for! It was the truest way to prove their personal power, faith, and devotion to the god they deemed supreme!"

He shook his head, a little awed by her knowledge, and calm recitation of something he knew would always bother him, deep inside. "Well...all I am is a cop! This talk about ancient religions, and human sacrifices...it makes me nervous! I think I've always felt that there was a lot more to it then everyone thinks! Let's get back to the things that are missing...what was so special about those three amulets you mentioned, Sandra?"

She leaned back in her chair, thinking. "I remember that part of their significance was what they were constructed of...certain gems, minerals, and metals held a sacred meaning for the ancients. As such, they were sought out when a talisman, or amulet was ordered made. The amulet of the Heart was usually made from carnelian, green jasper, basalt, or lapis-lazuli...these were the preferred hard stones, though others could be used, and often were. It goes without saying that the best ones were of pure gold, silver, or a mixture of the two. Since the heart was considered not only the source of all life, but of all though as well, its amulets were the most powerful. Even in the mummification process, the heart received the most special care. This amulet was often inscribed with a scarab, and specific formulae, or prayers, from the Book of the Dead, relating to the heart itself. This particular amulet was of green basalt, with a bennu bird also carved on it!"

David held up one finger, interrupting her. "A *what* bird? What's a bennu?"

"We know it as the phoenix. It was an emblem of resurrection, and also associated with immortality. The phoenix appears in many cultures, with a few variations...but almost always represented rebirth, immortality, continuation, and resurrection. It's frequently pictured as rising from the sacred flames, strong and forever young!" She took a page from her notebook, did a quick sketch, and handed it to him.

He scanned the brief sketch. "Kind of strange looking...and yet, it also makes me hopeful!" He wondered at his response...why *did* just seeing this make him feel better, and more than that…safer? "What about the other two?"

"The amulet of Life…the ankh. That was a commonly seen article…old and young, rich and poor. It was usually worn about the neck, either on a chain or a leather cord. Sometimes, with royal females, it was worn about the waist, on a belt. It was always included in funeral matters. This one was made of electrum, and had neferu carved all over its surface. Neferu were symbols that were especially used for good luck, wealth, and good life." Sandra sipped her coffee…she was in her element, discussing history. "The third amulet, the Eye, was made from all types of materials. It was either a single representation of the eye of the god Horus, left or right…or a double eye, even a quadruple. They were called ut'ats, and held great power. The one we had here was a double eye, made of hematite, with gold inlays…it represented the twin halves of the sun, north and south. According to the notes I made from the manifest, it had prayers carved into it that came from the 163rd, 167th, and 140th 'chapters' of the Book of the Dead. Basically…it was to insure good health, safety, preservation, and happiness for the wearer, or possessor. The god Ra was the protector…a very potent amulet indeed!"

"Well…from what you've told me, I think those amulets alone would be considered very much worth the effort breaking in here would take! But…I still don't know why none of the gold, silver, and jewels I saw all over that room weren't taken as well! You didn't note any jewels, and such missing?" David sat back, thinking things over.

"Nothing…except for what was on the chest, and the amulets. The amulets *do* have a monetary value, but nothing like the jewels and such still in the Tomb!" She threw her hands, palms up, in the air. "I don't understand it, either! I get the strong impression that whoever broke in had a very specific agenda they were looking for, David! And, for some reason, that makes me very uneasy!"

"Well, I guess we'll learn the reasons when we find the perps! I hate to ask this...but, did you find anything about that mark?" He leaned forward, elbows on the table.

"I think so...it *was* a religious mark! The head priest would paint it onto the forehead of the animal...or human...designated to be sacrificed! This particular mark was associated with either the temple of Set, or Sehkmet." She referred again to the notes before her. "Either one was a very powerful figure among the chief gods of the royal dynasties. Most of the ruling houses favored one of the incarnations of Ra, but Isis, Osiris, Horus, Ptah, Hathor, Thoth, Anubis, and Set were the other chief deities favored by the ruling families. There was one Pharoah who tried, unsuccessfully, to institute the worship of one god...Aten. But, his methods weren't exactly diplomatic...he was a bit of a fanatic...and after only a few years reign, he and his family disappeared. Some versions say the priests of the other gods allied with the army's generals, and assassinated this Pharoah...others say he simply stepped down. He was a member of King Tut's family...some say, he was an older brother." Sandra drew back...she was getting off the subject. "Anyway...Set was once worshipped as a very benevolent god...though, his worship turned evil later on, and Sehkmet was one of the most powerful of the goddesses Egypt worshipped! She was often portrayed as having the head of a lioness. She was the avenger of her father, Ra, and the armies always performed ceremonies to her prior to setting out on an engagement. She was not a goddess to underestimate!"

"You said she was an avenger...what exactly did that mean? What was she supposed to be avenging?" David found himself being caught up in Sandra's explanation of the ancient world's religious practices.

"There's a legend of how Ra sent her to punish mankind for turning from his worship, after all he'd given to them. In the form of a lioness, she searched mankind out amongst the deserts, and valleys they were hiding in, and she began destroying everyone she found. Eventually, Ra regretted his anger, and sent word to Sehkmet to cease her war of retribution. However, by that time, she'd developed quite a taste for bloodletting, and the power she found she now had over man. She refused to obey her father's request, and defied his orders. She is always noted as a very powerful, albeit dark, deity...not entirely evil, but not entirely good, either! Generals, wishing success in upcoming battles, made profuse sacrifices prior to their departure for war. Soldiers, wishing to gain her favor, would anoint her statue with blood from the wounds they suffered in the battles, and lay hands lopped from the enemies they killed at the her feet! A dark lady indeed, was the lion-goddess, but also one closely related to the light of the Sun. She was the power of the midday sun...the heart of the home hearth...and the deadliest of enemies to anyone who earned that title!"

He smiled, gazing at her. "You know, I always hated history in school...but, listening to you talk about this stuff is...I don't know, it's just fantastic! It's like all these gods, and such are real!...or were real! I think, from the way you talk about her, you're partial to this Sek...that lion-goddess!" David struggled with the ancient name...linguistics never was his strong suit.

"I'll admit it...she's always held a fascination for me. She's pictured in so many ways, in so many legends...some good, some bad! Though she was just a creation of the priesthood, I suspect there was a great deal of truth, about somebody who served as the role model for Sehkmet! Her uncle-brother, Set, or Seth...now, there was a real heavyweight!" Sandra had been smiling, but as she said the name of the centuries old god, her smile faded.

"You said Set started out benevolent...what turned his worship evil?"

"It's true...in the earliest writings about him, he was a popular god, and had a legion of followers! A number of rulers fashioned themselves, in their throne names, as the 'beloveds of Set'. He was the personification of the power of the sun's rays...but still, viewed as a god of the light. Then, for reasons not really clear...he became the embodiment of all that was evil, ruler of the darkness, and the sworn opponent of all that was good!" Sandra sighed a little, clasping her hands together on the table top.

"No clues as to what happened to make him a bad guy?" David was really getting into this stuff...or perhaps, it was the "teacher"?

"I don't think anyone's really cleared that little historical 'secret' up, David...I remember reading that somewhere between the XXIInd, and XXIVth dynasties, there was a violent outcry against his worship. A lot of his temples were desecrated, statues mutilated, and bas-reliefs either disfigured, or utterly ruined! Some think it was due to the story that came out about that time...the one about, Osiris, Isis, Horus, and Set!" Sandra smiled slightly, thinking again of Prof. Handradi.

"Well, don't leave me hanging!...what's the story?" David held his cup out, grinning his silent request for more.

She just shook her head, but poured some more of the dark beverage into the empty cup. "Sure this isn't boring you to tears?" She teased a little, thinking how a simple discussion about a symbol had led to a history lesson.

"Not a bit! Somehow...it's oddly important that I learn about all this!" He sat back a little, frowning, wondering at such an unusual statement. "Please...tell me about that story?"

Sandra tilted her head back a bit, feeling that warm current again. "Let's see...I think is goes something like this...Osiris, and Set were brothers. Isis was wife to Lord Osiris...Horus was their son. Osiris was worshipped as a wise, just, and good king...who civilized his subjects, and spent most of his rule trying to better their lives. Set was jealous of his brother's popularity, and plotted Osiris' murder. After the deed had been accomplished. Set cut the dead god's body into fourteen pieces, and buried the pieces all over the world! Isis, ever the faithful, loving wife...traveled the world around, seeking each hidden piece. She found thirteen pieces, and put the god back together...but he could no longer rule on the earth, as there was still one piece never found. He became ruler of the underworld...the one who led souls there, for their final judgements. He, with Anubis, and Isis, had a vital part in the weighing of the hearts! Horus, ever the loyal son, vowed vengeance on his uncle, Set, and their battle has been going on ever since. Since that story's conception...Set has been addressed as the supreme ruler of the darkness of the night...not the restful sleep, but the night that hides all manner of evils! All the forbidden, baleful, demonic, perverted things that creep, walk and slink about under the cover of darkness...these are his minions! It's their version of good versus evil!...the light against the dark! Osiris, with Isis and Horus, is always the positive...Set is the polar opposite, negative!"

David sat a few moments, thinking. "Sounds like even the ancients had their bogey-man, so to speak! Though, to me, he sounds like their answer to the devil! It kind of makes one wonder...you know?"

"Wonder about what?" Sandra was curious to know what he was now thinking, he had such an odd expression.

"It's just that...well, they say every legend has some basis of truth in its creation, and that's been proven true more times then the average person on the street realizes! I just wonder...how much is true where the 'devil', in any culture, is concerned?" David felt a little sheepish immediately after he uttered the words. Letting his inner thoughts out was not his usual routine. He decided to change the topic a little. "We're going to need to get fingerprints from everyone in the house...see if they match any of the ones we lifted from the Tomb. After we eliminate the ones that are *supposed* to be there...you know, like a housekeeper, etc...we investigate the ones that are left. This isn't going to cause any problems, is it?"

Sandra stood up, stretching a little. "Not a bit...I'll have Roland round up the house staff, and your men can get started. I'll call the stables, and have Tony get everyone there gathered up as well...okay?"

"Perfect...oh, we should also probably get prints from those guests you spoke of earlier...just in case they had been in the room! Would there be anyone else who might have been in there in the past few days?" David stood also, pulling his notebook out.

"Other than Garalynn, and Kristine?...no, I don't think so! As for our house guests...there's a problem there, I'm afraid! Our butler told me they received a call, from London, very early this morning, and they had to leave immediately!" Sandra gazed out the window, recalling how frantic her twin sister had been when she learned Tamara, and Sean had left. She thought, again, how strange it had been... considering how close they were supposed to be ...that Sean hadn't told Beth he had to leave.

'Well...maybe we can work around it...it will depend on if we're lucky enough to get some good prints. What are their names again?" David started writing in his notebook.

"Tamara, and Sean Dresden...he's Lord Dresden. Their family owns a business, in London, that our firm just concluded a very lucrative deal with. Beth, and Sean are quite...close! In fact, I'm sure their hasty departure is one of the reasons my sister is not feeling well!" Sandra replied slowly, still uneasy about her sister's relationship with the big man.

David sensed something behind her words, but didn't pursue the subject as he knew it fell under the category of personal business. "Sandra...do *you* know whether, or not, they were ever in the Tomb? Would your sister have shown it to them?"

She turned her head, frowning. "I know they had asked her, several times, to see the room! I think she may have!" She looked at him, chewing on her lower lip. "I honestly don't know, David!...I'll have to ask her. I have to say...I, personally, do not like the Dresdens, either of them! I am very glad they're gone, even though I don't like seeing my sister so upset! But, as much as I don't care for them...I can't see either of them as the ones who did this! I mean...why would they? They certainly don't need the money!"

"Sometimes...that isn't a consideration, Sandra! You just can't tell about people at times...we have to check every angle! If we do come up with unidentified prints, we just might have to have your sister's friends fly back here...we'll see what happens." He started to reach a hand out to her, but pulled it back. "Still...it is kind of funny that they'd leave just before you find that the Tomb was broken into!"

She shook her head, not convinced her departed guests had anything to do with the damage done in the Tomb. "I thought so, at first, also...but, Roland, our butler, was the one who took the call for them. I'm afraid it's just a coincidence!"

David sighed...he'd like to get some sort of a break here! "We'll just wait, and see what the lab guys bring out! I'm sure we'll fine something...even though it's probable the perps wore gloves!" He glanced at her, then fidgeted a bit. "Uh...Sandra, can I ask you a favor?" He seemed suddenly embarrassed, and awkward.

"Please...call me Sandy...everyone else does! What's the favor?" She was curious about what could be bothering him all of a sudden.

"Sandy...can I have another piece of pie? I'm still starving!" He asked, feeling like a little boy, begging cookies from his mother.

She burst out laughing, albeit a gentle laughter. She walked over to the table, cut another, larger slice of pie, and put it on his plate. She also poured the last of the coffee into his cup. "If you'd like, I can have Frances wrap the rest up, and you can take it home with you! Frances *does* make the best pies, and cakes, in this part of the state!"

Now, David felt a little silly for asking...he shrugged, holding his hands out, palms up. He sat back down at the table, and picked his fork up. "This is fine, Sandy...it's just that I usually eat out, in a restaurant, or a fast food place! I never get food, or coffee as good as this!" He lifted his cup in a salute. "I'll hurry!"

"Take your time...no one's going to rush you!" She sat back down, watching his obvious enjoyment of the food. "I take it there's no one at home to do the cooking? Or...do you just prefer eating out?"

He grinned at her words. "Is that a subtle way of asking if I'm married?" Then, he sighed, shaking his head. "Actually...I'm divorced!…about four years now! And, I have to add…there's no one in the picture at present time!"

She leaned forward, impulsively covering the hand wrapped about his cup with her hand. "Sorry…I have a bad habit of poking! I didn't mean to bring up any bad memories! Forget I asked anything!…none of my business anyway!"

He unfolded his hand from his cup, and turned it over, gently enfolding her hand within his larger one. "It's okay…sometimes, it's good to talk about things!…you know what I mean? I think it was the job that finally killed whatever it was we had…it just got to be too much for her! She loved me…I never doubted that for a second! But…the long hours, money tightness, and worst of all, the wondering if I'd be home at night! I had tried to explain it all to her, before we got married…everything a cop's life entails. She said she understood…and I think she did…at first! Then, when I got shot…well, then all bets were off!"

"You were shot?…oh, David! That had to have been horrible! Your wife must have been beside herself!…I know I would have been! What happened?" Sandra felt her cheeks warm as she realized what she'd just said…and implied!

He nodded absently, her slip unnoticed. "It was pretty bad…I was in the hospital for a long time! The doctors weren't too certain I'd have full use of my right leg. The three bullets they dug out of the leg had done a nasty job on the areas they entered. I know how much it hurt Lynn…that was my wife's name…but, she stayed right beside me all the time I was hospitalized, and after, when I had all that damn therapy to go through!" He sighed, absently playing with the fingers of her hand. "When I was finally able to go back to work full-time…that's when she told me she was leaving! I didn't get upset, or angry…she'd been so great up to that time. I told myself that I understood all the reasons she gave me for why she was leaving our home…our marriage! I still miss her…we shared a lot of good memories!" He looked at her, and she felt a twinge of pain at the sadness in those wonderful eyes. "Being married to a cop isn't easy…my mom raised three kids, mostly on her own after my dad was killed in the line of duty. I saw how hard it was for her…how hard it had always been. The family never knows if their cop is coming home each night…ah, I think this is where I need to turn off the memories, Sandra! I'm still a cop, on duty, and I've got a lot of work to get at!"

"I know what you're talking about, though…about the memories, I mean. I'm divorced also…five years ago, though we'd decided to try and give it another try a little over a year ago. We'd both gotten a little confused, about a lot of things, the first time…but we really thought it could work this time! Unfortunately, we were never able to honestly find out…he was killed in a car accident. I miss him, too…we'd had so many hopes for things!" Sandra's voice caught a bit at the last…Matt had been on his way to the manor house…to her, when his car mysteriously went off a curve, and shattered in a hideous explosion when it impacted in the rocks below.

He looked at her face for a few moments, then got up, and walked around the table. He bent down, and gently pulled her to her feet. "I think we both need to put the bad memories back where they belong…in the past! What about it?"

She was about to reply when another policeman appeared in the doorway…it was Patrick. He stopped at the sight of his partner standing very close to Sandra, and holding her hands. The burly detective's grin was broad. "Dave…sorry to butt in, but the lab crew needs to talk with you right away!"

David glared at Patrick, warning him to keep his mouth shut. "I'll be right there, Pat, so tell them to keep their shirts on!" Patrick nodded, his grin getting even wider, and then he left the two of them alone again.

David looked back at Sandra. "Guess I have to get back to work," he said. He turned, as if to leave, then looked back…she was still standing by the table. "Listen…this is one of the craziest things I've ever done, and I'll understand if you tell me to go to Hell…but I gotta do it!" He stepped closer, gazing into those fantastic eyes. "What I am trying to get out of my big mouth is...would you ever consider dating a cop?"

To his surprise, she smiled, soft and warm...the expressive ice blue eyes sparkling like diamonds. "I think that that's a consideration I'd have very little trouble with, David!"

"Is that a yes?...or a no?" He asked hesitantly.

"It's very much a yes!...I'd like it, very much!" She smiled again as she saw the way his face lit up when comprehension finally made itself realized. She looked him over very closely...gauging all that her eyes took in.

His wasn't the handsomest one in the world, and in fact, wasn't even all that close-shaven at this moment. But...it was easy on the eyes, with a rugged strength, and honesty that radiated cleanly from its strongly chiseled features. The dark-blue eyes gazing into hers were clear and bright, no hidden secrets concealed in their depths. His dark brown hair tumbled about his head in curls more riotous than her own. Yes...all in all, it was a face she liked very much.

At five-foot ten, she was a tall woman...he was six feet. He looked well-built, and gave the solid impression of quiet, understated power. He moved with the unconscious, but deliberate confidence of a man who knew his way, and could be counted on in an emergency.

"Good...cause, if you're serious...I'm asking!" He squeezed her hand, feeling as though he'd known her all his life. "Will you go out with me?"

She put her free hand over his, and smiled. "Yes...just tell me when, and what time! The where I'll leave to you!" She stepped back, breaking their connection, and the mood...not because she wanted to, but because she knew he had a job that needed him.

He cleared his throat, understanding. "Gotta go...I'll call you...real soon! Don't change your mind!" Then, with a wave, he hurried from the room.

She watched him go. "No fear of that happening, David...none at all!" She murmured aloud. She was still standing there, lost in thought, when one of the maids, Beth's personal one, came into the room.

"Excuse me for interrupting, Miss Sandy…but I think we should call the doctor for Miss Beth! I think she's really ill!" Diane had taken care of Beth's personal needs ever since Beth had been in grade school.

"Sick?…are you sure, Diane? I thought she was just upset about…let's go see what's going on, Diane!" The two women left the sun room, and headed for the stairway to the second level. "When I looked in on her this morning, she said she felt like she had a touch of the flu, that's all! How has she gotten worse?"

The older woman shook her head, her face creased with deep worry. "I know that's what she told you…she tried to tell me the same. But, she forgets I've practically diapered her!…both of you, for that matter! I *know* when one of you, especially Beth, is trying to put me off!" Diane scowled in mock anger at the younger woman. "It has to be either a bad case of flu, Sandra…or worse! She's been tossing, and turning for over an hour now! She says she feels like she's on fire…and her skin feels it! One minute she began sweating like crazy…now this! I'm worried, Sandy!…I'm really worried!"

Sandra felt a sharp pang of concern. She hurried up the stairs, followed by the other woman. They went down the corridor leading to Beth's bedroom, reached the door, opened it, and went in. Sandra crossed the room, and bent over the blanketed form tossing from one side to the other of the wide four-poster bed. Beth didn't even seem conscious to the fact that anyone had entered the room.

Sandra reached out, her fingers softly caressing the sweat-covered forehead, feeling her throat tighten at how hot her twin's skin felt. She bent closer. "Beth?…honey, are you okay? It's Sandy!"

Beth's eyes fluttered open, focusing with some difficulty on her sister's worried face. "Sandy?…oh, God…it hurts so much, Sandy! I'm so hot I can breathe right, and I can't get enough to drink! Every time I try to drink anything, I get sick to my stomach, and then I'm thirstier then ever!" She clutched at Sandra's hand, the unusual strength of her grip causing Sandra to gasp in real pain. "Sandy...make it go away! I...I don't want this! It's a mistake!...make it leave me alone!"

Sandra sat on the edge of the bed, slipping her arms around her twin's shaking, sweat-covered form. She nodded to Diane, who handed her a cool, wet cloth. Sandra put in over Beth's forehead, and spoke soothingly into her sister's ear. "It's okay, Beth...it's the fever! We'll get Dr. Hodges out here right away! He'll get you to feeling better...don't worry!" She nodded again to Diane, who nodded back, then left the room to summon the family physician.

Beth's eyes closed, her hand tightly clutching Sandra's, and she seemed to be resting a little calmer now. She continue to toss her head from side to side, though...mumbling indistinctly. Sandra rinsed the cloth in the basin of cold water, and replaced it on Beth's forehead. She wasn't sure what to make of this...Beth was so seldom ill at all! What could have caused this sudden sickness?

Sandra's forehead furrowed as she suddenly recalled Beth's feverish words...what was it that she'd been so anxious to get rid of? What didn't she want?...and how was it a mistake? What mistake? She gazed at her now sleeping sister, seeing the golden sheen of the perspiration on the skin. Suddenly, Sandra was scared...there was something in the room! She sat up straight, keeping a protective grip on Beth's hand, and looked all around the semi-darkened room. After a few moments, she relaxed, realizing there was nothing. She glanced back at Beth...with a sudden insight, Sandra knew that this went far beyond a simple illness...this was something that was likely to change their entire world!......

......Standing in the hallway, outside of Beth's door, Dr Hodges was speaking with Sandra, his voice low, and grave. "I'll be honest with you, Sandy...right now, I'm not sure what's wrong with Beth! From what Diane had said on the phone, I thought it was a case of that very virulent flu that's going around....but, it isn't! I'm going to call for an ambulance…I want her in the hospital! She's severely dehydrated…like she's been ill for days!…and that doesn't make sense if this just showed up this morning! I want twenty-four nursing care, and there's a few tests I want run! This, plus getting IV therapy started, can best be done in a hospital environment."

Sandra paled a little, glanced at the closed door, then back to the doctor. "If that's what you think is best…Jonathan, what is going on with her? At first, I thought it was just her being depressed at the Dresdens' departure…obviously, I was wrong! But…it came on so sudden, and so fiercely! What could it be?"

"The Dresdens?…who are they?" The doctor paused as he was dialing for an ambulance.

"Friends of Beth's…from England." Sandra looked away…she didn't want to say the next words, but she knew she had to be truthful. "Beth's is in love with Sean Dresden, Jonathan…and he'd left without telling her why, or even that he was going! I thought she was just being…well, a little melodramatic. We haven't exactly been in agreement about her relationship with him, you see!"

Jonathan Hodges was well aware of the twins' devotion to one another…he'd been their doctor much of their lives. He knew if there had been an argument, it had probably been a real winner!…especially since they seldom disagreed about anything in their lives! "Well…the hospital's the best place for her right now. We'll know more once the tests I'm ordering are done. I'm going downstairs, and meet the ambulance…see you in a few!" The doctor snapped his bag closed, and headed down the hallway.

Sandra went back into the room. She gestured for Diane to leave, then sat down on the bedside. Beth opened her eyes when she felt the bed move. Sandra smiled encouragingly, bending forward. "Hi there…feeling any better?"

Beth managed to shake her head...she felt so weak! Everything seemed to take a total effort on her part. "Not much...what did Jonathan have to say?"

"He's going to have you admitted to the hospital, Beth...oh, honey, please don't cry! You're so sick, Beth...if you get any worse, you could..." Sandra couldn't finish that thought. She wiped the tears off Beth's cheeks, then gently stroked the backs of her fingers over those same cheeks. "Why didn't you tell me this morning how sick you felt?"

Beth grasped Sandra's hand tighter, shaking her head weakly. "I only started feeling this bad a couple of hours ago! This morning...I was just down...about Sean's leaving!" Beth turned her head away, covering her eyes with her arm. "Oh, God...I wish he was here right now! I need him so much!"

Sandra tried to clam her sister down...and her own fear as well. What hold did that man have over her sister that reduced the cool, logical Beth Phelps into a weak, shaking woman who begged for him to return to her? Sandra shook the thoughts away...this was just the sickness talking. "Beth...you know Sean had to leave...he got that call from London, remember? Right now, you can't think about him...you have to get yourself well! Once you're better...if you still want to see him...than we'll go to London!" Seeing either of the Dresdens again was the last thing Sandra wanted...but if it would help Beth, Sandra was willing to do just about anything to get her sister well, and happy once more.

Beth raised her upper body up, bracing it with her elbows. Eyes wild, face flushed, she glared at her sister. "You're glad he's gone!...aren't you? You never liked him...or his sister! You couldn't stand the thought that I actually loved him!...or that he loved me back! It made you insane with jealousy that he picked me, and not you!...didn't it? Garalynn is just as bad!...I caught her trying to seduce Sean once, did you know that, Sandra?" She spat her fever-induced fears, and resentments at the astonished face of her twin sister. "You think I don't know you both wanted him?...and when he wouldn't respond, you plotted how to get rid of him!"

Sandra swallowed, throat suddenly dry. "Beth...you can't possibly believe anything that you're saying has an iota of truth to it!" She tried to take Beth's hand, but the other woman pushed her away, then slumped back down on the bed. Sandra bent over her sister, her temper surging. "I have had enough, Elizabeth! You damn well know I am *always* honest with you! I have never lied to you...and I sure as hell have never tried to take a man from you!...especially Sean Dresden! In fact...I wouldn't take him if you offered him on the proverbial silver platter! You want honesty?...well, here it comes, sister mine! Yes...I *am* glad they're gone! It would make me ecstatic if I never had to see either of them ever again! But...if that's what it took to make you well again...than I'd fly him here on my own back!"

Her eyes bored into Beth's, seeking to break through the barrier of illness, and make Beth see the truth. "There is something very wrong about them, Beth...they're hiding something! And get this clear!...if Sean were to walk in here, right this minute, and say he wanted *me*...I'd tell him to go straight to Hell! Get that through your head!...or the relationship we've had all our lives is in for big trouble!"

Beth stared at her sister, the force of the emotion behind Sandra's words breaking through. Filled with remorse at her hasty words to Sandra, Beth buried her face in her pillow, and began crying...bitterly, and very ashamed. Sandra's anger melted away, and she took her sister in her arms again, murmuring soft words in Beth's ear. She rocked her twin until Beth fell asleep. Gently, Sandra laid her back, cradling the precious head on the pillow. She touched her sister's cheek, feeling the wetness of tears. Jonathan Hodges had taken care of them a long, long time...he'd fix this. She resolutely pushed the thought away that her sister might not recover. With a silent, heartfelt prayer, Sandra placed her twin sister in the hands of the greatest physician, and sat back, waiting for the ambulance to arrive.....

…..Garalynn stood beside Sandra, on the wide front veranda of their home. They silently watched the ambulance pull away from the manor house, and head for the near-by city hospital. They would soon follow, in Garalynn's car. The lady lawyer had been summoned to the manor house by Sandra, after the doctor had called the ambulance. She now stood, by her sister, hands clenching and unclenching, her concern mounting.

After the emergency vehicle had vanished from their sight, Garalynn turned to Sandra. "I don't understand any of this! I've never seen Beth so wild!…and so incoherent, Sandy! I was really glad when that injection the doctor gave her finally kicked in! How did she get so bad?"

Sandra had her arms crossed over her chest, fingers rubbing up and down on her upper arms. "She's been like that, in and out, for over an hour! Jonathan said it was probably the fever…but, she was so irrational at times! It's almost like she was intoxicated…or high on something! And that's just an impossibility!"

Garalynn knew her next question would incense her already stressed out sister, but the lawyer in her knew it had to be asked. "Are you absolutely sure drugs *don't* play a part here, Sandy? I mean…we don't know what Tamara, and Sean were into…and Beth would do just about anything he asked of her!" Garalynn glanced in the direction the ambulance had gone. "I'm no expert…but, Beth acted like an addict who hadn't been able to get her regular 'fix'!"

Sandra whirled, fists clenched at her sides…a shocked, angry look on her beautiful face. "Are you crazy? This is Beth you're talking about, Garalynn!…your sister, in case you've forgotten! She doesn't even like to take aspirin, for God's sake!" She closed her eyes, taking a deep breath, trying to settle herself. Finally, getting control of herself, she put a gentle hand on her companion's arm. "Forgive me…I didn't mean to be so abrupt! I know these questions have to be asked, sooner or later! I just wish we knew what was coming next!"

Garalynn hugged her, understanding, and grateful Sandra's anger hadn't lasted any longer. "Forget it! Come on...let's get to the hospital!" She stepped back, looking at the mansion. "I just can't believe that the Dresdens are really gone!...and so suddenly at that! I had gotten the strong impression they planned never leaving!"

Sandra nodded in agreement as they headed inside the manor house, to get their purses, and Garalynn's car keys. "Well, whatever the emergency was that called them away...I hope it doesn't get resolved any time soon! I'll tell you something, Garalynn...as soon as she's well, I'm sure Beth will be heading for England! And, *that* thought scares me to death, Garalynn! I don't know why...it just does!"......

.....Sitting in front of her dressing table, Sandra slowly drew the brush through her hair, her eyes gazing off into space. Then, blinking her eyes, shaking her head, she brought herself back to the present. She was supposed to be getting ready for a dinner date, not day-dreaming...or nightmares might be a better word! It was a date she'd been looking forward to quite a bit...her first one with David. Yet...she couldn't keep her thoughts from the hospital, and the room her sister was now a patient in. Beth still didn't seem to be showing any signs of improvement yet, despite all the treatments, and drugs the hospital staff had pumped into her. At least, she thought...the fever, and periods of irrationality had vanished. But...Beth was getting weaker every day. Today, when she'd gone to see Beth, Dr. Hodges had informed her he'd called two specialists in, from Atlanta, to examine Beth. Sandra had agreed with the actions, tell him to do whatever deemed necessary to heal her sister.

She had actually considered canceling her date, despite how badly she wanted to go on it. Garalynn and Kristine had convinced her, though, to go through with the engagement...stating Beth would definitely want her to do so. They assured her they'd stay at the hospital tonight, and be with Beth. So, reluctantly in one aspect, but eagerly in others...she had gone home, and begun readying herself for tonight.

Satisfied with her hair, and make-up, Sandra stood up, and went to her double walk-in closet. She looked over the dresses, and suits, hanging there, wondering what would be best for tonight.

"I suppose it would help if I knew *where* he was taking me, but he said it was a surprise! I wonder...where does an off-duty police lieutenant consider a surprise?" She shook her head, hearing how condescending, and patronizing her words sounded to her ears. "Boy...do you sound like a snob! Get it together! Just pick out something that goes good for any situation, and get moving!" She grumbled at herself.

Squaring her slim shoulders, she peered at the line of clothing, and finally selected a very chic, but simple, dress whose blue color enhanced the amazing blue of her eyes. After twenty minutes, she stepped out of her dressing room, and walked to the full-length mirror. She nodded, pleased with the results. She picked up her purse, draped a lightweight coat over one arm, and left her room, headed for the stairway.

As she reached the head of the stairs, she saw Roland ushering David in from the veranda. As he entered the foyer, he caught sight of her, poised at the top of the stairway.

His eyes widened, and he let out a low whistle of appreciation under his breath, nodding his head. "Lord Almighty..." He began to grin as she came down the stairs.

Sandra saw the warmth, and appreciation in his eyes...it made her feel very nice inside. "Good evening, David...you're looking very handsome tonight. That suit style fits you very well."

He smiled back at her, feeling a little like a goldfish out of its bowl. Next to this poised, sophisticated, and beautiful woman, he was very aware suddenly of the vast difference in not only their backgrounds, but their lifestyles as well. "You look spectacular, Sandy! I've made reservations at The Poplars for dinner...then we've got tickets to that new play at the Arts and Science Pavilion. I hope that meets with your approval?"

He was thinking that perhaps this wasn't such a good idea...what could she possibly see in him?

Sandra sensed the tension behind his polite words, and guessed at the possible reasons. She placed a hand on his arm, and gazed into his darker blue eyes. "It all sounds wonderful, David...those happen to be two of my favorite spots! There's just one thing, though...could you please do me one favor before we leave?"

"Sure...name it!" He wondered what was coming...maybe she'd changed her mind.

She couldn't hold back the gentle laughter. "Will you please *relax*? I promise...I don't bite!" Her smile turned into a mischievous grin. "At least...not on the first date!"

Letting a deep breath out, he grinned back, silently thanking her for ridding them of the normal awkwardness of a first date. "That obvious, huh? Guess I do have to admit...much as I have wanted to take you out, the idea of actually *doing* it is still intimidating!"

She cocked her head to one side. It was a gesture she often used, and he found it a strangely endearing one. "*You* have no reason to feel nervous, David...any woman would be proud to be seen with you! Besides...you aren't the only one nervous here, you know!"

He smiled, taking her coat from her arm, then holding it open. "I guess I didn't think you would be nervous about a date! Why are you?" He slipped the coat up her arms, settling it comfortably on her shoulders...his hands lingering there after.

"I've never dated a policeman. Like you, I wasn't sure what to expect!" She replied, settling her purse in the crook of one arm, turning to face him.

For a moment, or two, they looked at one another, wondering. His hands still on her shoulders, David cleared his throat. "Tell you what...if you won't be nervous because I'm a cop, then I won't be nervous just because you happen to be one of the most eligible women in the state! Deal?"

Sandra looked at his face, the cerulean eyes dark, and thoughtful. "Is that the reason you asked me out, David?"

He gazed down at her, thoughtful himself. Then, with a gentleness that both surprised, and impressed her, he bent slightly, one hand tilting her chin up towards his face. The kiss was unexpected, but warm, and gentle. "No…that's not the reason." His voice was low, quiet, and full of meaning.

She stared at him, a little confused. She hadn't expected the gentle caress, not the response she'd felt within her when it happened. She finally spoke, breaking the moment, her voice very soft. "I guess we'd better be going…don't you think?"

Nodding, he opened the door, and escorted her out to where his car waited. He helped her into the passenger side, than ran around the car quickly, sliding in behind the steering wheel. He started the car, shifted gears, and the vehicle began moving down the sweeping, circular drive.

She looked at him, a thought coming to her. "By the way…has anything turned up yet about the break-in?"

He glanced over at her, then back to the road. "There's been a couple of weird things that have popped up. The lab boys found lots of prints in the Tomb, but every set has been matched up someone…you, your sisters, the staff, and your friends. There weren't any other prints found…and that's one of the weird things!"

"But…what's so weird about that? You said that the burglars probably wore gloves…they wouldn't leave any prints!" She wondered what he was getting at.

He shook his head, braking the car as they came to the drive entrance. He waited for the opportunity to slip into the traffic on the highway. "That's right…but we should have come up with at least *two* sets of prints we couldn't match up!…those guests of your sister's. At least…if they did go into the Tomb. Did you find out from your sister if they had, or not?"

"Yes...Beth took them in the day you found those three teenagers in the cave! Is that...I mean, why would their not leaving prints in the Tomb be so strange?" Sandra turned a little in her seat, so she could face him.

"It's just that I find it hard to believe *anybody* could be anywhere in that room, and not touch one single thing!" He stepped on the accelerator, easing the car into the traffic, settling in for the drive into Denver. He looked at her. "Being in the Tomb...seeing all that stuff...you *have* to touch them, Sandy! It's like being a part of all that history...that destiny! So...unless they wore gloves, I don't see how your friends could have touched anything without leaving prints! And if they *didn't* touch even one thing...then, they have no souls!" David had never talked so passionately before...Sandra knew there was more to this.

"You're very passionate...for someone who said they never liked anything historical! What's changed you so?" She asked, placing her hand on his arm.

He was quiet for a few seconds. Then..."It's hard to put into words, Sandy...but it's about this case, the murders, the feeling I got whenever I went into the Tomb...and you!" He stared out the windshield, getting his thoughts, and words, into order. "It's true...history always bored me! I could never understand what earthly good a bunch of ancient happenings was going to do for me when I went out on my own! And, frankly...I never had any reason to think otherwise...until this case happened!"

"And what happened then?" She sensed something very deep emerging within the scope of David's words.

"I found myself *believing* in the possibilities that these things were raising inside me! I know that doesn't make much sense...let me try it this way...I find myself more and more convinced that there *is* a definite reason behind things that have happened! I never felt that way before...and that scares me a little!" He looked at her, his easy grin coming back on his rugged face. "I think that's enough shop-talk! I don't know about you, but I'm hungry as a horse!...how about you?"

She smiled back, feeling good inside. "Ditto...I bet I can keep up with you, sir!...let's see, shall we?"

"You're on! Say...I almost forgot...how's your sister? She still in the hospital?"

She looked away, her smile fading. "There hasn't been any change...and, yes, she's still in the hospital! The doctor's calling a couple of specialists in for consultation, David. I hope they'll be able to figure this all out...she's so weak!"

He reached over, taking her hand, and squeezing it. "You know the old saying...things look darkest before the dawn. She's going to pull through whatever this is, Sandy! She's in God's hands, in a lot of people's prayers...she's going to be just fine!"

She smiled, eyes bright with unshed tears. "You seem to have so much faith, David...that's somewhat of a surprise to find in a policeman. With what you all see every day, you must get a little cynical! But...thank you for your words, and for being here, with me!" On impulse, she leaned over, and brushed her lips over his cheek.

He was surprised at the gesture, and the car swerved a little. He straightened the vehicle out, and grinned in apology. "I'll be here for as long as you'll let me be, Sandy...that's a promise!" He looked away from her lovely face, gripping the wheel tightly...not believing he said that out loud.

She smiled, feeling warm inside. She held his hand between the two of hers, believing that he really meant what he said! The day seemed a little brighter.......

****

VI

❀

.......Sandra stood by the window, staring out at the lights of night-time Denver, her arms crossed over her chest. She felt so empty inside. Bending her head slightly, she sighed, then glanced back at the still figure on the hospital bed behind her. She hated hospital beds...and hospitals. They were such cold, impersonal things...objects of pain, loss, and anger. She remembered standing beside her mother's bed, a child of ten...brought there at her mother's request. She could still feel the gentle touch of those beloved fingers as they brushed the curls off her forehead...hear that low voice telling her how much she was loved, and to always obey her father. She remembered standing by her father's hospital bed, holding his limp hand, telling him she loved him. He never responded to his daughters, never woke to tell them anything. She'd next stood beside a bed when her ex-husband had his accident. Then...she'd stood next to a death bed because Matt had died just minutes before she walked into the room. Yes...she hated hospital beds, and rooms!

Glancing to where Lynda and Leslie sat, she could see the worry reflected in their faces also. Sitting right beside the bed, watching Beth's every move was Kristine, her pretty face tired and drawn. Sandra didn't have to look for the final person in the room...Garalynn was where she always was, beside, and just behind Sandra. They were all waiting for Dr. Hodges to come in to give them any news. As she was thinking this, the door to Beth's room opened, and Jonathan walked in, closely followed by two doctors she'd never seen before.

Dr. Hodges walked to the bedside, and bent over Beth's still figure, checking her pulse, and looking into her eyes. He conferred with the other men, quiet and soft, then turned towards the silent women. He gestured towards his two colleagues. "Ladies, this is Dr. Carter, and this is Dr. Barrows. They're two of the leading specialists in the field of immuno-deficiencies, and neurological disorders. They flew into Denver this morning, at my request, and have been going over all the test results we have so far on Beth's case...they're going to do a physical examination now." He motioned to Sandra, and Garalynn. The two came over to the bedside where he stood. "Gentlemen...these are Beth's sisters, Sandra, and Garalynn."

Dr Barrows glanced at the sleeping Beth, then back to the two women. He extended his hand to Sandra. "Jonathan mentioned you were twins, Sandra...he didn't tell us you were *identical*, however...I think it would be incredibly hard to tell you both apart, when your sister is healthy! The illness does make it a bit easier. Tell me...to your knowledge, had your sister been exposed to any form of parasite?"

Sandra and Garalynn looked at one another in surprise. "Parasite?...just what exactly do you mean, Dr. Barrows? What's a parasite got to do with...has Beth got Lymes?" Sandra thought about the one disease caused by a parasite in this area.

"I almost wish it were that simple...no, your sister does not have Lymes disease...but her system *has* been invaded by some sort of parasitical infection!...or, something resembling such a disease!" came the grave reply.

Sandra turned to Dr. Hodges, her eyes wide with concern. "Jonathan...it's been over two weeks now since Beth was admitted here! Haven't you been able to figure something out to help here? She's getting weaker all the time!...even I can see that happening!" She looked at the other two doctors. "You said they were experts in immune disorders...you're not thinking...AIDS?" Her hand went to her mouth, covering the quivering lips, and smothering the little gasp of fear that tried to exit her lips.

Garalynn put a reassuring hand on Sandra's shoulder. "Dr. Barrows said Beth had some sort of parasite, Sandy...that means it's *not* AIDS!" She looked back at the trio of physicians. "Jonathan...you've kept us up to date with Beth's condition, and we're grateful...but, please, tell us now just what it is you're going after!"

"I'll do my best...we still don't have any concrete answers, just a lot of confusing, and contradicting data! You're correct about the AIDS...we tested her, and those tests were negative...though she'll have to be re-tested in six months to be one hundred percent certain...due to the HIV virus incubation period. Actually, her blood work has come back negative on just about everything! That's what has us going in circles, Sandra...Garalynn." He took his glasses off, rubbing the point on the bridge of his nose, trying to ease the tension there. "We've tested her for Mono, thyroid abnormalities, hepatic functions, renal functions...I even ordered a cardiac work-up to rule that out! I took the liberty of ordering pregnancy testing, after you told me about her relationship with her male friend, Sandy...and, everything is negative, or normal! I have also ordered testing for Lupus...she's had C-scans of every part of her body, and internal organs, including the brain! There is no evidence of tumors of any sort, anywhere in her body, and all the neurological testing we've done so far shows no disfunctioning areas of the nerves!" He was about to continue when the door opened, and a nurse came into the room.

"This lab result just printed out at the nurse's station, Dr. Hodges...I thought you'd want to see it right away!" She said, handing the computer print-out to the doctor.

"Thank you, Sherry." He replied, taking the paper, and slipping his glasses back on. He quickly read the contents, frowned, read them again, then turned, and picked up the phone on the bedside table. He dialed a couple of numbers, and waited. "Lab?...this is Dr. Hodges...I just got the lab results on Elizabeth Phelps. Are you sure about this result?...was it verified? Yes...I understand, but we'd just had this same test run a week ago, and the result was negative! Did you run a quantitative yet? Well, do so, and make it a STAT! Yes...I'll be in the hospital, so just page me with the results...thank you!" He replaced the phone, and held the paper out to his two colleagues.

"The levels must have been to low the last time you tested her...although it would have had to be *very* low, indeed! Is there a chance there was an error?...either with this one, or the first one? Would they still have the first sample?" Dr. Carter mused aloud, looking the paper over. "Not that this answers the questions...but it's good to know *everything* while trying to pinpoint the real culprit!"

"I'll go to the lab myself...make sure about the first sample. If they still have it, I'll have them rerun the test, and add a quantitative to that one also!" Dr. Hodges nodded, looking down at Beth.

"Hello!...remember us, the family?" Sandra waved a hand under Dr. Hodges' nose. "What is going on? What test are you talking about?"

The three physicians glanced at one another, silent consultations going from one to the other in their looks. Finally..."I had the lab run another pregnancy test on Beth, Sandy...it was just re-check to nail the lid down on that being a possibility. The first one, as I said, was negative...this one..." His voice died away...he really didn't want to tell the sisters this.

"What about this one?...is it now positive?" Garalynn had a feeling she knew the direction this was all going.

He nodded, slowly and firmly. "Yes...this one said she's pregnant!" He bent his head towards the very shocked Sandra. "Beth is going to have a baby, Sandy...and the reason I reacted so strongly to this result is that something should have shown up sooner with all the testing we've done! Granted...low levels of gonadotropic hormones sometimes get missed at first...until the level builds up in the system. And, that's a definite possibility here, with Beth! Still...I feel sure something else should have shown us this was at least a possibility! The test you heard me ordering...the HCG Quantitative?...will tell us how far along she is, and help pinpoint the due date! This is not the answer to Beth's condition...I want you all to understand that...on the contrary, it may make our job even harder then it's been so far!"

"I don't understand...why harder?" Lynda spoke up. She, and Leslie, had joined the group standing around the bed.

"With a fetus present, the degree of agressiveness we can use in treatment, or testing will have to be tempered a great deal...otherwise, we risk the pregnancy, and possibly increase risks to Beth's already compromised system! Knowing the stage of the pregnancy's development will help us know how to proceed...especially if termination becomes a necessary option!" Dr. Barrows answered, stroking his chin...this case was certainly offering aspects he hadn't seen before.

"Termination?...you mean, abort the pregnancy? No!...that will *not* be an option, doctor! My sister would never consent to such a move! And speaking in her place...I will not allow it, either!" Sandra bristled with indignation...she knew how her twin felt about such matters, and how she'd want Sandra to decide for her. Besides...that fetus...that *baby* couldn't speak for itself, so she had to! Despite who the father had to be, Sandra was secretly thrilled at the thought of being an aunt. Besides, her mind told her...no matter what, such a decision had to be Beth's, and Beth's alone!

"It may come down to an abortion being the only thing to save Beth, Sandy! I know how you both feel about this, but we have to think of Beth!...she could die if abortion becomes the only option, and we do nothing! Think about it!" Dr. Hodges didn't like even suggesting it...he didn't believe in abortion, unless there was no other way to save the life of the mother, and even then, he felt like a common murderer.

"Well...there's someone else who has a say in this...the father! I'll have to call London, and let him know. He's not even aware of her illness, let alone the...I'll call when I return home!" Sandra's entire body felt like it had hit by a truck...and the idea of calling Sean made her ill. Still, her sense of honor argued that he had a natural right to know...and also know how ill the mother of his child was now.

Kristine, trying to assimilate all this, looked at the three doctors. "You said her being pregnant wasn't the cause of her illness...but, is it helping to make her so sick? I mean...pregnancy causes so many changes in the body! And, this parasite infection you mentioned...how's the pregnancy going to affect that? What's this infection going to do to the baby?"

Dr. Carter looked at the earnest young woman...he could feel the concern, and affection, all the women had for Beth. "Her pregnancy, as such, is not in any way a cause for her illness. However, it *could* make it worse, in a number of ways. Her resistance is already low...being pregnant is going to tap that even more! Hormonal changes may alter the way the infection progresses...we don't know which direction it could suddenly go I because we don't know the causative agent as yet!" He tried to be as gentle, yet as open, as possible.

"Are any of you familiar with the term blood dyscrasia?" Dr. Barrows looked around the tight circle.

"That means an abnormal condition within the blood itself, isn't it?" Lynda spoke up. As everyone's heads turned towards her, surprise on their faces, she shrugged. "My husband's a vet...I've heard him use that word before! Don't look so shocked, everybody!"

Dr. Barrows smiled. "Well, your answer was correct. In the blood work that Dr. Hodges has had done, there are a couple of things that...well, quite frankly, we haven't an answer yet for them!"

Everyone started asking questions, all at the same time. Sandra held up one hand, silencing the hub-bub. "Exactly what did you find in the blood tests?"

"Her CBC...complete blood count...on admission, showed an elevated WBC, or whit cell count. But, that wasn't a surprise, as it went along with the high fever. The last CBC we did, after the fever left, showed the WBC level to be normal again. The thing that's odd, however, is how the differential changed, from the first CBC to the last one we did. A blood differential shows the types, and percentage, of white blood cells that are prevalent in the patient's blood. It also helps us know the status, and condition of the red blood cells, and platelets." Dr. Carter explained. Lifting her chart, opening it, and showing them the various lab printouts.

"And what did this differential thing show, on Beth?" Leslie asked quietly, almost afraid to hear the answer.

Dr. Carter took a deep breath…this was the area the three of them couldn't really agree on. "There's an unusually high monocyte level…that's a type of white cell, normally a very low number seen. You'll see an elevated mono count in specific diseases, like mononucleosis, and rare leukemias!" He held up a hand as the voices started in again. "No…were pretty certain it's not leukemia!…at least, not one that's ever been discovered before this! Her mono tests were negative, as was the Epstein Barr. Any liver tests already done were also negative for any disease conditions! We can do a bone marrow to eliminate any ideas of cancer…that should help narrow the field a little!"

Sandra turned away, and walked back to the window. "So far, all I've heard is all negative! She doesn't have this!…it couldn't be this!…she doesn't respond to this!" She turned back towards the group. "I don't want to hear any more negatives! Tell me something you *did* find!"

Again, the three doctors looked at one another. Then, clearing his throat, Dr. Barrows continued. "What we found in your sister's blood cells is called an inclusion body…something found within the internal structure of a cell itself! There are many types of inclusion bodies…some that are simply anomalous conditions that have no clinical significance…others that are definite harbingers of specific diseases. Malaria, anemias, etc…all have inclusions of one sort, or another. Some inclusions are also parasitical in nature…such is the case where

Beth's blood is concerned. However, what we've found in Beth's blood has not matched up with any of the known parasitical infestations so far. We've sent the information to the CDC in Atlanta, and also to the disease centers in Washington, D.C., Paris, London, and New Delhi. We're waiting for their replies…hopefully, one of them will have a match!"

"Beth has something in her blood that can't be identified…how is that possible in this day, and age? What could have caused it? What about the baby? Is it going to be infected as well?" Kristine was shocked.

"Well, until today, we didn't know there even *was* a baby, Kristine…we just don't know! Until we can determine exactly what it is that's infected her, we can't do anything more then treat the symptoms…keep Beth as comfortable as possible! Any information any of you can give us may prove very helpful!" Dr. Hodges looked about the group.

"What kind of things are you referring to, doctor?" Garalynn asked, looking at her stricken sister.

"Well, whether, or not, Beth has been around anyone showing the same symptoms…we know she hasn't been out of the country in the past year, so our search has to be limited to diseases here, in this country…an any exposure she may have had with persons of another culture!"

Sandra started, her mind bringing up a memory. "Jonathan…Sean! He was sick for a couple of days while they were here! Beth called you about it, remember?"

Dr. Hodges stepped closer to Sandra, his eyes narrowing. "That's right! She had wanted me to come right out to the manor house…then called me back, and said to forget it! She said everything would be fine…that the sister had the medication needed! Sandy, just how was Sean ill? What were any of his symptoms?"

"Both Sean, and his sister didn't feel a doctor's examination was necessary…they said it was a family disease, and Tamara…that's the sister…said she knew what to do to get Sean feeling better. I didn't see him myself, so I can only tell you what Beth told me, Jonathan. He was feverish, in great pain, sweating profusely, very weak, disoriented, and unable to keep anything down!" Sandra realized the symptoms she just described were a great deal like Beth's. "Look, I can't tell you what Tamara did, but Sean was his old self within a couple of days! And, according to Beth, that was a miracle because he'd been at death's door...again, that was Beth's description, because I never saw Sean!"

"I saw him when she brought him back to the manor house after their ride, Sandy...he *did* look like a man about to die! He was writhing, and screaming, in abject pain!...sweating profusely, and white as snow! Then, three days later...he looked the same as when he'd first arrived! It was amazing!" Garalynn declared, remembering that day.

"He might very well have been suffering from something similar to this. Now, I wish I *had* been able to examine him then!...it might have helped here! If I had a blood sample...we could compare its constituents with Beth's, and see if anything matched! If it did...we'd be a step closer to a possible cure." Dr. Hodges turned to Sandra. "Sandy, do you think this Sean could fly back here, and let me check him out? And the sister...would she let me see a little of whatever it was she used to help her brother? This could save Beth's life!"

"Save her life?...Jonathan...is it *that* bad?" Garalynn asked, her voice rising a few octaves as his meaning sank into her mind.

"Her condition *is* worsening...I don't have to tell any of you that! She's getting weaker all the time, and even the IV treatments haven't helped any. They should have been bracing her...at least a little, but nothing seems to have been the key!" The doctor turned as the same nurse walked into the room again. She handed a paper to the doctor, without a word, then quietly left. Dr. Hodges read the words printed on the paper, let out a gasped exclamation, and handed it to Dr. Carter.

"Are they sure about this?...that's an awfully fast turn-about time for this test, Jonathan...are they verifying it?" Dr. Carter frowned, shaking his head...this was too weird.

"See for yourself…they ran it twice! The automation our lab has is top of the line, Ted…it usually takes less time then…" Jonathan glanced at his watch. "It's been twenty minutes…more than enough time!"

"What's going on? What test is that?" Sandra pointed at the paper.

"This is the quantitative HCG I ordered…the test that tells us what stage the pregnancy is probably at. This confirms that Beth is indeed quite pregnant…according to the level of the hormone, she's about four months pregnant!" Dr. Hodges answered, waiting for the inevitable outroar.

Kristine stood up from her seat at the bedside, her right hand raised in disbelief, and shock. "Wait just a minute!…four months? That's impossible! If Sean *is* the father, how can it be *four* months? Sandy…you know that Sean, and Tamara were only here a few weeks!…barely five weeks!"

"Yes…and even counting the time she was over in London…three weeks…that sure don't add up to *four* months!" Lynda declared, doing some fast thinking.

"Eight weeks…versus twelve. It's close, but still hard to accept!" Dr. Barrows turned to Dr. Hodges. "I feel that it's essential we get a sample of this Sean's blood, and whatever it was that his sister used to treat him! They needn't come back here, if that's going to be a hardship…they can air-flight both the blood, and the treatment! We could have them here within a few hours, once they agree! Can we do it?"

"If they agree to it, it will be no problem at all…but, I'd rather they actually came back to Denver. I'd like to thoroughly examine this Sean!" Dr. Hodges stated, glancing at Sandra.

"Are you saying that Sean may have given this…whatever it is…to my sister?" Sandra stared at the physician, her jaw set…her anger beginning to grow.

"I don't think we can't say something like that at this stage, Sandy…but if we find the same inclusion bodies in his blood that are in Beth's, and we apply the same treatment his sister did him…then, we stand a chance to beat this thing!" Dr. Hodges replied, glancing again at the lab report the nurse had given him. "And it's imperative we get a sample as soon as possible! If this is anything like malaria, once the effects of an attack ar fully gone, it becomes harder to find the inclusions in the blood cells! And, as you said, it's been a few days since his illness…the longer we delay getting a sample, the harder the chances to finally identify this thing! But…either way, we'll never know unless he agrees to give us a sample!"

"Then…we'll call him! He loves Beth…he won't refuse such a simple request, especially when it could save Beth's life!…not to mention the baby's!" Kristine declared, not liking the idea of seeing either of the Dresdens again, but willing to endure it if it would help Beth.

"So…we bring Sean back from England…right?" Lynda asked, sighing…things had just started getting back to normal!

Sandra stared at her sister, lying so motionless in that hospital bed. The mere thought of having Sean around again was almost physically repulsive…but, *her* feelings didn't matter in the here, and now. "I see no other alternatives…we have to contact the Dresdens! I'll try, and talk them into coming back, rather than just sending the things you need, Jonathan. We'll see what they have to say!" She looked at Beth, then at Jonathan, a worried frown creasing her forehead. "Jonathan…what about the baby? How is all this going to affect it?"

"We'll schedule an ultra-sound, Sandy…that should let us know if anything's up with the fetus. It will also aid in determining the gestational age as well!" Dr Carter spoke up, looking to his colleagues for confirmation.

"Well, then…guess I'd best be getting that phone call done! The rest of you stay here, with Beth. I'll go back to the manor, and make the call from there! I'll be back as soon as I can!" Sandra bent down, kissed her sister's cheek, and then headed out of the hospital room.

As she was waiting for the elevator, she saw Garalynn approaching her. "You don't have to come along, Garalynn…it only takes one person to make a phone call, even an intercontinental one! One of us should really stay here!"

Garalynn nodded, but still stepped into the elevator after the doors opened. The doors closed, and the car began moving down. Sandra frowned, wondering what was going through her sister's mind. "Garalynn…what is it? I said you didn't have to come…why are you? And, why are you being so…so quiet? Garalynn…answer me!"

The other woman still didn't answer…just shook her head. In silence now, they rode the car down to the main floor, exited when it stopped, and continued through the

Hospital still unspeaking. As they went through the main doors, Sandra drew a deep breath, stopped on the stairs, and took Garalynn by the arm. "Okay…I've had quite enough! What's going on today? Why have you been making like the proverbial clam?"

Garalynn stopped at the edge of the top step, and stared out over the crowded parking lot for a few seconds. "I know I haven't had all that much to say today, Sandy…it's just that I'm so damned worried over everything that has happened recently, Sandy! I really wish we didn't have to make this call!…don't get me wrong, I know we *have* to…I just don't like it!"

"I don't like it, either, Garalynn! God…the last thing I want is them back, but it's out of our hands right now! And, don't forget…Beth isn't our only consideration anymore!" Sandra tapped her fingertips against the leather of her handbag. "I just hope we *can* count on Sean's feelings for Beth!"

Garalynn could hear both the pain, and the doubt in Sandra's voice. "Why do you say something like that? Why wouldn't he want to help not only the woman he loves…but, also his unborn child? What kind of man could refuse that?"

"The kind of man who could leave the woman he is supposed to love, without even telling her he's leaving, or why! The same man who hasn't contacted the woman he's supposed to be head over heels about since the day he left!" Sandra gazed dispassionately at Garalynn, her azure eyes dark with her inner emotions though her face was smooth, and calm.

"Sandy...you're hurting in so many ways...why not let me make the call? You stay with Beth...after all, she's your *twin* sister!" Garalynn squeezed Sandra's hand, smiling slightly at her. "Calling Sean is going to be hard enough for *me*...for you, it's going to be horrible!" She paused, seeing something glimmer for a mili-second in the azure depths. "It's the baby, isn't it? Sandy...what are you thinking?...please, tell me!"

Sandra stared at the other woman, her face tight...her eyes bright. "Yes...and it's so hard to know what to do, Garalynn! Both Beth, and I have always wished for children one day...Matt and I wanted a family so bad, and when we learned he couldn't...I told myself that it didn't matter, but...it did!" She turned away, closing her eyes. "It's all so crazy! Now...there's this precious little life, Garalynn! I almost don't care that Sean's the father! This is a dream come true, for Beth and me! The family continues...and all I really want right now is for Beth to get better...to be able to experience all that comes with being pregnant...good, *and* bad! To be able to see her sitting there, holding that baby in her arms...I can almost see the expression she'll have on her face! This baby is going to be important to both of us! I admit...the news of the pregnancy shocked the hell out of me!...I was even angry at Sean for what he'd done to my sister! But...all that's important right now is getting Beth well again, so she *can* enjoy her baby!"

Garalynn took Sandra by the shoulders. "Sandy...I know what the doctors are saying...why they want Sean back here. I can't shake this feeling, though, that having Sean back here is just *asking* for more trouble! And don't forget...where Sean is, can Tamara be far behind?" Garalynn stepped back, her hands falling from Sandra's shoulders, and bowed her head a bit, sighing deeply. "Look...I know we have no choice...we have to make that call! I'm just saying we *all* have to be on guard when they come back!"

Sandra was about to reply when a car drove up, stopped at the foot of the steps, and the horn beeped once, deep and echoing. The driver's door opened, and a tall man stepped out.

Sandra's eyes widened as she recognized the man. "It's David!...what on earth is he doing here?"

The two women watched as the tall policeman pushed the car door closed, glanced up at them, and grinned. He waved, and hurried up the steps. The sight of his rugged face made Sandra feel suddenly less alone...less mired in the barren lands her mind had started sinking into. Garalynn glanced at Sandra's face, and smiled, recognizing that dreamy, pleased expression.

Joining them, David unconsciously took Sandra's hand, and dropped a quick, light kiss on her left cheek. "Hi, you two! They told me, out at Blackmoon, that you all were here at the hospital Anything new on Beth?...she okay?" He nodded to Garalynn, who nodded, and smiled back. In the past three weeks that David had been seeing Sandra, Garalynn had come to know David fairly well, and liked him very much. She knew he was the one man who could bring that special light back into Sandra's expressive, beautiful eyes.

Sandra did feel her spirits lift a bit with David there now. "I guess so...if you call being pregnant okay! The thing that's got people confused right now is just how long she's been that way! They've got a couple of specialist in on her case now...we'll see if they can finally find out what is going on with Beth!" She gazed at him, the sight bringing a peace to her emotions. "Not that I'm not happy to see you, but I didn't think I'd see you before tomorrow night. Is something up?"

He shrugged his broad shoulders, slipping an arm about hers. He sensed the worry she held within her, and gave those shoulders a hug. "Nope...just felt like you needed a little cheering up, that's all. I thought maybe you'd like a little dinner. How about I take you out?...the two of you?" He grinned at Garalynn. "How about it? I don't often have the chance to take *two* beautiful women to dinner at the same time! The guys at the precinct will eat their hearts out!"

Garalynn smiled, shaking her head. "I have to pass this time, David…have a phone call that needs making. Why don't you take your fellow up on that dinner, Sandy, while I make that phone call to London?" She raised one hand as Sandra started to protest, and shook her head again. "No arguments now…go have dinner! I'll go to Blackmoon, and call the Dresdens!"

Sandra would have protested further, but the solid feel of David's arm around her shoulders stopped her objections. She needed to have her thoughts distracted. She nodded to Garalynn, her appreciation shining from the ice blue eyes.

Grinning, David nodded to Garalynn, gently pulling Sandra towards the waiting Stealth Probe, his pride and joy. Garalynn waved as the car drove off, and stood a few moments more, thinking. Breaking her train of thought, she headed for her own car. Like Sandra, she wasn't too keen on talking with either of the Dresdens, bit it was for Beth's sake, and that was the most important thing to remember………

………Tamara put the phone back on its holder, and stood there for a minute, fingertips lightly stroking the smooth plastic of the receiver. Hearing footsteps coming up behind her, she turned to see Sean entering the wide hallway. He had just returned from a hunt, and was filled with the sweet exhilaration such activities brought him. He stopped when he reached her, puzzled by the expression on her face.

"You timed your return well, Sean…I just finished talking to Garalynn Gagnon…about Elizabeth!"

He frowned, tossing his hat onto the phone table. His handsome face was serious now, an underlying expression of tension tightening the perfect features…dimming the glow of health, and power. "Why would *she* be calling us, Tamara? What's wrong with Elizabeth?" His face paled a little. "She's not ill, is she?"

"If Garalynn was speaking the truth, then Elizabeth is not doing well at all, my dear brother. She's not only ill, Sean…she's pregnant!" Tamara stared at her brother, watching the surprise, and guilt, slip over his features. "Yes…I was surprised as well, Sean! It would seem you did your job *very* well indeed, brother!…very well! You don't seem to be very surprised, Sean…why is that I wonder?"

Sean glanced away, chewing on his lower lip. Finally, he brought his gaze back to his sister. "Alright…yes, I knew there was a good chance she had conceived *before* we left Denver. And, yes…I *meant* for it to happen! I knew it would happen after the first time I took her, Tamara…she is the most receptive woman I've been with in years!" He swallowed, knowing the risk he was taking with his next words. "I wanted to give myself an edge, Tamara…a way to get my rightful place back! With what we had discovered about Elizabeth's family, I knew if I accomplished this, it would give me an invaluable weapon! I do not apologize for my actions…anyone in this family would have done the same, given the same set of circumstances!" He stepped closer. "You said Garalynn said Elizabeth was ill…what has gone wrong? Is it the child?"

Much as she wanted to take him to task for the unexpected pregnancy, Tamara knew there were far more important things to think about just now. She shrugged in answer to his query, and walked into the spacious den off the hallway. "Garalynn didn't give me too many details over the phone, Sean. She did say, however, that Beth's very weak, debilitated, and unconscious a great deal of the time. The hospital she's in has called in some specialists…who seem to feel a sample of *your* blood, and of the medicine I used to *treat* you with is what they require to cure Elizabeth! They'd like us to either return to Denver, or send the samples air mail!"

Sean followed her quickly, face set and pale, taking her by the elbow. "Why do they want my blood?…you know we can't allow them to have blood from either of us, Tamara! And, you most certainly cannot let them know about the *medicine*! I thought you said everything was under control when we left!"

She pulled her arm free, pushing against his chest with deceptive strength. Eyes flashing golden bolts of power, she stepped into him, backing him up a pace. "I would be extremely careful what you say to me, Sean! You're that close!" She held her hand up, forefinger and thumb pinched close together. "That close…to having your miserable existence terminated forever! Get back…keep your mouth shut…speak only when I indicate!" He stepped back two more paces, sensing his very real danger. She watched him carefully, her jaw tight with suppressed anger. "Good…continue to act cautious, Sean! Now…back to the matter at hand…Elizabeth's illness, and the doctors' requests for sample!" She walked slowly around the den, arms crossed over her chest, occasionally tapping one manicured fingertip against her full lips, her agile mind going over all possible scenarios, choosing and analyzing.

Sean watched her closely, knowing she was selecting the best way to handle this situation. Finally, she stopped pacing, and sat down in the plush sofa in front of the fireplace. The maid had placed a well-stocked tea tray on the coffee table a few minutes ago, and Tamara helped herself to its contents. Fixing a steaming cup of tea just the way she liked it, Tamara took a sip of the beverage, and sighed softly with pleasure. She glanced up at her brother, who hadn't moved from his spot in the middle of the room.

"Well, Sean…what do *you* think we should do?…return, deny their request with a well-thought out reason, send the samples through the mail?…which?" She asked quietly, stirring her tea.

Sean was startled…he didn't believe she'd even consider his opinions. "We can't ignore their requests, Tamara…it would drag up too many suspicions on their part, and that could prove to be disastrous for the entire family! But…returning could prove equally dangerous! How could we prevent their obtaining a sample of my blood? You realize what would happen if that happened? And, the medicine you gave me, with the 'treatment'...if their scientists ever had an opportunity to analyze the leaves, and herbs, Tamara...I don't even want to think about *that* scenario!" He actually shuddered at that thought.

"All good points, Sean...which I have already gone over, in my mind, and weighed all the pros, and cons, of each...reaching the conclusion I have...we will return to Denver immediately!" Tamara made her declaration calmly, and returned to her tea.

Sean sat down in the chair beside the sofa, staring at his sister. "We're going to return!?...deliver ourselves straight into our enemies' hands?" He shook himself, like a huge mastiff, and looked at her again. "This is the *best* solution?...the *right* answer? I don't understand...don't you realize the danger this will place us in?"

"If you follow what I am about to tell you, Sean...the danger will be minimal in all aspects!" Tamara refused to let his anxiety ruffled her usual calm.

"But, Tamara...look, I am worried about this illness of Elizabeth's! It must be quite serious if her family felt they had to call us! It's true, full expression has had a few side effects in the past...nothing as serious as this sounds, however! What could have gone wrong?" He spoke up quickly, afraid to hear what she had to say.

"Didn't you hear what I said about those unusual current of power that I sensed after your 'attack'? Obviously, they played more of a part in the scheme of things than I first believed possible! Things were complicated enough with your self-centered desire to father a child! Tell me one thing, Sean...is it possible you've allowed yourself to actually *love* this woman? How foolish, dear brother...and pathetic!" Tamara declared scornfully, looking at him with contempt. "That's a foolish concept mortals have lived with for centuries...and where has it led them? Love is only something to be felt, and used, when it is controlled!...remember that! It is best when used as a means to an end...but always under your power!"

His handsome face was dark, with anger and discomfort. "What if I *do* care deeply about her, Tamara? I can feel whatever I wish...about whomever I desire! It's my business, sister...not yours! I want to know she'll be all right!...and the child as well!"

"As do I, Sean...believe it, or not! I wish only to be certain nothing goes wrong where Elizabeth, and the baby, are concerned! We have to be with Elizabeth...before those doctors can find anything from her blood! The only way we can do any of that is to be there! Tell me, Sean...did you take into consideration the possible outcome of your thoughtless actions? What happens if these specialists are able to discover the secret to whatever it is they think they've found in Elizabeth's blood? And what about the baby, Sean?...what if they discover the truth?" Tamara's voice cracked with the sharpness of a whip's bite. "You made this situation dangerous...I'm going to minimize the damage your actions may have generated!"

"You never miss an opportunity, do you, Tamara? How well you enjoy twisting the knife, once you've jammed it into someone! I may not have figured this out completely, analyzing all the possible reactions...but at least I behave with emotion from time to time! I allow desire to fill my life with the beauties of all things...in short, I live, Tamara!" He snarled, shaking with a level of anger he'd never attained before. " You, on the other hand, choose to live as cold, and as calculating as those computers you admire so much! What I feel for Elizabeth, and our child, is something *you* will never experience, Tamara!...never!"

She stood up, fists clenched at her sides, and eyes aflame. "Enough!...sit down, and keep silent! There's no time for this! I will not allow these passions you hold so dear to ruin what we've established, or keep us from attaining the greatest goal ever dreamed possible! Now, shut up, and sit down!" She matched his angry gaze, and held it. Finally, unable to keep his righteous anger at the level he started out, Sean bowed his head, and sat back down.

Letting her breath out slowly, Tamara also sat back down, and with amazing calmness, and steadiness of hand, poured herself another cup of tea. She poured another cup, and silently handed it to Sean. Equally silent, he took the teacup, and settled back in his chair. Tamara took a deep breath, then let it out…pushing the last vestiges of the mind-deadening rage out of her head.

"Now, then…to the reason we're returning to Denver. First…we must check on this illness. If it's something I can tend to, than I will do so! We need to check on the baby's progress…*before* they realize something's not normal! We'll give them the blood sample they asked for…" She held up a hand as Sean started to object. "Peace!…it won't be *your* blood! I have an idea, and by the time we get to that hospital, the details will be all worked out! As for the medicinal herbs, and leaves…I'll allow them to have a small portion! That will allay any, and all, suspicions…and you know, when they're not on guard against something, it's that much easier to get what we want!"

"Tamara…I understand everything you've said…I acknowledge that your methods are best here…but, is you really *give* them a sample of the potion's ingredients, won't they discover its uses, *and* its potentials?" Sean was trying to see the logic behind his sister's words, but failed.

"You really believe they've the ability to identify something not seen by anyone, except our family, for over three hundred centuries? How can they find the true name to something even the greatest computer in the world doesn't even know?" She smirked, sure of her reasoning. "Put your mind at ease, Sean…even if, by the wildest stretch of their miniscule brains, they're able to identify the herbs, and leaves…they still have to determine the uses, and applications of the medicine. It will take them a great deal of time to do all that, Sean…and that time will be more than enough to accomplish what we need to where Elizabeth, and the baby are involved."

Sean nodded slowly, going over her words in his mind. "Tamara...what about the...other matter? Do you think it wise to return when *that* could still be all stirred up?"

She waved a hand over one shoulder, dismissing that point. "I've been kept well abreast of anything dealing with *that*, Sean!...they're no closer to discovering the truth there than they've been able to countless times before! If anything turns up, I'll know about it before they do!...my 'eyes and ears' are very thorough, and totally loyal! We have no problems in that area...trust me!" She smiled slightly. "Wipe that look of apprehension off your face, Sean! Concentrate on how happy you'll be to see your 'lady' once again! We need to enter the enemy's camp with unassuming airs, and no sign of guilt or tension! Keeping the upper hand, at all times, is the way *we* will always be the winner in all events!"

"As you wish, sister...but I am still uneasy inside!" Sean stated, downing his tea in a single gulp.

"Sean...you must learn to let these kind of things roll off your back...like a duck allows water to roll off its feathers! Think about it...if this illness is within my ability to cure, and I haven't found one yet that I couldn't overcome...then I affect a 'miracle' cure for our dear Elizabeth! Once she's cured, their happiness at her recovery will lessen the intensity of their desire to know the cause of the sickness! The urgency gone, our freedom of movement will increase! Be confident, dear brother...how many times have you seen me fail?" She was firm, and steadfast in her self-confidence concerning her many abilities.

He nodded, knowing she was right...however often that fact never failed to irritate his male pride. He looked around the big den, drawing comfort, and strength, from the familiar sights, sounds, and smells. He didn't relish the thought of returning to the States...memories of hid strange illness made him almost sick again...but he wanted to be sure Beth, and their unborn child, were all right. He sighed again, thinking of his home here. Their family had lived here for over five hundred years.

The castle here was considered among the finest family-owned estates in all of England. The main section of the castle, where the family actually lived, held eighty-four rooms, and a staff of twenty-seven. Its name was Winternight…named, according to legend, for the most important ancient Scandinavian festival that took place at the end of October, marking the beginning of winter. The legend said the ancestor who claimed the family's lands was a Viking lord, who'd fallen in love with a Saxon girl from a nearby village. She agreed to marry her pillaging, sea-roving adventurer so long as he would build her a home close to the central part of her native Britain. He'd found the right spot, on the day his people would be involved in the days-long celebration call Winter Nights…it corresponded with the Celtic feast known as Samain. The family that resulted from that union stayed in their new lands, right up through the present generation. The home was located about thirty-four miles southeast of the outer limits of London…close enough for the family's many business interests, and active social obligations, but far enough out to insure the privacy this family was totally committed to. Their lands were vast, and were bisected by the Medway river that flowed by the port city of Chatham.

    Sean looked up at the wall over the great fireplace. There, just catching the last rays of the setting sun and blazing like it was afire, was a great sculpture of an Egyptian sphinx-like creature. Made from gold, heavily embellished in cornelian, and a few rough-cut opals, it was a magnificent piece, and the family had had many offers to purchase it over the years…from museums, and private collectors. The experts, however, couldn't seem to agree what the head of the sphinx was supposed to represent. That it *was* an animal was agreed on…but it wasn't a lion, a ram, or any type of bird. It possessed a long, curved snout, and thick, square-cut ears. The eyes were of darkest obsidian, and seemed to sparkle with a gleeful malevolence, The sight of it did much to ease his feelings of misgiving.

He stretched out his arms, and let out a deep sigh. He looked at his sister, who was finishing up her tea, and smiled ruefully. "I really wish we didn't have to go back, Tamara...despite my eagerness to see Elizabeth, especially carrying our child! Things are always so much calmer, less confused here! I know it's vital we go, but...Tamara, are you even listening to me at all?"

"Yes...I am listening to you, Sean...you needn't yell! All this aside...you *know* we would have to go back eventually. We failed the first time, Sean...you know how the family reacted to that! We managed to get part of what we were sent after, and that's the only reason we remain living! This time...this time, we're prepared. What happened to you will not happen again. Those odd power currents?...we're ready for them this time, Sean! And, we also have an ace up our sleeve...the best of all possible allies to help us succeed!" Tamara looked at him, smiling with quiet satisfaction.

He stared, at first uncomprehending...then, it dawned in his mind, and he shook his head in reluctant admiration. "You...you planned it all this way! How you did it, I don't even begin to understand...but you made sure we'd be covered at every turn! You allowed even me to think we'd failed the main undertaking! But...in truth, you had already set all the wheels in motion, leading right up to now! I wish I had half your confidence in making plans!" It was the first time he could pay an honest, open compliment to his sibling.

She shrugged, smiling. "It was nothing...merely being cautious, dear brother...just making sure we couldn't be *too* surprised! Although, the pregnancy wasn't in my plans...and it sounds like the illness has progressed far beyond what I had intended it to be! That is why we must go back!...to see what unknown factors have been introduced!" She straightened her back, pointing a forefinger at him. "Your main problem has always been that you allow rumors to influence your judgements, Sean...I prefer acting only with factual data. Since we came home, you've said at least a thousand times that you're sure there was something there that was out to destroy us! Once, and for all, listen to me…what you fear is an impossibility! The only possible threat there has been immobilized for countless centuries! Please…disregard all the legends, and folk tales you've been told! Don't create more problems than what already face us! Do what I do…ignore folk stories! They seldom are based on fact, despite what the so-called experts feel!"

"There's one story *you've* listened to, Tamara, and you know which one I'm referring to! You're always so interested in…" He was cut off as she stood up, reached over, and viciously seized him by the front of his throat. He choked, gasping for air, his hands clutching at her grip as she stepped back, dragging him off the chair, and onto his knees on the floor.

She leaned over him, hissing her words out between her teeth. "You've been told repeatedly to leave that subject alone! If I didn't require your presence in Denver, I'd make sure you never had to fear anything!…ever again! Now…keep your thoughts to yourself, and do as you're told! Go tell them to get the Lear ready…I want to leave first thing in the morning! Do you think you can do that without making a complete mess of it?" She waited until the half-strangled man was able to nod his understanding, then she straightened up, releasing her death-grip on his throat, and dropping him back to his knees. "Good…we're making progress! Now…get out! Do as I said!"

He nodded again, coughing as his crunched throat tried to draw deep droughts of air through to his aching lungs. He pushed himself up to his feet, staggered a little, then left the room as fast as he was able. Tamara watched him leave, then walked to the huge all-glass patio doors. She gazed out the glass panes, seeing the gardens sitting stark, and empty in the cool autumn afternoon. Turning slightly, she looked up at the large golden sculpture. In the light, and movement of the flames in the fireplace, she seemed to see flashes from the distant past. The shimmering effects of the light on the jewels called up memories she didn't want to face right now.

She turned away, walking over to the grandfather clock, in the corner of the room, by the patio doors. She reached up, and twisted the carved owl at the right-hand corner of the clock's face. With a soft "whoosh", a concealed panel on the right side of the clock slid up, showing a concealed control panel array. She pressed down, in quick order, on three of the buttons, then flipped one switch down. She watched as a section of the corner wall seemed to disappear…sliding into a hidden recess. She walked quickly into the opening, flipping on a light switch as she entered. There were several shelves, and a long table, covered with scrolls, made of both leather, and papyrus. Tamara walked to one end of the middle shelf, and picked up a medium sized pouch, made from Egyptian linen. She wrapped her fist about the pouch, switched off the light, and exited the room. She reset the mechanisms, the wall closed, and she returned the wooden owl to its proper upright position.

She glanced once more at the sculpture, and sighed. "How glad I will be when this is all over at last! I will have no regrets, save one…and that cannot be helped! A great prize awaits, and *that* is what we must concentrate on at all times!" She gripped the pouch tighter, and nodded to herself. "And, now…back to Denver! To Elizabeth, the baby…and the final piece of the riddle!"…..

…..David looked around, still awed by all that was contained within this remarkable room known as the Tomb. He'd come back out to Blackmoon, to update Sandra on the investigation of the break-in. This was the day after their meeting at the hospital. He found that he was developing quite an interest in history, though he had a suspicion that it was his "teacher" that had caused the major part of this interest.

He turned to the woman beside him. "I see they've been able to fix up a few of the relics…I'm glad. This is one of the most unique rooms I've ever been in, Sandy! I hate to think it will never be able to be seen in its original glory because of some damned break-in punks!" He looked around again. "It's funny...how all this started with trying to locate the meaning of a small sign!"

Sandra glanced up, not quite certain what it was he was referring to at that exact moment. "What started? I don't understand!"

"Remember...we came down here, that first time, when you were trying to help me find out about that mark on that girl's forehead. That was when you discovered the break-in!" He saw her nod as she recalled that day. "I think that's when I first got hooked on this history stuff! It's like it's always been inside me, but I didn't know it until I came into this room! To tell the truth...before coming here, I used to think history, and the people interested in it, were...well, pretty stuffy!"

She cocked her head back, arms crossed over her chest, one eyebrow raised as she looked at him. "Oh?...stuffy, huh? Thanks!"

He grinned a little sheepishly. For a few moments, they both stood there, looking at one another. Then, clearing his throat, he moved away, walking over to the altar stone, and stopping there. "You know...even with things still all busted up, it's really quite the room, isn't it?"

She watched him as he gazed at the artifacts, her forehead creased. She knew something was going through his mind...what he'd come to tell her could as easily been related over the phone. She slowly came up beside him. "What else did the museum curator tell you about that sign?"

He straightened up, looking away from the carvings he'd been studying. "Not too much more than what you'd told me...by the way, he told me you're considered quite an expert...for an amateur, he said! It *was* a mark of sacrifice...and only a high priest could administer it! That came back to haunt me when the coroner told me we had another mark on another murder victim!"

She stared, suddenly gripping his upper arm tightly. "Another victim?...David, are you saying there's been another killing like those three kids? When did this happen?"

He shook his head, taking her hands, and holding them tightly. "Forget I said anything, can you, Sandy?...that's not for public knowledge. I don't know why, but I seem to always want to share everything with you." He took one hand , and softly touched her cheek. "Yes...there's been another murder like those three kids! I shouldn't be telling you *any* of this, but something tells me you need to know! I'm not telling you any details, but the murder happened about the same time as the kids. The coroner's pretty certain the same person, or persons, committed the second killing."

Sandra didn't say anything for a moment, than she just walked over to the steps of the large dais, and sat down on the second step. She bowed her head, covering her eyes with her hands. After a minute, she lifted her head, and looked up at David. He was surprised to see the tears rolling down the high cheekbones. He came to her, kneeling in front of her, and gently wiped the tears away with his thumb. "Say...what gives? Why the tears, hon?"

Holding onto his hand, drawing on the honest strength he radiated, she shook her head, trying to smile. "I'm sorry...it's just that I can't shake this feeling! It's one that scares me so much I can barely breathe! It's come over me, on and off, for the last two weeks now. With Beth's illness...David, I feel like there's something out there, just waiting to pounce! It's silly, I know...but I can't seem to shake it!"

He wiped the last of the tears away, then cupped one cheek with his large hand, his eyes warm and tender. "I don't want you to ever feel scared...about anything...when I'm around, Sandy. I promise you, as long as I'm able, I'll never let anything get close enough to harm you..." He grinned suddenly. "Unless it's me!"

She had to laugh, which was what he had wanted from her. She shook her head, touched by his concern. "So...*you're* the only one who can get close to me, huh? Don't you think that's just a tiny bit presumptuous, Lt. Collison?"

He turned serious, looking into the crystal blue depths that had entranced his soul since their first meeting. "No...just being honest! Give me enough time, and I'll prove it to you!" Feeling a little uneasy at speaking such a declaration aloud, he released her hand, and stood up. He looked down at her, sitting there, then looked away. He really hadn't intended letting any of his deep feelings come out right then.

David walked back to the altar stone, and ran his hand over the grainy surface, thinking. "The chief is convinced that what we're working with is a group of religious fanatics…like the Satanists we ran into about three years ago! They didn't commit any murders like this time, but they caused a hell of a lot of damage, and more than just a couple assaults! I just wish I could figure what out what triggered all of this now! I've checked with other precincts, here in Denver, and a few of the surrounding states…but nothing similar seems to be happening in any of them. Why here?…in Denver, of all places!" His rugged face showed all the frustration he was feeling. "I wish I was more familiar with this kind of stuff!…that's why I've been coming out here!" He glanced at her, suddenly aware of how that sounded. "Well, maybe, at first it was!…not now!"

Sandra slowly stood up, stepped down from the dais' steps, and walked to join him by the altar. "David, I said I would help you wherever I could…one thing you have to always remember is this: To the ancients, a sacrifice wasn't viewed in the same light as a murder! All over the world, in nearly every historical era, you'll find evidences of blood sacrifices…animals, *and* human! The peoples who practiced this were *not* mindless, blood-thirsty savages! They were, for the greater percentage, deeply religious persons who truly believed in the rightness, and the sacredness of their actions!"

He shook his head, finding it all fascinating, and appalling all in the same instance of time. "I can't help but wonder when it started that way…someone had to have made the first decision to shed blood as part of a religious ceremony. Who were they?…when did they even dare to think about sacrificing a human being? If blood had to be included, why not stick with animals? But, I guess I keep thinking the same thing…why blood at all?"

She spread her hands, and shrugged her shoulders. "I'm not an anthropologist, so I can't give you a cultural reason, David. I'm not even sure an anthropologist, or an archaeologist could really answer that!...or at least, agree on the reasons they would bring up as possible. I do think, however, that their religions, myths, and legends can give us a very good basis to start finding the answers!"

"Like the story you told me about Isis, Osiris, and Set?" He grinned at the surprised expression on her face. "See...I can remember things!"

"So I see...anyway, as I was saying...there's a great deal of information to be gleaned from their beliefs, and stories. Remember when I told you a little about the god Set?...that's a perfect example of what I'm saying." She nodded towards the altar.

"What do we get from that?...other then how *not* to win friends, and influence people?" David gazed at the symbol Sandra had shown him earlier that stood for Set...a wolf's head.

"Well...this is strictly a personal interpretation you understand...but I think a lot of it shows they held a similar belief in good and evil, like we do today. As Christians, we hold a belief in a being called the Devil...I think, to the Egyptians, Set became their version of the Devil! There have been writings that stated Isis was the contemporary of Mary, and Horus was her Son! It's an ages old story that I feel is still very active in the here and now!...good versus evil, light against the dark. Set, representing all the terrible evils and perversions the darkness can hold, is the Egyptian equivalent of Satan, the fallen angel. Osiris, Isis, and Horus, along with a few others like Thoth, Ptah, Hathor, and so on...represent the side of goodness and light, their version of Christ, the prophets, and the apostles. Eternal life versus servitude in Hell!"

"I can't remember...didn't you say this Set had blood sacrifice?" He never ceased to be amazed by the wealth of knowledge she possessed.

"Yes...probably more than most." She bent over, and gently picked up one of the unbroken vessels sitting around the altar stone. "Vessels, such as this one, were used to collect the blood...which was used later in more secret ceremonies in the deep sanctuaries of the temple."

David touched the exquisite alabaster vessel. "Hard to believe something so pretty could be used for such a grisly task! The chief wasn't surprised at the idea of these perps being religious fanatics...he always says the dirtier the deed, the crazier the doer! I guess sacrificing human beings for the worship of a god carved from stone...or the Devil himself would definitely be a nomination for insanity!"

"Why do we always jump to the conclusion that religious zealots are insane? It's a well-documented fact that the most zealous leaders in history were extremely intelligent, and totally focused on their beliefs! Their sanity may be as sound as yours, or mine...the greatest danger from such people is their absolute commitment to what they belief to be the right, and true way to worship their god, whoever it may be, and see his religion grow into the only true worship!" Sandra had never been able to understand why everyone, herself included, always chose to believe the worst instead of trying to see all possibilities in the world's peoples. "The irony of history is always so sad...some of the worst atrocities committed by one culture against another...or one on one...have been in the name of religion! Everyone believes their religious beliefs to be the right one, and the only one! And Heaven help anyone who says differently!" She shook her head, a terrible sadness deep within her.

"I don't think my chief is going to agree with your views, Sandy...he's a staunch Catholic, and makes no bones about his church being the only one that counts! He's always spouting...say, how did this turn into a debate on religion?" David scowled in mock anger. "All that stuff's past history...hasn't got anything to do with today! I really don't see , no matter how interested I may be, knowing all that is going to help solve a murder today! There has to be a better explanation, Sandy!"

She took his arm, shaking it a little to make him listen. "Don't you understand?...it's *not* just in the past! My family has known, for generations, that there is little difficulty in locating peoples who still live by the old ways...practice the beliefs of their ancestors, who died thousands of centuries ago! In every country...no matter how modern, or technologically advanced...the practitioners of the ancient ways can always be found, if you only know where to look! If you want to stretch a point, the three major religious faiths in the world today...Islam, Christianity, and Judaism...are carry-overs from several centuries ago. But...I'm really referring to the really ancient sects...the Mayans, the Incas, the Atzecs...their descendants still hold to the old ways, even though they're Christians. In Africa, the multi-deity cultures are rich with the legacy from times beyond written history. I could give you a hundred more examples...but it all comes down to the same point...the old ways are not dead!"

David pointed at the altar, eyes wide, and jaw set. "You're trying to tell me that these kind of things happen today? Sandy...how can anyone believe in something that's made from stone, and has the head of an animal? They'd have to be crazy!...or ignorant!"

She shook her head...she thought he had started to understand. "David, you just don't understand. It's not up to you, or me...or anyone to say that how a person worships, or what they believe in is all wrong!...even if it's a religion long thought vanished! It shouldn't be so hard for you to believe that...those Satanists you mentioned? The religion they adhere to is one that has been around since the days of the ancients. It may not have been called by the names it is today...but it existed as much as the pyramids, and has lasted in the same way! The same goes for the truly ancient faiths, David...and their practitioners use the same words, and rites that those priests of long ago used."

He stared at her, then shrugged his shoulders in defeat. "Sorry, Sandy...I was being a bit of a jerk! I've never had to think about things like this before, and I'm not sure what to think now! It's all so...so unreal!"

She understood what he was trying to say, and that he was baring his innermost feelings to her...something, she suspected, he seldom allowed himself. She stepped closer to him, wanting to return that kind of trust. "Sometimes lately…I've found myself wondering about the ancient rituals…wondering if there wasn't more truth in their words, and actions than the experts today realize! Especially the rites, and prayers they performed to protect themselves against evils!"

He reached out, gently taking her by the shoulders, and turning her so he could see her face. "Why?…what was so special about those?"

Low and quiet, her voice nonetheless seemed to be coming to his ears from every corner of the room, evoking echoes in his mind…of past events, so long ago, he never realized he held the memory within himself. "Powers of darkness, and evil…the things we call the Devil, and his minions. I believe, with all my heart and soul, that true evil is very much a reality, and the powers of darkness ever present! People today tend to shrug such things off…putting them down to over-active imaginations. They say that the movies, TV, and the media are responsible for all the bizarre, and terrible things that have happened in recent years. They say that such things are just creations, in stories and legends, that were made up to scare children, and the weak-minded…to keep them in line so they didn't disobey!" Sandra looked up at his tired, tense face. "The real problem is far more complex, David…and yet, so simple! The ancients truly believed…no matter who, or what was their governing deity…their faith in that god, and the beliefs that went along with it, was complete! Today, the number of truly faithful persons is small…and that's why our world is poised on the brink! We believe more in self, science, and technology than something purely spiritual! Don't get me wrong…science and technology are necessary ingredients to our world, and some of them are only hope for cures, peace, an end to hunger, etc. But…there *has* to be the spiritual factor as well, David! For our 'armor' against evil to be failsafe, there has to be spiritual belief!…total, absolute faith, David! The ancients had it…and they survived!…even if only in memory! We don't really have it today…and I fear for *our* survival! I fear we give evil too many opportunities to find that chink in our 'armor'!"

He shook her a little, smiling tenderly at her. "Come on now…you're saying what's going on here today is a battle between good, and evil? Kind of corny, don't you think?"

She pulled away from his grip on her shoulders, irritated by the tone of condescension in his voice. "Don't treat me like a child, David! What I'm talking about is true!…and I'm not alone in feeling that way! Tell me, Mr. Police lieutenant…you have a better idea?"

He bent his head a moment, then looked up at her again. "No…no, I don't! I will tell you this, though…I am beginning to believe that whoever, or whatever, we're after here is like nothing we've ever come up against before! That thought scares the crap out of me, Sandy…but it's not going to keep me from doing my job! The only certainty I have right now, where any part of this case is concerned is this fact: I have to find this killer, or killers, and make sure they're put away for a very long time, if not forever! If I don't…well, I don't want to think about that possibility!" He smiled, a trifle lopsided.

She looked at him, knowing he'd leave nothing unturned, or untouched in his pursuit of the truth. She could feel the determination oozing from him…he would bring these ruthless killers to justice, or die trying! That thought caused shudders to course throughout her form, and she gripped both his arms tightly. "You be careful, do you hear me? Don't try to be the hero in this, David! I don't think I could stand anything happening to you, too!"

He pulled her up tight against him, liking the way her body seemed to mold itself so perfectly to his. He stroked her hair, leaning his chin on the top of her head, rubbing it gently against the fragrant softness. "Take it easy, honey. This is one cop who always makes sure nobody gets a piece of his hide!" He lifted his head, and looked down into those intoxicating blues. "Kind of nice to know you'd care, though." His voice was husky, though he was trying hard to hide the emotions he was feeling.

Her eyes were bright with unshed tears. "Of course I care!...don't you know that by now? What did you think I was getting at?"

Looking down at her, feeling her secure within his arms, David felt all that he'd kept hidden inside come surging to the front...threatening to explode. He tightened his arms around her, and bent his head over hers, seeking the softness of her lips. At first, the kiss was gentle, warm...filled with first discovery, first expression. Then, it began to deepen as the guards they'd both erected slowly fell, one by one. He felt a sense of exaltation growing within his heart as he felt Sandra returned his kiss, matching his intensity with her own fire.

Her arms slipped around his neck, and her slender body arched closer up, and into the lines and curves of his. David could feel his senses begin to swim...he wanted to take her right now, right there! His grip on her lithe form tightened, pulling her even closer...he wanted their bodies to melt into each other. He wanted this to never end...to go on through eternity, with her ever in his arms. Then, with a smothered gasp, he pulled his head back, and pushed her way, at arm's length. He saw her love, passion...and confusion, clean and honest on her shining eyes. He dropped his hands from her arms, steeping back, shaking his head.

Sandra didn't understand...she could see the desire, the hunger in his eyes. Why had he pushed her away? "David...what's wrong? Why did you push me away? Did...did I do something wrong?"

"No!...of course not! And...I'm making sure *I* don't, either!" He took a deep, somewhat shaky breath...he had to try, and make her understand. "Look, Sandy...in a short period of time, you've become a very important part of my life!...in a very special way! I don't want anything, especially me, to spoil that in any way!" He could still she the confusion in her eyes. "Sweetheart, if you were any other woman, I wouldn't hesitate taking you right now!...right here! And, I'll be honest...it's taking every ounce of self-control I have to keep from doing that this very minute!" He bent his head, gritting his teeth. "This may sound corny, and I'm probably going out on a very shaky limb here, but...when something *does* happen between us, I want everything to be just right!...can you understand, and accept that?"

She stepped into his body again, hiding her face against the leather jacket he was wearing. The scent of the leather, and the clean herbal cologne David was wearing sank deep into her nose, completing their connection. Her voice came to his ears, muffled against his chest, but still audible. "I *do* understand, David...and I feel so flattered, so utterly blessed!" She lifted her head up, an unmistakable twinkle in her eyes. "Of course, I'll wait until you feel it's right...however, I don't promise that *I* won't try anything!"

He groaned a little, feeling her move against him. He had this very bad feeling that there were going to be a lot of cold showers in his near future. "Mercy, please, Sandy!...come on, honey...give me a break!"

She his her smile as she snuggled deeper into the circle of his arms. She thought of how much he'd come to mean to her...the devastation if she were to lose him. She moved against him, grinning suddenly at the low gasp she heard. "I guess I can think about it!" She couldn't quite hide the giggle in her voice.

He was about to say something when the sharp ring of the phone cut into the warm atmosphere of the room. Sighing, Sandra broke the embrace, and walked over to where the hidden phone was kept. After a few moments of quiet conversation, she hung the phone up, and came back to where he stood, slowly and thoughtfully. She stopped in front of him, and looked up. "That was Roland...he just took a phone call from Tamara Dresden. They're about to leave London, on their private jet, and will be here in a few hours."

He wanted to say something...he could feel her pain. Instead, he took her in his arms again, and held her tight. He hoped contact with him would take her mind from the fear for her sister. He suddenly had this very strange feeling, and was suddenly afraid...for her, and for all of them!...

****

VII

❀

.......While this exchange between Sandra and David was taking place, Garalynn was hard at work, in her condo in mid-town Denver. She looked at all the papers, and books spread all over the desk, coffee table, and scattered on the large sofa. She rubbed her eyes, more tired then she could ever remember being, and sighed. She'd been poring over all this for over four hours…her head ached, and her neck was stiff.

She muttered to herself, pushing some of the papers away from her. "This is utter madness!…going through all this just because of some wild dream! I don't even know what I'm trying to find!"

She leaned back in her chair, stretching her arms high over her head, trying to get some of the stiffness out of her back. She thought back over the past few nights, to the unexplained dream she'd had every night, and shivered involuntarily. She closed her eyes, putting her head back against the headrest.

For the past few nights, she had vivid dreams…of a golden hawk, a golden lioness, and two glittering eyes shrouded in darkness. She knew they were somehow all connected, and it was her task to find that unknown connection. She always seemed to hear a deep voice, in her mind, telling her that it was up to her…she had to find the key that would save them all! But…what key? And, what was it a key to?

She come home this afternoon, tired and wanting nothing more than to sleep. It seemed as though she'd hardly lain down, on the sofa, before she was once more in the throes of the dream. When she'd finally awakened, it was with a strong sense of danger, and urgency. She'd gone to the university library, and checked out some books...wondering how she knew what books to look for. She was going to figure this all out...though she wasn't sure what it was she was trying to figure out.

She'd returned to her residence, and started going through the volumes she'd selected, searching for something she wasn't sure about. A fact soon became evident to her, as she leafed through all the pages of Egyptian legend, and religious practices...she became convinced that she'd known all this before...long before. How was that possible, she asked herself. What she knew, she knew through her family's interests in such things, and her sister, Sandra's, obsession with history. But, some of what she'd read went even beyond Sandra's knowledge...so where had she picked this all up?

With a sigh, she leaned forward, resting her elbows on the desk top. "Whatever it is that I'm supposed to be looking for, I sure wish it would make itself known! Dear God...make this all go away! I'm losing whatever sanity I have left!"

She'd no sooner uttered those few words when a tremendous wave of feeling swept over her senses. She reached for a volume she'd shoved aside. This one dealt with translations from the Book of the Dead, and the Papyrus of Ani. She leafed through it quickly, stopping when she reached the section that discussed the prayers necessary for a soul to speak to the gods when in the lower world. She sat back, arms on either side of the open book. She closed her eyes, and suddenly heard a voice intoning the words she'd just read. It was her voice, speaking a language she'd never known before, and speaking it with a familiarity that bespoke prior knowledge of such a language. She wanted to stop...get up, and leave. Instead, her voice went on, growing in volume...reaching out, beyond the room, beyond this world...reaching for things long past, and yet to come.

As she finally finished the words, a silence fell over the room, and she felt the presence of another in the room, with her. She opened her eyes, and looked around where she was sitting...there was no one! Then, a voice began to speak...that same deep voice that awakened echoes of the past. "Very well done, my sister...thy power has not been dimmed by the long years. Fear not...thy sanity is ever intact. Thy safety, and that of thy loved ones, is not so blessed, I fear. The darkness is close, my sister...its fingers reach out to grasp all that thee holds most dear! Listen well to my words, and stiffen thy spirit, Death's touch is too close! What lies before thee, and thine, will require all the strength, courage, and power thou possesses!"

Garalynn shoved the chair backwards, knocking it over in her haste to stand. In a state of near panic, she whirled around, searching the entire room with her eyes. She was still alone in the room, but the voice still spoke, clean and precise. She knew her doors, and the windows were secure...she'd locked them before she started reading. Had she really heard that voice?...or was her mind finally surrendering its hold on reality.

She clenched her fists, getting angry. "Look...I'm getting very fed up with this crap! Enough is enough! This asinine joke has gone too far too long! Who is responsible for this?"

There was the soft echo of a deep sigh, than a low chuckle. In slow, even tones, the rich low voice began speaking again. "There is no time for hysterics, my sister...the danger is all too real! I am real as well! Look behind thee!"

She turned slowly, looking into her living room. At first, there was nothing...then, faintly at the start, she saw a small nimbus of light begin to grow. It spread out, reaching the size of a volleyball, outshining any of her lights. Garalynn approached it, slow and cautious...intrigued as well as fearful of what it could portend. She looked closely, for any signs of hidden electric lines, switches, etc. She'd been a lawyer long enough to know a lot of the tricks con artists used to confuse their "marks". She saw nothing...save the gently undulating sphere of light.

She reached her hand towards it, feeling the gentle warmth that came off it. It was a warmth that was oddly compelling...soothing. The longer she gazed at it, the less she feared it. She felt herself becoming relaxed inside. She didn't drop her guard completely, preferring to stay very alert. Her fingers went through the ball of light...connecting with nothing that was solid...yet her fingers told her she had touched something incredible.

"Is that not better? Now thy eyes will have a frame of reference, I believe thee would call it. Put fear from thy mind...all will be made clear, in a way that will leave thee with no doubts of any kind!"

Garalynn pulled her hand back. "This isn't possible!...there's no such thing as...ghosts?"

"In point of fact, using the definitions of thy world, I am not exactly a ghost, or spirit! They are both supposed to be deceased...I am not! The words that thou read...they allowed my mind to converse with thee. My body lies quite a ways from where thou are at this moment in time. I have been attempting to contact thy mind for several days now, but couldn't really use a true voice. All I was able to accomplish was the implanting of things thee has seen in thy dreams!"

Garalynn looked around again, still not sure she wasn't being tricked. She didn't want to accept a supernatural explanation, either. "Who...or what, are you? What do you want with me? More to the point...*why me?*"

"I desire only thy continued safety, and long life. My sister...thee must listen well to my words, and take the necessary actions. The time grows short, and the dangers ever greater!"

Garalynn suddenly realized something...she recognized this voice! It was the same one that had warned her that day, in the forest, when they had seen the police in that clearing near the cabin. "You said you haven't been able to speak to me before today…but that's not true! You spoke to me once before…in the woods by the cabin!"

"Think back…it was not speech, such as this we share now…my words registered in your mind that day. The speaking of minds is easier, and faster…but the duration of accessibility is of a far shorter time! This way…no restraints." The disembodied voice was calming, and unhurried. "Thou must learn to curb any further impatience…thrust away any doubts! Thou must learn silence, and acceptance!"

She put one hand to her temple, feeling a little unsteady, with a slight pain in her head. "I don't believe I'm doing this!…standing in my own living room, talking with a bouncing ball of light! This has to be some sort of dream!" She lowered her hand, and looked back to the desk, half expecting to see herself sitting on the chair, sound asleep, and dreaming. "That's got to be it…this *has* to be a dream!"

There was another deep sigh. "Thou are very much awake, and this is reality, my sister! Listen well…there is a task that must be done, and done this very evening. The dark one will soon have his people among you again!"

Garalynn sat down on the sofa, her legs suddenly a little rubbery. "Tonight?…I don't think you have any idea how late it is! It's after six p.m…everything will be closed for the day! What do you want me to do?…or get?"

"Thy mind lives with only one concept of what Time truly entails! To those that truly know, Time's possibilities cannot be measured. Go to thy family's home, to the room of history…seek thy sister out, and have her help you find the fourth key. It is within that locked room, and is known to be there by only one other person in this city of thine! I will tell thee where to look…and what to look for! Trust my words…as more time passes, thy mind will begin to find the answers within thyself. That will make this all easier…but, it will also make it more dangerous! Are thou ready?"

She stood up suddenly, throwing her hands up. "Sure! Why not? Hell…it might even be fun!" Her jaw set in a stubborn line. "Not!"

"Trust me…listen to my words. There is not the option to offer thee a full explanation at this precise moment! All eventually will be mad e clear…but, for now, a leap of faith is required, my sister!"

"No way…not until you answer a few more questions! Then…then I'll make my decision as whether, or nor, I decide to help you!" Garalynn felt she had to stand her ground.

The light moved until it was hovering just in front of her. "Sit down, and open thy mind. Relax…I will tell thee all that is needed…at this time! Thy spirit will soon break free of the fetters this time has placed upon thee, and doubt will never be a word spoken by thee again. Now, sit…lean back, close thy eyes, and listen well!"…….

…..Still half asleep, Sandra watched as Garalynn moved across the Tomb's vast space. She wondered what it was that seemed to be driving her adopted sister. Sandra yawned, putting her hand over her mouth, and thought back over the night's very hectic chain of events. It had started nicely, in late afternoon, when she learned just how David felt about her. Then, early this morning…the household had been awakened by the arrival of Tamara, and Sean. Sandra had talked very briefly with them, then told Roland to show them to their same rooms. She had just fallen asleep again when Garalynn had arrived, breathless, wide-eyed, and wired tighter than Sandra had ever seen her.

She cleared her throat. "Are you about ready to tell me what's going on here, Garalynn?…or, do I have to guess? What on earth is so vital that you have to comedown to the Tomb this early? Garalynn…will you stop poking around, and answer me?"

Slowly, the other woman turned, and faced Sandra. Sandra almost stepped back a pace, shocked, as she gazed into her sister's, and best friend's, eyes. These were not Garalynn's eyes!…rather, the piercing gaze of a stranger!

Slow and clear, Garalynn's voice broke through the haze of confusion in Sandra's mind. The low tones of her voice were almost regal, but somewhat distant. "I don't know where to start...to tell you everything that's happened to me in the past few hours. I know now that there's so much I never realized...couldn't begin to understand...before all this took place! Now, though...it's so clear that I can't see how I could have missed it! I wish I could tell you how...make you see what I do now, but there's not enough time! I only hope you'll come to understand, in time, and then forgive my abruptness!"

Sandra moved closer to the tall, nordic beauty, and looked directly into the incredibly bright eyes. "What is it that you know now that you didn't before, Garalynn?...tell me. What are you here for?"

Garalynn smiled slightly, knowing all the thoughts that had to be tumbling through Sandra's mind at that moment. "It's taken several hours for me to get a grasp on what was shown me, Sandra...right now, though, I do not have that same option with you!" She reached out, taking Sandra by the shoulders. "If you have ever trusted me, or believed in me before today...than do so, with all your heart, right now! I do know what I'm doing, Sandra...and what I'm after! Please...believe me, and don't ask me any further questions! Now...is what Roland told me true? Are Tamara, and Sean, here once again?"

"Yes...they arrived here about five-thirty this morning." Sandra glanced at her watch ring. "It's almost eight now...they'll be leaving for the hospital shortly...I guess Sean's very anxious to see Beth." Sandra put her hand over one of the two gripping her shoulders. "I'll trust you, Garalynn...as always! But, please...at least tell me what it is that brought you here so early! You look as though you haven't slept in days!"

Garalynn stepped back, breaking their connection, and smiled ruefully. "You're right...I haven't slept! I can't really tell you why I'm here, but I can show you!" With that strange pronouncement, she turned and walked towards the dais' steps. She went up the steps, to where the giant sarcophagus rested, Sandra close behind. Garalynn knelt by the side of the marble coffin, her fingers lightly caressing the smooth stone, rippling over the carved picture characters running along the bottom edge of the sarcophagus. When her fingers reached a large, jeweled carving of a seated bennu bird, with a solar disc on its head, they stopped…then pressed into the carving of the disc, hard and steady.

To Sandra's surprise, with a soft grating, a small drawer slowly slid out from the bottom of the sarcophagus, near its head. She continued to stare, bewildered, as Garalynn reached into the drawer, and pulled something out. Then, the lady lawyer pushed the drawer back into its hidden position, stood up, and turned to face her sister. She raised the object she'd removed from the drawer…Sandra saw that it was a small, leather pouch, tied closed with a ribbon of a strange, glittering fabric. "This is part of what I am after, Sandra…the rest I will retrieve later. This is going to protect, and save all of us! But, for now…I have to get going! It's essential I leave before anyone, other than you, knows I've been here…especially here, in the Tomb!"

Sandra couldn't grasp all this…things were moving too fast. "Why leave now?…and not letting others know?…what's that all about? Garalynn, what's in that bag that's so important? How did you know about that secret drawer? I don't think even father knew it was there! What is this?"

Garalynn's impatience to depart was becoming quite evident. She held the pouch up, shaking it a little, the dust dropping from its leather. "If you really trust me, like you said…ask me nothing! If you must see what is in here, then do so now! But, know this…if you see the contents, you put yourself, and Beth, in mortal danger! Your best safety, for the two of you, is in your ignorance of this! The choice is yours!"

Sandra wanted to gab that ominous pouch, and tear it open…but an inner voice told her to listen to Garalynn, do what she requested, and trust in her. She gazed at the other woman, her expression calming, and she slowly shook her head. "No…I do trust you, and I'll let this pass. But, Garalynn...I fully expect a complete explanation later, do you understand?"

Garalynn stepped into her, hugged her tightly, then hurried towards the door. As she reached the twin doors, she looked back. Seeing Sandra still standing upon the dais, she raised one hand, waved, and left. Sandra had watched her leave, not speaking a word, not making a move to stop her. She felt a cold wind sweep over her...a wind she'd felt several times before now, and it always meant trouble. She hoped it wouldn't be too long before Garalynn explained all this. She'd wait for her sister, and friend, to give her the answers...but, not *too* long!

She sighed, feeling like everything about her world was beginning to go into a tailspin. Why had Garalynn been so intense that she almost seemed a stranger? Why did she feel like Garalynn's presence here this morning had been some kind of warning?...but, about what?

With a groan, she put her hands to her temples, trying to press away the sudden throbbing there. She drew a deep breath, rubbing her temples, allowing the motions to distract her thoughts, albeit briefly. When the pain eased, she dropped her hands, opening her eyes with another sigh. She'd think about this later...right now, she needed to get ready to go to the hospital, then on to the firm's main offices. It was still somewhat dark outside, but she knew the sun would be up fully in about an hour...she wanted to be on her way by that time.

She walked out of the room, locking everything as she went. She couldn't get Garalynn, and her odd behavior out of her mind. She hoped everything was going to be all right with Garalynn...she didn't want another sister to worry over!.......

.......Garalynn drove her Porsche Turbo along the twisting, turning mountain road, at high speed, handling the powerful car like a seasoned professional. Her eyes never left the pavement ahead, the twin beams of the car's headlights cutting through the gray dawn like double silver knives. She'd left Blackmoon, and the city, far behind...heading for the private road that wound its way through the forest, to the family's cabin compound.

She had almost asked Sandra to come with her...that would have been a very big mistake. Sandra's place was with Beth right now...not serving as an emotional bolster to Garalynn's faltering spirit. In her heart, she knew that it was not the right time for Sandra to be given *all* the answers. The stage had been set, so to speak...all the players were in place, awaiting their predestined cues. It was too late foe changes...simply time for the "play" to go on as it was always meant to do.

She gripped the steering wheel, knuckle white with the force of her hold. Her foot pressed harder down on the accelerator, and the turbo-engine car seemed to leap forward in a surge of speed as its powerful motor shifted gears into over-drive. The wheels appeared to barely skim over the pavement, hugging each turn with precision, and strength.

Spotting the familiar turn-off, Garalynn whipped the wheel hard to the right, and the car spun off the main highway, and onto the paved road that led to the cabin. About twenty minutes later, she brought the car to a stop inside the cabin area. The dawn was almost fully realized as she got out of the car, and approached the cabin itself. She took a breath of the cool, fresh morning air. Then, she punched the security code in, and opened the door. As she entered the hallway of the spacious cabin, she reset the alarm codes, and shut the door. She headed for the den, slipping off her jacket, and tossing it over the back of one of the easy chairs as she passed it. She walked over to the fireplace, and checked to see if the gas was still turned on...it was. She flipped a hidden switch, and the fireplace came to life with a soft "whoosh". The flames played in the cool air, doing a graceful dance as they flickered about. Garalynn turned, and sat down in the chair nearest the fire, watching the flames' movements for a few minutes.

She looked up as she heard the sound of the back door opening. She twisted around in the chair, and looked up as two men entered the room, guns out, and a large German Shepherd straining on a leash. They stopped when they saw Garalynn.

"Ms. Gagnon?...sorry, ma'am. We thought we had a break-in...no one told us any of the family would be coming up here so late in the year!" The security guard put his gun away, as did his partner. "Is everything all right, ma'am?"

She smiled softly. "Everything's fine, Tim...I just needed the privacy...to work out some tricky details on a case. I'm sorry if I alarmed everyone...I honestly forgot to let anyone know I'd be in the cabin! Sorry."

"No problems...we'll reset everything on our way out. Buzz us if you need anything...remember, the caretaker's cabin is only a few hundred feet away." The guard nodded, then he and his partner left, dragging a very anxious dog with them...the animal clearly wanted to stay.

Garalynn turned back to the fire, watching the play, the give and take of color in the flames. She thought back over everything that had happened, in the past few weeks, and especially the past few hours. Strange how so short a span of time could so irrevocably alter the lives of so many individuals! It seemed that the stability that been the mainstay of her life the past few years was now just a vision from the past.

She slipped from the chair, kneeling on the plush rug directly before the fireplace itself. She had always loved this particular article...her real father had given it to Richard Phelps as a gift so many years ago. Touching it somehow kept the connection with her dead parent. She shifted around, until she was sitting on the rug. She brought her knees up, resting her chin on them, hugging her arms about them. Closing her eyes, she felt unbidden tears begin coursing their way down her cheeks. Dashing them away with her hand, she angrily told herself that this was neither the time, or place for this...but, the tears wouldn't stop. She cried, for all the times she hadn't in the past few weeks...and for all the pain, and fear she knew lie ahead!

Finally, the flood of tears abating, she straightened up, and wiped the tears from her face. She had things to do. Getting up from the floor, she went to the well-stocked western-styled mahogany bar, and poured herself a generous snifter of brandy. Then, she went back to the chair by the fire. She sat down, gently cradling the snifter in her hands, watching the dark amber liquid swirl around in the crystal container. She drew her legs up, tucking them to one side. She sipped the brandy, letting its warming qualities seep through her tired, tense body…easing the tensions.

When she finished the brandy, she sat the snifter down on the end table, and leaned back, closing her eyes. She was starting to feel the effects of the liquor, her breathing becoming slow, and deep…her senses beginning to swim. She began to feel as though her spirit was trying to detach itself from the form that housed it.

She began breathing even slower, deeper…willing her mind to let go. Where this knowledge of how to induce a meditative state came from, she didn't know…it was simply there. She was losing connection with the surroundings, entering a limbo, void of all sound, and touch.

She felt an uplifting of her spirit, as if she'd actually risen from her seat. Opening her eyes, she was surprised to find she *was* truly standing. Turning…she became a little uneasy, seeing herself still sitting in the chair, asleep. She realized she must be in the state called astral body…though, how she knew this was yet another unanswered mystery added to all the others. She turned back, facing towards the French doors that led onto the wide deck outside.

Moving forward, she seemed to weigh little, or nothing…like floating on the surface of an utterly calm lake. She reached for the door handles, only to see them open all by themselves. She passed through them, and out into the early dawn. She stood there, on the deck, feeling so many sensations from the air about her. Though the stars were fading, she could make them out so clearly…as if night were still in full state.

She looked around her. It was all so familiar...yet, so odd. The wind seemed to not only caress her skin, but to actually go right through her body. She was aware of every sound, and scent present in the area around the cabin...and, in some strange way, she was part of everything she sensed. She should have been chilled...the wind was coming directly from the north, off the already snow-capped mountains. Instead, she was very comfortable. She felt a small "tug" at the back of her head, near the occipital bone, and cocked her head in an effort to pinpoint the odd sensation. She looked at the mountains, looming still black in the rising sun. The feeling seemed to be telling her that these same mountains were where she had to go now.

Garalynn spread her arms wide open, and let the wind swirl about her, lifting her gently into the air. It gathered her up, like a lover's gentle arms, and bore her swiftly up to the mountains. It was as effortless as an eagle's flight, coming to the foothills, and then swooping straight towards the Dark Eagle's Nest...the mountain of the Joshua Phelps story, and legend. She was a little surprised to see where she was headed, but she didn't feel any sense of fear, or apprehension.

She went ever higher...higher than anyone had ever gone on this ominous, and often treacherous peak. The "call" was much stronger now. She could almost make out words, and the odd sensation of a deep, throbbing accompaniment...the muted beating of great drums. She came to a large jumble of rocks, and loose debris, very close to the summit of the peak. Here, on a wide ledge, her strange journey came to an end. She stood there, looking around, awed. She looked back down the mountainside...the shadows of early dawn were still deep...she couldn't even make out the trees that surrounded the cabin. She reached out to touch the great boulders, only to see her hand pass through the solid granite like it was mere air.

She pulled her hand back, wondering where she was to go from this point. There didn't seem to be any paths to follow...or a cave to enter. Then, the "call" came once again, and she found herself stepping into the face of the boulder itself before her mind had time to protest that this action would only get her a broken nose! To her shock, it was like diving into water, and about as difficult as swimming for a professional. She moved through the cold stone until the granite dropped away, and she found herself in a dark, dank tunnel. Her eyes, in this state, seemed extremely sensitive…for instance, she was able to perceive, even in the darkness, that this tunnel was not a natural formation. Hands other than nature's had fashioned it. She went forward, seeking the source that was calling her…guiding her. Finally, she entered a vast cavern, and stopped there, surprised at how bright it was there.

It was a natural cathedral, awesome in its measurements. On either side of where she now stood, out of the tops of tall rock protrusions, were burning lights…like natural gas geysers, yet glowing with an unearthly brilliance. They gave off neither smoke, or odor…neither did they emit the crackle natural flames did when one was close to them…they simply shone. The stalactites sparkled as though encrusted with millions of tiny jewels, some of them so long that they joined with their compatriot stalagmites, forming huge pillars of a majesty surpassing anything man-made.

Slowly, Garalynn walked forward, letting the silence of this place take hold of her, pushing away any lingering doubts, or fears. She looked from side to side as she went deeper towards the center of the cavern. She knew she'd never been ion such a place before…and yet, it was so familiar. When she reached the central area of the stone room, Garalynn stopped, gazing at a stone formation that made her think of the dais back in the Tomb. She could see signs that its natural shape had been enhanced, and polished by the skilled hands of Man. She reached out unconsciously, and was surprised when she could actually *touch* the smoothed stone. She drew her hand back, and that was when she saw the scattered piles of bones on the other side of the dais. She paled a little, not really having been mentally prepared for something like that. She shook herself, collected her focus, and looked closer, trying to determine the source of the bones. She saw scraps of rawhide…a few arrows…a shattered bow…three knives, and at least four flintlock pistols, two in such mint condition a collector would have died in ecstasy. Obviously, she thought…there had been visitors to this spot in days gone past. She wasn't as good as Sandra at gauging the age of things…but she was certain that these were artifacts from a few hundred years ago.

Garalyn stepped closer to the dais. She ran her hands over the polished top…it felt so strange…cool to the touch, but smooth and soft as velvet. The top was perfectly smooth, and unblemished…that fact made her feel much better inside. Its shape had made her think of an altar stone, and she knew what transpired on top of a lot of ancient altar stones. She looked closer, searching for signs that the ceremonies she despised had been performed there…the sight of the bones had prompted such thoughts. To her great relief, there was nothing to indicate any such rites were consecrated upon the smooth surface.

As she was leaning on the edge of the altar stone, she was surprised as it tipped, almost making her fall. She bent closer, tugging on the stone with both hands…it moved every time she tugged. She could see now that it was actually some kind of lid, covering the base of the shaped altar…there was an opening she could fit three fingers into. She straightened up, looking for something to serve as a lever. It had become important that she see what this stone covered.

She searched all around the cavern, but was unable to find anything that would be strong enough to force that lid up. She'd found an old lance, but she knew the age of the wood would never stand up to the weight of the stone. She returned to the altar, and stood there, staring at it. She noticed, for the first time, that there was tiny engraved characters along the sides of the base stone…and they looked inlayed in gold! Garalynn frowned…this definitely meant someone had been in this cave, and was probably responsible for all that was in it. But…she couldn't figure out…why here? And why was there evidence, that even her inexperienced eyes could tell, of an ancient culture that originated in an area of the world several thousand miles from this spot?

Garalynn stepped back, suddenly not at all certain she wanted to know any of the answers to her questions. She wasn't the impassioned amateur archaeologist Sandra was, but she'd picked up enough to recognize one, or two of the markings on the altar. The presence of these marks made her both uneasy, and oddly comforted. She stepped back, beginning to wonder why she was here. What had she been thinking, anyway? Why had she allowed herself to follow a disembodied voice's impassioned instructions? She looked down at her body, seeing the shimmering quality her flesh had now…and the unreal feeling to everything around her. How could any of this be?

A sudden wave of panic swept over her. "God…I'm losing it! This has to be some sort of nightmare! I've got to be dreaming all this!…back at the cabin!" She clasped her hands to both sides of her head, muttering…there had to be a way to wake up, to regain the reality she was used to. It was then that she became aware of a heaviness around her neck…a weight that she didn't recall being there before.

She put her hand slowly to her throat, her fingers tracing along a heavy metal chain that encircled her neck, and hung down between her breasts. She looked down, puzzled. Her hand cupped the unknown object, and lifted it up. It was an amulet, made from gold, and formed to resemble a large scarab…a sacred image from Egyptian antiquity. The detail work, inlays of electrum and lapis, was delicate, precise, and astounding. It really looked like the actual insect. She turned it over, recalling something she'd heard Richard Phelps remark about such amulets. In their use as a source of protection, they frequently would have this potent power enhanced by a carved text, or scene, on their undersides. Sure enough…the underside of this golden scarab bore many minute, though clear, carved hieroglyphic symbols. She couldn't decipher the entire message, of course…merely a word, here or there.

She fingered the amulet, wondering where it had come from...was this what had been in that bag? When had she removed it?...and why, all of a sudden, couldn't she remember any of the words that had been spoken to her? As she continued to handle the amulet, her memory suddenly kicked back into gear. This *was* what had been contained within that pouch she'd removed from the Tomb. Somehow, before she'd begun this odd quest, she had removed the amulet, and slipped it about her throat. It was the key that had brought her to this spot...to do what she'd always been destined to do. Prompted again by her recollected memories, Garalynn removed the heavy chain, and wrapped it about her left wrist, holding the amulet itself in the palm of her left hand. She stared at the writings on the scarab's underside, willing herself to read them. Slowly, her mind moving like the tumblers of a safe's lock, letter by letter...the symbols resolved themselves into words in her mind...the words into chants, and prayers.

In what seemed forever, but was in truth but a few minutes, she had successfully translated the entire text. The ancient picture writing was becoming as simple to read as the English she'd used every day of her life. She stood to her fullest height, holding the scarab over her head. She began to speak the words written on the scarab, but in a language she'd never heard before! Her voice gathered strength with each word, reaching into every nook, and cranny of the stone room. It awaken echoes of the cavern's past, from times long vanished into the limbo of mankind's collected memories. There was an aura of power building in the cave...gathering its strength into a crescendo of tangible energy. Her words ended, the last one still a ringing echo in the cavern, and she brought her arm down, suddenly very tired, and drained. She drew a deep breath, waiting...for what she really wasn't too sure.

Then...a calm, deep voice reached out to her, embracing her with the warmth of its tones, and the strength of its depth. "Well done, my beloved sister...it is enough! The first of thy tasks has been accomplished!"

She turned, feeling the presence of another behind her. To her great surprise, a man stood just behind her, smiling gently at her. She stepped back, bumping into the altar stone. She knew she'd never seen him before...she'd have remembered someone who looked like this man! Yet...he had that inexplicable aura of familiarity about him.

He smiled again, stepping closer to her. He held out a hand to her, and she slowly took it, feeling the solid strength, and warmth it radiated. She looked up at him, puzzled but unafraid. He nodded, pleased that she didn't draw away from him, or still seemed frightened.

"There is much within thy mind...questions beyond number that need to be put at rest! Be patient, my sister...I will answers all, and soon."

Garalynn gazed at him, feeling so at peace. He was the tallest man she'd ever met in her lifetime. And, to look into his eyes was like gazing fully into the sun itself, light radiating from them as he smiled down at her. His skin was a dark hue, like a deep bronze tan, but with the tactile appearance of crushed velvet. It seemed to shimmer...she started as she remembered that both Tamara, and Sean had similar characteristics to their skin as well. His features were classic, flawless, and well-balanced. His physique was like a Greek statue brought to life, clean and powerful lines in perfect symmetry. She was sure he had to be the handsomest man she'd ever been fortunate enough to meet.

His dress was also far from common. His broad chest was bare, save for a golden pectoral formed into twin wins, open as if in flight, touching the top of each shoulder with the golden plumes. About his neck, hanging down to the top of the pectoral, was a silver ankh, with a large rough-cut cabochon of feldspar at the crosspieces of the ankh itself. He was clad in a simple, though elegant kilt, of pleated linen...each pleat tipped in gold leaf. The kilt was held in place with a wide belt of silver links, festooned with lapis lazuli...it hugged his trim waist snuggly. On the proudly-held head was a headdress, like ones worn by the ancient Pharoahs, of yellow linen with black striping. A black headband anchored the headdress to his forehead. In the center of this headband was the uraaeus...symbol of royalty, or godhood. This particular uraeus held a blue-white gem, secured between the figures of the cobra, and the vulture. Roughly triangular in shape, the jewel pulsed visibly with a cool light.

Without conscious thought, she reached towards that gem. As she touched it, it seemed to glow brighter at the contact, and she felt something pass from it to her, through her fingertips. She jerked her hand back, shaking her head to clear it from the sudden onslaught of thoughts, and memories. She looked at him. "Who are you? Why did you bring me here? What's this all about?" She swept her arm around, indicating the cavern, and what it held.

His smile widened, a glint of pleasure in the shining eyes. "To begin...in a very real sense, I am *not* here, nor are thou! Our *physical* forms are still where we left them...thine in the cabin below, and mine within the grips of this stone prison!" He pointed at the altar itself. "I have rested inside the cold embrace of this stone coffin for nearly two millenium! My spirit was awakened by certain events taking place outside this cavern...what exactly I will tell thee later! The words spoken here today are what was needed to allow my *ka* to appear before thee, as thy *ka* was freed to come here. Now, we can converse on a more normal plane."

"You call this a more normal plane? Let me tell you, your idea of normal, and mine, are worlds apart!" She stared at him. "You were the one who talked to my mind...in the woods, and my apartment...aren't you? Why? Just who *are* you?"

He lifted his noble head, gazing off into space, seeing things she couldn't. "Yes, I was the one whose voice thou heard. My *ba*, and *ka* have slumbered for such a long time...when I realized they had become active once again, then I knew certain things had been put into motion. I knew that my time of release was soon to be realized!"

Garalynn held up her hand. "Just a minute...just what is a *ba*, and a *ka*?"

"Simply put...a *ba* is a soul, and the *ka* is the vital force all living things possess, a spirit as it were...both gifts from the Creator." Came the quiet reply.

"So...what I'm talking to is the spirit form of a living being...right?" She asked, trying to settle everything in her own mind.

He nodded. "In thy terms, yes. Basically...the spirit form is the power of the mind...the vital force that animates life. The spoken word...written down in times long shrouded in darkness...gave voice to that force, and an energy created by those same words granted a form to that same force...that is the *ka*." He looked down at her from his impressive height, and smiled again. "It is very good to actually speak to another. It has been a very long time since last I conversed with one of thy kind!"

"How long?" She was getting used to this...how odd.

"Over a hundred and fifty of thy years...approximately. At first, I wasn't sure why I had awakened. The dark powers that had imprisoned me so long ago never intended for me to be able to use *any* of my powers with the outside world. I thought, at first, it was a sign my connection with the living realm was about to resume. Then, I realized it wasn't to be...their presence was so close, that all I could envision was more torments. That feeling also passed...my mind realized that *they* had very little, indeed, to do with my mind coming back from its long sleep. I am not certain yet what really did awaken me, but the fact remains I *am* awake again. Soon...I will once again take my place in the fight I am sworn never to concede!"

Garalynn was having a bit of difficulty grasping all that he was saying. "Just who was it that put you in that thing? Why would someone do such a thing to another living being?" She realized the irony behind her words. "But, then, you're not exactly the *usual* living being...are you? I mean...most people don't live over a hundred years, do they?...let alone, being imprisoned in stone, with no food, no water...no air?"

He could "see" the confusion in her mind...the doubts. "There are forces in this world that thou has no comprehension of yet, my sister!

Some of these forces are of such unspeakable evil that thy race could barely grasp the reality of their existence! Such forces were behind the reality that trapped me in this stone...as they have trapped, or destroyed, others! They seek to overcome that which is the salvation of all life...the Light we all are born from, and will return to one day! This evil is without scruples...remorse...seeking only that which will *serve* them best! These forces are in no way human, beloved sister...though they seek to enslave humanity, infusing the soul with a darkness that is total! Any means to an end...this is their credo. Any measure that will achieve their ultimate goal, that is acceptable!" He turned sideways, gazing at the stone altar. "Imprisonment was *not* the choice they held in mind for me...it was the one they were *obliged* to select! And...so they did, that fateful day more then a millenium ago!"

She frowned, placing a hand on his arm, feeling the hidden power emanating from the spirit from. "You've called me your sister several times now...what do you mean? I don't have any siblings, save for my adopted sisters. Besides...if what you've told me so far is true, and you *have* been trapped in that stone for almost two thousand years...there's no way we're related!"

He turned back to face her, touching her temple lightly with the fingertips of one hand. She felt something flow from those fingers, like an electric current...going deep into the farthest reaches of her mind. "Think back..." His voice was low. "Ever back...deeper than thee thought possible. Look into that hidden place all minds possess, dear one...the very core of all collective memory! The answers are there, waiting to be accessed...to be awakened!"

She gasped, feeling an odd sensation as her mind seemed to be tumbling backwards, at the speed of pure thought. She found herself in a time of memories she never knew she held within her mind. The memories were so clear...so real, it was almost a physical sensation! She opened her eyes after a few more moments, and gazed at his beautiful, calm face. There were bright tears in her eyes...a sense of awe, and joy in her soul.

He nodded, smiling with perfect understanding at the expression on her face. "I know...thou has seen with thy inner 'eye', and now some of thy memories have started to awaken as well. The rest...all that still sleeps...will soon come forth, and there will be no more doubts, no more questions!" He touched her cheek gently. "Thy world...thy upbringing...all these have caused the suppression of these memories. Every living creature possesses these thoughts...they are simply unaware of their existence. Thy world has a term...race memories. Few accept this as a reality, choosing to put the term down to misguided speculations. They do not know there is so much more to the concept...that, to open one's mind to this possibility, is to open a door to complete knowledge...complete awareness! Opening thyself...giving thyself a chance to join with these memories is granting thy soul connection with all living things! And, such a connection is that much closer to the Creator! It is all there, within thee! I will help as much as I am able, in this state...to fill in any gaps thy mind finds too difficult to call up, or accept!"

She touched his hands with an eagerness she'd never felt before. "Please...tell me now! I feel as though I've awakened from a long sleep! Tell me everything!"

He made her close her eyes again, than began speaking, very quietly. "To try, and *tell* it all would take more time than we have now. Allow me into all thy mind...to tap the power there. Then, thee will be able to see, and know all, within but a few heartbeats! Be silent now, and let thy mind open unto all it holds within it!".......

......"In the times of the dim beginnings, we were masters of all. Our homeland had been isolated from all other land masses since the great cataclysm that wrenched us from the others. In this aloneness, instead of stagnating, our race developed itself faster, swifter than the outside world…something experts would say was a miracle, that we should have been slower then the rest because of our isolation. I do not say they are wrong…I merely allow thy mind to see what truly transpired.

Our race began to evolve…to actually mutate away from what the outer world races were heading towards. We went in another direction altogether. We developed to a greater intellect, a greater technological level then thy world today has yet to reach! Our homeland became the center of the world…the hope of all living things. Thirty-three thousand years *before* Christ came into your world, we ruled as gods! The age of the demi-gods…that is what thy learned men today call that time. Thy history would begin to record our names, and the legends ascribed to us, some fifteen thousand years B.C.E. The Book of the Dead has reference to us. The Aztecs, Incas, and Maya had their legends of the divine race that taught, and ruled them. We were the absolute rulers of all! Our quest for power was unquenchable…but, this was also the time of our greatest shames! We had not always been thus, however…and that is where the history of this world really began to alter itself for the first time, when *we* allowed ourselves to change!

Once…ours was a race that had been truly blessed by the Creator. Our culture had reached a zenith of development even *we* had only *dreamed* possible. We'd overcome almost all sicknesses, of mind as well as of body! Physical imperfections had long been eliminated from our people…life expectancy was nearly immortal! There seemed to be nothing our scientists could not create…no problem for which they could not find a solution. The powers of our minds had evolved to such a degree that many were actually able to alter their shape, or appearance, with a single thought. This shape-shifting became a popular pasttime for those able to achieve such a degree of mental control.

We'd reached ever outwards with our minds, expanding the limits. The ability to communicate with a mere thought was common-place, as was the ability to move things, or envision the future…with a moment's concentration. We were at the pinnacle of our young adulthood...everything possible to us. Than, like so many since that time...we allowed ourselves to think forbidden thoughts...we erred!

Until this moment, we had been governed within our spirits by the force that we had worshipped as Creation itself! Never, no matter how powerful it seemed we were becoming, had we ever forgotten this, or failed to give the Creator the homage deemed right, and true. All that we were, all that we had become, or been given...all came from Him. This was primary among our all our laws! After all...even a 'god' must abide by a higher law!

First among those laws was that the supreme force in our lives *was* the one, and only Creator. To willingly harm another living thing, other than that which was necessary for food, was to go against all we'd been given...to go against the Creator itself. To desire more than one had already been given was to show the basest of ingratitude! To break any of the laws, deemed passed down from the Creator, was considered an act of defiance, and punishable by eternal banishment! We were His creations...even the oldest elder among us didn't clearly remember where, or when our race appeared...they only knew that the supreme force had caused our development, and had continued to guide, and succour, us until the day of reckoning arrived. If only that fact had stayed uppermost in our minds when that dark time came over our minds!

At this time, when all was possible...those selected as our leaders fell under the influence by something that had reached into our isolation...from the outer world. A tall stranger walked into our principle city-state, and we were never the same! His countenance was beyond words to describe...his voice, and words were like the purest ambrosia, holding within them the power to block our ears, and minds to those things that had always guided us. Even the oldest of laws, and beliefs, began being pushed aside for the doctrines, and promises he preached to us!

More and more, the leaders, and those about them, fell under the subtle spell of his words, the strength of his personality...the power of his will! He told us we *deserved* to be masters of the world, not just this little hole we'd built for ourselves. The Creator, he said, was jealous of our powers…our potential. We should go forward, he said…claim the rightful destinies…to rule the world, and all within it! We had viewed ourselves as a perfect race, held up by our Creator's hand…but, inside, we knew this was not so. There is nothing that is totally perfect!…to truly understand, and appreciate, all that one is, or has, there must be some small *imperfections* present. How does one ever hope to know what ultimate happiness can be…if you've never experienced loss, or failure? True…our level of failure was minute, but it was still a fact of life! And that fact had always caused us to honestly appreciate, and be thankful for all that we *did* have, or were able to do. We forgot that…it was pushed away, because he awakened the desire…the belief, within us, that we *were* the only ones who *could* accomplish world domination! He told us…made us see, and believe…that all we had was due to *our* hard work! It had been *our* personal efforts that had brought us to this pinnacle…not some unseen, untouched force! So, since it was *our* work that had brought us this far…why share it with someone, or something that we'd never seen among us?

As for the rest of the world…it was up to us to bring them out of their darkness, and teach them the *right* way to live, and believe! It would be for the greater benefits of their lives, he said…and their gratitude would be to worship *us* as their rightful, and true rulers! As I have already stated…we were *not* a perfect race, though many among us thought this to be true. More and more of us succumbed to his words, and ideas. More and more, the given laws…those that had governed us since time unknown were being either subtly altered, or utterly ignored! Soon…many among us *did* feel the manifest destiny of our race *was* to be the absolute rulers of all!

We began to create armies…a fact never deemed vital before. These armies were unlike anything ever seen before…or since! Behind the force, and overwhelming power of these armies, we came out of our centuries old isolation, and moved to overcome everything in our path! The brutish, backwards 'children' we came upon...they were no match for us, in any way! Most of them cowered before us, believing us to be supreme beings. They quickly became nothing more than glorified 'slaves'...at the beck, and call of their 'gods'! They never questioned, doing whatever was told them. Under our guidance, they constructed dwellings for us to live in...to be worshipped! These dwellings were similar to what we inhabited within our homeland...made us feel better to be out among the 'savages'.

As time passed, and our realm grew, these 'slaves' grew, and developed also. We taught them all the basics, a little at a time...of agriculture, medicine, science, mathematics, prophecy...and government. We encouraged their institution of religions all over the world...though *not* the one we had learned, and practiced those many years past...of the Creator. These peoples were encouraged to develop new worships...and many did, basing their new beliefs on their rulers...us! These 'children' should have been acknowledged as our 'brothers', and 'sisters'!...given every chance to learn all that we had been taught! Instead...they became servants, chattel...playthings! Loved, yes...but only on *our* terms, never allowed to go forward save on our terms, and limits!

We'd become so certain of ourselves...of the rightness of our positions in the scheme of things...so secure in our right to rule. To those who'd become *true* followers of his words, the stranger had granted even more, select powers! Many of these 'powers' were of a dark nature, unfamiliar to most of us...but, at that moment in time, we neither saw, or believed the true blackness behind these 'powers'!...sensed the *real* dangers their possession would raise. After all, were we not masters of all? Where, in all the world, was there anyone who could compete with us, or against us? Vainglorious, and misled...fools! We'd forgotten out own roots...trodden underfoot like so much useless chaff!! We had forgotten that we were children of Mother Earth, as much as were those we'd enslaved, conquered...or killed! How had we allowed ourselves to fall so far?

As time passed, we'd created positions of rule, and power among the more intelligent of our 'slaves'. They became the kings, and generals over the various groups...cultures that had spread out all over the world. They would be the ones to pass on the laws we'd set up...the religious practices we'd encouraged...to the generations yet to come. Most of these kings, and despots were actually our own off-spring...sired on, or by, selected members of the lesser people, as we now called them. These off-spring, sworn by blood to obey us, swore to always follow our doctrines, and laws. We set a pattern of growth for them to follow...deviation from this pattern was punishable by banishment...or death!

We thought we had everything under our firm control...but, we were so very wrong! We overlooked one very small fact. While safely secure in our isolation, we had little, very little that distracted us from the goals we'd set out to accomplish. There had also been no need to suppress certain urges, or needs that always been a part of who, and what we were. These urges, needs...they'd been tended to in a very practical, humane way...those ways were no longer feasible! It was as though, moving from our original homes had left us vulnerable...we'd left behind the things that made these urges simple things, little more than an annoyance. Now...they were becoming serious problems, even addictions for those who chose to freely follow the stranger's ways.

Also, when we came among those who dwelled in the so-called outer world, we unknowingly opened ourselves to their influences, virtues...and vices! As unlearned as they were, in comparison to us, their basic, sometimes brutish natures contributed to the downfall we had unknowingly already started towards.

Our ability to alter shape had been observed by some of them, and they had indoctrinated this into the various worships they'd come to practice. Our people were spread all over the world by now, in small groups, to better govern our blossoming world, and it many peoples. We gradually lost full contact with each other, weakening those links necessary to maintain a strong rule. Each individual group began to develop its own seat of power, building up their own ideals, adjusting their laws to fit *their* own particular situation, and location. Individual cultures began appearing...personal, and political empires started to spread their feelers, looking for other areas to conquer, and incorporate. The world was rapidly changing...too rapidly! The seeds had already been sown...the germ of an idea had begun to expand, and mature. Though we didn't realize it, until too late...the struggle for dominance was upon us! We had grown so far from what we were...what the Creator had intended for us. We had become exactly what we had been told we should be...gods! Not gods that were to benefit, lead, and care...no, for the most part, we had become vain, glory-seeking, power-hungry, selfish, and immoral! A very wise man once said that one should never forget from whence they came...or what they had been given. A 'god' should remember this as no other could! Even a 'god' should remember where they came from, and *who* they come from! Compassion...love are the greatest things within a true human...never forget that. Without love, or the ability to feel for another, we lose a important part of ourselves...the part that allows us to truly grow.

    The struggle began...at first, small strivings within the groups themselves, settling out their individual hierarchies. Then, the struggle expanded, as the various groups jockeyed for supreme power...to make their particular group the highest ranked. There were also those who felt we needed to return to our base...to what we had been *before* this world conquest. They were hounded, and ignored at every turn. As we had gotten used to being treated as 'gods', worshipped as such, expanding our knowledge, and power...we'd become less flexible, less willing to acknowledge any power greater then our own! At the time, we didn't know it, but the small struggles we were experiencing were laying the basis for the *true* fight. The dark power that had subtly turned us into the conquerors we now were...despite our protests...knew it would require great numbers of followers, to increase its own power. The fight was starting...the struggle between darkness, and the light...a struggle, I might add, that continues in thy time as well!"

He paused in his epic narrative, looking down at the seated Garalynn, whose eyes were still closed, viewing the scenes his words evoked, her expression intense, and enthralled. He smiled, "reading" the thoughts in her mind.

She slowly opened her eyes, sighing deeply. "It's like nothing I could ever have imagines! Such promise...such greatness. How could anyone have allowed all that to be lost to the world? Your race...all that's known of it any more is all attributed to folk stories, and myths!" She looked up at him, reaching out to him. "Please...help me to see more! I need to know what happened...and why!"

She was shocked to see pain, stark and clear, flit over the perfect features. He looked away, sighing himself, than looked back at her. "Forgive me...it is still quite painful, even after all these centuries, to talk of the end of most of my race! As I have already told thee, we had been cajoled down a path totally alien to the one meant for us to follow. The stranger who'd come among us?...he was more powerful, more insidious than any of us could have imagined! It would appear, that despite all our accomplishments and powers, we were innocents where true evil was concerned! To be honest...evil wasn't a concept a lot of us grasped in its full entirety! In truth, he was manipulating us...continuing to do so even today, with those he seduced to his cause! As I have related, he granted special powers to those of my race who chose to follow him absolutely! They continue to help him towards his true goal...regaining his total dominion of this world!"

She shuddered suddenly, not knowing why. She looked at him, thinking about what he'd shown her, and what he'd said. "I think, in a very real sense, your people just got 'confused'...like my world today! We all want so many things...peace, harmony, freedom, justice, equality...and love. But, most of us haven't a clue as to the right way to achieve any of that! We think we have a way...it blows up in our faces! Or, another way seems good, but in the end, it takes the rights away from others in order to give us what we want! It' a real mess!"

He gazed at her. "Strange, is it not? Centuries separate our times, yet the basic desires, and needs remain the same! Thy time, and world, face a challenge as great as that which nearly destroyed my people utterly! My race almost perished from the face of the world…due to our own blindness, our own refusal to see, and accept the greater truth! So, we were unprepared to keep the darkness from flooding over us!…and with all that we had been, we should have been prepared!"

She shifted her position on the rock she was sitting upon. "What happened? How were you almost destroyed?"

He bent down, touching her temple again, making her close her eyes. "See for thyself…thy memories are awakened now. Allow tem a free rein, and they will answer all thy questions."

She clasped her hands in her lap, eyes tightly shut…eager to see more of the fantastic, impossible revelation of his race's history…her history. He couldn't help but be touched by her eagerness. He pushed away again the sadness these memories always brought forth in his heart. He took a deep breath, and induced the memories to begin once again…….

……"At a time thy world denotes as approximately nineteen thousand B.C.E., our homeland was destroyed…engulfed by a great flood, and lost to the ocean depths that had protected it for centuries. All over the world, the groups left of my race faced the same threat as the peoples they ruled…destruction of their homes, kingdoms, and death from the engulfing waters of the great flood. Undeniably, we 'gods' had an advantage over the lesser peoples…as long as we were in our human forms, we were virtually immortal, indestructible. However, a great number of my race *did* perish…though, we're not certain as to the true cause. Even after all these ions, our wisest members are not totally clear about the changes shape-altering causes within those who practice it on a regular time-table. In any case…when the world regained itself after the waters had receded, some of us still survived. True, we were fewer in number now, and scattered even further around the world…but our power over the lessers was still strong. The friction between the various groups, and cultures intensified. Open warfare erupted here, and there…the losers being absorbed into the conquering group's followers. The base had been set for the one great battle…the one which would determine the world's ultimate fate…then the time of revelation came, and everything changed…forever! Even today, it is amazing that such a simple thing saved an entire world!

What thing was that?…a man. He came into this world, in such a simple way, but one that had been prophesized for centuries, in cultures all over the world. He came from simple parents, from an ancient race, and in a part of the world history has deemed as a section of the cradle of civilization. He was not a general, nor a king, in the accepted sense of the word. But, to look into this man's eyes was to see the ultimate truth! To see those eyes was to *know* he was a sending from the greatest power…one that surpasses all that had come before, or anything that has yet to come! From time to time, we had heard of how some of our off-spring had fostered a new belief, different from any of the ones we'd given them over the centuries. It was the belief that all was one…one law, one life, one god! It was the Creator all over again! And, this one man was the epitome of this new belief…this new, yet old faith! I was unsure, but desired a return to the old ways…the ways that had brought peace, and satisfaction to my heart, and soul. I wanted to belief in what He offered…but was not willing to be deceived yet again.

But, when I finally confronted Him face to face, looked deep within those eyes…then, I knew! I saw the proof of His powers. He could calm a lunatic with but a glance from his eyes. His touch could heal the infirm, grant sight to those in darkness, and even bring life back to that which lived no longer. He looked deep into *my* eyes, into the core of my complete being…my body, soul, heart, spirit, shadow, power, and name!

He touched me, telling me I was a true solider in the army of the Light. He forgave me all that I had done in my immortal life, telling me my task now was to go out, and do His work among those I had once ruled as 'slaves'. He wanted me to forever turn my back on the dark path I had once trod…to accept that I was loved, and cherished as a son by the Creator. He wanted me to become a true servant, as He was…to treat everyone as an equal…as a 'brother', or 'sister'. I saw the truth of the message He was to bring to the world. That message was that we are all members of one great family…all brothers, and as such we must love, and care for one another always. And, that we must honor the Creator in all aspects…for the true path was towards the Light, and that path was through Him, and Him alone.

For a time, I followed Him…watching over Him. I had been told that there were forces working to destroy Him, and all that He'd started…that among these forces were some of my own race! I knew I had then power to guard Him…save Him from what they wished to do. I had to…what would happen to the message He was trying to bring to all the world. I didn't realize, at the time…that *was* the plan. He *would* die, for all the peoples of the world…paving the way for true eternal life, after death! He died…and I, who had not wept for centuries, cried! I wept for this man, for all that my own people had lost, for what the world had killed…and for myself!" He released the hold on her temples, and she opened her eyes, tears sliding down her cheeks. She felt his sorrow, and stood up, putting a comforting hand on his arm.

"It's incredible…to have actually met, and been with…with Christ! But…you said you saw His dying! Didn't you also see His Resurrection? The miracles you say you saw Him do…didn't that tell you that death had no power over him?"

He smiled slightly, pleased at her feeling for him. "At first, my grief didn't allow me to understand…to see the greater plan. Later, I learned all had proceeded as it had been ordained!…prophesized by many, in many tongues, and many lands. I saw, for myself…the eternal life sought by man was now a reality. The lands that *my* group had ruled over had always believed that there *was* a life after death…the second life. The life we lived here, in this world, is meant to be a preparation for the second life…the true life we are meant to have! I thought how amazing it was that two such diverse cultures believed in the same end…eternal life after death! Those of my group, who'd joined me in the teachings and beliefs of our chosen Leader…they all realized now just how great a task we had before us, and all who embraced this new, yet old way!"

"You said there were others, like you…members of your race…or your children?" Garalynn asked quietly, sensing he really wanted to talk about this event in his time.

"I have sired countless children in my lifetime…seen *their* descendents grow old, and die! Most of the time, I can recognize those of my own bloodline, and that is a happy occasion. The time I spoke of, however, dealt not with any of my off-spring, but actual, full-blooded member of the group I had been part of…the faction to which I belonged, and survived with. We felt great joy, and honor being with the Teacher. A few of us went on to spread His teachings…after His rebirth! Those of us who seen the wisdom, and worth of his words, began to change, or do away with, the laws, and customs we'd lived by, and taught to those we called 'slaves'. It was a bitter truth we had to admit to ourselves…how foolishly we had been led astray by the words of the dark stranger! I vowed never to allow the darkness that close to my heart, and soul ever again! Some of us have learned, also, just how treacherous it can be to listen further!"

She cocked her head, hearing ominous undertones in his words. "What do you mean?…what happened?"

He shook his proud head, lips tightly compressed as he recalled that past. "Some of my people were tricked!…cajoled in ways we didn't think possible…imprisoned, or destroyed! It was true that *now* we know evil, and the darkness…know now what it is capable of doing...we didn't know that *then*! We didn't realize how it can corrupt even the most well-meaning...or, the depths to which it will go to achieve its monstrous goals, and desires! We still trusted those of our own race who'd gone over to the darkness...even if that trust was at best, infinitesimal!" He looked back at her, striking his clenched fist against his broad chest. "*I* will *never* go back to what I was!...what the stranger tried to make of all of us! To do so would be the gravest of insults to the one who tried to raise us *all* above the darkness! However...some of my race saw no shame at all in bowing to the honeyed words of the stranger, and accepting the powers he offered, the gifts he gave! They became, and still are, among his greatest, ablest servants! Their sole goal in their immortal life is to advance the cause of darkness, seeking to overcome the Light, and all who follow it!" He lifted a hand to his forehead, rubbing it.

She saw how tired, and strained his face looked just then. She shook her head, beginning to feel the twinge of a headache herself. "You still haven't really answered an earlier question of mine...why did you call me sister? You also mentioned some urges, and desires that couldn't be controlled outside of your homeland...what did that mean?"

He touched her chest, over her heart, and the slight pain she was experiencing left her. "Go back...along the lines of thy family's collected memories. There, thou will find that a woman of thy bloodline was once impregnated by he who was *my* sire. We are, in truth, blood related. That was why our minds could so easily connect...why thee was able to come to me, and help!"

"I think I understand what you're saying. It seems like I'm remembering more, and more, as every minute goes by! It's almost too much to take in all at once!" She bowed her head, feeling the memories growing within. "And the rest?...those urges you mentioned?...nothing's come to me about them!"

He gazed at her, grave. "It will come to thee...soon! I think it best if thee wait for that, and talk with me then!"

She was about to protest, but than her mind began to get a glimmer as she was concentrating. She pushed the thoughts away as the barest hints started to be known...she wasn't ready for that direction as yet. Changing the subject, she pointed at the near-by altar stone. "Why were...*are* you imprisoned inside that thing?" She had to remember this was just a spirit she was talking with, as was she herself right now. "If your powers are as strong as I suspect, *how* could they trap you? And please...tell me why you were hidden *here*, in Denver? This spot is thousands of miles from Egypt, which is where I figure *your* race came from! You have to admit...it's a very strange, to say the least!"

"As I have already stated, we are immortal...for the most part! But...we are as human as thy race where our emotions are concerned! And, for a reason I am not conversant with...certain types of stone *can* hold us prisoner...immobilizing even the great strength we possess, and rendering our other powers to their lowest levels. Thus, the reason for the amulet, and all the rest. My enemies wanted me out of the way, but they had never been able to trap me in an animal form!...I knew better. So...they devised a very clever trap...a *very* clever trap!" He looked at the altar, resting his fingertips lightly on its top. "They designed it so well!...even *my* intellect, and caution were successfully clouded for the few seconds they required to spring the trap! As for *why* my prison is here, in thy city...well, it has been moved many times, during my long imprisonment, to prevent my friends, and companions from finding me, and possibly freeing me. I have been awakened many times, only to find the time was not right...there was none close enough, as thou was, to contact."

"Well, I guess I understand all that...but, I still don't get why here?...in Denver? I

feel like I'm part of a science-fiction movie!" Garalynn shrugged her shoulders, flinging one hand up to express her confusion.

"Ah...that is quite a story in itself. In the time that those known as the Aztecs ruled in the Yucatan area, three members of my race finally located where my coffin was hidden…in what is now called England. Securing it, they headed out, far across the ocean, to where they knew the great Aztecs dwelt. They had tried, unsuccessfully, to open the stone sarcophagus, but had been unable to accomplish this. They decided to conceal the coffin somewhere, until they could gather up all that they learned was necessary to crack the locks on the coffin. They wanted it to be a place none would ever think to look…and the new World, as it was called then, seemed perfect! It was entrusted to members of the ruling royal house of the Aztecs, who swore to guard it with their blood! And, a great many died protecting its discovery from the invasion of the Spanish conquistadores. Though their great empire fell, they managed to get word to word to the members of the secret society who'd brought the coffin to them. They told of how they'd sent the coffin far away from their realm, out of the reach of the Spanish invaaders…to a safe place."

Garalynn looked around the cavern. "They brought it here!…concealing it within this cavern."

"Yes…with a guard of honor, to protect it through eternity!" His arm swung out, indicating the human bones. "They were buried with the coffin…executed just before the rocks were brought down over the entrance, like all their kings, and priests! Their beliefs stated that the spirits would then be on guard for all time!" He shook his head. "It wasn't anything I could have prevented…though, I wished I could have somehow let them know such things were *not* desired!"

"It happens, though…even in ancient Egypt! Tell me…why not just destroy, or kill you? I mean…I know you said you can't be killed, in your human form…but it seems like a lot more trouble planning a trap, that *might* not work! They obviously considered you a threat…why not eliminate the threat altogether? After all…no matter how good a prison, somebody can always find a way to crack it!" Garalynn asked, glancing again at the stone.

A great sadness came over the beautiful eyes. "They *did* try to destroy me…as they will continue to try! They are followers of the darkness...the dark path they follow will always seek to keep the Light away. Remember...the Light will always triumph over the darkness. I think, in their hearts they also know this...but they are unwilling to admit it, and that just makes them even more dangerous...because there is nothing they won't attempt to keep that enemy at bay as long as possible! Even eternity isn't long enough for them! And, if trapping even one of the servants of the Light helps achieve that goal, then so be it! With each servant, or believer they can coerce...or destroy...their side of the struggle gains in power, and strength!"

"So, what you're saying is...by trapping you, they were trying to weaken their enemies...right?" Garalynn asked.

He smiled, a little ruefully. "Yes...in a way. Though, if the truth be known...they didn't have to work *that* hard to get me into this prison! I fear I helped them in all too many ways! I helped them trap me within that stone prison...allowed them to use my own feelings to attain their goal! I still feel the shame...I had always been the one who berated my group about the necessities of staying alert, and being on guard against their trickery! And yet...I let them capture me as easily as one would a brainless fish!"

Garalynn gazed at him, seeing not just the physical perfection, but the wisdom, strength, and intellect...how had they been able to capture such a man? "How?...how did they trap you? I wouldn't think *anyone* could coerce *you*, against your will!"

"Ah...thy words are the key! Against my will...but it wasn't! At least...not entirely! They used the love I felt for one of my own! I did not realized the depth of her belief in the stranger's words...her commitment to his ways. I couldn't not believe, because of the extent of our love, she did not feel as I felt! I should have recognized the signs, I suppose...but even a 'god' falls to the blindness of love!"

Garalynn almost felt like she was prying into his personal affairs, but she also felt it was necessary to know all she could learn! "Tell me what happened between you...please?"

He looked up at the ceiling of the cavern, sighing. "Those who turned to the dark, and stayed there...did so because they'd come to truly love, even crave the powers such a path had acquired for them. They had come to believe in, and seek out, all that such an alliance would bring to them. They had also come to believe in their status as 'deities'...as the powers that be to the peoples who worshipped them! They began to show *all* the traits, and tendencies their followers had attributed to them, in their worship of them. The use of blood sacrifices became more, and more prevalent in the everyday rituals to these 'great gods'...an intoxicating elixir, akin to the finest of wines! They learned that the awe, and terror their shape-shifting abilities could generate caused the potency of that elixir to become even more intense, as did their love-making capabilities as well!" He was interrupted here as Garalynn raised one hand, her face tight and pale.

"Wait!...you're saying that they began to *like* the blood sacrifices!?...that they actually did things to ensure such things continued to happen?"

"Yes...to our unforgivable shame! You see, they...*we* discovered a great secret during this time. Though our life spans *were* close to immortal, being in the outside world had weakened that somehow...but once the secret was learned, true immortality became a physical reality!" He held out his hand, palm up, as he spoke...slowly closing it until his fist was tightly clenched, emphasizing his words.

"What secret?...what did your people discover about blood?" Garalynn couldn't believe she was asking this, but she had to know!

"You have heard of endorphins?" He waited until he saw her nod. "Secretions from the brain, released in specific circumstances, each with a specialized effect upon the workings of the body. The ability to withstand excruciating pain...great bursts of physical prowess...enhanced vision...expanded mental abilities...great courage where there was usually only fear...physical dexterity, and flexibility where none had ever been present...unbelievable pleasure, and sexual fulfillment....all these, and more are possible with the right amount of one, or more of the endorphins...secreted at just the right time, and in the right situation! We discovered that there are two times when certain endorphins are released into the system, in such a combination, and strength as to produce a substance that gives the cellular structure of the body the greatest gift of all! It gives the truest form of immortality possible anywhere! This pure essence, as my race has come to call it, regenerates the very cells into a structure that completely resists all sickness, all forms of disease...even the aging process...beyond anything your race could begin to understand! To be honest, this was something we had discovered even before we'd left our isolation, and come out into the world. But, then it had been controlled...administered with control, and wisdom...no one had to die, or even suffer any form of pain, or torture. Our scientists had developed ways for us to replicate these endorphins, and administer them in a safe, oral form! But...the dark one found ways to make it seem more exciting...more intense, and this is what began to appeal to those who chose his way."

"What are the two ways you said?...what makes it more intense, more desirable then an oral administration?" The moment she asked, Garalynn knew, and looked away.

He nodded, thinking back. "Yes...sexual gratification, and absolute terror! At no other time does the body release such strength of concentration, or amount of secretion as these! At the time of orgasm, the endorphin that allows such pleasure, such completeness floods the body's senses...the euphoria is carried within every blood cell, to every part of the body. It is not without reason that many feel as though, in those few milliseconds, they have achieved virtual paradise! Their bodies are washed with the purest of essences, and every cell invigorated with new life. The same with absolute terror...many have stated they've never felt more alive, than when they've been in the greatest of dangers! It heightens every sense we possess...every power we're capable of feeling. Invoking either of these, then partaking of the blood which is bursting with such richness…that is to infuse thyself with all that power! Immortality is the reward for such actions! My race discovered that developing unbelievable ways to terrorize was one way to achieve the pure essence. Becoming consummate lovers, unrivaled anywhere in time or space, was the other way. Some used both methods…it was all to one end, the attainment of the essence that gave us eternal life! There was one drawback, however, for those who chose the darkness…they require this essence on a very regular basis…daily, weekly, monthly, it varies from one to the other. For those who chose the Light, such a necessity became null, and void. The essence became inherent within our bodies on a permanent state…a reward, I think, for being true, and faithful servants."

She smiled, glad that she didn't have to have the thought of blood use, about him, in the back of her mind. "It's not so hard to grasp…the reward of eternal life, as long as you believe in the way God has set out for you, has long been the lost sought after! It's ironic, though…even those thought of as 'gods' sought the way to perfect immortal life! I wonder if….oh, well, it's not important now! This person they used to trap you…you must have really loved her!"

"I did…I do! She was once considered a great goddess in the land our group ruled over…one whole villages, and cities prayed to for guidance, and success. Kings and generals…yes, entire armies…would make great sacrifices to her statues, to gain her favor, and success in their up-coming battles. They would dedicate entire treasures, prisoners, even their own life's blood…hoping to curry her favor, and her guidance…to pledge their undying dedication to her royal spirit! She was viewed as the daughter of the Sun…the embodiment of the power of the Sun's rays, and his avenging arm!" He looked at Garalynn, and she was surprised at the depth of pain in those glimmering eyes. "I didn't see any of this whenever I looked at her…I saw only the woman I was destined to love! The other half to my soul…the completion of my spirit! She knew that I had made my choice…to turn my back on the darkness that had invaded us, and turn back to what the Creator had truly intended us to be. I thought she had understood, had accepted that this was meant to be…that *we* were meant to be, in this way, as well. I believed, with all my heart, that she would stay with me, share the love we had found…for all of eternity, and beyond! I could not believe she would *want* to stay in her position of a goddess, with all that mindless, bloody adulation…that dark, self-serving power! She would see the truth one day, as I, and others had…this I kept telling myself…and stay with me, to advance the Light's ways, and enjoy the promise of this world. I told myself that love would be the way for her!" He sighed, looking down at his clasped hands. "How wrong I was ultimately proven to be! She was too enamoured of the position she'd achieved…too accustomed to the worship, reverence…and fear! These things…they become like a drug to which one is addicted! It is one that is almost impossible to live without! She reveled in all of it! She was not about to give any of it up…for something she deemed a mere emotion. She'd tried to sway me from my decision, and when that had failed, she used my attraction for her…as a weapon to achieve her dark master's wishes! She kept me off-guard, and that allowed her minions to spring the trap on me!"

She put a gentle hand on his, understanding the sense of loss, and betrayal he must have felt. He looked up as her thoughts came to his mind. He smiled, interlacing his fingers with hers. "No…I bear her no hatred, my sister. I've forgiven her the actions she showed towards me…they were the result of the evil that has her in its grip! My love for her is still within my heart. I still hope to see her freed from the life she has chosen. In many ways, she is more trapped than I!"

Garalynn could only be awed by such a love…she wasn't sure she could be as forgiving. "When will it come?…the time you will be freed, I mean! I wish I could do something to help!" She looked around the cavern, noting again the bones, and other artifacts. She thought a moment, than looked at him. "I understand what you said about these bones…that the Aztecs executed the guards so their spirits would always guard your hiding spot. But…the stories of The Dark Eagle's Nest, specifically the one concerning Joshua Phelps…they tell about the mysterious warrior the native Americans called Dark Eagle, and how he challenged the warriors to come up here, during a lunar eclipse, and try to win the great prize! Who was that warrior?…he couldn't have been one of the Aztec guards…they were all killed?…weren't they?"

"These human guards were not the only guard placed over my coffin…The king's chief priest conjured a living eagle warrior, originally a follower of the ancient Toltec god-lord of life and death, Texacatlipoca who later became replaced by the Aztec Sun God, Huitzilopochtli. The Aztec royalty saw themselves as the chosen ones, the ones to continue the old Toltec traditions…and somehow they viewed the mystery of my coffin as worthy of this same consideration. Therefore, a 'special' sentry was deemed necessary, besides the spirits of the slain Aztec warriors. This eagle warrior was an immortal being, who grew bored with his solitary existence. From time to time, he would go out among the tribes that dwelt in the area at times, and interacted with them. He was, actually, a positive force in many ways. He taught them much that improved their lives, and helped them better defend themselves. But…he also challenged them! He was, after all, a warrior…and had a warrior's desires. He developed the challenge to coincide with the lunar eclipses over the centuries, heightening the mystery, and sacredness of the entire situation. He would talk with me often…letting me 'see' what his plans transmitted themselves into over the years. Many young, brave warriors came here, seeking that which had been stated to better their tribes' standing…but, they had no comprehension of what they were facing. They were ill-equipped to battle the powers stacked against their valiant efforts. This went on for centuries…until one man came up against the warrior, and succeeded in over-coming his powers!" H paused, staring at Garalynn, making her see the seriousness behind his next words. "That one man was of great vision, and even greater faith! He actually defeated the ancient warrior, sending him back to the limbo from which he'd been summoned. His mine was able to touch mine, telling me of our connection in blood! He pledged his strength to my freedom…to seeing that my place of imprisonment would be guarded, until the true time of my emergence! I instructed him to take some of the gold the Aztecs had concealed along with the coffin. He did so, setting in motion all the events that have led to today! Many times, in his lifetime, he came here, and we 'talked'. I had told him of those responsible for secreting me here…the ones who'd taken me to the Aztecs. He told me he would find if any of them still existed, and if so…he would let them know what had happened. I can only assume he did, though I do know he put down everything that happened in a secret journal. When his visits stopped, I knew his mortal life had ended, and I felt the long sleep come over me once again!"

Garalynn had put all the pieces together in her mind. "That man…he was Joshua Phelps, wasn't he? That was when the family's fortunes started to rise…when the legend of Blackmoon first began!" She shook her head. "All my life, that story has fascinated me like no other story! Joshua was quite a man!"

He sighed, feeling more tiredness creep over him. "Yes…a good man, with the spirit strong within him!"

"I don't understand one thing…why didn't *he* free you? I'm sure he could have thought of a way to move that top slab! Why didn't he?"

"There is a scheme…a plan to all in this world, my sister. And it is those who are foolish, or impatient enough to try, and hurry, or alter this plan that cause the chaos thy race lives within now. Despite his desire to free me, Joshua knew it was not the right time! Let me put it in terms that might be easier to grasp…think of this as having a time lock! Only when the time is correct, will the 'lock' on my cell be opened. The dark ones who entrapped me thought they had imprisoned me for all eternity…but Fate frequently steps in, and deals a different hand."

Garalynn held up her hand, her confusion showing. "Wait…they put you in that thing, with a lock that was supposed to last forever, and you say that wasn't so? Why would they put a *time* lock on the coffin? They wanted you out of the picture for all time!...why run the risk of you're getting out by doing such a dumb thing?" She waved her hands in front of her face, clearly showing her disbelief. "None of this makes any sense at all!"

He suddenly grinned, a wide boyish grin that somehow became him. "No, they never meant such a thing! But...what they didn't know was that the one they had construct this stone prison, and the locks that secured it...his sympathies secretly lay with our side! He couldn't set me free, but he did what he could to make my freedom a definite possibility in the future!"

"Well...I guess I understand part of what you're saying...but, how was Joshua going to guard this place? He was mortal...and how did he hope to contact a secret society that had existed hundreds of years before he was even born?" Garalynn was beginning to think she'd never be able to get all this straight.

"He *was* able to contact them...how I do not know. They still existed, their beliefs and goals passed down, from father to son to son over the years. Joshua became a member of this group." He rubbed his temples again...the pain was growing. "The journal...Joshua's secret journal. He put it all down...everything that had happened between us. The things that were needed for success in the future...things that would eventually lead to my being freed...he wrote it all down, or hid them when he hid the journal! All that is needed...it is contained in, or with the journal! This is what thou must locate, my sister!...*before* the agents of the dark! Time is not a friend to thee right now...they have an edge now, for they possess three of the necessary items already. It is the journal that is the final piece...what is written within it, and what is hidden with it, such as the amulet thee wears now! Without that journal, they have no hope of achieving their goal...preventing my emergence! Find it!"

"Find it?...no one's seen that journal since Joshua died! It's part of the legend of Blackmoon...the lost diary of Joshua Phelps! How am *I* supposed to locate it now?" She stared at him, completely shocked. "Even those so-called agents of the dark haven't been able to find it, and they've had over a hundred years to look for it! Wait a minute!...you said they were after it...are you telling me that the ones after this are like you? I mean...like your race?"

"Yes...of *my* race, but under the rule of the darkness! Listen...begin thy search where I told thee to find the amulet!...Joshua would have hidden them close to on another! And, a word of warning...thy memories have almost completely awakened, and this will give thee an edge against thy enemies! But...it will also give them a weapon against thee! Thou will be able to recognize any of our blood now, and it will not take thee long to develop thy own ways to know those of the darkness as well! The danger...now, if they try to 'read' thy mind, they will know thy memories have come home! They will know how great a threat thou are to their plans, and they will act accordingly!" He took her by the shoulders. "My beloved sister, be most cautious in the world thou returns to now! Remember...the enemies thou faces will stop at nothing to obtain the secrets! Be careful...use the knowledge thee now has, but be cautious in thy thoughts! If thou can mask thy thoughts, it will help delay their discovering thy true

being! Move among them with great care!"

"Can you help me?...tell me who they are?" Garalynn begged.

He shook his head. "I am aware of many things, when awakened, within my cold prison, my sister...but I cannot tell thee what the dark agents may look like today! I have been able to sense that one, or more have been in the area recently...are, in fact, here at this moment!" He saw the expression of fear come, and go in her eyes. "I will try, and remain in contact with thy mind as much as possible...though, from time to time, I will have to terminate the connection. Even our minds require rest, and recharging. While we are connected, I will try to guide, protect, and warn thee. Understand this, however...each time I try to actively contact thy mind, they also may 'hear' it! Thy senses will be exhausted when thy spirit rejoins thy body…stay far from others for a time, until thou feels thy mind is ready once again! And…may He who watches over us all be ever with thee!" He touched her temple.

Garalynn felt her senses swim, and she grew extremely disoriented. She was falling, spinning…then everything seemed to come to a crashing halt. She slowly opened her eyes, letting her vision clear. She was a little surprised to find herself flat on her back, on the plush rug in front of the fireplace…back at the family cabin. She pushed herself up into a sitting position, more than a little shocked at how weak she felt! When she could finally sit up, she leaned back against one of the chairs, and glanced at her wristwatch, her eyes very tired, and bleary. She was surprised to see that only ten minutes had gone by…it had seemed like hours! She still found it hard to comprehend all that had taken place…all that she had been told. And yet…the memories were so clear, so precise, inside her mind. She lifted her hand to her neck, a sudden thought coming to her slowly clearing brain…the amulet was still there. It was all real!…she'd actually been there, and talked with him.

"And…I never even learned his name!" She suddenly shivered, awed and scared by all that had happened…all that she knew now.

She tucked the amulet in, under the collar of her blouse. She had to get going…there was so much to do! But…her body wasn't ready to move from the spot it was in right now! It was taking all her efforts to just remain upright!

Okay, her mind sighed…we rest, until everything's back to the norm. Then, no more wasting time! She knew the time was short…she had to find that journal, and whatever might be with it! She was only too aware now that she was treading a delicate path, between danger, and possible death! And, somehow…she knew she wasn't the only one doing so! Her adopted family was in very serious danger as well! She would return to the city…to Blackmoon, as soon as she was able. She would be more on the alert than ever…her newly awakened senses told her she'd already met the enemy! She knew now, without a shred of doubt, why she'd been so on edge around them…the Dresdens! She *had* known them before…in a time long gone by, she'd gone against them, and lost! She was determined that the outcome *this* time would be a far different one than that which *they* planned! She knew she had no choice…however great the fear she felt within her heart right now! Sandra, and Beth were at risk…especially Beth! She'd already been affected by them…who knows what they planned for Sandra? She…Garalynn…was the only one who could hope to protect them now! For everything now…for all that had gone before, and all yet to come…she had to try, no matter what the costs!……………..

****

VII

❀

..........Earlier that same evening, while Garalynn was having her unusual experience, the coroner shoved his head into David's office. "Hi, Dave...you leaving now? Need to hold you up just a minute, or two!"

David paused in putting on his jacket. He stared at the coroner, his eyes narrowing in fatigue. "Okay...but it better be a good reason! I've been here too long today as is! So, what's up, Jim?" He indicated one of the chairs, and sat back down behind his desk.

Jim came in, and sat down, stretching a bit. He rubbed his eyes, leaning back in the chair. "Boy...I am beat! I sure hope things get back to normal around here soon, my friend! This overtime is about to kill me!...not to mention what my wife's threatening to do to me!"

David leaned forward, resting his elbows on the desk top. "Jim...forgive me, buddy, but I *do* have a date tonight...and I've made her wait too often as it is! So...do me a big favor, and cut to the chase here, okay? You got something new for me on any of the murders? The chief's getting agitated...when do we get the results of those special tests you said you were ordering? You know...those one with the gas chromo-whatever!"

Jim looked up, surprised. "Hell, Dave...I sent you a copy of that yesterday, when the results came back from FitzSimmons General!" He glanced at the paper pile covered desk. "Course...I don't see how you could find anything in that mess!"

David began rummaging through the paper flood. "Everyone's got to be a comedian these days! There's got to be…ah, here it is!" He pulled a large manila folder out from under the debris.

Jim sat back, satisfied now that the missing report was located. "I'll save you a look, and give you the condensed version, Dave. You already had the preliminary reports on all the deaths…this was just to clear up a few inconsistencies I came across! There were traces of cannabinoids in what little urine we found in the boys' bladders, but with teenagers these days, that's hardly a shocker. We found minute traces of alcohol in their tissues as well…the girl had neither alcohol, or marijuana in hers. The cuts that were along the boys extremities was made along established nerve pathways…in other words, they were put through excruciating pain just prior to their deaths!"

David lifted one finger. "I'd still like to know *where* all the blood, and bodily fluid went to, Jim! You know we didn't find any blood in that cave!"

"We haven't found the girl's heart as yet, either! We find that, and we might also find the answers about the blood! Oh, remember that mark on the girl's forehead?…we were able to match up the pigments. They're from plants in Egypt!…used to make dyes, and paints for over two thousand years! A friend of mine at the university was able to help pin that one down!"

"Two thousands years…why does everything about this case seem to be in terms right out of the Dark Ages?" David snorted, running his fingers through his hair in frustration.

"More like the era *before* Christ, Dave!" Jim was about to say more when Patrick walked into the office.

"Hey…don't you have a date with Sandy tonight? Saw the light, and wondered why you were still here! Hey, Jim…what's the coroner doing up here?" Patrick asked, stuffing loose papers into the manila envelope he had in one hand.

David glared at his partner. "Jim was filling me in on those special tests he ordered, Pat. And, you don't have to remind me about my date, Pat! Jim...you got anything else that's pertinent?"

"What do I say that hasn't already been said? Systemic failure, due to complete fluid depletion. Cardiac, and respiratory failure...death due to heart being removed! I put that all down in the first reports you got from me!" He looked down at his hands, then back up at the two of them. "In the past few weeks, we've had the strange fortune to find five mutilated bodies turn up in our jurisdiction! All the mutilations resemble one another...impression?...the same person, or persons are involved in all five deaths! Is there anything else in common?...so far, no! I take it back...there *is* one thing! There's little, or no blood at any of the crime scenes! Impression?...they could have been killed somewhere else, then dumped where they were found!...but so far nothing's turned up to indicate *where* else they could have been murdered! All I know is that this is getting really spooky, guys...and I'm getting real tired of it!"

David stood up, tossing the folder back on top of the pile. "There's nothing that ties any of these victims together...nothing that can help our profilers figure out the type of killer we're up against, or any kind of pattern that would help us figure out which way the killer might go again. I feel like we're suddenly in side one of those old TV serials...you know, the way out, creepy ones? Either that...or, we're dealing with something not exactly human!"

Jim glanced at Patrick, then leaned forward in his chair, shoulders slumped, and tight. "Funny you should say something like that, Dave...I've got something to tell you, and I honestly don't know how to tell you, or how to explain it! What I'm about to tell you guys *isn't* in any report...I just couldn't bring myself to write it down! And, I tell you plain...I wouldn't tell this to anyone, but the two of you! If anyone else finds out about this...well, let's just say I'm sure I'd be facing early retirement!" He looked at both the men...friends he'd known for years...took a deep breath, and let it out with a loud whoosh. "What you said just now, Dave…I think there's more truth than lies in that statement! I don't think what we're looking for is…human! At least, not entirely human, as we know it to be! I mean…well, not all human!"

Both David, and Patrick stared at Jim for a few moments, then gazed at one another for a few. For a few moments, there was absolute silence in the small office, so deep you could hear their separate breaths. David cleared his throat, trying to speak, but the words didn't seem to want to leave his lips. He swallowed hard, feeling all stirred up inside. Finally…"Do you have any idea of what you are trying to say? You're right about one thing, Jim…if you had tried to tell anyone else, besides us, about this, they'd have measured you for a padded cell! You have anything to back this wild idea up?"

"Yeh…and it better be good, or I'll get the straight jacket myself!" Patrick grumbled, eyes narrowed, and beads of sweat on his brow. This case was getting worse all the time!

Jim got up, crossed to the door, closed it, and locked it. He returned to his chair, and sat down, reaching into the inside pocket of his suit jacket. He pulled out a folded envelope, and handed it to David. The officer took it, then looked a silent question.

The medical examiner's voice was low, flat…and deadly. "I found something under the fingernails of Douglas Traylor, one of those teenage boys, and the security guard. I didn't mention it before, because I honestly wasn't sure what it was. At first, it looked like some kind of tissue…like the victim might have scraped the skin of his killer with his nails…but it didn't really match up with any tissue I'd seen before. I sent some samples out to CDC, in Atlanta…that report is what they found."

"So…what did they find? What kind of tissue is it?" Patrick asked.

Jim pointed at the folder. "In there, you'll also find pictures I took, off my microscope. All three victims came into contact with the same…thing! Something that has characteristics of both human DNA…and some other type of living tissue that they have so far not been able to identify! Whatever killed these people…wasn't human, but was!"

Patrick scowled, unconsciously clenching his big fists. "Not human?...what are you saying, Jim? What the fuck is he saying, David?"

David held up his hand, silencing his long-time partner. "Jim...you're not going to sit there, and tell me we're looking for *aliens*...are you? Or, some kind of monster from outer space?"

Jim grinned suddenly, loosening his tie. "No...that is not what I'm saying! I am trying to say...look, it boils down to this...what we found *is* living tissue, taken from a living being! But...it's not one-hundred percent *human*! Its composition, and DNA patterns have a lot of matches that say *human*...but there are a lot that don't say anything of the kind! These are the ones that say it *isn't* human! It's human, and...and something that is neither animal, or human...but a mixture of both! I've sent samples, and pictures off to Mayo Walter Reed, and a few research labs we've used in the past. I also took the liberty of asking the investigative labs at Interpol, Scotland Yard, and the DeBrance Tissue Research lab in Paris. I figured we ought to get some help from one of those places...*if* it's something that's been identified before, that is!"

David sat back, staring at the other man, shaking his head. He couldn't believe it!...the longer this case went on, the worse, and more bizarre it got! Then, making a decision, he stuffed the folder inside his jacket, and stood up. "Look, Jim...you do whatever it takes to find out what we're really up against!...even if it's just an incredible hoax! Nothing goes outside this room, until we're all sure of the facts, right? We're not going to say anything...are we, Pat? Jim...you keep on being quiet about anything relating to this, okay? Whatever comes up about that tissue, I want only *my* office getting any feed-back...at least, until we can take it to the chief, with proof of what you suspect!...don't want to give him any reason to put us all away! Especially if we're going to tell him, and everyone else there's some kind of monster among us!" He shook his head. "I can't believe that I just said that...out loud! Get going, Jim...keep us posted, okay?"

Jim nodded, and left the office...he felt a lot better having gotten all that off his chest. For a couple of seconds, Patrick sat there, thinking. Then, he spoke up, quiet, and strangely saddened. "Boss...I can't help thinking back to when I said there was something about this case that make me real uneasy...I'm getting that same feeling again, and I don't like it! Maybe...maybe, it's all true! Maybe...there *is* a nightmare out there, just waiting to come true!"

The tall police lieutenant didn't answer right away. He went over to the one window in his office, and looked out over the lights of downtown Denver. He just stood there, watching the come and go of the busy traffic...settling things in his mind. Finally, his voice came back to Patrick, low and meaningfully. "Pat...you ever have a dream that was so real, so intense that no matter what you did when you woke up...you just couldn't shake it? You keep telling yourself...it's just a dream...that there's no way it could be real...but, it won't go away!"

"Yeh...sure. The kind of dream that makes you sorry you had all that beer the night before?" Patrick tried, unsuccessfully, to lighten the air in the room.

"Cut the joking around, will you? I'm serious here!" David glared over his shoulder at his partner. "I'm scared, Pat...and that's not something I admit, to anyone, very easily! I don't think I've ever felt as scared as I do right now!...except when..." His voice died away as a memory surfaced.

"What?...when? Hey, Dave...you okay? What are you remembering?" Patrick stood up, and walked over to where David was standing.

"A nightmare...when I was about eight years old! Funny...I thought I'd forgotten all about it! I remember it so clearly now...I was in a dark place, with trees and a lot of wind blowing. I had a target pistol in my hands...my dad had been teaching me how to shoot it, I remember. I was shooting it at something, but not a target! I remember glittering eyes, and dripping teeth...then, I woke up, shaking and crying. I can still feel how vivid everything was...how scared I was! And now...I feel like my nightmare is about to come true!" He looked back at Patrick. "I feel as though someone is trying to tell me something…to warn me to do something before it's too late! But…I don't know what it is! I think I'm going a little bananas!"

Patrick put a hand on David's shoulder, a concerned look on his face. "I think, Dave, that we're both a little too involved with certain aspects of this case! That's part of what makes a good cop, though…you know? You gotta learn to leave the case behind, though, when you leave the office. That's the only way to keep your sanity…at least, part of it!" Patrick was doing all he could to pull his partner out of the funk he seemed settling into. "I just hope you don't talk shop when you're around that special lady of yours!…that would be a real waste!"

David had to smile. He shook his head. "The truth is, Pat…I can't think of much else other then her when she's around! *She's* the one who brings work subjects up, but usually it's only when she senses I need to get some things out of my head!…she's really special that way!…in all ways! I really love her, Pat…and that scares me almost as much as this case!"

Pat grinned, slapping the younger man on the back. "Being in love scares the bravest men, Dave!…if they're being honest, that is! I'll tell you one thing, though…you let *this* one get away, and you're a bigger fool then any I've ever met!" He patted David one last time on the back. "Look…I have to get going before my wife sends the hounds out after me! Dave…I can't say anything to get this nightmare you're talking about out of your mind…except to say that we can't let this case take over our lives! If we do…then the 'bad' guys win, no matter what happens! Think about your lady…that's enough to keep any nightmare at bay! See you tomorrow!" With a shake to the shoulder, and a wave, Patrick was gone.

David turned away from the window, looking after Patrick. His partner was right, and he had to shake these feelings before they got control of everything. He sighed, leaning on his desk. He reached inside his jacket, and pulled out the folder he'd put there earlier. He stared at it, wondering. Finally, he shoved it underneath all the other papers.

He stood up, looking at the pile of papers, jaw set. "Come on, damn you!...talk to me! Show me what it is I'm missing! It's there...I know it is! We're so close I can taste it!" He slammed a fist down on the pile. "Talk to me!...help me!"

He lifted his head, looking up towards the ceiling. "This is kind of a new thing for me...this praying stuff, I mean! It's not something I'm in the habit of doing...and I can't say I've really had much faith in it, either! But...Right now, I don't know which way to turn, and I need to know! It might be crazy, but I *know* we're in danger! I've got someone very special in my life now, and it's her family that is in danger...though, I can't help but feel we *all* are as well! Please...just help me to find this killer, or killers! Let me stop the killing...once, and for all! And...please, let my dream be just that!...a dream!"

Maybe...it was just his imagination, or he was more tired than he thought...but, as he stood there, he got a feeling. It was clear, and distinct...his words had not gone unheeded. Someone...something was stirring, and getting ready to come to his die!......

......Sandra stood towards the back of the hospital room, watching the radiance that shone from her sister's face. She still couldn't get over the change in Beth's condition in just the two days since Tamara, and Sean's arrival back in Denver. The marked change began with the Dresden's first visit to the hospital. They doctors couldn't explain it...they were still working on trying to figure out what had nearly killed Beth in the first place. As yet, they hadn't been able to do the further blood, or tissue, tests on either Tamara, or Sean Each time they'd tried, Tamara had intricately put them off, turning their attentions to other matters. Then, the unexpected reversal of Beth's medical condition kept their attentions off the Dresdens momentarily. For a time...the tests were forgotten.

Seeing how happy her twin was, Sandra felt a pang of regret that she couldn't share in that happiness...she really didn't want them here. She sighed, thinking about that...and her concern for Garalynn, and her odd behavior of three days ago. She hadn't heard from her since that day in the Tomb...and that thought made her even more worried.

Tamara's soft voice broke into Sandra's thoughts. "I am very glad that out returning here has helped our Elizabeth recover so quickly! And the news about the baby...I can't remember seeing my brother so happy, or excited! I admit...we were a little concerned when we had to leave before...she looked so frail! She's one hundred percent now...isn't she?"

Turning, Sandra looked at the other woman, still uncertain as to her true motives in this situation. "Yes, she is definitely better! To see such an improvement when she was...all I can do is thank you again, Tamara! Having Sean close seems to have been the key to getting Beth better. I have to thank you, also, for that family remedy you brought back with you...it worked a miracle! What is it exactly?"

The smile Tamara flashed was wide...and smug. "Just something that's been passed down in my family for more generations than there are records for!...I'm glad we were able to be of help, Sandra. After all...we're all family now, aren't we? I knew we had to get back here immediately, after we received Garalynn's call. By the way...I haven't seen her since our return...is she away on business?" She glanced back at the hospital bed, seeing Beth sitting up for the first time in days, Sean balanced on the edge of the bed, caressing her cheek with one hand. "Have the doctors been able to determine what made her so ill, Sandra? Are there any sort of problems with the pregnancy?"

Sandra didn't want to appear ungrateful, but the old familiar tensions were beginning to re-emerge within her. "They'd be closer to the answers if they could analyze a blood sample from Sean, Tamara. You've put them off several times about it...why is that? They need a comparison between his blood, and Beth's, to help work the true cause out. Why is it so hard for you to do that?"

Tamara's smile grew broader. "As a matter of fact...we gave them the blood, and tissue samples just this morning! There were other things that were more important before…we'll just have to wait, and see if anything comes up! Getting back to Garalynn…why isn't she here, Sandra?" Tamara's attention suddenly shifted back to her brother, and Beth. Her sharp eyes detected something about the glow that surrounded Beth. She excused herself to Sandra, and went to the bedside. Putting a hand on her brother's shoulder, she stared at Beth. Sean, wrapped in a cloud of happiness that was new for him, looked up, a broad smile on his face. Seeing his sister's expression, though, that grin began fading…to be replaced by a dark expression of concern. A barely perceptible shake of her head caused him to turn back to Beth.

Tamara bent forward slightly, smiling gently down at Beth. "You really seem so much better this morning, Elizabeth! How are you really?"

Beth smiled up at her. "It's like a miracle, Tamara! Ever since you, and Sean, returned…I feel like my health is getting better by leaps, and bounds! I feel more vital inside than I have in a long time! Whatever was in that herbal stuff you gave me worked wonders, Tamara! You should really see about distributing it, Tamara…it's really a miracle sure!" Beth looked up as a man entered the room, and came to the bed. "Ah, Jonathan…I feel so good this morning! Thank you for never quitting on me!…*and* for allowing Tamara to give me her herbal concoction!"

The physician squeezed her hand, smiling down at her. "I can only take credit for part of this, Beth…it was really that herbal mixture that turned the tide, so to speak! I'm afraid we're still in the dark as to the real cause of your illness. But hopefully, those blood samples we took will point us in the right direction…or show us nothing at all! I am glad you're getting stronger, though…you're eating for two now, don't forget! The baby is going to be as strong as you are…remember that!" He nodded over at Sandra, who was approaching the bed. "We hope to have at least the preliminary tests done by this evening. Hopefully, it will shed some light on things…we can only wait, and see what happens. I'll check in on you later, Beth…take it easy, and don't overdo! I know you might feel pretty good right now, but you came very close to dying! So…one step at a time, okay?" He gave her hand another squeeze, and then left.

Tamara gazed after him, a smirk playing about the corners of her mouth. Then, she brought her gaze back to Beth. Beth wondered about the odd expression, looking up at Tamara. "Is everything all right, Tamara? You seem…kind of distracted! What is it?"

The tawny blonde shook her head, dismissing the subject, then looked at Sean. He alone could read something in her eyes. It caused him to pale, glancing down at Beth. He lifted her hand, kissing the palm. She smiled back at him, her eyes shining with the love she felt for him.

Sandra sighed…why couldn't she let go of this? She could see how her sister loved this man, could see how his being here helped save her life…why couldn't she just accept? Just then a nurse walked in, came up to Sandra, and whispered something in her ear. She nodded, and looked at her sister. "I'll be back in a few minutes, Beth…there's a call for me at the nursing station." She was about to leave when Tamara spoke up.

"Is there something wrong, Sandra?…who would be calling you here?"

"I had told the office I'd be here for most of the morning, Tamara…that's who is probably is…I'll be back, Beth!" She gave a cool nod to Tamara, then left.

Tamara watched her to go. "She's a very busy person…your sister. She seems to always be on the go about something!"

Beth agreed, squeezing Sean's hand, smiling at him. "Yes…I'm afraid she's had to handle an awfully lot during my illness! She's done quite the job! But, then…everyone really likes Sandy…she's always been able to get more out of all our employees than any one else! I don't even like to think about my life *without* her in it!"

Tamara was about to remark on that last statement when an attendant walked into the room, carrying a well-laden breakfast tray. He placed it on the bed-side table. "This is for you, ma'am…but the head nurse says not to eat anything until the lab gets up here to draw your blood first."

Tamara frowned. "More blood?...I thought she'd already had blood drawn this morning!"

"She did...but the lab called, and said there had been an accident...something about the blood samples being broken in the centrifuge. That's all I can tell you." The attendant replied, leaving the room.

Tamara stared after him, her mind working...she'd taken care of the problem of the blood samples already...further samples could prove a complication. She looked around the room...only she, Sean, and Beth were left in it. "I really can't believe such incompetence, Elizabeth...breaking the blood sample in such a careless way! If it were me, I'd refuse being drawn again!"

"It was just an accident, Tamara...besides, it's no bug thing having your blood drawn! There's nothing to get upset over!" Beth shrugged her shoulders, wondering why her friend seemed so tense.

Tamara looked away, then back. Beth's smile faded when she saw the golden eyes shining with a strange radiance. She shrank back against the pillows.....

.....Sandra stood at the nursing station, waiting as the nurse brought he phone to her. She lifted the receiver, turning away for a little privacy. "Hello?...Garalynn? Where on earth have you been the last two days" I've left messages all over the city! The cabin?...why were you up there? It's all closed up for the...well, why didn't you get in touch with us when you got back in town? What do you mean...too dangerous? You haven't even been to see Beth! She's fine...an almost miraculous recovery, but she wonders where *you* are!...so do I! I have a right to know what's going on, and I...what do you mean, you can't tell me over the phone? Garalynn...I'm getting just a little fed up with all this! My patience has come to...what? Your apartment?...alright, alright, I'll come there! But,

I'm telling you...there had better be some very good answers for everything that you've been doing! Yes, I understand...I won't let anyone, even Beth, know where I'm going! Don't even *think* about it?...what's that supposed to mean? What did you say?...*who* can read my mind? Garalynn, I want to...yes, I trust you! It's not a question of trust, or even of...okay, I promise! No...I don't understand what you mean, but I will trust you! I'll be there as soon as I can!" Sandra was about to say something else when the phone went dead.

She slowly replaced the receiver, and just stood there a moment, trying to straighten it all out in her mind. Garalynn had sounded so odd!...and what had she been trying to say?...someone reading her mind? She walked down the hall, heading back to Beth's room. She began to let the lyrics to a song go through her mind...over, and over, keeping her thoughts masked. She re-entered the room, and told Beth she had to leave on business.

"It must be very important business to pull you away from the hospital, Sandra!" Tamara's voice was soft.

"It is...you could almost call it critical!" She bent down, and kissed her sister's cheek. "I'll be back soon, sis...you just rest, okay?" Then, she hurried from the room, determined to get some mysteries cleared up.

Sandra had been too distracted herself to notice that her twin sister had made very few comments to her sudden departure. Beth had simply lay back, propped up on the pillows, her eyes never leaving Tamara. The tall blonde nodded, and Beth closed her eyes, snuggling her head deeper into the pillows. In a few minutes, she was deeply asleep, and unmoving. Tamara turned to the nurse who'd come into the room while Sandra had been out. "You can go now...see that my orders are carried out! See that we're not disturbed in any way for at least the next hour!"

The nurse slowly nodded, and left. Sean stood up, glancing at his sister with concern on his handsome face. "You're taking unnecessary risks again, Tamara! What if that nurse hadn't been available to you earlier? Then, our giving them our blood, and tissue would have been suicidal!

Now…they want more blood! How do you intend handling that? They can't keep having laboratory 'accidents', without someone getting very suspicious! Every minute we stay in this hospital, we risk discovery! And what about Elizabeth?…was that really necessary?…putting her under? What if Sandra had noticed her sister wasn't herself? What if that doctor comes back, like he said he would?"

"Oh…be quiet! I have things well under control…I promise you! If I didn't know so, I never would have allowed their taking our blood! I knew they'd order more tests once the original specimens had been destroyed…I just didn't anticipate it being so soon after the 'accident'!" Tamara declared, glancing towards the door. "I wish I knew where Sandra has gone to!…her thoughts were so chaotic, so inane! It was almost as if she were deliberately trying to mask her thoughts from me!…but, *why* would she do that? I wonder…" her voice died away, her left hand absently tugging at her chin.

"Don't make any more problems for us, Tamara! That call was probably just what she said it was…business! What connection could it have had with us?" Sean stated, his right hand stroking Beth's cheek.

'Perhaps…we'll see." She looked down at the sleeping Beth. "Let us hope that your sister is not trying to get herself into a situation she shouldn't, Elizabeth. She may find the outcome one she is unable to accept, or handle!"…….

……Sandra sat across from Garalynn, looking at her adopted sister, and best friend in silence. She'd spent the last three hours listening to what Garalynn had to say, and reading the brief notes she'd written. She wasn't sure anymore if Garalynn still had a hold on the real world…or if her sister had finally lost her grip on reality.

Feeling very quiet and sad inside, certain that Garalynn was seriously troubled, Sandra stared at her. Finally: "You believe everything that this guy told you?…that it's all the truth? You believe everything happened just as you told me?" Sandra held out one hand, pleading for her sister to listen. "Garalynn...wake up! This kind of thing only happens in the movies, or on television! Look at what you've told me, for God's sake!...voices from nowhere, flying out of your body, and talking with the *spirit* of some guy who claims to be over forty thousand years old! He tells you some story that's right out of science fiction, warning you of some ancient evil...and you buy it all! Let me ask you this...if *I* had told *you* something like this, what would you think?"

Garalynn smiled...a response Sandra found slightly disconcerting. "I would probably be thinking the same thing you're thinking...that I had lost it!" She leaned forward, reaching over the coffee table, and grasping Sandra's hands. "Listen to me, Sandy...all of what I have told you *is* true! If you'd only allow your heart, and mind to be open to what I've said...you'd find yourself believing it because it reaches into the deepest part of you, and triggers something there! If you think about it...you'll find it clarifies so much!"

Sandra shook her head vehemently, jerking her hands away. "I can't accept any of this, Garalynn! You ask me to think about it...have you listened to your own advice? The man told you he met Jesus...how can that be true? How can it be anything but some sort of scam...or your mind showing just how troubled it has become? Garalynn...this is either your mind completely going over the edge...or the most tasteless joke I've ever heard! You have to face facts!...how can any of this be real?"

Garalynn sighed. "Why is it so hard to allow yourself to see the truth? Why would anyone make all this up?...what do they stand to gain? Where did they get all the details, not to mention the fantastic, involved special effects? Why would anyone dream up the details that explain all the murders?...especially if none of it could be proven? You're the history expert...how much of what he told me is documented fact?"

Sandra squirmed in her chair...she was being boxed in, and didn't like it. "I guess I'd have to admit those facts, for the most part are very good...except for where he said he came from! There's nothing, anywhere, documented about a race of demi-gods conquering the world, and laying the basis for countless other cultures all over the world, Garalynn! He's delusional!…and so are you if you continue to believe all of what he told you to be the truth!"

"To use a well-stated phrase…what is truth? He caused me to 'see' all that he told me, and even more he didn't!" Garlynn straightened up, her gaze firm and steady. "I have spent the last two days letting all my memories come out…I have seen the end of countless civilizations…the rise of countless more! I saw all the lives I have lived throughout the centuries, Sandra…all my loves, families, enemies, and deaths! The part of me that is of his bloodline has passed from incarnation to incarnation, seeking the one that was to be its last…me! Listen to me…we're best friends, family, and have you ever known me to talk like this?…or act like this? Remember one thing…I didn't *have* to tell you *any* of this! I could have simply gone back to Blackmoon, gone into the Tomb, and find the journal…and you never would have known a thing! I *wanted* you to know…so that someone could carry on if I…if something happens to me!"

Sandra stood quickly, feeling the walls closing in on her. Her voice came out as tense and strained as she felt inside. "Will you stop…please? Use that wonderful intellect God gave you, and look at all you told me…can't you see how utterly impossible it all is, Garalynn?" She could see her words, and pleas had had no affect…Garalynn's belief, and conviction was still strong in the depths of her green eyes. Sandra slumped back into her chair, trying to maintain the strength of her protests…she couldn't. Deep within her own soul, she felt the ancient and irrefutable truth of her sister's words. "Alright…let's say, for argument's sake, that I believe you! Let's say that everything he told you was the honest, logical truth! Answer me this…if *he* was imprisoned, how do we know it was the 'bad' guys who did it? All we have is *his* word for that! What if it's *him* who's the real villain here, and he's trying to trick you into releasing him? How do we know?"

Garalynn stood up, walked around the coffee table, and pulled Sandra to her feet, gripping her by the upper arms, and shaking her. "Listen to me...he's *not* the enemy here, Sandra! Joshua's journal will tell us everything...once we find it! The keys wouldn't have been taken from the Tomb the way they were if the ones who'd taken them were the *right* ones! You have got to believe me...before it's too late for all of us, but especially our dear Beth!"

Sandra pulled free, angry. "Why is it so damned important for me to believe?...tell me that! Like you said...you could have done all this without me knowing a thing! How does this concern me, you...or Beth?"

Garalynn calmed herself...she couldn't afford the luxury of temper. When she spoke again, it was quiet, soft, and calm. "You believe in the existence of God, don't you, Sandy?...in Jesus having been a real man? Why?...other then what's in the Bible, no one's been able to prove He really lived! So...why do so many believe?"

Sandra wanted to snap back, but she couldn't. Her words, when she finally began to speak, were slow, and resigned...accepting. "We believe...because of faith! And, because of what we're raised to believe! Mostly...it's based on faith...accepting something even though we can't see, hear, or touch it! It satisfies something inside each of us...a comfort of a sort, a need realized." She looked at Garalynn, anger gone, her eyes calm, and warm. "So...what does that have to do with the here, and now?"

Garalynn smiled...she knew she had Sandra's interest now. "You said it yourself, Sandy...faith! Do you remember what the Bible says faith is?...'it is the substance of things hoped for, the evidence of things unseen'! Our belief, whether it is Christ, Allah, Buddha, etc...lies within our hearts, where it truly matters! If we can hold the belief, the faith of eternal good within our hearts...then why is it so impossible to believe as firmly in an evil that has existed throughout all time? Archaeologists have found proof that Troy was more than a city mentioned in a story by

Homer...that the tower of Babel had basis in fact, as well as mention in the Bible. The seven wonders of the ancient world have been documented so that we know of their greatness...the pyramids have existed for over four thousand years, along with the Sphinx...why would it be so heard to *think* there's a possibility that this man's people may have once existed! If we accept the lives of Christ, and all the saints as having been true...people we have never seen, and yet accept, on the basis of faith...why not a force that actively seeks the elimination of all that is related to the Light? I know this is a lot to digest at one time...all I am asking right now is that you keep an open mind! Let me show you all that I have...to let you see the truth! Is that too much to ask of my sister?"

Sandra stepped closer, hugging Garalynn. She held her out, at arm's length, looking at her. "No...it's not too much! Alright...make me see the truth! Give me something concrete to hold onto!"

Garalynn reached into her slack pocket, and drew out the pouch she'd taken from the Tomb. Silent, she handed it to Sandra, and waited. Sandra opened it, curious, and dumped the golden amulet into the palm of her hand. She stared at it in awe, then looked up at Garalynn.

Garalynn nodded, understanding what Sandra must be thinking just at that exact moment. She, too, had felt that strange electricity when she'd first touched the ancient piece of jewelry. "You see? Sometimes, there are things we simply cannot find the answer for right away! Sometimes...we merely have to accept the reality!"

Sandra looked back at the amulet. "You were right...this amulet is definitely *not* the norm! But...what about the rest, Garalynn? How can you prove that?"

Garalynn came up to Sandra, so close they were almost nose to nose. "I'll start by asking you another question...Can you tell me, honestly, that over the past few weeks you *haven't* felt the brush of a powerful force?...one of such malevolence as to defy explanation? Can you tell me you haven't experienced the return of fears, and nightmares from your childhood?"

Sandra wanted to yell at Garalynn that she was wrong, that there was another explanation…but, she couldn't. She *knew*, in the very depths of her heart and soul…Garalynn was right…about everything! She bowed her head, giving in…her voice was soft, and resigned. "You're right…on all counts!" She lifted her head again, and looked at Garalynn. "Alright…I'll believe you! I may turn out to be as crazy as you…but I'll go along with you!"

Garalynn let her breath out…she hadn't even been aware she'd been holding it. "I thank you, Sandy…you've done the right thing! We have a lot of work ahead of us! The first thing is for me to get back into that Tomb! I've a pretty good idea where to look for the journal, but it may take a little time…and right now, that's something we don't have in abundance!" She looked at Sandra. "We have to be the first ones to find it!…we have to, Sandra!"

Sandra nodded, then paused. "Garalynn…about these enemies you said were also after the journal…do you know *who* they are?"

"I've a pretty good idea…I'll know for sure when we see them. I also know that they'll may also realize that I know about them when we are together! It's the risk he warned me about. Once they realize the truth…my destruction will become their ultimate goal!" came the quiet reply.

Sandra grabbed her sister's wrist, stepping closer. "I want to know…who are they, Garalynn? Tell me!"

Garalynn turned away, returning to the chair she'd been sitting in. She sat down with an air of sadness. "Sandy, there are some things I shouldn't *have* to say aloud! If you just stop, and think over everything that has happened…you'll find the answer all yourself!"

Sandra sat down on the couch, facing Garalynn…her lovely face a mixture of anger, suspicion, and fear. "You mean it's *them*, don't you? It's Tamara, and Sean!…isn't it? Why, Garalynn?…why our family? How?…how can they be involved?"

"That would take too long to explain...simply put, they are here to prevent his being freed! His being at liberty would be a danger to their plans going through. As for why it has involved our family...I don't have all the answers there! It's not really clear!"

Sandra spread her hands...this was so confusing! "How can *they* be part of the group that imprisoned him? That was nearly three thousand years ago!...no human being can live that long? Are...are they children of the old race?"

Garalynn shook her head grimly. "That's just the point...a *human* being couldn't live that long!...just as a human couldn't have existed in that tomb he's in all this time!"

Sandra's eyes widened, her face paled. "You're saying they're...they're not human beings? But...they look...I mean, they act...dear God, Garalynn, what *are* they really? Garalynn...Beth, she's pregnant by Sean! For the love of God...what is our sister carrying inside her? If he's not human...oh, God, how can this be happening?" Sandra buried her face in her hands, wishing it would all go away.

Garalynn understood. "He's human, and something else...that's the only way I can describe it to you, Sandy. The race he comes from is very like us, yet incredibly different...a different species of human. Homo superior as opposed to Homo sapien!...in almost every way, they're better physically, and intellectually! And, what's worse...those of his race who chose the side of darkness are even more complex, more different inside then our race. They have given up those things that linked the two races...the humanity, the compassion, the love that has always placed mankind above the animals." Garalynn drew another deep breath. "They *look* human, Sandy...in every way, they are a perfection of human appearance! But...for the dark ones, even the appearance doesn't make them human inside! Look...for want of a better term, call them demons! They come straight from the depths of the Hell we've heard about since we were children!...right out of the darkest nightmares we've ever had!"

"Demons?...are you serious? There's no such thing...except in stories! They aren't real!" Sandra waved her hands, trying to push it all from her...Garalynn *had* to be wrong! This sort of thing couldn't be true!

Garalynn couldn't believe how stubborn her adopted sister was being...she had to make her accept it, and believe! It was the only way to successfully combat the enemy they faced now! "How many times, growing up, have we all heard...in fact, you've even said it yourself...that *all* legends, folk lore, myths, and such had some sort of basis in fact within them? Sandy...you're a student of history. You possess an ability within yourself to sort fact from fiction...that's what makes you a good historian. And a good historian knows that too often what we've thought were stories often become facts! Wipe any doubts from your mind...this *is* truth!"

Sandra shook her head. She couldn't believe this!...it was all too much! If she allowed herself to really believe all of this...she'd opened herself to a wave of fear she wasn't sure she could handle. And what about Beth?...what did this mean for her if is was true? She burst into tears, hiding her face in her hands.

Garlynn gazed at her sister, knowing how painful this had to be. "I know how hard this is, Sandy...to let go of yourself, to open yourself to accept things you thought could never be true! I had to go through all that myself! I promise you...accepting the truth makes you stronger...gives you a weapon against them they won't expect! It does get easier!"

Sandra lifted her head, ice blue eyes bright with tears. "All I want to know now is what about Beth? How do we keep them from hurting her any further? I want to know that we're going to beat them!" Her eyes widened, the pupils completely hiding the cerulean blue. "Garalynn...they're the killers, aren't they? They killed those kids...and Doug!"

"I think so…at least, everything I've learned so far say it was them! So, you see…I have a *personal* stake in the outcome here! We'll win, Sandy…because we can't afford to lose!" Garlaynn clenched her fist, emphasizing her determination.

"First things first…we have to find Joshua's journal, and that's somewhere in the Tomb. I understand why the Tomb was vandalized now…they were looking for the journal, and whatever else was needed to prevent the opening of your friend's stone prison! The things that were missing…it all makes sense now! Why did they stop looking, I wonder?"

"For some reason, they appeared to have been pressed for time…they had to leave before they could find everything! Why…I don't know! Something strong enough to make even them nervous! Maybe they felt their part in the murders was about to be made public knowledge…I don't know! The only thing that's important is that they *didn't* get everything they should have…that means we still have a chance! So, we go to the Tomb, and we find it!" Garalynn felt a thin tendril of something alien brush over her heightened senses. She sat erect, turning her head towards the windows of her living room, narrowing her eyes as she concentrated. Try as she might, though, she couldn't locate the feeling again…it must have been just another sense reaching its peak. She'd felt similar twinges as her newly awakened memories, and senses had continued to develop.

She looked at her sister again. "No one living knows the Tomb as well as you do, Sandy…put your imagination to work! Where, if you wanted to hide something, would you put it? We have to find it…have to set him free!"

"Garalynn…why is this one man so important? Why is his being freed…or kept imprisoned worth all that we've had to endure? He's from the same race as they are…you said so…if that's true, *should* we set him loose?" Sandra was still a little hesitant. The more she thought about it, it made certain things make more sense…but, she still couldn't shake her doubts.

"His being freed has more to do with the *time* it happens than anything else, Sandy…though his powers *will* be more then a thorn in their sides! His chief role is to help the Light overcome the Dark! It's a proven fact that eventually all darkness will relinquish itself to the Light…no one's arguing that, even them! But…just suppose that they could find a way to *delay* that happening? A small portion of time, for them, could be several eternities for us. Given enough time…I think the powers of darkness feel they *can* find a lasting solution! But…even a delay would allow the power of the dark to go on, causing mankind untold pain, and suffering! They would have time to find a way!"

"A way?…to what?" Sandra asked.

"To make night eternal! To rob their enemies of that which gives them strength…the eternal Light!" Came the quiet, firm reply.

Sandra stared, a little awed by her sister. "Where did you get all this knowledge from, Garalynn?…from that one time with…with whoever that guy is?"

Garalynn sighed, leaning her head back. "A great deal of it *did* come from the memories he's awakened during our time together…the rest seems to be coming from my own subconscious! It's like a faucet that's been turned on, and just keeps gushing! I think he called them 'race' memories. He said once they started, they'd just keep growing, and emerging! It's unbelievable…the things that are coming into my brain, Sandy! I wish I could share it all with you…then you'd really understand!" Garalynn's enthusiasm faded a little as she thought about the consequences of this knowledge. "It's unfortunate that my new-found knowledge may also be the death of me!"

"I knew there was something I didn't like about them!…or trust! I just still find it hard to believe they're…they're what they are!"

"That's the exact attitude they count on, Sandy!…it gives them their greatest power, the freedom to move among us freely! The inability, or refusal of the human race today to accept their existence feeds their strengths…keeps their powers strong! Demons and monsters…human and inhuman…impossible to believe, but the truth nevertheless!"

Sandra drew a shaky breath…but, she could feel a strength growing within her, a conviction…they would not fail! "So…now what? Where do we go from here?"

"Back to Blackmoon, and the Tomb. Once we find the journal, I'll take it back to the cabin, and make contact again! Did you come in the limo, or your own car?"

Sandra shook her head. "I came by cab. As far as anyone at the hospital, even Beth, is concerned, I'm tending to family business…which isn't that far from the truth!"

Garalynn seemed preoccupied…staring into space, her eyes wide. She slowly brought her attention back to her sister. "Sandy…I think you need to get back to the hospital! I have a very bad feeling where Beth is concerned! Once we know everything's fine with Beth, than we'll head for the Tomb!" Garalynn was listening to an inner voice…one that was saying all was not well at the hospital.

"Why would she be in any danger?…she's carrying Sean's child! He's not going to let anything happen to her!…is he? Garalynn…you're beginning to make me a little scared!" Sandra glanced towards the door…she had the sudden, overwhelming urge to run.

Garalynn began to pace…the sense something was very wrong was growing. "I don't mean to…but I can't shake it! Yes, Beth's important because of the baby…but I can't help but think there's some other reason…and that reason involves Tamara! I think she's got big plans for Beth…and our entire family! I doubt Beth has any idea of what's in store for her!" Garalynn stopped her pacing, and looked at Sandra. "You still need to check on her, Sandy…and right away! We can't leave her alone with them…she's already too far under their control!"

Garalynn had stopped by one of the windows of the living room…one that faced out onto the street in front of the large condominium. A movement caught her attention, and she brought her full gaze to the window. A large limousine was just coming to a stop at the curb across from the entrance to her home.

Seeing how quiet, and tense Garalynn had become, Sandra came up beside her, looking out the window. When she saw the big automobile, Sandra gasped. "That's *our* limo!...what's it doing here? I left it at the hospital, with strict instructions to take care of Tamara, and Sean! How could they have known where I went?"

Garalynn didn't answer...she was to busy thinking. She glanced over her shoulder, at Sandra, seeming to come to a decision. She went to the couch, picked up the amulet pouch, and Sandra's purse. She then came back to where Sandra was still staring out the window. "Listen to me...get to the hospital!...make sure our sister is all right! I want you to take this with you...keep it with you always, do you hear? But...don't even let Beth know you have it!...remember that! Don't forget what I said...she's not to be trusted any more...she belongs to them! Now...get going! I'll meet you at Blackmoon later! Go!" She pushed Sandra's shoulder, pointing to the door.

Sandra looked at the pouch in her hand, then back to Garalynn. "What's this all about? Why are you sending me on without you? I don't understand!" Her heart began to beat faster, and she felt an ache within her souls start to grow...and she didn't know why.

Garalynn took Sandra by the shoulders. "I *have* to stay here, for a little while!...don't you understand? They must have picked up on me somehow...or else maybe they're just here to try, and see if I know anything! Maybe...they're just here to get you, which means they somehow found out you came here! There could be any number of reasons...but it doesn't matter now! You have to go...before they know you're still here! If I stay, they won't be able to follow you...and you can go look for the journal! But...check on Beth first, okay?" She could see the hesitation in Sandra's eyes, and feel the reluctance. "Look...if we both go, then they can follow us, and find the journal! If they haven figured me out yet, then we have an ace up our sleeve...so, you have got to go!...now!" Garlynn looked out the window, seeing the parked car, the tinted glass preventing anyone looking inside. She turned towards Sandra, pushing her towards the door. "Go out the back way...I'll call a cab, and have them pick you up on the corner by the party store! Take the alley, and stay out of sight until you get to the store. Don't forget what I said...check on Beth, go to Blackmoon, and keep that pouch hidden! I'll see you soon!" She gave her sister a tight hug, then pushed her to the door.

Sandra held her by one arm, looking deep within her sister's eyes. "You're trying to use yourself as a decoy...aren't you? I won't let you, Garalynn!...you're my sister!...I can't leave you here alone! You said they were capable of anything!...and I already know what they *have* done! If you stay here...they'll find out what you know...what happened in that cavern! They'll kill you if you don't tell them what they want, Garalynn! They'll kill you one way, or the other! Please...you have to come with me!"

Smiling gently, tears in her eyes, Garalynn shook her head. Loosening Sandra's grip on her arm. "I'll be fine...I promise! I can keep them off-balance far better, and longer if I don't have you around to worry about! If you stay, my concentration will be compromised! Please...go! Make sure Beth is safe!"

Sandra still hesitated...she didn't feel right leaving Garalynn alone. "You'll meet me at Blackmoon? You promise you're going to be okay?"

"I said I would, didn't I? How many times do I say something I don't mean? Get out of here...do what you have to do! Look...for all we know, they're just going to sit there, waiting for one, or both of us to leave, then follow us!" She hugged her sister again, and whispered in her ear. "Leave now...and stay safe!"

With a last backwards glance, Sandra opened the door, and left the room. After she had gone, Garalynn quickly dialed a number on the phone, and ordered a cab. Once that was done, she replaced the receiver, and just stood there, hand still on the phone, thinking about what she had said to Sandra...and how angry her adopted sister would be when she had to break her promise to her. She lifted her hand, irritated with herself when she saw the hand tremble. She walked back to the window, and peeked out...the limousine was still parked across the street. She let the curtain drop back in place, and slowly walked over to the sofa. She sat down, and leaned her head back, her eyes closing, and blocking any further tears from dropping. She'd done the right thing, she knew, in sending Sandra away. That move ensured at least one of them getting to the Tomb ahead of any of their enemies...but she wished she wasn't alone right now. She sighed, settling herself...allowing her mind to shift gears, and begin to produce the necessary thought patterns that would make it very difficult for anyone to probe her thoughts.

She murmured a silent prayer, asking for the inner strength vital to be able to handle everything that was coming her way...especially if the ultimate choice had to be made. Then, like a cold breath on her neck, she felt the small hairs at the nape of her neck lift, and chills spread down her spine. The air in the room suddenly chilled, and became still, and lifeless. Muscles taut with tension, Garalynn slowly opened her eyes, and looked all around the room. It was still empty, but she now felt a sense of urgency she'd not experienced before now. She grabbed the notes still laying on the coffee table, and threw them into the fireplace, watching as the paper blackened, then burst into sharp, bright flames.

She looked around, making sure there wasn't anything in sight that could compromise Sandra, or her task. She relaxed a little, knowing her sister, and the amulet was safe...her mind was still spinning, keeping up the barrier to her thoughts. She could still feel the abnormal sense to the room...and it was growing in intensity! She drew in a deep breath, through her nostrils, then let it out through her parted lips, her eyes continuing to roam the room.

"You actually sensed my coming!...how astute of you, my dear Garalynn!...and how so un-human! Congratulations...there are few indeed who've been able to accomplish such a feat!" The silken voice purred throughout the room, echoing like the slow pealing of a deep bell.

Garalynn slowly turned towards the fireplace, staring at the tall figure now standing there, a self-satisfied smirk playing about the full lips. Garalynn felt her throat constrict, her mouth go dry as Tamara tilted her lovely head to one side. Garalynn was sure that the other woman could actually hear how hard, and fast her heart was beating at that moment. She also couldn't help but noticed how like a coiled serpent the tall blonde was…beautiful in her outward appearance, but deadly in her intent!

Garalynn swallowed hard twice, took a deep breath, than faced her enemy fully…tall, proud, and firm. "I supposed I should say how surprised I am to see you, Tamara…but I'd be lying! I think I've been expecting *you* for a long time! I *do* admit to being surprised how easily you got into my condo, though…how did you manage that little trick, in a *security* building?"

Eyes never leaving Garalynn's, Tamara smiled again, but this one never reached her eyes. "Getting into a place has never been a problem…for me! But, then…you should already know that fact, Garalynn! You've been foolish, my dear…and that's a mistake that will cost you dearly!"

Garalynn moved to her left, keeping the sofa between her, and the other woman, knowing that was the only way to be around Tamara now. "If I have been any kind of hindrance, or bother where your plans are concerned, Tamara…then I'm happy! It's worth almost anything to see you fail! I promise you one thing, Tamara…I will *never* submit myself to you! Don't even try to make me!"

Tamara walked a step, or two, closer to the sofa, then perched gracefully on the sofa arm, one arm lying along the top edge of the sofa's back. She observed the lady lawyer with amusement…and increasing interest. "You talk so strangely, my dear Garalynn…why would I be here to *harm* you, or anyone? Is it such a reach to believe I'm here just to *talk*? I just want to clear the air between us...let you see what it is I am really trying to accomplish...what *I* can offer *you*! Really...all I desire right now is to talk!"

"Do you honestly expect me to swallow that?...to believe you came here just to talk?" Garlaynn scoffed, determined not to allow the will of this woman to override her own. "Tell me you wouldn't relish the thought, or chance to do me great harm?...as you already have by Doug's death!" Garalynn hadn't meant to let that slip, but now that it was said, she was glad to confront Tamara with that knowledge.

Tamara sighed, shaking her head slightly. "I wish you'd listen...I would never desire any harm to *you*! I would more greatly appreciate compromise, or sweet surrender to the alternative of force! There are, I admit, times when force *is* the most warranted of choices." She lifted her arm off the sofa back, elegantly stretching her fingers to their widest width, and length. "I tell you this, Garalynn, in the hopes it will make you see the futility of refusing me...if you force things between, I can cause you the most exquisite of pains, and torments! That is not my wish, however...I'd much rather grant you your heart's desires! Please...do not fight me on this! Willingly give me what I seek...and you will know only satisfaction, and pleasure all your life!" The voice was pure seduction...silken honey-sweet caressing for the ear.

Garalynn could almost feel the sensual power of that voice...tripping along the skin of her arms, and shoulders, like a physical touch. She shook herself, fighting to keep her confidence up, and walking to the end of the sofa. "There is nothing I have to tell, show, or give you, Tamara! Nor, is there anything you have that I would possibly want!...even if my life depended upon it! You've wasted your time in coming here!"

Tamara's eyebrows arched upwards, her lips twitching in amusement. "Oh?...I think I'm a little disappointed in you, Garalynn. Do you really think you can resist me, my dear? Countless thousands have tried, over endless ions of time…all failed! In what way do you hope to succeed where they did not?"

Garalynn knew she was being goaded. She bent her head slightly, her eyes never leaving Tamara's face. "Whatever I say, you'll have a comeback, I'm sure, Tamara…I will not allow you to goad me into losing control! You've admitted who you really are, Tamara…whether you meant to, or not! You speak of thousands of people, and thousands of years…and in a way that states that you *were* actually there! You're not going to win this time, Tamara…I won't let you! Wheels have been put into motion now, my dear Tamara…wheels that neither you, or Sean can stop!"

Tamara threw her head back, the rich laughter echoing throughout the room, vibrant and powerful. "Sean?…do something on his own? Please…the man is ruled by his passions, and his desires! He doesn't possess the true intellect necessary to carry great plans to completion! The very idea if beyond amusing!" She leaned towards Garalynn, the golden eyes strangely warm, and compelling. "Between us, Garalynn…my dear brother is only of any use in matters of the bedroom, if you understand my meaning! I admit that once, he *was* viewed as a terror, a power to be obeyed, and feared…but, even the best lose some of their skills as they age, don't they?"

"You really don't have much respect for your own brother, do you? Does he love my sister at all, Tamara?…and, the baby…what about it? What part does Beth, and the child play in all this?" She somehow knew she could get answers from Tamara…for some reason, the tawny woman seemed almost eager to please Garalynn.

"The baby was actually all Sean's doing!' Tamara grinned as the double meaning of her words struck her. "Satisfy my curiosity for a moment…*how* did you become aware of our true identities? You had no clue at all when we first meant…I know that! What led you to the discovery?"

Garalynn smiled…she'd been a lawyer too long not to recognize the change in tactics. "Nice try, Tamara…but no gold ring! Tell you what…I'll make you a trade! You answer my questions, and I *might* tell you how I came to understand *what* it is I'm dealing with, alright?"

Against her will, Tamara found herself becoming intrigued. She'd always admitted to a great interest in the tall nordic beauty…it was fast turning into an obsession she wanted fulfilled at all costs! She particularly admired the way the lovely lawyer's mind worked…she especially wanted to find out how she had learned the way to block her thoughts from Tamara's skill at reading minds.

"It's not exactly a *fair* trade…I give you facts, and you give me maybes! Still…I find myself eager to do anything to prove how important it is to me that you are…shall we say…happy? Go ahead…ask what you will!"

"Alright…you are obviously someone with great skills, and power…why would someone like that allow herself to be *used* in so dark a way? How could you *want* to be what you are today? Is it worth all you've given away?"

Tamara held up one hand, two fingers raised. "You said *a* question…that was really two! Still…I find myself inclined to reply. But…do me one favor, please? Forget the pious lectures of good versus evil! Don't tell me how my immortal soul is in danger because of the way I *choose* to live! You know, I can stomach almost anything from your people…but *not* their hypocrisy! How can someone with your intense intellect be so gullible as to *accept* that religious tripe?"

Garalynn shrugged. "I don't choose to view it in that light…and I will not get drawn into a debate with someone like you on the merits, or demerits, of following a religious belief! So…let's get back to my question…shall we?"

Tamara waved one hand, dismissing Garalynn's seriousness. "Oh, very well…if you insist on an answer! The truth?…we were the finest race this world has ever seen, or ever will see! Why, with all our gifts, skills, and powers, shouldn't we rule? It has always been, and always will be, our manifest destiny to rule, Garalynn…and we shall!" She leaned closer. "You really have no conception of the power you're attempting to challenge, my dear...I'd advise you to take care! I have no true desire to harm you, or see you suffer in any way! I'd rather you join me...of your own will!" She smiled, arching one slender eyebrow up. "Like the old saying...don't knock it until you've tried it!"

Garalynn's nostrils flared. Against her will and common sense...she was beginning to lose her focus, and temper with this being. Memories of her slain lover moved through Garalynn's mind, and her eyes narrowed. "If you honestly think I'd have anything to do with you...in that sense...than you're more insane than I could ever have dreamed! You killed the man I loved!...tore him to pieces like so much trash! How could you even think I'd let *your* hands touch any part of me! You're obscene, do you know that, Tamara?...beyond anything I've ever known! Some people view gay persons as perverted...that's wrong because I know several, and they're wonderful individuals who simply choose to love in a different way! But...their relationships are as good, or bad as heterosexual ones! I've never used the term perverted in respect to any of them...but you are a different case altogether!" Garalynn could feel all the emotion, and feeling she'd bottled up since Doug's death surging to the surface. "You have so much...you could be so great...and you chose to immerse all that potential under the stench and filth of corruption...and evil! Join you?...not in all the time left until eternity passes away!"

"Don't be so self-righteous! Why is it you homo- *inferiors* always want to debate, or prove your self-worth with us? You can talk a good talk, Garalynn, but the truth is...for all your good words, and intentions, your subsequent actions usually fail to back up everything you've said, or claimed to believe! It's the fatal flaw in your race, and always will be!" Tamara studied her nails with a nonchalance that was annoying. "You people always talk, such beautiful and passionate words...about having faith, and believing." She glanced up at Garalynn. " Living in the true way of faith is something very few humans have been able to accomplish, Garalynn. The only way Faith is successful is when it is *unshakable!...unstoppable!...unending*! Few indeed have been the number of humans who've been successful in staying with such a demanding, unyielding way of life! And that is why *our* lord, and all who follow him will ultimately always triumph! That is why we will always survive...far beyond your race! We will always be the ones left standing!"

"Don't *you* talk about how much better than we your race is!...you betrayed all that your Creator intended you to be! You chose the darkness...you had your chances, with everything my people can only dream about, and you failed! My race may not be so all-powerful, and we're far from perfect...but we do possess a capacity to care, and a desire to better the world around us! Our efforts may not always be the best ones, but we at least try! Your kind *had* their day in the sun...it's gone now! Now...it's our turn, and though we might stumble, and fall...we'll pick ourselves up, dust ourselves off, and keep on trying! One day...we *will* succeed! And, despite all your powers, Tamara...there's nothing you can do to stop that! It is as inevitable as knowing the sun will always rise the next day!"

Slowly, the smirking smile gone, Tamara rose to her feet, facing Garalynn. "Look at you...so full of righteous indignation! Your eyes have been blinded, Garalynn...as were my own once! It has always been the right...the destiny of the mighty to rule over the lesser peoples! That is in the natural order of things...even among the animals, it is the strongest, the most powerful and intelligent who leads the pack! Your race today is no better than when we first ruled over it! Oh, yes...you've advanced a great deal, technologically and intellectually, since that first era...but you're still no closer to our level than an amoeba is to a DNA matrix! Listen to me, Garalynn...even your race possesses its 'dark' side!...deny it though you may! And that fact is the key to our strength against you! You may not want to admit it, but your race craves that darkness...and the power that comes with it! History has always been nothing more than a struggle between the strong, and the weak! Power is what it is all about, Garalynn…power makes kings of beggars, and paupers of kings! Power raises great civilizations and dynasties…power is what destroys them!" Tamara held out one hand towards Garalynn, fist tight and strong. "Hold the key to power, and you hold the key to the world! Control all that power is…and you will rule forever!"

Garalynn could only stare, open-mouthed, and wide-eyed. "You really believe all that…don't you? I feel a great pity for you, Tamara…you may have all the power you seek one day…and you will be the loneliest, most wretched person alive at that same moment!"

Tamara was beginning to lose patience. " Listen to me, Garalynn…put all this trivial matter aside…allow me into your life! Join me…be with me…and the greatest desires of your wildest dreams, and of your heart will be realized instantly! No matter what that desire may be…you need only voice it to me, and it will be yours!" She held out her hand, palm up, her eyes warm. "Please…come to me. Let me show you what real power can be…even in the realms of love…and if you still desire not to be with me, then so be it! But…at least, give yourself the chance to weigh, compare…and choose! Is that asking so much?" The voice was soft, compelling…reaching into Garalynn's very soul, and tantalizing it with the fulfillment of ecstasies beyond comprehension.

Garalynn's mind was a little confused by the hypnotic gaze of those golden eyes, and she tried to shake off the touch of that formidable will. She turned away, repulsed by the sensation., shaking her head. "Nothing *you* can offer me, Tamara, could ever make me change my beliefs…or my allegiance! Even if I could ever remotely entertain such a thought…do you think I'd surrender myself, physically, or otherwise, to the creature who murdered my lover? Why can't you see that?"

Tamara drew a breath in, settling the thread of her thoughts *before* they tore apart, and gazed at the object of her current frustrations…and obsession! "Have you ever been revered as a goddess, Garalynn?…of course not! You have no idea the intoxication, the absolute warmth such adulation, and devotion can bring! King, princes, generals, entire empires...once all bowed their heads, and might, to *me*! Was I to give *that* up to return to a way of life whose time had come, *and* gone? I think not! My time as a goddess will return again...it has been so promised!" She sighed, and looked at Garalynn again. "If you open your eyes...you will see that the demise of that man you claimed to love was a necessary step to re-establishing the way it should be! You will see your place in the true plan of things, and know where you should be standing!...at my side!"

"Can't you see that you're as much a slave as the thousands you once ruled over!...you're not a goddess! You're a servant! I may not ever possess the powers you do, Tamara...but I'll forever be freer then you! My lifetime may be a mere sweep of a clock's minute hand compared to yours, but I wouldn't trade it for the shackles your immortality carries with it! Tell me...if I were to join you, would I also be a slave?"

Garalynn saw anger come, and go in those bewitching golden orbs. Tamara stepped a pace closer. "You would never be treated, or judged as a slave! I would not allow such a thing! And, despite what you think...*I* am slave to no one! I serve the one I do out of free choice, not bondage! All that I am, all that I will be is due to *my* efforts, and self-worth! I will always have a great sense of gratitude to my lord for all he has given me...and I acknowledge a debt because of this. But...I am not a slave!" She held out her hand once again, but her eyes this time were not warm. "Make this easier for everyone, Garalynn...join me willingly...tell me what I want to know! Than...everything will proceed as it has always been meant to!"

Garalynn appeared to be thinking...Tamara knew a slight thrill as it seemed that the lovely lawyer was leaning the right way. Then, Garalynn looked up. "And what exactly is it that you would have me do?" She realized, however distasteful it may be to her personally, she did have a power over this powerful woman...if she played it right, she might be able to win this.

Humming a little tune of satisfaction to herself, Tamara came ever closer, reaching out, and softly running the back of her right hand over Garalynn's left cheek, smiling. Garalynn held herself in check, hiding her revulsion at the other woman's touch.

"It's so simple, Garalynn...all you need do is answer a couple of questions! Once that is done, we can get on with our life together...and you will never want for anything in your life again! You have my word on that!" Tamara's fingers slid down the cheek, along the jaw line, and settled on the slender neckline, over the pulsing artery.

"And what might those questions be?" Garalynn knew she wasn't going to be able to hold her emotions down much longer.

"Where is the amulet?...and where is the journal of Joshua Phelps?" Tamara breathed, her lips bare inches away from Garalynn's. She was bringing the full force of both her telepathic powers, and sensual powers to bare on Garalynn's senses.

Garalynn senses were reeling a little...it was a little difficult to keep clarity in her thoughts, but she fought back, her eyes blinking with the effort. She shook her head, and looked directly into Tamara's eyes. She could feel the warmth of the other woman's breathing on the arch of her neck. "Tamara...you, and I both know that you have no intentions of keeping your so-called word! Once you got all that you needed from me...I would be beyond expendable! Your kind doesn't know the meaning of the word honesty, or integrity! There's nothing further I have to say to you! I will not betray everything, and everyone dear to me!"

Tamara cocked her head to one side, a slight smile playing about the full lips, but a murderous rage flaming in the golden eyes. The hand that had been caressing Garalynn's neck continued its movements, but now with a strength that was far from loving. "Do you honestly believe I would let you leave here?...after refusing *me*? I could have taken you any time I so desired, Garalynn! But...I wished to give you the chance to come to me on your own! I could destroy you with a single motion of my hand!' Her hand slipped around the column of Garalynn's throat, and the lawyer found herself suddenly unable to move. "A single squeeze, and it would all be over! How strong is *your* will, Garalynn?...how steadfast *your* faith? Tell me...what would it take to tempt you? I repeat my offer...join me, and you will live a life people only dream possible!"

Her flesh shivering slightly at Tamara's grip, Garalynn tried to pull away, but failed. "What have you done to me?...I can't move!"

Purring like a cat playing with a mouse, Tamara stroked the fingers of her free hand over the shoulders, and throat of the woman she held captive within her grasp. She ran her hand up the arm of Garalynn, and slipped into the long blonde tresses when reaching the shoulder. She brushed the hair back, exposing the back of Garalynn's neck, the bared skin breaking out in goose bumps at the cool air striking it. Tamara leaned forward, murmuring into Garalynn's ear. "Tell me what you would give to be free of this situation, my dear Garalynn. What would you want?...your price, as it were? No matter how extreme...name it, and you will be freed! By my word...all I desire is your happiness! Just tell me what I need to know!"

Heart pounding, Garlynn weakly shook her head...her voice was harsh and raspy due to Tamara's grip on her throat. "I want nothing from you, Tamara...and I will not tell you what you want, if only because I do not know where those things you asked for are at this moment!" She managed to glare fiercely into Tamara's eyes. "No matter what it costs me, I will always defy you! I will never give into, or join anything that is connected to you, and yours!"

With a hard jerk, Tamara pulled Garalynn up tight against her own body, her hand tightening about Garalynn's throat. "You stupid fool! You could have ruled like a Queen, at my side! You would have had everything in life that would pleasure you! But...you couldn't allow yourself to 'see' the truth!...so be it! You made this choice on your own!...remember that! You will be mine, in the end...know that as fact! You wanted to really know me?...look well, *human*! See the face of your deepest fear, your greatest hidden terror! Look well, and let me see that faith…that courage you were talking about so bravely! Let your last conscious thought be how this could have been avoided! You could have had it all, Garalynn!…now, you will have only darkness!" The hissing voice became deeper, more powerful, and more menacing in its timbre.

Through the red haze trying to smother her senses, Garalynn saw a change coming over the features of her enemy. She blinked her eyes several times, trying to clear her vision. She tried to push against that now rock-hard body, hoping to break free…but, to no avail. She tried to speak, to scream her protests of disbelief at what her eyes now were seeing. But…nothing came out of her mouth, just a hissing of strangled breath. She felt the fear surging, the terror taking over her entire body. Her heart was going too fast, trying to burst free of the chest that imprisoned it! Her breath was going too fast, and her senses began swimming from lack of oxygen. Her legs were trembling, threatening to buckle under her.

She used every bit of strength left to her, forcing her tortured throat to work, and croak the words out of her mouth. "God in Heaven…grant me thy strength! Into thy eternal keeping, I place my immortal soul!" The words were uttered in the language long vanished, but remembered by Tamara. She shrieked in anger, bringing her other hand up to Garalynn's throat…she was determined to break this person, and bend her to her iron will. The last thing Garalynn saw, before the blackness took her sight, was the contorted rage of Tamara. She felt the enraged woman's breath searing her throat, felt a stinging pain, and than………

****

IX

❀

……..Sandra stood at the nurse's station, staring at the head nurse in disbelief, her eyes wide, and her mouth open in shock. "What do you mean…my sister's not a patient here any longer? She was here just a couple of hours ago! Who had the authority to over-ride Dr. Hodges' orders? When did she leave?"

The nurse was uncomfortable, and concerned about the situation…she knew they could be in very big trouble. "*She* checked herself out, ma'am! Every patient has the right to check themselves out, unless they've been classified incompetent…even if it's against doctor's medical advice! She requested to leave about twenty minutes after you had left…you know, when you received that phone call? The couple that was in her room with her were the ones that took her away. I tried to delay them until we could either get in touch with you, or until Dr. Hodges got back from the cancer center in the city! She wouldn't stay, and we couldn't refuse to let her go! If it's any consolation for you…she was in good condition when she signed herself out! I checked her over myself before she left! I'm very sorry…but, didn't she go back to your home? You didn't see her there?"

"I haven't been back to the manor house since I left here earlier! I know you don't like cell phones used inside the hospital building…so, can I use your phone again? I'll call, and see if she's turned up there!"

She could hear the words she spoke, could hear the nurse's replies…but, her mind was swimming in numbed shock. She was remembering what Garalynn had said about keeping Beth safe…how emphatic she'd been. Why had Beth left?…without letting Sandra first? Who was behind this?…and why?

The nurse handed the phone over, and left Sandra to her call. Sandra quickly dialed her home number, and waited for someone to answer. "Roland?…it's Sandra, and I'm calling from the hospital. Is Beth there, with the Dresdens? She's not?…well, have you, or any of the others, heard from her at all today? I'm asking because Beth's checked herself out of the hospital…against the doctor's wishes!" Sandra's voice rose an octave as her control slipped a bit. She gripped the receiver tighter, and settled herself back down to a more normal tone. "I'm sorry, Roland…I'm just worried! Beth didn't say a word to me before she left!…no, I wasn't in the hospital at the time! Listen…I'm going to check a couple of things out…if you see her, or hear from her, contact me! Yes…I've got my cell-phone with me! I'll check back with you soon!" She placed the receiver back on its rocker, and tried to convince herself that there was a logical, normal…*safe* reason for her twin sister's actions….so, why couldn't she come up with any?

She put her hands in her coat pockets, and felt the lump in the right one. Her fingers closed about it, seeking some kind of comfort. She picked up the receiver again, and rapidly punched a few numbers. She listened to the ringing, willing for someone to answer…that someone being Garalynn! She pushed the reset button, and redialed. She waited through several more rings…still no answer. She slowly replaced the receiver, staring off into space, her eyes wide and her throat tight. She felt a gnawing fear growing in her gut…what was happening back at that condominium? Sandra turned, and ran down the corridor. Her mind kept repeating over, and over…"Please, God…let it be all right! I can't lose her, too!"……..

.......David sat on the edge of one of the three sofas in the living room, his elbows resting on his knees, his hands dangling between them. He felt sick at heart, and angry as all hell! Once again...he'd responded to an emergency call, and found yet another scene of carnage, and insanity! Only this time...he knew the owner of this home! He'd been here, more than once, with Sandra. He really liked the lovely, charming woman who'd lived here...and he hadn't already been deeply involved with Sandra, he'd have been only too glad to date the lady lawyer who was her adopted sister.

He bent his head, staring at the floor between his feet. Around him, his men were quietly going about their respective tasks. He couldn't believe the wreckage! He'd thought he'd seen a trashed place when he was in Douglas Traylor's place...but this made that look almost immaculate! There was one big difference also...at the Traylor place, there'd been little, or no blood. This wasn't the case here, at Garalynn's condominium...here, blood was everywhere! And, the coroner had said there was more then enough blood to fill a human body, and then some! But...that was the unsettling point...there was no body to be found! At the Traylor apartment, he had a body, and no blood...here, it was tons of blood, and no corpse! As insensitive as it sounded, he wished he did have a body! At least then, he could have a body to give Sandra, and Beth! A poor consolation, at best...but far better then not knowing! He looked around, his chest aching with emotion...what had happened here? Why would someone want to...to what, his mind asked?...no one was even sure yet what really *had* happened here! Was this blood Garalynn's...or a victim not yet known?

He stood up slowly, looking towards the fireplace. One of the lab guys had told him they'd found fresh ashes in the firebox...he thought it was some papers that had been burned, and that there were a few small sections still unburned. They'd know more when they got the ashes back to the lab for testing. They'd also found a few tiny tufts of what looked like some kind of animal fur, over by the largest sofa, which was literally soaked in blood.

The sound of a loud gasp drew his attention to the doorway. His eyes widened when he saw Sandra standing there, being restrained by one of the uniformed police officers. David hurried to the door, taking her in his arms regardless of the gawks, and grins, and pulling her away from the scene he'd just left. "Shut that damned door, and keep it shut!" He snarled at the officer, and ushered Sandra a few feet away from the door.

He held her tight, feeling her trying to get away, to go back to the door. "Honey, no! You don't want to go in there, believe me! Besides…it's a crime scene, and you're not official personnel!" He wrapped his arms tighter about her, keeping her trembling, struggling form against his. "Come on, baby…please, don't fight me on this! Sandy…listen to me! You can't go in there right now!"

She threw her head up, glaring at him with tear-filled eyes. "You let go of me, David Collison! This is *my* sister's home, and I have every right to know what happened in that room! Where is Garalynn?…what happened in there?" Sandra pushed against his chest with frantic strength. "Let go of me!…tell me where my sister is!"

He cradled her against his body, trying to keep the tears from falling himself, and wishing he had something concrete to tell her. He let her rage, knowing she'd never be able to handle what was yet to come if she bottled her emotions up inside. She stormed at him for a few more moments, then finally went limp in his embrace, clutching at the broad shoulders with fingers of iron. She cried as though she'd never stop, the tears soaking the front of his shirt…she could hear the deep heartbeat increase as he hugged her close…murmuring softly into the dark wealth of her hair.

Finally, she lifted her head, a shuddering breath escaping her parted lips, her cheeks awash with fresh tears. Her lips trembled, and the incredible blue eyes mutely asked questions. "David…please, tell me…what has happened here? Why does that room look like a…a slaughter house!? Garalynn...where is she, David? This doesn't make...I don't understand any of this!"

He pressed his lips against her forehead, allowing them to linger there as a sigh of deep regret escaped. "I wish to hell I could tell you, sweetheart...but the honest truth is...we just don't know right now! We're not even sure if all that blood *is* from a human being! The lab boys will be able to tell us soon...and if it is human..." He took a deep breath, steeling himself to continue. "If it *is* human, then we still have to prove it's Garalynn's, Sandy! We don't have a body...so, if someone's been killed...well, again, we have to prove it's Garalynn! I was at the station when the call came in, and I recognized the address! Look, all we know so far is that it's a pretty good chance that something very bad took place in that room! This being Garalynn's condo...well, it's a good bet she's somehow involved...either as victim, or...we don't know any of that yet, honey...and you're being here isn't going to help us! All you can do, right now, is tell me all you know about Garalynn's movements today. The neighbor who called it in said the noises that caught her attention happened about two hours ago! Do you know if Garalynn was home about that time, Sandy? Maybe...she was at a meeting, or maybe the hospital, or Blackmoon?" He was hoping she'd give him information that would prove that the lovely lawyer wasn't involved, in any way!

Sandra shook her head, chewing at her lower lip. "No...no meetings! She *was* here...at least a couple of hours ago! I was here, too, with her! She'd called me at the hospital, saying she had to see me right away! We hadn't heard from her for a couple of days...everyone was worried because it's not...wasn't like Garalynn to keep away from the family, especially with Beth having been in the hospital! I asked her where she'd been, and she said she'd explain everything when I got here!" Sandra leaned her forehead against David's chest. "We were talking...about Beth, and things! She was warning me about..." Her head jerked up, and she gripped the fabric of his shirt with both hands, staring into his eyes. "She knew what was going to happen!...that's why she sent me away! She promised she'd be okay…that she'd see me later!…but, she lied! She knew we'd never see one another again! She sent me away from her…to keep me, and Beth safe! God damn…Garalynn, you knew what *they* were capable of!…you told me all about it yourself! You sacrificed yourself!…you promised me you'd be okay…but you went ahead, *without* me, and now…" Her voice gave out, and she buried her face into the hollow of David's left shoulder again.

He could feel the gulping shudders that racked her body as she cried again. He rubbed a gentle hand in rhythmic circles over her back, the other cradling the back of her head, keeping it supported against his shoulder. He thought about what she'd been saying, and it had thrown him. He had to get her calmed down, find out what she'd meant by her wild statements…there might be a clue that would help them. He gritted his teeth, irritated with himself for being so…so a cop! But…right then he knew, he was the only one who could get Sandy through this…and he knew she'd expect the best effort from him. So, he pushed his own personal grief, and anger down, and gently lifted her chin up until she was looking into his eyes.

"Sandy…tell me what you meant by all that just now. What did Garalynn sacrifice herself for?…what was so dangerous that she'd do such a thing? And, what did she want to warn you about? Who, or what meant her *that* kind of harm?" He motioned towards the closed room with a jut of his chin. "Who is this *they* you mentioned?"

She sniffed, wiping at the tears on her cheeks. She knew she had to confide in David…but where to start? Her entire world felt like it was crumbling down about her shoulders. "It's…complicated! I'm not sure I've got it all completely straight in my own mind!…let alone try, and explain it to you! She had so many really strange, and unbelievable things to tell me before I went back to the hospital, and…the hospital! I almost forgot!…David, Beth's missing! She left the hospital, against medical advice, and I don't know where she's gone! Oh, God…Garalynn said we had to keep Beth safe! I don't know what to do!" She turned away from him, trying to think...her heart was pounding, and she felt like she was going to pass out! She closed her eyes, trying to slow her breathing, and keep from panicking altogether.

"Whoa!...slow down! Beth's left the hospital?...why?" That didn't sound like the Beth Sandra had told him about. He'd met Beth several times, of course, but her being a hospital patient kept him from really getting to know her well. "Sandy...why were you here today? What did Garalynn want?" He wanted to ask more about Beth, but he knew he had to get things back on track right now.

"She wanted to let me...I mean, to tell me about some things she'd discovered that could both explain a lot of things that had happened lately, even the murders! She was so intense...so different than her usual self! I didn't want to believe anything she told me, David!...it was too incredible!" She slowly shook her head again, tucking her clasped hands up under her chin. "I began to believe her, a little, when she showed me a few things...I should have believed her all the way! If I had, maybe..." She lifted her head, staring at the ceiling. "Forgive me, my dear friend...my sister! I was so wrong!" She whispered softly.

She pulled herself together, as much as she was able, and turned back to face the anxious policeman standing close behind her. "David...I have to know...was she mutilated, like those kids?"

"Baby...we don't have a body to know that, remember? Listen...we don't know, for sure, that the blood is hers...do we? We'll have to wait for the tests...you know what type she was, don't you?' God...he hated asking questions like this, at a time like this...but he'd rather it be him asking the questions, then one of the other officers.

Sandra nodded, feeling drained. "Yes...she was O negative! And, I seem to recall that she said they found some type of antibody in her blood...what did she say it was?...I think it's something like Anti-Colton, or something like that! It's rare, I do know that...she said it was really rare!" She sighed, just wanting to be far away just at that moment...far from all the pain, anger, and fear. "She's dead...isn't she, David? I mean...all that blood...it can't be good, can it?"

"Sandy...look at me! If there's something you know, that you might be keeping from me...you've got to tell me, love! What did she tell you that was so unbelievable?...that makes you feel it's connected with this? Honey...you've got to talk to me! If only for the fact I'm the investigating officer on this case!"

She pulled back slightly, her eyes never leaving his. She was suddenly afraid that the knowledge she carried within her could harm him. She gazed at him, wondering what he would think if she were to tell him all the fantastic things Garalynn had told her. How would he react if she did tell him? Wouldn't he respond the way she did?...with scorn, and disbelief? How could she tell him? And, yet...what if she said nothing, and the killing continued?...the terror went on, as it had for centuries!? How could she face him then?...face herself? What would Garalynn *want* her to do? She squared her shoulders, and looked directly at him...even if he laughed in her face, she had to tell him! She had to make him see...before it was too late for him, too!

David had seen this mental battle being waged, watching the emotions come, and go over her beautiful face. He had the feeling that what she held within her was exactly what he was looking for...the evidence he could use to end this horror. He reached out, touching her gently on the chin. "Sweetheart, I'm not going to bite! Come on...tell me what's going on? What happened today, with you and Garalynn? What is it that you're afraid to tell me?"

She shook her head, confused, hurting, and angry. "If I were to tell you what Garalynn had told me today...I know you'd think I had lost it entirely! It's all a whirlwind inside my head right now!" She looked at him, her eyes begging him to believe her...to understand what she was feeling right then. "At first, what she told me was so confusing...so fantastic...I just couldn't take her seriously! Then...I *did* begin to believe, little by little! It all began to make sense...cold, hard, *terrifying* sense! I'm afraid you'll...you won't believe it, either!"

He took a deep breath, gripping her shoulders. "Look...I hate coming across like a hard-nose...but there's already been several homicides, and this is a probable! I have to be the one to find the answers, Sandy...and right now, I'm telling you that *you* could be considered a possible suspect!" He nodded, seeing the expression of shock on her tear-stained face. "Don't be so surprised...it's only logical! After all, you were here, and so was she!...you said she was acting funny, and that you were probably the last one to see her! So...until you're questioned, and they can rule the possibility out, you become a suspect!" David knew he had to push her...he knew that an eager assistant district attorney wouldn't hesitate to grab her, and wring whatever she knew out of her...regardless of the consequences. David knew he couldn't allow her to be put through that...he had to get her to talk to him!

She stared at him, then suddenly reached up, cupping his face between her hands, and kissed him soundly. She gazed at his infinitely dear face, caressing one cheek with the fingers of one hand. "I want to tell *you*, David...I just don't know where, or how to even begin! It's all so unbelievable!...you're going to think both Garalynn, and I are completely crazy!"

He shook his head, pulling her close. "Haven't you learned by now that you can tell me anything?...that anything concerning you, or your family is vitally important to me? There's nothing you can't tell me, Sandy...nothing! If I'm pushing, it's because I care, and I don't want you to go through anymore than you already have...I don't want you hurt anymore!" He looked away, weighing the merit of telling her the next thing he was about to say, then looked down into her face. "Sandy...I don't want whatever happened in that room to happen to you...don't you see?...it could have been you! Now, tell me!"

Sandra made up her mind, and glanced around. Satisfied no one was close enough to overhear them, she leaned into David, whispering into his ear. "I can't tell you here, David! They may still be around...or have someone watching us! We've got to go somewhere private...someplace they don't know about!"

He went a little pale, staring at her. "Who, Sandy? I don't follow...who, or what are we talking about here?"

She shook her head, refusing to go any further on the subject right then. "There's too much to tell you...and I don't feel safe speaking about it here! I want to tell you...but I can't do it here! Please...try to understand!" She looked at that closed door, and her eyes filled with tears again. "It may turn out that my family has had to pay a heavy price for the knowledge we carry...but there's too much at stake now for anything but the whole truth! Please...lets go somewhere else!"

He looked down at her, taking inner counsel with himself. Then, decision made, he turned from here, and strode purposefully to the closed door. He spoke a few quiet words to the officer standing there, looked back at her, then went into the room, closing the door after him.

Sandra leaned back against the wall, closing her eyes, feeling the tears slip out under her lids, and down her cheeks. "Why did you send me away like that, Garalynn?" She whispered to an unseen spirit. "You were the one who told me what they could do to you! I should have stayed with you...or gotten you to come with me!" She brought one hand up to her mouth, choking back the scream that threatened to erupt. She was consumed with an anguish she hadn't felt in years...the same tearing of heart, and spirit that she'd experienced at the deaths of mother, father, and ex-husband. "Oh, God...I can't take this!...please, let them find her!"

She opened her eyes as she heard the door opened again. She watched as David walked towards her. "All taken care of...so, let's get going!"

He took her hand, and briefly touched her cheek with his free hand. She smiled crookedly at him, and they headed down the corridor, towards the main entrance. He glanced once, or twice, at the silent figure beside him. He wasn't sure what it was she had to tell him...he wasn't even sure he really *wanted* to know. He did know, however, that it was something he had to know!......

.....Sean sat in the limousine quietly, not daring to even move around in his seat, or speak a word. He wished himself anywhere, but here. He especially didn't want to be anywhere around his sister...the mood she was in was deadly for those about her. He could only remember one other time like this...when Tamara's rage was so intense, so public...so out of control. This time, she actually had him very scared! All she had done, since they'd left Denver's city limits was rant like an insane woman! He kept glancing at the driver, separated from them by a sliding glass pane. He was sure that the man had to have overheard the majority of Tamara's tirade...he'd glimpsed the man's eyes looking at them in the rear view mirror. The driver had been reluctant to leave the hospital, and then the city...he had said Sandra had given him precise orders about staying close, and keeping available, and he really didn't want to make his boss angry. Tamara had screamed at him, telling him he'd better do as he was told, or he'd be worse than just fired!

Sean finally gathered his nerve, and leaned forward slightly. "Tamara...you have got to settle down! If you keep on like you have the past half hour, the driver's going to really get suspicious, and probably turn back to the city! Even worse...he could use the car phone to call Sandra!...or the police! Please...control yourself!"

She threw a small pillow at him, narrowly missing his head. She picked up one of the heavy lead glass tumblers, and hefted it in the air. "Another word, Sean...and it'll be *this* instead of a pillow! And, what do I care *what* that idiot driver thinks?...he'll do as he's told, or he'll be as dead as the rest! The same goes for you as well!...don't tell me what to do!"

He reached out, imploring her to listen to reason. "Tamara...we have things to sort out, and your present state of mind is *not* conducive to making the best decisions! I think we need to find some place that's safe, and plan out our next moves!"

She grabbed his hand, bending the fingers backwards, while squeezing the knuckles tightly. Even with his powers, Sean felt the increasing pressure. "I said…don't tell me what to do! For your insignificant information, I've already decided where such a place may be, and gave the driver orders to go there! Anything else?"

Sean grimaced in pain, sweat breaking out on his forehead. "Tamara!…let go of my hand! You're breaking the bones! No…no more questions, just let go!"

She flung his hand back into his face, and sat back in her seat. Her lovely jaw set, and eyes hard, like crystalline amber, Tamara watched Sean shake his hand gingerly, wincing as the fractured bones raked over irritated nerves. "You have failed to grasp the most basic of facts in this situation, Sean! I can handle almost anything…except an act of defiance! And that is what she dared to do, Sean!…she defied *me*! She actually stood there, despite knowing the price, and refused me! I promised her the world…riches, power, pleasures beyond anything she could ever dream of! But…no matter what I offered, promised…or finally, threatened!…she refused to give me what I demanded of her! I still cannot believe that she did that!…that she would take death over me! No one has ever done that before, Sean…not to me!"

Sean was really getting concerned…she wasn't even trying to be rational! She was keeping the level of her rage high by letting it consume her emotions, and he wasn't sure she could regain control at this point. Of course, his inner voice whispered…if she *does* lose it altogether, then this would be *his* chance to regain his position as the most favored! But…the logical side of his psyche argued…was it worth having his sister as a full-fledged *enemy*, instead of a reluctant ally? Besides…for some reason, he wasn't as interested in seeing this through as he had been! "Tamara…did you find out anything about the amulet?...or the whereabouts of that journal?" He finally spoke up, hoping the tone of his voice didn't betray his inner turmoil.

"She had the amulet...I saw it in her mind before she died! But...it wasn't anywhere in that place of hers!" Tamara replied in a flat voice...staring out the side window. "I was so sure, Sean...she *should* have given into me! We should be celebrating the success of this mission...together! How could she so defy me like that?...where was she getting that strength?...that knowledge?" She brought her gaze back to the worried, and cautious face of her brother. "I am on fire inside, Sean...I can't settle my mind, and heart! I want to curse her!...curse her soul to all the depths, and shades of hell itself! I want her to feel the pain of rejection, and lost love as she has given them to me!...and I thought I had done that!...that when I felt the heat of her blood on my hands...in my mouth, it would all be over! But...I was wrong! And that makes me want her even more then I did before!...only, now it's too late for anything!...for hate, for defiance, for retribution...for love! Curse her!...I still don't believe it!"

Sean spoke firmly, slowly, and with great caution...he wasn't sure just how far she could be pushed in this state of mind. "Tamara...I've given this a great deal of thought, and I'm convinced she was *not* an ordinary mortal! She couldn't have, and withstood all you...I mean, no regular person would...I just think there was more to her than you thought when we first came here! Perhaps...a descendent? That possibility *could* answer a great many things, don't you think?" He could see she was barely listening to him, and this further agitated him...he had to reach her! "Tamara...this outburst has gone on long enough! Do you *want* them to find us?...to win?"

Her head jerked around, and she glared at him in shocked disbelief...he knew the extent of her rage, and he still dared to speak like that! She slid forward on her seat, teeth bared. Sean tried to keep a firm gaze, but finally shrank back, acknowledging her the superior position. She leaned across the space separating them, hissing her words out between the clenched teeth. "Don't think to take advantage of my lapse of control, *dear* brother!…you don't have the power necessary to destroy *me*! At this moment, brother or not, I would gladly add you to the list of victims!…don't push your luck!" She held him motionless for a few moments with the intensity of her gaze. Than, with a slight wave of her hand, she dismissed him, and sat back with a loud sigh. "I, too, have thought about that, Sean! When we came to Denver, for the first time, I was on the alert for anything like that…a descendent, even a sensitive! I was also on guard against the enemy here, or their agents! I found nothing!…I felt nothing, until just after your strange illness! And then, what I felt didn't come across like any of those! I'm still not entirely certain what that feeling really portended even yet." She looked at her brother, and he could see that her usual control was beginning to re-assert itself. Her voice was calmer, more its normal sultry depth. "When we returned this time, however…there *was* a difference! But…I wasn't able to clearly access her thoughts. Somehow, she was able to block most of whatever it was she now knew…that was when I began to take a greater interest in her, Sean…and that turned into something else!"

"What was the difference you sensed, Tamara? What did you 'see' that hadn't been there before?" He asked quietly, breathing a little easier inside as it seemed she'd calmed down to her normal self once again. He was still very much on his guard, however…with Tamara, it was the act of a fool not to be vigilant!

"When I first met Garalynn Gagnon, there was something I couldn't fathom, but I put it down to simple attraction. But…the next time we met, there was suspicion, an awareness…she knew about us! How this came about, I'm not certain yet…but that it was there, I knew without a doubt!" She looked out the window again, her voice un-customarily soft, and Sean was shocked to hear an underlying current of sorrow in those dulcet tones. "I was so sure she'd turn…I wanted that more than I've wanted anything in centuries, Sean!" She just didn't understand why things hadn't gone the way they usually did, and what bothered her most was the depth of the intensity of her final response to the situation. She leaned her head back...she hadn't reacted with such emotion in a very, very long time!

"How?...how could she have known? Who...what is there here with the knowledge sufficient enough to be able to discover the truth? Tamara...she had to have been a sensitive, or a true descendent! That's the only possible answer!" Sean looked about him nervously, seeking the unknown enemy.

Tamara shrugged her slim shoulders, her outrage finally over, and her icy control back. She reached over to the third side seat in the limousine, and pulled the blanket back from the shape it covered. She gazed in quiet satisfaction at the sleeping features of Beth Phelps. She replaced the blanket, and sat back, looking at her brother, a slight smile playing about her lips. "The reason behind her knowledge doesn't really matter any more, Sean...her threat has been neutralized! And, when we finish with the next step, it won't matter *who* knows!...they'll all be taken care of, one way , or the other! We have the upper hand in every way that matters, Sean...as it was always meant to be! Everything is going to be ours again...as promised! Our family will once again be the greatest of all the families...and the ultimate goal is nearly ours!"

Sean looked at the sleeping woman, then glanced again, over his shoulder, towards the driver. "I'm still unconvinced that taking Beth from that hospital was the correct method of response to this situation! We were in the clear, Tamara...this is going to complicate things greatly! I don't understand...you'd taken care of the blood samples, and without arousing suspicion. And, with your curing Elizabeth, they really weren't that eager to keep after us! You even had Sandra's suspicions eased...she was profuse in her gratitude to you. Why take her from the hospital?...wasn't that an unnecessary risk?"

Tamara sighed...sometimes he was so blind, never seeming to grasp all the needed facts in a situation. She couldn't help but remember how strong, unyielding, and brilliant a strategist he once used to be...she shook her head. "Yes...we'd seen to the immediate dangers, Sean, but when I saw Elizabeth...really *saw* her I knew it was only a matter of time before everything would be in the open! This way...*we* are still in control of things! Yes...they'll soon figure out whom Elizabeth is with, but by then it will be too late! Don't worry...I know Sandra Phelps better then she knows herself!...she won't allow anyone to step in, and possibly cause harm to her beloved sister! She'll negotiate with us alone...and she'll give us what we seek!...if she ever hopes to see Elizabeth again, alive and well!" She nodded at him. "As for the threat from other sources...I suppose it *is* possible for Garalynn to have been contacted by, or herself contacted a member of that accursed group...but I don't think so! It wasn't easy to get any information from her mind at the end...but what little I did get held no signs of that! It is a possible explanation as to why I didn't sense anything the first time."

There was an audible tremor in his voice as he sat up straighter. "But, Tamara...we know there *is* such a group in this area! We know some of the members, and where there are a few, there are many! But...how could they have any idea we had been here? We...you were so secure on everything! Do you think they had something to do with her...with Garalynn's defying you?"

She looked at him, mildly exasperated with this continuing fear. "You don't live the life we do, Sean, without learning to expect *anything* coming at you!...especially where any of our enemies are concerned! I don't know that *they* did have anything to do with Garalynn...but I do not rule such a possibility out! Humans are like the basest of insects, brother...but, like insects, they can be swatted away, or crushed underfoot! I am not about to let them sway me from what I seek, Sean!...they'll do so at their own risks!"

"Tamara...don't you understand? This is not about your opinion of humans, or anything else like that! This is about what's going to happen when Sandra Phelps discovers her sister has left the hospital! And when what happened to Garalynn comes out, she's going to begin to put things together…not a difficult task, by the way…and she'll be after us will all she can throw together! And, with her money, and family's status, the force she'll gather will be a formidable one!" Sean was trying to put it all together. "You haven't really tried to cover our tracks this time…why? If they're able to put things together…how can we ever go home? We will have failed the family, even if we *do* somehow get the things we were sent here to obtain! And, you…you're making it unerringly clear for them to follow! Taking *this* automobile, which is high profile…no matter where we go, someone is bound to see us! And your actions at that house…was it necessary to be *that* violent?"

She snarled, angry again. "I told you…don't question my actions, or my motives, Sean! I told you…she refused, and defied me! It gave me great satisfaction to completely destroy all that intellect, beauty, and skill!…to make sure no one ever experienced it ever again!" She calmed herself, the poise as shocking as the calm after a tornado. "I will forever regret not turning her…she would have been a beautiful asset to have around!"

"I don't think it would have been a good thing, even if you had been able to convert her, sister. I don't think you could have ever really trusted her! She would have always been a subtle threat to our family!" Sean sighed, though…the thought of that beautiful woman being around was a very tempting one. "But…as you said, it's of no matter now! Answer me this…why the cabin? I would think that Sandra would think to look there right away!…she's hardly a stupid woman! Besides…there's the driver, and the security guards at the compound…what about them? They're sure to either call the police, or try and stop us!"

Tamara's smile was arch, and deadly. "Why *not* the cabin? It's private, well-stocked, and from what Elizabeth has told me, quite comfortable! Why not be comfortable while we have to wait? As for Sandra sending the police after us…we'll be contacting her *before* she figures it all out! Don't worry…she'll do as we bid! As for the driver, and the security people...I'll handle all that." She glanced at her watch. "We'll be there in about twenty minutes. Tell the driver to stop after we turn onto the entrance road, alright? There's another good reason the cabin is the ideal place to stay...we need the seclusion, Sean...especially now!" She pulled the blanket over Beth back again, and lifted one of the window shades, allowing the sunshine in. It flooded over Beth's sleeping face highlighting the sculptured cheekbones. Sean glanced at her, then looked up at Tamara, not understanding what she was trying to get him to see. He looked down at Beth again, and hissed in a quick breath as he suddenly saw what his sister had meant.

Beth looked completely recovered...a miracle in itself when one remembered that just a couple of days ago, she'd been quite literally at death's door. Rose bloomed in the high cheekbones, and the dark curly hair shone like it was pure silk! The supple, firm flesh was soft as a breeze's caress, and the tanned skin was a gleaming bronze...certainly not belonging to someone who'd been deathly ill. Sean recognized the soft, velvet-like shimmer to her skin...it was the same as his, and Tamara's! He raised his eyes, asking a silent question of his sister.

She nodded, tossing the blanket back over Beth's shoulders. "Yes...that's the reason I had to move her from the hospital! When I realized what was really happening to her, I knew it would be but a small matter of time before the doctors made the determination that there was more to Beth than an unidentifiable illness. I'd been able to stall them where *our* blood was concerned...*her* blood was another thing! There would not have been any logical way I could have blocked them taking more of hers without really rousing suspicion! They were already alerted enough, trying to identify what they'd discovered thus far in her blood samples...if they got a sample of that blood now, it would be all over! Taking her, or rather, convincing her to sign herself out of the hospital seemed the best way out!"

Sean leaned forward, touching Beth's cheek with the back of one hand. "I don't understand what happened, Tamara...it's never done this before! I did everything you said!…to make her compliant to our every wish! Yes…I admit I tried to advance my own agenda by getting her pregnant!…which, by the way, I didn't know was successful until Garalynn called us in London! But, even *I* didn't plan this!" He pointed at the sleeping woman. "This wasn't supposed to happen!…turning her into one of us! How?…a true morph is nearly impossible to achieve! You know that, Tamara!…it's something that's rarely seen because it takes *two* of our race to realize its completion! I was one…who was the other? I can swear Elizabeth was not with anyone else since we first started! So…how can this have happened?"

She leaned back, her eyes always on Beth's face. "Honestly?…I don't have a clue, Sean!" She looked at him. "Why did you have to complicate matters by impregnating her, Sean? You were told to make her compliant, obedient…*not* pregnant, dear brother! How did you think this wouldn't be found out?…or, the attempt on your part to put yourself first?"

Sean was shaking, certain he was about to be destroyed as she had so many others who'd disobeyed her direct orders. "Does it matter now, Tamara? I was wrong!…no matter what I hoped to gain! But…you seemed to know even *before* I did!…how?"

She just shrugged…it wasn't that important to her. "The fact that I did know is all you need to know…or worry about, Sean! I will tell you this…you are *very* lucky we're so close to our goal! If we weren't…your continued existence would not have been a solid certainty! The family is still deciding your punishment, you know…they were not at all pleased about the pregnancy!"

He closed his eyes, swallowing hard against the gorge threatening to overwhelm him. He opened his eyes, gazing at her, so golden, so sure. "Tamara…when we finally get to the cabin…what are your plans?"

She frowned. "What are you getting at, Sean?"

He gestured over his shoulder, towards the driver. When he spoke next, it was in the ancient language of their family. "The driver of this car…will he not require dealing with?…as well as the security guards? What are thy intentions for them?"

"The driver is as nothing…as are the guards. They will become 'servants', willingly, or not! Do not worry further over the insignificant, brother…if they become a problem, their existence is terminated! Cleanse all further doubts, and fears from thy mind, dear brother…they sap thy strength! Prepare thy mind, and thy strengths!" She replied in the same tongue.

He bent his head, ashamed he could no longer control his fears. "Would that it were as simple for me as it is for thee, Tamara! This I know, however…thou must take care as well, my sister! Thy pride, and rage may blind thee to dangers ahead!"

She jabbed a finger towards Beth, then out the window, indicating the approaching night. "There are no dangers ahead we cannot deal with, Sean! The darkness will shield, and protect, as always. We hold all the odds in our hands at the moment, and this means Sandra will have to do whatever we deem to get her beloved sister back! The fact that that sister is now becoming one of us isn't necessary for her to know right now…nor that Beth will *never* return to her!" She nodded, confident as always. "As for going home…there is a contingency plan for situations such as this, so don't worry about such things! Soon…all this will be behind us, and we shall return to our beloved home, and the strength of the family! Keep that thought uppermost within thy mind, brother…it will be thy strength!"

Sean nodded, gazing at Beth once again…she was so beautiful, so desirable. He shook himself as the familiar stirrings began going through his body. This was not the time…he sighed, bringing himself back to the present. "I still want to know what happened with Elizabeth…what could have caused this?" He asked, switching back to English.

Tamara stared out the window, thinking hard. "Those forces I've sensed from time to time…they are, in some way unknown to me as yet, responsible for all the strange events here! You know that one of the reasons we were sent here was to form an alliance with this family. The Phelps hold a *very* unique position in history's chapters, past, present...and future! It was desired that they become members of our family...and that was to be achieved through *your* specialized talents, Sean! You succeeded admirably where Elizabeth was involved...Sandra was yet to be influenced, however...Garalynn was an unknown factor, which I chose to work on."

"Sandra is not like her sister, where personality especially matters, Tamara! I was not allowed sufficient time to work on her...and Garalynn was the same, though I think I could have reached her sooner then Sandra. Why was it so important that this alliance as you called it become reality?" This was the part he still didn't understand. True, the Phelps family were powerful, influential, and wealthy beyond rich...but what was it that his family so desired as to instigate such an alliance?

"That's not important now...I'll explain it all at a later time. For now...ah, here's the road to the cabin. Tell the driver to stop about a mile in...I'll take it from there!" Tamara smiled...one of such dark intent that even Sean shuddered involuntarily.

Sean nodded, and gave the required instructions. Then, he sat back thinking...he shivered again, then shook himself angrily. He tried to keep the negative thoughts out of his mind, but they refused to be ejected. Tamara was right...he had to get himself under control, and prepare his forces for what lay ahead...or he would be finished!......

.......Hunched up in a chair, David gazed at Sandra, his eyes quiet and thoughtful,

his expression bland. He rubbed the stubble on his chin, wishing for a second that he'd had time to shave before this. With a sigh, he looked again at his lovely lady, and waited for her to continue. Sandra stared back at him, waiting also...for his snort of scorn, disbelief, or the expression in his eyes that would say he thought her insane. She'd just finished telling him everything she, and Garalynn had discussed that afternoon. She'd shown him the amulet, watching him closely as he fingered the shining gold. Now, she wondered what *was* going through his mind...why he was so silent.

"Well?...aren't you going to say anything?" She finally couldn't stand the quiet any longer.

He straightened up, still very quiet. "You've told me everything she told you?...there's nothing you might have forgotten, or thought not important?"

She nodded, not understanding this reaction...she'd expected far different. "Yes, that's all of it! Now do you see why I said you'd think I'd flipped? If Garalynn were here, she'd..." her voice choked as she thought of her sister's grisly fate. She looked away, her eyes filling.

His voice cut into her thoughts. "Why do you think I don't believe you, Sandy?"

Her head jerked around, and she stared at him in disbelief...and relief. "You mean...you *believe* me? How?...why? Other then the amulet, I don't have a thing to prove anything I told you! How can you say you believe me?" She'd been so prepared to be disbelieved she wasn't sure how to respond to any other actions.

He stood up, walked to the refrigerator in his small kitchen, opened it, and took out a beer. He came back into the living room, twisting the cap off the bottle as his walked. He sat back down in his chair, and took a long swig from the bottle. He held the cold bottle against his forehead, sighing slightly as the cool glass soothed the heated skin there. Then, he looked at her, and smiled slightly. "The fact is, hon...though there's no concrete reason, I *do* believe all you told me! I'm not just trying to humor you, so get that expression off that pretty face!" He held out one hand, palm up, trying to get his point across. "Look, I can't give you a why...the fact remains that I believe that everything Garalynn told you is the truth! Maybe it's what they call a leap of faith!...or just a gut feeling! I don't know...only that, inside, I believe! The question now…where do we go from here?" He sat back, taking another drink of his beer. "Taking any of this to the authorities is out…no one would believe any of this! I haven't been entirely open with the chief about everything we've found on these murder cases…I can't go to him without tipping my hand! Besides…the captain, the chief, and the commissioner are hardly the type of men who believe in fairy tales, dragons, demons, and bogey men! So…what now?"

Sandra lifted her hands, showing the frustration, and helplessness she was feeling at that moment. "I don't know! Garalynn was the one with all the knowledge…the memories, she called them! She was the one who was to find the things we need…and what had to be done once we'd found them! Well, *I* don't have those memories, David…I can only go by what she'd told me, and with whatever help this thing can give us!" She held the amulet up, from its resting place around her neck, hidden by her blouse collar.

He put his beer down, stood up, and came to where she was sitting. He bent over her, lifting the amulet gently in his hand. He looked at the bird image on the front side, then turned it over, and gazed at the tiny hieroglyphics there. "This is one of the keys she told you about? What, exactly, is it a key to?"

"I'm not a hundred percent sure!…it's involved with the journal, helping to set free whoever is in that stone coffin she talked about, and also to help prevent some great catastrophe from happening! David…how are we supposed to find that journal when I'm not sure my interpretation of Garalynn's words is the correct one?" She bent her head, wrapping her fist around the amulet in frustration. "What am I supposed to do?"

He knelt down beside her chair, tugging on his right earlobe…an old gesture he did in moments of decision, or great stress. "Well…let me think like a cop here…if we take everything she said as true, then we have to believe that the race of people who made this amulet were as technologically advanced as she indicated…right?" He paused, waiting for a response from Sandra…she nodded slowly, her eyes on his. "Okay…so, if this thing is necessary for some sort of…let's say, ceremony, alright? If it's needed for a ceremony, then there's got to be something, maybe written down, that tells what the exact role it plays is supposed to be! In other words, this thing may look like a piece of jewelry to everyone else…but, to the right people it's much more!"

Sandra leaned forward, a hand to his cheek. "David…I'm impressed! You've hit it on the nose!…I should have thought of that earlier, if my head wasn't so messed up right now!" She reached up, and slipped the heavy chain over her head.

She turned the amulet over, bringing it closer to her face, and studied the picture writing all over the amulet's back side. David watched her for a few seconds, then leaning close, he said softly, into her ear. "What are you looking for so intently?"

"The ancients had ceremonies for just about everything, David…and prayers as well! They especially used prayers where the dead, and their peaceful rest in the other world were concerned! They wrote all these down, on walls, stellae, monuments, etc…but, to them, it was the *spoken* word that held the greatest power! To speak the words of prayers, blessings, or supplication was to grace those words, and the ceremony that might accompany them the deepest meaning, and honor!" She stared at the amulet, trying to calm her rapidly beating heart, and bringing to mind everything she'd ever learned, or been taught, about the deciphering of the hieroglyphics. David stayed where he was, kneeling beside her, watching her face as she concentrated.

"That's it!" She declared after a few moments, and pointing at the carved picture language's symbols on the amulet. "This is why she didn't want the amulet to fall into their hands!"

He looked at the spot her fingertip indicated, then shrugged his shoulders…he had no idea what she was trying to show him. "I don't get it…what does all that stuff say anyway, Sandy?"

"I can't make it all out, but the few words I can translate seem to indicate this amulet is needed in a ceremony of opening the mouth, or something like it!" She slapped her hand down on her slack covered thigh. "I wish I was better at this!...David, what we need is someone who's more skilled in translating hieroglyphics! That would give us the full meaning of this...I am convinced this amulet is the way to go!"

He shook his head...she was amazing. "You think this is all tied in with Beth's disappearance from the hospital, don't you?"

"Yes...it's all connected somehow...especially if Beth is with the Dresdens, and I believe she is! If she'd shown up at the manor house, or any of her usual haunts, I would have been notified by now!" She held up her cell phone. "But...nothing so far! I also believe that whoever it is that has my sister...again, I say the Dresdens...is also responsible for Garalynn's disappearance, *and* all the other killings here lately! And, David...I know, in my heart, that Garalynn *is* dead!" She stared at him, jaw set, and the incredible crystal blue eyes like hard diamonds. "I am going to find the monsters responsible for turning my world up-side down, David...and they are going to pay!"

He leaned forward, still on his knees, slipped his arms about her waist, and pulled her close. "Sandy...I know I said I believe you, and everything you said about what Garalynn was trying to do...but, I got to tell you, this talk about monsters, and ancient evils is beginning to get me a little spooked! I'm just glad Pat, or the captain can't hear me right now!...they'd be measuring me for the loony bin!" He kissed her on the forehead, staring off into space.

She shook her head strongly, looking up into his eyes. "Not just monsters, David...demons! Beings right out of the nightmares of our youth...with all the powers of darkness at their command! The thought of my sister being in their hands...the thought of what she's carrying inside her, pregnant by such a...a thing!" The sky blue eyes clouded over. "I can't bear to think what Garalynn must have gone through at their hands! I wish she hadn't sent me away!" Her eyes filled with hot tears as the pain, and anger roused within her again.

"No!...no, she did what I would have done, Sandy! The thought of you being...if you had stayed, you'd have been killed as well! She knew that, and she couldn't let it happen...so she sent you away...to save you! I don't think I could stand it if you had been there, with Garalynn, and they...God, Sandy!" He clasped her tight against him, his stomach lurching as the thought of her death went through him.

She cuddled close, enjoying the feel of his arms around her body. She closed her eyes, willing away everything except the feel of this man, and the clean scent that was uniquely his. She wanted to stay like this forever, but her rebellious mind nudged her, reminding her of the tasks ahead. "David...we have to go now! We've got to find someone to help us with the amulet!"

He lifted his head, twisting so he could see her face. "Do you know someone?...they're going to have to be trustworthy, as well as skilled, Sandy! If these people are as dangerous as you've said, they're bound to have others helping them! You have to be careful who you talk to now! You also need to know whether, or not, this person is going to believe us...and not think we're completely wacko!"

She smiled suddenly, wide and hopeful. "As a matter of fact...I do! He's an old professor of mine, and a good friend of my father! This is just the sort of challenge he lives for, David! I'll call him right now...he'll see us tonight, I'm sure!" She pulled away from him, and went to use the phone.

David turned, slipping from his knees to sitting on the floor next to the chair. He watched her as she talked quietly on the phone, and remembered how chilled he'd been thinking of what could have happened if Garalynn hadn't had the foresight to send Sandra away. He realized in that single instance just how important she'd become in his life...and he whispered a silent 'thank you' to Garalynn's spirit, and the unseen forces that watched over them all. He knew that he had to say something…even if it wasn't exactly the right time, or place. He shook his head…he couldn't take the chance that something could happen to one of them, and he'd never told her what was in his heart.

She hung the phone up, and turned to say something to him. She saw him staring at her, such an odd expression on his face. She walked over to him, and looked down at him. "David?…are you okay?"

He looked up at her, and rose to his feet. He cupped her left cheek in his right palm, and gazed at her so intently she began to get a little nervous. "I'll tell you in a bit…that professor willing to see us?"

"Yes…he said to meet him at his office at the university in about an hour!" She cocked her head to one side. She wondered why he still looked so odd…so distracted. A thought occurred, and she paled a little, wondering if this was why he seemed so absorbed in thought. "David…if you don't really want to come with me, to see the professor…you don't have to!"

"You trying to ditch this cop?" He growled, scowling to hide his surge of fear at the thought of her out of his sight.

She shook her head, the fingers of her left hand fiddling with the bottom edge of his tie. "That's the one thing I will never want to do, David! I know how weird things are right now, but when this is all over…and we're still able…" She looked up at his face, the azure of her eyes seeming to surround him as he looked back. "David, I want you to listen, because I intend telling you this for as long as I am alive! When this is all over, we're going to have a very long, private talk…because, you see, I happen to be very much in love with you, Lt. Collison, and I want you in my life forever! Do I make myself quite clear, sir?" She stood on tiptoe, and kissed him, softly and warmly.

His arms slid around her, and pulled her tight against his body, feeling her curve into him, filling all the spaces all along his length. He nuzzled into the crook of her neck, not wanting her to see the glint of tears that suddenly appeared in his eyes. "Would you mind repeating that last part, please? I think my ears are in shock!"

She placed her hands on either side of his head, and lifted it up so she could see it clearly. She wound her fingers deep into the thick curly hair over his eyes. She couldn't remember her heart being so full, even with all the pain, loss, and anger. "I said…I am in love with you, Lt. David Collison! Do you need to hear it again?" She said in mock sternness.

"If I have anything to do with it, you'll be saying it everyday, for the rest of our combined lives!" He gazed down into her uplifted face…a wide grin on his face. "God, how I wish I didn't have cases to work on…or, that we had this thing to resolve! I can sure think of how I'd like to spend the next few days!" His eyes involuntarily drifted towards his bedroom.

Her body arched into his, and she wrapped both arms about his neck. "When all this is behind us, I'm going to hold you to that idea, sir! I won't let you back out, so don't even think of trying!"

His grin got even wider, and he held her close, sharing the warmth and tenderness of the moment. It had been a long time, this special feeling…for both of them. He bent his head over hers, and sealed the moment with her lips parting under his, and their tongues caressing, and seeking. Sandra moaned softly, his mouth capturing the sound, and giving it back with his own, deeper groan. His large hands, fingers splayed wide open, pressed into her back, and buttocks, pulling her in tighter. She responded by grinding her hips once, hard, against his. He groaned louder, feeling the sweat break out on his forehead. Reluctantly, he gripped her by the shoulders, and put a little space between their bodies.

Sandra sighed, though it sounded more like a whine…she understood, but still didn't like it. "I guess we'd better get moving…the professor will be expecting us!" She looked at David, her eyes clearly showing the love, and desire she was feeling. "Just so you'll know…that idea you have?…I've got the same idea!" She purred in a low, sultry voice.

"Good…things are always better when everyone's in agreement!" He joked, kneading her shoulders gently. Then, his expression went serious.

"Just remember...no matter what lies before us, you are not alone!...got it?"

She could feel his strength, his love, enfolding her with its power, and helping her to face the future. "Got it...and, thank you! " She kissed him, quick and soft. "That thought is what's keeping me going...that, and getting Beth back, safe and sound! Come on...let's get going!"

He nodded, digging his car keys out of his pocket, following her out the door, squaring his shoulders for whatever was out there waiting for them....

.....Professor Yusuf Hanradi, head of the Department of Antiquity at the Denver Metropolitan Museum, and professor of Ancient History at the University of Colorado, raised his eyes from the study of the golden amulet, and gazed at Sandra, and David, an enraptured expression on his bearded face. "This is simply marvelous, my dear! One of the finest examples of amulet workmanship I've ever had the chance to examine! And its condition...absolutely mint! This is priceless...beyond monetary worth!" He lovingly ran his gnarled fingers over the surface of the amulet. "You say your sister found it in the Tomb?...in a concealed drawer? Amazing!...I've been in that room countless times, and never suspected there was something we hadn't inventoried already! And...this is supposed to help you locate Joshua's missing journal?"

"That's what I was told...exactly how, I'm not sure of yet. Can you make out the hieroglyphics?...I was able to make out a few words, but I guess I'm a little out of practice." Sandra leaned forward in her chair. They were in the professor's office at the university...surrounded by artifacts, scrolls, piles of papers and folders, and the professor's beloved expresso maker. Sandra had smiled, discreetly, when she'd seen the battered, but still working coffee maker. She remembered how, even in classes, the Egyptian-born teacher was never without his favorite mug full of the hot beverage.

"Yes...I believe so. They appear to be mostly a series of prayers, and intonations taken from the Book of the Dead...see this?" He pointed out a small sun symbol. "That's a prayer to Ra...asking for the god's guidance in being able to speak freely in the land of the dead. I've only had a quick examination of the words, but to give you, and your young man a condensed version...these prayers deal with rebirth, being able to visit the land of the living, raising the dead, and the granting of the powers necessary to achieve all of the above! For the ancients, there was...*is* a great deal of power contained within these few passages, Sandra!...a great deal, indeed!" The sixty-eight year old scholar stroked his beard, bemused.

Sandra nodded...that was the kind of answer she'd been expecting. "Would it be safe to assume that such an amulet would be necessary in a ceremony?...such as raising the dead, or freeing someone from imprisonment?"

He looked at her sharply. She had been one of his best students, and he knew how keen her insight could be at times...where historical subjects mattered. He suspected, though, that this time something beyond history was on his former pupil's mind. "Yes...it could play a vital part! Remember, Sandra...the spoken word was all-powerful to them, my dear! It is a documented fact that even the king had his favorite prayers, spells, talismans, and amulets! To be without was considered by them to be open to attack from enemies, and the forces of evil!" The professor sat back in his chair, pulling his glasses down so that they balanced on the end of his nose...a favorite gesture Sandra remembered him using to intimidate a student. "Sandra...I'm a little confused on one point. You said this is to help find the journal...how is that going to happen? To my knowledge, based on what your father had told me several times...no one in the family has seen that journal since the time of Joshua's death! Supposedly, it will stay hidden until needed...according to the legend...and then, it will appear to help defend against a great danger! What makes you feel this is the time the story speaks about?"

He looked at her closely, reading the expressions that came, and went over her face. David had the keen impression that this teacher knew more then what he'd let on. Then, he shook his head...he was thinking too much like a cop!

Sandra wasn't really sure how much to reveal to her old teacher, and friend. She trusted him completely...that wasn't the problem. She wasn't sure it was right to drag him into a potentially fatal situation...she cared a great deal for the old scholar, and didn't want to see him in any danger because of her. She shrugged, hoping her tone of voice was calm enough. "I was told it would be a help...that's all I can tell you, Prof. Hanradi. As for the journal...I don't know. I only know I have to find it!...and fast!"

The professor looked long, and hard at her, then he looked at David. He held the amulet in one hand, his thumb smoothing it absently...his thoughts hidden, his expression blank. Then, he lifted his head, and Sandra was surprised at the look in his eyes. She'd never seen such firmness, such determination of purpose, in those eyes. "I think, my dear Sandra...that it is time for total honesty between two old friends...don't you?" He held the amulet up. "What is the truth on how you came to have this? Why is it so important for you to have me see this...that you come in the night, with your own police escort? I know there is something you have not told me, Sandra...and you must tell me everything! I am your teacher, your friend...and I swore an oath to your father that I would protect you, Beth, and Garalynn with all my strength if something should happen to him! You three are like my own daughters! Now...what great terror is it that you're keeping from me?"

"She's told you what you need to know, professor...what are you getting at?" David spoke up, his voice low and firm.

"What I have been told tonight, David...it is but the tip of the proverbial iceberg...isn't it, Sandra? I have know this woman since she was but a child...and her sisters as well! I know when she is in great pain...as she is now!...and when she is consumed with anger...as she is inside at this very moment! I know that there must be something very deadly to make her this way, and the fact that her two sisters are conspicuously absent tells me that danger is very real!" He held up the amulet again, and looked directly into David's stern, yet worried eyes. "This *is* one of five items documented as being hidden by the high priests of Amun-Ra, and Isis! It is believed to have first been used, indeed created, by the followers of Horus…mythological semi-divine beings who ruled thousands of years ago…long *before* the Pharoahs came into power! It is said to possess the power of the seventh level of the Seer…a being legend says will bring the Light back into the world!" Yusuf sat back, a little breathless from his impassioned oration.

"Who…or what is the Seer, Prof. Hanradi?…I don't recall that being discussed in your classes!" Sandra frowned, strangely intrigued.

"I never brought it up in class, Sandra…it is not common knowledge…indeed, few are the number who know of the amulet's existence, or of its vast, and terrible history, my dear! It, and the Seer, are secrets long guarded for over ten thousand years, my friends. Since the Age of Leo…10,500 BCE…it has fallen to the Keepers of the Seer to protect all things connected with that most complicated of secrets! Even today…all over the world, the keepers stand ready to fight the dark powers. These forces seek to possess, in their entirety, the powers of the seventh level!" The professor's voice had gained in both volume, and strength as he talked.

David glanced sideways at Sandra, and was gratified to see she looked as confused as he did. He leaned forward, pointing a finger at the professor. "Who are these Keepers, professor? And what the hell is the seventh level?" David wondered if it could be these mysterious Keepers who were his unknown killers.

"I remember reading something, somewhere, about the Followers of Horus…a French archaeologist first put the story forward about ten years ago. But…I didn't think there were many American archaeologists who bought into that story!…I especially didn't know *you* were one of them, Yusuf! This amulet…why is it you're so familiar with it? Yet…that wasn't the impression you first gave when I handed it to you!" She gazed at the old man. "Yes…I think you're right…it's time for complete honesty between old, and dear friends! I'm going to tell you *everything*, Yusuf! Then…I think…you have some things to tell us!"

David put his hand over hers, causing her to look at him. "Sandy…do you think that's wise? I mean…I think the fewer people who know about this, the better! We don't know who could be working with…well, you know what I'm getting at, don't you?" He was feeling a little left out here…like the professor, and Sandy were on a different level then he.

She looked at him for a few moments, then leaned over, and kissed his lips softly, and briefly. "Trust me, David…we're among friends here. I think we're also going to learn things vital to accomplishing what we must!" She looked back at the professor, and smiled. "I'm correct, aren't I, Yusuf?"

He nodded, smiling cautiously. "Yes…it *is* time you learned certain things, Sandra…things only privileged persons have been privy to over the centuries. And, things that have involved *your* family as well…in ways you could only dream of! Yes…I think it's time! First, though…tell me everything that has happened to bring you to me!"

Sandra took in a breath…she wasn't sure if she really was ready to renew the pain, and anger within herself…but it had to be told. "I guess the best way to tell you is to start with Beth…and her involvement with what I realize now are some very dangerous, and highly unusual people!"

"Tell me precisely what you mean by that, Sandra!…how exactly are these people unusual?" Yusuf was immediately interested…leaning forward, resting his hands, and elbows on his desk top.

Sandra looked at David, who slowly nodded, then she looked back to her old teacher. She squared her slim shoulders, took a breath, and started to speak, beginning with Beth's trip to London, and all the events that trip put into motion……..

.......Beth stretched, rolling over on one side, and opening her eyes as she let out a wide yawn. She felt incredible...refreshed, renewed, and vital. It had seemed like a very long time since she'd felt this good...this complete. With a sensually deep sigh, she sat up in the bed, and looked around. With a start, she realized she wasn't in the hospital any longer...so, where was she? This room looked familiar...large, and airy....

"What the...I'm at the cabin! How on earth did I get here?...an why? The last thing I remember...I was at the hospital, getting ready to leave. Tamara, and Sean were with me, and...what is going on here?" She muttered, standing up. That was when she realized she was utterly nude! Her eyes widened...she never slept in the nude! She leaned over, picking up the green silk robe draped over the foot of the bed, and slipped it on.

As she fastened the belt around her waist, her fingers brushed over her softly rounded abdomen. To her sensitive fingertips, it seemed as though her stomach had gotten larger...a point emphasized when her wandering fingers received a gentle bump as they went over the area of her navel. Beth's eyes widened...it was too soon for this feeling...wasn't it? She crossed the room, and sat down in front of the dressing table. She picked up a brush, and began bringing some order to the dark curls. As she brushed her hair, she gazed at her reflection in the mirror. She was pleasantly surprised to see that all signs of her former illness were gone. Now, she had a glow of well-being she thought she'd never see again!

As she was finishing her hair up, she heard heavy footsteps from the hallway, headed for her door. She turned on the bench seat, and gazed at the door. In a few moments, it opened, and Sean came into the room. He was dressed merely in slacks, with the broad chest bare, and his eyes warm as they looked at her. He grinned at her, seeing she was awake.

"You're finally awake, my love...good!" He came to her cupping her chin, and kissing her gently. "How do you feel?...better?"

She felt that surge his touch never failed to awaken in her. This time, though, there was something else...uneasiness, and a sense of loss. "Sean...what am I doing at the cabin? The last thing I remember is being at the hospital, with you, and Tamara! I don't recall leaving, or coming up here! Why are we here? And, why don't I look, or feel sick any more?"

He took her hands, gently pulling her to her feet. Once she was standing, he slipped his arms around her waist, and pulled her close. "Tamara, and I brought you here last night, Elizabeth...don't you remember? Tamara had given you some of her medicine in the hospital...an old family remedy. She felt that what you needed was complete quiet, and privacy while your recuperation progressed." He looked down into her crystalline eyes. "You agreed with us, Elizabeth...even suggested coming here. Surely, you must remember our discussion prior to leaving the hospital? You said the cabin was one of your favorite spots to get away from things, and rest!" He used his considerable will to make her believe the story Tamara had decided they'd tell her.

She moved away from him, unsure...still feeling unexpected doubts, and filled with many unspoken questions. "I honestly don't remember anything about last night, Sean! Is Sandra here, too?...or, does she know I'm here?"

Sean jerked his head towards the door, keeping the gentle smile on his lips, though her words caused his insides to tense. "No...to both questions. There wasn't time enough to inform Sandra...you can do that later. Right now...Tamara wanted me to bring you to her as soon as you woke up, so let's go down, and get you some breakfast, shall we?" He held up a finger to her lips as she was about to speak...finding himself strangely troubled by the shocked expression in her eyes. "She'll answer all your questions, Elizabeth...don't worry, everything's all right! Now...let's eat, okay?"......

....Tamara glanced up as Beth, and Sean walked into the sunlit breakfast nook just off the kitchen. She smiled slightly, seeing the bewilderment in Beth's expression, and the way she moved. She waved them both towards the empty seats around the table she was sitting at, and reached for the filled coffee-pot.

Sean looked at the two still smoking filled plates, then back to his sister. "Why are there only two plates, Tamara? Surely, you haven't eaten already? I thought you'd be joining us?" He asked, sitting down, and accepting the cup of coffee she held out to him.

"I have already eaten, Sean...earlier." She replied, then looked over to where Beth sat, just staring at her food. "Elizabeth...you're looking much more yourself this morning...how *are* you feeling really?" Tamara could sense a tension emanating from the other woman.

Beth gazed at Tamara, wondering. "I guess I'd have to say...physically, I'm very good! It's just that...Tamara, Sean says you're the one who actually cured me. I'm very grateful, but...how did you do it, Tamara? What was it that you gave me that worked where the doctors' medicines didn't?"

Tamara shook her head gently, hand up, forestalling any further questions. "In time, my dear Elizabeth...you'll soon understand everything. You won't require any explanation from me, I think...merely open your eyes, and really see things around you!"

"What are you getting at, Tamara? Look...whatever it was that you did, I am grateful! But...all I want now is to go back to Blackmoon, and see my sisters! And, what I also want from..." Beth's voice died away as she stared hard at her own, out-stretched arm. She just realized her skin had that odd shimmering quality to it that both Tamara, and Sean's possessed. She touched her skin with the fingers of her other hand...there was that familiar velvet texture she'd felt so often on Sean's flesh. But...her mind was reeling...when had such a thing happened, and how?

Tamara sighed, rose from her chair, and walked around the table to where Beth was sitting. With an uncharacteristic gentleness, she knelt beside Beth's seat, taking one of the now frightened woman's hands.

Beth looked at her, eyes wide. Tamara nodded, understanding the silent query. "I know…your flesh is just like ours now! As time passes, Elizabeth, you'll begin to see other similarities appearing. It will take some time for your mind to grasp it all, but you *will* learn, and accept! You're in the final stages of a great change, Elizabeth…your illness was the beginning of this most remarkable alteration! I will explain what you need to make your acceptance of this complete…though, in truth, there are a few aspects even I don't fully understand!" She touched Beth's cheek with her free hand. "The end result is that you're becoming one of us!…in fact, your transformation is very nearly complete now!"

Beth tried to push away her rising panic. "What do you mean…becoming one of you? I can see that my appearance is changed a bit, Tamara! But…how does that make me one of you? And, just exactly what do you mean by that? I don't like double-talk, Tamara…you're a human being, just like me! So…what's going on?"

Tamara rose from her kneeling position, and stood beside Beth's chair. "This is the truth, hard as it may be for your mind to grasp it, Elizabeth! *You* are no longer fully *human*!…any more then we have ever been!" Her hand gestured from Sean to herself, willing the shaken woman beside her to accept the physical reality. "To be utterly honest, my dear…you ceased to be 'human' the first time Sean 'infected' you!…that first time in his bedroom!"

Beth turned to stare at Sean, horror and accusation clear in the cerulean gaze. He reached across the table, and wrapped his hand around her limp fingers. "I meant only to make you pliable to our wishes, Elizabeth…and to express the feelings I had within me for you! Something went beyond even our intentions, dear one…something even Tamara hasn't been able to fully explain! You'll find your life to be a far superior one now, my darling…one that…" He was cut short as she jerked her hand away, and stood up, eyes flashing her indignation, and rage at him. He heard the sharp hiss of breath from his sister, and instinctively turned towards her. Her golden eyes were bright with irritation, and determination.

Beth felt like her entire body was about to explode, and her brain was spinning like someone was physically twisting it. "I want to know just what the hell you two are talking about! I want to know how I got here…how I was cured…and why I can't see my sisters! And I want to know all this right now! No fancy words, or phrases…just plain old English!"

Tamara made a gesture with her hand, and Sean knew he was being dismissed from the room. He stiffened, not sure he wanted to leave Beth alone with Tamara…his sister was so unpredictable these last days.

Tamara glanced at Sean, wondering what was keeping him from obeying her silent command to leave the room. "Elizabeth is correct, brother…she deserves to know the whole truth, and right now! Why don't you take yourself off for a walk? Elizabeth and I have a great deal to talk over, and it doesn't require *your* presence!"

Knowing that it would be useless to argue, Sean nodded, clenching his fists at his sides. Then, without a further word, he turned on one heel, and stalked from the room. It was oddly quiet now…the two women gazing at one another. Tamara seated herself, poured another cup of coffee, and settled back…relaxed, and confident.

"And now…there's a great deal you have to learn, and accept, Elizabeth. There isn't much time, so you will sit there, and listen…without interruptions, do you understand? So…listen carefully…understand who, and what you are becoming! See the world as it was meant to be seen!" And, softly at first, Tamara began the explanation of Beth's metamorphosis…………

………The professor leaned back in his chair, still cradling the amulet in his hand, smiling slightly at the two people in front of his desk.

"Well...have you been able to digest everything I've told you, my friends? It would seem we've talked the night away...look!" He pointed out the picture windows of his den. They'd left his university office, and traveled to his spacious home on the outskirts of Denver.

David glanced at Sandra before speaking...he could see the still shocked expression she wore, and knew it had to mirror his own. "I'd just like to know when this nightmare is going to end! I've taken in more information today, and last night, the I ever did in any class I took! And you know what?...I still don't know what the hell is going on here! I mean...I do, but...I'm not sure of anything any more!" He ran the fingers of one hand through his thick hair, and sighed deeply. "Sorry, Prof. Hanradi...but, you have to admit that this is an awful big mouthful to swallow at one sitting! It's incredible!...frightening, inspiring, and fantastic! If I didn't know it was all so God-damned real, I'd say it had all the ingredients for an Oscar-winning movie!"

The professor slowly nodded, agreeing. "Yes...I would be among the first to agree with you, my friend! I have lived most of my life with this knowledge, and still...each time I deal with any part of it, it never fails to awe, and terrify!" He looked at the third member of this group, who up to this time had been silent. "Sandra?...you've been very quiet! I know how disturbing all this must seem to you. Are you certain you've understood everything I said? Perhaps, you need a little more clarification?" He bent forward, holding a hand out towards her.

Sandra had been just staring off into space. With a jerk, she forced her attention back to the two men. "No...no, I'm fine with what you said, Yusuf...just stunned with the extent *my* own family is involved with all this, and I never suspected any of it! Not in any way, shape, or form was I even suspicious of such activities! Why hadn't my father, or grandfather ever told any of us?" She looked at him, then at David. "Tell me...how does someone go about reconciling the fact that, for generations, members of their family have been involved with what has to be the biggest cover-up in history? How did they manage to keep it so secret? And why was it decided that only *one* member of each generation would possess that secret?"

"It has never been an easy task...protecting mankind from the darkness that has always sought to overwhelm this world. But, as time unfolded over the centuries, mankind became more aware of the world they lived in, and developed their technology to a higher degree...they left behind the teachings of their ancestors, deeming them no longer necessary for everyday living. That was all the powers of darkness needed, and they began to expand their abilities, using the growing ignorance and apathy of mankind to facilitate their power base." Prof. Hanradi gazed at her, fully understanding her reluctance to accept all he'd said...how it shattered existing belief parameters, and shook the roots of one's family beliefs to the very core. "Once, Sandra...our race, the world over, was very versed in the knowledges needed to fight evil, in all its forms! Our faiths, whatever they have been called over the centuries, were stronger...purer, then they are now, for the majority of people! We moderns...so many of us are so sure of ourselves, our abilities...we don't need anything, or anyone! And though we go to church, synagogue, mosque, etc...the true belief, the true faith is something very rare in most humans! Our sciences, technology, and computers can solve most of the problems we nay face today...the old ways aren't necessary any more. After all, the kind of evil our ancestors sought protection from doesn't exist! Devils...demons...monsters, they're the stuff of books, plays, and movies! They have no place in reality!...so say the sophisticates of the world! Not accepting the reality of evil is to give that evil a way in the back doors of our lives!" He looked at Sandra keenly. "What you, your family, and this city have been experiencing the last few weeks is an example of just how real this danger can be! This is just such a situation that led to the Keepers being created!"

David reached over, taking Sandra's hand, and squeezing it tight. "What you've told us...that there are groups of people all over the world whose sole purpose is to keep alert for anything unusual...supernatural, occult, and unexplainable! And, if they determine the source of this happening *is* these dark powers, then the nearest group of Keepers kick into gear, and set out to fight it, hopefully destroying it! Is that about the gist of it?"

The old scholar smiled, and nodded, packing a fresh plug of tobacco into his favorite pipe.

****

X

❀

..........The professor leaned back in his chair, still cradling the amulet in his hands. He looked back at the confused, concerned couple across from him, sitting on the couch, hands clasped...he smiled to himself. "Well?...have you been able to finally digest everything I have told you, my young friends? It would seem we've talked the night away!" He gestured towards the big bay windows...at the first glimmerings of the dawn coming, and the first searching rays of the rising sun. At his suggestion, they'd all come here, to his home outside of Denver, to continue their discussion.

David glanced at the quiet woman beside him before speaking...she was just staring off into nothingness, letting all that they'd heard wash over her. He looked back at the professor. "I just want to know when this nightmare ends! I've taken in more information, on things I never dreamed possible, today then I ever *never* wanted to learn, professor! And, I still don't understand what's going on! I mean, I do, but...this has got to be a dream! These things *can't* be real!" He ran the fingers of his free hand through his thick hair, and sighed. "Sorry, Prof. Hanradi...but even you have to admit, this is quite a mouthful for one sitting! It's all so incredible!...and terrifying all at the same time! If I still had my sense of humor, I'd say this has all the ingredients of an Oscar-winning movie!"

The old teacher nodded his head, agreeing. "Yes...it most certainly does, my friend! I have lived nearly my entire life with this knowledge, David...I've had to use it to combat things your imagination would have trouble believing! Each, and every time, it never fails to awe, and terrify! And, yet...I know if we don't strive against the enemy, our world will never survive!" He looked at Sandra...after all she'd told him, he understood the beautiful woman's silence. "Sandra...I know how angry, and sorrowful you are at this moment...I can't believe Garalynn is gone, and in such a horrible manner!...or that Beth has allowed herself to be so coerced! Although...if anyone should know the skills the enemy possesses, it is I!"

"Professor...these keeper groups...are they all the same? You're one of them...aren't you? Does that mean there's a group here, in Denver?" David spoke up before Sandra could reply to the old teacher's words.

Yusuf gazed at David, wondering just how much to reveal to the policeman, then he sighed...the time for holding back was gone, absolute honesty was the only thing that would save them all now. "Each group is different, David...largely due to geographical factors, and the ancient beliefs of each area. And, the things that caused their formation also differ, yet each are Keepers in their determination not to let the darkness become the victor. We rely on the old ways to show us the way, and the faith of our conviction to keep us going! All the groups have sought to keep connected...an easier task now, with computers, and other technological tools. That's one thing that has bothered me since you told me what was going on...none of our groups were even aware there was a concerted effort by the darkness to get these items! We had no warnings at all!...our spies, and sentinels have all been fooled! Whoever is behind this attempt is clever indeed!"

"Yusuf...I have to know...how did my family get involved in this? How could they...we be part of this Keeper network, and keep it such a total secret?" Sandra felt herself getting angry with her father...why hadn't he told her?

"It actually started with Joshua Phelps…he was the first in *your* family to discover the secret. That is part of what's contained in that journal, Sandra…it deals with what he found when he went up into the mountains. He knew that the knowledge he'd recorded into that journal had to be kept as safe, and secret as possible. That was why he declared only one member of each generation would be empowered with that all so important secret…the location of the journal! He never told anyone, not even his eldest son to whom he told the location what exactly was in the journal….just that the hidden location was to be passed on." The professor pointed at her. "I have been a member of the Keepers since I was eighteen years old, Sandra…my father passed on the knowledge, and his position within our particular group. Like you, I was confused, and shocked…until, the year before his death, my father took me to a zenith gathering when I was twenty-one years old. A zenith is held once every three years…to allow all the groups to touch base with each other all at the same time…to discuss any problems needing resolving. It was there that I finally realized what was at stake…the importance of the Keepers' work. I have served with enthusiasm ever since…as did your father!"

Sandra looked away, her throat tight. "He was a member?…I never knew, never suspected!" She stared at the professor. "He never said anything to us, Yusuf…why didn't he let us know? And the journal…he didn't tell me about it! I know he didn't say anything to Garalynn…oh, my God!…they have Beth! If he told her, and they know about the secret being passed on…they'll kill her to get that knowledge, Yusuf!"

He shook his head, waving his hand slightly. "Ssh-ssh…calm yourself! He wasn't able to tell Beth either! The reason I know this is Richard and I were talking about it a week before his accident. He had held off because he wasn't sure about laying this on either of your shoulders…but he knew he had to, and Beth being the elder of the two of you, she was the logical choice. But…I talked with Beth after the funeral. I could tell, after I'd asked a few subtle questions, that she knew nothing about the Keepers...which meant she knew nothing of the journal...unless she was a master at hiding things."

"Point of fact...she *is* an expert at hiding things, Yusuf, or at least, she was before the Dresdens! But...I think you're right that she doesn't know anything about the journal's location. We've never been able to keep things from each other...I would have known if she had been keeping a secret from me." Sandra sighed, her head hunching down between her shoulders. "That means the journal's location went to the grave with my father! It's still missing...and whatever knowledge it possesses is also!"

"That's just it, Sandra...it's not really missing! It's still in your family's possession! And, with this..." He held up the amulet. "Along with what Garalynn was able to tell you...just might give us the edge!" Yusuf looked up as David rubbed one hand over his eyes...he could see the younger man's agitation. "Yes, David?...what is it?"

"I'm just trying to get it all settled here, professor!" He jabbed a finger at his temple. "I can't reconcile having a centuries old secret popping up here...in Denver, of all places! It's insane!"

"It's not that hard to figure out, David. When Sandra's great-grandfather unearthed that tomb in Dahshur, Egypt...the Egyptian official assigned to the dig, and he found signs that there was knowledge in that tomb that the Keepers would appreciate, and know how to protect. Both the official, and Sandra's great-grandfather were members of two different Keeper groups. It was that official who convinced the government in power then to go along with an idea he had...and that was how your family ended up with all the relics found in that tomb!" He smiled at Sandra. "Everything that was in that tomb is what is now in the Tomb, in Blackmoon! Everyone involved with this felt that a private collection would be more secure than that of a public museum. Everyone knows the security system at Blackmoon is finer than any museum in the States! The leaders of the various Keeper groups agreed unanimously to move the tomb contents, before our enemies became aware of the find!"

"The things you told us about the seventh level…this is where your people got that knowledge?" Sandra was beginning to put things together.

"Yes…after the artifacts were safely moved, and installed in the Tomb, your family, selected archaeologists, and Egyptologists began working over the relics, one at a time. In the course of their work, they found a few scrolls that shed a great deal of light on the prince who was buried, the cause of his death, and the fears of the priest who'd been his greatest friend, and who had himself buried along with his prince, and friend. It talked about the curse of the dark one, and the reprisal of the lion goddess! This priest, one Khamose, wrote about how his friend, the prince, dared to challenge the dark ones, to save the nome over which he ruled, in the Pharoah's name!" Prof. Hanradi explained about the way the relics had been brought to their present location. "When the experts working over the relics here realized that there was mention of the seventh level, they contacted other groups, to collect as much data as possible about this mysterious state of power. You see…up to this time, the seventh level had been considered merely a folk story…a legend lost in time. Now…we know it is all too real, and its coming could mean the rise…or fall of all mankind!"

"Did…did my father ever say anything to you about the journal?" Sandra's voice was quiet, thinking back to when her father was still alive.

The professor shook his head slowly, fingering his beard. "Richard told me many things in the years of our friendship…not surprising as we were also fellow Keeper members. But, other then our discussing the legend of Joshua's journal…your father stayed true to his family's vow, and never once even hinted at the hidden location, my dear Sandra! I came to understand the wisdom behind that tactic…fewer people knowing the whereabouts of that journal meant fewer people the dark ones could coerce into disclosing its hiding place. The group leaders agreed with it as well, and made protection of your family members a daily task." Yusuf grinned at the lovely woman. "Since the day you were born, you, Beth, and later Garalynn have had a Keeper bodyguard assigned to you...as well as your cousins, and their family!"

"You know...maybe I've been a cop too long, but there's something that doesn't smell right!" David broke in, rubbing the back of his neck with one hand. "It's been bugging me ever since you said Sandy's dad was a Keeper. Now, I've got just one thing to say...isn't it real convenient, for these dark guys, that the girls' father died so suddenly? Kind of removed a big obstacle for them, didn't it?"

Yusuf frowned...he'd vaguely toyed with a similar feeling when Richard Phelps had died, but there had been no proof of foul play...no sign that the dark forces were involved in that sad event. "You feel there's a connection, David?...our group found no connections at the time of the...his death! Of course...it *is* possible we didn't investigate as deeply as we should!" The professor was shaken to think his group had been lax in their sworn duty.

"Whatever...look, it's just a little too pat for me!" David looked at Sandra, who was dazed, and confused. "Look...if your father died, *before* he could pass on the secret of the journal, then that would work to the dark ones' advantage...give *them* more time to search for it themselves! Also...with him not around, they probably thought they'd have a better chance convincing one of his daughters to give them free access to the confines of Blackmoon, and thereby, the Tomb!"

"And, once into the Tomb, they could work on locating the things they desired, including the journal!" Yusuf finished, his fist clamping around the bowl of his pipe, angry that they could have missed such a vital clue, and maybe, as a result, be responsible for the events of late. "I begin to see what you're getting at, David...and I don't like it! I think we allowed our guards to drop when they shouldn't have done so! This could be bad!...very bad, indeed!" He began to drum his fingers on the desk top. "I begin to see where we could have been misled...where they could have...yes, they could have done it, and all too easily!"

"Done what, Yusuf?...what are you getting at?" Sandra looked from one man to the other. Her eyes began to widen as a thought began creeping into her mind.

The professor looked at his former protégé, a bleak look in his dark eyes. "It is possible, now that David has made me look at things from a different angle, that your father's death *wasn't* an accident, Sandra! It could be that they used our own emotions to...they blinded us! We were all too shook, too shocked at your father's passing!...we didn't investigate because we were too upset! We let...*I* let my old friend down! They are devious indeed!"

Sandra stood up slowly, fists clenched at her sides. "Are the two of you trying to say that my father's death was no *accident*?...that they murdered him, because of the journal?"

David stood up, stepping in close to her, putting one hand to her cheek. "I'm a cop, Sandy...I have to see *all* possibilities, and find the correct one! What I'm saying now is that it's a real possibility his death wasn't an accident!" He gently stroked the satin skin of her cheek, his eyes searching hers. "It's just a thought, Sandy...but one, I admit, we'll never really know for sure! I don't want to hurt you, but keeping our minds open to all situations, and chances is what's going to save us!"

The professor held up a hand, getting their attention back. "I think David is correct, Sandra...we'll never know for sure! But, from now on we keep even more alert, more on guard to every possibility! Murder is a viable path for them, and they have no regrets at using that path to achieve their goals! However...if what David has stated truly *did* happen, it could mean the dark ones had gained knowledge we'd been trying to keep hidden from them over the years!"

"What do you mean by that?" Sandra sat back down, feeling the pain of her father's death wash over her again.

In answer, her old mentor reached over, to the left hand corner of his massive desk, and slid a panel to one side. This hidden panel revealed a small switch, which the professor flipped up. A hidden drawer opened, and he reached inside. Removing something they couldn't make out, he then rose, and walked over to one of the wall sized bookshelves. He removed two small volumes, and then held a silver key up so they could see it. He slid the hand holding the key into the space created by removing the two books, and inserted it into a concealed lock. He twisted the key, and they looked up, startled, as the opposite wall began sliding open. It kept opening until a room almost as large as the den they were in now was revealed. In this room was an elaborate computer set-up, complete with satellite up-link.

He headed into this special room, motioning for them to join him. Sandra looked around as they came in...she'd never seen a set-up like this, since her own father's set-up back in his office, now hers, back at the manor house. He'd shown it to her, telling her she could use it to run the horse business, and for whatever needs the running of the estate entailed. "Yusuf...this is incredible! You could contact anyone, all over the world, with this! My dad had a set-up like this. He..." Sandra's voice died away as she realized that her father must have used his computer link-up for his business as a Keeper. She reached out, and touched her old teacher on the shoulder. He looked up from his seat, wondering at the expression she had now. "Yusuf...who, or what is the Seer? What exactly is it that the Keepers...keep?" She asked softly...firmly.

He leaned back in his chair, his hands resting, palms down, on the pine wood desk he was now sitting at. He gazed at her, seeing her father in the resolute set to the jaw, and shoulders. "The Seer is what we, the Keepers, have been guarding for centuries, awaiting the time when it would be finally re-awakened, and set free...to do the task assigned so many ions ago!" His voice was quiet...so quiet that the two people with him had to lean in close in order to hear. "You see, those people who know our organization truly exists think that what we stand guard over is a seer...a psychic, or worker of the occult forces, Sandra. But...in truth, it is just what the word implies...a see-er! A personage whose vision is greater, deeper, more profound than anyone could ever dream!

He is the one who will 'see' the truth, the way...the Light! He is the one who will help defeat the darkness, and banish it forever by helping mankind walk into the Light! This was set forth in scrolls long before man, as we are today, walked upright, and held cognizant thought, and speech! These scrolls, and clay tablets, and papyrus parchments...in endless cultures, all wrote of the time the darkness would seek to overwhelm, and conquer...to control all aspects of life on our world! Many gifted men, and women, throughout all time, have sought to warn human kind by predictions, visions, and writings of what lie ahead...and how to avoid, lessen, or combat it!" Yusuf's voice was almost hypnotic in its low tones, and David felt his eyes grow heavy...if only he could just lie down, and sleep!

"And, this Seer...he is one of the weapons against what's trying to conquer us all?...is that what is in the journal?" Sandra asked, her hand gripping the professor's shoulder gently.

"A weapon?...not exactly. More like...a leader, or teacher!...someone who can show us the truth behind our enemies, and the truth behind ourselves!" He looked up at her, his dark eyes warm, and encouraging. "A teacher who can help us find again what the Creator wanted us to be, and to do! His *knowledge* is what is the true weapon, as you will, my friends! He was a great leader once...a Prince, and a God! He knows, in ways we can only guess at, just what the enemy's strengths, and weaknesses are...and how to use them! What is in the journal about all this?...I honestly don't know! All any of our groups know is that the journal is the most important item of five that are needed for the seventh level! If it falls into *their* hands...everything, and everyone is lost!"

David cleared his throat...things were getting decidedly too heavy here, and it was really getting him down. "Look...that's all well, and good, but let's get back to things at hand now, shall we?" The tall police officer pointed a blunt finger towards the computer set-up. "What did you bring us in here for, professor?"

"Right…back to things! I'm going to try, and bring up what facts we have, on record, about your father's death, Sandra…to see if there *was* something we missed! If there was, and we can find it…it may help us out now!" The old scholar pushed a key on the elaborate keyboard, and the monitor hummed into life.

Yusuf tapped in his password, then his fingers flew over the keyboard, calling up screen after screen of data, columns, and pictures, interspersed with charts, and cryptic symbols. After a few moments, he nodded his head. "Here's what I was looking for…news articles about your father's death…the funeral, and all the information our group had gathered concerning it." He pointed to the seventeen-inch screen, and the newspaper articles now on the monitor.

In silence, the three of them read the items as the professor slowly scrolled the screen down, bringing up even more information. Sandra felt like she was experiencing one of the worst times in her young life all over again as she read the large amount of media coverage the death, and funeral of Richard Phelps had engendered. Then, as a picture went by, she jerked forward, grasping Yusuf's shoulder tightly. "Stop!…go back a little! Yes…there!…stop there!" Her finer jabbed at the screen. "Look at that picture!…my God, I can't believe it!"

David bent forward, peering at the highlighted picture closely. It was from one of the local papers, showing a particularly nasty accident scene. "That's nothing to do with your dad's funeral, Sandy…it's about some car wreck! Hey…wait a minute!" He leaned closer, his eyes widening at what he read underneath the main picture. "Sandy…that's the wreck that killed your ex-husband!" He looked over at her, surprised at the look of horror, and anger on her beautiful face. "Honey…what is it? What's wrong?"

"Can't you see?…look there!" She pointed at the picture again. Both David, and the professor looked again, but still couldn't see what it was that had their companion so agitated. They looked at her, their mutual confusion very clear.

Sandra tossed her hand up in frustration, and tapped her fingertip on the monitor screen, emphasizing her words. "Look there!...this woman standing back in the crowd surrounding the scene! See...you can make her head, and shoulders quite clearly!"

I see what you're indicating...a very attractive woman, even with the grainy photo, but so what? Who is she?" David shrugged, still not understanding.

She was about to scream her frustration at him, then remembered. "That's right...you haven't met her yet! David...that's Tamara Dresden! She was there that day!...at the accident! She was there!" Sandra slowly backed up until her spine was pressed against the nearby wall. "She was there the day he died! But...how is that possible?"

The professor looked intently...staring at the exposed head and shoulders of the tawny beauty. He stared at her image, feeling something surging throughout his mind, and finally coming to the front. Memories crowded over him, his eyes widened, and his breath caught. "No...it cannot be! How could we have overlooked such an obvious thing as this? My God...it was there, all along, and we all missed it!" He slumped back in his seat, fingers tugging at the ends of his neatly trimmed beard. He glanced at David, who was by this point very baffled. "You were right, Sandra...in everything you ever told me about this woman! Forgive me if I doubted you in any way!"

David looked at him, then strode over to where Sandra was slumped against the wall. He took her arms in harsh, strong hands, and pulled her to a standing position in front of him. "You say that the woman in that picture is Tamara Dresden?...but, you said she'd *never* been to Denver before visiting you, and Beth! Why would she not have told you she'd been here before?...especially at the accident that killed your ex? Did your family know them then?"

She pulled away from his grasp, hissing her words out between clenched teeth, angry and scared. "No!...Beth, and my father *had* met them, in London, a few years ago, but only as business associates! To my knowledge, they'd never come here until the merger deal, and they came back with Beth! Look...maybe her being in that picture means nothing at all! I don't know any more!...except that it *is* her!"

The professor stood up, slamming his hand down onto a book sitting open on the desk. "Enough!...you must both listen to me now!" He stepped nearer to Sandra. "You are quite sure the woman in that picture, and this Tamara you spoke of are one, and the same?"

Sandra nodded, having no doubts. "I know I'm not mistaken!...that is her!"

The professor looked away, shaking his head, and muttering under his breath, in his native Egyptian. He fiddled with some papers, and tapped a few more keys, bringing up more screens of information...it was obvious he was searching intently for something that was clearly bothering him. Finally, he brought his attention back to the couple sitting across from him once again. "That woman...she has gone by many names, Sandra! If I am right, and she is who I think...we could be in even greater danger then any of us could have realized!" He looked back at the news photo, then reached over to the convenient bookcase. He selected a thick volume, and blew the dust off it.

He sat the book on the desk top, and leafed through its pages quickly. Finding what he needed, he swirled the book around, and pushed it towards Sandra, and David, his finger pointing at the picture shown. "That's the lion goddess of Thebes...better known to history, and folk lore as Sekhmet! That's the name she's known best by...do you see what I mean?"

David stared at the picture of the intricately carved statue of the Egyptian deity, then at the picture on the computer screen...his eyes narrowed. "There is a resemblance, I guess, professor...but I'm not going to go so far as to say they are the same woman! I just can't...I mean, she would have to..." David looked away, feeling his fears, and beliefs crowding in on him once again.

"I know, my boy...I know!" Yusuf's voice was low, and understanding. "That woman has gone by many names, and they all mean death! She has been a scourge of mankind for centuries, and one of our bitterest foes since we first became aware of her kind's existence! I didn't see it...we *were* lax here, not expecting them to send one of their most powerful agents to an out of the way place like Denver!" He looked around, and smiled slightly at the exasperated expressions. "Well, as you said it yourself, David...why a place like Denver? The answer is so clear...because it's wide open, and no one would ever expect anything here! Even the Keepers...well, we are human, after all!"

"And her being at the accident scene?" Sandra asked, not sure she really wanted to know the answer.

"I can only answer that question in this way...if that woman was there, then that accident wasn't an accident! In some way we don't know...it had to have been part of a plan!" The professor bent his forehead down, resting it in the palm of his left hand. "It proves that they had a plan in effect back when your ex-husband was killed, Sandra...and it doesn't take much to believe that it's a good possibility your father's death wasn't as clean as it appeared either!"

"Somehow...they must have put a few facts together, and figured out about the journal, and the other items, being somewhere here! But how?" David slipped an arm about Sandra's shoulders, feeling the tight muscles trembling slightly.

"It doesn't really matter now...they're here, and I must alert the other members! I only hope we find what we must soon...and first! They have been one step ahead of us all this time, and we haven't known it!" The old man stood up, back straight with the determination, and sense of purpose now coursing through him. "We need to get organized!"

David watched as the old teacher began to glow with his inner fire, and then he looked at Sandra, who was still sitting, hands clasped in her lap, shaking her head at all that had been disclosed. He looked at the computer, and with a muffled oath, shouldered the professor aside, and sat down behind the computer keyboard, and monitor. His fingers stabbed at the keyboard with powerful strokes, and when he found what he was looking for, he stared at the monitor for a few seconds. He leaned back, and looked at Sandra, his eyes dark, and filled with regret. "Sandy…" His voice was soft. She raised her head, eyes questioning. He held out his hand. "Sweetheart…I don't want to cause you any more pain…but, you need to see what I've found! Come here!"

She slowly stood up, and came to his side. He stood up, and motioned for her to sit down. Then, looking at both her, and the professor, he tapped his fingertip gently against the monitor screen. Sandra gazed at his face for a few moments more, then looked at the screen…it held an account of Richard Phelps elaborate funeral, and showed several pictures of the people attending the funeral ceremonies. She stared, mouth dry and throat tight, at the unmistakable profile predominate in one of the graveside service photos…the proud lift to that classic head, and the cold beauty of that one of a kind face, with the golden eyes gazing into space…and time. Tamara.

"She was there, too…at Dad's funeral, and I know none of her family had been asked to attend…they were simply business acquaintances." She looked at the professor, her gaze hard and searching. She looked back at David…he winced at the pain, confusion, and anger in that cerulean gaze. "I don't understand…is she involved with everything bad that's happened to my family in the past few years? Why? Is it all because of that journal?" Her voice began to rise, her hand flinging out at the monitor. "Is all this because of a journal, supposedly written over a hundred years ago?…a journal that no one's seen since it was written? A journal no one knows where it is today?…if it still exists?…or ever existed?"

"Sandra!…get control of yourself! Falling to pieces now is exactly what they will count on us doing!…giving into the fears, and terrors we all hold deep within our minds, and allowing them to rule our passions!" The professor declared, gripping her shoulder, and forcing her to look into his face. Seeing the pain, and shock there, he smiled slightly, caressing her cheek with the hand that had grabbed her shoulder. "I know how much it hurts…how angry you are, and how much you want revenge! I have felt all you're going through now, Sandra…but you must push it from you! To allow that anger…that rage…that hate to rule you is to hand them the victory on a silver plate! We are all to blame for what has happened…we allowed ourselves to become over-confident, and too self-assured. Our guard dropped, our faith wavered…and the enemy is now here!"

He turned from the other two people, and slowly walked to the bay window, and gazed out at the early morning sky. Normally, this was one of his favorite times of the day…when everything was new, and anything was possible. Now…all he saw was the results of their failures, and it sickened him. He looked back at his friends, and his jaw tensed…there was no time for self-pity. "Yes, Sandra…this is all because the journal *does* exist, and they know its power! They want it…and somehow they learned of the secret that your family has kept possession of it all theses years! I truly believe that is why they have singled out your family!"

"Why kill, or cause the deaths of Sandy's father, and ex-husband? What did that gain them, professor? And what about the killings here?…and…Garalynn!?" David asked, wanting there to be a logical reason…one his mind could accept.

"I can only speculate…but, if it were only Beth, Garalynn, and Sandra that had to be dealt with, it made things all that much easier! As for the murders here, in Denver…the way they were committed, and all that you told me you found at the scenes, David…they were a necessary part of some ritual necessary for them. What, or why those ceremonies…I don't know!" Yusuf looked at Sandra. "As for our dear Garalynn…I don't have a reason there, unless it was to make you understand how serious they are, and that Beth could suffer the same fate if you don't cooperate with all they want!"

"But...Beth is carrying Sean's child, Yusuf!...they wouldn't harm her! They'd hurt the baby if they did! I can't believe Sean would allow Tamara to harm my sister in any way because of the baby!" Sandra shook her head, hands over her ears...she didn't think she could take much more. Her sanity felt as though it was ripping apart, from the inside out!

"Get this through your head, both of you!...these beings will do anything...anything at all to achieve their goals, and desires!" Yusuf didn't have the time to be gentle, and to argue with them. They had to see the truth, and accept it...or they were doomed to fail before even starting! "Murder, terror, torture...blackmail, and extortion...these are the tools they use every day, without a blink of conscience, or compassion! Believe that...file it away in your minds, and keep it always clear!...and you just might make it through this, with at least half of your sanity still intact!"

Sandra wanted to scream...she wanted to mourn the grisly death of her sister, and friend...to demand justice, and revenge for the deaths of her father, and ex-husband! She wanted to stand up, and yell that she'd had enough...all she wanted was for the pain, and the rage to stop! She bent her head, and the tears began...it would never be over until they found the journal...until they could put to rest all those who'd given the ultimate sacrifice.

Sandra lifted her head, smiling at the man who was now kneeling beside her, his hands stroking her curly hair, tears in his eyes as well. She leaned into the strong body, feeling the arms wrap around her. "I'm so scared, David!...I want my life back the way it was!...and I want Garalynn!" She whispered into the crook of his neck, where she snuggled her face. "But...it can't be that way again!...can it?"

He held her closer, wishing he had the strength to keep her from any more pain, or danger...but he'd seen what these beings were capable of, and now he felt his resolve harden, and he taunted the enemy in his mind, daring them to try, and take his lady from him! "It's going to be okay, honey…I promise you! We'll get through this, and have our life together! Just hang on to me!…don't let go!" He buried his face in the dark hair, inhaling the scent of her deep into his lungs, feeling the firmness of her body against his.

Yusuf watched them, knowing how afraid they were, and how doubly things were impacting on them, as they discovered the depth of their feelings for one another. "I think we have talked enough for the moment, my young friends…there is much we have yet to do!" He patted Sandra's shoulder. "I've a couple of phone calls to make…gather up some additional forces for our side. Then…we'll set out to do what our dear Garalynn wished you to do, Sandra…and before our clever friends make another move!"

"And we keep our determination high, and fast!" David wasn't sure why he'd felt compelled to say that, but once uttered, he wasn't going to take the words back, or apologize for saying them. He looked at the professor. "Like you said, Prof. Hanradi…unless we have our faiths strong, we'll lose! Right?"

The old man nodded. "Yes…yes, you're right, my boy! And, David…it's Yusuf, alright? We're going to be going through too much to be formal amongst ourselves! And, now…Sandra, you said that Tamara, and her brother are at Blackmoon, is that right?"

She shrugged. "They were…but, where they are now, no one seems to know! I know they have Beth with them…and that's what's got me so worried!…especially in light of all you've told us, Yusuf!"

"Understandable…but, I truly believe she's in no immediate danger from them, Sandra…right now, she's far too important to their plans, whatever those are! Worming their way into your family's good graces…in this case, Beth's affections…was necessary to achieve their goal, which we now know is to obtain the journal, and the amulet." The professor fingered the amulet…it seemed to call to him, seeking his touch, no matter where he placed it on the desk.

"They already have the things they took from the Tomb...the amulet, and the journal are the last ones. Garalynn told me that they needed all of them to accomplish two things...setting someone free, and the other preventing that which would change the world forever!" Sandra could hear the lovely low voice again, in her mind, and her eyes closed, willing the fresh wave of pain, and loss away.

"But, she told you about this guy locked away in some stone prison...that it was her task to free him! Is it him who they're after?...but that doesn't make any sense!" David declared.

"They're not out to free him...from all that Garalynn said, he's one of their bitterest enemies! I sooner think their interpretation is to *prevent* his being freed! That would be their idea of preventing a disaster! No...the one they seek to free is obviously someone the world could ill afford being free! Remember...when dealing with the dark forces...with evil incarnate...learn to use reverse logic. I believe that whatever is contained within the pages of Joshua's journal is beyond our comprehension of judging, beyond the meaning of power! I think that they need the journal for what it can tell them...the final key to accomplishing their nefarious goals! This information, whatever it may turn out to be, coupled with all the other items will enable them to succeed! All the prayers inscribed upon those relics, and what is written in that journal...they must be powerful words indeed, Sandra...for them to risk so much!"

"Yes...as you always taught us, the spoken word carries the deepest power, especially if they come from the Scroll of Thoth...the Book of the Dead!" Sandra took a deep breath. "You know, I'm beginning to make sense out of some of the stories Grandfather, and Papa used to tell us when we were growing up." She looked at the old teacher. "They were more then just stories, weren't they? It was their way of preparing us, wasn't it?"

"Probably...you yourself know the importance the ancients placed on the telling of their legends, and lore. It was their way of keeping their history alive…and passing on the ways, and customs of their ancestors. Passing their beliefs on, orally, was their way of preserving the things that would keep them strong, and safe! It was a way to educate their children." He glanced at her. "Dealing with this woman, and her brother, is not going to be easy! Are you sure you want to go along? It might be easier for you if you allow me, and my friends to handle them!"

"Forget that! This is my family these bastards have fooled with!…and they're going to pay for everything they've taken from me!" Sandra's eyes flashed with a potent blue fire as she stood up swiftly, every inch of her lithe frame shaking in anger.

"Hey…settle down! This is no time to be a loose cannon!" David took her hand, gently coaxing her back into her seat. "We're all in this…together! Profe…I mean, Yusuf, there's something I meant to ask…what *is* the seventh level?"

"Well…to put it in the most basic of explanations, David…the seventh level is one step removed from total, and complete power over *all* living things, dimensions of time and space, and death itself! There have been stories, and legends, in numerous cultures, about the attainment of such power…but, there's never really been any proof it actually existed, until they found that tomb. That's a simplification, but I think you get the meaning?" Yusuf replied. "Let me add one thing…according to the legends, the ultimate power…the eighth level…can only be achieved with possession of the seventh!"

"Now, we understand what they're really after!…virtual command of all life, and all death! The stuff that dreams are made of…nightmares, that is!" Sandra's voice was harsh, and sarcastic…more then ever, she wanted her revenge on the Dresdens, especially Tamara!

"Yusuf…you said you knew this Tamara…who is she, really?" David heard himself asking the question…but, he wasn't sure he really wanted to hear the answer.

"I have never met her, face to face…but I do know her, David! She has been called by many names throughout history…all of them involving blood, sacrifice, and unrelenting power! Seeing her photograph on the computer screen caused the memories of some of her descriptions to re-emerge, and I realized who we're up against!" Came the firm, low reply as the professor opened his phone number rolodex, and started searching for a couple of numbers.

"Are you saying that she's...Yusuf, look at me!" Sandra demanded as he continued fiddling with the rolodex. When he looked up, in some surprise at her tone, she pointed at the computer monitor. "You are actually telling us that the woman I know as Tamara Dresden is really a...she's an immortal?" He slowly nodded, and she slowly dropped her outstretched hand. "I...I know a lot about the legends of immortals...every great culture had them. And, I figured there was some basis of fact behind these stories...but, to actually *believe* immortals could truly exist..." Her voice died away as she realized the stories she'd heard had become reality.

David stared, his hand absently rubbing up and down on his jean covered leg, as he digested what this meant. "A real immortal...someone who can't die!" He looked over at Yusuf. "How...professor, how old is this woman, and her brother?"

"That I cannot say...a good guess would be several *thousands* of years! That is why we must be alert, and at our best, my friends. The knowledge these creatures have accumulated outweighs that of most computers today! And this one...here, let me read you something written over two thousand years ago, by a high priest of Thebes." He tapped a few keys, and brought up the historical section. A few key strokes later, and he pointed his blunt finger at the screen. "Listen...'She is beautiful in her rage, the lioness of Ra's wrath, the bringer of war...member of the triad, most terrible in her pursuit of the blood of man...the slaying power of the Sun God's countenance. May she live forever!'"

Sandra listened, then sat there, in silence for a few seconds. Then, her voice muted, awed, and deliberate, she spoke, saying but one word..."Sekhmet!"

Yusuf glanced at her, a small smile of pride playing about his mouth. "Yes…the mighty Sekhmet…the lion-headed goddess all generals prayed to before going to war, whom the ordinary foot-soldier anointed with their own blood, from wounds received in battle. Here's more written about her…'golden death falls from her eyes, and swift is her arm with the lance. Immortal goddess…come to punish. Lay before her trophies gained in battle, for most pleasing to her is the sweet blood of man as sacrifice. Let the blood of the enemy be given her, for favors desired in war. The nectar of life is her sacred brew, and her greatest power. Be cautious, and most diligent in her worship…great the rewards for the faithful…swift is her anger upon those who defy her!'" He finished his narration of the data, and looked at his two companions. "There ware many other such recitations of her, some more flattering then this…but they all have one common thread, that this is a most powerful being! A deity worshipped by millions, who reveled in war, and all the destructive powers associated with battle!…who also held the power of the Sun's greatest power, the destructive heat of the noon sun's rays, granted her by her immortal father, Ra, the greatest of the ancient Egyptian godhead. In short…a very dangerous foe!"

"But…she wasn't always viewed in such a dark light, Yusuf…you yourself told us, in class, that she was also viewed in the same light as Hathor, a goddess of love, and birth, and family. Dark, and powerful, yes…but truly evil? And how could Tamara be…I just can't grasp that fact well!" Sandra declared, her heart sinking as she began to really see what they faced…how do you fight against that which cannot be killed?…cannot die?

"Seeing this as an impossibility is what gives them more strength, Sandra! You must keep your mind open!…to all things, and all solutions! There is nothing that is truly impossible!…put that in your mind, heart, and soul…and believe!" Yusuf was stern…there was no time for the nicety of gentle persuasion.

"That is why they have remained hidden all these centuries, my friends…even though they live among us! The disbelief of most humans that such creatures, or beings could ever exist…it gives them the edge, a strength that we never have been able to possess. That was what that man in the stone prison was trying to make Garalynn see…what she did finally grasp! As long as no one believes in their existence, they remain entrenched among us, and always will!…safe, hidden, and powerful! When the time comes that the human race once again accepts their reality, and begins to battle them as our ancestors taught us…then we will begin to actually win a few of these silent battles! That's one of the things that make the journal's possession so vital!"

David leaned forward, laying his forehead on his knees. His voice was somewhat muffled, but Sandra could still make out the words. "I want to wake up now!…this dream has gone on long enough!…just let me wake up now…please!"

Sandra bent forward, wrapping her arms about his shaking body, cradling her cheek against his. She murmured softly, causing his head to rise so he could gaze into her eyes. Their lips came together slowly…for a few moments, the fear was gone from them as their spirits bonded together. The professor said nothing, simply smiled, watching them, granting them this small niche in time.

Finally, he cleared his throat. "We have a lot of work ahead of us tonight…and the first thing is Elizabeth! Do you have any idea where they may have taken her?"

"There's so many places…all over the country! I wouldn't think it would be too far…Beth was still quite weak! I guess we'll have to wait…until they contact us! I don't think they'll leave the country, but I'm sure they're not without resources!" She replied, her left hand weaving lazy circles on David's right cheek.

"Why do you think that? They have to know that we'll have the authorities hot on their tails…once we get the proof, of course!" He was puzzled by both the statement, and the calmness of her voice.

"They have to know I'm not about to do anything to risk my sister's life…including notifying the police about this! Besides…everyone else will say that she left voluntarily, so where's the crime? No…they'll get in touch with me, and soon. As for leaving the country…they don't have what they came for yet, do they?" She looked at him, cocking her lovely head to one side…a gesture he always found endearing.

"They're going to use Beth as a form of blackmail…that's what you're counting on, isn't it?" He shook his head, clasping her left hand, and kissing the palm gently. "I had a thought…what if they've already been able to locate the journal? This could all be for moot!"

"They do not have the journal!…trust me when I say that, David! If they had it in their possession right now, the entire world would know! There would have been little reason to take Elizabeth…or kill Garalynn…if they already had it! No…I sooner think Sandra's assessment of the situation is correct…they'll use the threat to Elizabeth's well-being as a lever to coerce Sandra to do their bidding! Going after them gives their side the advantage of prepared response. Letting them come to you…that gives us the home court edge!" The professor looked at Sandra, thoughtful and concerned.

"Yes…so all I can do now is wait. I really think our efforts need to be in trying to locate the journal first! That's what Garalynn wanted!…what I promised her!" Sandra's throat tightened a little, and she spoke around the lump her emotions created.

"Yes…we must go to Blackmoon! We will search the Tomb as it has never been searched before! I will call my friends, and have them meet us there!"

"Whatever you say, professor…you're better versed in these things then I!" The tall police officer declared, standing up.

The old teacher nodded, and reached again for the phone. Sandra stood also, leaning against him, the solid feel of his muscles the anchor she needed as her thoughts zoomed ahead…to the possibilities the could open before them……….

.......Tamara stood on the wide rear deck of the cabin, letting the chilly wind from the mountains swirl her long hair about, in silken ripples. A glance behind her showed Beth still crumpled up in one of the chaise loungers, an expression of shock, and disbelief on her beautiful face. It had taken a few hours, but Tamara's will had finally prevailed, and Beth had, reluctantly, accepted all that Tamara had to tell her. Tamara was now giving her a little more time to get her emotions under control...to adjust to all she'd been given to digest.

It was while she was standing there that something softly brushed her sensitive inner powers. She frowned, instantly alert, reaching out with her own mind...seeking that which had caused the disturbance. To her surprise, and concern...though she was able to ascertain something *was* there, she couldn't pinpoint its location. It wafted from one section to the other, never lingering long enough in any one spot for her to definitely secure its location. She leaned on the deck, eyes narrowing, as she gazed out over the darkening landscape. Very few indeed had been the enemies who'd been able to successfully surprise Tamara over the years...she was not about to allow that rare occurrence to happen again!

Rousing herself from her near-stupor, Beth noticed the stiff posture of her companion, and wondered what on earth could have caused such a state. "Tamara, what is it? What are you looking at?"

Her thoughts preoccupied, Tamara spared the younger woman a cursory glance, and merely shook her head. "It's nothing for you to worry about, Elizabeth...I just thought I heard something, that's all!" She finally turned, and gave the other woman her full attention. "Are you fully calmed down now?...or, is there still something that has you unsettled?"

Beth stood up from the lounger, slipping her wind-breaker tighter about her shoulders...the evening wind was getting crisp. "I guess everything's straightened out in my mind, Tamara...for now! If it weren't for the fact that I can...well, everything you've told me is pretty fantastic!" She glanced down at her slightly protruding abdomen, her left hand gently rubbing it. "I guess, for now, I really don't have much choice, but to accept! The next question is...where do we go from here? And, why did we come here, to the cabin, instead of back to Blackmoon? After all...that's been my home for my entire life, Tamara! I'd like my child to know it as well!"

Tamara looked a little surprised...hadn't this woman been listening? "What do we do?...you really weren't listening, were you, Elizabeth? We can't go to Blackmoon!...at least, not to live! You will learn very quickly, my dear...we're different from the ordinary mortal! And, when they have learned just how different, their first response is to try, and destroy us! So...we strike first!" She shook her head. "I'm getting distracted...we are here, Elizabeth, because we seek to stay out of the reach, and knowledge of the authorities! At least, until we get what we came here to get!...the journal, and the amulet are still out of our grasp!"

"But...I've told you...no one told either Sandra, and me where that damned journal was hidden! I don't think anyone's known where it's located for years! It's just a legend that's been in my family for several generations!" Beth tried again to make Tamara see how futile this quest was for them. "Why do you think my sister would be able to find something no one's even seen for ages?"

"I think, to save you any harm, and get you back...Sandra would move heaven, and earth to find that journal, and give it to us!" Tamara was smug, tossing her head a little to re-settled some locks of hair back over her shoulders. "I think we should make that phone call now, don't you? It's been almost thirty hours now since we left the hospital...more then enough for your sister to have gotten my 'message', I think. So, let's make that call...and don't forget what I told you to say!" The tall, tawny blonde leaned closer, her eyes golden points of fire.

Beth looked away, her heart clenching at the mention of her sister. She knew Tamara would not be pleased if she realized Beth's feelings for her two sisters hadn't altered along with all the other changes. Tamara had told her that her feelings of love, and compassion would gradually fade completely away...the human side of her altered psyche would cease to exist. But...nothing had changed at all where her regard for Sandra, and Garalynn was concerned. Beth knew, deep within her heart, that no matter what the changes were that she was going through...her loyalty to her family had to stay constant! She was afraid for her sisters...especially Sandra. Whenever Tamara had mentioned either of them there had been a clear menace in that silken voice. She thought about what Tamara had instructed her to say to Sandra when she called...she wasn't sure she could go through with it.

Tamara sensed the hesitancy, and it irritated her. "There is no more time to make you understand, Elizabeth...simply do as you are told! Emphasize to your sister the consequences of bringing the police into this! If she refuses to listen, simply say this to her...the condo was merely a warning! Refuse to go along with our 'request'...and the next 'message' will be closer to home!"

Beth frowned. "What's that supposed to mean, Tamara?"

"Let's just say that it's a private 'joke' between Sandra, and me! Now...shall we make that call?"

Beth found herself shaking her head. "I really don't want to call her, Tamara. I don't see what good that's going to do...she doesn't know where it is!"

Tamara seemed to move like a shadow, and seized Beth by the wrist. She pulled Beth in closer, and bared her teeth. "You'll do as you're told...because I say so! Never question me again, Elizabeth! There is always a reason for anything I do, and your only responsibility is to do what I have said to be done! Remember that...and also remember, moving swiftly, before your enemy can act, is the best path to success!" She released Beth's wrist, standing tall, regal...and dangerous. "Your sister has something we want...or, knows where to get it! Either way...she will bring it to us, or she will pay a greater price then she already has paid!"

Beth wasn't sure what the older woman meant by that last statement...and she wasn't sure she *wanted* to know! "I wasn't trying to upset you, Tamara...I'll make the call, but I still don't know what good it's going to do!" She raised her hands, attempting to placate the tall blonde. "Besides...I'm sure Sandra, and Garalynn are both worried about my leaving the hospital. I'll be surprised to find out they haven't called the police by now. Once they both know I'm okay, and everything else is fine, they'll relax. I'm sure they'll want to help us out by trying to find the journal!" Beth still really didn't see the danger, and the complexities of this new existence she had crossed over to embrace.

"You are still allowing those human emotions, and foibles to control your mind, and powers, Elizabeth...get over it! Those emotional deadweights are only an asset when they can get the best for you! As time goes by, and the changes within you become permanent, and final...you will find that such things are merely passing interests, when they can serve your desires best! The things that seemed important, in your old life, will be as meaningless as an empty canvas! Persons you once thought vital are mere servants, existing solely to serve your simplest whims!" Tamara declared, satisfied that Beth seemed more compliant now.

"If you say so, Tamara. Should I make the call now?" Beth simply wanted to hear her sister's voice right now...she was beginning to get a very uneasy feeling inside, as if her very soul had suddenly been gouged with red hot daggers.

Tamara nodded, pleased at the outward signs of obedience. It was as she had so often stated...a little show of force, now and then, tended to make things much more beneficial to one's plans. She followed Beth inside, to the den, and stood close by as the other woman picked up the cellular phone, and tapped a few numbers into the phone's sleek body. She allowed herself a brief second of sweet triumph...things would soon be fully realized.

Beth called Blackmoon, and spoke with Roland. She learned that neither Sandra, and Garalynn had been home yet that day, or the day before. All Roland knew was that Sandra had called late the day before, and told him she was going to see an old professor of hers…and that if he needed her, she had her cell phone with her. Beth instructed Roland to have Sandra call her, on her cell phone, if she checked back in with him. He promised he would, then asked if everything was all right.

Beth slowly replaced the phone, then looked back at her companion. She shook her head, knowing that Tamara understood she hadn't gotten in touch with Sandra…after all, the other woman had heard the entire conversation. Beth was beginning to feel as though she was being pulled in a thousand different directions. She felt a very strong pull towards Tamara, especially after these metamorphic changes…but, Sandra was her twin, and Garalynn was as dear. Beth *did* feel that invisible bond to her family, and friends diminishing very gradually…and she fought it. Sandra was her twin sister…how could she ever turn her back on that fact?

She walked over to the sofa, and sat down, feeling suddenly very shaky. She almost wished she could be sick to her stomach…maybe she'd feel better. How could this really be happening? How had she allowed this to go so far? She bent her head, knowing it was her *obsession* with Sean that had started things on the road to this place. But, knowing that fact didn't lessen its impact any!…she still was intoxicated by the thought, scent, and feel of the big man. She lifted her head, cheeks awash with a sudden flood of hot tears…staring into space, and wondering when it would all end!…if it *could* end!……

……Sandra switched her cell phone off, lowering it to the desk top, and then looked at the men in the room with her. "That was Roland…he just spoke with Beth, and she told him to have me call her. She told him she was fine, and had left the hospital on her own…that she was going to spend a few days resting, and would be home after that."

"Did she tell him where she was?" David asked, knowing she was hurting inside.

She gazed at him, and shook her head. "No...but there's only one place I can think of she'd go to be alone." She bent her head a bit, deep in thought. Her voice came to him, low and abstracted. "She's at the cabin...and they're probably with her! We'll have to wait, and see what she has to say when I call her."

"Sandra..." The professor's voice cut into their conversation. She looked at him as he continued. "When you talk with Elizabeth, remember one thing...she is most probably under *her* influence! Everything she may say, or do will be under their control at all times! Do not allow yourself to be swayed in any way! This means you're going to have forget your feelings for your twin sister, and use only the logic, and intellect you've been graced with since birth!" He stepped closer, putting a gentle hand on her shoulder, squeezing lightly. "If you forget that, you may find yourself suffering a fate similar to...to Garalynn's!"

She nodded, and picked her phone back up. She looked once at David, then quickly tapped the number she wanted into the cellular phone's memory. Lifting it to her ear, she waited a few seconds, and then..."Beth? It's me...yes, I just talked with him. I'd like to know what the hell you were thinking of, leaving the hospital the way you...I didn't say that! Of course, you're more then capable of making your own decisions! We usually talk it over with one another first, though! I've been worried sick about you, and where you were! Speaking of which...just exactly are you? What do you mean...it's none of my business right now? Did Tamara, or Sean tell you to say that? I can so ask something like that, Beth!...you're my sister! I am not prying into your...Beth, this is getting us nowhere! What did you want to talk with me about?" Sandra drew a deep, shaky breath, remembering what Yusuf had cautioned her about where her twin sister was concerned.

For a few moments, she stood in silence, listening to what her sister was saying, the two men watching the expressions come, and go on her face. Finally..."Yes, I understand everything you've told me, Beth...but I have no idea where the journal is hidden! And what amulet are you talking about?" Sandra couldn't believe she was actually lying to her sister. "Yes, I know Garalynn took something from the Tomb, Beth, but she never showed me what it was before she left!" Well...at least, that statement was the truth...after all, it was much later when Garalynn had shown her the piece of jewelry.

"Beth...be serious! *Why* would I lie about that to you?" Sandra was trying to stay calm.

At the cabin, Beth was about to say something more when Tamara took the phone from her. "Sandra?...how very nice to hear your voice again! Of course...both Sean, and I are here, with Elizabeth. Where else would we be, my dear? Now...let's keep things on a simple level, shall we? Elizabeth has spoken of what we want...now it is your task to follow through, and bring us what we desire!"

"And if I can't deliver it, Tamara...what then? What about my sister?" Sandra's voice was cold, and sharp.

"Elizabeth's well-being is no longer any concern of yours, Sandra...she belongs to us now! If *you*, however, do wish to see her ever again..." Tamara's voice was like a caress of molten silk...soft, and deadly. "I tire of these mind games, Sandra...bring me what I want! If you don't already have it...find it! I'm sure dear Garalynn told you whatever is necessary to locate the items! You have forty-eight hours from this moment, Sandra...or you can forget ever seeing Elizabeth again! Oh, by the way...as a sort of incentive for your searching...did you get my 'message' at Garalynn's condominium yesterday?" Digging the knife a little deeper, Tamara smiled, and hung up.

Sandra stared at the phone, the nails of her free hand digging deep into the palm of her hand. She finally looked at David, and the professor. "They want the amulet, and the journal...or we'll never see Beth again! We have forty-eight hours to find the journal, and turn the two things over to them!"

"Well…everyone's cards are on the table now, aren't they? They've tossed their ante in, and now it's our turn! So…what now?" David said quietly, looking at his two companions.

"We find the journal…not to give to them, but to see what it was that Joshua felt had to be kept secret at all costs! We do that first, then we see!" Yusuf declared, tapping the bowl of his pipe against the edge of an ashtray. "When we have all the keys in our hands, we'll know better how to deal with these people!"

"If you say so!" David looked back at the lovely woman beside him. "Sandy…did Beth let on where she was when she called?"

"No…but my cell phone has caller ID…she's at the cabin! They're with her, obviously! She said she was fine…that it was *her* decision to leave the hospital, and she went to the cabin just to have a private place to rest! Knowing my sister…she's probably saying what she believes to be the truth! But…I'm sure she was coached to say the words she did! There was so little emotion behind her voice!" Came the quiet, firm reply. David felt long, tapered fingers seek his, entwining with them.

"Things are getting very serious now! We must concentrate all our efforts on locating that journal! That must be first!" The professor waved an admonishing finger in the air, needlessly reminding them all about the situation.

"I need to check in with the station first…I want Patrick to send a couple of units up to that cabin…" David was interrupted by Sandra's grabbing his arm. "Hey…what's that for?" He glared at her.

"No police at the cabin, David!…I mean that! That will have to wait until we find the journal, and then deal with Tamara, and Sean…and Beth!" Sandra shook her head, the azure gaze never leaving his. "You have to trust me on this, David…please, darling, do this my way for now!"

It was the softly whispered endearment dropping from her full lips that tipped the scales. David drew her close, nodding slowly, and claiming those lips with a tenderness even he wasn't aware he was capable of showing.

Yusuf put his arms around the couple…they would need the closeness of each other to get through what lay ahead.......

......Sandra straightened up with a slight groan, rubbing her lower back, trying to ease the sudden spasm that had struck. She'd been bent over this one chest for nearly thirty minutes, searching every inch of the structure. It was when she'd twisted to the left that she'd felt the muscles contract. With a sigh, she felt the cramp ease, and she looked over at where the others where involved with moving one of the larger statues, in order to search the area behind the monolithic figure. She sighed again, feeling the fatigue, and frustration, seep into her body. They'd been searching in the Tomb for over five hours now, and it didn't look any closer to locating the object they sought. She'd shown everyone the hidden drawer Garalynn had taken the amulet pouch from, but a thorough search there didn't turn up any further clues. The professor marveled that the amulet had been there for all those years, and he hadn't a clue to its existence.

Sandra glanced at the two individuals that the professor had called to help them…one of whom she knew personally. Angela Wainwright had been a former classmate of Sandra's at the university…in fact, they'd shared the class taught by Prof. Hanradi. The other friend of Yusuf's was a man…Jacob Pintz, a well-known, and respected restaurant owner in the local Denver environs.

Sandra walked over to where Angela was resting, sitting on the bottom step of the dais. "How's it going? Anything?" She asked quietly, sitting down beside the other woman.

Angela looked over at her friend, stretching a little to ease the tired muscles in her back, and arms. "I'd almost forgotten how pains-taking the work can be in any archaeological undertaking! Repetitious movements never were my favorites!" She smiled wanly. "In answer to your question, however…nothing's turned up so far!"

"Same here…God, I wish my father had said something before his death! I am still having a few difficulties with this whole damned situation!…you know what I mean?" Sandra rubbed the back of her neck, trying to keep her agitation under control.

"Yes, I do…and the longer you work with this kind of happening doesn't make it any easier, I'm afraid! It just makes it a little easier to accept the reality!" Angela looked around the vast room. "You know, Sandra…I've heard, and read tons of things about this room…but, you have to really *see* it to understand! Your family should be very proud of what they accomplished here!"

"It sure is something…makes one's eyes pop!" Jacob stated, coming over to where they were sitting, in time to hear the last statement. "When Yusuf told me we'd be working *here*…well, it was almost like a surprise gift! I've wanted to see this room every time I read anything about it." He looked around them, wiping his forehead with a handkerchief. "You know, I used to think your family should open this to the public…like they did the formal gardens a few years ago. But, after seeing it…I understand the caution, and the privacy! In fact, knowing now what Yusuf has told us…I applaud their precautions! Can you imagine it?…items of the seventh power, here! I would never have dreamed that *I* would ever be looking for anything to do with that!…an especially here, in Denver!"

"Well…someone not only dreamed about it…they somehow broke in here, and took three of the items away! It was only through God's grace they didn't find the most important ones!" Sandra glanced up at the marble sarcophagus. "I wish I'd listened fully to my instincts! They were telling me, all along, that there was a hidden truth about these people, but I chose to believe I was reacting merely out of a…a jealousy! I wouldn't listen to what my inner senses were saying! Maybe…if I had…" Sandra couldn't finish that thought. She ran the fingers of one hand through her dark hair, swallowing hard…trying to keep visions of Garalynn, and Beth out of her mind's eye.

"Don't…don't do that to yourself, Sandra! Allow yourself to grieve, yes…even to rage if you must! But don't let those feeling overwhelm you to the point your defenses are dropped even a little bit!" Yusuf came up, his dark eyes filled with compassion, and determination.

"He's right, Sandy…I know, I've been there! Until I'd had a near death experience, I was skeptical of people like Yusuf, and Jacob. I put them in the same category as those people you read about in the tabloids…you know, the ones who talked about their abductions by aliens, and such stuff!" Angela glanced up at Jacob, who smiled, and squeezed her shoulder comradely. "Now…I keep my eyes open in a way I never thought, and my mind as well! There is so much out there, Sandy…things we don't understand because we never thought them even remotely real! I've learned that ignoring something simply because it seems impossible is leaving myself open to attack! Keeping an open mind…being willing to look at something as possible, until properly researched, is the only way! To shut ourselves off, in any way, is to give our enemies a very big hold on our being…our souls!"

Sandra was curious as she reached for one of the bottles of water she'd had Roland bring them down. "Angela…what *did* happen that changed your mind?"

The other woman grew thoughtful, her eyes staring into space. "I was in Greece at the time…working with my dad's salvage group. We'd been asked to help out with a new discovery, just off the shoreline of the island, Cephalonia, in the Ionian Sea. A team of archaeologists, from Greece and the US, had located what looked like a small fleet of sunken vessels…merchant ships. There was an unbelievable number of intact amphorae, as well as a lot of other artifacts to be salvaged, and brought to the surface. My dad was friends with one of the American scientists in the team, and agreed to send his best divers, and equipment over to help bring everything to the surface. They all got really excited when they saw the first amphorae that the nest, and divers brought up."

"What was so special about them?" Sandra looked up as David sat down beside her, reaching for one of the water bottles. She smiled at him, then brought her attention back to Angela.

"They all had a very distinct seal on their caps...of a situla. You remember what that was?...from class?" Angela remarked.

"I think so...a mark, in the shape of a milk churn that was supposedly constructed of metal. It was used to designate something that was used in a sacred ceremony, like holy water, or sacred wine." Sandra frowned. "You said *all* the amphorae had that particular seal? Did they ever determine where these ships were from?...or going?"

"Well, the situla were most common during the Third period, but not usually in Grecian lands! That was part of what was so intriguing...here were what was clearly Greek ships, carrying amphorae that were nearly a hundred years *older* then the time the ships themselves had been constructed! The wooden fibers of the ships' hulls revealed that fact after they were tested. The amphorae tested much older!"

"Wait a minute...first off, what *are* these amphorae?...and secondly, how could they be so much older then the ships?" David wasn't sure he'd heard correctly.

"Amphorae are bake clay pottery vessels, usually large, that were used to transport, and store a number of things...like wine, grain, water, etc. As to why they were so much older...that was a question that never got fully answered! It became another part of the mystery that surrounded those ships! After all, what good to transport anything sealed up in a clay vessel for so long? I mean...any wine, or water was sure to be spoiled, wasn't it? As for grain...why save it for such a long period, other then possibly for an anticipated siege?" Angela answered his questions, smiling slightly.

Sandra stared, an annoying feeling snipping at the back of her mind. "Did you open any of the amphorae, Angela?...find out what they were indeed carrying?"

"Yes…we brought up a total of thirty-seven intact vessels. The head of the team selected, at random, five amphorae to open. The very first one we broke the seal on was only one third full…of a blackish residue later determined to be ashes. It was amazing that no sea water had leaked into that vessel. The next two held what looked like water, which it did turn out to be…but water of like we'd never seen before! Again, there was no contamination by salt water, but the water was as pure as if it had been drawn out of a fresh water spring mere hours before! A remarkable fact in itself…then, the experts declared that it possessed an incredibly high mineral composition, with high healing qualities." Angela stretched her back a little, then accepted some water from Jacob. They were all sitting now, enthralled with this tale.

"That's wild…mineral water that heals, still potent after a hundred years! What was in the last two?" David was getting so he really liked this history stuff…though he knew the real importance was what history could teach in this battle against evil.

"That was where we all nearly died! We opened the last two jars at the same time, in the army hut we'd set up as a field lab. There was eight of us present at the time, myself included. When the seals were broken, the entire hut was flooded with an over-powering scent…of a cloying sweetness that all of us were immediately rendered unconscious! When we finally came to, a few of us were quite ill to our stomachs, and one member of the team was dead!"

"What happened?…some kind of gas?" David asked, leaning one hand on the stone under him.

"We never really found out…evidently, within a few minutes, the sweet scent dissipated, and when we searched the amphorae later, they were completely empty! There wasn't even a trace left to tell us what they could have been holding! We decided then not to open any more until they were in a sealed room. It was later, though, when I returned to Denver, that the real effects began!" Angela looked away, suddenly afraid she may have said too much. Talking about that incident was something she didn't do often at all.

"Real effects?...what do you mean, Angela? What happened after you returned home?" Sandra felt she had to know everything that had happened.

Angela clasped her hands together, and bowed her head. Jacob leaned closer, placing his large hand over hers, and squeezing. "It's okay, Angie...tell them. The only way people are ever going to really believe is if they're told about others' experiences!"

She nodded, knowing his words were true. "I started having these dreams...sometimes while I was still awake! They were so real, so vivid...it was like it was actually happening! I also began hearing things...inside my mind! It was a voice, speaking in a language I'd never heard before! I finally went to a therapist, but there was little he was able to do for me! It was becoming a daily, and nightly torture! I could hardly sleep anymore, and being outside my apartment was becoming sheer hell!" The woman shuddered, remembering the terrible time she'd lived through. "I finally went to see Yusuf...why I'm not sure, except he'd been an old teacher of mine, and deep inside, I felt he could help...and he did!" Angela smiled at the professor, who nodded slightly, and smiled also. "He saved my sanity!"

"I was fortunate to be where she needed me, that's all! When she told me what had happened, I knew she'd been exposed to powers of extraordinary levels, and that they'd brought forth something hidden deep within her own subconscious. I called Jacob, and assigned him to Angela as a sort of bodyguard, and guide, until we could investigate this fully. We were able to end the dreams, and allow Angela to get on with her life" The professor said, nodding his head...that was one of the reasons the Keepers were created.

"I was only too happy to help...becoming a Keeper has been the shining moment in my life...besides, what better way for an old man to meet, and take care of such lovely young women?" Jacob grinned, hugging Angela.

"Jacob...sometimes I think you never take anything seriously at all!" Angela admonished good-naturedly, waggling one finger at him.

"That's just Jacob's way, Angela...something we have all become used to over the years. Going back to what Angela said about her experience...we were able to find out something about what had happened, utilizing the world-wide Keeper network. Ages ago, some priests of the goddess Ceres, in ancient Rome, discovered that a certain combination of herbs, and chemical bases created a substance that would induce a high state of awareness, and sensitivity. It was similar to the peyote used by the Native Americans to summon visions, and guidance. The dark powers used this substance exclusively to converse with their lord, and master!"

Sandra started as she heard these words...why hadn't she thought of that? What had Garalynn told her?...yes, that *was* it! "Yusuf...the amulet!"

Everyone turned towards her, wondering if something was wrong. David couldn't understand why she seemed so excited...though, he had to admit, excitement looked very good on her face. He shook his head, pushing such thoughts away...time for that later, he told himself.

The professor frowned, shaking his head. "I am afraid I don't understand, Sandra...what about the amulet?"

"Don't you see?...that was one of the things Garalynn was trying to get me to see! The spoken word...it carries the most power, right?" She waited until she saw them all nod, albeit slowly. "Right...Garalynn kept talking about the prayers on the amulet...sayings from the Book of the Dead. She said something that I didn't understand at the time, but maybe it makes more sense now. She said that the chants would help her communicate with that trapped spirit...by speaking the prayers aloud!"

There was silence for a few moments. Yusuf stared at her, then at Jacob, whose eyes had begun to glow as his excitement mounted. Angela put a hand to her mouth, as if to hold in the rising she felt within her own soul. David looked at all of them, and shook his head...he didn't get this at all! What were they all getting so up-tight about now?

The professor's eyes glowed...he stared at Sandra, holding her hands tightly as he digested what she'd been suggesting. "You may have hit on the only way, my dear!" He reached into his pocket, and drew out the golden amulet. Holding it up, it twirled slowly, picking up the hidden track lights, and throwing out glistening rays. "This just might help us to do the impossible!"

David hunched his shoulders involuntarily...a sure indication to him that something very big was about to take place. "Are you by any chance suggesting that we say these prayers aloud...again? Do you recall what happened the last time someone said these? It was Garalynn...and she's missing, probably dead!" David turned at the soft gasp from Sandra. "God...Sandy, I'm sorry!" His dark blue eyes were filled with remorse, and something much, much warmer.

"It's all right...it just took me by surprise, that's all! I have to learn how to accept it, you know...if I can!" Sandra touched his cheek briefly, then turned towards the others, looking at the professor. "Yusuf...you had better be the one to attempt this...you're more versed in the occult, and religious practices."

The old teacher held the amulet reverently, and glanced around at all his companions. "Thank you, my dear...I'll do my best. But, first...I want us all to have the most protection possible! Jacob...would you take care of that matter, please?"

The olther man nodded, and went over to where he'd stored a large brown leather bag, and knelt beside it. Opening it, he removed a large deerskin pouch, and four large white candles. Rising, he once again rejoined the group. "If you'll select the proper spot, Yusuf...I'll get things set up!" He nodded at his old friend.

The learned scholar nodded his consent, and walked to the center of the room. He stood perfectly still, his head slightly cocked to one side, as if listening to some sound that the others couldn't hear. After a few moments, he turned back to the others. "I want everyone to come over to the area in front of the altar to Horus…it appears to be the one spot that's the least marked! I think that's the best spot, Jacob!"

"Marked?…what do you mean?" David came up behind Sandra, slipping a gentle arm around her waist. She smiled softly up at him, then looked back at Jacob, and the professor.

"He means it's the one spot in this room that has the least amount of spiritual upheaval, or contamination, David. That's where I'll set up a spirit circle…it's to protect us from any force, or power, that means us harm!" Jacob walked to the place Yusuf indicated with his finger.

First, he opened the pouch, and pulled out a handful of what looked like white salt, or sand. Using this, letting the grains slip slowly out between his close fingers, Jacob traced the outline of a large circle. He used almost all the powdery substance in the pouch, and finally closed the pouch by the drawstrings…satisfied with the pure white, unbroken circle he'd made. Then, he set the four white candles at the four points of the compass, and lit them…all the while muttering words that David strained to hear, but couldn't clearly. The tall policeman sniffed…a sweet, ethereal fragrance was beginning to waft around their heads. It was from the myrrh concealed within the candles, being released as the flame burned the wax down slowly. David glanced around the room…his police sense kicking into gear again.

The professor ushered Angela, and Sandra into the confines of the circle, cautioning them against touching, or disturbing the circle in any way. Once the women were within the spirit circle, he motioned for the other two men to follow him, and he stepped into the circle as well.

Once they were all within the circle's expanse, he lifted the amulet up, and peered at the inscriptions on the back of it. In a slow, deep cadence, his voice reaching into every corner, and crevice of the room, Prof. Hanradi recited the prayers carved into the golden amulet, translating the characters into the Egyptian language the ancients spoke in the days of the amulet's conception. It only took a few minutes to complete the chants, then all was silent in the room. Indeed, the last spoken word's echoes seemed to roll about the room, never completely dying away, as did true echoes.

Angela hunched her shoulders a little, her hand curling around one of Jacob's...she knew something was about to happen. "Jacob...can *you* feel it? Like the hum of an electrical current in the air! Something's going to happen?" She whispered softly.

He squeezed her hand, reassuring and steady. "Yes...I know. Now, be still, little one...and don't break the circle in any way!" He cautioned, his free hand clasping the silver Star of David he always wore.

"Thou has summoned my spirit...what would thee have of me this day?" A deep, resonating voice was suddenly heard in the room...coming from everywhere, and nowhere. There was no hint of malice in the voice...just an almost overwhelming calmness, underscored with a deep sorrow. David knew it wasn't a trick...the faces of his companions told him they heard the same thing he did, and that, like him also, they could understand every word, even though it was a language he'd never heard before.

"I charge thee, by all the powers of the Light...by the blood of the Lamb...in the name of the all-seeing Ra...be truthful only in thy speech! Keep thy intentions open, clear, and honor bound!" Yusuf declared, firmly clutching the amulet.

"By all that is Truth, and Light...in the name of He who never dies, I will speak only what is true, and free of all evil intentions! Ask me thy questions!" The voice answered, serene and clear spoken.

"Do I address the one who granted knowledge of this amulet to our sister called Garalynn?" The professor asked slowly. "Are thou the One?...he called the Seer?"

There was a pause of a few seconds, then the voice began speaking again...the deep sadness clear in the deep tones. "I can answer only the first part of thy question; learned scholar...yes, it was I who granted that knowledge to Garalynn. It was she who first used it to free my tongue, that I might communicate with thee! For this...I fear she has paid a heavy toll!" There was another long pause. "As for the query about the Seer...for now, that must remain unanswered! Until the designated hour, no one may reveal, or know, that sacred secret! For now...believe that I am a friend! I am to help thee defeat the evils now confronting thee, and thine!"

"What do you mean by a heavy price? What has happened to her?...is she..." Sandra closed her eyes, and drew on her inner strength. "Is my sister dead?"

"Be strong...yes, thy sister is no longer of this world! But, her spirit will always be with those she loved best! Do no ever forget this...think of those who have passed over before will always be able to hear thy thoughts!" came the slow, sad reply.

Sandra stared wildly about her, then collapsed into David's arms, grief overwhelming her. Up until now, though she'd stated she knew her sister was probably dead...she'd never totally given up hope. Now...now there was no alternative left. Now, she had no choice but to accept the cruel fact that Garalynn *was* dead!

"David...stay with her...make sure neither of you touch the circle's rim, though, alright?" Yusuf then straightened up, and looked around the room. "We desire thy help, to find that which will save our entire world from a great catastrophe. Time is growing short, which thee must already know! If within thy power, point the way! Help us keep the eternal darkness at bay!"

"The Light will ever defeat the dark, my friend...seek the truth, and the way, where the Light is born!" Came the reply, then all was silent. The electric feel to the air was also gone, and they realized they weren't going to get anything further today. Jacob, moving swiftly, used his foot to scuff a break in the white circle's border, then snuffed all four candles out as quickly. He straightened up, and looked at the professor. "Well...did you understand that, Yusuf?"

The old teacher began pacing back, and forth…muttering to himself. "Where the Light is born…where the Light is born!" He stopped, looking at Sandra. "Sandra, I can't seem to pull the memory up…which altar had the chest that held the Sun Stone fragment?"

She gazed at him, choking back a last few tears. She pointed at the altar of the falcon-headed god, Horus. "It was over there, before the break-in, Yusuf…it's in behind the god's statue now. But…it's not there any longer…it was one of the things taken during the break-in!"

The professor's shoulders slumped. "Perhaps…the stone itself isn't really what we're after, Sandra. Where the Light is born…what if that means *where* the stone was, *not* the stone itself!" He was beginning to feel like he did in his younger days, when he took part in a great many field operations that came before the Keeper council.

"We've searched all around the altar, and the statue…looking for the journal! I really can't believe we would have missed anything really significant, Yusuf!" Angela wasn't sure her old teacher's interpretation of the cryptic message was correct.

"No…I am sure you didn't, Angela. What I'm thinking about wouldn't have been something you'd think to look into!" The professor knelt down, and tugged on the heavy chest wedged in behind the polished sandstone statue.

"Here…let me help, professor!" David added his arm and back strength to the professor's, and the two men dragged the chest out in front of the altar itself.

Yusuf opened the chest and took out another, smaller, more ornate chest. In this was a thick scroll, which he carefully removed. He checked the inside of the chest thoroughly, then placed the small chest inside again. He turned to his friends, and held the big scroll up. "This is a scroll copied from the original Scroll of Thoth…if I remember correctly, there is a passage in here that refers to the birthing of the Light, and the sacred items consecrated to it! I think this is what our spirit friend was referring to, my friends!"

Sandra was about to speak when she felt the distinct sensation of something brushing her cheek. She turned towards the direction of the feeling, eyes wide with a sudden fear...no one was there...and at that moment, none of her companions were close enough to touch her. She was about to turn away, but that brushing sensation came again, stronger this time, and her head jerked around again. It was when her head came around that her eyes spotted the strangest thing. Across the room, by the door, was a floor to ceiling panel, completely covered with carved, and painted hieroglyphics. She could have sworn she saw one of those carvings glowing with an eerie, pulsing green-blue nimbus.

She slowly walked across the room, her attention solely on the tall panel. She felt drawn to that panel. She stopped directly in front of the carved panel, and lightly skimmed her fingertips over that area that had appeared glowing...which it wasn't now, she also noticed. She felt the fine granules of stone under her fingertips...fingertips that were now lingering over one particular spot, as if drawn to it. The character carved there was that of a large bennu bird, painted white and black, with gold accents. The eyes, however, were not painted...but created, rather, by small turquoise stones, a rarity prized by the ancients. She wondered if this wasn't what she'd seen glowing.

"What's up?...looking for something?" David asked, coming up behind her.

"I'm not really sure...I felt drawn here. Actually, I thought I saw something glowing over here! I think it was just the lights reflecting off the stones in the eyes. I thought..." She paused, not sure what she was about to say. "You know...I'm not at all sure what it was that I was going to say! What connection could this bennu have with what the voice said?" She mused out loud.

"A what?...did you say bennu? What's a bennu?" David asked just as the others joined them.

"The bennu was a sacred symbol, found in many tombs, David...it was also referred to, by some, as the phoenix! It represented many things to the ancients...renewal, resurrection...immortality. It was considered a symbol liked directly to the Creator...and very important for a safe journey to one's second life, in the Western land!" Angel stated, smiling at the surprised look on Yusuf's face. "Didn't think I'd remember all that, did you?" She teased gently.

"It's not your memory that surprises me, Angela...it's the fact that you were actually listening to my lectures on that subject! Very good...I am impressed!" Her old teacher grinned back at her.

"Are all you guys this up on the history stuff?" David made a circling motion with one hand, indicating the entire group.

"Comes with being part of the Keepers, David...you turn into a permanent history student!...*all* history!" Jacob smiled, touching his Star of David again. "My work is as a restaurant owner...but since I was a child, I've taken every opportunity to learn about the world around me, and especially its history! My father believed, and I have come to agree, that to be well learned was to have many weapons at your disposal, at all times, for any situation! Knowledge...it is fascinating, and powerful!"

Yusuf had opened the scroll while they were talking, and had been scanning the text drawn there. His sudden exclamation drew everyone's attention back to him. He stabbed a finger at a passage, about halfway through. "This is it!...I knew I had remembered right!" he looked at them eyes bright. "Angela...Sandra...Jacob...what else can the bennu mean? I used to talk about it often in my classes, when we dealt with the Egyptians beliefs on the Creation...the ancient beliefs! Remember?"

Sandra stared at him, then glanced at Angela, and Jacob, her mind trying to think back to her time in the professor's classrooms. The women could tell by his expression that the professor was serious in his questions...but what exactly was he after?

"Okay...let's run over what we already know." Angela began. "The bennu was the phoenix...which was a symbol of immortality...which went through an eternal cycle of life, death, and rebirth!"

"And...it was also a symbol of creation!" Sandra added.

"Very good, girls...you did listen! Now...knowing all that, what does that give us?" He looked at each of them in turn.

Sandra held her hands out, palms up to denote her bewilderment. Angela shrugged, one eyebrow rising, then looked at Jacob. They were all stumped at what he was trying to get them to see. Then...it began first with Jacob, then the two women. They looked at the professor. He nodded, and pointed at the open scroll he was still holding, smiling broadly. "As it is written...may the sky-eyed lord of the rebirth forever point the way to the god's light..." He read aloud.

"Would one of you be so kind as to let this ignorant cop know just what the hell is going on here?" David was more then mildly exasperated right now.

"You've heard what a bennu bird is?" Sandra waited until she saw him nod before she continued. "Well...if the bennu had eyes made from the sky stone...turquoise...it meant two things! One...the tomb was that of a member of the royalty! And, two..." She turned, and pressed her forefinger, and middle finger, in hard on the two eyes of the carving. She wasn't surprised when she felt the stones give way under the pressure of her fingers. She was startled, though, when, with a grating, raspy sound, a large section of the panel slid open, displaying a deep niche. "And, two...the eyes would point the way, or direction, the burial chamber laid." She almost whispered.

Yusuf stepped forward, and reached a trembling arm into the shadowed recesses of the hidden spot. He brought his hand back out, grasping a medium sized wooden box, about the size and width of a large telephone book...secured with an ornate, old-styled padlock. The professor held it in both hands, and looked at Sandra.

Slowly, with great reverence, he handed the box to Sandra. "Here...it belongs to your family...you should be the first to see it!" He said quietly to her, clasping his hands over hers that now held the ancient box.

Sandra stared at him, then at what she was holding. She walked slowly over to the largest altar, and sat the box down. The others crowded around, forming a circle about the stone. She unhooked the catch, and lifted the lid of the box. Reaching into the shallow box, she lifted out a leather bag. This, she opened, and gently slid a large leather-covered journal out of its covering. Sandra held it in both hands, staring down at the black leather, unable to really believe they had actually found the lost journal of Joshua Phelps. She held it out to the professor. "Here, Yusuf…you see what's inside!" She smiled slightly, knowing how eager her old teacher was to see the book from the Blackmoon legend.

He hesitated a moment, looking at all his companions, then eager hands took the journal, and opened it. He scanned a few pages, his eyes growing wider as each page was turned. "This is quite wonderful, and quite surprising as well!" He glanced once at Sandra, a smile on his bearded face. "Your ancestor had excellent penmanship, my dear Sandra…unusual for an ordinary man of his times! He appears to have been a highly educated man…also a rarity for the times!"

"Yusuf, I can hold it in any longer!…what's it say?" Jacob had heard about this journal for such a long time…the thought of actually seeing what was contained within its pages had his heart pounding.

"What I've skimmed over so far deals mostly with his travels west, and everything he came across, and what he hopes to find. He also talks about this feeling that's driving him onward." The professor skipped a few pages ahead. "Here is where he met Two Feathers, the shaman…and first learned the legend of the Dark Eagle's Nest…it's going to take some time, I can see that, to read everything here." The professor looked up, one hand resting reverently on the aged pages.

"I think we should retire to your home, Yusuf…it's a better protected place for such an undertaking!" Jacob suggested, looking around the Tomb room.

"Why not just read it here? We don't have all that much time, you know!" David declared, wondering why they'd risk yet another delay.

Prof. Hanradi nodded, sliding the journal back inside the leather bag. "Jacob's right, David…we need the special protection of certain items I have back at my home before we start reading this! Right now, we must put this room back in order before we depart to my home. Everything must be in its proper place before we leave."

Angela, and Jacob nodded, and went to start putting things away. Yusuf also left the altar stone, heading for the obsidian dais. David looked after him, then over at where Sandra still stood. "Why are we doing this now?…cleaning up, then going to the professor's house? This isn't a coffee party, you know! And how is the professor's house better protected then here?"

Sandra cam to him, slipping her arms around him, and hugging herself tight against his body, her hands stroking the strong back. She knew how confusing this had to be for him, yet he'd been nothing but supportive, and loving. "What Yusuf, and Jacob were getting at were spiritual protections…the ancient ways of guarding the home, and everything inside it. I've been to Yusuf's home before…he has a collection of ancient talismans, and amulets second to none!" She lifted her head, and glanced over to where the other three people were gathered, putting some chests back in place. "They want us to leave here because our having found the journal, and removed it has upset the psychic bonding of this place. When we actually take it from here, there will be a void that any psychically sensitive individual will be able to sense! By replacing everything in the room, into the spots they were we are putting the psychic bond back into place. See, they're even putting the box the journal was in back into its hiding place. It's not much, but it may buy us a little time before our enemies discover we do indeed now have the real journal!" She tried to explain things as best she herself understood.

"But…the journal will be gone! Won't that still leave that void you spoke of…even if the box is replaced, the journal won't be in it!" David looked down at her, still within the circle of his arms.

"The dark powers *have* been within the Tomb, David…that's true! They will have taken a psychic imprint of everything they could…but they're limited in that their imprint can only be of what they can actually *see*! They didn't see the journal, or its hiding place, so by replacing the box, we should delay their discovering anything has indeed been removed…other then what they themselves took! The journal's hiding place was also protected from detection by the symbol it was behind…they should not have been able to get any kind of sign that the journal was even in this room. They things they'd already taken, they knew *were* actually here! The journal…well, they probably figured it *was* somewhere in the room, but not for a certainty! The longer we can delay their knowledge, the more chance we have to come up with a foolproof plan against them!" The professor cam up to them, placing a reassuring hand on the younger man's shoulder.

David shook his head. "I know I've been going along with all of this so far…but I got to tell you all, this is getting way too deep for me!" He ran his fingers through his hair, pushing it back from his forehead. He looked over to where Jacob was cleaning up the remnants of the white circle. "Professor, there's something I wanted to ask…what is that stuff he used to make the circle? And why did he rush to break the circle after that spirit voice stopped speaking to us? And why did you seem so disappointed when it didn't answer your question about the Seer?"

"First, that substance Jacob used is pounded virgin wheat…the first wheat taken in a harvest, and milled on a brand new millstone. It represents purity, growth, strength of body, and soul. By using it as the matrix material of a psychic circle, it affords optimum protection to anything, or anyone inside that circle, from any form of evil influences. By breaking the circle immediately, Jacob was assuring that none of us would be assaulted by any lingering evil forces still outside the circle. You see, even a good person can be harmed by stepping out of an unbroken circle…it acts like a magnet for the dark forces, to roam on the outside. Once the circle is broken, however, the magnet is defused, the psychic energy immediately dissolves, and the danger is dispersed!" The professor replied, motioning to Angela, and Jacob.

"And the Seer?" David persisted...he felt he had to learn as much as possible, in the short time he felt they had left to them. His policeman's instincts were on over-load right now...the enemy was very close!

"No one really knows exactly who, or what the Seer is, my boy...save that it *is* a vital key to the salvation of all mankind, and the world! Beyond that...unless you are a Keeper, there's not much I am allowed to say further! Now, come...we have much to get done, in a short amount of time!" He motioned to all of them.

Sandra looked up at David, and smiled sadly. "He's right...we'd better get things taken care of, and then get going! I still have to figure out what I'm going to say when I see Beth, and Tamara! I hope Yusuf, and the others can find something in that journal before that!"

He hugged her, suddenly afraid for her. "You told me that Joshua said there *was* something in the journal's pages that would help the right person, at the right time! The professor will find it, don't worry!" He shook his head, still wondering about the mysterious Seer...friend, foe, or an even greater danger? He pushed the dark thoughts away...he had to be strong for Sandra right now.

She lifted her head from his chest. "Where did you get such strength of faith? Or,

Have you always had it?" She asked quietly, gazing at his rugged face...her eyes caressing every line.

He shrugged, tightening his hold on her a little. "I'm not sure if faith is the right word. I just know I can't give up, or give in...to anything! If I do...I know it will be all over! And now, with *you* in my life...well, let's just say I'll do whatever it takes to keep you safe!...and that goes for Beth, and your friends, too!" He grinned down into her suddenly anxious face. "And, if that means fighting a demon, or two...then, bring them on, I say!" He tried to sound funny, and confident...but there was a little break in the deep voice that gave his inner feelings away.

Sandra hugged him close, her eyes shut, willing the world to depart, and leave them alone for a while. There was no certainty of what would take place in the next few hours…or, who would be the final victor. For this moment in time's passing, all she wanted was to be with him………

…….David sat up with a yawn, stretching his arms out at shoulder level, trying to ease the kinks in his back from sleeping on the sofa. They were all camped out in the professor's den, waiting while Jacob, and Yusuf worked over the journal. Sandra had also been helping, albeit in a lesser role then the two older men. David had curled up on the sofa, watching his lady do her history thing. He frowned now as he realized she was no longer around the table, with Jacob, and Yusuf. He saw Angela curled up in the big easy chair by the table, sleeping fitfully.

He stood, stretching his entire body once more, then walked over to where the others sat. He glanced at the clock on the fireplace…three a.m. The older men looked up at him as he came near. "Sleep well, David?" Jacob smiled up at the younger man, pouring him a hot cup of coffee from the thermal pitcher on the table. The older man's face was lined with fatigue, but his eyes were still bright with excitement, and anticipation.

"Thanks…guess I slept okay, though I feel like shit!" The tall policeman took a big swig of the coffee, his eyes widening with appreciation of the blend. "Where's Sandy?" He asked, looking around the room.

I sent her to the guest room, to get some sleep! She was exhausted, and with what she's got facing her…well, I thought a few hours of safe sleep would do her a world of good!" The professor took his glasses off, rubbing the bridge of his nose. "Why don't you go check on her, David? It's the third door down the corridor…on the left side!"

David nodded, took a couple more drinks of his coffee, put the cup back on the table, and left the room. He walked a few paces down the long corridor, and stopped at the indicated door. He opened it gently, and walked inside. It was dimly lit, the only light being the small bedside lamp. David walked slowly to stand beside the bed, gazing down at the sleeping woman there. Sandra was sleeping on her left side, one hand cradling her head, under her left cheek. David knelt by the bed, leaning his folded arms on the edge of the bed, his head resting on them as he stared at her face.

"I wish I knew how all of this is going to turn out...that I could promise you that everything's going to be all right...but, that's just not possible! I can't even promise any of us will even be alive when this is all over!" He said softly, tenderly wrapping one lock of the dark hair about the tip of his right forefinger...caressing the silken tress. "There's only one thing I *do* know, and can promise solidly! You are the best thing that has ever been in my life, and if...no, *when* we survive all this, I'm going to make sure you know that every day of our lives!" He bent closer, his lips a mere inch, or two, from her right ear. "I love you, Sandra Usher-Phelps...and I want you for my wife!"

"Is that a proposal?" the low voice was still heavy with sleep, but clear, and very serious. He looked down as her eyes opened, and she gazed at him. She didn't speak any further, just maintained contact with his eyes. Then, her right hand reached out, slipped behind his head, and drew it closer to her. Their lips met, softly at first, then the intensity grew as the kiss deepened.

Her lips moved against his. "I love you, too, David...and the answer is yes! I want nothing as much as I do to be your wife!" She twisted her body to the right, pulling him along with her, until he ended up draped half-way on top of her body. "Please, my love...make love to me! I need you so much...I love you so deeply!" Her lips moved from his mouth to the sensitive skin under his left earlobe. "I want you!...now!"

He pulled back a little...thinking they were rushing things a bit, that she was still half-asleep, and didn't realize what she was saying. Though his entire body was thrumming with desire for her, he didn't want to take any sort of advantage. But, she arched her body up tight against his, wrapping her arms securely about him. He groaned, feeling his carefully maintained controls slipping rapidly...he loved this woman so much, and he'd desired the lovely body under him for what seemed an eternity…how much more could he take?

She nipped his earlobe, sucking the bit of flesh deep into her mouth. He shuddered, feeling the muscles in his groin tighten with a liquid fire. He twisted his head, pulling his ear away from her avid mouth, and claimed her mouth with a passion he hadn't allowed himself prior to this. His hands slid up her arms, over her shoulders, then down her chest to the hem of the sweater she was wearing. Those hands slipped under the soft material of the sweater, and slid ever so softly over the warm, silken skin, until they cupped the full breasts enclosed in the sheer lace bra she wore.

Sandra moaned, feeling her nipples become erect, pressing through the bra's material, into the palms of the hands caressing her. Her hands slipped up, sinking their fingers deep into the thick hair of the man holding her so lovingly. She pulled the head down, bringing the lips that had left hers just moments again back into contact. Her lips parted, inviting…his tongue slipped in, exploring, and tasting. As they learned about one another, Sandra's left hand slipped down, and began fumbling with the buttons of his shirt. The knot in the tie he wore, though, gave her fingers problems as it refused to loosen. He drew back a little, fighting back a deep chuckle as he saw her frown.

Cupping one cheek, he smiled, sitting up. "Here…let me help!" He said softly, yanking the tie off, then quickly stripping his shirt off. He kicked his shoes off, then stood up, and slid the jeans he was wearing off, tossing them to the floor. He knelt back on the bed, wearing only his silk boxers. He didn't say anything, just stared at her, his eyes conveying all the love, and passion he was feeling at that precise moment.

She smiled, happy and seductive. She sat up, watching his eyes all the time. She took hold of the bottom of her sweater, and pulled it over her head, letting it drop to the floor once it was off. Still watching his face, she reached behind her back, and unfastened her bra. She brought the straps forward, letting it slide down her arms, and drop to the bed. She sat there, a little shy, but allowing his eyes to roam over her unclothed upper body. She, in turn, let her eyes rove over his broad chest, with its erect paps, and thick thatch of dark hair.

They slowly leaned towards one another, their lips seeking each other's. Once, twice, she brushed his mouth, and cheeks with her lips…her warm breath causing his skin to come alive with sensation. His hands worked their way up her back, massaging and arousing as they went. Her right hand rested on the soft curls of his chest, feeling the strong, rapid beat of his heart. Her fingers slipped around the nipple of his left chest, caressing it…feeling the small piece of flesh harden, and rise. She felt the pectoral muscles tighten, and felt the small shudder he gave.

He buried his face in the curve of her neck, inhaling the scent of her skin, and her arousal. He gently pushed her back, until she was lying on the bed, his body draped atop hers. They continued kissing, their bodies moving against each other in a sinuous, sensual dance. Her arms slipped about him, pulling him close in a sudden rush.

He lifted his head, and was surprised to see the tears. He gently wiped them away with the tips of one finger, and looked down at her, cradling her head and shoulders in the crook of one arm. "What is it, sweetheart?…what's wrong? Look…if you've changed your mind about this, I'll understand…it's okay!" He said quietly, not wanting her to feel like she *had* to go through with anything.

She shook her head, momentarily unable to speak past the lump that was in her throat. "No…I'm just so…David, I'm scared, and happy! I love you so much, and I want you so much! I *do* want to make love with you…to you!" She swallowed, blinking her eyes to clear away new tears. " It's just…that we don't know what lies ahead! I'm selfish…I want a *whole* lifetime with you! The thought that that might not even be a possibility because of what's facing us…" She didn't finish…she pulled him back on top of her. "I love you!" She finished breathlessly, her fingers digging into his back.

He cradled his head in the valley between her breasts, smoothing his cheek against their soft firmness. "I want to be able to promise you everything will be fine, Sandy…but you know I can't! What I do promise, though, is that I will love you, and only you, for as long as I am alive! If we're together, there isn't anything we can't face, and win! I swear I will do everything in my power to keep you, and yours safe! Whatever the Fates have in store for us…we'll face it side by side! For as long as there is life within my body…and even beyond death…I will love you!" He bent over her, kissing away her lingering doubts, and paying homage to the beauty that was her body. He lifted his head a little, and grinned. "I can't believe I'm talking like this…you must bring out the poet in me!" His teasing was gentle, and filled with the love he was trying to show.

"Whatever it is…I love it! The way your hands feel on my body…the way your lips make me feel like I'm on fire, and only you can put that fire out…" She buried her face into his chest, gripping his body with an urgency she'd never known before. "David, please…I need you so much right now!" She kissed his lips, biting the lower one gently, and rubbing her nose along his jaw line. She found the pulse point at the apex of his shoulder, and neck, and bit down. "Take me!" Her whispered words stoked the flames within her lover, and he bent down, capturing her wrists, and stretching the arms up above her head.

"I love you." He whispered, claiming her mouth. "Whatever happens, I will always love you…and you will always be mine!" His voice was hoarse with passion, and his mouth a little bruising as it moved over the lithe body beneath him.

Sandra arched up into his body, her arms still held above her head, and wrapped one long leg about his hips, pulling him in tighter against her body. The contact caused her to moan softly, and her hips moved sinuously against the hardness she felt growing between their two bodies. He released her wrists, and his hands cupped around her hips, pulling her warm wetness tight against him. In a swift movement, they were joined, and began the ancient dance.

Their bodies moved together in an ever increasing rhythm, with the smooth fluidity of classical dancers...each attuned to every sensation, every desire. The air was sharp with the scent of aroused passions, and mellow with the deepening heat of full-blown sex. Unseen, or sensed by either of them, a soft radiance filled one corner, ebbing and flowing from that spot. There was a warmth from that unearthly glow...not of danger, or threat, but of love. Its supernatural glow added to the sensual atmosphere, and deepened the feelings both lovers were experiencing right then. And, there was an overwhelming sensation of gentleness...a wistful, poignant aura that made each touch, each caress more intense, more meaningful. The glow continued for a few minutes, then faded away...and from the corner, if they'd been aware of things about them right then, the two lovers would have heard a soft, deep sigh……..

****

XI

❀

.......Jacob sighed, setting back in his chair, rubbing his eyes with the knuckles of his hand, He looked at the clock, and saw that it was nearly eight a.m. He replaced his glasses, and looked at his old friend. "Well, Yusuf...it's almost eight o'clock. We've accomplished more than I thought we'd be able to by now! There's still more to decipher, but we've found what we were after, I think!" He looked down at the desk, at the pile of papers that were scattered all about the open journal. "I am still astonished at the wealth of information this Joshua managed to cram into the pages of this journal! And, the wording...where do you suppose a man of his times came to learn so many diverse languages? I mean...it wasn't as if he were one of the great scholars of that era!"

The professor looked up, wiping his glasses with his handkerchief. "I would say that this person...or thing...he discovered on that mountain was largely responsible for that feat, Jacob! It was also most likely the source of all this great knowledge he put down in the journal. It is no small wonder that Joshua took the pains he did to conceal its whereabouts from all, save the one destined to find, and use that fantastic teachings!" He put his eye glasses back on, and placed his open palm face down on the pages of the journal. "Can you imagine what could...*would* happen if this were to fall into the wrong hands? What they wouldn't...what they haven't already done to possess this...this treasure?" He rolled his neck a bit, groaning a little as he felt a vertebrae pop back into place. "I'm going to put another pot of coffee on...you'd better wake Angela, Jacob. You want more tea as well?"

"Thank you, old friend...yes, I would. And, I think she will as well. Do you think I should go awaken Sandra, and David, also?" The restaurant owner stood up, pausing as he turned towards the chair Angela was curled asleep within.

"Let them have this time together...we'll give them a little more time, then awaken them. I'll put that kettle on now!" The professor rose from his chair, unconsciously closing the journal, and slipping it into the large pocket of the smoking jacket he had slipped into earlier.

Jacob was still standing in the same spot...his expression thoughtful. "Yusuf...are you going to tell Sandra everything it said about her family in there?"

At first, the professor didn't answer...just stood there, absently tugging on his beard, his thoughts deep, and far away. Eventually, his eyes cleared, and he looked back to Jacob. "Jacob...I just don't know *what* I should do about that part! Some of it, I don't think is relevant in any way, so why tell her? The rest may help her deal with this situation with Elizabeth, but it may also bring up feelings best left sleeping! I'm just not sure what is the right way to go here!"

"Let me make it easier for you all, Yusuf...simply tell me *all* that was in the journal!" A clear, strong voice broke into their reverie, and they both turned to see Sandra standing in the archway to the long hallway.

She entered the den, and walked up to the desk. "Please...don't start keeping things from me just because you think they'll upset me! I need to know everything that's in there! Keeping things hidden is part of what caused all the things that have happened to my family, and friends of late...I don't want that to continue!" She leaned her hands on the desk, bending forward a little, gazing at the professor. "Please, Yusuf...for the friendship you've had with my family all these years...tell me what the journal said!"

"By rights, that journal *is* her family's property...she has a right to know what it says!" David added, coming into the den, and stopping directly behind Sandra, his right hand slipping forward to clasp her right hip. "Tell her, professor...tell us!"

Yusuf gazed at the younger man, seeing the determination etched on the rugged features...but he also saw the great depth of the love this man held for the woman between them. He nodded, and motioned towards Angela. "Wake her up, Jacob...we might as well make sure everyone hears this! I'll get the coffee, and tea!" he looked back at Sandra, and David. "Pull up a chair, and make yourself comfortable...there's a lot to tell you all about!"

In a few minutes, everyone was awake, and seated, complete with hot coffee, or tea, grouped around the fireplace, with the professor sitting in his favorite, battered old easy chair. He looked at Sandra as he began. "We haven't got all the way through the journal as yet...but most of it has been translated so that we now have a pretty good idea of the main topics."

Sandra interrupted, one hand raised, palm out. "Wait a minute...translated? That journal should have been in English! What would you have had to translate?"

"That was one of the first surprises we came across, Sandra. The first few pages are indeed in old style English, and the grammar was a little hard to understand, but that was to be expected. However, what we didn't expect was to then some into sections in Hellenistic Greek...Doric, to be specific...as well as cuneiform Old Persian, nineteenth dynasty Egyptian hieroglyphics, and the real shocker, a few Mayan glyphs, and Aztec characters! This journal is almost like an encyclopedia of some of the oldest forms of writing known to man! It is absolutely an amazing volume...simply amazing!"

"Why would that stuff be in the journal? Where would someone like Joshua Phelps learn all that, especially if he didn't know it before?" David leaned forward on the footstool he was sitting on, situated right beside where Sandra was sitting, in one of the other easy chairs. "This

Joshua was just an ordinary guy, right? I mean…he wasn't some sort of scholar, or scientist, was he?"

The professor smiled…he understood the other man's confusion. "Yes, you're right, David…Joshua wasn't a scholar, or a scientist! He was a bit of a dreamer, and a visionary…but more importantly, he *was* the right man! When he went up on that mountain, during that lunar eclipse, he did so with the confidence that what he was doing was right! It was that confidence…that faith, that enabled him to do what no one before him had been able…discover the secret of the Dark Eagle's Nest! That is what started the long line of events that has led to this exact moment in time!"

Jacob stood up, and walked to the bar. He picked up some of the toast Angela had made, and poured himself another cup of hot tea. "Joshua knew all about the legends…the old shaman had told him. He figured, as the journal stated, he would try at the next black moon. He wrote how he felt certain he would succeed…as if something was leading him right to that spot, and would show him the right things to do! He'd had a vision that showed him he would be the victor! That was the first clue we found that there was more then mere human involvement here!"

"A vision?…that was never part of the legend, or the story I've heard all my life about Joshua's travels! Did he write down what that vision was?" Sandra asked, frowning a little.

"Not in anything we've come across thus far! He speaks of what he found when he went up onto the mountain, however!" Jacob replied, rejoining the group.

"When Joshua left the village that night, he states that it was the horse who led him the right way. It went directly to a hidden tunnel that led up the center of the mountain, until it ended in a great cavern, deep in the center of the mountain itself!" The professor pulled the journal out of his pocket, and lay it on the desk top.

"The interior?…I wasn't aware there *was* a way to get into that particular mountain. Even today, that peak's one of the most treacherous to climb! I certainly don't recall any stories of tunnels, or caves!" Sandra declared, thinking hard. "Where exactly is this spot?"

"He doesn't go into detail about where it can be found…only about the cavern he ended up finding! He speaks about the size of the cave, the torches that seemed to burn eternally, and a carved sarcophagus concealed within a great altar stone!"

"That reminds me of the cave we found those kids in!…I can't get it out of my mind!" David said quietly…bitterly. Sandra's hand stroked his cheek, conveying the love he needed to push the painful memory away.

"What Joshua found in that cave is the main secret to his journal. He met the danger, in the form of a spirit guard, and was able to defeat it. Though, if I've understood his words correctly…it wasn't much of a contest. He states that the guard offered only token resistance to him…as if it had expecting him all along." Yusuf continued the narrative, pausing only to re-light his pipe.

"Expecting him?…but, the legend spoke of countless warriors who went up that mountain…never to return! What happened to them?" Sandra wondered, feeling a slight chill go down her spine. "Was that just a story? And, what about the eclipse?…was that merely an added detail to make everything more colorful?"

"Nothing about the legend of Blackmoon, and the Dark Eagle's nest was just added details, Sandra! As for the eclipse…there is a great deal of arcane power released during a lunar eclipse, my dear…that is something that has been known by practitioners of the arts since the days of the first men! Joshua's 'defeat' of the spirit guard was a preordained fact…that was why he succeeded where the others did not! The others that attempted this?…probably all slain by the spirit guard. Harsh, I know…but the supernatural is never easy, on anyone! The spirit guard knew that Joshua was the one foretold…that was why his test was relatively easy!…he was always meant to win!" The old teacher nodded, emphasizing each word with a wave of his fingers.

"I would have thought that *his* test would be the hardest because he *was* the chosen one, so to speak! You know…make sure he was the right one." Angela remarked, cocking her head to one side, warming her hands about the cup of tea Jacob had handed to her.

"Remember…one of the things that gives the darkness part of its powers is our way of perceiving it. We think of it, if we think at all, taking something very complex, and devious to do the trick. Simplicity is often the best key to success for the dark! I want you all to always remember that! We mortals think to achieve the best, in any situation, the plan must be ornate, multi-faceted, and devilishly clever! They know this, and come up with the simplest of ideas!" Jacob was quiet, but firm as he thought back to times when such tactics had been used successfully by generals, armies, kings, and even in the contests of athletes.

"Who, or what was this spirit guard you've mentioned?" David asked, wondering about what must have taken place on that mountain so long ago.

The professor leaned forward in his chair, his elbows resting on his knees. "That is one of the most unusual parts, David…that section is in Aztec characters! Here, I admit, we are on somewhat shaky ground…neither Jacob, or myself, possess a great expertise in the Mayan, and Aztec wordings! We each know a few of the glyphs, and such…so we were able to make out a lot of the translation, but not all! If we're right, the Aztec ruler who'd sent the sarcophagus up this way to begin with, had also sent along one of his greatest priests. The party with the coffin was to find a lasting place of protection, until the rebirth! There seems to be something about the priest having a vision…then something about a white-skinned god, with long hair, and a beard telling the priest something….then they're here, in the cavern…there's some garbled stuff about a ritual, and the guardian called forth to be in the cave…and then, something about the chosen one coming!" He looked at the journal spread open on the coffee table in front of all of them. "That's about all we were able to glean from that section…anything more will have to come from a real expert in that particular script!"

"So…this spirit guard was conjured up by the Aztec priest…to guard the cave until the chosen one…Joshua…came to claim the prize! So…the guard was a…what, a ghost, a demon?" The big policeman said, frowning as he took this all into his mind.

"Well…not exactly. Most likely, from what I *do* know about some of their rituals, it was most likely one of the warriors that had accompanied the priest. It wasn't unusual for a warrior, from one of their elite groups, and one of the aristocracy, to volunteer to die, and be buried with the deceased, especially if it were a king! He died a ritual death, usually on an altar, at the hands of the high priest…then was brought back to 'life'…in a spiritual sense only…to stand guard over the ruler's body, and treasures for all eternity! It would have been considered the highest honor, and the ultimate way to prove his loyalty to his dead king! I think that's a real possibility for what happened here!" Yusuf replied, settling back in his chair, taking a deep draw on his old pipe.

"And what was the little 'game' this guard had going with the indians then? I mean…what was all this about the Dark Eagle's nest?" David had wondered about that ever since this had all started.

"That we're not too clear on, David…we picked out a few words that stated something about setting the wheels in motion, then there was what looked to be a sign for the fire bird rising…a reference, I think to the phoenix rising reborn from the flames that it died within! Until I can get someone else to read this, we may never know any of the rest!" Jacob spoke up, drinking his tea, the fatigue in his face stark.

"Then, there was a shift in the writing, and the next few sections were in Greek, and the translation was much easier! That was when we picked up a clue as to what could have happened when Joshua went into that cave. It states…'by his divine choosing, he defeated the sentinel of eternity, and was granted the gift of knowledge, and prosperity that would continue on through all his line until the last'…this prosperity would include things spiritual as well as material! We know that because of another passage that went like this: 'and to the destined liberator would be forever given the power of the uraeus, or iaret, and also the shen, or shenu…and this also to the bloodline that follows'…in other words, the temporal, and spiritual power that was deemed granted only to the ancient Pharoahs, or a god!" Yusuf stated, pushing his glasses back up on the bridge of his nose.

Sandra's head jerked back a little…what was she hearing? "What exactly does all that mean?" She had a pretty good idea, due her own extensive knowledge of the ancient cultures…but, she couldn't believe what those words implied.

For just an instant, the professor hesitated, realizing the burden this would place on his young protégé, if their translations were correct. "We think that what was being stated here was that whoever freed the prisoner within the sarcophagus was destined to receive great gifts…the protection of the Sun, universal power, and control over the direction their lives would take. In short, riches, personal success, protection from most, if not all, the dangers we mortals face every day…and a singular power to ensure their lives being full, and rich! Very potent inspirations indeed for someone to go against a spirit guard, don't you think?"

"And the evidence is right before you, my dear Sandra!…look at the history of your family…it's one of the most fulfilling of any family in the country! All because Joshua fulfilled that ancient prophecy!" Jacob finished, gazing at her with respect, and admiration.

David could feel how shaken Sandra was…he knew she needed some time to take all this in, to understand what it meant. He stepped forward, distracting everyone from what had just been said. "That's all well, and good…but what's in that book that these people are more then willing to kill for? Why are we all in the middle of some gothic nightmare right now?" he demanded to know if they'd found the true secret of Joshua's journal.

Jacob stood, coming around to stand by the younger man, placing a strong hand on one shoulder. "David...there are so many secrets we've come across since we started reading the journal...one deals with how to avert the catastrophe the dark powers *want* to take place! Another deals with the time, and way to release the one trapped within the sarcophagus in the cavern...the one Garalynn described to Sandra! In some way we don't know as yet, Joshua shared a strong spiritual link with the prisoner in the cave...one of the reasons he wrote all that he did in the journal. He knew the time of the great confrontation was far in the future...a time he'd never see! He wanted to make sure that someone would know the secrets in that far off time...and that someone was destined to be a member of his family!"

"All that my family has achieved through the years...everything they've come to stand for...it all comes from Joshua's going into that cavern! From his receiving some sort of...of *powers* from whoever is in that cave, and passing it on, in some way, to his descendents!" Sandra's voice was flat, almost bitter. Her cerulean eyes stared into empty space, seeing none of her companions, or her surroundings. She was feeling a great surging of emotion...anger, and resentment. "Everything that's happened *now* is due to all of that! My father...my ex-husband...my adopted sister...all dead because of what my ancestor did!"

"Sandra...you're getting angry, and you shouldn't! Your family has been responsible for some of the greatest advances in science, medicine, industry, and the arts...to name but a few! Your contributions to Archaeology, and History are without number...and I can't begin to name the number of colleges, and universities all over the country that have been the recipients of your family's generosity!" Jacob took her by the arms, looking into her face with a gentle smile. "You're upset by what has happened...and you should be! You should be angry that good people's lives were cut short by the greed, and dark motives of the greatest evil the world has known! Mourn them...grieve that their light has been taken from your life...that's what we should do when we lose a loved one! But...remember also what their light gave to us...and also, that, even unknowingly, they died for the greater good! Your father was a Keeper, as was his father before him...they knew what they might have to give up their lives to protect! I don't want you to dwell on their deaths...remember instead what was really the cause of that death! That evil is still out there, Sandra...and we have to find it, and defeat it! If we don't...and they do get their hands on this journal...the entire *world's* population will be the ones to suffer! Remember that...and think of how cheapened your family's sacrifices would then have been!" The older man was very gentle, but firm as he spoke...his people, the Jews, were experts on sacrifice...and fighting on for the greater good.

Sandra's eyes were filled with hot tears, and they streamed down the high cheekbones as she stared at Jacob. She could feel her anger easing as the truth behind his quiet words...and knew he was so right. "Jacob...what *is* the secret? What did my family members die for?...what is it that they want so desperately they'd risk public exposure like this?" Her voice was soft, empty of the bitterness from before. Her hand came up, covering one of his that still held her by the arms. "Please...I need to know!"

"What we have been able to translate thus far deals with the secrets of true rebirth...the essence of the Phoenix! Freedom from pain, disease, physical and spiritual perfection...immortality in its purest sense! But...there was also a warning!" Jacob answered without hesitation.

"A warning?...what sort of warning?" Angela asked, putting her teacup down on the coffee table, leaning forward in her concentration.

"That such a gift could prove to be more of a curse then a blessing!" Yusuf saw the blank looks on the faces of the three younger members of their group. "Let me put it this way...imagine the secret as if it were a special narcotic substance! It helps to heal, makes you feel better, stronger...more able to do what has to be done! But...like that narcotic...it has side effects after too much time, and use!" He stared at them, willing them to really listen, and understand. "Eventually, the guards the brain holds on emotions, and behavior could break down, and the dark side we all have within us can come forward! That was stated like this: 'and the dark could kill forever the light of the eternal soul!'"

"If that's true...then how could this secret be considered a blessing? It sounds to me like it's nothing more then a super addiction!...complete with all the hell an addict goes through, or puts others through!" David declared, remembering all the cases he'd been called in on that involved drug use.

"It's like most things given to us, David...it's all in *how* it's used! All things in moderation...remember? But...how many of us practice moderation in anything! I think I begin to see what he was trying to tell us, and why!" Sandra said, her eyes seeing the real reasons Joshua did what he did.

"Indeed...how many of us are able to balance our light, and dark with a freedom of choice?...the *right* choice!" Jacob nodded.

"The true secret is hidden in the Eye of Horus, the journal states...instructions on how to blend certain herbs, and certain spiritual 'codes'...I think they meant prayers, or chants here...creating a sort of psychic, or spiritual 'toddy' that brings about the state of physical perfection, and immortality. But...you need the journal also, as it contains the final prayer that seals all the rest! We haven't come across that part as yet, and there may even more secrets as we've still a lot of reading to do! You understand the implications, my friends?" Yusuf declared, placing his hand over the journal again.

"Implications?...other then the immortality claim, what else are you talking about?" Sandra wasn't really sure she understood her old teacher's serious expression...what else did Yusuf mean?

"If the dark powers get all that they're after...including the amulet, and the journal...they'll seek to make sure that 'toddy' will be created, and to as many persons as possible!" Yusuf was about to continue when Angela broke in, forehead furrowed, and eyes puzzled.

"Wait a minute now...you're saying they *want* to give the gift of immortality to humans? Why on earth would they do that, Yusuf? The more immortals there are, the more their plans can be defeated!...especially if people like the Keepers are made immortal. They'll have an eternity to find ways to defeat the darkness! I don't understand you!" She was sure they'd misread their translation.

"I am quite serious, Angela...believe me! Look...Joshua, and this being he communicated with, obviously realized the pitfalls a state of immortal life could raise for an individual. How many people are really capable of living forever?...watching friends, and loved ones age, and die. Never being able to cherish anything, because sooner, or later, they're going to be gone! The way of life you come to love, and desire...gone forever as time changes. Sooner, or later, however desirable...immortality, and physical perfection could create a psychotic state within the individual. Again...the darkness comes forward, and rules! This is what they want...to create a world where they would truly be supreme...true immortals reigning over the darkness of a population gone completely over the edge! They would once again rule the earth, and their dark lord would once again have regained his dominion! After all...who could stop them if sanity, and true faith were no longer a strength in the world? Now...do you understand?" The professor looked around, watching the slow nods as each member of the group realized the true dangers they faced.

"What you're saying then is...you know, I'm not sure what it is you were trying to say!" David's head hurt...the beginnings of a very bad headache...this was getting to be too much! No matter how often it seemed they had things cleared up, another turn, and they were back in the middle of the maze again!

"David...my boy, all I am saying is that the ancients have granted us a great gift, but they understood the dangers, and thus also gave us a warning! Like Sandra said, in moderation, all things are well, and good! We humans must learn that also in our inner selves! If we learn to balance our emotions…learn how to combat our dark sides with a freedom of choice, then we'll be ready to accept what they offer! Until then…all we can do is keep the secrets protected, and out of the wrong hands! The risks, and dangers are far too great!" Yusuf sighed, feeling fatigued, but knowing it wasn't time for him to rest yet.

The word "protect" reminded David of something he'd wanted to ask Yusuf earlier. "You told us once, professor, that Sandra, and her sisters each had Keeper assigned to watch over them, right?"

Yusuf was sure he knew where this was going, but felt honor bound to answer with only the truth…no excuses. "Yes…since they were babies! Why?"

"Then, answer me…where was this so-called Keeper protection when the Dresdens first showed up? Why were they allowed to get so close to the girls? And, what about the deaths of their father, and Sandy's ex-husband?…where were the keepers then, huh? Joshua Phelps was the chosen one…he, and *all* his descendents were supposed to have the protective powers for being the one to defeat the spirit guard! Where was that protection when Garalynn was killed? Why wasn't somebody doing their job, professor?…answer me that!" David's realized love for Sandra made him want to know why his lady, and her family had to go through what they had suffered so far.

"That is enough, David!…sit down!" Yusuf waited until the angry man had seated himself again. Then, the professor turned his attention to Sandra. "Sandra…what David says is unfortunately true! We failed in our job…we didn't protect your family the way we were supposed to! We allowed ourselves to become lax…too complaisant! The dark powers had seldom, if ever, made an appearance in our area…no reason to drop one's guard, but we did! We should have been more alert! We weren't…and the family of one of our longest, dearest members paid the price!" The old man's eyes were bright with unshed tears, and sharp with his inner pain. "We can't change that lapse in attention, my dear! Nor, can we ever bring back the ones sacrificed because of it! All we can do, in their names, is go forward!...never give up, never let them win! If we do...their loss will have been in vain indeed!"

Angela wiped some tears from her eyes. "He's right, Sandra...it's the only way we can keep them from winning! It's the only way to avenge the deaths so far! We're all feeling the pain...in different ways, and degrees, true, but pain nonetheless! But, we can't let that pain hold us back...to cripple our efforts!"

Sandra was emotionally exhausted by this point, but she understood what both Angela, and Yusuf were trying to get across. She looked across at David's pale, angry face, and smiled slightly, reassuring him she was all right. Something touched her on the cheek, and she turned in the direction of the touch, thinking Angela had been the one to touch her. She stared at the point of light she saw glimmering over the other woman's shoulder. Her slight gasp brought everyone's attention to the mysterious glow.

Yusuf muttered an oath under his breath, reaching into his pocket He pulled out a large silver ankh, and held it up in the palm of his hand. "By the Light that created all, I charge thee...if foe thou be, then depart! If friend, then speak...let thy intentions be known! I command thee, in the name of the Light...speak, or leave!" He moved to the center of the room, motioning all his friends to stand behind him. As they moved, the glowing sphere of light remained hovering a few feet above the floor...as if silently watching them.

The nimbus of light grew, slowly shifting its position until it was in the corner where the professor's desk sat. The light grew until the entire corner was bathed in a now bright, almost blinding shine. Sandra found her initial fear fading away as she gazed at the light. If she peered intently enough, she could almost make out a central orb of light, holding just about the desktop. David's arm was about her shoulders, as he stared at the gently wavering light...what was after them now, his mind was wondering.

Everyone stared, waiting for something...anything to happen. Sandra felt something reaching into her mind...gentle, and warm. Her eyes widened as she realized what was going on...it couldn't be! She stepped forward, before David could realize her intentions, and stop her.

"Sandy...no! Get back!" David cried, lunging after her. To his surprise, and horror, something stopped him, inches from her. He couldn't see anything, or anyone...but he couldn't move forward any further.

The other also found they couldn't reach the tall woman as she walked towards the unknown light. She didn't act as if she heard any of their yelled entreaties, but continued her forward progress. Finally, she stood directly before the center of the light, and slowly reached a hand out. The light seemed to quiver, and suddenly swooped forward, and engulfed Sandra. She disappeared from the collective sight, in a burst of bright light.

The professor slowly lowered the arm that had held up the ankh, staring at the shimmering wall of light. Jacob, standing beside him, gripped Yusuf's shoulder tightly, also still staring at the corner. David was about to say something when Angela grabbed his arm, pointing as she cried out. "Look!...there she is!"

The light faded rapidly...then was completely gone, leaving Sandra standing before the desk, her back to them. She turned slowly towards them, and when they saw her face, they all gasped. Her eyes were wide, with a hint of bewilderment still in the azure depths...but her expression was one of joy. She looked towards David, and simply held out her arms. He found he could move forward once more, and in three long strides, he'd crossed the space between them, and scooped her up in his arms. He kissed her soundly, his face wet with tears...hers, and his mixed.

The professor, and Jacob went up to them, Angela close behind. The teacher took Sandra by one hand, and looked hard into her face, intently probing what he saw. He came closer, until their foreheads touched, and their eyes stared only into each other's, pushing everyone else out of their minds for the time being. "You are well, my young friend?...nothing is wrong?" He asked softly, using a dialect of Egyptian only he, and she would be familiar with.

David put her down, keeping hold of one shoulder. She smiled at him, then looked back at the professor, a puzzled expression on her lovely face. "I'm fine, Yusuf...why wouldn't I be? I do admit to being a little confused...why was I standing over here? The last thing I recall was you were talking about the deaths in my family, and apologizing...then things a re a bit fuzzy! The next clear thing...I'm in the center of the room, no one's talking, and you're all staring at me as if I'd sprouted wings, or something!" She looked back at David. "What happened? What's going on?"

The professor held up a hand, silencing them all before anyone could say even one word. He held the ankh out to Sandra, who took it in her left hand, blinking as she stared back at him, wondering what this was all about. The professor motioned to Jacob, who approached, pulling a small, though ornate engraved flask out of his jacket pocket, and giving it to the professor. He looked at the flask for a few moments, then back at the woman before him. He held it out to her, nodding for her to take it. Shrugging, she took the flask in her free hand, then stood there, hands out, items clutched within them...looking at him, frowning.

The old teacher smiled, in relief, and retrieved the items from her. Handing the flask back to Jacob, he clasped Sandra by the upper arm, and nodded. "It's all right...she's clear! Nothing tainted, or marked by evil can hold either of those two things, let alone both at the same time, without being in excruciating pain! The ankh has been blessed, by both a Christian bishop, and an Egyptian mullah. The flask holds sacred water, from the Ganges, the Nile, and the Jordan rivers...and it has also been blessed, by representatives from the faiths of Christ, Buddha, Mohammed, and Abraham. These two items hold much in the way of spiritual power, my dear...they are infallible!" He looked at Sandra, seeing the horror in her eyes that they would have thought her one of the evil they strove against. "Forgive me, my dear...our enemies are clever, and would think nothing of taking one of us right in the middle of the entire group! I had to be sure...you understand?"

"I...I think so! It's just...I don't remember anything of the past few moments, professor! What was going on?" She asked, looking at each of them in turn, wondering.

"Let me ask you this first, Sandra...why did you walk into that light? What happened to you while you were in it? Do you remember any of that at all?" Jacob spoke up, replacing the flask in his pocket.

She looked at the restaurant owner, and frowned, thinking hard. "I think that...there was something that I needed to do, but it's..." Sandra glanced at David, her eyes widening. "I remember now...David, I have to go to the cabin! That's where they're waiting...for me! It's the only way I can get to Beth!"

They all stared at her as thought she'd suddenly started speaking a foreign language. David shook his head vehemently. "That's just plain stupid!...putting yourself in their hands voluntarily! Do that, and you might as well give them what they wanted...gratus!" He didn't mean to snarl, but the fear he was feeling, for her, made his voice rough, and sharp.

She stared at him, blue eyes flashing like chips of pure crystal. "I have no intention of giving them anything, Lt. Collison!...and that includes my twin sister! I know she's carrying Sean's child, but that doesn't mean I turn my back on her! I am probably the only one she'll listen to right now, David! There is still a chance she can be turned back, to our side! I have to go!...can't you see that?"

In utter frustration, David turned to the others, holding out one hand. "Can you get through to her? Make her see what she's risking!"

"Sandra...what good do you think your going to her is going to accomplish? I think it's obvious she's gone over to their side...she's not going to listen to you! I think she'd betray you to them in the time it took a second to split! Do you want to give the darkness another member of your family to corrupt, or kill?" Jacob's voice was quiet, and flat...he wasn't going to try, and talk her out of her plan...simply try to make her see the probable results.

To everyone's surprise, Sandra smiled, easy and relaxed. "I understand all your concerns, and I thank you for caring! But, believe me...I am in no danger from my own sister!...no matter what it may look like! I also know if I don't go...I will lose her forever, and that's a risk I won't take!" She held her hand out to David. "Please, David...help me to save my sister's soul, if not her life!"

He gazed at her, arguing all the right points in his head...finally, giving in at last, knowing he couldn't hold out against her! He took her hand, and kissed the palm. "I'll help, in any way I can, Sandy...on one condition. When you go to the cabin, I go as well, and no argument!" He glanced at her face, and knew she was about to refuse him. "It's got to be this way, honey...or nothing! Look...they won't even know I'm around! We'll fit you up with a wire! That way I can listen, without their knowing I'm anywhere around, and get to you if something goes wrong!"

The professor shook his head. "I don't know...this seems wrong, Sandra! At the very least, it puts you within their power circle! At the very worst...you could be going to meet your own death! Have you considered all aspects on this?"

"Yes...I have, but I don't have to worry, Yusuf! I can't explain it, but I know I'll be in no real danger when I go there!" She looked back at the man standing so close to her, their fingers entwined. "If I can't go without you , then so be it! We'd better get things rolling...our time limit is fast approaching!"

The professor looked at Jacob. A silent message passed back, and forth between the two men. Jacob nodded, understanding. Yusuf looked back to Sandra. "If that is your final decision...then we must support you in every way we can, Sandra! Before you go, though...allow me to show you a few basics in protection measures. They should help you, if something comes up! We'll keep reading the journal...maybe we'll come across something else that will help before you have to leave!"

"Go with Yusuf, Sandy...it will take w little time to get everything arranged so we can go. I have to make a couple of calls...can I use your phone, professor?" David turned towards the old scholar. He nodded, and motioned towards the desk. Then, he brought his attention back to Sandra.

He gestured for her to sit down, and then Jacob, and Angela joined them. The professor opened the journal, and turned to a section they'd already been over. "Do you remember anything about the so-called Lost Books of the Dead, Sandra?...or the Chronicles of Atlantis?" he asked her.

She was a little surprised at the question. She glanced at Angela, who shrugged her shoulders...as puzzled by the question as Sandra. "Well...I'm not sure. I believe the Chronicles of Atlantis are supposed to be a collection of teachings, philosophies, and prophecies written down by the priests of Ra, and Thoth. They're supposed to have been dictated to them by the High Priest of Atlantis himself!" She frowned, trying to pull details from her memory. "As for the Lost Books...all I can recall is they were more prayers, and chants for the soul's journey to the Western lands."

The professor leaned forward, looking at them all. "That's basically what the experts, and scholars have believed over the years...though some feel the volumes don't exist at all!...just more legends attributed to the mysteries about the pyramids! I confess...I myself felt they were just stories, grown into legends...but no facts! That is...until we read this!" he jabbed a blunt finger at the journal.

"What did you find, Yusuf?...what does it say about them?" Angela was almost afraid to ask.

"In short...what they do contain, according to what's in the journal...prayers for eliminating all obstacles to one's deepest wishes! There are said to be chants, and prayers for obtaining control over all forms of life on this planet! Prayers, and instructions to achieve the destruction of all illness, and terminal diseases!...to bring unbelievable powers, and abilities into one's possession! In short...anything ever desired, or prayed for by all people of the world...throughout all time!"

"The dreams of a lifetime…the three wishes of Aladdin's lamp!" Angela sat up, staring into space…visualizing all that Yusuf had spoken about. "But…am I wrong, Yusuf, if I say I get the feeling that obtaining such things comes with a high price?"

The professor smiled, proud of his former pupil. "Your perception is as sharp as always, Angela. Most people would read about such treasures, and powers, and go no further…ask no questions as to what this would mean, or cost. And, if they did read further into these pages…would they ignore the possible warnings about a deadly source, in their obsession to find the gifts of the ancients?"

"What is the cost, Yusuf?…what did they journal say about that?" Sandra asked softly. "What is the source the ancients are trying to tell us about?"

"Scholars, historians, and archaeologists have been disputing this very thing for as long as science has argued with faith! They'll do the same thing about what's in this journal…should we ever allow this knowledge to be made public! Some people…scientists and experts…don't believe the Lost Books ever existed, the same way many people don't believe the things in the Bible ever really happened! Some persons…experts…believe that theses same Books are really prayers for summoning the dark forces, not the good!" The professor leaned back, putting his now unlit pipe back in the corner of his mouth. "They believe that all that man holds to be evil…powers that rule the night, and the dark…demons, and all forms of evil beings…they believe all this to be *one* entity! One power that corrupts, and enslaves all it touches, or coerces…turning these cursed souls into the servants it requires to breed its evil, to spread it throughout the world…and all time!"

"What we today refer to as…the Devil!" Sandra's voice was so soft, so small…feeling as though a bitter cold wind suddenly was blowing through the room. She suddenly had a vision, in her mind…seeing Joshua furiously writing all this fantastic, exotic knowledge down, then seeking a way to protect it. He must have spent countless minutes, even hours trying to come up with the right way to secret it...until it could be used in the correct way. She had to be sure what he wanted was made reality...no matter what her personal feelings, or those of others. "It has to be for the greater good...or, not at all!"

The professor looked at her sharply, then continued. "I suppose that is one name that modern man would understand...though again, there are many who don't believe in the Devil, any more then they believe in the existence of God! They acknowledge the process of evolution, as a natural happening...not as the result of a divine force putting all the wheels into motion. Therefore, if they don" believe in a supreme being of love, compassion, and good...why believe the opposite, that of true evil, exists? But, getting back to the journal...it has a reference to a hidden place in the valley of the Kings, in Egypt. At least, I think that's what it is referring to! It states : 'seek in the hidden place, near the eastern end of the holy resting places of the living gods!'"

"Yes...that could be talking about the Valley of the Kings, outside of Thebes...but, it could also be referring to the tombs at Giza as well! Remember...for some time now, the leading archaeologists in the world have been aware that there is a large, secret room deep within the body of the great sphinx itself! A number of experts believe that, if they truly exist, that it is in *this* secret chamber! Other experts think this chamber may be one of the lost tombs of a great ruler of the Egyptian history! The only way to know, of course, would be to open this chamber! But...a lot of people feel that to open this room would be to destroy the fragile environment of a few thousand years...and whatever would be within that room as well! Even scientists, and archaeologists from Egypt itself aren't allowed to do anything beyond x-rays, and special sounding equipment...we may never know!" Jacob sighed, tugging on one ear...a sign of his inner agitation.

"So...if we're to believe Joshua's journal...these Chronicles, and Books really do exist! And they hold within them more than anyone ever dreamed possible!" Sandra sighed, the weight of all this heretofore unknown knowledge beginning to make itself all to clear in her mind.

"Yes...and one thing more that I haven't told you all!" Yusuf paused...this part had been very unsettling to him as he'd translated it...did he dare tell them? He thought about the up-coming confrontation...they would need every scrap of knowledge on their side to stand a chance. He had no choice...he had to tell them! "Imagine a prophecy that tells about the final battle of all life...light versus dark, good against evil! This is a battle that has been going on, silent and relentless, throughout all recorded time! Imagine now...a scroll that would tell mankind the right path to take...the correct ways to protect against the ultimate evil! In short...how to defeat, for all time, the darkness that has always stalked the people of this world!"

No one spoke a word when the professor finished...they couldn't. What Yusuf had said...had suggested possible...it was beyond anything any of them to grasp. David came back, finished with his phone calls. He'd caught the last part of what the conversation had been...he didn't know if he wanted to believe it, or not.

"What you said, professor...you're talking about things people have been looking for since...since forever! It's the dream people have spent entire lifetimes searching to fulfill! I know people who'd give their very lives to find the location of what we've been talking about here today." He looked at the older man. "This is the sort of thing the keepers were formed for, isn't it? To find these kind of things first, and keep it from the wrong hands...right?"

"Partly...the things deemed dangerous, by the combined council of the world keeper groups, are put into a place of safety. Those things deemed mere historical value, or of potential good, are allowed public exposure. There are government officials, rulers, scientists, experts, religious heads, and archaeologists whose family has been Keepers for generations...these decisions are not arrived at in a rush, David. They are made after many hours, even months...years...of deliberations, by the finest minds in all fields of science, religion, and archaeology!…not to mention anthropologists as well!" Jacob took this opportunity to try, and explain the Keepers to his young friends.

"The Keepers, David, are pledged to defend, protect, and prevent…we serve the peoples of the world…race, religion, and way of life are things we don't look at when we set out to help someone. There have been entire villages helped by our members…sworn forever to fight the darkness. True…some of our 'weapons' are of ancient origins, and many outsiders would consider them 'witch-doctor' medicine! But…we have learned the folly, over the centuries, of dismissing something because it's ancient!" The professor, sighed, rubbing his bearded chin. "We have stood against all forms of evil that have threatened mankind…eternal vigilance is our oath! We have won many battles…and lost some crucial conflicts…but the war still rages! We cannot relax, or that final battle will finish in a darkness more black then any can imagine!" He looked around. "Well, this has turned out to be quite a dissertation! Come, we have much to do, and little time! This is what we still have to do!" He motioned them closer, and began explaining what lay before them............

****

XII

❦

……..Getting out of her car, Sandra stood beside it for a few moments, staring at the cabin. She looked about the compound, wondering where the security staff was. They should have been outside by now…they would have received an alarm when she turned onto the driveway leading to the compound. There wasn't a sound to indicate anyone was there, but her. She lifted one hand, brushing some wind-blown hair out of her eyes. She looked again at the cabin itself, wondering if she was being watched…she didn't sense anything like that, but she knew she had to be on guard every second she was here.

She closed the car door, and started walking towards the cabin's front door. She stopped half-way…something was nudging her to go around to the back, and enter by way of the back deck. She followed that nudging, and was soon standing on the rear deck, looking at the rear patio doors. There was still no sign of anyone else being there, and that fact was making her nervous. She opened the left set of patio doors, and stepped into the den. She looked around the room…no one. The room was being warmed, however, by a roaring fire…so someone must be around, she mused. She crossed the room, and headed for the main living room.

She stepped into the living room, and stopped at the sight of Sean, standing by the fireplace, and gazing into it. He looked up as she entered, and smiled, lifting the glass he held in salute. "Welcome, my dear Sandra! You have no idea how wonderful it is to see your lovely face once again!"

Sandra glanced around, then looked directly at the big man. She squared her shoulders, and stepped up behind the sofa. "You'll understand, I trust, if I don't return your greeting, Sean? I'm here to see my sister…now! Where is she? And, while we're at it…where is *your* sister? I can't imagine Tamara missing out on all the…fun!"

His grin got wider as he shook his handsome head. Sandra was a little surprised to see how warm, and sincere was that grin. "You may not believe this, Sandra…but I do understand your reluctance to be around either me, or my sister!" He took a deep swallow of the whiskey in his glass, then looked back at her. "I'm forgetting my manners…could I get you a drink of some sort?" He walked over to the nearby bar. "I must tell you how magnificent a bar your family has in this cabin! The cabin itself is a wonder…such peace, and richness of the surroundings!"

She waved away the offered drink…she wasn't going to risk anything that would dull her senses in any way. "I want nothing from you, or your sister, Sean…except *my* sister! Now…where is Beth?"

He walked over to her, standing too close for her liking, gazing warmly, and purposely down from his impressive height. Despite what she knew about him, she couldn't help the surge of attraction. She shook her head…focusing her thoughts on David, and their love. She knew she had to keep this thought uppermost in her mind…it was a protection for her.

Sean gestured towards the sofa. "Please…have a seat. I believe Elizabeth is with Tamara at the moment, but I expect her joining me shortly. Wait with me?" He asked softly, leaning closer, taking her by the elbow, his fingers caressing the smooth skin of her forearm. "I really think you're over-reacting, dear Sandra. There's no reason we shouldn't be friends, now is there? After all…we'll soon be family, won't we? And, I believe family members should be close, don't you?…very close!" He leaned towards her, dark eyes glittering with a dark purpose. She suddenly realized he'd been drinking…and heavily. Her sense of apprehension increased.

She drew away from Sean, pulling her arm free, and walked around the sofa. She sat down in the over-stuffed chair next to the sofa, not wanting him sitting next to her right at that moment. She stared pointedly into the flames of the fireplace, hoping he'd take the hint, and leave her alone. She shook her head a little, not believing she was behaving this calmly…these people were dangerous, and she was acting as if they were passing the time of day!

She glanced at the tall man. He'd walked back to his original place beside the fireplace, and stood there, back to the flames…drinking his whiskey, his dark eyes raking over her. He never realized just how identical she was to Beth, in appearance at least. She wasn't at all liking the way he was looking at her…like a buccaneer about to ravish a maiden. She shifted in the chair a bit…now, why did she have to think that?

After a few minutes, she looked up at him, irritated as well as nervous. "Do you mind not staring at me like that? It's not as though we've never met, you know!" He didn't reply, simply kept staring at her. "Well?…answer me, damn it! I said don't stare at me like that! Why are you looking at me like that?"

He sat down opposite her, and leaned forward, his grin widening. "Is it so wrong to enjoy looking at a beautiful woman? I never realized, until today, just how much you, and Elizabeth look like one another! You both are quite incredible!"

She frowned, crossing her arms over her chest. "We're identical twins, Sean!…we're supposed to look alike! Look, I want to see my sister! I do not care to bandy words about with you any more! Where exactly is my sister?" She stood up, preparing to continue searching the rooms of the cabin.

He stood up quickly, and came over to her. He looked at her, the grin gone, intent clear in the dark eyes. She shrank back a bit, then stood her ground, determined not to let him shake her focus. He swayed slightly towards her, his eyes seeming to grow in intensity, and size. Sandra felt her senses begin to swim. Then, her anger rose, bolstering her will, and she stared back in defiance. She stood straighter, and faced him so strongly that he actually took a half step backwards.

She glared at him, eyes like blue ice, snapping at his like living lightning. "I don't know what you think you're going to do…but whatever idea you have in that drunken brain…forget it! My sister may love you…but I'd sooner let a leper touch me before I'd let you touch me like that! I want my sister, and I want her now!"

Taken aback at first by her defiance, Sean then started grinning again…he liked nothing better then a challenge. He held a finger up, waggling it a bit. "Don't be so quick to refuse, Sandra! You might find out you'd like it as much as Elizabeth…and believe me, she *begs* for it!" He reached out, intending to caress her jaw line.

Sandra couldn't hold back any longer…with all the power she could call up, she whipped her right hand around, and connected with his jaw. He tripped backwards a couple of steps, dropping his glass with a crash. Hand to his bleeding lip, he stared at her, disbelief mirrored in his eyes…that changed swiftly to a black rage. With a speed she didn't believe possible, he grabbed her by the offending wrist, and jerked her up against his body.

He bent over her, twisting the imprisoned wrist cruelly, grinning darkly down into her pained face. His voice reminded her of the deep purr of a big cat. "That was so foolish, my dear Sandra! I don't take that from anyone…especially a mere female! Your only worth is the pleasure you can bring to a man…and I will show you exactly what I want from you! You can't refuse me again…I won't allow that! Try hitting me again…and the price will destroy you!" He imprisoned her within his arms, and nuzzled her throat.

His tongue trailed along her pulse point, and she felt her senses go swimming once again. Sandra fought to free at least one of her hands, but his grip was like an iron manacle. Sean's lips were slipping lower, pushing the vee neck of her lightweight sweater down further, coming closer to the tops of her breasts.

She drew on all her strength, and brought her right knee up, swift and hard, right between his legs…connecting with his groin like an atomic explosion. At the same time, she heard the patio doors side open quickly. Sean , gasping harshly, had released her, and stepped back a little, bending forward in his pain. He lifted his head, in time to see the clenched fist of Lt. David Collison come roaring at his head. The hand contacted powerfully with Sean's jaw, and dropped the big man to his knees. He didn't go all the way down, but knelt there, one hand to his jaw…the other at his crotch. He stared up at David, shock in his dark eyes.

"You dare to strike *me*?…mortal, your days are few indeed!" Sean's voice was still harsh from the attack Sandra had dealt on him…but everyone in that room knew he was far from being down for the count!

David towered over him, both fists still clenched. "Touch her again…and even if I was dead, I'll rip your throat out!" He turned his back on the kneeling man, and held out his hand to Sandra. He pulled her to him gently, and cradled her trembling figure within the circle of his powerful arms. He glared back down at Sean. "We're leaving now…and we're taking Beth with us! Where is she?"

Sandra, still a little shaky, clutched the front of his jacket. "David…be careful! You remember what Yusuf warned us about!"

David never took his eyes off the other man, who was still trying to get his breath back to normal. Secretly, the tall policeman was a little unnerved by the fact that Sean was still conscious, after two blows that would have most normal men writhing on the floor in abject pain, or our cold. "I remember everything he told us, Sandy. I also know he better not even think of trying that again…or he just might be missing some vital body parts!" He leaned closer to the still incredulous Sean. "I asked you where Beth was, jerk!…I expect an answer! Don't make me ask again!"

"No need to carry on so belligerent, David…I'm not far!" the cool, quiet voice was like a splash of ice water in the face. They all turned, and saw Beth in the doorway, shock and dawning anger on her lovely face.

Sean slowly stood up, rubbing his jaw, and taking a very ginger step. His eyes were deadly as they gazed at David. "You need to have a little talk with your sister, Elizabeth…let her know that it's wiser to be nice to a future family member! Next time, I expect her actions to be…nicer then today's! And, trust me, dear Sandra…there will be a next time!" He shifted his gaze solely to David. "I owe you, lieutenant…and I never forget my debts! We'll continue this another time, I promise!"

"Any time, jerkoff!…any time!" David was still to aroused, and angry to choose his words with caution.

"I think you are the one who should apologize, Sean…I overheard your highly suggestive words to my sister, before the lieutenant made his appearance! I think David was well within his rights to object the way he did!" Beth glared at the big man, then looked at her sister. "Sandra…you should have let us know you were coming! What can we do for you?" Beth's eyes held a quiet blue fire burning within her eyes. Even David could see how ell Beth looked now, and how pronounced her pregnancy was now.

Sandra took a couple of steps closer to her twin, one hand out. "I came here to get you to come home…I need to talk to you, and I can't do that here! I want the doctors to check you out…make sure everything's all right, with you, and the baby!"

Beth didn't answer right away…she was watching closely as Sean approached her in the doorway. He stopped when he reached her, gazing down into the angry, troubled blue eyes. He could easily see the confusion, pain, and anger there…but he merely smiled, lifting her chin up.

"Don't look so glum, my love! At least, I keep it within the family! You will always be first in my heart…if not in my bed! Remember what Tamara told you, Elizabeth…accept what you cannot hope to change!

Push these remaining human emotions out of your life, my sweet...they are only good when they can be put to your personal gain! Your loyalties are to *this* family now...not your old! Remember that...and your life will be sweet indeed!" He caressed the bulge of her abdomen, softly kissed her cheek, and then left the room...in no hurry at all!

Beth looked after him, still not saying a word. Sandra could easily see the hurt, and confusion in her sister's body language. She crossed the room, and enfolded Beth in her arms, hugging her close. "Beth...please, come to your senses! Can't you see?...he'll never love you the way you want! Come on...let's get out of here!" She drew back, looking into her twin's face. "You *are* okay, aren't you?"

Beth nodded, breaking away from her sister, and going to the sofa. She sat down, her back to Sandra, speaking calmly, quietly. "Of course I'm all right, Sandra! Don't be so quick to jump to conclusions!" She looked up at David, and Sandra. "You'll have to forgive Sean...he's not at his best when he drinks! He gets a little amorous...but, he doesn't mean anything by it!" She turned her head away, gazing into the fire. "You'd better go, Sandra...before Tamara gets back! She's taking a walk right now...and I'm not sure what her reaction to David's being here may turn out! Especially since he, and Sean had their little...discussion!"

Sandra came to the sofa, sitting down nest to her sister...staring at Beth in utter disbelief. "I don't believe you! This is the man you love...the one who professes to be in love with you! He tried to seduce me, Beth...and if David hadn't showed up when he did, I really believe Sean would have tried to rape me! He tells you, in so many words, that he'll probably go to bed with others...and you excuse it as he's drinking!" She stared into her sister's eyes, not understanding the blankness she saw there. "Beth...you have to know, by now, that these people are not normal! You let them take you from the hospital, and bring you up here. They make you call me, and tell me to bring *our* ancestor's journal up here, as well as a priceless amulet! And, if I don't, they threaten me with never seeing *you* again! Please...come with us! Let's go...before Tamara gets back!"

Beth shrugged, looking away. "As usual...you're making too much of things, Sandra! It was just a *harmless* pass...just the whiskey talking! Why must you always over-react?"

"Was she over-reacting about Tamara, Beth? You yourself said she'd be irritated to see me! And why is that, Beth? Wasn't she the one who threatened Sandra?...your twin sister? Or, should Sandy just shrug that off also?" David asked, his tone flat. He wasn't sure he trusted his love's sister any more...there was something that wasn't right any longer!

Beth regarded the man, eyes calm and brilliant. "Tamara asked Sandra to bring her something she needed...Sandra refused, and of course, Tamara got angry. She was just reacting to her anger, that's all...she'd never really do anything to harm my sister, David. Besides, what could be in that journal besides useless dates, and places. What earthly harm would there be to just let her look at it?"

"Just let her...have you lost all claim to sanity, Beth? Don't you realize they wouldn't want the journal, or the amulet unless they could get something from them? I don't think you realize just how *evil* these people are, Beth! They killed our father!...and my ex-husband!...and Doug!...and Garalynn! Can you shrug *that* away?"

Beth frowned, staring at her sister. "What nonsense are you talking, Sandra? Are you saying Garalynn is...I don't believe you! What possible reason would either Tamara, or Sean, have to do such terrible things? Who told you these things?" Beth looked up at David. "Did he tell you those lies? Sandra...he's so desperate to solve those murder cases he'll pin the blame on almost anyone!"

"That's enough!" Sandra glared at Beth. "You just crossed the line, Beth! I think we'd better drop this before things are said that can't be forgotten, or forgiven!" Sandra took a deep breath, trying to quiet her surging anger...and fear. "Are you going to come with us?"

"Before I answer that, tell me…did you bring the things Tamara told you to bring?" Beth' voice sounded so much like Tamara's that Sandra had to suppress a shudder.

"The amulet is with me, Beth…but I will never allow Tamara, or Sean anywhere near Joshua's journal! You're the one who's deluding herself if you think Tamara wasn't serious about the journal, and the amulet! I don't know if you really are as naïve as you seem, or you're just refusing to look at the truth!…but she's going to be your destruction if you don't wake up!" Sandra was aching inside…that she now had to be wary of her own twin sister was almost more then she could take.

Beth closed her eyes, and shook her head. "You're the one who's deluding themselves, Sandra…she was very serious about the journal, and the amulet!" She leaned close, her eyes suddenly alive, and flashing. "You're the one who doesn't realize what you're up against here! Why couldn't you just follow instructions?" She leaned back, her eyes resuming their blank expression.

"She's quite right, Sandra…you should never have come here without the items I told you to bring! This is an ill time for attempted heroics…unless you think I possess a sympathetic side, which is an even more foolish dream!" The cold tones cut into the room like the teeth of a buzz-saw. Turning quickly, Sandra, and David saw Tamara poised within the doorway. Sean stood behind her, wearing a wide, sinister grin on his face.

Sandra stood up, a restraining hand on David's arm as he had started to pull his police issued revolver from its hidden holster. She wasn't sure his gun would be effective against the tawny blonde. He turned his head, speaking softly into the hidden wire he also wore. "Stand by, Pat…things are getting a little hairy in here!"

He started to turn his head back, but suddenly found himself seized by the throat, and lifted off the floor, his feet dangling a few inches off it. Sean had moved with blinding speed, moving across the room before anyone had even a thought to stop them, or get away. Sean shook David, grinning with maniacal glee as he saw the other man only a step away from blacking out from his grip on his throat.

Tamara had moved just as swiftly, and now had Sandra in a similar grip. Sandra tried to kick her way out of the hold, refusing to submit to Tamara. The tall blonde pulled her close, snarling into her face. "You insect!...you would defy *me*? You still don't understand who, or what you're trying to fight against...do you? Now...no more stalling, Sandra! I want that journal!...give it to me now!"

Trying to loosen that steel grip, Sandra felt the room beginning to go black. Her blows had no apparent effect on Tamara, though she kept trying. Finally, only partially conscious, she hung in Tamara's grip like a rag doll. Tamara sneered, tossing her onto the sofa. Tamara looked over to where Sean had tossed David's unconscious form, down by the fireplace. She tossed her head, her lip curling back in a satisfied smirk. She could hear the gasping as Sandra tried to fill her lungs with fresh air.

Tamara then turned to Beth, who hadn't moved from her seat on the sofa. She pointed at David, then Sandra. "You see, Elizabeth?...they're no match for us! We are always going to be the supreme...the superiors! It is only in the natural order of things that *we* rule this world!"

Sandra rubbed her sore, and constricted throat. Her voice was harsh, but filled with anger. "What have you done to her, Tamara? Why does she act, and look like one of you now?" Sandra looked towards the fireplace, relief flooding her as she saw a groggy, but alive David sit up, rubbing his throat, and shaking his head. "David!...are you okay?"

"Stay right where you are, Sandra!...or I'll tell my brother to finish him! He won't be able to take Sean by surprise this time!" Tamara warned, stabbing a finger at Sandra. Fearing for David's life, Sandra did as she'd been told. Seeing her compliance, Tamara straightened up, standing tall, and proud. "Your sister ceased to be human, in the normal sense of the word, the first time she made love with my brother! She has, shall we say, moved onto a higher plane! Her existence as an insignificant mortal has come to a well-deserved ending! She no longer needs you, Sandra...she belongs to us now, as does the child she carries within her! She will move up, with us, as we take back the pinnacle we lost so many centuries ago!"

Sandra pulled herself upright, feeling better as the pain of her choked throat faded from memory. "Oh, yes...her life will be like a fairy tale...so long as she pays the piper's price, and does what she's told!...right, Tamara? Tell me...has the price you've paid all these eons been worth it?"

Tamara's eyes narrowed...the cheek of this impudent woman! "My life has been, and always will be...my own! My loyalty is given of my own free will, Sandra!...not because it is ordered! Take care...you tread on very shaky ground here!"

Beth stirred into action at last, standing up, a hand held out to Tamara. "Let me talk to her, Tamara. I'll make her see the error of this kind of continued behavior!"

Looking deeply into Beth's eyes, Tamara finally nodded, and stepped back from the sofa. She motioned to Sean, who stared angrily. He was about to object when she shot him a glance that warned him not to speak. He moved towards the doorway, then stopped, waiting for his sister's next instructions.

"I'll give you some time, Elizabeth...see that it's put to good use! My patience where your sister is concerned is waxing thin! You have one hour to make her see the way of things!...one hour!" Tamara glanced again at Sandra. "I trust you'll then make the right decisions, Sandra! If not...if you persist in this vein of action, you will learn how 'persuasive' I can truly be! If you don't think I'm serious...ask Garalynn the next time you see her! She learned how 'dead' serious I can really be!" With that parting barb, Tamara turned and left the room, her brother trailing after her.

"David!" Sandra ran to him, kneeling beside him, and cradling him close. He was still a little groggy, but he was aware of who was holding him. "Darling...please speak to me! Let me know you're all right!" Sandra held his head against her bosom, She looked at Beth. "If he's hurt in any way, Beth…that bitch! How dare she throw Garalynn in my face!"

Beth merely looked away…an air of sadness about her. When she finally did look at her sister, Sandra was shocked to see the blue eyes so like her own filled with bright unshed tears. There was a remoteness…an emptiness there Sandra had never seen before this. "Sandra…you must listen to me, and do exactly what I tell you! No arguments…no interruptions!…I mean it!" Beth sighed, knowing her time was all too brief. "I know Tamara…in a way you never will! She is serious beyond anything you can imagine! I don't know what that remark about Garalynn meant…but it's not the issue now! You have two choices, no negotiating or substitution! You either give her what she wants…and I mean, all of it! Or…you get the hell out of here…now! You needn't worry about me! Sean won't let her harm me in any way!"

Beth was about to turn away, when Sandra grabbed her by the arm. "You want to know what she meant by that crack about Garalynn?…well, I'll tell you! She's dead, Beth!…our sister is dead, murdered! And I am almost certain Tamara is responsible! And, you want me to give her things that will enable her to become even more dangerous, and murderous? You're the one who's not thinking clearly!" Sandra shook her sister's arm, sharp and firm. "Wake up, Beth!…while you still have the humanity to do so! They are not the beautiful people they appear to be! They're monsters!…demons from hell itself! And if you don't open your eyes soon…you'll be one of them!"

Beth jerked away, and went over to the bar. She leaned against its polished wooden rail, trembling, trying to regroup her emotions. What Sandra had said about Garlynn…it couldn't be true! After a few moments, she turned back to face her sister, and the silent man now standing close behind her. "I don't believe it!…Garalynn's not dead! Why would Tamara want to do such a thing to her? Do you have any proof of this?"

Sandra walked slowly to the bar, her eyes never leaving Beth's. they stood there, staring into each other's eyes. Sandra shivered a little, seeing the remoteness again in the depths of her sister's eyes. With all the love, and tenderness she could call up, Sandra touched Beth's cheek softly. "Honey...you've got to wake yourself from the nightmare you're caught in, don't you see? If you don't...if you allow things to go on like this, more people that you love, and care about are going to pay the price!...maybe even me! Is that worth your new life? And, what about the baby?...is this what you wish for it?"

Beth was about to say something when the patio doors opened, and Patrick slid into the room, gun drawn, and at the ready. He looked around, then stopped next to his partner, putting a hand on David's shoulder. He saw the reddened marks on the younger man's throat, and scowled. "Sorry I'm late...couldn't find the back door! You two okay now?" Sandra nodded, and Patrick looked at David. "Sounded like you got a good right cross in, Dave...of course, it also sounded like you got sucker punched, too!"

"Why is everyone has got to be a critic?...or a comedian?" David grumbled, rubbing the back of his neck. He looked at Sandra. "Well?...what now? We have got to get moving, one way or another...and soon!"

Beth looked from Sandra's face, to David's, then back to her sister's. She smiled slightly at what she saw in both faces...a sad, knowing smile. "You'd better leave now, Sandra! Tamara meant what she said by one hour!" She watched as Sandra slowly turned towards her, eyes wide as she realized what it was that Beth was saying. "Yes, Sandra...without me! It's too late, for me, or the baby!...way too late! I'm changing, Sandra...becoming one of *them*! And it's not the type of change that can be reversed! I have to stay here!" She came closer to Sandra, looking directly into the eyes so like her own. "The thing is...I don't think I *want* it changed!...not if it would mean giving Sean up! I love him so deeply...no matter what, I still love him! And as strange as this may sound to you...I owe Tamara my life! Whatever it was she gave me in the hospital, it healed me! You take your David, and his friend, and the three of you leave! I have to stay…if only to make sure they don't come after you!" She gazed at her twin sister, then touched Sandra's cheek briefly, with her fingertips. "And, Sandy…don't come back!…not for any reason! Let this be good-bye!"

Sandra couldn't believe this. Her hand came up, capturing the one that Beth held to her cheek. "You know what she'll do to you when she finds out you've not only permitted us to leave…but let us take the things she wants with us? Beth…you can't mean this! Please…come with me! You're my sister!…my *twin* sister! I love you!"

Shaking her head, Beth stepped back, breaking the physical contact. She glanced over at David, Patrick standing close behind him. "David…I know that you love this bull-headed sister of mine…and I'm glad for that! Keep her safe…take her from here now! I don't want any of you to try, and come back here! Nor, do I wish any further contact! I mean it…now, leave!"

"Beth…" Sandra started to protest…she wasn't going to just give her only living sibling up so easily.

Beth shook her head, holding one hand up, palm out, halting any forward motion Sandra might have made. "I will always love you, Sandy…no matter what happens to us next, remember that if nothing else!" There were silent tears slipping down Beth's high cheekbones, and her use of the nickname told Sandra how deep were her feelings. "If that doesn't sway you, then remember this…the welfare of the majority is more important then any one individual's! Remember…Dad always use to tell us that! It was how he lived his life. I'm not him…but maybe, in this one small way, I can be the daughter he always thought I would be! Please, Sandy…let me do this!"

Sandra had pulled the amulet pouch out of her jean pocket, prepared to give it to Beth. Now, after hearing her sister's words, Sandra wasn't sure what to do. "Beth…here is the amulet! Take it…if you give it to Tamara, she'll forget about the rest! Please…take it!" She made a quick decision, and held the pouch out to her sister.

Beth shook her head again. "David...take her, and your friend, and get out of here! My control is ebbing, and Tamara will be back soon!...I can't take that, Sandra! If I were to do so...please, just go! When Tamara, and Sean return, my resistance will be totally gone!...I won't be able to help myself!"

David walked over to where Beth stood, and took her by one shoulder. They gazed at one another for a few moments...he saw the painful truth behind her words, shimmering in the azure eyes, eyes so like the ones he loved to desperation. His heart lurched, knowing she was right...they had to leave her behind! He took her in his arms, and hugged her close. She wrapped her arms tightly about his tall form, and murmured softly in his ear. His head nodded, and when he drew back a little, he kissed her...tenderly, sadly. He turned, and looked at Sandra...all his love, and devotion there, in his gaze.

He looked at her for a few more moments, then turned to Patrick. "You got the car close by?"

"Yeh...down at the corner of the rear deck...hidden by that small grove of poplars. I couldn't tell what was going on in here, but it was beginning to sound heavy...then, all of a sudden, everything went dead, on both your wires! That's when I decided I'd better get my big ass in here!" Patrick glanced at the doorway. "Look...can we get going? I really don't want to be here when they get back! I got a real bad feeling about those two!"

David nodded, walked over to Sandra, and took her hand. "Come on, sweetheart...we got to go!"

She shook her head, her eyes bright, and wide. "I can't just leave her here, David...I can't! She's my sister!' Sandra looked at Beth, who looked away. "She's my sister!" She whispered, the tears flowing heavily now...she knew what she had to do, but her body wouldn't move. "Beth?" She reached for her sister.

Beth shook her head, and walked over to the fireplace. She stood there, arms folded over her chest, staring into the flames...her back to the others. Sandra swallowed hard, knowing her sister had made her decision, and she was going to be able to change her mind. She had to do what she knew what the right thing…no matter how much it hurt inside. She nodded, and took David's hand. He squeezed it, nodded to Patrick, and the three of them headed out the patio doors. As she went through the doors, Sandra cast one longing look back at the woman she'd shared her entire life with, her eyes filled with pain, and love. Then…they were gone.

Beth slowly walked to the patio doors, and gently closed them. She held the doorknobs in both hands for a few brief seconds, head bent. Then, squaring her shoulders, she went back to the sofa, and sat down with a deep sigh. She closed her eyes, getting her emotions back under tight control…and pushing them back into the deepest recesses of her mind. She lifted her head, opening her eyes…prepared now for the return of Tamara, and Sean. She knew the tall blonde's rage would be akin to a full-fledged explosion. She could already picture the scene when Tamara realized the situation…her enemies freed, and the things she'd murdered, and schemed for once again beyond her reach!….

….."What do you mean they're gone?" Tamara stared at Beth, her customary calm utterly gone. "You just stood there, while they walked out, and made no move to stop them? Why didn't you at least call for me?" She walked, slow and deliberate, to the sofa where Beth was sitting. Behind her, Sean was standing in shock, unable to believe Beth had actually betrayed her instructions.

Beth just sat there, hands clasped together in her lap. She watched as Tamara came closer. There was no sign of fear, or remorse in her gaze…just simple resignation, and sadness. "I know that I should have at least called you, Tamara…it was wrong to just let them leave. I realize my life now belongs to another plane…another way of thinking, and doing. But…she is still my sister, and she still means something to me! I cannot allow anything to happen to her...not even for your benefit!" She said quietly, her eyes darkened with her conviction.

Tamara wanted to destroy the woman sitting before her...rend her flesh, and utterly terminate her existence...but just as she felt herself giving into that rage, she also felt the tiniest brush of something else. She paused, lifting her head, and letting all her senses reach out...seeking the essence that had triggered her alertness. It was gone...but only very recently, leaving behind it the distinct aura of its presence. Her eyes narrowed, and she turned slightly, looking towards the patio doors. Her eyes widened, and she felt the tips of her nails dig into her palms as her fists clenched in sudden spasms...her enemy had been in this room, and she'd never known it until now! That meant they'd learned how to mask their presence, or at least delay her detecting it right away...this presented a potential threat she couldn't ignore.

She glanced down at Beth...she'd have to wait to settle with this one's defiant actions. Her head clearer, she realized if she'd pursued her original desires, both Beth, *and* the baby would probably be so much history right now. That thought caused her a slight wince...not out of any concern for either party, but because she knew her family would not be pleased. They *wanted* this child to be born!...so, her desire for revenge would have to wait.

"I should destroy you right this moment!" Tamara saw Sean's movements out of the corner of on eye. "Stay where you are, dear brother!...or I will make good my threat against your woman!" She warned, watching him closely. Satisfied he would stay put, she turned back to Beth. "Don't be so misguided as to think your becoming one of us will save you from my wrath, Elizabeth! Sean is my brother by blood, and he's felt my rage on more then one occasion...isn't that true, brother?" Sean nodded slowly, face set, and angry. "You see?...I always make sure everyone knows who is in charge! Never think I won't punish a traitor, or anyone who defies me! Your adopted sister thought she could do that, and get away with it! She found out just how wrong she really was!...and she'll never do so again!" Tamara bent slightly closer to Beth as she spoke.

"What do you mean?...what has happened to Garalynn?" Beth stiffened, remembering what Sandra had told her about the fate of their adopted sibling.

"Happened?...she's dead, Elizabeth! Dead because she defied me!...she could have had the riches of the world, and more power then anyone could ever dream of possessing! But...she chose instead to defy me...to refuse me! And she paid the price for such unthinkable acts!" Tamara's actions were becoming a little agitated as she remembered how Garalynn, even to the last, refused to give in...to join with her. Truth be known...Tamara hadn't wanted to destroy the tall nordic beauty, but her rage at the rejection had taken control, and before she realized what had happened, Garalynn's life was no more.

"Then...Sandra was right! You *did* murder our sister!" Beth stared at the other woman, feeling her own rage beginning to build. But...she knew she couldn't allow it to take away her focus, and she pushed it back down. She'd wait...though she knew her human controls were weakening as the final changes took place within her body, and mind. She'd hold on, with every once of humanity left her...she'd play her ace card when it was least expected. But...even as her mind said this, she could feel yet another control slip into the oblivion that was taking her over. Her time had to be soon...or it wouldn't be at all!

Tamara clenched her fists, raising them up in front of her. She stared at her hands as her brow furrowed, and her lips drew back in a snarl. "You are both insects!...she didn't understand, but you will! I have ruled over millions in my time, Elizabeth! All over the world, in countless eras of time! Kings, and their armies, lay the riches of looted cultures at my feet, begging my favor! They drenched my royal robes in the blood of their own wounds, supplicating my attention! The blood of their victims was the sweetest of the wines, and beers they offered me to drink! I was the chosen, of my father Ra, to punish mankind for their legions of sins against the godhead…for forgetting all that that godhead had done for them! I was a god!…and she, an insignificant *mortal* refused all that I offered!" The waves of rage flying off Tamara's now strangely shimmering body were causing shock waves to shake the room's walls. Sean hurried over to Beth, and picked her up in his arms, cradling her close…stepping back a few steps from Tamara's proximity.

Tamara saw this, and it was like a splash of cold water that brought her back to her senses. She straightened up, once again in control…but determined to let her brother know how she felt. "Sean…are you attempting to interfere here? She betrayed us, Sean…am I to simply overlook such action? Don't forget…she also let them leave with the things we need! What should I do about *that* fact?"

"If anyone knows the price of failing, it's me, Tamara! And, believe me…I am not telling you to forget that at all! I am simply saying…you cannot harm Elizabeth in any way! Not now…while she carries my child!" He drew the woman in his arms closer to him. "You leave her alone!"

Tamara stared, eyes wide. "Did you just say…did you just tell *me* to leave *her* alone? Do you realize what she's done? And you want me to let her go unpunished?" She wasn't going to punish Beth…but she wasn't about to let her brother think it was because of *his* actions!

For the first time since she'd known him, Beth saw Sean stand up to the terror that was his sister. "You already know the answer to that, Tamara…the baby! Even you cannot harm one of our unborns!…especially this one! You know what the family said…what they would do if their edict was broken! We can still get the journal, and the amulet…who has ever kept anything from *you* when you truly wanted it? We need that journal to succeed…but we also need this baby! To regain our full power, our ranks need to swell again…as they did those centuries ago!" Sean wasn't an orator as a rule, but he poured all his meager skills into convincing his sister to leave Beth alone…at least, for now.

Tamara lifted her head, gazing at her brother, analyzing his words…impressed in spite of herself. "Very well, Sean…you're right…now is not the time! I'll overlook her disobedience…for now!" Her smile was sweet…but filled with menace. "Keep her under control, Sean…and out of my way! If she interferes again, I won't be held in any way responsible…regardless of the family's edict!" She switched her attention to Beth. "Keep yourself within the rules from now on, Elizabeth…child or not, I won't hesitate to act should there be a next time! Now…come, we must catch up with those foolish enough to think they can escape me!"

"Tamara…what good will it do to go after them? They don't have the journal with them! Sandra told me she didn't bring it…only the amulet is with her!" Beth spoke up, motioning for Sean to put her down. Once back on her feet, she looked back at the other woman. "What do we do now?"

Tamara sighed…some days she wished she had free rein again. "Say your good-byes, brother…then join me outside! We have work to do!" She looked pointedly at her brother, then Beth. "Your sister, and her friends will not get away, Elizabeth! She may not have the journal, but I'd be willing to venture a guess that she knows *where* it is! And, she does have the amulet! That will make this at least somewhat bearable until we do get our hands on that journal! I promise you…they will not suffer! In fact…they'll never know what hit them!" With that, Tamara turned, and hurried out the patio doors.

Sean helped Beth to the sofa, his touch consoling and supportive. She looked up at him, tears beginning to shine in her eyes. "Sean…please. Don't go! Will it really be so bad if they just left?" She gripped him by his hands. "Please…you love me, I know that…you love our baby, I know that, too! I know what you really are, and I don't care, Sean! Please…let them go!"

He shook his head. "You don't understand, Elizabeth…and I really don't have the time to try and explain it right now! Actually, though…I don't understand myself why I tried to back my sister down!" He straightened up, drawing to his full impressive height as he gazed down at her. "It's time for the hunt, my love!...the night approaches, and that is my domain! Stay here, Elizabeth...our child is now your only responsibility, and it would do well to remember that! I will not try to back Tamara down a second time...don't push her again, Elizabeth!" He grinned suddenly, and Beth saw the dark eyes flash with an intensity she'd seen only when he was making love. "The prey awaits, my sweet...and the hunt is the passion I value the highest!" With a wave, he turned, and hurried after his sister.

Beth sat there, not sure of anything...of what to do now. She'd always been the sensible one of the twins...look where it had brought her! She had thought Sean the ultimate love of her life...she knew now, deep in her heart, that even the fact they created a child together would never make him completely hers. That there would be others who'd strike his fancy, she had to tearfully acknowledge...yet, it wouldn't drive her from his side! Her pride was nothing next to the driving passion...obsession she had concerning him.

With a shaky breath, she leaned back into the pillows on the sofa. She'd been horrified, then awe-struck as she realized what Tamara, and Sean really were...then learned she herself was becoming like them. She couldn't believe she was actually pregnant...or that this pregnancy was progressing at an alarming rate. There were times she'd truly felt she was actually communicating with her unborn child. She wasn't sure what this child was really going to be...except that it also was a result of her obsession with Sean...the same obsession that was even now leading to her twin sister's destruction, and worse. Was immortality, and power worth what she was paying? Was the passion she thought she'd won everything she'd thought it? It was a bitter pill indeed to realize that the true love she'd thought she'd gained hid a brutality, and evil few knew existed, or could cope with. Passion, to be pure and soul-lifting, had to be tempered with the purity of love's spirit, and the soul's commitment...if not, it became the shackles of the fallen from grace.

Beth knew she'd never see that sort of purity again...but she couldn't give in just yet. She looked at the patio doors, and wondered what was now happening, out there in the darkening woods, as night came into being....

.....When David, Sandra, and Patrick had run out of the cabin, they'd all headed for where Patrick had hidden the squad car. In only a couple of minutes, they'd reached the car, gotten in, and Patrick had started the car. He shifted the gears, and the tires dug into the dirt, spraying it up, and out in a cloud.

"Hurry up, Pat! They'll be coming any time, and I don't want to meet those people out here in the woods!" David yelled, glancing over his shoulder at the fast fading cabin as they drove away.

The burly sergeant nodded, gripping the wheel tighter, and pushing the gas pedal to the floor in a sudden lunge. David saw how the sky was darkening, and instinctively knew they didn't have much time. "Great...that's all we need!" he brought his gaze back to the shadow covered road just in time to see another car lurch around the curve,, and head directly for them. "Pat...look out!" He cried, bracing himself with his feet hard against the floor boards.

The sergeant wrenched the wheel hard to the right, and their car flew off the road, into a grove of trees nose first. There was the sound of brakes grinding, breaking wood, and the shrill screaming of metal bending ways it was never meant to bend...then there was only silence. Patrick sat back, arms trembling from the intensity of his grip on the steering wheel. He reached down, and turned the key off, adding to the silence by shutting the motor off. He shook his head, and turned to his companions. "You two okay back there?" His voice was a little hoarse...this case was getting even weirder then when David first tried to explain it all to him when he called about getting the wires.

"I think so." David leaned forward, twisting to look into what he could see of Sandra's face in the growing darkness. "You okay?" When she nodded, he got out of the car, and helped her out. He walked around to the front of their vehicle. He shook his head when he saw the abnormal tilt to the right wheel well, and the wheel itself laying on the ground beside the car. "Wheel's been sheared off...axle looks cracked, if not broken altogether. We ain't going anywhere further in this car!" He muttered, pulling his gun out, checking it, then returning it to its holster.

"David...are you all unhurt?" The voice startled them all. Sandra turned, staring as Jacob, and the professor came up to them...it had been them in the other car.

"What the hell are you two doing here? We agreed we were going to handle this, Prof. Hanradi! This is police business now!" David was furious the older men hadn't listened to his orders. He didn't want the two men in danger...he'd come to respect, and admire them greatly in the very short time they'd known one another.

"David...we *had* to come! Sandra, after we'd finished the journal's translation, we had no choice !...we had to make sure you all were all right! However...we didn't plan on meeting you almost head on, as it were! Are you sure you're all right?" Yusuf hugged his former student, anxious to be sure they were all fine.

"I'm fine...I think! Yusuf...do you have any idea the danger you, and Jacob have placed yourselves in by being here? She's after us!...or soon will be when she discovers we left the cabin! Not to mention, taking the amulet with us!" Sandra glanced back up the now shrouded road, shivering a little...her adrenaline was wearing off now. "Yusuf...you should have seen her! She was yelling, and scared the crap out of me! I really thought she'd kill me given half the chance! I tried not to let her know how she was getting to me...but you should have seen her eyes! God...I've never seen anything like those eyes, Yusuf! I don't even want to think what she's going to be like when she finds out Beth let us go!" Sandra buried her face in her hands.

"Elizabeth let you go?…why? I thought she was under their influence too deep! Is she all right?" The professor was worried.

"She looked fine, but how she really is…I just don't know! Sometime, she seemed like her old self…other times, she was just like them! She let us go when Tamara had threatened us…she said she couldn't leave, but not to worry because she'd be all right! They wouldn't do anything to her because of the baby!" Sandra replied, choking back a sob.

Jacob came up to them. He'd been examining the squad car with his flashlight. "I think we're all going to have to ride out in my car…that axle's history!" he pointed up to the sky, where the first stars were just becoming faintly visible. "Yusuf…full night's only about an hour away! We'd better be a long way from this mountain when it does get here!…unless we come up with a very good plan!" He shifted the backpack, hanging from his left shoulder, to a more comfortable position on his right shoulder. "I feel they're close, my friend…very close! We have to go!"

The professor motioned to them, and they all headed for where Jacob's Land Rover waited. David, and Patrick had removed all the weapons stored in the squad car, and loaded them into Jacob's car. Jacob started the vehicle, and had just started it in motion when Tamara suddenly appeared in the road ahead of them…her tall figure illuminated starkly in the car's lights, her smile menacing, and filled with intent.

"Jacob…get us away from her! Quickly!" The professor stared at their adversary, awed as well as appalled. Know what they now did about her, he still couldn't help staring at her in the same fascination one would a coiled serpent.

Jacob swerved the vehicle sharply…first to the left, then just as sharply to the right, then flooring the pedal. He shot the car past the surprised woman, and into the darkness of the road beyond Tamara. The car swerved, and screeched around a couple of more curves in the road, hitting top speed in the straight sections. After a few minutes,

Jacob slowed just a little, glancing into the rear view mirror with a quiet satisfaction. "I think we're okay now...there's no way she can catch up to us now!" He stopped speaking, eyes widened in shock, as Tamara stepped out into the road before them, and stood there, tall and regal...waiting for them.

Jacob gripped the wheel with all the strength he could muster...he was going to ram her. He mashed the gas pedal to the floorboards, and yelled to his companions as he hunched his shoulders together. "Hang on!"

The car screamed towards Tamara, who made no move at all to get out of its way, but just stood there, her glittering eyes never leaving it...a snide smile playing about the full lips. She stared into Jacob's eyes, and he stared back into hers. His thoughts were all too clear on his face...to see her broken body flying through the air, her evil finally finished once, and for all time. His family had been involved in the battle against evil, and its minions, for generations...this was the chance to destroy one of the ultimates of darkness!

Closer the car roared, and still the tall blonde didn't move. Then, with the sound of a distant thunderclap, the car seemed to smash into something unseen just as it reached Tamara. Like slamming into a brick wall, the front end of the Land Rover folded in onto itself, like so much tissue paper. Then, once again...there was the silence of the deepening darkness, even the usual night sounds were strangely absent. The superbly constructed vehicle was only a crumpled remnant of its former self. Tamara still stood in front of it...untouched, unharmed, and still smiling. Inside the car, everyone was stirring, trying to take stock of the bumps, bruises, and other injuries, if any.

Suddenly, the driver's door was ripped open, and off its hinges. Tamara reached in, and grabbed Jacob by the collar of his leather jacket. With the ease of someone taking something off a shelf, or out of a closet, she yanked his body out of the car. Holding him up in the air, at arm's length, feet dangling a good six inches off the ground...she grinned up at his shocked face.

"You wished to see me dead, old man?" Her voice was a silken ripple of sound, almost caressing to one's ear. The softest of smiles graced her lips, and the golden eyes seemed lit by an inner fire that shed a gentle light over Jacob's terrified face. Tamara jerked him closer to her, his body now hiding her face from those still struggling to get out of the car.

"Jacob!...look away! Don't look into her face!" Yusuf cried out, trying to get out of the wrecked car...to reach his old friend.

He heard a choked scream, then some hastily spoken words...in Hebrew...then, there was a scream of such heart-wrenching terror that they all shared that terror, for a few brief seconds, in their own hearts. They couldn't see much more...the darkness was becoming too intense, there within the heart of the forest.

"Jacob!" The professor made it out of the car, and hurried to the front of the car, heedless of his own possible danger...his only thoughts were of his dear friend. Blood trickling down one cheek from a gash in his forehead, Yusuf stared at the ground. One headlight still worked, and bathed the ground in front of the car in a pale luminance. He saw the backpack on the ground...but nothing, and no one else. Both Tamara, and Jacob were gone! The professor gripped the side of the car, where the door had once been, and felt his heart thudding painfully in his chest. He forced himself to breathe, deep and slow...this was no time to court a heart attack. "Jacob...no...no!" Was all he could say, over and over...his friend was gone.

David was now out of the car, as was Patrick, their guns out. Neither of them was hurt any more then a good shaking, and a few bruises. They both looked around, aided by the flashlight David dug out of the backpack...he'd seen Jacob put it in there earlier. It was hard to believe they were still alive, still able to move about.

"Where'd they go?" Patrick growled, holding his .357 Colt up beside his ear, looking all around. He glanced at the front of the Rover. "How the hell does someone take a hit like that, and still be able to rip a car door off its hinges?...let alone yank a grown man out of a car like he weighed nothing!? What the hell kind of people are we dealing with, Dave?"

David was helping a slightly dazed Sandra out of the car. "Didn't you listen to the wires? Didn't you hear anything that they said?"

Patrick shrugged, keeping his eyes roving over the area around them. "Yeh, I listened...I just thought you'd all lost it, that's all! When you first talked with me, about getting the wires, I figured you'd taken one too many hits to that thick skull!" He glanced over at David. "How the hell was I supposed to know you were telling the truth!? I mean...come on, man...demons? Would you have believed me, not knowing what we do now?"

Sandra moaned, leaning against the side of the car, shaking her head to clear out the few cobwebs still lingering. She winced as the movement hurt. She felt slightly dizzy, and a trifle nauseous. She put a hand up to the left side of her head, just behind her ear, and found a good-sized lump there. Her head had banged against the roll-bar base when the car struck Tamara. She opened her eyes, and looked at the spot she'd last seen her nemesis standing. She saw the professor moving off towards the woods. "David...we can't let him go alone! He's in no shape if she's still out there!"

He nodded, knowing the truth of her words. He left her by the car, and hurried to catch up with the old teacher, grabbing his arm just as Yusuf was about to step into the heavier foliage. "Come on, professor...we can't do this right now! Running off half-cocked like this, in the dark, is just playing into their hands!" He understood the older man's feelings...he'd have acted the same if it had been Patrick who'd been the victim.

"But...Jacob...she has him! He's out there, somewhere...in the grips of a horror you can't even begin to understand, David! I can't just abandon him! He wouldn't if it had been me! We have to go after him!" The professor pulled against David's grip...he had to find his old friend...save him. Though, his brain was telling him it would be a futile effort, at best...Jacob's fate had already been sealed. He shook his head, refusing to accept that.

"I do understand, professor...if it had been Pat out there..." David shook that picture away...he had to keep focused. "But...ask yourself this...if we go after him, are we doing what he believed in?...the greater good!"

The stunned old scholar stared at him at first, not comprehending what the younger man was trying to say. Then, his shoulders slumped...David was right, though every cell in Yusuf's body wanted to continue searching for his lost friend. He knew Jacob would tell him to do his job...the job every Keeper vowed to carry on, even at the cost of his own life...to fight evil wherever it appeared. If he kept on, and went off into that darkness, then the cause of the Light would be lost.

He looked at David, then back towards the ruined car. "Yes...yes, you're right, David...we must leave! The best thing I can do for Jacob is make sure the things he died for don't fall into the wrong hands. She'll be back...like a cat playing with captured mice, she'll be back! I just wish..." His voice died away as he looked once more towards the woods.

"I know...I didn't know Jacob very long, but I do think he'd want us to save ourselves right now...so we can fight the *good* fight later! He said it a lot, professor...the greater good is the only thing that can never be allowed lost...or sacrificed. If a single life can save countless others, then so be it! Though every single life was to be cherished, there is no greater love then..." David was cut short as Yusuf gripped his shoulder.

"Yes...I know, my boy...as the saying goes, no greater love hath a man that he lay down his life for a friend! Come...let us leave!" The older man said.

"Look at it this way, professor...You, and Jacob are the only ones who really know how to fight these...these persons! You're going to have to be the one now to show us the right way out of here!" David didn't like sounding so callus, but there wasn't time for finesse...they had to get out of this forest, and right now!

Yusuf heard the words…knew they were true, but his heart was still numb. He'd lost so many loved ones, and friends in the battle he'd willingly taken on so many years ago. Jacob had been one of the best…one of the closest. The wise, witty, and charismatic restaurant owner had bee beside him in several confrontations with their unearthly antagonists over the last forty-three years. It would feel very strange to turn around, and not see that roguish grin. He shook himself…this was a time for action, and avenging lost friends, not self-pity.

He looked once again at the tall police officer, and squared his shoulders. "Yes, I believe you're right, David! My old friend would be upset that I was fretting over his welfare when the chance to destroy such evil is before us! Let's go!"

The group gathered themselves, and headed down the road, keeping in the center of the road, as much in the moonlight as possible. Yusuf had cautioned them to do so, explaining that any pure light was a form of protection against the ranks of those who dwelt in the darkness. Sandra was still feeling the effects of the hit to her head, and leaned heavily against David as they walked along. Patrick brought up the rear, continually looking over his shoulder. He expected some sort of attack, and couldn't believe that one hadn't materialized as yet. The suspense was beginning to get to him.

David, too, was wondering about the seeming lack of pursuit, or attack. He had the feeling that Tamara wasn't the type to just give up…especially when she had things going her way! He looked down at Sandra, seeing her face in the moonlight…seeing that she was struggling to keep moving, though every step was obviously becoming harder, and harder. David was sure she had a concussion, and should be resting…but for their safety, he had to keep pushing them on. If he figured correctly, they had about half an hour's walking, and they should hit the entrance to the cabin road. From there, the main highway was just a few minutes walk, and they could catch a ride into the city. It was still early so there would be a lot of traffic. They just had to keep moving…they'd make it, and then he'd return, with lots of help. They'd tried to use the radio in the squad car earlier, to call for assistance. But...for some inexplicable reason, it had refused to work.

Suddenly, David stopped, tightening his hold around Sandra's shoulders. As they had left the site of the wrecked Rover, the usual night sounds, of birds, frogs, and insects had started up again. Now, with an abruptness that was chilling...everything was silent once again. He had the intense, urgent feeling to seek shelter...protection. He looked down at Sandra, who had glanced up when his arm tightened its grip. She was startled to see how pale his face was in the moonlight.

Patrick, and Yusuf had also stopped...Patrick because he'd seen his partner stop, and the professor because he sensed the same things David had...they needed to find a place of shelter. "David...we must find a place! They're coming!" His whisper was loud, and urgent.

David nodded, looking around, shining the flashlight's beam as he searched for something to fit the professor's need. The light beam settled on a very dense looking thicket of bushes, and trees...maybe that was what they were looking for right now. He pointed the light in that direction. "There...that way!"

Patrick went in first, followed by the professor, then David, and Sandra. The group pressed into the dense underbrush, looking for some sort of haven. After a few minutes, the brush suddenly gave way, and they found themselves in the center of a wide clearing...complete with a small cave just beyond the clearing. The professor led them into that cave, instructing David, and Patrick to gather as much firewood as possible. He sat Jacob's backpack on the ground, and started digging among all the items his old friend always kept with him. He soon had a fairly large fire going at the opening of the cave...effectively blocking anyone coming into the cave, and locking them inside its sheltering confines. The professor had found another of the special pouches Jacob used to construct mystic circles, and soon had created such a circle. It took in the entrance to the cave, the fire itself, and went all along the inside of the cave, effectively protecting them in all directions.

"It's not quite the same as the one Jacob created within the Tomb...but I feel confident we're fairly safe." He commented to the others, sitting the backpack down, and sitting on one of the two blankets he'd found in the back half of the pack. He'd also taken a bit of chalk he'd found within the pack, and drawn a few intriguing designs on either side of the walls of the cave entrance.

He smiled at Sandra, recalling the puzzled expression on her face as he scratched the designs out on the stone walls. "You don't remember my lectures on the talismans, and amulets of the ancients? Look close at the symbols I've drawn, and see if anything jogs your memory!"

Sandra peered at the drawings, studying them intently, glad to have something to distract her mind. The drawings on either side of the cave entrance were the same, and were very familiar to her. They each resembled a large human-looking eye, with brow drawn in above, and lines denoting the makeup known as kohl. She smiled as a memory surfaced, and looked at him.

"Those are *wedjat*...the eyes of the god Horus. They can be singular, or double...like you've drawn them here! The right eye represents the sun...the left is for the moon. In a drawing together, they stand for the power of all light! It's generally conceded that the *wedjat* are one of the best forms of a protective talismans, probably because it invokes the favor of the god, Osiris!" She grinned at her old teacher. "I think I just scored an 'A'...right?"

He laughed, patting her hand as he looked at the two other men. "She was the best student I ever tutored! I always regret not convincing her to go into archaeology as a full-time profession!"

David stroked her cheek, agreeing with the professor concerning Sandra's skills, and attributes. "Professor...you never really answered my question...what were you, and Jacob doing up here? I'd told you that we'd handle this!"

At the mention of his friend's name, the professor bowed his head, murmuring a few words that David couldn't make out. He looked at Sandra, an unspoken question on his eyes.

"It's a prayer...rather, a prayer, and a chant. It's for a soul that has crossed to the western horizon. Yusuf used to teach a lot of things based on the Books of the Dead when I was in his class, as well as the religious customs of other faiths. I recognize the one he's using...it's a Hebrew prayer to allow the departed an easy passage." She whispered, watching her old teacher, feeling the pain he was bearing. She leaned forward. "Yusuf...there wasn't anything you could have done to prevent this. She is just too much for any one person to withstand!...I should know! Please...don't let her beat you down! Jacob wouldn't have wanted her to win that way!"

The professor lifted his head, his brown eyes gazing at her, with respect, and a great deal of affection. "You know...I was there, with your father, the night you, and Elizabeth were born! Your parents were so proud...two beautiful daughters, and they were so much in love! It made me so happy to see my dear friends so blessed!" He reached into his coat pocket, and drew the journal out. He held it out towards the lovely woman, motioning for her to take it. "Having finally gotten through all that Joshua had written there, I understand fully now the feeling I had the night of your birth!"

Sandra stared at the worn journal she held. "Why? What's in here that makes you say that?"

"You know all about how the Aztec High Priest had arranged for the sarcophagus to be brought here...the summoning of the spirit guard, and Joshua's defeat of that same guard in order to win the prize?" The professor waited until the others all nodded. "Well, it seems that Joshua was intended all along to be the chosen winner...all others failed, and perished! This we all know...what we didn't know was that Joshua was getting visions about this long before he actually went up onto that mountain! He wrote that it was if this One that was hidden away was *sending* him these visions. He wrote down everything these vision dreams told him...in all the languages written down in the journal we have here! Once he had overcome the spirit guard, Joshua found the amulet...right where the visions had told him to look. He used this to be able to converse with the being trapped inside that sarcophagus. That was when he learned all the secrets that the dark powers wanted!"

"Okay...we pretty much knew all that already, like you said. So...what else is in there that's important to Sandy, and her family." David asked, slipping an arm about the shoulders of the woman sitting next to him, leaning against his body. Patrick, on the other side of Sandra, grinned reassuringly at her.

"It's not so much what we found, David...as it is what we did find implies! There was a section where Joshua wrote down some predictions that his visions showed him...concerning some of his descendents. It practically set forth the exact *dates* of the deaths of her father, ex-husband...and a sister not of her true blood!" The reply was soft, but firm. The old man gazed at Sandra, wishing they'd been aware of what the journal actually contained long before this day...maybe they would have been able to avert those deaths.

"You mean...Garalynn?" Sandra turned her head away...the pain was beginning to get too intense. Then, she felt that gentle brush of...something again. She raised her head, eyes wide, and looked around. Patrick saw this, and lowered the cup he was drinking from...frowning, but deciding not say anything, the big policeman kept an eye on his partner's lady.

Yusuf also noted the sudden alertness, but decided not to comment. "The other thing written here section stated that Joshua was told his bloodline was a direct descendent from one of the greatest of the immortal demigods mentioned in some sort of ancient story. We weren't able to decipher the rest of this part...it switched from Greek, and hieroglyphics, to Mayan, and Aztec glyphs. Anyway, this lineage carried with it a 'special' gift...that would be passed from generation to generation, and would make itself known when the time was right! Now...what this gift is, we don't know. It's highly possible that Joshua knew, and chose not to put it into the writings of the journal! It's also possible that this gift was something passed on, orally, from father to son to son, etc. I doubt know any time soon!...at least, not until we get some other experts to examine the journal!" He sighed, rubbing the back of his neck. He sipped from the cup of tea he'd made from the pan of water David had warmed at the edge of the fire. Patrick offered him some more tea, but Yusuf shook his head.

"You said it mentioned a *demigod*?...Yusuf, are you saying that somewhere in my family's history, there was...was an *immortal*? That's impossible!" Sandra realized the irony of her words as soon as they left her mouth. She waved a hand, the gesture showing her confusion, and upset. "Okay...okay, I should know by now that *nothing* id impossible any more! What I am trying to say is...if there is such a thing as immortality, and I guess after what we've seen, that's no longer an if! Okay...let's say what Joshua was writing in that journal was all true, and not any kind of artistic license, or creative exaggeration...right?" She leaned forward, wincing a little as she did...her head reminding her it still hurt. "Yusuf...if there is the influence of an immortal's blood...power...whatever!...if it's there, in *my* family, why hasn't anyone ever noticed?"

"How does one *notice* someone may be an immortal, Sandra? Your family has always been blessed with exceptionally long, healthy lifetimes!...barring accidents, of course! Why is that? Have you ever wondered about it?" The professor chuckled a little, seeing how exasperated his former protégé was getting.

"Cool it, both of you!...we've more important things to think about right now, you know!" Patrick spoke firmly, not wanting to offend, but knowing they couldn't afford getting too side-tracked.

Sandra nodded absently...her mind distracted. She had the sudden sensation that she'd had this conversation long before this...what did that thought mean? She looked at her old teacher, seeing him staring at her intently as though he was waiting for something more from her. She came to her knees, balancing herself with one hand on the rock beside her.

"Yusuf...this gift Joshua hinted at...what if it were some kind of psychic ability, or power?" She asked, looking out the cave entrance, past the fire's flickering, into the darkness of the looming forest.

The professor nodded slowly. "That's a very real possibility...especially considering the success your family has had over the years. But...I just don't know if that's what Joshua meant, Sandra!" He was about to say something further when he noticed her eyes were distant, her head cocked to one side, as though she were listening to something else...something he somehow knew neither he, or David would be able to see.

He reached out, nudging David with the side of his foot, then doing the same to Patrick, who was already watching Sandra. When the younger men looked at him, he jerked his head towards the still silent Sandra. The two men inched a little closer to the still figure, instinctively realizing something was happening. "What is it, Sandy? Do you hear something?" David asked softly, reaching to take her by the hand, but the professor stopped him, shaking his head.

"Don't!...it might break whatever connection she has right now!" The professor said in a hushed tone. Then, he leaned forward. "Sandra...tell us...what is it you're hearing, or feeling?"

She held up a hand, gesturing for him to be silent, her head still cocked to one side...as though she were listening to her own body as it was listening to the unseen, and unknown. After a few more moments, she turned back to the three men who were watching her every movement. "They're here!...at least, one of them is out there right now! The fire, and Yusuf's signs drawings are keeping them out so far, but it won't last forever! Its powers are too strong for the ancient symbols...at least these signs! It will find a way past the signs, and the circle!...sooner, or later!" She looked back outside, her jaw set, and her expressive eyes narrowed. Yusuf had a sudden insight…she really *was* hearing, and seeing whatever it was that lurked out there in the darkness. And, not only hearing it, but somehow tracking it, and "reading" its thoughts with her senses.

His eyes nearly popped from their sockets as he realized what it was that was really going on now with his former student. He crawled over to her side, and kneeling next to her, took her by the shoulders. He shook her a little, making her look at him, a puzzled, remote expression on her beautiful, pale face.

"Sandra…that's it! That's the gift!…you're using it, right now! This is what Joshua was talking about!" He was practically breathing in her face in his excitement.

"Hold on…you mean she really *is* listening to something out there?" Patrick stood up, drawing his police special, peering through the darkness past the fire, and cave opening.

"Yes!…as Joshua wrote, the 'gift' will appear when it is needed the most! She has been unconsciously sensing their presence with heightened sensory powers! Those same powers 'masked' their presence within Sandra's mind, and body…so that the Dresdens couldn't know, and act on that fact! The stress we've all been under the past few days, and especially during the last few hours…it triggered something within her, and the power awoke!" The professor gazed into Sandra's eyes, seeing the confusion…but also the strength growing as the dormant psychic power began to "spread its wings"!

Sandra looked at him, then her attention went back out to the woods surrounding the cave…it was coming closer! She almost recoiled from the malevolence her mind was touching…it was more then evil, more then an understandable anger. The feeling of rage…of rending flesh, and bone…of the utter destruction of all that was good, all that lived, and by, the light. She took a few deep, cleansing breaths…attempting to keep tight control over her suddenly nauseated stomach. She knew, with every once of her being...what was prowling around out there, unseen and reeking with livid danger...meant to kill them! And more...it meant to destroy their very souls as well!

She understood, in a flash, what Joshua had been trying to tell the descendents who would read the journal he'd written. She looked up at the professor, awe, and comprehension clear in the azure orbs she lifted to his face. "Yusuf...do *you* understand all this?" She looked back outside...her attention focused again. "It's getting angrier!...I don't think it's going to wait much longer! Oh, God!...the hate, and the rage!...it's more then I've ever seen, or felt! If it gets in here...David!" With a cry, she whirled towards the man she loved, seeking the solace of his arms.

"You're feeling the sensations true evil can generate within us, Sandra. Don't fight them...learn to know, and recognize your enemy! Can you tell if it is either Tamara, or Sean?" The professor asked, pulling the backpack over to his side.

She shook her head. "Not really...except that it is male! What are we going to do when it finally figures how to get past our protection symbols?"

"That's why I'm checking to see what all Jacob packed in his bag...he believed in being prepared for all situations!" Yusuf answered, opening the multi-pocketed backpack, and beginning his search. His fingers closed about something with several points, and made of metal. He wondered what it was, and pulled it out to check it out. He saw that it was attached to a silver-looking chain. When he let it dangle from its chain, he saw that it was a silver Star of David. He stared.

"Jacob...you left the Star in your bag...you knew what was going to happen tonight, and left this to help protect us! You knew a sacrifice was needed...that's why you didn't try to save yourself!"

"He *let* her take him?...why?" Patrick glanced at the slowly revolving Star, catching golden highlights from the fire.

"Jacob was very skilled in the occult...perhaps he felt he could use that against her...I don't know! I can't think of any other kind of reason to explain it! I only know Jacob never took this off! He knew to do so would leave him open to an attack!" Yusuf closed his eyes, and in his mind, thanked his friend, and bid his spirit farewell. Then, opening his eyes, he pulled the chain over his head, and settled the Star of David on his chest. From now on, he would wear this in memory of his long-time colleague, and dear friend.

At the professor's instructions, David and Patrick moved to positions on either side of the cave's narrow opening. This gave each one of them a clear view of the entire cave interior, the entrance...and a clean shot at anything that tried to get into the cave, no matter how fast it may move. The professor pulled his ankh out from under his jacket, and let it hang next to the Star. He then pulled a small flask out of the backpack, and secured it in his right hand, flipping the hinged lid open. With his left hand, he pulled out a small, worn-looking book, and sat it on the blanket he sat on...opening it, and beginning to thumb through the pages.

Sandra watched the three men for a few moments...then, her charged senses took over again, and she looked back out the entrance. She could feel her breath quickening, and her heart rate accelerating...something was close, and about to make its move. She tried to concentrate harder, to see if she could determine who it was that was out there, stalking them. But, no matter how she tried...she couldn't identify their antagonist. In fact, she was having a great deal of trouble picking up on anything *human*! Granted, using these kind of powers was really a new thing...but the more she used them, the easier, and more familiar it became to her.

She lifted her head quickly, sucking in a swift breath...it was suddenly very, very quiet. The night sounds were totally silent...and the air of anticipation was getting so thick it was almost a physical reality, threatening to suffocate like a thick blanket. She shivered, moving closer to the fire, seeking the protection it offered. The silence grew, becoming sinister, foreboding...the shadows reaching for their haven, desiring to engulf, and obliterate their small zone of security. Sandra had a thought, and it made her shiver even more…was this what it had been like for Garalynn before…she shook her head, not able to complete that thought. She lifted her head, lifting her right hand to her forehead…it felt as if someone had just caressed her there, placing the gentlest of kisses in the middle of her forehead. She looked up, her heart surging…she came to her knees, and reached towards David, intending to call out to the tall man…she never got the chance.

With a roar that chilled, and curdled their blood, a dark shape exploded from the darkness, leaping past the circle, and the cave entrance. It landed just before the fire, and took a swipe at the blaze. The burning wood was scattered, dropping the light in the cave to dim shadows, and obscure shapes. David, and Patrick had been both pushed aside by the force of their still unseen enemy's entrance. David was struggling to his feet, searching for the gun that was knocked out of his hand as he fell backwards. He rose to his feet once he located his weapon, free hand dashing at the blood trickling down the left side of his face…his head had hit against a rock as he'd gone down. He looked to where his partner had been standing.

Off to the other side of the fire, Patrick was fighting for his life. The dark shape that had plunged into their cave had him pinned to the ground, and was tearing at his struggling form. Sandra, knocked down by something unseen, sat back up, her head turning in the direction of that screams, and roars now echoing throughout the cave. Her eyes popped wide open…she began trembling, shaking her head in denial. It wasn't real…what was attacking Patrick couldn't be real! The big sergeant was using all his strength, hitting and pushing at the shape over him, trying to save his life…his screams were filled with fear, and unbelievable pain…cries for help. She covered her ears, turning away. Beside her, the professor was searching for the small flask he'd dropped.

Just as he found the flask, and stood up…David was lifting his gun, and running towards where his partner was fighting. Yusuf was going to call out for him to stop, but it was too late…David had reached the pair, and dove into the melee. He managed to get a fairly good tackle grip on Patrick's assailant, and pull it partially off his friend. The thing turned its head in David's face, and snarled...blood dripping from a gaping mouth, and murderously sharp fangs. David's eyes widened in shock as he got a clear, good look at what he was fighting.

The eyes were dark, with no pupils...filled with a rage, and bloodlust he'd never seen before, not even in the eyes of a mad man. The face, illuminated in the dim light, was in no way human! Snarling lips drew back, baring deadly teeth in what could best be described as the muzzle of some form of beast! Elongated canines dripped with blood-tinged saliva, and David could feel the hot breath wafting across his face. What he was staring at now was a perversion of both animal...and human!

His shock caused his grip to loosen a bit, his horrified mind registering only the fact of blood everywhere, screams that were growing in intensity, and sounds of rage that threatened to rupture his eardrums! As he stared, in those few milliseconds, an arm came sweeping back towards him. His brain recorded that the arm was rippling with fur-covered muscles...fur? Then, his body was flying through the air as though he was nothing but a rag-doll. He impacted with the cave wall, and he felt a sharp pain explode in his right elbow. The pain was a blessing...it snapped him from that stupor his shock had been sinking him into so deeply.

Ignoring the painful fact of a badly fractured elbow, David managed to shove himself up on one knee. He lifted his left hand, a little awkward but determined, and aimed his revolver at the dark shapes moving around.

At the same time, Yusuf had located the small flask, and stood up, moving towards the still fighting pair. "David...don't shoot yet! Wait until I can get this on them!" He held the flask up to. He lunged forward, and splashed what was left in the flask over the back of the dark shape on top of Patrick. "David! Now!" The professor yelled, throwing himself out of the direction of fire.

David took a deep breath, steadying his left hand as much as possible. He saw the dark thing roar, and straightened up, arching in pain as the liquid from Yusuf"s flask struck its back. "Hey, you son of a bitch!...this way!" He yelled, tightening his finger on the trigger.

The inhuman thing swung its head towards him, snarling, in anger, and pain...as if it desired his blood next. David had it clean in the sights of the gun...and hesitated, feeling the power of those dark eyes.

"David...do it! Don't think!...don't reason! Just aim, and fire! Think only how right this is, and shoot!" The professor cried, lifting both the ankh, and the Star...holding them in the direction of their enemy. "In the name of the most High...make his arm strong, and his aim unfailing!"

David heard the words, felt strength, and determination flow back into his body, and he pulled the trigger. Screeching, clawing at its face, the thing fell backwards...a highly visible expression of disbelief on its demonic features. For a few seconds, it thrashed about the floor of the cave, gnashing its teeth, and tearing at the dirt. Finally, all movements ceased, a bloody froth about its mouth, bubbles slowly popping in the thick liquid. Then, even that stopped...and everything was silent again.

David slowly lowered the gun, and painfully rose to his feet, swaying a little. He walked over to where Patrick lay, hearing the tortured rasping of the injured man's breathing. He knelt down, grasping Patrick's hand. "Patrick...you okay?" Even as he asked the question, he thought how stupid it sounded.

"Sure...why would having your gut tore up make you feel bad?" The badly hurt man tried to cheer his also injured friend up...Patrick was in a deep shock, but he knew just how bad was the damage inflicted on his body. He gripped David's hand, feeling a sudden coldness sweep over his limbs...he had to tell David something. "Listen...pal of mine...get your lady, and the professor out of here! She's still out there, and it won't be this easy to stop her!" He gasped the words out, grinned once more, than suddenly went very still.

David stared for a few moments, then, putting his friend's hand down, he felt for a pulse in the neck…nothing. Yusuf knelt beside Patrick's body, and also checked a couple of places for a pulse. He looked up at the man kneeling across from him. "He's gone…I am very sorry, David! Your friend was a good, brave man!" The professor said in a low, stiff voice…this was turning out to be a very bad night.

David didn't answer…he simply stood up, and walked over to where the thing that had killed his best friend lay. He stood over it, staring at it. He drew back one foot, and delivered a vicious kick to the kneecap…an old Green Beret trick to check to see if an enemy were shamming. When there was no response, he drew a deep breath. "Just what is this thing? Professor?" He turned towards the other man.

The professor shook his head…he'd never seen anything like this. Half covered in glistening scales, the other half in thick, luxurious black fur…it was both repulsive, yet strangely beautiful. Sandra had joined the man, and turned away, one hand to her mouth, and choking back a large sob…she'd been genuinely fond of the big man who'd been her David's partner, and best friend.

David went back to kneel beside his dead friend. His police-trained mind made note of that slashes, and wounds that covered his partner's body. They were almost exactly like the ones he'd seen on Douglas Traylor's body…was this what had killed the man then? He felt something sweeping over him…he couldn't hold it back. He dropped to the dirt, on both knees, and hands dangling at his sides. A throat-tearing, gut-wrenching sob ripped its way out between his lips, and the tears coursed their way down his dust-covered cheeks. Sandra came up behind him, wrapping her arms about his body, and murmuring in his ear. He turned towards her, burying his face in the softness of her breasts, feeling the warmth of her body push back the cold within him. She began to rock in gently in her arms, crooning softly to him…feeling the loss almost as deep as he.

Finally, after a few moments, he gathered himself, and straightened up, feeling the pain of his fractured arm once again. "No one deserves to die like this! That's what Pat said about Douglas Traylor's deaths...and he was right! I can't believe this!" He wiped the tears off his cheeks, and squared his broad shoulders...they were still in a lot of danger. He took Patrick's cooling hand, and squeezed. "At least I was able to take it out for you, buddy! It won't kill anyone again!"

Sandra helped him to stand, then noticed the abnormal twist to his arm, and the wince of pain on his face. She went to look for something to use as a temporary splint. He moved his gaze to the dead creature. "Is that what they really look like, professor?...Tamara, and Sean, I mean. Are they really some sort of demonic beasts that take human form?"

The professor shrugged, shaking his head. "I honestly don't know, David...but I don't think so! I think that's just a form they take to terrify, and kill! For what purpose, I don't know as yet!...but I will before this is all over, I promise you! We can't really say that this thing is one of the Dresdens...though, if it isn't, it's surely connected to them! I can't believe I'm actually seeing the body of a demon beast! Amazing!"

David nodded, wincing as Sandra carefully placed his injured arm in the makeshift sling Sandra made out of a ripped off section of blanket, wrapped about two foot long sections of wood. "Professor...I think we need to pack up, and get out of here before someone else shows up! I'd like to get to a phone, and get some help up here! I don't intend leaving...leaving Pat's body up here!"

The professor nodded...he knew the danger was far from over. "I think that is an excellent idea, my boy! Whether, or not that is either Tamara, or Sean, is really not the point right now! We need to get out of this forest, and get help! That is the only way we can hope to finish this...and rescue Elizabeth, despite what she told Sandra! Angela is still at my apartment...we need to call her, and have her contact the other Keepers in this area! We can do no further good trapped here, and they have been paid for only a small portion of their debt to us!" He declared, jabbing his finger towards the beast's corpse, and looking at Sandra, and David. "They may have paid for our good Patrick's death, with this death!" He said, feeling a righteous anger. "But…they still owe us, for Jacob, and Garalynn!"

"And, my father, and my ex-husband! And poor Doug!" Sandra spoke up, feeling that same righteous anger coursing through her body.

They gathered by the cave's opening, and listened…Sandra using her new-found powers to scan the near-by woods. The usual night sounds were back, but they heard nothing else. Sandra sensed nothing else…in fact, she frowned as she realized she wasn't able to utilize the power as she had before. It was if it had abandoned her.

"Yusuf…it's gone!…I've lost it! The power…it's no longer with me…inside me!" She clutched at the professor's arm, swallowing as she felt exposed to the dangers out there. "What will we do?"

"Don't worry…when you need it again, I think it will be back! Now…come, we must get going!" The professor patted her shoulder, and nodded to David. As they started out of the cave, David turned and looked at the still figure of his friend. "I'll be back for you, Pat…I won't leave you out here! I swear!"…….

……She knelt inside the cave, one hand resting on the unmoving figure, a his slipping out between clenched teeth. Unbelieving, she ran her hand over the still silky fur, feeling the limbs hardening into stone hard angles of death.

With a muttered oath, she slipped into her family's true language, jerking her head up, scanning the area. "Thee cannot be dead!…not now! This cannot be!…it is impossible for them to have known *how* to kill thee! Curse them!"

Having flung her anger to the heavens, Tamara looked once more into the dead face of the fearsome beast. She reached down, covering the face with one hand, and murmuring a few words. When she removed her hand, she gazed at the forever stilled features of her brother, Sean. She touched his cheek once more, feeling the flesh now cold, and rigid...with the texture of dried leather. She knew, within a few hours, that same flesh would become as dry, and hard as the stone that surrounded them now as death extracted the final life moisture out of the shell that was once her living brother...that was their curse. Once seriously injured, while in their beast, or creature form...death would quickly follow, and the ages would catch up with the flesh that had defied it for so long. All that would remain would be the rock hard images of once living flesh, and bone.

"I told thee to locate Sandra...and tell me! Thee should not have attempted an attack without me! How could thou have allowed this to happen?...how did they know what to do to accomplish thy death? Why did thee alter thy shape?...thou knew the risks are greater when in beast form! Thy arrogance...it has always been the thorn that caused thee conflicts. Despite thy faults...I will miss thee, my brother...I will miss thee!" Her hand slipped down his head, and reached under his body, intending to take him back to the cabin. To her shock, she felt a searing pain, and when she jerked her hand out, she was surprised to see that shiny, raised marks of a severe burn. The pain ran up her entire arm, causing her to clench her teeth. After a few moments, her will had the pain under control, and she opened her eyes again.

"Holy water...someone is very versed in the right weapons. This may prove a bit harder then I anticipated...but, I do so love a challenge!" She glanced at Patrick's body, and her lip curled into a feral smile. "One of our enemies has paid for their defiance, my brother...I will see that the others meet a similar fate, and especially Sandra! Her punishment will especially creative!...Elizabeth will see that further incorrect behavior on her part will promote an equal ending for her! I will protect her as long as she carries thy child, Sean...per the family's orders, but after it is born...well, than we shall see!"

She touched his cheek, leaning closer. "I must leave thee here...for a time. But, thy shape is in its true form now, should anyone discover thy body. I will return to take thee home, Sean…after I tend to those who caused thy death! I go now to find them, exact my vengeance, and take from them that which is ours! Until later!"

She stood up, and strode from the cave, her stride long, and purposeful. Her grief was pushed to the rear of her mind…her focus centered on the task at hand. Turning towards the towering darkness of the mountains, and took a deep breath of the cool night air. She twisted her head slightly…they were headed in the direction of the main road, seeking help no doubt. One, or more of them was injured…the scent of fresh blood was sharp on the night wind. It was time to bring her greatest powers to bear.

She knelt in the middle of the clearing, leaning forward until she was resting on knees, and hands. She lifted her face to the sky, seeing the stars bright, and clear. "By all the powers that are mine…by all that is contained within the darkness of the night…by all that has been, is, and will be…let it begin once again! Powers of darkness, enter again into this form, and make it thine!" She smiled, thinking of her revenge upon Sandra, and the others. "Run while thou may, my enemies…there will be no escape tonight! There is no way, or place to run from thy deepest, darkest terrors!"

She lowered her head, channeling all her concentration inward, closing her eyes as she began. She could feel the upsurge within her body as the awesome powers at her command took control. Giving her will entirely over to those powers, she also let her mind go, taking in a deep breath as she felt it leap outwards. The changes were beginning, and she smiled in anticipation. The sense of well-being, of power, and strength such times as this brought to her created a feeling of elation she felt at only one other time…when she made love.

The long, tapered fingers clenched together, beginning to flow into one shape…that of a clawed paw, enwrapped in thick, silken golden fur. Joints, and sinews altered their basic structures, and alignments…twisting, and compressing, pulling the muscles they were fastened to, changing the usual shapes, and forms of those muscles.

Her lower jaw began to elongate, jutting forward...the upper one also stretching from its flattened position. Tamara arched her neck, feeling it contract, settling deeper between her shoulders. She drew deep breaths in, steady and rapid...feeling the sense of smell becoming more acute by the moment. Heart pumping rapid, and steady...arteries pulsating with the power of that heart. Chemicals, released into the blood from the brain, caused the changes to accelerate...become more acute. There would be no stopping the flood now...not until the final goal was reached....

.....Sandra, David, and the professor were resting in a small, moon-splashed clearing, just off the cabin road. Their progress had been slower then they wished, frequent stops dictated because of injuries. Sandra's head still throbbed like a drumbeat, David's arm was swollen, and painful. He'd been fighting bouts of nausea, and dizziness, insisting he was fine. The professor feared his compound fracture was beginning to be inflamed. Yusuf himself was feeling a tightness in his chest...the combination of the thin mountain air, and the stress of first Jacob's death, then that of Patrick was bringing the old scholar dangerously close to severe cardiac problems. He knew this, but didn't see a different way to pursue right now.

David sat on the ground, leaning against a tree. He wouldn't admit it to his companions...but, he felt terrible. He knew he had a nasty gash on the side of his head, and a badly broken arm. He also was afraid he had a concussion...like Sandra. He knew she was also experiencing some difficulties traveling the way they were. He figured they were only a couple of miles more from the main road...maybe less. Once there, they could get the help they needed...he'd make those bastards pay for all they'd done. He looked at Sandra, sitting beside him, her head on his uninjured shoulder. "Hey…how you doing, honey?" He asked quietly, touching her hair with the unhurt hand.

She lifted her head, gazing into his eyes. She tried to smile, but only managed a weak one…her head hurt too much. "Okay, I guess…considering everything. I wish this headache would go away! I sure wish I had an aspirin right now!" She saw the professor rubbing the left side of his chest. "Yusuf…is there any aspirin in Jacob's pack?"

"I believe so…but, Sandra, you shouldn't take something like that with a head injury! It could be dangerous!" He looked into the backpack, and saw that Jacob had indeed packed a bottle of extra-strength aspirin tablets.

"No…not for me! I think *you* should take one…just in case!" She said, touching her chest lightly.

"Ah…yes, perhaps you're right! At any rate…it wouldn't hurt!" The older man smiled ruefully, and shook a tablet out from the bottle. He took it quickly, washing it down with a sip of water from the one canteen they had with them. He knew she was worried about him keeping up with them. "I'll finish right beside you, my dear…never worry about that! But, the two of you are hurt…and getting worst! Perhaps I should go on alone, and bring the help back?" Yusuf wondered if that wouldn't be the correct path.

David shook his head. "No way, professor…for all we know, another one of those things is waiting for us out there! No, sir…we stay together!"

"He might be right, though, David! Isn't it better if one of us gets through, and brings back help?…rather the all of us maybe never making it?" Sandra looked up at the man she loved, using his nearness, and warm strength to keep the waves of fear, and panic away. David could see the wet tracks of tears in the moonlight shining down into her up-turned face.

He took her in his good arm, and hugged her close. She wrapped her arms about his neck, wetting the top of his jacket collar with her tears…her breath on his skin causing him to shiver delicately.

"I need you so much! I'm so afraid, and all I really want to do is run away! I just want everything to be like it was before all this started!" She whispered in his ear, the nearness of her mouth causing another shiver.

He held her close, his own face wet with tears. In the middle of this dark, and terrifying night, he'd come to know exactly what she meant in his life. "I love you...now, and forever! I will spend the rest of my life telling...no, showing you just how much you mean to me!" He whispered back.

The professor smiled sadly, watching over them, allowing them this moment, and praying they'd all make it through the rest of the night. He bowed his head, closing his hand tight about the Star he wore around his neck...Jacob's Star.

It was Sandra's gasp that brought his head back up, and caused David to open his eyes. The policeman tightened his arm about Sandra when he saw what was waiting across the clearing. Just a few yards away, crouched in the moonlight, tail lashing, was the biggest lion he'd ever seen...and yet, it wasn't like any lion he'd ever seen. The creature watched them, golden eyes unblinking, gigantic fangs showing, a low, almost continuous rumbling issuing from its throat. David stared...again, he had that feeling of watching something so evil, and yet so beautiful. The golden fur moving slightly as the great muscles rippled was like watching a wind blowing over a field of ripe wheat, seeing the waves come, and go. It was like watching a living sculpture.

Sandra shrank back against David, seeing no mercy in the cold, hard eyes that stared at them. She stared back, feeling something brush against her back...something murmuring in her ear. She lifted her head, turning so she could whisper in David's left ear. "David...it's Tamara!"

He swallowed hard, remembering the last time they'd been tracked down. "How can you be so sure? We're still not sure who it was that attacked us back in the cave!" He whispered back, glancing at the crouching animal.

Never taking her eyes off the creature, she shook her head. "Who, or what that was back in the cave, I don't know! That *this* is Tamara Dresden...that I know beyond any doubts!"

Struggling a little, David finally pulled his gun out, and brought it up, aimed right at the lion. The rumbling increased at the sight of the gun, but the animal still didn't make any kind of movement. To David's surprise, the professor reached over, and pushed the gun down.

"Don't waste your bullets, David...they'll do little harm to this one!" He shook his head, staring at the lion.

"What are you saying? Look, I know you said they're not able to be hurt in their *human* shape...but I was able to kill that one back in the cave because it was in *animal* form! We have to get this one before it gets us!" David pulled away from the professor's grip, and aimed his gun again.

"That was also because we had the blessed water, David! Remember...I told you to wait until I splashed it on that creature's back? Then...I yelled for you to shoot! It was the holy water that made it possible to deal it a *fatal* blow! Without it, we wouldn't have been able to defeat that creature!" The professor explained, trying to make the younger man understand everything that had happened.

"Okay...so where's that water? We'll do it the same way here!" David declared, looking back at the professor.

In answer, the old teacher held up the small flask he'd carried the water in...upside down, with the hinged stopper open. Nothing came out. In silence, the two men gazed at the flask, and each other. Sandra watched the lion, feeling her throat swell with fear...they wouldn't be able to trick this one. She stood up, slow and deliberate, swaying a bit as her head gave a twinge of pain. She felt a warm brush against her back, like someone helping her stay erect.

She began to walk towards the lion, her cerulean eyes never leaving the unblinking golden orbs watching her. David gasped, bringing his revolver up again...useless or not, he had to try to save the woman he loved. But, as if reading his thoughts, Sandra stepped directly into the line of fire. He couldn't shoot...he didn't dare for fear of maybe hitting Sandra. "Get out of the way! For God's sake, Sandy...get away from there! Are you crazy?" David struggled to get to his feet, but a wave of nausea caused him to wrench to one side, and empty his stomach yet again on the forest floor.

"Sandra...no! She'll tear you to pieces!" Yusuf felt the tight band across his chest tighten again.

Sandra disregarded the pleas from both men, and slowly advanced on the dangerous creature. "It's all right...both of you stay there!" Her voice bespoke a confidence both men heard, and were puzzled by. Sandra took another step towards the lion, and the clearing suddenly echoed with the rumbling thunderclaps of the creature's roars. Sandra stopped, never taking her gaze off the animal.

David was still trying to maneuver around, looking for the spot where he could get a clean shot. But, Sandra kept in front of him. Her eye contact with the big cat never wavered, but she did stop walking towards it. She smiled, grim and sure, feeling something gathering within her again.

"Here I am, Tamara...waiting for you! Face me, on an equal basis!...or, are you unsure of those special powers you bragged about? You probably prefer old men, and those persons helpless against your type of evil! What's wrong?...can't stand against someone who might have a power equal to you?" Where were these words coming from? It was like someone else was saying them.

Staring, David wasn't sure his concussion wasn't acting up. He watched as the animal seemed caught up in sort of convulsion...twisting, and writhing, stretching its limbs like they were made of rubber, or putty. In a few minutes, he was gazing at the tall, exquisitely curved form of Tamara Dresden. She stood on the edge of the moonlit clearing, tall and impressive. She gazed at the trio, a smirk playing about her full lips, and her eyes strangely warm. But, Sandra wasn't fooled by that expression…she could feel the hostility coming off the other woman's body in powerful waves.

This was the first time David had seen Tamara, and he had to admit…she was an incredibly beautiful woman. But…he shuddered a little as he also sensed an air of death, destruction, and evil surrounding her. He lowered his gun, and looked at the professor, who was staring at the tawny blonde. Yusuf's fingers fiddled continuously with the ankh, and the star about his neck…staring at the incarnation of evil he knew Tamara to be.

Tamara nodded to Sandra, the gesture as full of sarcasm as a slap in the face. She smiled…one of contempt, and great anger. "Does this make you happy, Sandra?…to see your death full in the face? Do you have any other wishes I could grant? I want you to meet your end with nothing left unfulfilled!" The silken purr was like gratings on a chalkboard to Sandra…her hatred of this woman was so great. That was when she realized that that emotion was going to get her killed…she had to focus all her feelings into a plane of non-emotion, make all that power work for her, not against her.

"What did you do to my sister? I know you had to be furious she let us leave the cabin, Tamara!…is she all right?" Sandra took a step closer…easy, her mind prompted, one step at a time…don't let her "read" your intentions before you can get close enough, it cautioned her.

"Elizabeth?…why, she's fine, Sandra. I wouldn't do anything to her…she's carrying my brother's child. You remember my brother?…Sean? The man you all murdered!" Tamara dropped the light tone she'd been using. She stepped closer to Sandra, the golden eyes like lethal spears. "Forget about your sister, Sandra…her transformation is complete…she belongs to us now! She won't help you again, so don't count on that! In fact…I'd venture to say that when she learns her own sister had a hand in the death of her baby's father she'll want in on whatever I finally decide your fate should be!"

"You go right on thinking that, Tamara...Beth may surprise you! I'm sure Garalynn did!...that's why you had to kill her!" Sandra's voice was even, sure, and strong. In her eyes, Tamara saw no sign of fear...or anger. All there was, in fact, was a calmness that was unsettling...even for Tamara.

"This farce is over, Sandra!...it all stops here! I am the power here, and you *will* bow to my wishes! There is no longer anything you, your damned family, or friends can do to further interfere! Accept this as fact...surrender to destiny's inevitability! Give me what I seek...do so, and I assure you all, you will never feel a thing! It will be over in less than a second!"

Sandra's upper lip curled in disdain. "If you honestly believe I'd give, or do anything to help you carry out your plans, Tamara...then you're delusional, as well as evil incarnate!" She stepped even closer, keeping Tamara's eyes locked with hers. "I make you this promise, Tamara...whatever it takes, whatever I have to do...even if it means my death, I will die knowing I have been the thorn in your side, that kept you from realizing your plan's fulfillment!"

Tamara went very still, her eyes expressionless. "I see I have misjudged you, my dear Sandra...there is an awareness within you now, an awareness you didn't have before this! Garalynn was like that...she wouldn't tell me how she found out, and I very much suspect neither will you! A most intriguing woman, your adopted sister...but an uncommonly stubborn one also! A pity she couldn't, or wouldn't see things for what they were, Sandra. If she'd been able to expand her 'vision', she'd be here today! Of course...that wouldn't be an asset for you...because her being here would mean she'd chosen me over you!" Tamara tilted her head, gazing over Sandra's shoulder. The brunette was surprised to see an almost wistful expression on the blonde's face.

"I truly disliked eliminating such beauty...I admit, I had great plans for her! But, she left me no other recourse!...just like you! Of course, there was only one choice where you were concerned, Sandra!...no one messes with *my* family without paying the price for such action!"

The mention of Garalynn, and the way Tamara was referring to her was the breaking point for Sandra. She didn't lose her control...kept her mind calm, and detached, but very determined to make this woman before her pay. "I'd say damn you, Tamara...but that would be redundant! I'll see you in Hell...that's a given! The difference is...I don't plan on staying there, while you have an eternal lease! You won't win!...the odds are all against you!"

She spoke with such calmness, such conviction that Tamara was taken aback for a few seconds. She tried to "read" Sandra's thoughts...and found herself blocked at every side. "I have had enough of this dribble! If you have the faith you say, then make your peace with your God...you just ran out of time!" She snarled, reaching for Sandra.

"No!" David cried. "Sandra...look out!" The professor yelled.

Sandra had braced herself for a frontal attack, her hands curled like claws, waiting to feel Tamara's flesh under their grip...she started forward as well. Both women seemed to go headlong into an unseen barrier between them. Sandra stepped back a pace, looking up as she did so. Tamara was also taken off balance, looking around for the unknown assailant. The two men, forgotten by the women for the moment, could only stare...their limbs in the grip of a strange lethargy. All four persons could see the heavy mist that was growing...at first just between the two female antagonists, then spreading out until the entire clearing was blanketed in the thick, swirling fog.

It had developed at an alarming rate...and seemed to pulsate with a bluish radiance. Seeing the physical reality of the enveloping fog, Tamara peered intently into the center of the mist cloud. Her face went deathly pale, and she staggered back a few paces, raising one hand in a defensive reaction.

She kept shaking her head, unwilling to accept what she saw in the depths of the strange fog...something as yet unseen by the other three people in the clearing. "No...it can't be! That's a physical impossibility! You can't be here!...you're dead! You've no more power over me! You can't stop me any more!" As if answering her outburst, the mist's radiance intensified, and its density also grew. It wrapped itself about everything, and everyone. Tamara held up both hands now, as if shielding herself, fingers crooked in a sign of power, and surprisingly enough...protection. "No...get back! Stay away from me! You can't touch me!" Her voice echoed within the cloud that hid each of them from the others.

David, and the professor had managed to find one another in the denseness, but no matter how heard they tried, they couldn't see Sandra, Tamara...or whatever it was that had so effectively rattled the tall blonde. Within the swirling rolls of the odd cloud, Sandra stood perfectly still, an odd smile playing about her mouth. She could hear Tamara's protests...could almost feel the confusion, and yes, fear coming from the other woman. She felt an incredible feeling of safety, and warmth within that cloud...and a perverse pleasure in Tamara's discomfort.

David, and the professor were both trying frantically to find Sandra, moving barely a foot at a time. They, too, had heard Tamara's words, and wondered what could so rattle such a powerful woman. David was trying to remain calm...but his every thought was for Sandra. Suddenly, two very soft, warm arms slipped around his neck...and the softest lips he'd ever known caressed his. He wrapped the tall, lithe form within his arms, and pulled her closer to his body. He forgot about the dangers around them...forgot Tamara was close at hand. All that existed for him, at this moment in time's passing, was the physical proof of the woman he held in his arms.

When he finally lifted his mouth from hers...only to take a much needed deep breath...David was surprised to see the clearing free of the pulsating fog. No, his mind told him...it hadn't completely left. It was still there, but now only as a small mist cloud that hovered near the edge of the moon-washed clearing. Yusuf moved up beside them, his hand gripping David's shoulder. He stared at the lingering cloud, still trying to see what it was about this phenomenon that had shaken…"Tamara…where is she?" He whirled about, seeking their deadly foe…there was no sign of the lithe blonde woman.

"Where'd she go?" David asked, his gun up, and ready. He glanced to all sides, fearing a sudden flanking movement…still no sign of their elusive enemy.

"She's gone…she won't be coming after us again!…at least, not out here! She's gone back to the cabin…and Beth! We have to get there before she can leave, and take Beth with her!" Sandra declared, feeling a sense of urgency now.

"Ah…what about that? If it was able to scare off someone like Tamara Dresden, I don't think I want it coming after me!" David pointed at the still present fog cloud.

"Yes…it's quite obvious that we've been in the presence of a very potent power, my dear Sandra! I am not sure if our 'friend' there is on our side…or merely toying with us!" The professor stated, still unable to discern anything clear about the mysterious "visitor".

Sandra looked over her shoulder at the cloud, smiling slightly. "Trust me…I don't think we'll have any reason to fear anything about that! Yusuf…do you feel anything dangerous about that fog?" She asked, one hand gently caressing David's cheek as she gazed at the gently undulating cloud.

The older man stepped closer to the cloud…it didn't move. He studied it closely, noting the pulsation was steady, and continuous. The delicate blue radiance intrigued the scholar…he couldn't recall any story, or legend that spoke of such a cloud. "I think Sandra's right this time, my boy…I get no hint of danger, or malevolence!" He looked back at the cloud. "There is something, though…something very familiar! I'm not really sure that…Sandra, what are you doing?" He stiffened as he saw the beautiful woman approach the cloud again. "Don't!...even though it's made no move against it doesn't mean it's not dangerous!"

David shook his head, and started after her. She stopped him with an up-raised hand. She stood directly before the cloud, which had now brightened in its radiance as she had neared its position. She gazed into its center, a soft smile on her face. A tendril of the cloud drifted towards her, touching her right cheek...a touch so light it was like the caress of a gentle wind. Her eyes widened, the azure turning into a brilliant sky blue, and her smile was warmth itself.

David and Yusuf, watching her, found their apprehensions fading away. They looked at one another, confusion clear on their faces...what power was at work here? It was feeling less and less like any form of danger as every second ticked by...and it certainly wasn't evil in any way. They watched as Sandra pulled a small pouch out of her jean pocket. Yusuf gasped as he recognized the pouch that held the golden amulet...his gasp echoed as he realized she was holding it out to the eerie cloud. "No...not the amulet! Has she lost her mind?" He breathed out-loud.

The radiance grew and grew, and they were forced to turn their heads away, the light too bright to stand. They found themselves once again wrapped within the fog's embrace...but as before, there was no sense of fear, or danger. The two men found that they felt safe, warm, and protected...infused with a sense of well-being neither had experienced in a very long time.

David jumped a little as he felt someone take his hand, and lift it to press against two soft, warm lips. He smiled, knowing who it was, and then looked about him, seeing only the dense cloud that had imprisoned them. He felt a wave of affection wrap about him, and he could have sworn someone kissed his forehead. It wasn't Sandra...he still held her by the hand...was this some sort of angel?

He was surprised to hear a giggle as he thought that. He felt Sandra lean into him, standing on tip-toe to kiss him on the mouth. "Is this heaven?...are we dead after all?" He said softly, brushing her ear with his lips.

She snuggled against his strong body. "We are all very much alive, my dear love...and this world is getting better all the time!" She glanced up, seeing the stars clearly again. The fog had vanished...this time completely.

Yusuf, and David also realized their strange benefactor had gone. The professor found himself a little disappointed...he'd have welcomed the chance to examine such an unusual happening. He wondered, though...what was it about that seemingly gentle fog cloud that frightened a powerful woman like Tamara?

"Sandra...I think it's time you told us a little about what just happened! What, or who, was within that strange cloud? Why was Tamara so frightened about it?" The older man came up beside Sandra, gently taking her by the hands. "It saved us because we were with you, didn't it? We were never in any kind of danger from it...were we? Tell us about it, please!"

She squeezed the old teacher's hands lovingly. She smiled at the other man hovering close behind her, anxious to be close, and be sure she really was all right. "I can't tell the two of you anything just yet! But, I promise...very soon, you'll understand everything! What I will tell you, however is that we have got to get to Beth!...before Tamara can take her away! We have to go back to the cabin!" She looked into David's eyes, silently pleading with him to understand, and agree.

He gazed at her, his policeman's mind telling him to stick with the original plan...go, and bring back more police. They needed help...more then what the three of them could accomplish. He looked at the other man for a direction. Yusuf could only shrug...this had to be David's decision.

David looked back at her, and slowly nodded his head. He might have made the wrong decision...he probably would live to regret this, but he also knew her heart would be broken if she didn't try one more time to save her twin sister. "We'll probably all get ourselves killed…but, if that's what you want us to do, we'll do it! You're right…we do have to at least try, and save Beth!" He stroked her hair, smiling slightly.

"Well, it's decided then! I have only one question…Sandra. Do you still have the pouch, and the amulet?" Yusuf asked gently. He wasn't surprised when she slowly shook her head.

"What happened to it? Sandy?" David asked, not sure he wanted to hear the answer.

She slipped an arm though his, and smiled up at him. "I'll try, and explain everything to the two of you as we go! It's vital we get there before they have a chnace to leave! Come on…let's go!"…….

…….Beth was silent, watching Tamara pace back and forth in the cabin's living room. She sat in one of the easy chairs, hands clasped together in her lap. She'd never seen Tamara so worked up. She wanted, very much, to ask what had happened, but she wisely kept silent, and out of the way. She wondered where Sean was, but again, prudently didn't ask.

Tamara stopped mid-stride, throwing her head up, listening with all her senses on the alert. Satisfied that all was well for the moment, she turned as Beth was about to speak, and stabbed an accusing finger at the younger woman. "This is your fault, Elizabeth! None of this would have happened if you hadn't allowed them to leave here when we had them! I will never forget that fact!" She dropped her arm, her eyes never leaving Beth's face. "I promise you…if there was the time, and you were not pregnant, things would be quite different! Prepare yourself for a long journey, Elizabeth…we'll be leaving as soon as I tie up some loose ends!"

Beth nodded, sitting very still, and thinking hard. She'd discovered a very short time ago that her sixth sense was developing at a faster pace to a finite degree…a fact she'd been able to keep from both Sean, and Tamara. She tried it now, while Tamara seemed distracted with her rage.

Her mind tentatively reached out, seeking that of her twin sister. She felt her senses brush something, like the touch of a butterfly's wings...then, it was gone. She smiled to herself...she was learning! She looked over her shoulder...where *was* Sean?

She glanced back at Tamara, beginning to pick up some disturbing feelings from the blonde as she brought her concentration to the woman before her. "Tamara...where is Sean? I thought he went out when you did...hasn't he come back yet?"

Tamara waved her hand impatiently. She turned away, gazing out the window at the night sky. Her voice came back, distant and blunt. "He won't be back, Elizabeth!...nor will he be going with us when we leave here! Sean is dead, my dear Elizabeth!...dead! Murdered by your loving twin sister, and her friends!"

Beth slumped back in her chair, stunned and disbelieving. "Dead?...killed by Sandra? What are you saying? You said your kind...*our* kind was immortal, that we can't die!" She stared, wide-eyed and trembling. "Why on earth would Sandra kill him? I know they didn't get along the best, but...Tamara, what was he doing that would cause my sister to react so strongly? What are you *not* telling me, Tamara?"

Tamara whirled, snarling. "You little idiot!...do you ever listen? When I told you the history of our family, I told you we were immortal, and invulnerable so long as we remained in this *human* form! If wwe change shape, then we risk death! Sean had altered his shape, and even though killing us is difficult even then, he played the odds...and lost!" She stepped closer to her sitting companion. "How, or why isn't important now, Elizabeth! What matters is that my brother...the father of the child you now carry...is dead! And your sister is responsible! My brother was a *god*!...and an insignifant *mortal* killed him! They'll be on their way here now, to finish matters, or so they think!"

Beth lifted her head, unconscious of the hot tears slipping down her cheeks. She'd felt that brief connection...she knew her sister was close.

She turned her head, gazing at the French doors. She rose, and walked gracefully over to the fireplace, where Tamara stood, with crossed arms...staring into the fire. She gazed at the golden blonde, calm despite the loss of her lover, and father of her baby. "Sandra is anything but a fool, Tamara. If everything happened as you said, and Sean *is* dead, then my sister would never willingly come back here! Why?...just for me? I told her...my place is here now, not with her!" Beth took a deep breath. "If Sandra *is* responsible for Sean's death...I refuse it was in any way, but self-defense! I know my sister!"

Irritated by the questions, and the confidence Beth still possessed concerning Sandra, Tamara glared at her. "Do not push me too far, Elizabeth! I've taken far too much from members of your family today as is!...any more, and I'll begin exacting payment!...beginning with that irritating sister of yours!" She pointed a level finger at Beth. "Stay out of my way...let this race run its course! Simply do as I tell you, and when it is finished, I will take you to a place of safety, to await the birth! Interfere, in even the smallest way...and I will hesitate no longer! Is that clear?"

Beth nodded, eyes blank. "Perfectly...and I will say nothing more, if you'll answer just one question?"

"Make it the last one, Elizabeth...we haven't much time now! I want to concentrate on 'welcoming' our guests in the style they so deserve!" The deadly beauty glanced at Beth, then back to her study of the flames.

Beth walked around so that Tamara had no choice, but to look directly into her face. Tamara was a little surprised at Beth's boldness. Beth slowly reached out, and gently tapped two fingertips to Tamara's forehead. "Why are you so afraid of my sister, Tamara? You're never frightened, by anything...or anyone! With all your skills, and powers...how could you be so nervous about one mere mortal? How could they hope to defeat you?"

Tamara pushed Beth's hand away, the gesture imperious and irritated. "Never touch me like that again, Elizabeth!...unless I have granted you the privilege to do so! I am hardly *afraid* of your sister! True...they surprised me, out there in the woods! But, it's hardly likely to happen twice in a row! If that's what they're counting on, then they'll learn just how fast I *adapt* to situations!...to their ever-lasting dismay, and pain! Go back to the sofa, Elizabeth...sit down, and wait! IT won't be much longer now!"

"As you wish, Tamara!" Beth turned, and went to sit on the sofa. Tamara used her mental powers to scan Beth as she sat down...searching for any chinks in the other woman's loyalty to her. She felt nothing that would smack of betrayal, or such...she smiled, confident of her hold over the lovely woman.

Beth watched Tamara as she waited...noting the concentration, and readiness evident in every line of the long, powerful body. She knew the hunter was ready for her prey to enter the trap. Beth lifted her head, and spoke up. "Tamara...what are your plans once you've taken them?"

The tall blonde raised her eyes, the lids half closed. "My plans are simple...they pay for what they did, for all the trouble they have created! Your sister's lover will die before her eyes...so she can feel every minute sensation of the pain I will inflict on him, and that old man foolish enough to be with them! If hearing that fact causes you some concern, then I suggest you shed any remainders of that human compassion...it is not logical! Persist in keeping this annoying quality, and it will ultimately lead to your own destruction! You still have much to learn about this new life you've taken on, Elizabeth...as well as knowing the powers yet coming. I am the only one who can properly prepare you...be wise, and remember that!"

Stiffening at the more then implied threat, Beth managed to look calm, and unruffled on the outside. "And just what more do I have to learn, Tamara? I'm not certain I care for any further 'surprises' about our life!"

At first, Tamara was not going to tell the other woman anything, then, she changed her mind. Beth was more able to support Tamara if she knew what awaited her in this new life style. "The changes within you are finished, Elizabeth...all that remains is your learning how to adjust to the powers within you now. You're a child again, Elizabeth...learning how to walk, talk, and reason, as you did in your *human* infancy those years ago! When your child is born, those powers will come to their fullest level, and you will be ready to take your place within the family hierarchy! You will require the guidance of another family member...to show you all that is possible within you, and how to tap into it! You need to know how to survive, to maintain your body's youth, strength...and immortal status! Living apart from us will only cause you great agony...and deprivation! Without the correct guidance, you could end up suffering great pain, and eventual madness!" She gestured towards the patio doors. "You will discover that your human sister will become a source of irritation, even pain, for you. You have a choice to make, Elizabeth...make it now, and make it the right one!"

Beth raised her head, her eyes level with Tamara's. "I made my choice long before today, Tamara...it was made the first time I made love with Sean! The fact that I am still here should tell you that fact!"

Tamara was about to say something when her sensitive powers picked up on an entrance by person, or persons unknown, into her personal sphere. "They're almost here now! Soon, I'll not only have my revenge...but the keys to the ultimate prize! We'll return home with more power then anyone has ever seen since this world began!"

"Is this prize so precious?...must it be purchased in blood? Why can't we just leave before they get here?" Beth wasn't so sure she could go through with this.

"Because I want to be here when they arrive!...I want to see their faces, look into their eyes as their life ebbs away! I want the heat of their blood on my hands, Elizabeth!...and no one is going to cheat me out of that! They have what I need to reach my goal, and I am not going to turn my back on that! I have done too much, given up to much...I will not be denied what is rightfully mine!" Tamara relaxed a little, a smile of cruel humor playing about her lips. "Besides…I've never been one to deny myself pleasure, Elizabeth…and destroying your sister, her lover, and that annoying old man will afford me one of the greatest pleasure I've had in centuries!"

"Well…never let it be said I denied someone their pleasures!…even if that someone is a bitch of your ranking, Tamara!" the clear voice carried into the room like an exploding bomb.

Both Beth, and Tamara twisted around…staring at David, and Sandra standing in the doorway. Tamara went white with the force of her anger, and shock. "How did you get inside without my knowing? What sorcery is at work here?"

Sandra smiled grimly. "Sorcery? Why, Tamara…are you acknowledging the existence of a power higher then yours?"

Tamara regained her control quickly, and lifted her head, gazing directly at the woman she desired vengeance upon. "I know of no power greater then mine, Sandra! I admit you took me by surprise in the forest…but, tricks like that will not be successful again!"

Sandra shook her head slightly, smiling darkly. "That was no trick, Tamara!…at least, not one of my doing! It was real, Tamara…and so was the fear on your face! You met your match out there…and all you could do was run away! Someone was able to stand up to you…and you ran away!"

Eyes wild, teeth bared, Tamara was a golden fury held in the briefest of checks as she stared at Sandra. "I chose to regroup, Sandra…a sound strategic maneuver, my dear Sandra!" She lifted her left hand, pointing three fingers straight at Sandra. "I want the amulet, Sandra…and the journal! You will give them to me, right now…or I will rip this pitiful lover of yours to pieces before your very eyes! I promised myself that pleasure!…but, I'll forgo it if you do as I command!"

David pushed forward, his injured arm in its make-shift splint tucked into his middle body. "Take one more step in this direction, and it will be your last!" He declared, lifting his good hand so Tamara could see the gun he held. "I'm placing you under arrest, Tamara Dresden...for more murders then I can say right now! Surrender peacefully, and that will be so noted in the arrest record!" David hoped, with all his heart, that she'd give in without any further show of force. His body was just about at the limits of its endurance, and pain thresh hold as it was right now.

Tamara glanced at Beth, who'd walked back to the sofa, and was now sitting down, a calm expression on her face. She brought her attention back to the couple before her. "You know...I'm actually quite pleased you cam, Sandra...I wanted you to see how your sister is doing with us...that her choice was of her own doing, and how she will do nothing to help you, after knowing you killed her lover!...the father of her child!" The tall blonde took a step forward, and held out her hand. "Give me the amulet, and the journal, Sandra...I will wait no longer!"

Sandra spread her hands, palms out. "Search me if you wish, Tamara!...search David! You won't find anything on either of us! We don't have the artifacts any longer, Tamara...nor do I know where they are right now! I couldn't tell you where they were to save my life...or anyone else's! So...I guess you'll have to do your worst, bitch!"

Suddenly, the patio doors slid open, and Yusuf stepped into the room. He slowly approached his friends, never taking his eyes from Tamara.

She knitted her brows together, staring at the old man. "What is this?... a school reunion? Old man...I don't know who you are, but interfering in my business will be the last thing you have the strength to do! Coming here, with them, has made your ending a physical fact!" She started towards the trio, her rage radiating from her body like a living flame.

The old scholar shook his head, keeping eye contact with Tamara. "I think not, lady of darkness. Where the battle of good and evil is fought, that is where the Keepers must always be found! I have trained, and studied since my childhood for such a day as this...I will not walk away now that has come! I will not desert my friends in their fight against you!"

Tamara chuckled, her amused gaze raking over the frail-looking senior. "You would fight me?...an amusing, if misguided, thought, old man! You must be insane if you're serious about this!"

David saw her step in the professor's direction, and he aimed his gun. "Hold it, lady! Keep away from him! If you don't stop, I'll be forced to shoot!"

She turned an amused face to his. "Shoot then...get it over! Perhaps then you'll understand when I say it is futile to struggle against me! Go ahead, policeman...shoot me!"

Sandra reached out a hand, intending to stop the tall man from doing what he'd threatened. "David...don't listen to her! She's just trying to goad you into wasting bullets on her! It won't hurt her!...not like this!"

David ignored her...all he could see was the woman responsible for so much pain, and death. His gun roared into life, and three quick shots sped their bullets on their deadly way. When the noise cleared away, he lowered his gun, staring. All three bullets had struck Tamara's body...there wasn't a drop of blood spilled...even the entry, and exit points of the projectiles couldn't be seen.

"What the..." He couldn't finish...he'd blown it, his mind shouted...now what?

"Forget this, my boy...in this form, she's impossible to harm!" The professor patted David's shoulder gently.

The big policeman looked at the professor. "It strikes me that we had agreed that you'd wait outside the cabin! What are you doing in here?"

He cast the two of them a side-long glance, a grin of mischief on his bearded face as he did so. "You really didn't think I was going to let you, and Sandra have all the fun, did you?"

"If you think this is going to be fun, you meddling old dolt...you're more senile then I thought possible!" Tamara declared. "However...if it's fun you're after, then allow me!" She raised one arm, her fingers pointed in a straight line, directly at the professor.

He quickly raised the ankh in his left hand, and grasped the star about his neck with his right. His voice rose, echoing throughout the room. "By the Living God, I adjure thee, demon!...step back, and show thy true face before the Light! Refuse, and feel the wrath of the righteous!"

As if she'd been struck across the face, Tamara gasped, and stepped back, clutching at her face. Nostrils flaring, she looked at the old teacher angrily. "That mumbo-jumbo doesn't work on me, old fool!...other then giving me a good sinus headache, that is! Keep out of my way!"

The professor smiled...he felt as though he were twenty years younger, his heart pounding strong and sure...the adrenaline coursing through his body, giving it new strength of purpose. "You're the one who needs to have a care, my dear! You call me an old fool, and that may be...but, I'm an old fool who knows many of the old ways of fighting evil! I know the words of power, and the chants necessary to call forth the gods' assistance! You know my words are true...you have only to look inside me to find that I am speaking the truth! Deep within the twisted depths of your dark mind...you know I can beat you!"

Sandra couldn't believe this determined, embattled old man was her impassioned, gentle teacher from her college days. She'd never seen him alive with such purpose, and faith. She reached over, taking him by the hand. "Take it easy, Yusuf!...don't push too much!"

"Don't you see, Sandra?...that's just the way they want us to behave! Doubt, hesitation, uncertainty...a lack of true faith...these things give them the opening they need to creep into our lives, and undermine them! They keep us from believing the way our ancestors did...making us reluctant to accept anything we cannot see, or touch! But, isn't that what real faith is?...a willingness to believe no matter what, even if we can never see, or touch? We are all born with a spiritual armor, Sandra...regardless of the belief s we may be raised in as we grow. They use doubts, and fears to pierce that armor, and open us to their attacks. They keep us from learning, or remembering the things that have been there since time began to help us keep our faiths strong, pure, and right!...as the ancients did before us!"

Tamara snarled silently at him, gathering her strength again. Then, abruptly, her expression cleared, and she smiled...almost seductively. "You are obviously a man of great learning, Yusuf Hanradi...surely we can discuss this as persons of great intellect, and desire to know the truth? All that I require is the things I came for...give them to me, and I will depart without further harm, or death! Isn't that better then more warfare?...more deaths? You cannot win this, Yusuf Hanradi...walk away, and live!"

"You're not going anywhere, Tamara...nor are you taking my sister anywhere away from here! This is her home...she stays here! As for the amulet, and journal...I have already given you your answer there, Tamara!" Sandra knew she had to keep Tamara's attention off the men...there were many stories of seduction attributed to the legend of Sekhmet, like those of Venus, and Aphrodite. She wasn't going to allow her even the slightest chance to try anything with David, or Yusuf.

Beth rose from the sofa, and came to stand just behind, and to the side of, Tamara, gazing at her sister. "Sandra...I have already told you I wouldn't return with you! That part of my life is over now! Now that Sean is dead...yes, I know all about that, Sandra, and despite your part in that, I hold nothing against you! I do hope, however, that you understand I really don't want very much further contact with you for a little while! I just want to concentrate now on having my baby, and making a life on my own! I'm going away with Tamara, Sandra...I wish you'd understand, and accept that!" Beth looked at her twin for a few more moments, then looked away, her indifference like a slap across Sandra's face.

Even David, and the professor were staring at Beth now...no one, except Tamara, could believe Beth was acting this way, or saying the things she was saying. "How can you say things like that, Beth?" Sandra was unable to believe that Beth was acting on her own volition. "As for what happened to Sean...Beth, you weren't out there, in the woods...you don't know what really took place. He killed Patrick, for God's sake, Beth!...and tried to kill us! She..." Sandra jerked a finger at Tamara. "She killed Jacob, and nearly got the rest of us by causing a car wreck! And you have the nerve to stand there, and tell *me* you don't blame me! Thanks...but no thanks, Beth! I make no excuses for any of *our* actions out there, sister of mine...we were fighting for our lives, and yours, I might add! If I had to do it all over again...I'd do it again!" Sandra stared at her sister, willing her to turn, and look at her...Beth acted as though she hadn't heard a word Sandra had just said.

"You see?...she's not being coerced, or forced, Sandra! She simply wants to be with her true family...and not with any of you! Now...enough talk! Give me what I want!" Tamara stepped closer, until she was mere inches away from Sandra. "I am not going to ask again, Sandra!...don't make me have to use force! Believe me...you wouldn't like that one little bit!"

Sandra gazed into Tamara's eyes, her own like chips of blue ice. "No...you go to Hell, Tamara!...again!"

Tamara stood there for a few seconds, looking deep into Sandra's eyes, trying to impose her considerable will over the younger woman's mind...only to find herself blocked at every corner. Finally, her golden eyes turned hard, and her lips drew back in a guttural snarl. "Aargh!" She roared out, seizing Sandra by the shoulders, and jerking her close against her own tall, lithe body.

Taken off guard, Sandra didn't have a chance to fight back. A little dazed by the speed, and strength of the attack, Sandra stared into Tamara's face. In only a second, or two, as she stared into that face...Sandra saw subtle changes taking places. She swallowed, her breathing shallow and rapid...she was having to struggle to keep from screaming…this wasn't possible! But…she couldn't scream, couldn't make any kind of sound…her mouth moved, but nothing came out.

Yusuf, and David had been standing there, as if entranced…which indeed, they had been, in a half-second of her will, before Tamara made her move. The older man was finally able to shake himself, rubbing a hand over his face. When he felt more like himself, his mind clearer, Yusuf moved to push his body in between the two women, breaking Tamara's hold on Sandra. The lovely brunette staggered backwards as her old teacher slammed the silver ankh he held into the inhuman apparition of Tamara Dresden's face…the contact of the precious metal causing a sizzling noise as the skin it touched began to actually burn like so much raw meat.

The creature that was Tamara, though a far sight from the beautiful blonde at this moment, stepped backwards, lifting one hand to the cheek that had been seared. David's eyes widened at the sight of that hand…long, deadly claw had replaced her finger nails, and the hand itself was larger, and powerful in its appearance. Sandra lifted her right hand to her throat, feeling the slight cut there from one of Tamara's fingers…she'd hadn't even felt the flesh being broken. She stared…she didn't expect Yusuf to be so aggressive. She moved to one side, wanting some distance between her, and Tamara before the blonde recovered her composure. The professor also moved, keeping himself always between the two women. David moved quickly, coming up, and slipping an arm around Sandra's waist.

In pain, but still dangerous, Tamara gathered herself, and made to go after Sandra again. "This time…this time, you are finished, Sandra! I'll find what I need, without your help, or interference! I'll do everything I was meant to do…right after I destroy all of you!" With lightning movements, she moved around Yusuf, and pushed David to the floor. Her right hand closed around Sandra's throat, and lifted the other woman completely off the floor. Sandra's eyes seemed as though they'd burst from their sockets, and she brought both hands up, trying to break that steel hold.

Tamara grinned gleefully...she would finish this meddling irritant, then enjoy herself with the two men. She pulled Sandra closer, slowly tightening her grip...her eyes gleaming with pleasure. Suddenly...she found herself jerked backwards, and tossed aside like so much trash. She stumbled over the footstool behind her, and fell to the floor with a crash. With a pain-filled roar, she leaped back to her feet, and whirled on her unknown attacker. Her eyes showed the shock she felt when she saw Beth's lithe figure standing there, in a half-crouch, waiting for a chance to deal Tamara another blow.

Tamara's rage burst forth, in full expression, and she leaped at the waiting enemy, determined to punish. The other woman met the head-on assault as best she could, but she didn't possess the experience, or cunning that Tamara had acquired over her long lifetime. It became evident almost immediately that she was no match for Tamara, and she was soon gasping with the efforts she'd been exhibiting. Tamara seized her head, hands on either side, and swiftly wrenched it to one side in a sharp, twisting movement, the snap clear to everyone in the room. Suddenly, everything was deathly still, and Sandra watched in unbelieving horror as her sister's limp body slid to the rug-covered hardwood floor.

Her chest heaving with the force of her emotions, Tamara turned, stepping over Beth's unmoving form, and faced the trio behind her. "I have taken all I intend taking from you, or yours, Sandra! I'm going to finish it all now, and take great pleasure from doing so!" It was almost hypnotic...hearing that silken voice issuing from the mouth of an apparition from Hell itself. The glistening fangs, the strangely beautiful, luxuriant fur, the deadly clawed hands, and those eyes...they no longer reminded Sandra of a cat's, but rather some twisted combination of both feline, and reptile.

"Before thou will deal with them, thee must face me!" The deep voice, speaking a long dead language, was slow, and clear, seeming to come from all parts of the room.

Tamara stopped, her features calming from the mindless rage...beginning to alter back to the features they once were. "What trick is this now, Sandra? Where did you get a recording of *that* voice, in that tongue?" She hissed, balling her fists at her sides.

"I had nothing to do with any of this! I have no idea who did...but I think I welcome it!" Came the quick, anger-filled voice.

The professor seemed to start, turning his head sharply, wondering who'd just touched his shoulder. His eyes widened, and his head cocked, as though listening to some unseen person. Then, lifting his head again, he grabbed Sandra, and pulled her behind the large chair next to him. He hollered at the still standing, mesmerized David. "Get down!...behind something, and hurry!"

It was the tone of voice, more then the words, that finally galvanized David into action, and he dove behind the other chair. He found he was close to the spot where Beth's body lay in a crumpled heap. He crawled part-way out from behind the chair, and as gently as possible, supporting her neck, and head stiffly, the big policeman slowly got the unconscious woman to a place of some safety. Once he had her behind the chair, he rolled up a throw from the chair, and used it to rap around the head and neck, forming a sort of support holder. He felt for a pulse...it was slow, but very steady, and she was breathing, also slow and steady. He looked around the chair, only to jerk his eyes away as the brightness of the light now in the middle of the room was too much to look into for even a brief second.

He clapped his hands over his ears, hearing the sounds, and feeling the vibrations of what sounded like a fierce battle. It was deafening, nerve-wracking...and seemed to be going on forever. David risked another look around the side of the chair...his eyes popped as he seemed to see gigantic figures struggling within a nimbus of unearthly, incredibly bright radiance. What was so unbelievable was what was in the center of that light…two clearly visible figures, one that resembled a great lion, the other a huge bird of prey. They were circling one another, lashing out here and there with a clawed paw, a taloned foot, a viciously curved sharp beak, a heavily muscled long leg. The last thing he was able to see before having to turn from the brightness again was the great bird leaping onto the back of the beast, sinking its large talons into the golden back. He buried his face in his arms, and prayed. There was a final, reverberating roar…then nothing. The silence that followed seemed almost as deafening as the noise before.

    The three humans slowly lifted their heads, peering out from behind their separate shelters. They saw Tamara, fully human again, gazing across the few paces that stretched between her, and a tall, powerfully-built man. He was dressed in the royal raiment of a king…an ancient Pharoah. Sandra was shocked to see how much he resembled Tamara…the height, the facial features, and the far-seeing eyes. She also noted the velvet-like, shimmering quality to the golden, tanned skin. He was looking at Tamara, a gentle smile hovering about his lips…sad and yet happy.

    He held a hand out to Tamara, his eyes warm…forgiving. When he spoke, it was in a strange language that only the professor understood, though Sandra picked out a word, here and there. "It is over, my love! Come…acknowledge this, and join me at long last!" He seemed oblivious to any other presence in the room, except Tamara's.

    She, also, had seemed to forget both her rage, and the other people hidden in the room. When she began to speak, all the others were surprised at the warmth, and sadness in her voice…even if at least two of them didn't understand the words she spoke. "After all these millenium…thee are free again! It fills my heart with joy to see thy face again…my love! And, it fills me with a great sorrow as well!…remembering why thou were condemned to thy lonely prison those long centuries ago! Who set thee free?…why are thee here?"

David shook his head, cradling his injured arm to his chest. "Now what do we have here?...another headache?" He grumbled, watching the scene unfold before them. "I just want my old life back!...drunks, thieves, and old-fashioned murderers! Sounds like a slice of heaven after all this!"

The tall, golden man stepped closer to Tamara, his smile almost glowing as he gazed at her. "That reason should be obvious, beloved...it has not changed in all these long years! This battle is over...the prize thou came for is now forever out of thy reach, my love. There will not be another chance to find it...it lies in the grasp of one forever beyond thy reach! There will be no triumph this time for the lion of war! I ask thee...surrender to me, join my circle. Do not return to thy family...darkness, and pain await there. Do not force yet another confrontation between us...my being here should tell thee how it is meant to end!"

She stepped back a couple of paces, shaking her head slowly. "I cannot!...too much time has past! I am too used to things as they have been...and are! I cannot...will not concede to thee, now, or ever!" She drew herself up to her full height, looking like a mighty queen, regal and dangerous. "I will not go back to being merely another face in the flow of humanity! I have tasted too often the sweetness of power...it is a nectar I refuse to live without! Thy love, and thy caresses were my life...but the intoxication of being worshipped became my soul! The pure essence within the blood of humans has been the sustaining rhythm of my heart!...and my eternal life! I can no longer live without the mixture of worship, fear, power...and blood! I was a goddess once, my poor love...and I will be so again when the darkness I serve becomes the ruling power of this world once more!"

"The darkness will never truly overcome the light, my heart...it can only delay the inevitable conclusion. Remember the prophecy...it cannot be forever pushed away, dear one! Please...join me!" He stretched his hand closer to her, urging and gentle.

"I remember well the prophecy...the one the humans have misread, or misunderstood for centuries, even today. The third millenium has begun...and the change destined to happen will soon be upon the world. Not when the so-called experts of this world predicted it would come...but when it is least expected! It only remains to determine the *direction* that change will take! The darkness wishes one way...the light another. The one who holds the final strings of power will wield that change, and that one will be they who gather the greatest number into their sphere of power!" She declared, squaring her slim shoulders, facing him with a slight curl to the corners of her lips.

"Perhaps...but remember, the words of the prophecy state that which *may* be...not what *will* be! Many are the things that can, and will influence the final outcome, my love! Please...allow us to be together once again!" He was saddened that she seemed still so wrapped up in this quest for power...and the desire to once again be the center of a frenzied, savage worship.

She tossed her head, the blonde tresses rippling like strands of shimmering liquid in the lamplight. "Is that all that matters to thy mind now? *We* were here, long before *they* developed enough to articulate aloud in coherent speech! We have always been superior...the ones destined to rule!...as *he* told us!" Tamara calmed herself, looking into his warm eyes...wanting him with all the fire, and passion she had experienced those centuries ago, when first they loved. He could sense that aura of pure seduction beginning to grow stronger about her. She held her arms out to him, moving closer until her fingertips slid ever so softly over the muscles of his chest.

"Come...be with me again, dearest heart...as we were those glorious days so long ago! Take thy place at my side again...be the god thou once was, my love! Let us recapture that shattering passion again...let the power live once more, within our grasp as it was ever meant to be!" She whispered, the tips of her fingertips digging into the skin of his chest.

Her words, and touched reached responsive chords within him…but, he shook his head, stepping back, his eyes sad. He knew now…she would never give in, and willingly join him, or follow what was now his commitment in eternity. She'd had become too enamoured of the base, materialistic, sensuous, powerful aspects of the world…she would see no benefit in living to serve, to love without reservation or hope of rewards, to put the welfare of other before self-serving. He sighed. "So long as my chosen way remains as it is, our paths will never be the same, or seek the same end! To go with thee, believing and feeling as I do, would be an impossibility! Darkness will always lose before the Light, heart's jewel…thou knows the truth of this! Do not fight me!" He held his hand out once again.

Tamara flung her hand up, finger pointing accusingly. "Words!…always words for you! They are nothing but empty sounds! There are no chords of power within the words thou speaks! Words will have no place in the new way of things, my love…without the strength of power behind them! I have offered thee my love, power, and position! Thou offers me thy hand, and words! I will not become less then I have been!…not even for thy love!"

He frowned for the first time since his appearance. "I would have thee return once again to the glorious creature the Creator gave me to love, honor, and cherish! We must all become as we were meant to be…teachers, doers, and givers! Even in this vein, thou could still be the ruler thou desires to be, if that is what will please thee! We must move forward, into this new third millenium! The fifth age of man is near, and we must help those deemed our brothers, and sisters by the Creator's words!"

Tamara turned, and gestured towards where the professor, in his fascination with this amazing conversation, had come out from behind the chair to stare. She jerked her arm up, curling the fingers back towards her…the professor's body jerked towards her, like being yanked by a string. He stumbled to her, with broken, jerking movements, and then fell to his knees before her...still struggling to break free of whatever mysterious force had gripped him.

Tamara pointed at the kneeling man. "You see...I can make even one of their learned men bow at my feet! And I am supposed to kneel to them?...power does not kneel, or concede! Tell me true, from thy heart's wisdom...was thy life as a non-god as rich, and full as when the masses worshipped thee as god of all the sky?"

With a sweeping gesture of his hand, the man released the professor, who quickly scrambled back to the safety of his chair. The tall man turned back to Tamara. "As thy words to me once were...that was a time that will never be again! The world has moved on, as any child will...it is growing all the time, and as a child must, it was time to forget the old ways, and go on to a new way! The things that were given us at the beginning have come full circle...it was their again! The time of ruling, and power are no longer what must be! Thou knows what is written, and what will be said! Once it is said...thy darkness must forever retreat! This is the way it is destined to be!"

"No!...we are smarter now, thanks to his leadership! We have become too powerful!...and enough power *can* alter what has been predicted! That also is the way of things! We have learned much over the eons, my love...and we will learn even more! In the fifth age of man...knowledge will be the power that will proves the strongest...and we will be the victors!" She was too confident...he could see, deep within her eyes...she would never give in.

He smiled slightly, spreading his hands wide. "Has thou really learned? I was imprisoned, supposedly for all eternity...how did I gain my freedom? The dark forces were in control of my release, or non-release...who freed me? The outcome of this act of the play was already written...who changed the steps of the play?" He gazed at her, his own golden eyes trying to look into her inner soul...where the true light of all living beings is supposed to burn bright, and strong. "Thy master has misled thee...the rewards will never be as great, with him, as they are elsewhere! Thy brother has already paid the price for refusing to push his darkness from his life. I do not wish to see thee follow his pathway.

She was growing angry again. "I will not debate this further with thee! I have chosen my way, freely and with eyes open! And...my way will be the death of the one chosen by thee!...one day this *will* happen! It is so written, and will be fact! I know not what force freed thee...but it will not sway my path, or the final outcome of this war!"

"Listen well...leave here now, and I will make no move to stop thee! Forget this senseless quest...leave these humans to live their lives as they were meant. That one step will lessen the torment of later times!" He said softly, trying another way to reach her.

Tamara turned away from him, seeking control of her surging anger again. "It will be as thou has said...to a point! I will leave, but know this well...we will meet again, and the outcome then will be as different from today as the Dark is the Light! The next time I will not forgo the battle...for any reason! Farewell, until next we cross paths! Remember this...no amount of memories, or useless emotions will sway my resolve in any way! The time of our loving is truly gone forever! Thou will mean nothing to me then!" With a wave of her hand, Tamara seemed to wrap herself in a cocoon of pure, pulsating energy...blinding everyone in the room. When everything returned to a normal lighting, the woman known as Tamara Dresden was gone!

Sandra pushed the professor's restraining hands away, and rushed over to where David was now kneeling beside Beth's unmoving form. With trembling fingers, Sandra felt all along her sister's neck, and down under the back. She didn't detect any obvious fractures, but she knew that could be misleading. At least, Beth was still breathing, and her pulse was steady. Sandra cupped Beth's cheek...hoping that this strange metamorphosis her sister had been going through was strong enough to sustain her from this severe of an attack. She should have know Beth wasn't really going to go off with that witch, Tamara! Her twin had just been playing "possum" until the time was right for her assault on Tamara. Sandra couldn't believe the surge of relief that went through her.

She glared up at the mysterious man who'd just walked over to where they were crouched. "Why the hell didn't you take her down? You obviously have the power, and God knows you had more then one opportunity! But...you did nothing! You actually let her go! Why didn't you stop her? Do you know the havoc, and pain she has caused here, especially in my family!? Why didn't you stop her?" She raged at him, one fist raised towards him, the other hand still touching Beth's cheek.

The golden man knelt beside her. When he spoke, it was in clear, concise English, without a trace of an accent. "To forgive someone, even if they never change the way we wish...is to take some of their power from them. I fulfilled my role...keeping her from getting that which would have destroyed an entire world, and all its peoples! I wish I could have prevented the death, and pain...that was out of my hands, Sandra! It was not written in the great plan of Life...pain, death, and evil are as much a part of Life as breathing, eating, and loving!" He looked down at Beth, and put his large hand over her forehead, concentrating, closing his eyes as he murmured strange words. After a few moments, he opened his eyes again, and looked at Sandra. "I have done what I can for thy sister...she is gravely injured, but she can make a full recovery, if she desires to do so!"

"I don't understand...what do you mean, *if* she desires it? We have to get a doctor out here right away...David needs medical help also! And, the...oh, God, what about the...the baby?" Sandra reached out towards David, seeking contact. He smiled slightly, taking her hand in his good one, and squeezing. He glanced up at the strange man with them, and wondered if they *were* out of danger.

The golden man shook his head, rising to his feet with grace, powerful muscles rippling under that shimmering skin. He knew it was not his place to explain what he'd meant...that was Beth's right, and place. "In time, Sandra...thy sister will make everything clear!" He looked at the now empty space where Tamara had been. "I wish she'd had listened…that she had wanted to listen!"

David had had enough…he got to his feet awkwardly, and stomped up to the other man, sticking his face right into the other's, and jabbing a rigid finger into that broad chest. "You're in big trouble, mister! I'm placing you under arrest!…the charge is obstruction, aiding and abetting, and anything else I can come up with! You realize that you allowed the killer of seven people to just…well, just leave! I should yank you down to the station, throw your tail in a cell, and forget where the key is! Who the hell are you?" He stormed, then took a good look at the individual he was threatening with arrest, and bodily harm. Nearly seven feet of well-muscled male gazed down at him, and David suddenly recalled that this man had powers he could only dream of possessing. He drew a deep breath, and lowered his voice. "Just who the hell are you anyway?"

"A friend, I assure you! I understand thy anger all too well, my friend…but understand, it was not the time for her to be taken! If she would not come to the Light of her own will, she had to simply leave. I still hold hope for her change of heart." The big man sighed, then looked back at David. "If thou must have a name to address me…then use Horus…my proper name is beyond thy ability to pronounce." The smile he gave them was like basking in the sun's warmth.

The professor came up to the man who'd said to call him by the name of an ancient Egyptian god. "You said Horus? Are you, in fact, the one worshipped as the hawk-headed sky god?…son of Isis, and Osiris?"

The man simply nodded. "That was the most common name attributed to me, Yusuf Hanradi…in my lifetime, I have had many others! Despite the tales, and legends, however…I am no god! I am an immortal being, yes…and I possess powers mortals do not, but I am not a god! Thy bravery is great for one of thy advanced years, Yusuf…few indeed are those who dared face she once known as the lion-goddess!"

The old teacher shook his head. "For all the good it did…she escaped justice!…and answering for all the evil she has done!" he looked into Horus' golden eyes, and saw only patience, serenity, and love. "Tell me…why didn't you stop her?"

"In this, as in all things, Yusuf…there is a great scheme to things, set forth long before the world, and us were alive! It is when we, as men, try to alter, or hasten that scheme that chaos comes that much closer! *I must abide by that divine plan, as must all, my friend!* In all good time…for now, see to the care of those injured!" he inclined his proud head towards Beth, and David.

"Please…there is so much I want to ask of you! You have told us you're not a god…and Garalynn told Sandra all that was revealed to her, and that also said that your race were not gods! If you are, in truth, just men like the rest of us…how can you be an immortal? What is it, within you, that is so different then humans?…that allows you the powers you have, and to live the centuries you have? What?" The professor felt he had to know, and right now…this information could help the Keepers fight the evil they'd combated all these years.

Horus frowned, thinking…taking council with a higher power. He reached up to the pectoral spread over the broad chest, and pulled a small pouch from behind the central section of the ornate armor. "This should help thee to understand…but understand this…when thee reads this, thou will be the possessor of a knowledge few others have ever seen, much less know! Use it wisely…use it prudently, in the battles yet to come, dear friends…and never in a self-serving manner!" He smiled, and looked at Sandra. "I must tell thee…thy ancestor, Joshua, was as strong in spirit a man as I have ever met…as was thy Garalynn! She loved thee greatly…even beyond death, she will be with thee!"

Sandra bent her head, closing her eyes to hold back the sudden urge for tears. The professor looked at her, feeling her pain, and wishing he could take it away. David reached out, and touched the wealth of dark curls with his good hand. Yusuf turned back to Horus, then stopped, staring with open mouth…the golden man was gone.

"Hey…where is he?" David looked around the room…no way that guy could have moved that fast.

"I don't understand…why did he leave without saying anything?" Yusuf lifted the pouch Hours had given him…was this really the answers the immortal had promised?

Holding her sister's hand, Sandra slowly shook her head. "I think his task here was done, Yusuf…and he had to move to the next! He's gone to fight the good fight…in what ever places it is now fighting! I'm only really beginning to understand what Garalynn was trying to say about what he'd told her in that cave! I didn't understand when she told me, but I do now…and will understand even more tomorrow!"

David knelt beside her. He looked into her tired, saddened face, trying to read what was hidden there. "What did she try to tell you, Sandy? What do you understand now that you didn't just a few days ago?"

She placed a gentle hand on his cheek, feeling the stubble and dried blood, then leaned forward, and kissed him, slow and tender. "That, my wonderful man. She was trying to tell me…make me see what the beings we would have called demi-gods had forgotten in their quest for power, though some did remember. That the one right way for all of us is through love! And that love must never be allowed to have its light taken away!" She gently kissed him again, then bent over, and kissed Beth's forehead. "She gave herself for us, David…for all of us! In her love for us, she suffered unholy terrors, and unbelievable pain! She has no regrets about that part…none at all!"

David nodded, getting to his feet, with the professor's help. He went to call for an ambulance, and back-up police help. He wasn't really sure what reason he was going to come up with for the police, but decided to simply say it was in conjunction with the on-going murder cases. He also worked through, in his mind, what he was going to tell the chief about what had happened to Jacob…and Patrick.

As they waited, each was involved with his, or her, individual problems. David was still working out the words of his explanations…Yusuf was trying to read through the small scroll he found inside the pouch Horus had given him…Sandra sat with her still unconscious sister. She brushed the dark curls back off the forehead, seeing Beth's beautiful face so pale, and still. She shifted around, laying next to Beth, snuggling the limp body close. She heard again Horus' cryptic remarks about Beth…that the state of her health was up to Beth…what exactly had he meant?

She started thinking back, over everything that had happened, and the tears began to flow. She closed her eyes, trying to stop them…but the memories continued to fall, and she cried…for all the times she hadn't, and for all that she feared still lay ahead, some of these tears wetting the side of Beth's quiet face……………………………………………..

****

Epilogue

❁

........Sandra stood by the patio doors of the library, looking out over the snow-covered gardens. She felt at peace inside…for the first time in several months. Taking a deep breath, she smiled slightly, thinking. She looked back into the quiet room, checking the clock on the fireplace mantel…nearly seven p.m. David hadn't called her back yet, though his meeting with the police chief, and David's captain, was over three hours ago, and she wondered if everything had gone all right. There had been quite a hullabaloo a couple of months ago…when they'd had their fateful confrontation with Tamara, and Sean. When the police had finally reached the cabin, it had been quite a time as she, David, and Prof. Hanradi had tried to explain everything that had happened…the way the three of them had decided to explain it as they waited for the police, and ambulance to arrive.

She sighed, still not comfortable with the story they'd come up with…but, how could anyone have ever believed them if they *had* told the true facts. She was sure, in her heart, that the police commissioner, the District Attorney's office, and the police chief didn't really believe what they'd been told, but they didn't have any evidence to prove they were being lied to by the three. Beth, who'd been in a coma-like state for so many days, simply told the authorities she'd been unconscious all the time, and didn't know about any of the events that had taken place. She shook her head, deliberately pushing her thoughts away from her sister…she'd let those emotions roll over her another time, just not right now.

She walked over to the fireplace, to the wide, ornate armoire set in the recessed space to the left of the mantel's end. She opened it, and took out a small, jeweler's felt box. Sandra held that in her hands for a few moments, then slowly opened it. She gazed at the golden Horus amulet, glistening brightly against the royal blue velvet background of the box. She ran her slender fingers over its surface, feeling the unusual warmth of the gleaming metal, and jewels. As always, its touch seemed to bring Garalynn's presence into the room, and Sandra smiled wistfully. Looking at the ancient amulet brought back all the things that had happened…made what often seemed a dream of the worst kind a terrible, but oddly calming physical reality. And, one of the strangest things, at least to David, was finding the amulet suddenly back in Blackmoon, in the library that had been Garalynn's favorite place.

As she held the amulet, her gaze fell on the picture of Beth, Garalynn, and her, taken down at the stables the year before their father had died. She closed the velvet box, and replaced it in the armoire. She reached out, and touched the picture frame. She could feel the tears threatening again…the memories of the final moments at the cabin sweeping over her mind again.

She closed her eyes, hearing Beth's soft voice, when she'd finally come out of her coma, there in the hospital. Sandra had filled her in on what had happened after Tamara had so viciously attacked Beth. The two sisters had embraced, washing all the bad times, words, and memories between them away with their tears, and love. Sandra had no need to tell Beth the extent of the damage done by Tamara…Beth could tell the moment she regained conscious thought.

Sandra choked back the lump rising in her throat…why couldn't she get that last visit in the hospital out of her mind? Why hadn't she realized what Beth had been trying to tell her that day? She could hear that soft, clear voice telling her not to cry, that everything would work out for the best…for the right. She had shook her head when Sandra told her she had the ability now, within her own body, to heal herself completely, and keep the baby safe, too. Beth had acknowledged that, and simply repeated what she'd already said, squeezing Sandra's hand. She said she was tired, and wanted to rest. Sandra had kissed her on the forehead, and left, to meet David, and Kristine.

"Oh, Beth…why? Why couldn't you have talked this out with me? Why this way, and what about the…oh, God, Beth…what about the baby?" She leaned her head on the fireplace mantel. She tried, again, to tell herself she understood the reasons her beloved twin sister chose *not* to heal herself…not to use her fledgling powers to keep herself, and her unborn baby alive. The doctors had told Sandra, and David that it had been a miracle Beth hadn't died immediately after sustaining the injuries…that what had taken place three days later was an inevitable reality. Sandra heard herself talking the night before her sister's death…coming up with all sorts of reasons for her sister to use that power. Beth had asked Sandra three questions. One, what about the child's unnatural father? Two, if it were her, would Sandra *want* to become like Tamara? And, three…what would this baby turn out to be? "If it were you…" Beth had whispered gently. "Would you want even the remotest possibility of loosing another such creature on this world's population?" Sandra didn't know how to answer that…or, rather, how *not* to answer it.

She lifted her head, gazing with tear-filled eyes at the now blurry picture. "I didn't even get to say good-bye! I think that's what hurts the most…I didn't get to say good-bye to either you…or Garalynn! Neither of you gave me that chance…and I'm angry at that fact! But…that anger won't get me my sisters back! I love you both…and I pray to God you've both found the peace you didn't have here!" She whispered, stroking the picture frame.

"Penny for your thoughts?" A deep voice said softly in her ear as a strong arm wrapped itself about her slim waist. She turned, a soft smile slipping over her lips. The man behind her drew a sharp breath at the sight of the tears, and cupped the side of her face, his thumb wiping the tears away. "What's wrong, baby? Why the tears?" He asked, his dark blue eyes scanning her face.

She shook her head, slipping her arms about David's neck, sighing as she snuggled her head in under his chin. "My thoughts are worth more then a penny, sweetheart…but I really don't want to talk about them right now!" She looked up at his rugged face, lightly drawing a slender fingertip along his jaw line. "I expected you to call before now…how did the meeting go?" She glanced down, and saw that the heavy cast was gone from David's arm. "David…your arm! When did you get the cast off? Is everything okay?"

He grinned, lifting the mentioned arm, and wiggling his fingers under her nose like a mischievous boy. "The doc took it off this morning…I didn't say anything to you before because I was afraid he'd change his mind! I have to undergo a little physical therapy, to test out the tendons, but otherwise, I'm good to go back to work!" His grin faded into a grimace. "Desk duty, that is! The captain says it's protocol for on officer injured on duty…but it still bites!"

"That means you'll have to spend more time at home…what a burden!" She tried to make her voice sound firm, stern…but that slid into a loud giggle. Then, she sighed, taking the now un-encumbered hand, and kissing the palm. "I have to admit…I've missed the feel of *both* your hands!…more then I have words to tell you! I love you so much!"

As close as they had become, He could pick up on her thoughts every now and then when he held her like this. He gently tilted her chin up, gazing into a sea of cerulean blue. "Been thinking, haven't you? Everything okay?"

She shrugged, slipping out of his gentle grasp. "I just can't seem to shake it, David…the pain, I mean!…the sense of loss!" She looked back, smiling through the tears now slipping softly down her cheeks. "Having you in my life now has helped greatly, I admit. You've been a life-saver, both for my sanity, and my heart!" She sighed again, turning away again. "I just can't get them out of my mind…Garalynn, and Beth! I miss them so much!"

David gathered her back into his arms, trying to push some of the pain, and shadows, away with his presence…angry with himself for not being able to keep them away from her heart altogether. "Honey…it's okay to feel like that!…it's only been a couple of months, for God's sake! They were your sisters…no one expects you to be all bubbly this soon! Besides, remember what Yusuf told you…as long as you think about them, they'll always be here, with you!"

She smiled at that. "Yes, I remember…that's always been a pet belief for our dear old Yusuf! I wonder if he's finished with all the translations yet, including that scroll Horus gave him at the cabin?"

"Hard to tell…Angela said he's been shut up like a hermit since he got back to his house, except for a couple of VIP's last week." He looked down at the face that was his whole world now…he could see the real pain inside her soul. "Sandy…you're going to have to come to terms with this sooner, or later! I'm not trying to be unfeeling, love, but I can't stand seeing you in so much pain! What's going on today?"

"I don't know…I guess I was just thinking what things would have been like if Beth had…" her voice died away…she couldn't bring herself to say the words aloud.

He nodded, still a little thrown by the final outcome himself. "It was her decision, honey…no matter what we thought was the right thing to do. She was the one who would have had to live with it…so she made it! She did what she thought was right…and I have to admire her for that, even if I don't agree! What would *you* have done?" He looked at her, not sure he wanted to know, but knowing she needed to talk this out.

" God, I just don't know!…I'm glad I didn't have to make it! I wish she hadn't…I wish she was still here…that they both were here!" She turned away, and walked over to the sofa…all the peace she'd felt earlier gone. She sat down, and leaned back, sinking into the over-stuffed cushions. She looked up at him, still standing by the fireplace looking at her.

"How could she have done it, David? How could she just allow her body to completely shut down?...how could she die? Horus told us his race was immortal, couldn't die in their human form! But, Beth did die! She could have used that power she had to heal, and lived!...but, she refused to do so! Why?"

He came over, and sat down, taking her hand in his. He leaned forward, taking in the fresh scent of the dark hair. "I know you're hurting, baby...and I wish I could take it away from you, but I can't! Look, Sandy...stop thinking about just the bad times!...focus on all the good times the three of you had! Use that to get you through the bad times! As for why Beth did die...don't you remember what the professor said?"

"Yes...he felt it was because she hadn't been *born* that way! That being fully human once gave her an advantage over their race...he felt it was the endorphins we humans produce in moments of extreme emotions that were the keys, according to some things he found in later entries in the journal!" Sandra answered absently, her mind retreating into its memories again.

David noticed this, but didn't comment...he knew this was her way to deal with some things. "Right...something about the endorphins *their* race produced, and how they mixed with ours." He leaned back, his tired body relishing the soft cushions. "You know, I wonder just how the ancients put it all together...you know, the stories about immortals, vampires, and such. They didn't have it all right...but, if Yusuf is right about what they *have* translated, it answers a lot of questions, about folk lore, and some legends!"

She nodded, looking at him with an inquisitive expression. "You could be right...he said the entries talked about how their scientists discovered how at the height of extreme emotional states...such as absolute fear, or sexual climax, the endorphins released into our blood are the strongest dosage, the purest strength...then any other times we may experience. This 'pure essence', as they termed it, when mixed with the high complex amino acids...the so-called 'building blocks'...to form a substance capable of extending the lives of the blood cells, and therefore the tissue cells! In short…immortality! Not one hundred per cent, perhaps, or entirely perfect…but good enough to give their kind a life-span hundreds, thousands of years longer then ours! So, they became gifted seducers, lovers…and creators of terrors beyond comprehension! All to ensure their long lives!" Sandra's voice sharpened at the last…her eyes glittering chips of suppressed blue flame. It would many years before her bitterness faded…her anger completely doused. She understood all that the Keepers were about…and from what Yusuf…and Garalynn…had told her about the race that sired the Dresdens, and the regal, enigmatic Horus, she knew that not *all* of them were evil…like Tamara! But…her wounds were still too fresh…too sensitive. She needed to mend, inside…and regain the still-torn vestiges of her faith. The man beside her, by his love, physical presence, and solid strength, had helped her get this far…and would always be therein the future they were about to share. But…her heart still said it hurt!

"Are you okay?" He asked quietly, seeing the lines of stress, and pain ease a little from her lovely face, and the cerulean gaze was again free of that hardness…that sharpness.

"Yes…for now, I think. Angela told me, earlier today when she was over, that this is far from over, you know." She snuggled into the familiar shoulder, sighing softly. "She was trying to explain more about the Keepers…that we must always go forward. She told me that's what both Beth, and Garalynn would tell us to do if they were here!" She looked up at his face, wondering again how she could be so lucky to have found this kind of love in her lifetime.

"I know…I was talking with Jacob's wife…she took the news of his…disappearance more calmly then I could ever have believed! I hope, one day…that we can find his body, so she'll have that, at least!" He sighed, draping an arm about Sandra, pulling her in close. "She supported him all the way where the Keepers were concerned…that it was a necessary work! She said she knew how the dark ones were…that there were still many of them out there, doing their mysterious 'lord's' devious work! She said it was the work of all who knew they really existed to fight them!...at every turn, and in every way!"

"David...do you think we'll ever learn all there is about this?...about them and how it all started? Can we ever learn *all* the forms their evil can take?...or, all the ways to fight them?"

"I think...if we're vigilant, and take advantage of every opportunity to learn, that we can hold our own, at least! I do wish we knew more about this mysterious Seer...or that gut, Horus! I wonder if we'll ever see him again?" He mused, leaning sideways until he was partially laying on the sofa, pulling her along so she rested half on top of him.

She arched up, kissing the base of his chin. "Like you said...we'll have to wait, and see!" She sighed, leaning her head on his chest. "I got the amulet out again...I couldn't resist! I *had* to look at it, touch it one more time!"

He took a deep breathing, trying to still the sudden surge in his heart rate...it happened every time either of them mentioned the amulet. "I still can't believe we have it back again!" he looked down at her, tightening his hold. "When you finally told us that it was Garalynn's spirit who'd created that weird fog, and surrounded us all to protect us...well, I honestly thought you'd gone over the edge! Then, when you, and Beth said her spirit was also at the cabin...I started getting a little spooked!" He declared, a little shudder going through his body.

She felt it, light as it was, and understood. "Horus told us she'd always be with me, remember? I was so surprised when she appeared to me, in that fog cloud...but she explained it was all part of a plan, and not to be frightened of her. I told her how angry I was...because she's sent me away! But...I also told her I loved her! She took the amulet, and told me what to do." She smiled up at him. "That's why I insisted on going to the cabin...I had to delay Tamara until Garalynn could carry out the ritual necessary to set Horus free!"

"Okay, I finally got that through my thick skull…but why, and how did the amulet show up here, in this room?" David sank the fingers of one hand deep into the dark, silken hair…he loved the feel, and scent of her hair. It always made him think of a subtle mixing of something clean, citrus, and slightly spicy, like cinnamon.

Sandra shrugged. "I'm not sure…except this room was Garalynn's favorite one in the manor house. Somehow…I think Horus wanted us to have it, use it against the next 'bad' guys we meet up with! Though, *how* we're to use it…I guess we'll learn when it's necessary, I guess! I don't want to talk about that anymore, David." She sat up slightly, her hands braced on his chest. "How did the meeting go?" She asked, changing the subject.

"Okay, I guess…they said they were closing the book on the murders, although, I could tell they're not completely sold on the story we gave them! The news will be released to the media tomorrow morning! At least, there ill be some sort of closure for those kids' families…Pat's, and Jacob's as well. Sean's name will be given as the killer, the story being that he'd gone a little crazy, that he was on one of the exotic drugs, and was a member of a cult group that practiced human sacrifice. That was why those three kids, and the museum security guard were murdered! He kidnapped Beth, because of the baby, and was aided by his sister, Tamara. The rest of the story deals with how they had been plotting to get control of Phelps Industries by controlling Beth…with drugs! It will say that Pat was killed in the line of duty, trying to take him, and Tamara down…and that she was the one responsible for Jacob's…and Garalynn's disappearance, and possible murders! The papers will also say Sean was the one who killed Doug as well!" He finished, still not happy about having to concoct such a weak, contradictory explanation for his superiors…no wonder they acted so unconvinced! And yet…they hadn't pushed him for further explanations, or proof…it was as if they didn't want to know the truth! It was like they suspected the real reasons...and wanted to keep it from the public, as badly as he, Sandra, and Yusuf.

"You think they'll catch up to Tamara?" She rested her head back down on his chest, thinking about the deadly blonde.

'Well...there's an international warrant for her arrest on the wires! She's not at her family's home...Scotland Yard, and the army surrounded their castle, and searched every inch of the place...she wasn't there! In fact...no one was! The servants said they'd all received their severance, and were in the process of locking the entire estate up when the police arrived! They said the only family members who actually lived in that particular house were Tamara, and Sean...and they hadn't seen either of them since their trip to the States! Funny thing...there wasn't anything in that house, of a personal nature...you know, mementos, books, awards, etc. The detectives who'd searched the place said it was obvious things had been removed from the house...yet the staff maintains no one has been there since Tamara, and Sean left for here! It's weird!" He didn't believe the servants...someone had to know something!"

"They'll never find her!...she's had centuries to perfect the skills necessary to continuously escape justice! She's far too good a 'weapon' for the 'lord' she swears allegiance to, David!...unless it would serve his wishes, she'll never be brought in, to answer for all the evil she's done!" She stared at the ceiling. "One good thing has come from this...the journal's once again where it can be used to help the fight! Once Yusuf has the complete translation, we'll decide what's to be done with it! I wonder how much he's been able to get from the scroll!"

'Funny you should ask that, my dear...I came over to tell you, and David about that very thing!" Came a cheerful, deep voice. Looking up, the couple saw the professor, and Angela in the doorway...he was wearing the kind of expression one would see on someone who'd just won the lottery...shock, and disbelief!

"What are you two doing here?" David sat up, frowning. He was getting to be a bit of an alarmist whenever he saw the old scholar any more.

"Yusuf finished reading the scroll...I agreed with him that you should hear what was in it as soon as possible!" Angela replied, coming into the library, and sitting on a chair opposite the couple.

"So...what is it? What does the scroll say?" Sandra sat up, and leaned forward, looking intently at the professor.

"So many things, my dear Sandra...and if my friends, and I have done our work rightly...things that could mean the fate of the world! Tell me...are you familiar with the chapters in Revelations, or the mythological poems of the Scandinavian Edda...or the Mayan Prophecies?" Yusuf asked.

Sandra stared, as did David. "I know a *little* about Revelations, but absolutely nothing about the Edda...and my knowledge on the Maya is very sketchy, at best!" She replied, wondering where this was all leading.

"Well...don't anyone look at me! My Bible knowledge is rusty...I'm afraid I really haven't read the good Book since I was in college! As for the others you mentioned...never heard of either of them!" David answered.

"That's nothing to be ashamed of, my boy...it took me, and three other experts to decipher what we did of both the scroll, and the journal! Let me explain, one at a time, alright?" He looked at the group, and they all nodded. "Alright...first off, you must realize just how shocked we were to see mention of these things, in both the journal, and especially in the scroll! And, even though we've translated everything...we don't know the real meanings behind a lot of the sections, or chapters."

"So...what *can* you tell us then?" David felt his frustration level rising.

"Listen to these stanzas...and tell me what your impressions are...your very *first* impressions!" he pulled a thick notebook out of the briefcase he was carrying, opened it, and flipped through some pages. He stopped, his finger in the middle of the page, and began to read..."In one of the Mayan prophecies...'when the Love Goddess's star dips below the western horizon, and the seven sisters rise in the east, and the Hunter rises with the Sun God's sleep...the last age of Man will end, unless the kingdom of the God arises again from the depths of the seas.'" Yusuf paused, looking around at his friends. Then, taking a deep breath, he read on..." In the Scandinavian Edda...'when the All-Father, and the hosts of Valhalla approaches the Vigrior, the great Yggdrasil will tremble, and the nine worlds, including Midgard, will bear witness to this passing. The music of heroes will fill the air, and the Otherworld fruit will be harvested for those deemed most deserving. The Jotunheim, led by dark Loki, will seek the waxing of the sun, moon, and the very stars...golden fruit will keep the forces of Asgard, and Vanaheim strong!'" The professor paused again, pushing his glasses up on the bridge of his nose again. "And, finally, in Revelation, it tells about seven angels, seven Spirits of God, and seven vials containing the last plagues to be visited upon the world of man. The entries dealt with the sixth angel, and a third of the armies of the king named Abaddon, in the Greek called Apollyon being laid low as the angel's trumpet sounds. But, because the men of these armies still do not repent their worship of devils, their idolatry of Mammon, their murders, thefts, and other evils set before them as the way to true freedom by the ruler of the bottomless pit...they are given warnings of the coming of the seventh angel, and told to heed the prophecies of the witnesses, which will be for a period of a thousand two hundred, and threescore days!"

After the professor finished, there was a profound silence...everyone was trying to take all this in, and understand it. Sandra got up from the sofa, and walked over to the desk at the far end of the library. She opened the right hand drawer, and lifted a small, metal box out, shut the drawer, and returned to the group. She handed the box to the professor, not saying a word. He looked at her, a little confused, then took the box, and placed it on the coffee table before him. He opened the box, and looked into it. He looked at Sandra, surprise on his face. He reached into the box, and pulled out another papyrus scroll, this one tied with a faded yellow ribbon.

Everyone in the room was still silent…all of them almost afraid to break that silence lest it bring down some sort of terrible retribution on them. Yusuf opened the scroll, and read the few lines of script there. He lifted his eyes to Sandra…they were wide with shock.

"Where…when did you get this scroll?" He finally asked in a hoarse voice. "Why have you waited to give it to me?"

"What are you talking about?…Sandy, what is that?" David frowned, trying to understand what was going on.

"It was delivered to the house about ten this morning…Roland found it tied to the doorknob, *inside* the main door of the front foyer. He has no idea who, or when it was put there! However, it had to have been after nine-thirty this morning because I walked Angela out the front door at precisely nine-thirty!…and it wasn't there then!" Sandra said quietly, sitting back down. "It was addressed to Yusuf, so I didn't open it! I have absolutely no idea what it says!"

"Yusuf…what *does* it say? Who's it from?" Angela asked, worried about the pallor of the old teacher's face.

The old man finally shook himself, his hands still gripping the open scroll, trembling with the force of the emotion coursing through him. He looked at Angela, then back at Sandra. He drew in a deep, shaky breath. "It's from Jacob!…but…that's impossible! He's dead!"

"We haven't found a body, professor…or, even a sign to show that your friend *is*, in fact…dead!" David said gently. "Maybe, somehow, he was able to escape Tamara?"

"Hardly likely, David!…she wasn't one who let men like Jacob simply get away from her! Yusuf…are you sure that's from Jacob? If it is from him…where's has he been for nearly two months?" Sandra took her old friend's hand. "What does he say?"

The professor looked back at the scroll. "He says not to grieve…he's better then he's ever been, but he can't come to me again!…at least, not for a little while! He says we must be very careful...the dragon never sleeps. He doesn't want us to disclose the contents of the journal, or the Horus scroll..." the old scholar stopped, and looked at his friends. "How could he know anything about the Horus scroll? He wasn't with us when we received it!"

Sandra was about to say something when she felt that eerie brushing again. She turned her head, looking into the corner nearest the fireplace, and saw a familiar radiance there. She started, then began to smile...suddenly things made sense. She heard a faint laughter, and shook her head. She looked back at Yusuf, and patted his hand. "Trust me, my dear friend...there's a way he would know everything that's happened after he was taken from us, there in the forest! This is his way of telling you not to worry about him any longer! That he wants you, and us to concentrate on what we must do to make sure the darkness never wins!"

He gazed into her eyes for a long time, then slowly nodded his head. He drew himself up, and put the scroll into his shirt pocket. "Yes...yes, I understand. Now, then...back to the journal entries." He drew a deep breath, trying to get himself back to normal.

"The journal, and scroll entries...Yusuf, are you okay?" Angela asked softly, concerned for her mentor.

"Yes...I am now." He looked at the young woman, and smiled his gratitude for her concern. Then, he was all business again. "So...any questions about what I've read to you?"

"Any questions, the man asks!? How about...everything?" David stated, his head aching from the concentration.

Yusuf laughed...the sound startling, but reassuring as well. "Let's take it one thing at a time. First, the Mayan...the prophecy tells about the planet Venus dipping below the western horizon, while at the same time the constellation known as the Pleiades, or seven sisters, rises...at the same time, the constellation Orion rises, as the sun sets. This is to signal the end of the fifth age of Man, and hopefully to herald the beginning of the new age…or the new millenium!"

Angela interrupted. "But…we're already into the new millenium! I mean…it's the year 2001, for God's sake!"

"By *our* counting, yes…but the Maya measured, not in millenium, but in ages, and their next age is set for by the positions of the stars, and planets! In this case…approximately the year 2012!" The professor looked around, and proceeded with his narrative. "As far as the Scandinavian…it's talking about the final battle between the forces of good, and evil. The Asgard, and Vonahiem refer to the gods, and the Jotunaheim refer to the frost giants, their eternal enemies! Midgard is their name for Earth, or the world of Man. Yggdrasil is the tree of all life, and it is the fruit of this tree, the golden and silver apples, that promote healing, freedom from sickness, and immortality! And, finally…the sayings from the Book of Revelation…all talking about the last stage before the end of the world, the end of Man, the defeat of the Devil, and the birth of the new World…the kingdom of the Most High! It deals with the warnings mankind will receive…and must heed before the coming of the seventh, and final angel!"

"They're all dealing with the end of the world…either in righteous battle, from which can rise a new, and better world, and human race! Or, in flames, death, and oblivion! The immortality of the afterlife, however you believe in it, could be lost to us if we don't heed the warning signs, and fight the good fight! We can either be free, and leave such a gift to our descendents…or end up a broken, enslaved race under the heel of the lord of darkness himself!" Sandra murmured, looking at David, her eyes filled with a desperation of the very soul itself.

"Yes…that's what we thought as well. Of course, others can come up with other interpretations…it will be argued, and debated for years, as other such readings have been so treated! The question is…what do we do now, especially in view of what this scroll from Jacob has said?" The old teacher shrugged his shoulders.

"I think that's a decision best made when our minds are much more calm then they are right now! Yusuf...you, and Angela stay for dinner. We'll talk further after dinner, alright?" Sandra stood up, after pushing a button on the coffee table.

"I think that's a good idea...it will give us all a little time to digest all this...besides, I never could refuse a free meal!" Angela laughed, standing also.

Roland appeared in the library doorway, and Sandra instructed him to take her friends to where they could relax a little, and freshen up for dinner. When her friends had left, Sandra turned back to where David still sat, a confused expression on his rugged face.

"What's wrong, honey? You look like you swallowed something backwards!" She asked, smiling as she sat down beside him.

"I think I did...and it's stuck! You know...everything I think I'm beginning to get a handle on all this, somebody does something to knock me off my seat! And, here I was foolish enough to think we just *might* have a more normal life ahead of us!" The tall man slumped back into the cushions, shaking his head.

Sandra nodded absently, thinking. She glanced at him, a smirk tugging at the corners of her mouth. He caught the expression, and frowned...what was she thinking about now? "What's so funny? What's going on in that pretty head of yours?" He asked

Cautiously.

Her blue eyes sparkling wickedly, she leaned towards him, one hand caressing the soft cotton of his shirt. "Oh...nothing much! Just recalling a promise made to me a couple of months ago. A promise, I might add, that hasn't really been followed up on as yet by the police lieutenant who made it!"

"Promise?...what promise did I make?" David frowned, trying to think back.

She shook her head, sighing extravagantly. "I seem to remember someone telling me he knew a better way to spend time...and that he'd prove it to me! Of course, that *was* a while ago, and he *has* been awfully busy! Still, if he really meant it…" She never got a chance to finish as she was pulled down, and landed on top of the now broadly-grinning aforementioned police lieutenant.

"I thought I'd already made good on *that* promise! However, if you think another *payment* id required, guess I'll have to do something about that!" he burrowed his nose into the hollow of her throat, kissing the pulse point there.

She sighed, a throaty, purring sound, and slipped her arms around the strong body of the man under her. "Well, if you think that will help…I do hope, however, that you plan to keep that particular 'account' open, Lt. Collison…forever! Those are the only conditions I would be able to 'deal' with you!" She giggled, the vibrations pounding against his lips.

He lifted his head, running his fingers over her high cheekbones, then down the side of the slender neck. "Oh, I think I can positively state that that account will never be closed…Mrs. Collison!" He kissed the left corner of her mouth, the tip of his tongue flicking lightly over her lower lip. His hand lifted her left hand, and he kissed the wide golden band on the third finger.

She drew his head down, and they lost themselves in their closeness. Their hearts flowed into each other's, igniting their passions higher. The terrors of the past dark events receded from memory, for the present time, and the light of their love, and souls shone brighter then the day before…and not as bright as the days yet to come. As they slipped down onto the sofa, exploring the joys, and mysteries of each other again, neither of them heard a soft, joyful laugh weave through the room…then it was gone………

The end of the 2nd…the beginning of the 3rd…..

Bibliography

❀

The Holy Bible, *Book Of Revelation*, The National Bible Press, King James Version, 1963

Collins, Harper, *Past Worlds, An Atlas of Archaeology*, HarperCollins*publishers*
(Binders Group, Inc)   1997

Davidson, Hilda Ellis, *Lost Beliefs of Northern Europe*, Barnes & Noble(Routledge) 1993

Gilbert, Adrian, and Cotterrell, Maurice, *The Mayan Prophecies*, Barnes & Noble
(Element Books, Ltd.)   1995

Hancock, Graham and Bauval, Robert, *The Message of the Sphinx*, Three Rivers Press 1996

Morenz, Siegfried, *Egyptian Religion*, Cornwall University Press, 3rd Printing   1996

The Egyptian Book of the Dead, (The Book of Going Forth by Day)
Translation by Dr. Raymond Faulkner, Introduction Dr. Ogden Goelet, Preface Carol Andrews, (2nd revised edition) Chronicle Books, San Francisco   1998